PRAISE FOR

"This heartfelt, lingering tale of friendship, family, and forgiveness will captivate children and adults alike, especially those who have experienced loss."

SCHOOL LIBRARY JOURNAL

"...a smart story about friendship and grit."

PUBLISHERS WEEKLY

"Brenna Thummler presents *Sheets*, an incredibly endearing and heartbreaking story that uses a cute exterior to mask grief, economic hardship, isolation, and many other issues that children of today are dealing with in ways they didn't have to before."

ADVENTURES IN POOR TASTE

"5 stars out of 5"

ICV2

"Brenna Thummler's graphic novel [...] is an overwhelming tribute to the power of friendship in challenging times. *Sheets* is a triple threat of charming characters, honest writing, and spellbinding artwork. [...] Indeed, *Sheets* explores the ways we remember loved ones and rebuild our homes. Even when we feel all alone, there is hope."

COMICSVERSE

"And the colors are exquisite, absolutely exquisite, the neon pinks of the senescent leaves striking a contrast with the yellow-green lawn they've-fallen upon. [...] Very affecting, and fine for all ages."

PAGE 45

"Brenna Thummler's first solo work for young readers, *Sheets*, is a subtle, gentle work that expresses empathy and warmth even while depicting life's more painful experiences. *Sheets* shows the versatility of the graphic novel medium as Thummler uses color palette and the shape, size, and solidity of panels to evoke emotions both pleasant and upsetting."

SHELF AWARENESS

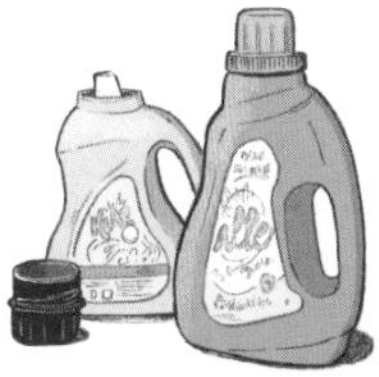

For Aunt Shary and Uncle Joe

SHEETS

Brenna Thummler

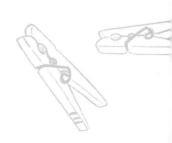

AN ONI PRESS PUBLICATION

It's difficult to list, in order, the things I hate. But I can say with no uncertainty that laundry and ghosts are currently tied for first.

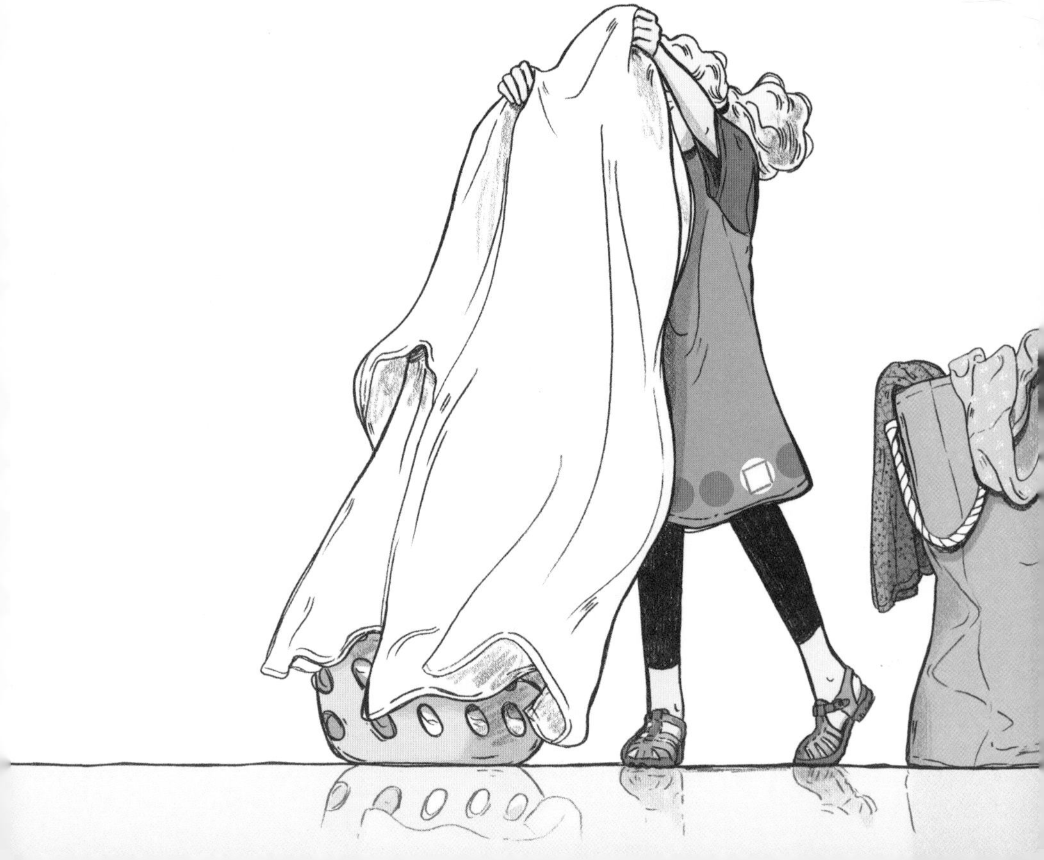

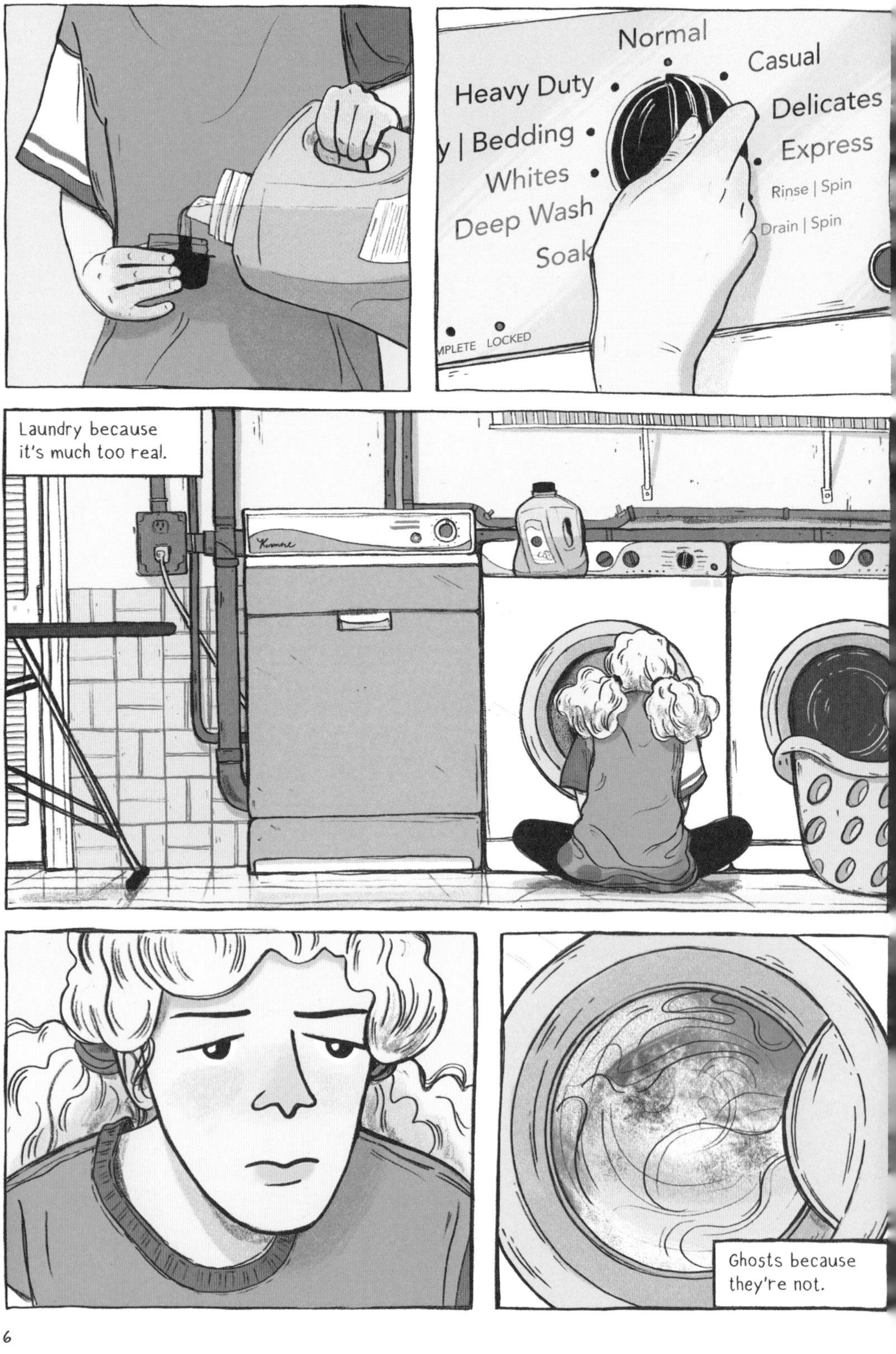
Normal
Casual
Heavy Duty
Delicates
Bedding
Express
Whites
Rinse | Spin
Deep Wash
Drain | Spin
Soak
LOCKED
Laundry because it's much too real.
Ghosts because they're not.

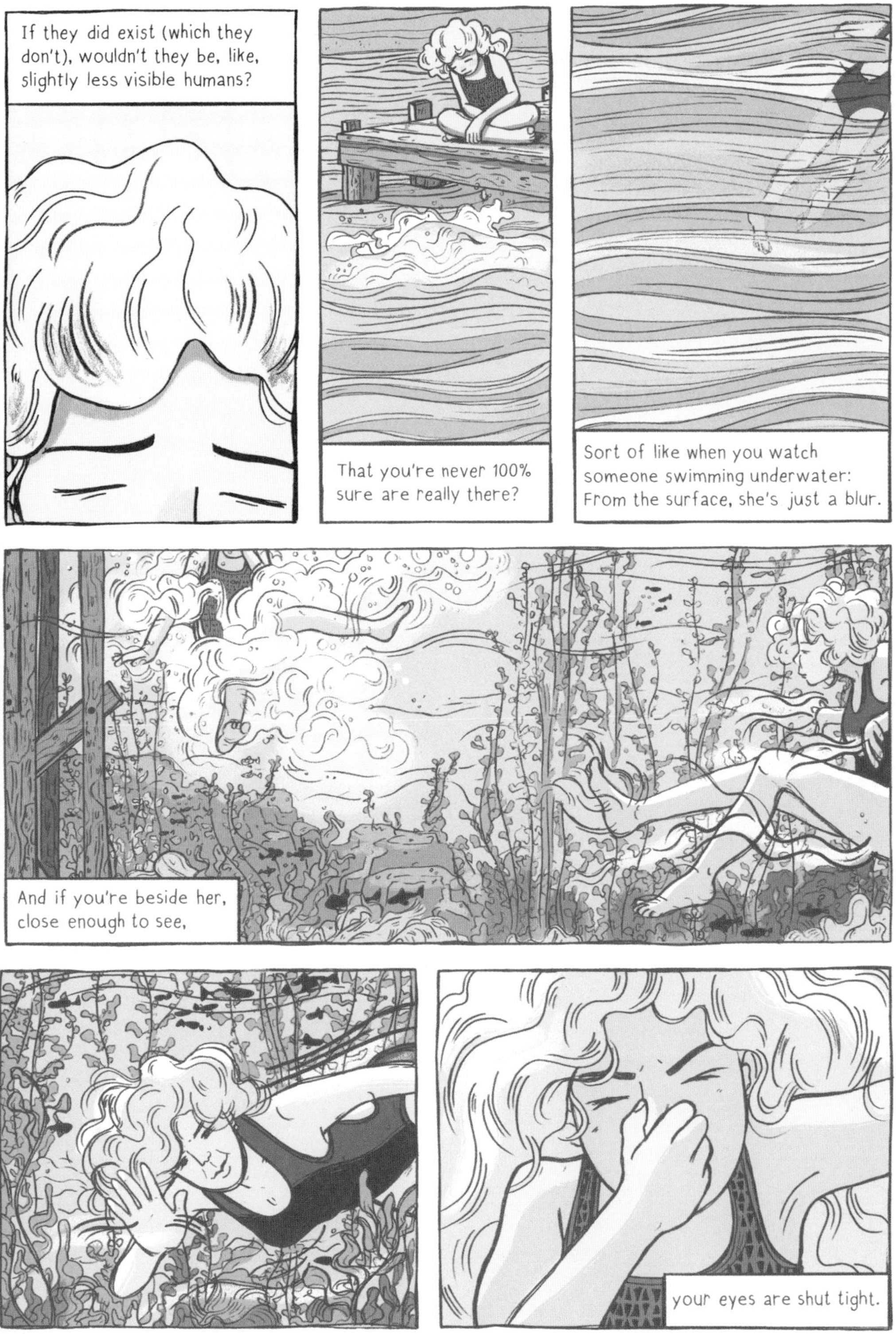
If they did exist (which they don't), wouldn't they be, like, slightly less visible humans?
That you're never 100% sure are really there?
Sort of like when you watch someone swimming underwater: From the surface, she's just a blur.
And if you're beside her, close enough to see,
your eyes are shut tight.

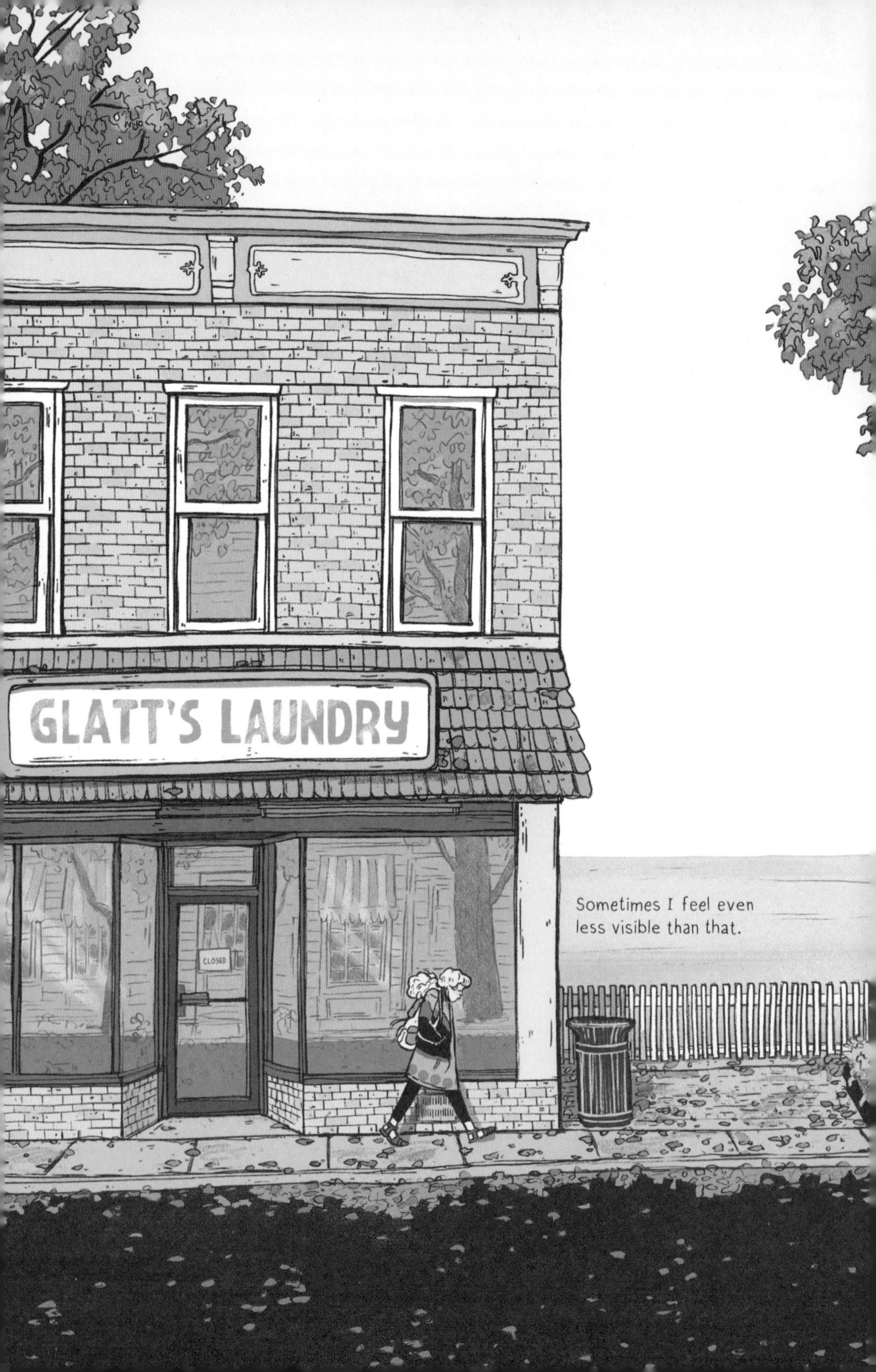
GLATT'S LAUNDRY
CLOSED
Sometimes I feel even less visible than that.

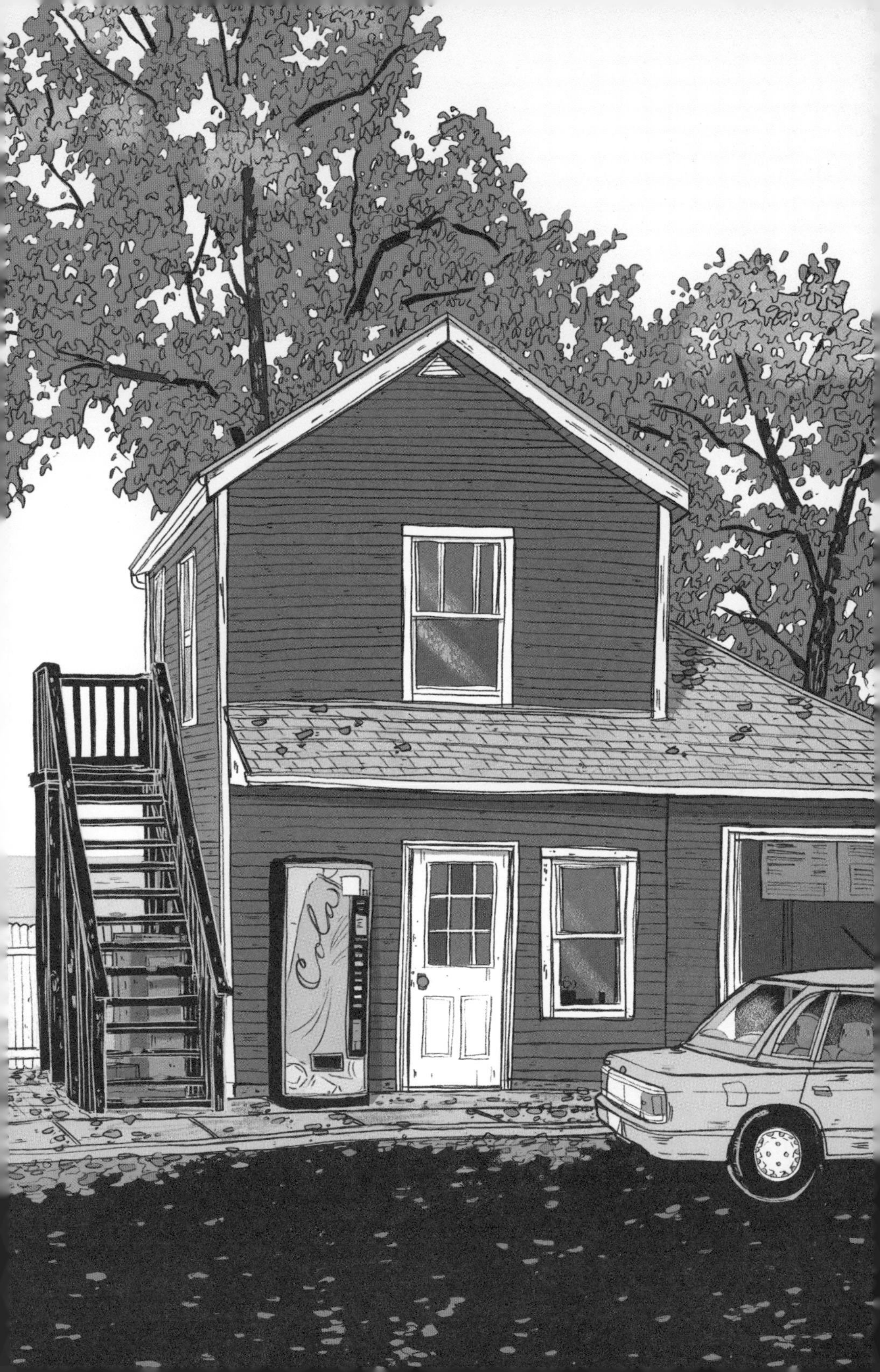
Cola

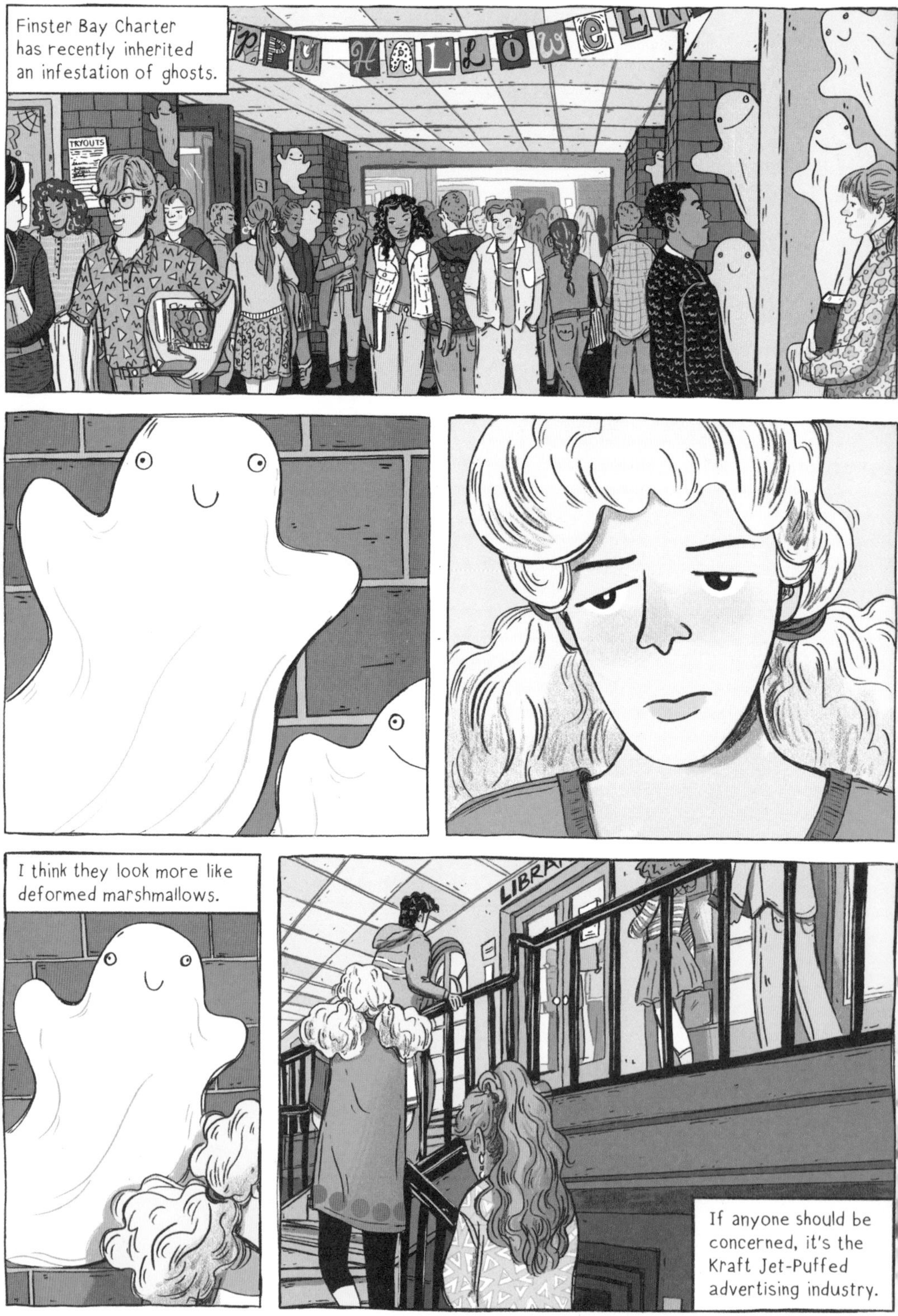
Finster Bay Charter has recently inherited an infestation of ghosts.
HAPPY HALLOWEEN
TRYOUTS
I think they look more like deformed marshmallows.
LIBRA
If anyone should be concerned, it's the Kraft Jet-Puffed advertising industry.

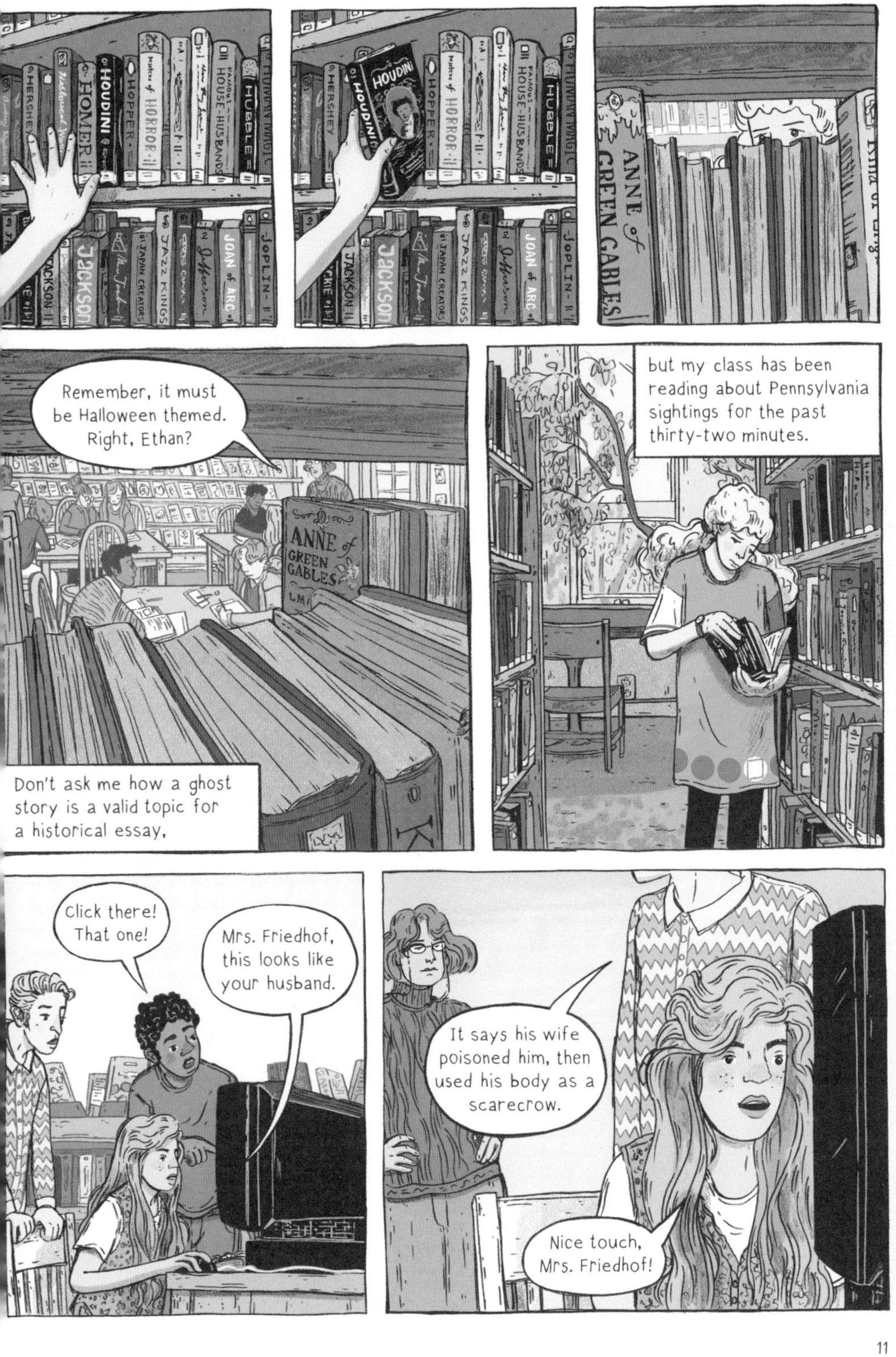
HERSHEY
HOMER
HOUDINI
HOPPER
Masters of HORROR
FAMOUS HOUSE-HUSBANDS
HUBBLE
JACKSON
JAPAN CREATORS
JAZZ KINGS
JOAN of ARC
JOPLIN
ANNE of GREEN GABLES
Remember, it must be Halloween themed. Right, Ethan?
Don't ask me how a ghost story is a valid topic for a historical essay,
but my class has been reading about Pennsylvania sightings for the past thirty-two minutes.
Click there! That one!
Mrs. Friedhof, this looks like your husband.
It says his wife poisoned him, then used his body as a scarecrow.
Nice touch, Mrs. Friedhof!

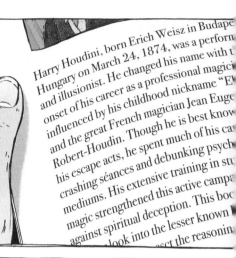

Harry Houdini, born Erich Weisz in Budape Hungary on March 24, 1874, was a perform and illusionist. He changed his name with t onset of his career as a professional magici influenced by his childhood nickname "E and the great French magician Jean Euge Robert-Houdin. Though he is best know his escape acts, he spent much of his ca crashing séances and debunking psych mediums. His extensive training in stu magic strengthened this active campa against spiritual deception. This boo look into the lesser known the reasonin

Harry Houdini died on Halloween, so sure, it's holiday themed.

I'm not interested in Ernie Hempstead, who skulks in corners of the Chestnut Street theater, or the sad granny who can only find pleasure in the afterlife by rearranging her furniture.

Umph!

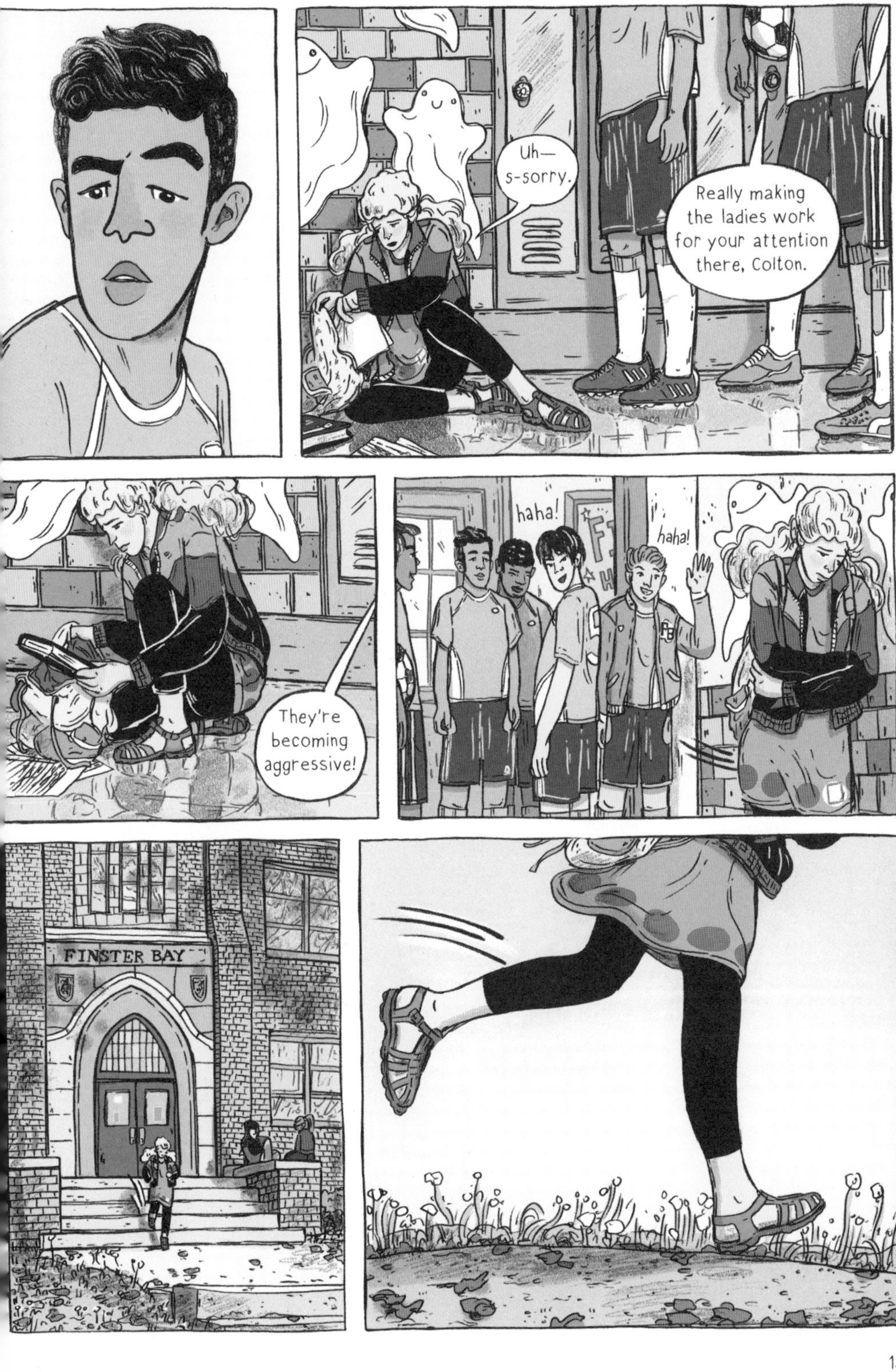

Uh— s-sorry.
Really making the ladies work for your attention there, Colton.
They're becoming aggressive!
haha!
haha!
FINSTER BAY

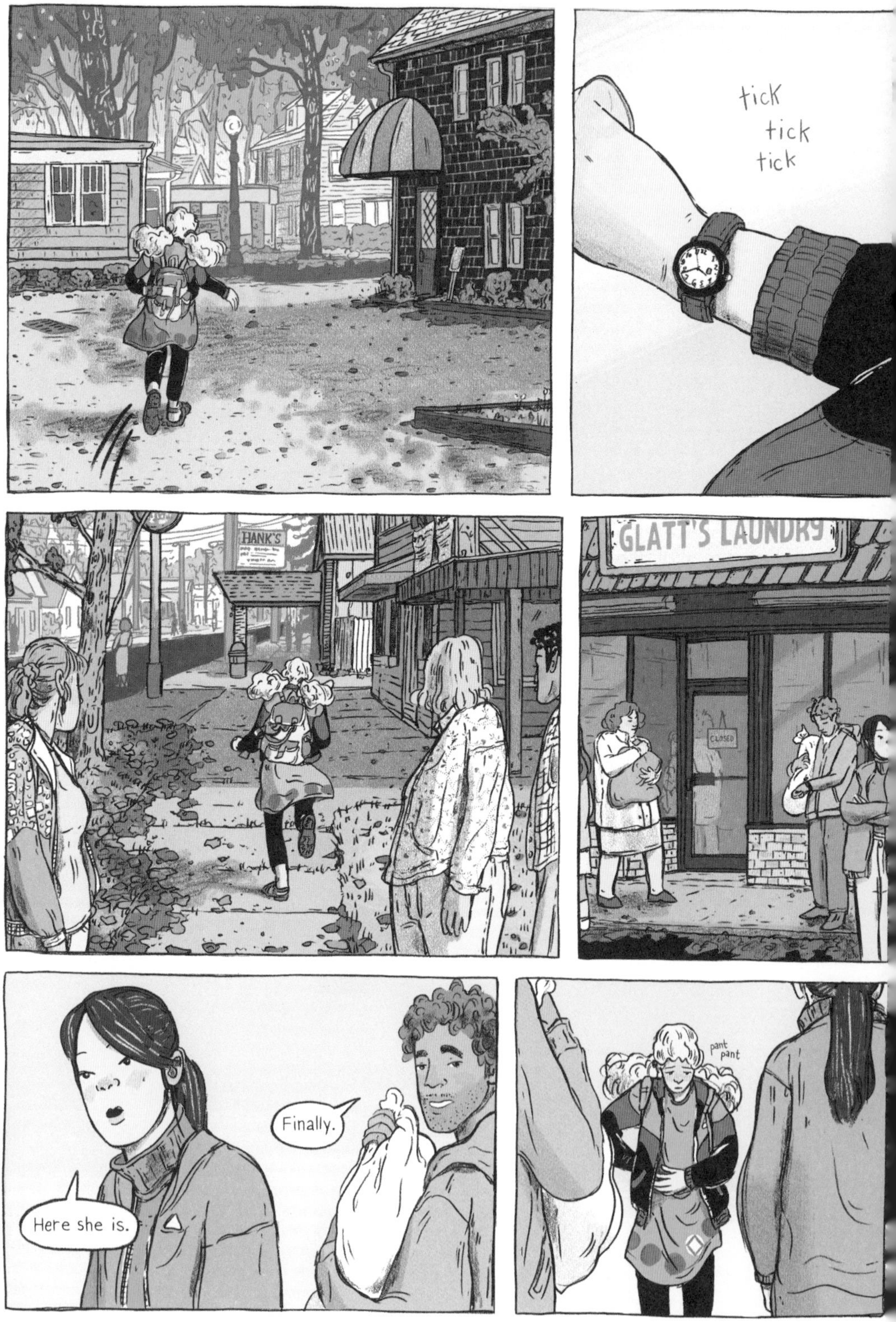
tick
tick
tick
HANK'S
GLATT'S LAUNDRY
CLOSED
Here she is.
Finally.
pant
pant

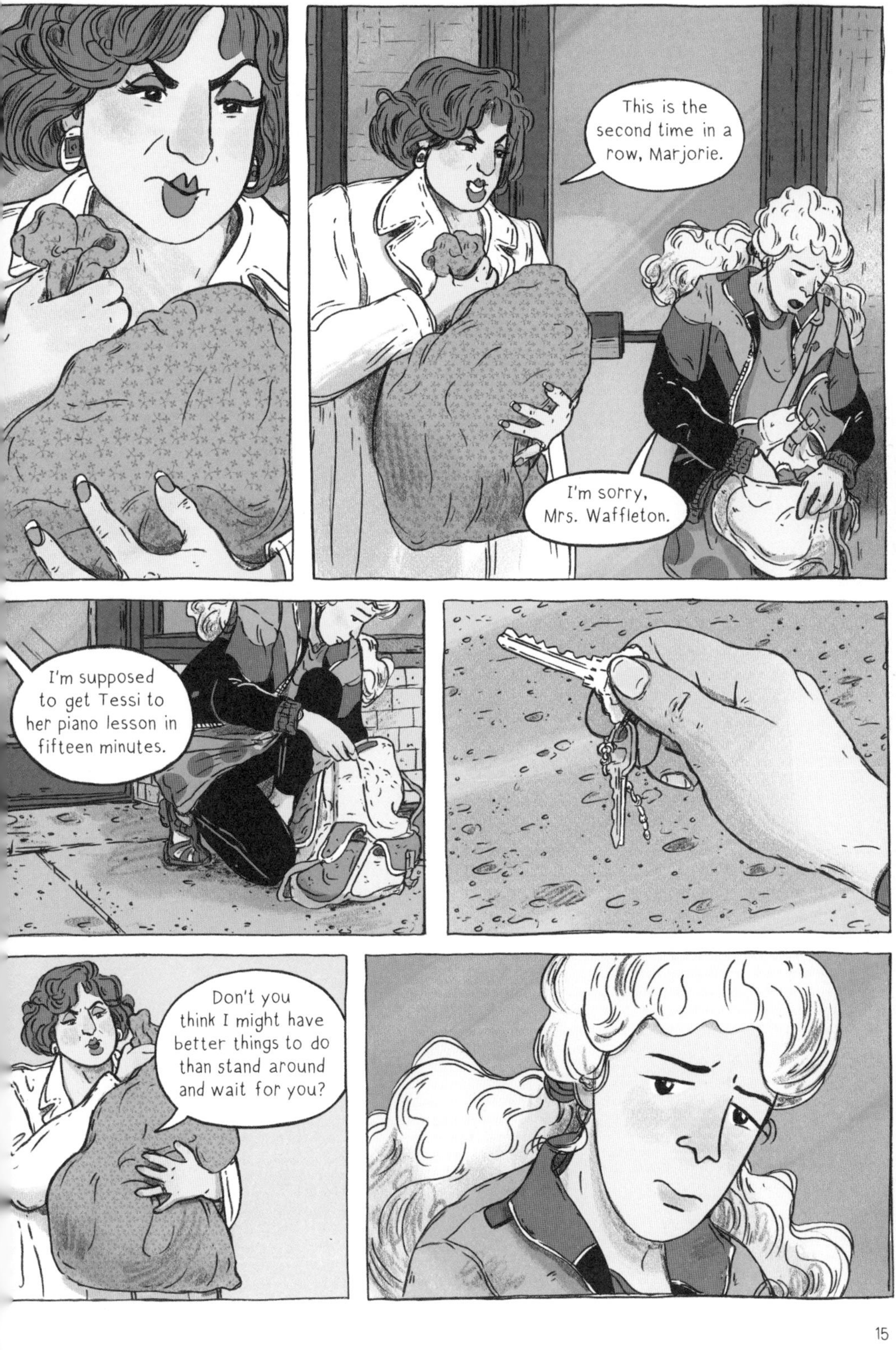
This is the second time in a row, Marjorie.
I'm sorry, Mrs. Waffleton.
I'm supposed to get Tessi to her piano lesson in fifteen minutes.
Don't you think I might have better things to do than stand around and wait for you?

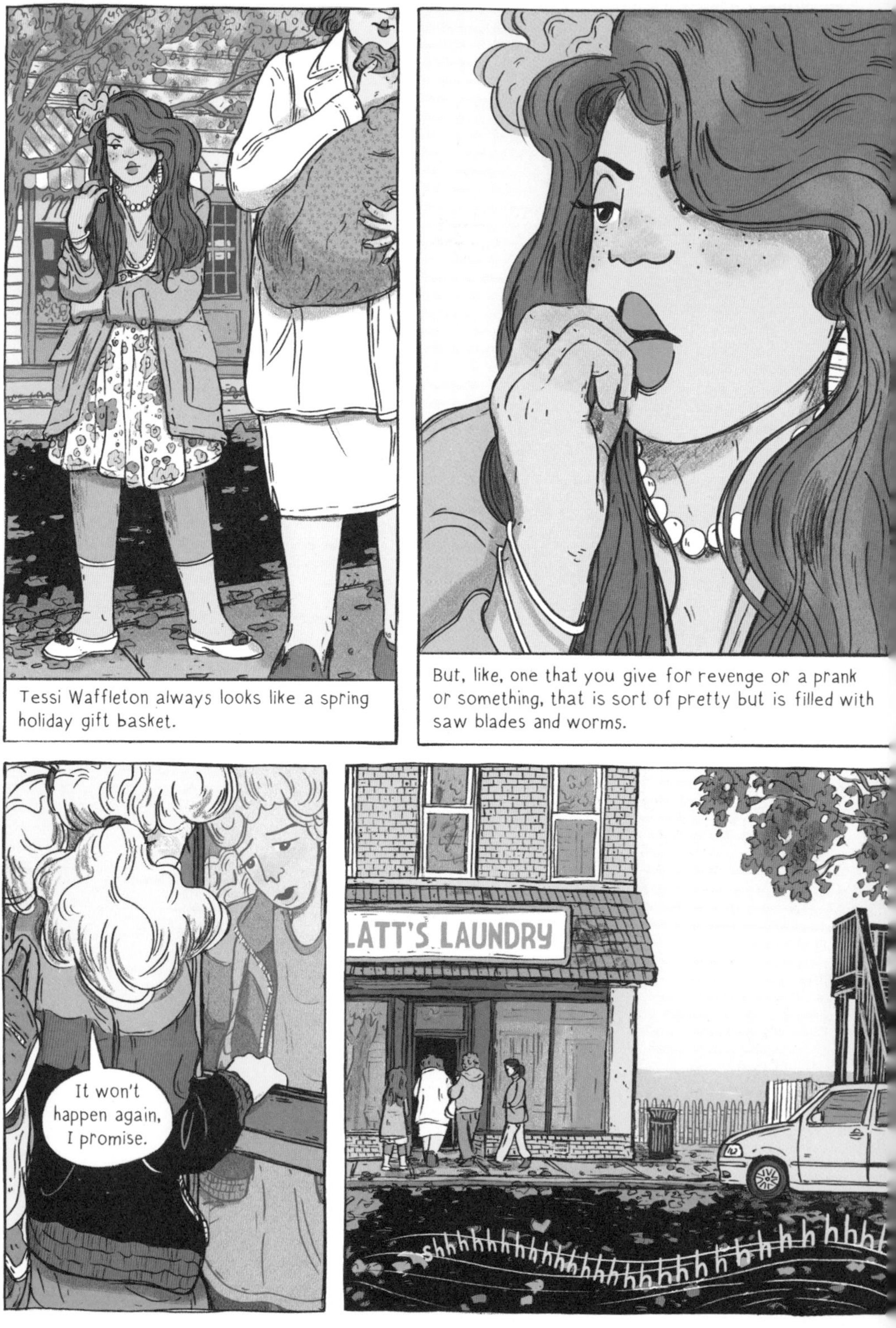
Tessi Waffleton always looks like a spring holiday gift basket.
But, like, one that you give for revenge or a prank or something, that is sort of pretty but is filled with saw blades and worms.
It won't happen again, I promise.
LATT'S LAUNDRY

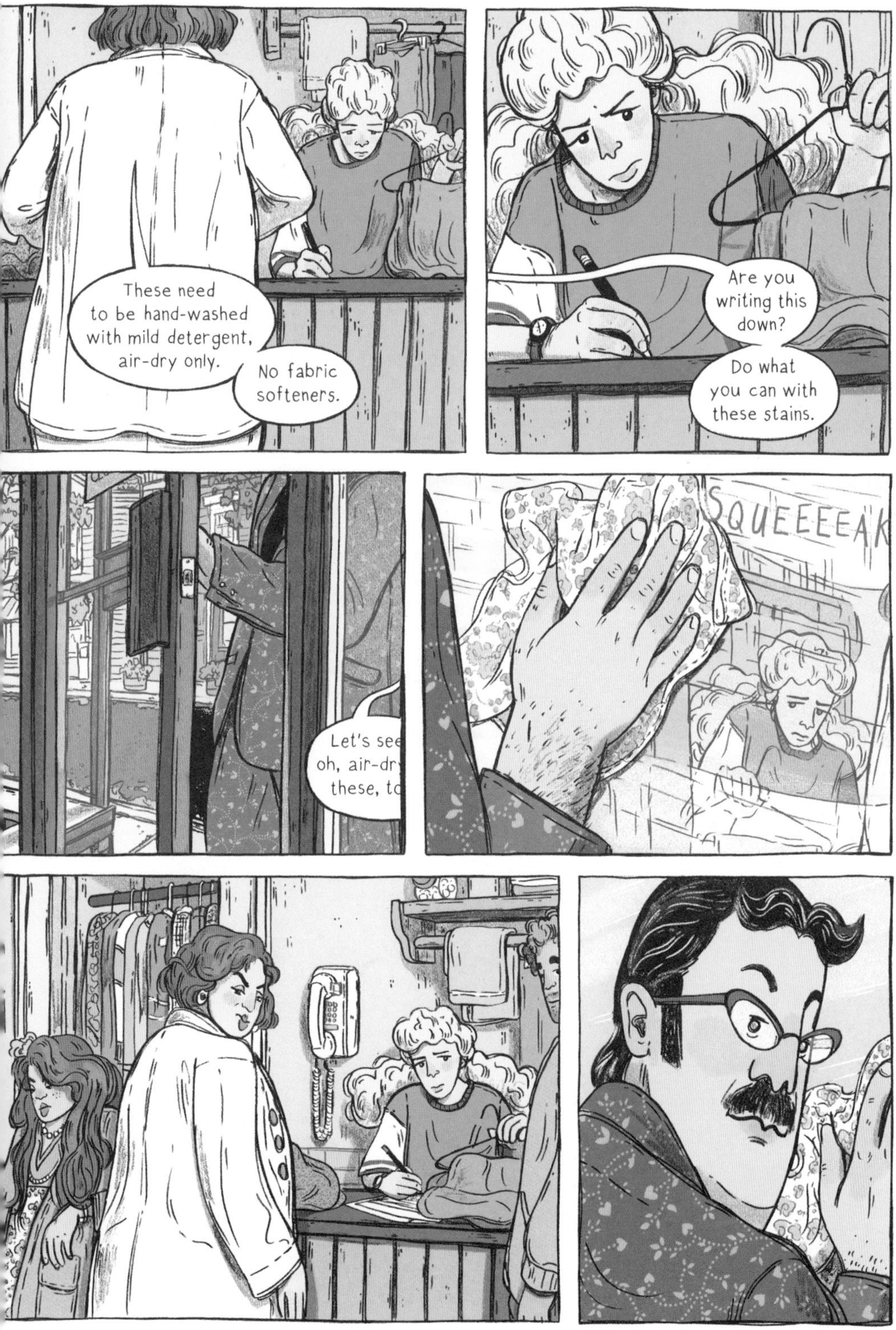
These need to be hand-washed with mild detergent, air-dry only.
No fabric softeners.
Are you writing this down?
Do what you can with these stains.
Let's see
oh, air-dr
these, to
SQUEEEEAK

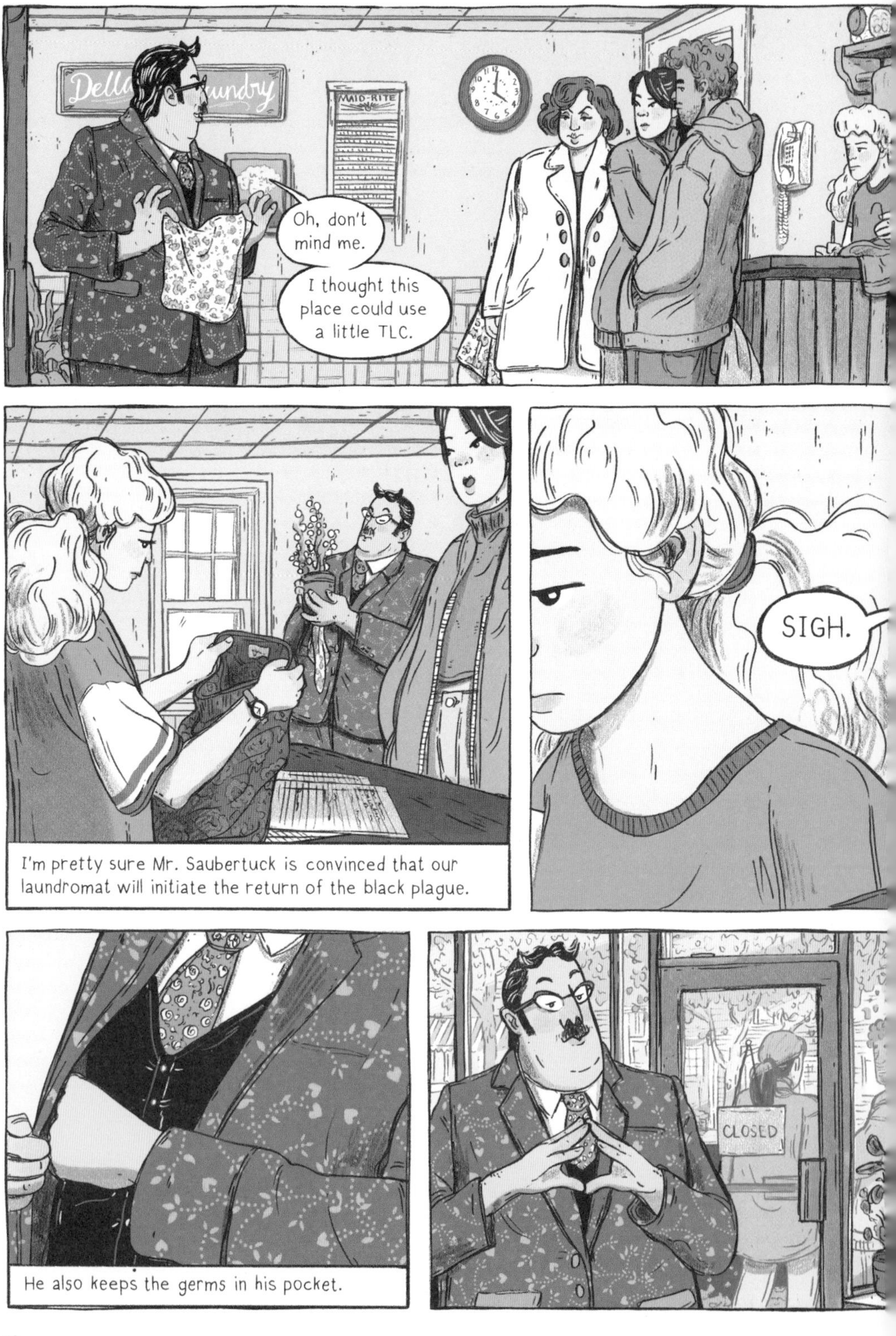
MAID-RITE
Oh, don't mind me.
I thought this place could use a little TLC.
I'm pretty sure Mr. Saubertuck is convinced that our laundromat will initiate the return of the black plague.
SIGH.
He also keeps the germs in his pocket.
CLOSED

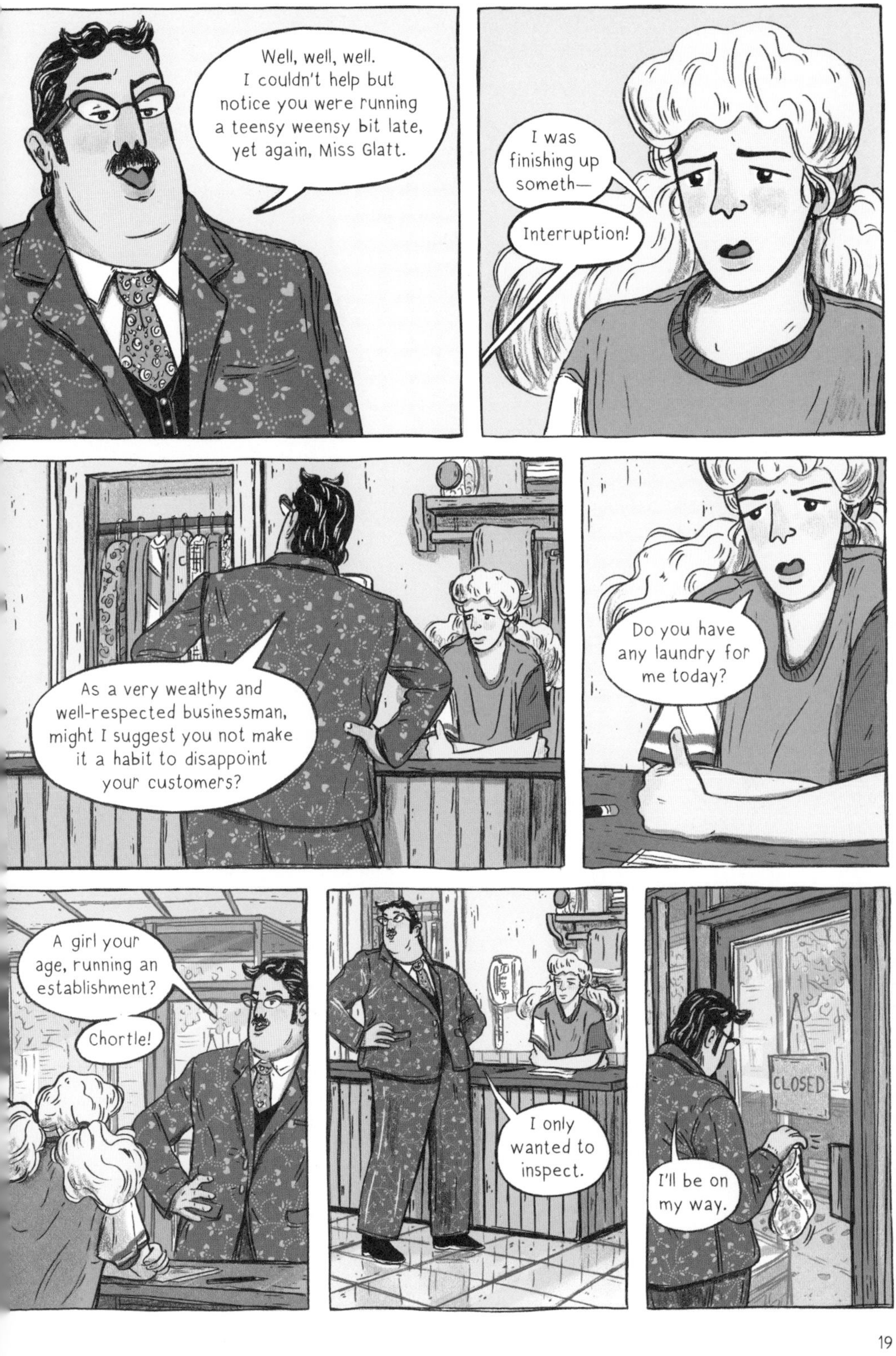
Well, well, well. I couldn't help but notice you were running a teensy weensy bit late, yet again, Miss Glatt.
I was finishing up someth—
Interruption!
As a very wealthy and well-respected businessman, might I suggest you not make it a habit to disappoint your customers?
Do you have any laundry for me today?
A girl your age, running an establishment?
Chortle!
I only wanted to inspect.
CLOSED
I'll be on my way.

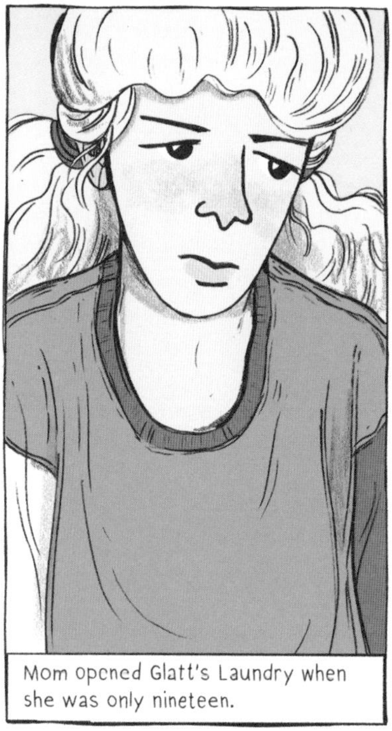
Mom opened Glatt's Laundry when she was only nineteen.

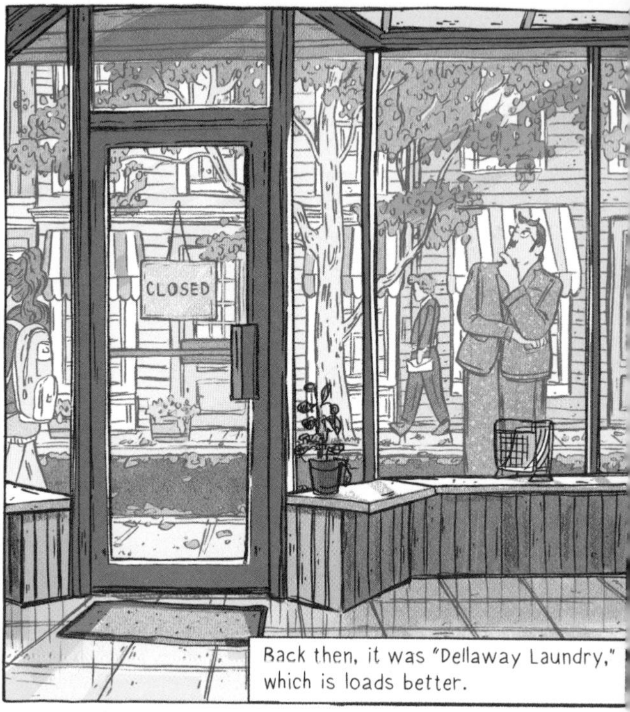
CLOSED
Back then, it was "Dellaway Laundry," which is loads better.

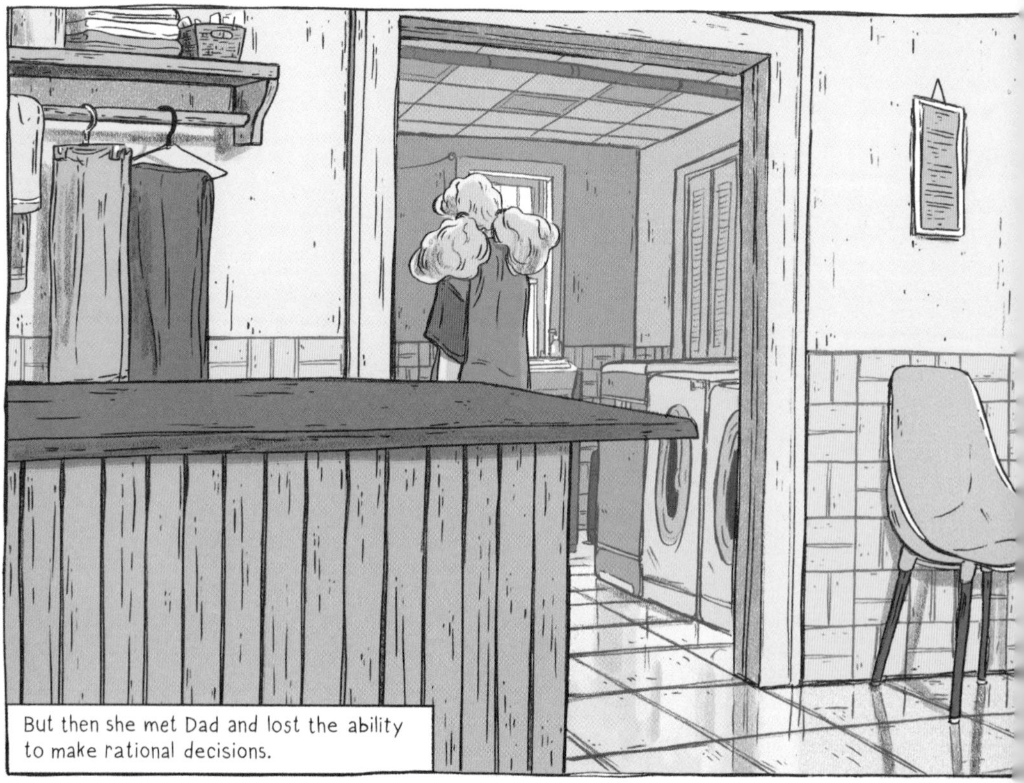
But then she met Dad and lost the ability to make rational decisions.

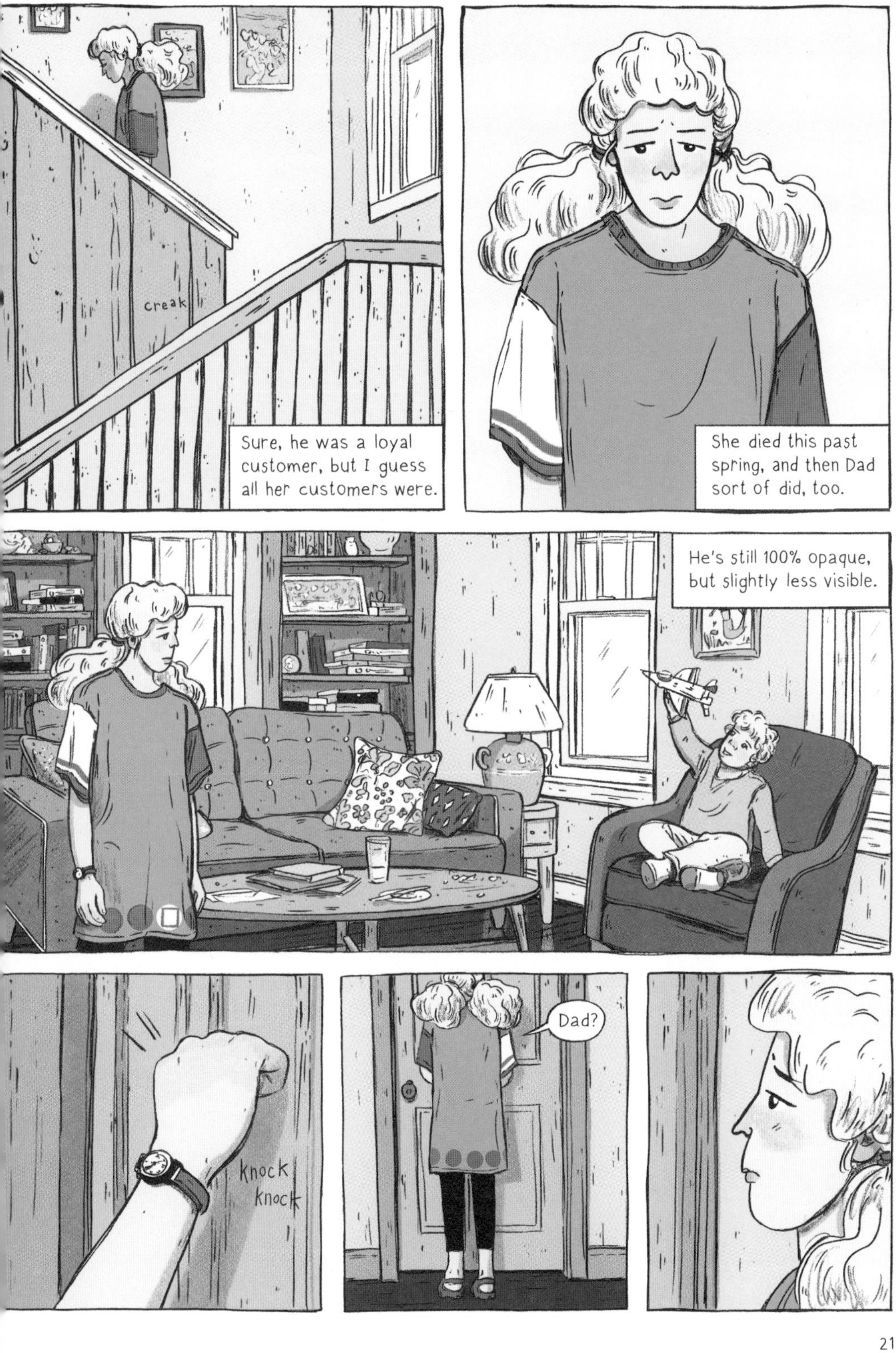
creak
Sure, he was a loyal customer, but I guess all her customers were.
She died this past spring, and then Dad sort of did, too.
He's still 100% opaque, but slightly less visible.
knock knock
Dad?

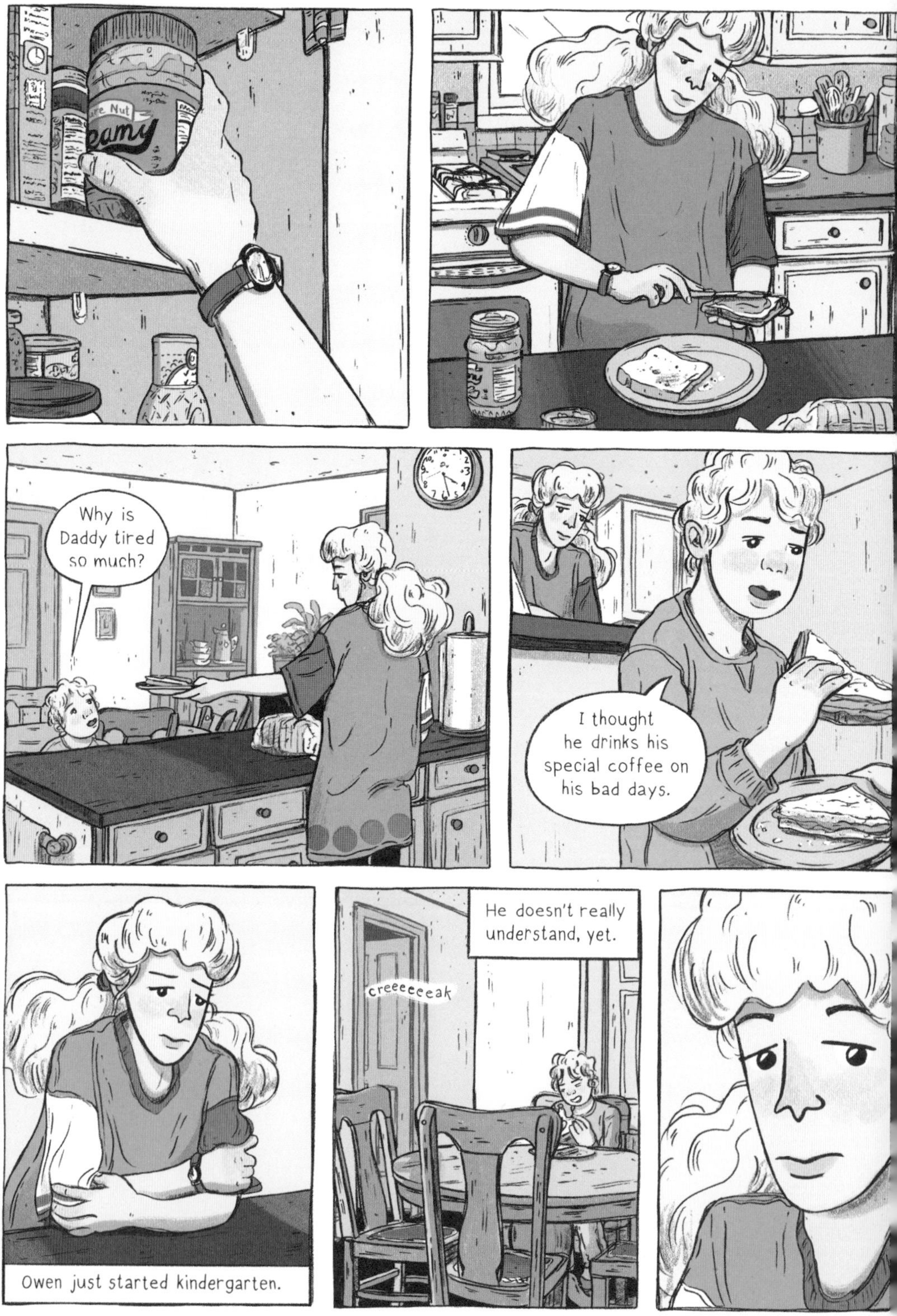
Why is Daddy tired so much?
I thought he drinks his special coffee on his bad days.
Owen just started kindergarten.
He doesn't really understand, yet.
creeeeeeak

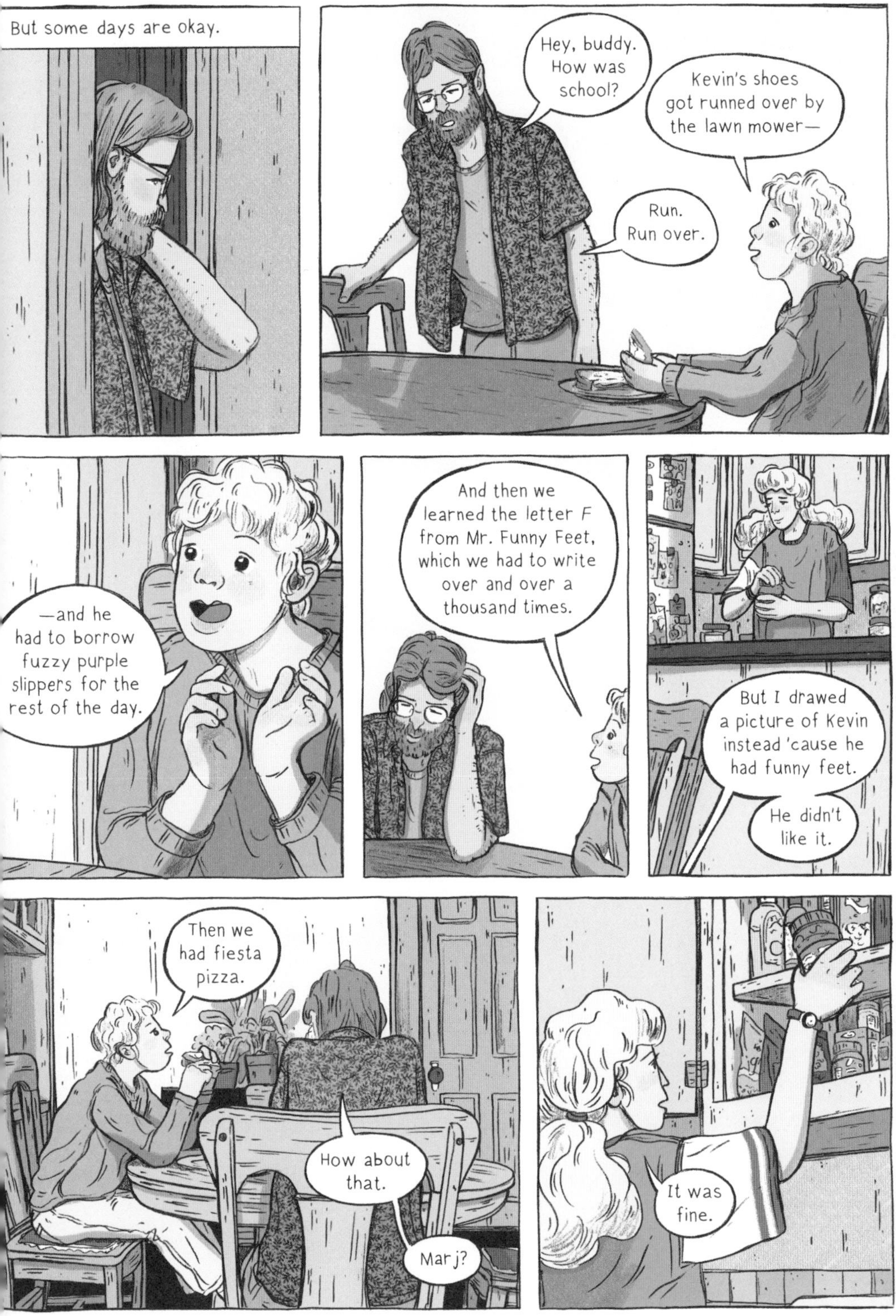

But some days are okay.
Hey, buddy. How was school?
Kevin's shoes got runned over by the lawn mower—
Run. Run over.
—and he had to borrow fuzzy purple slippers for the rest of the day.
And then we learned the letter F from Mr. Funny Feet, which we had to write over and over a thousand times.
But I drawed a picture of Kevin instead 'cause he had funny feet.
He didn't like it.
Then we had fiesta pizza.
How about that.
Marj?
It was fine.

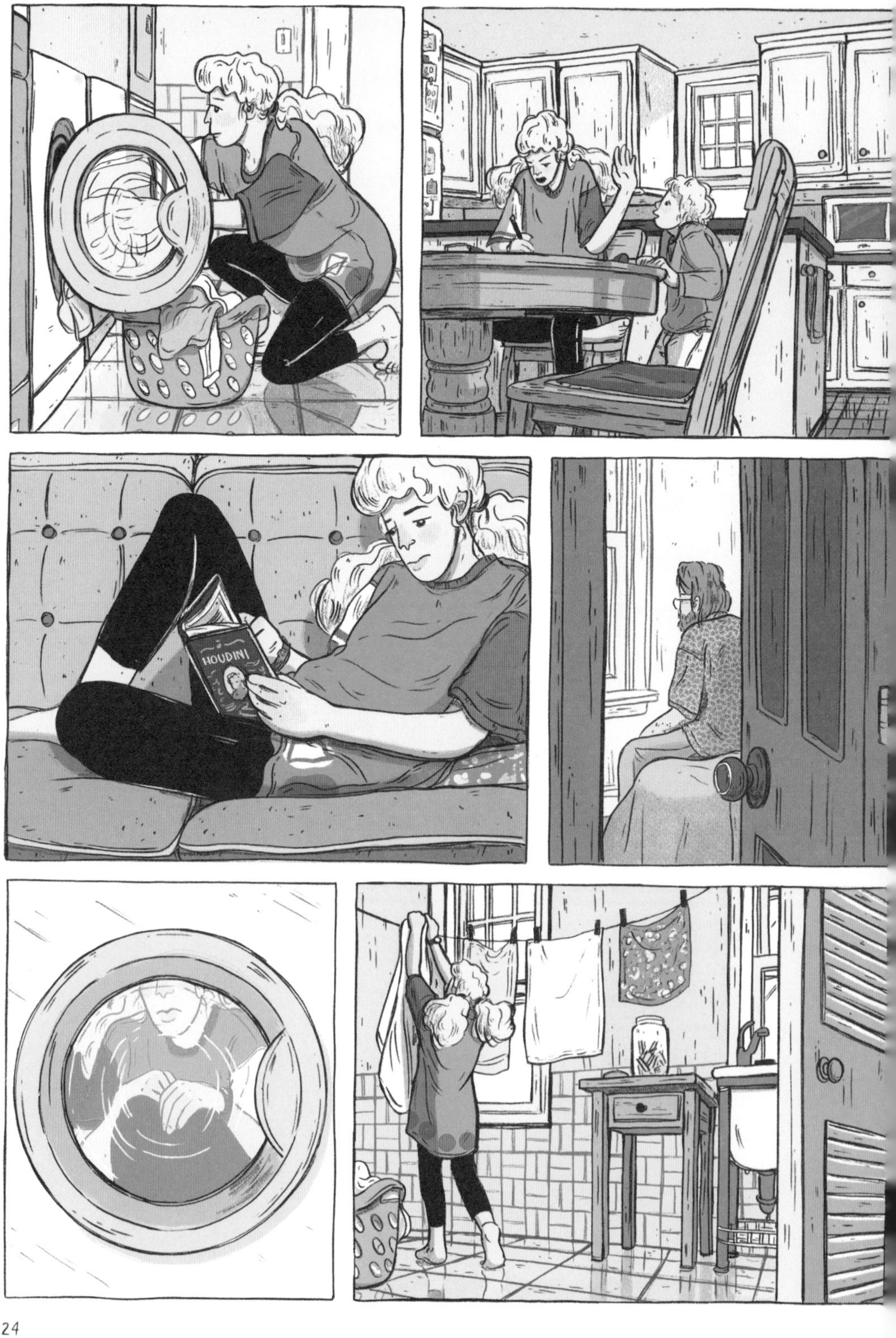
HOUDINI

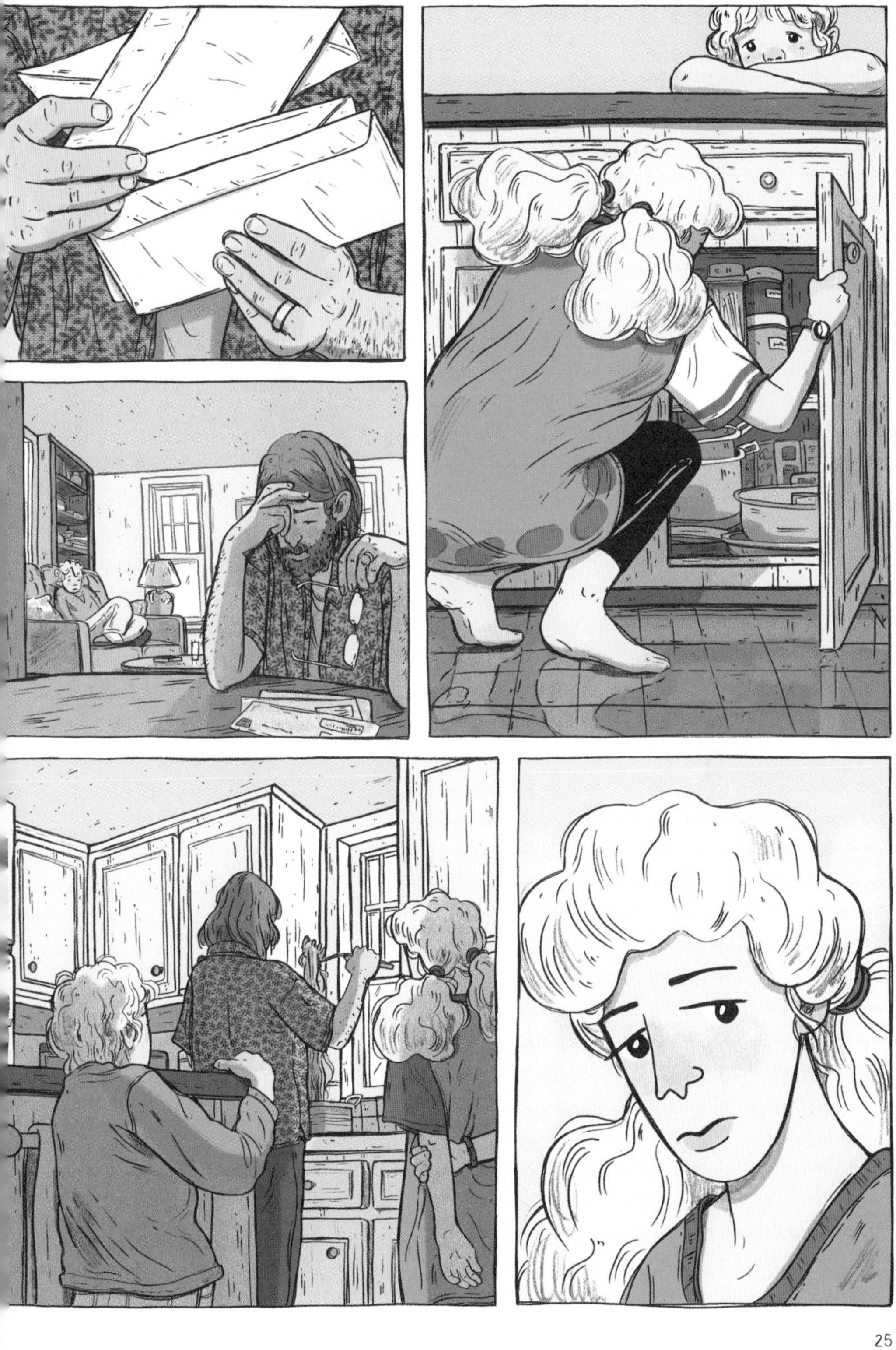

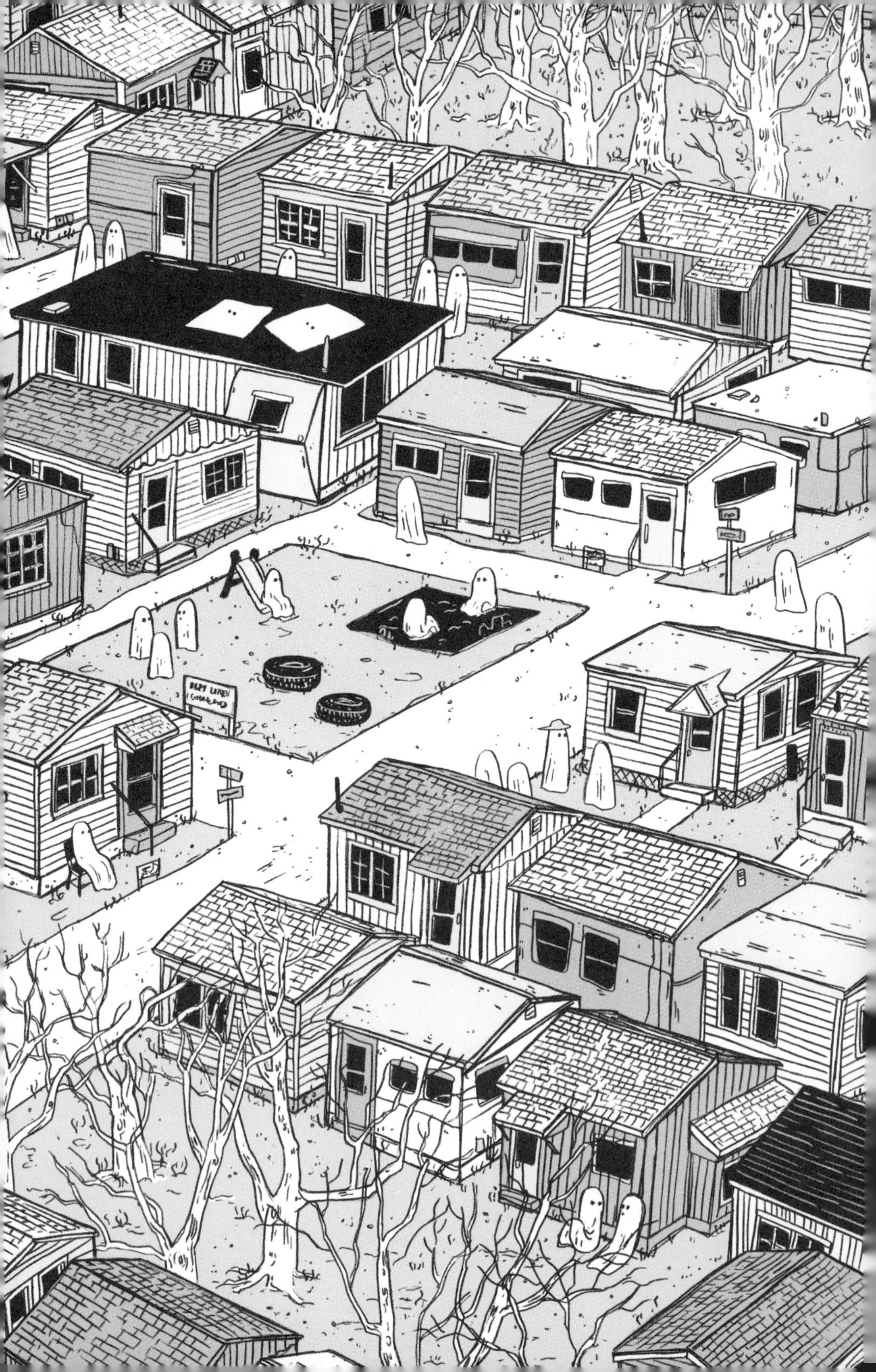

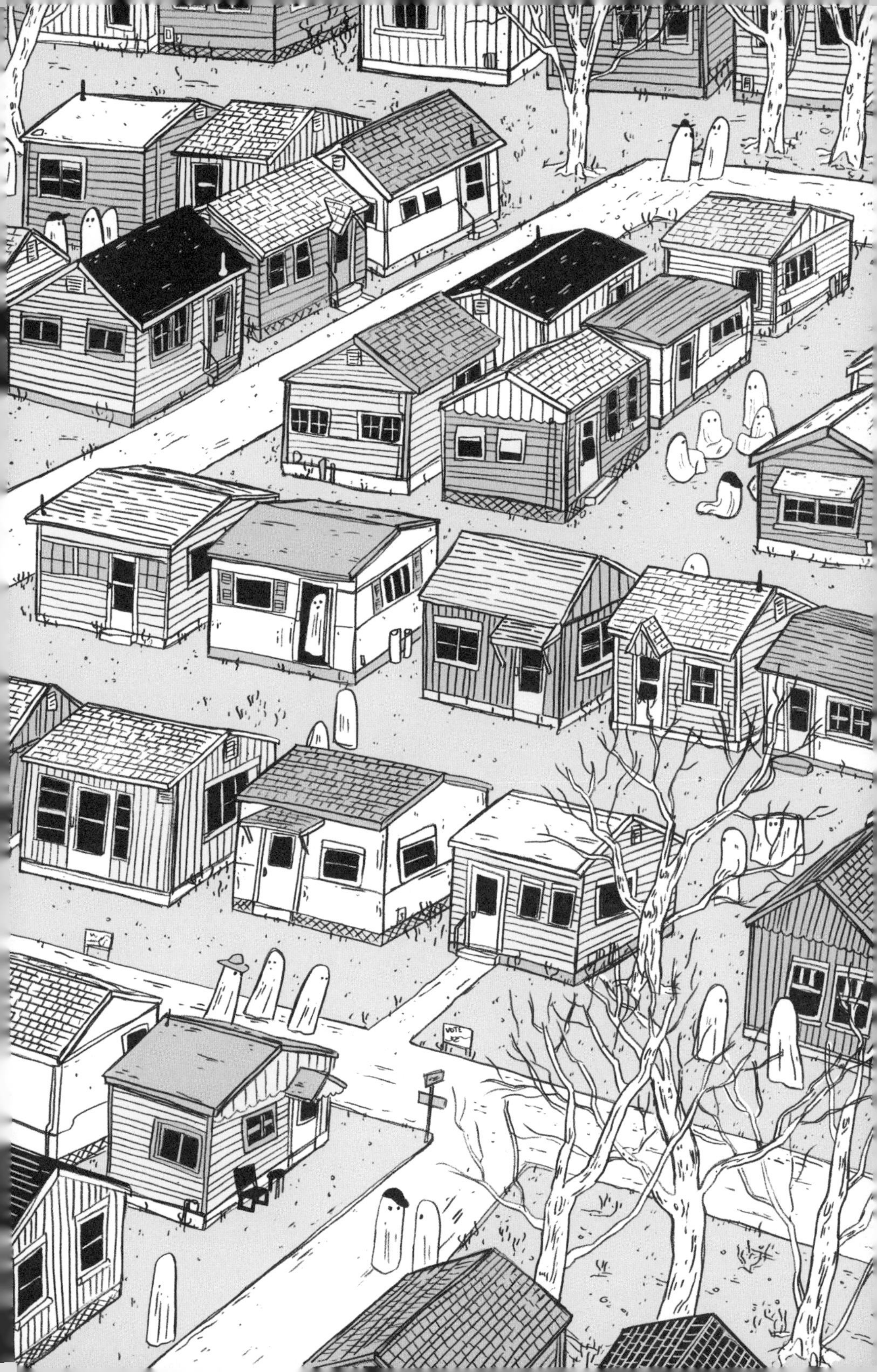
VOTE

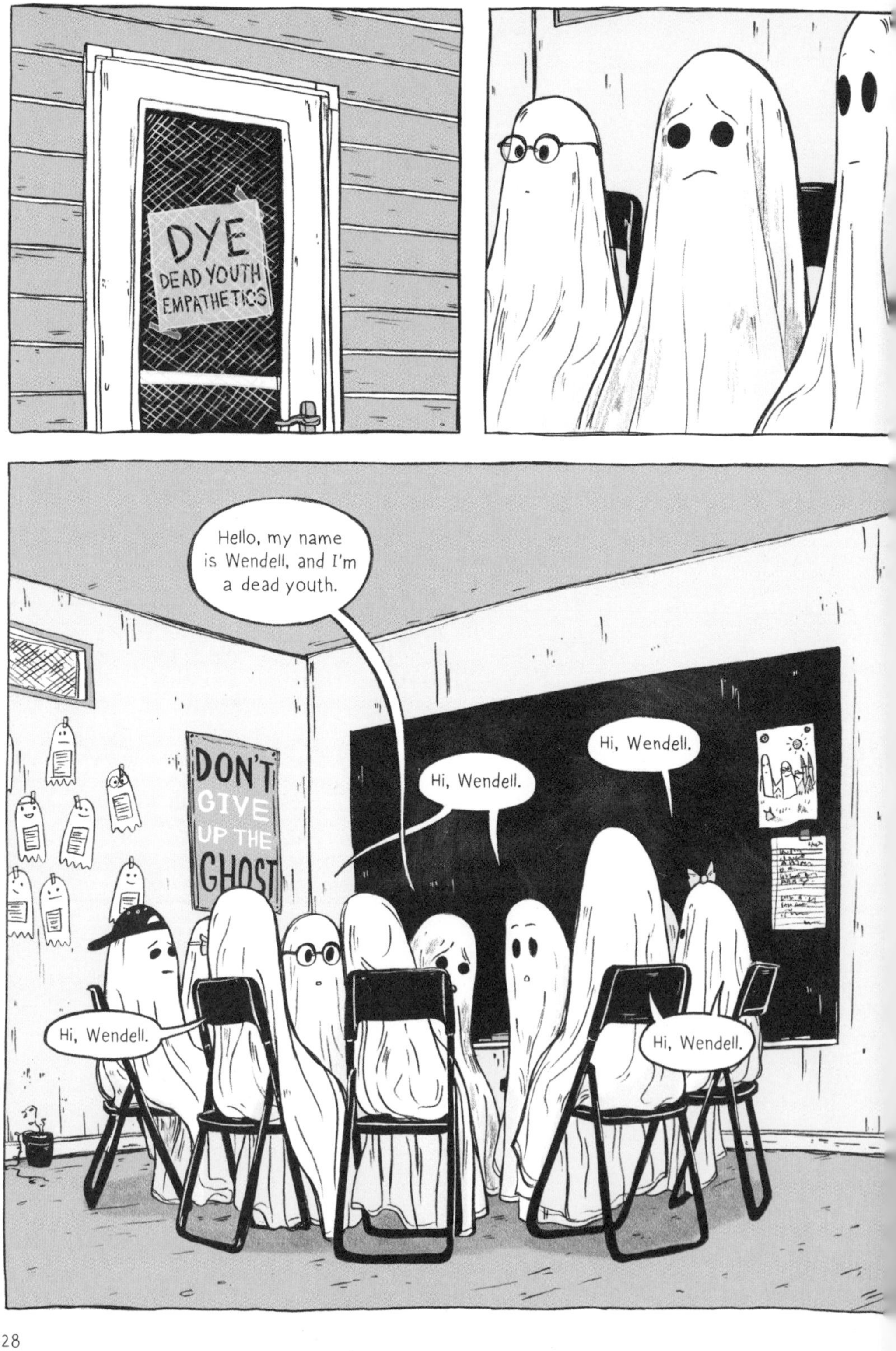

DYE
DEAD YOUTH
EMPATHETICS
Hello, my name is Wendell, and I'm a dead youth.
DON'T GIVE UP THE GHOST
Hi, Wendell.
Hi, Wendell.
Hi, Wendell.
Hi, Wendell.

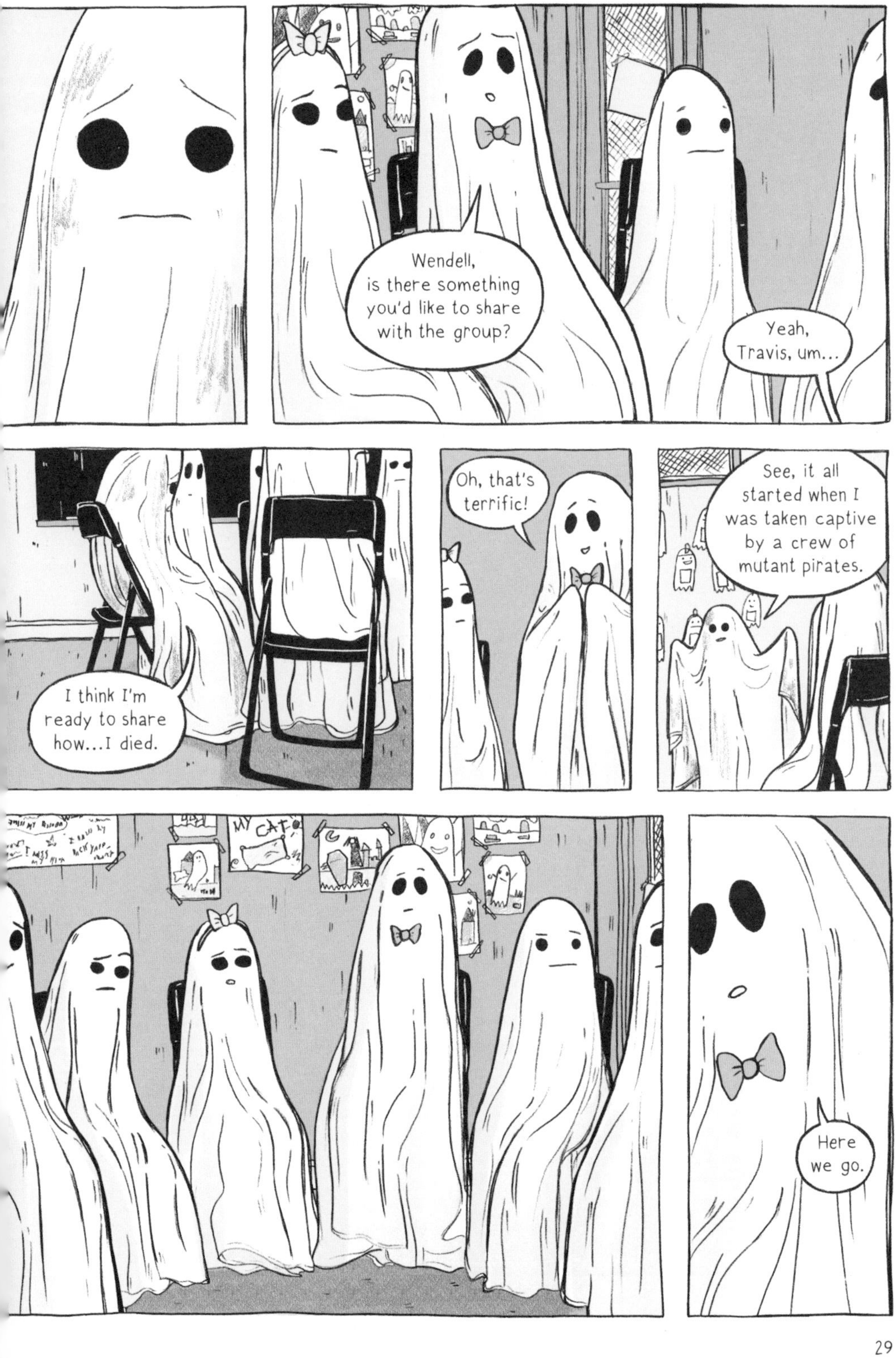
Wendell, is there something you'd like to share with the group?
Yeah, Travis, um...
I think I'm ready to share how...I died.
Oh, that's terrific!
See, it all started when I was taken captive by a crew of mutant pirates.
MY CAT
Here we go.

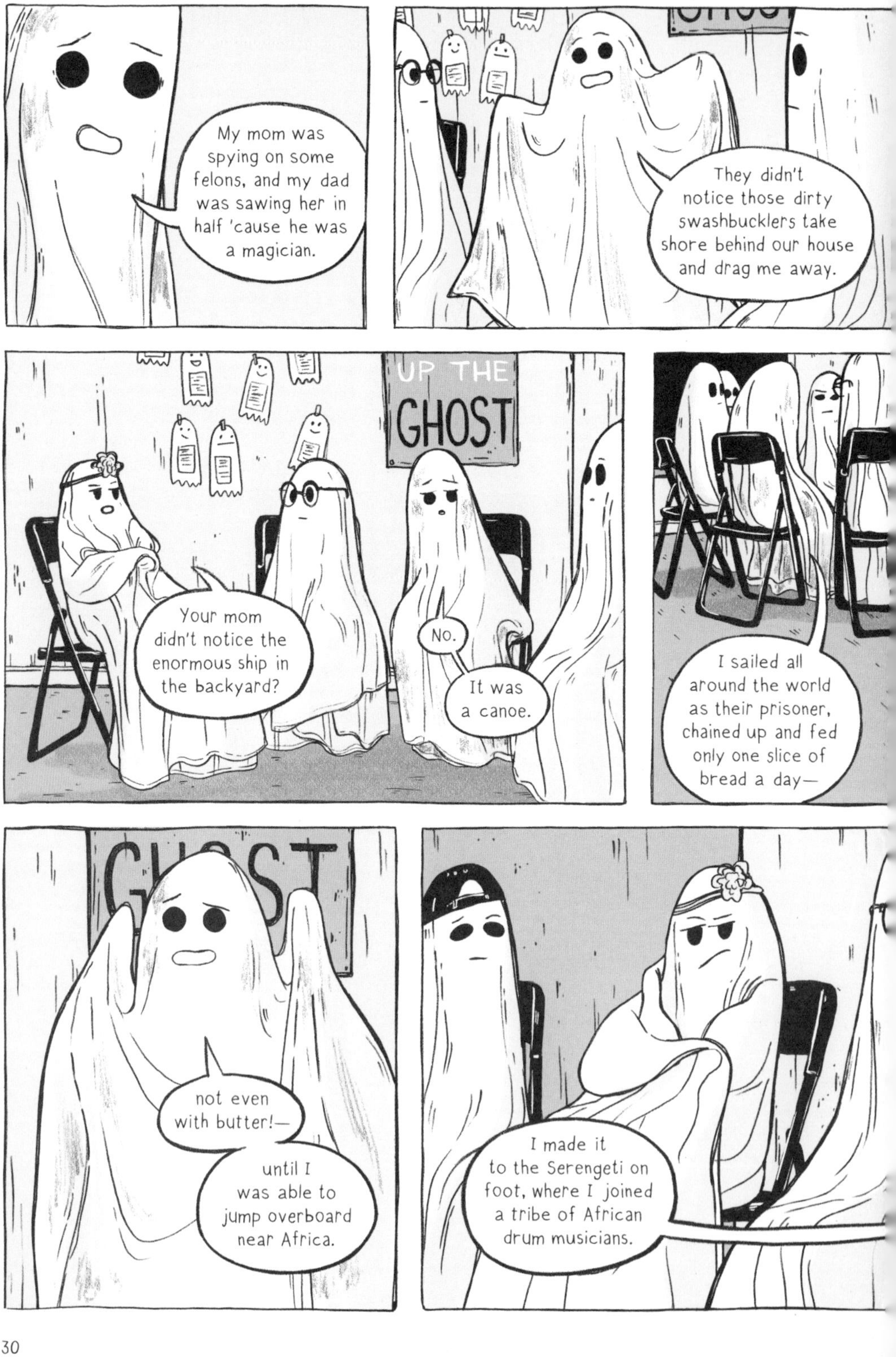
My mom was spying on some felons, and my dad was sawing her in half 'cause he was a magician.
They didn't notice those dirty swashbucklers take shore behind our house and drag me away.
UP THE GHOST
Your mom didn't notice the enormous ship in the backyard?
No.
It was a canoe.
I sailed all around the world as their prisoner, chained up and fed only one slice of bread a day—
not even with butter!—
until I was able to jump overboard near Africa.
I made it to the Serengeti on foot, where I joined a tribe of African drum musicians.

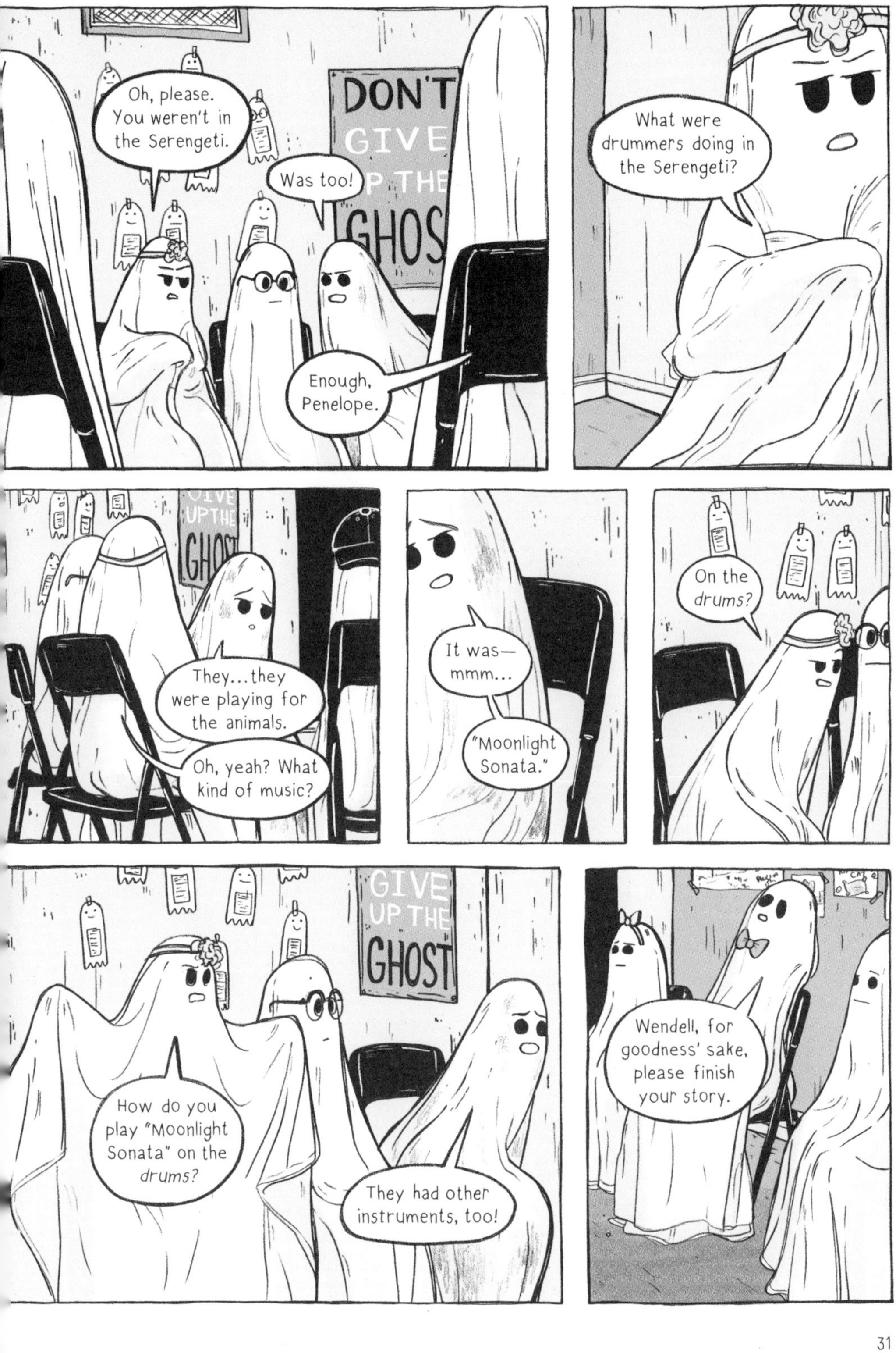
Oh, please. You weren't in the Serengeti.
Was too!
DON'T GIVE UP THE GHOST
Enough, Penelope.
What were drummers doing in the Serengeti?
They...they were playing for the animals.
Oh, yeah? What kind of music?
It was— mmm...
"Moonlight Sonata."
On the *drums?*
GIVE UP THE GHOST
How do you play "Moonlight Sonata" on the *drums?*
They had other instruments, too!
Wendell, for goodness' sake, please finish your story.

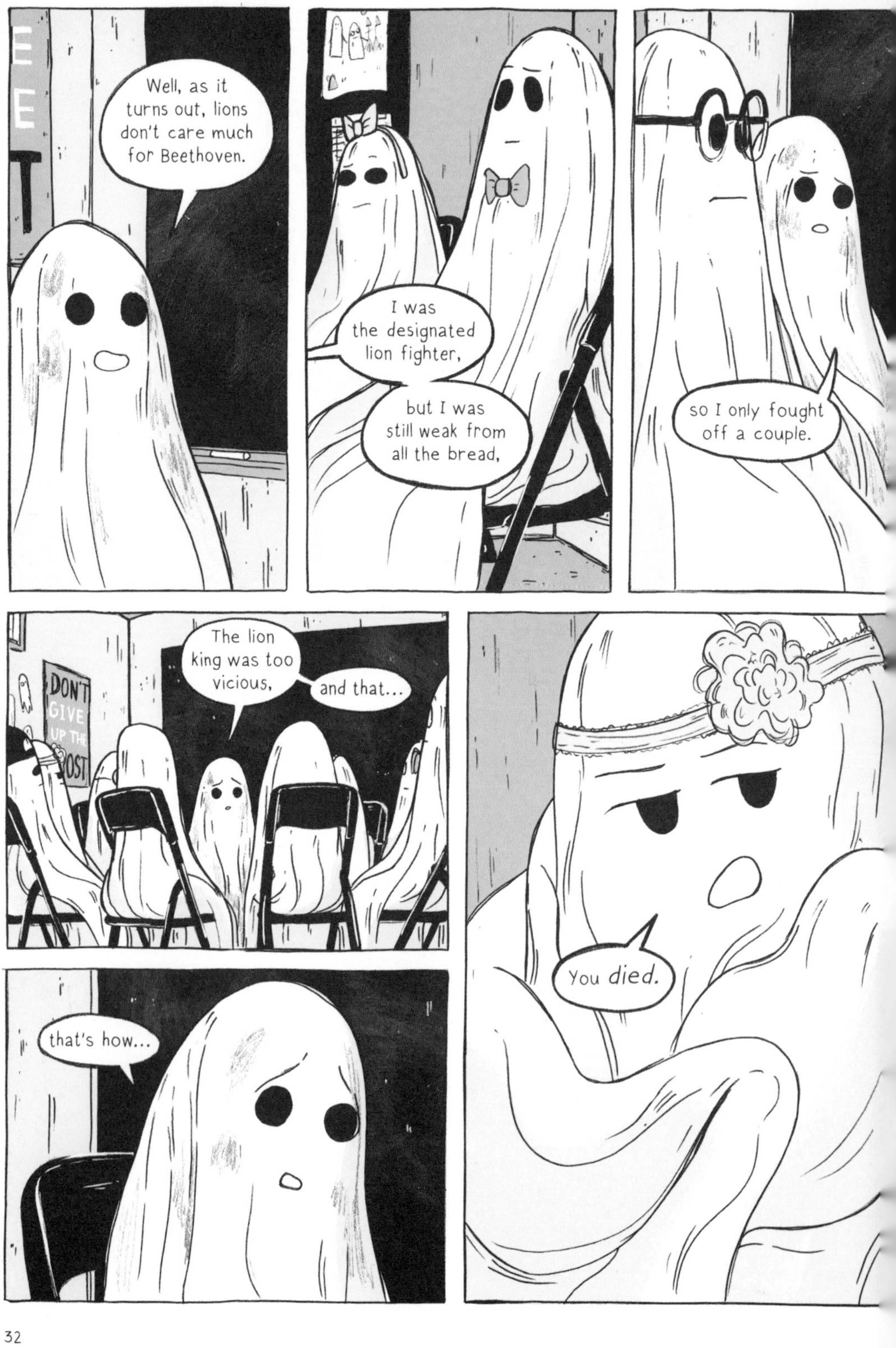

E
E
T
Well, as it turns out, lions don't care much for Beethoven.
I was the designated lion fighter,
but I was still weak from all the bread,
so I only fought off a couple.
DON'T GIVE UP THE GHOST
The lion king was too vicious,
and that...
that's how...
You died.

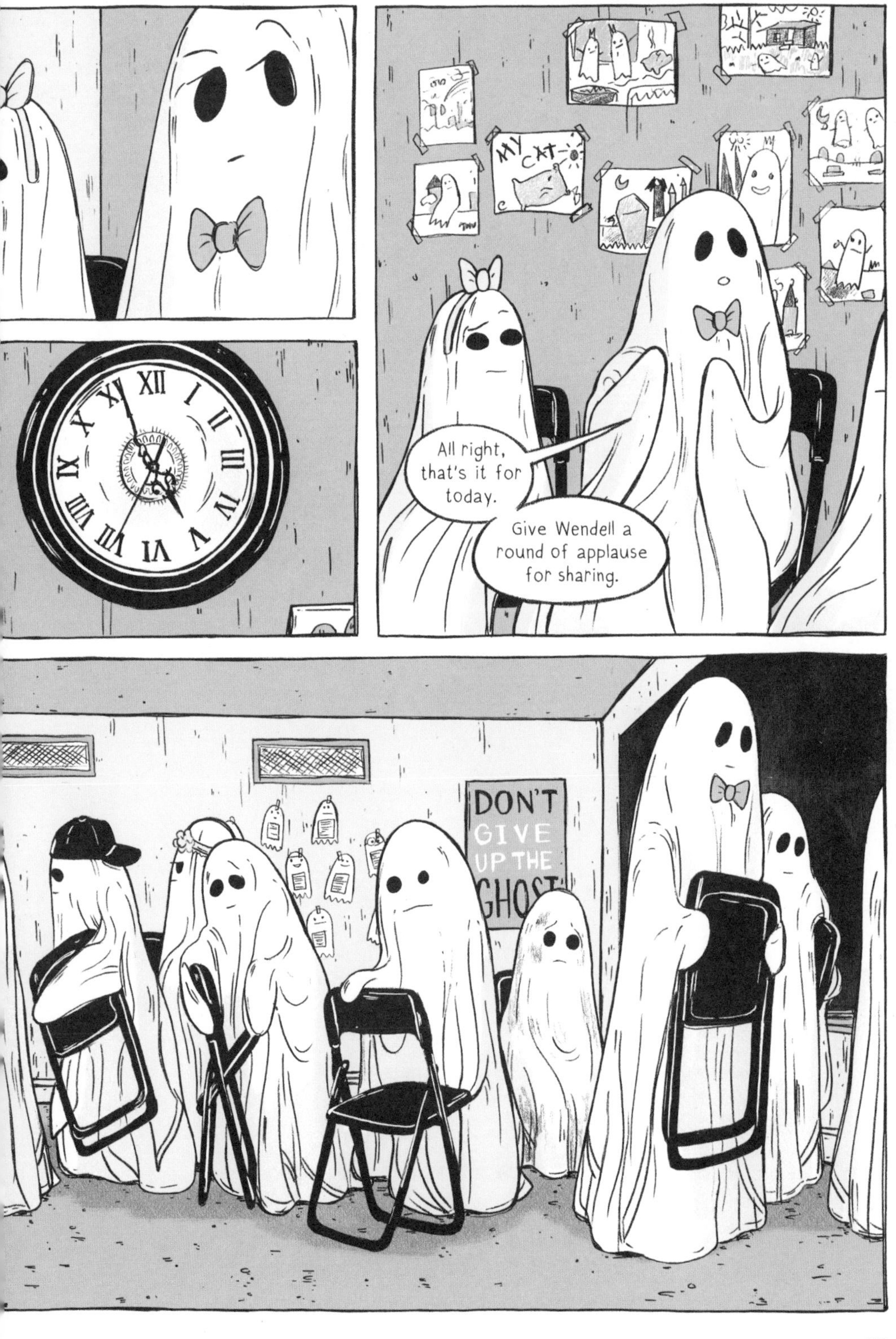
MY CAT
All right, that's it for today.
Give Wendell a round of applause for sharing.
DON'T GIVE UP THE GHOST

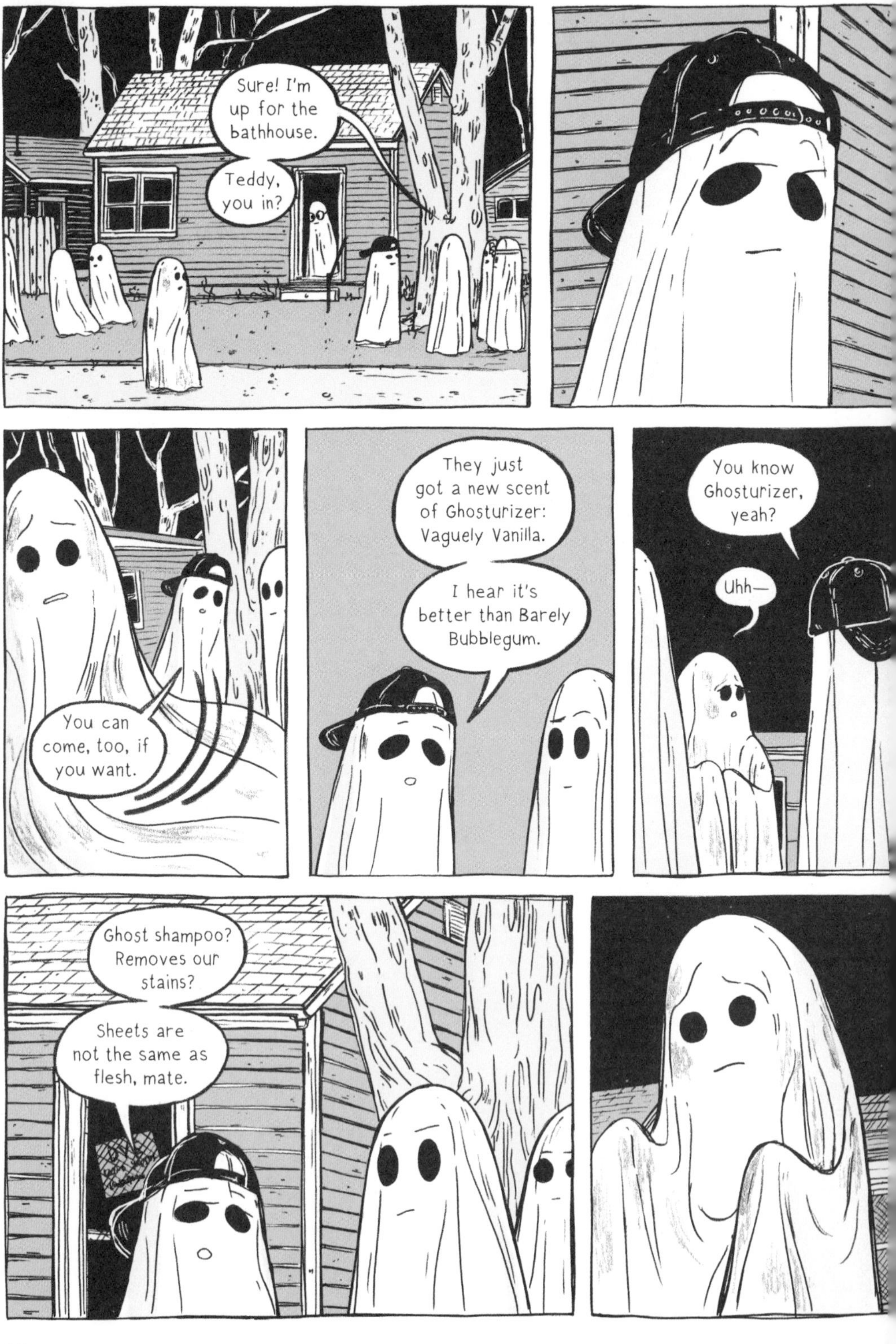
Sure! I'm up for the bathhouse.
Teddy, you in?
You can come, too, if you want.
They just got a new scent of Ghosturizer: Vaguely Vanilla.
I hear it's better than Barely Bubblegum.
You know Ghosturizer, yeah?
Uhh—
Ghost shampoo? Removes our stains?
Sheets are not the same as flesh, mate.

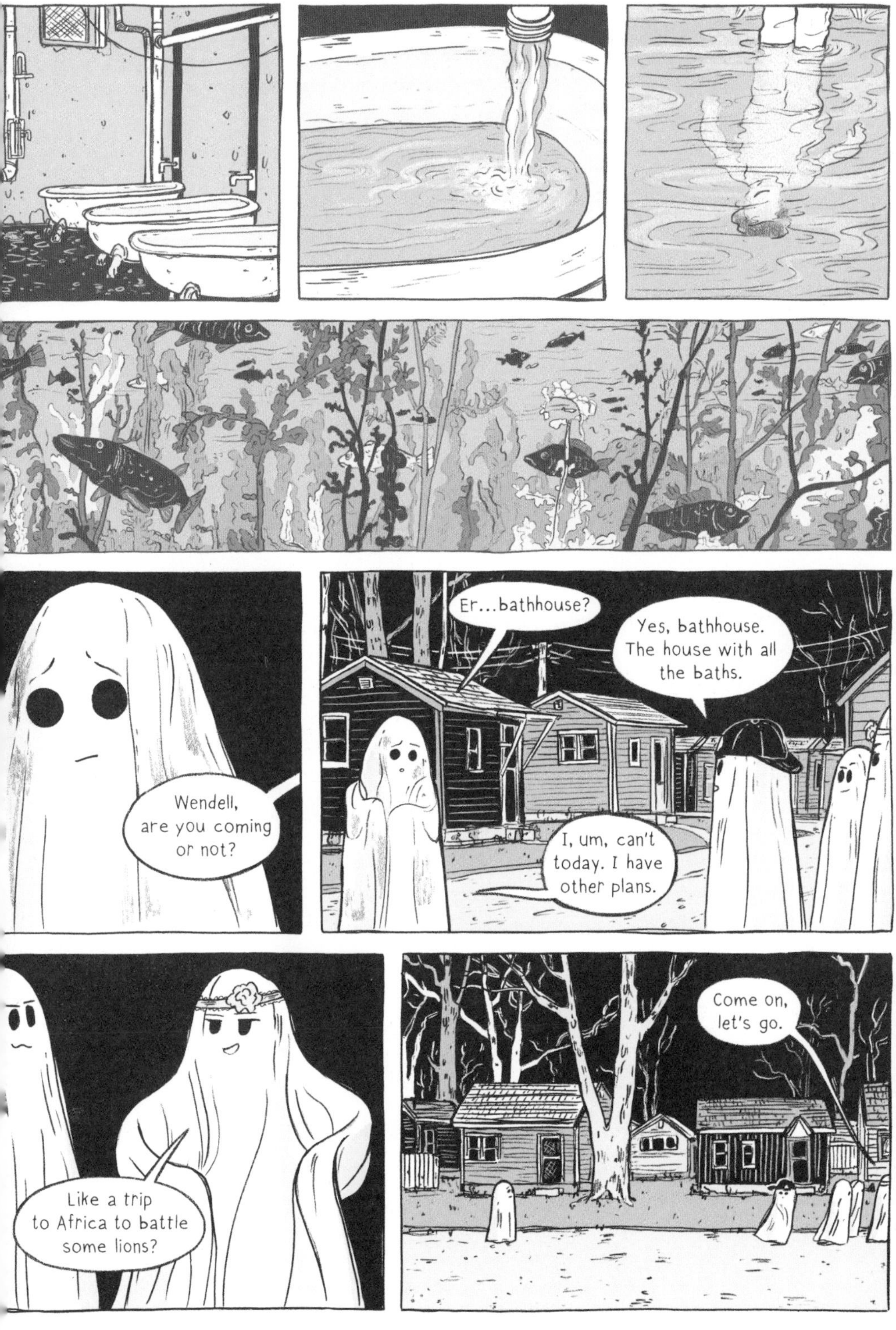
Wendell, are you coming or not?
Er...bathhouse?
Yes, bathhouse. The house with all the baths.
I, um, can't today. I have other plans.
Like a trip to Africa to battle some lions?
Come on, let's go.

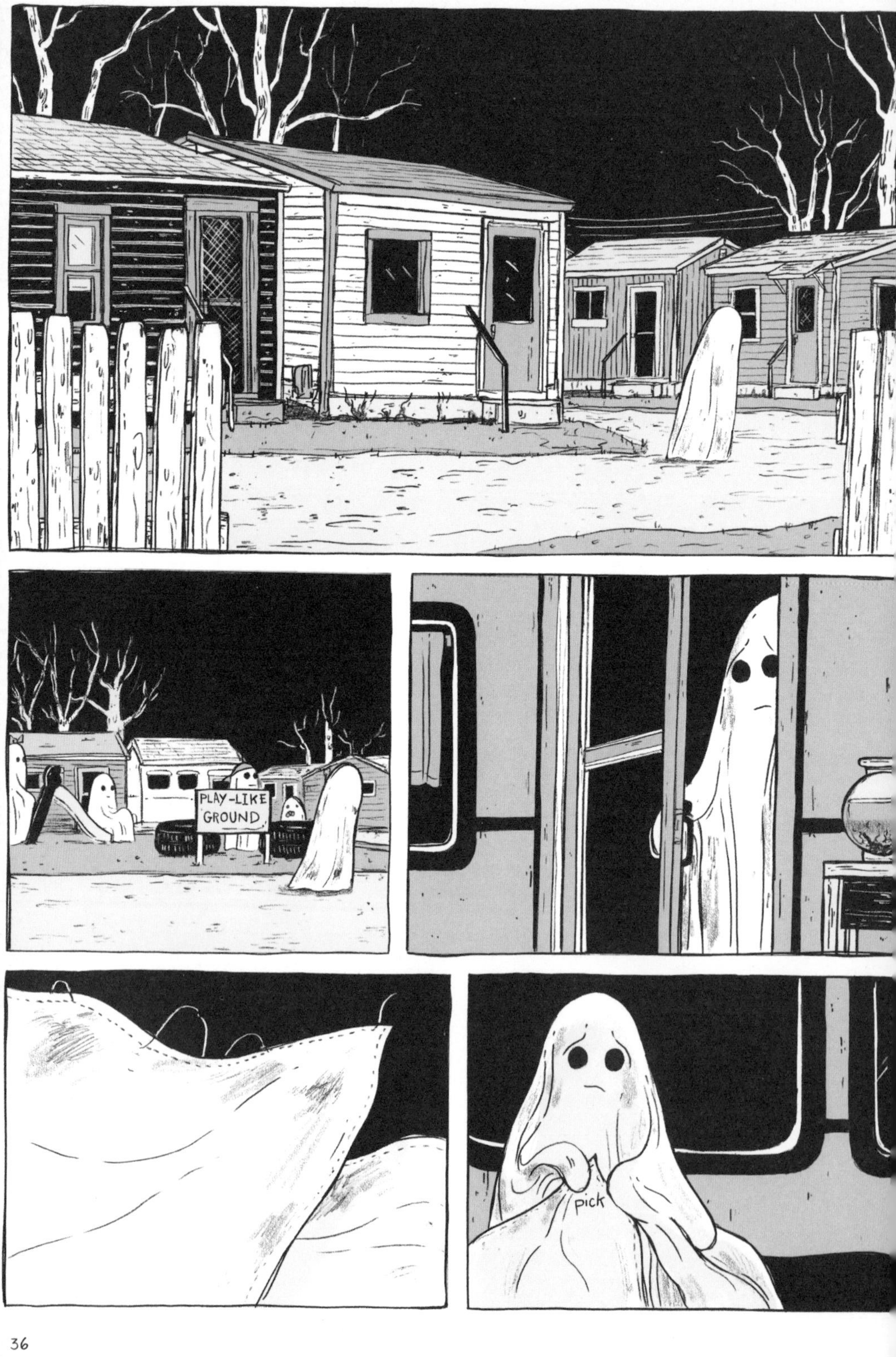
PLAY-LIKE GROUND
pick

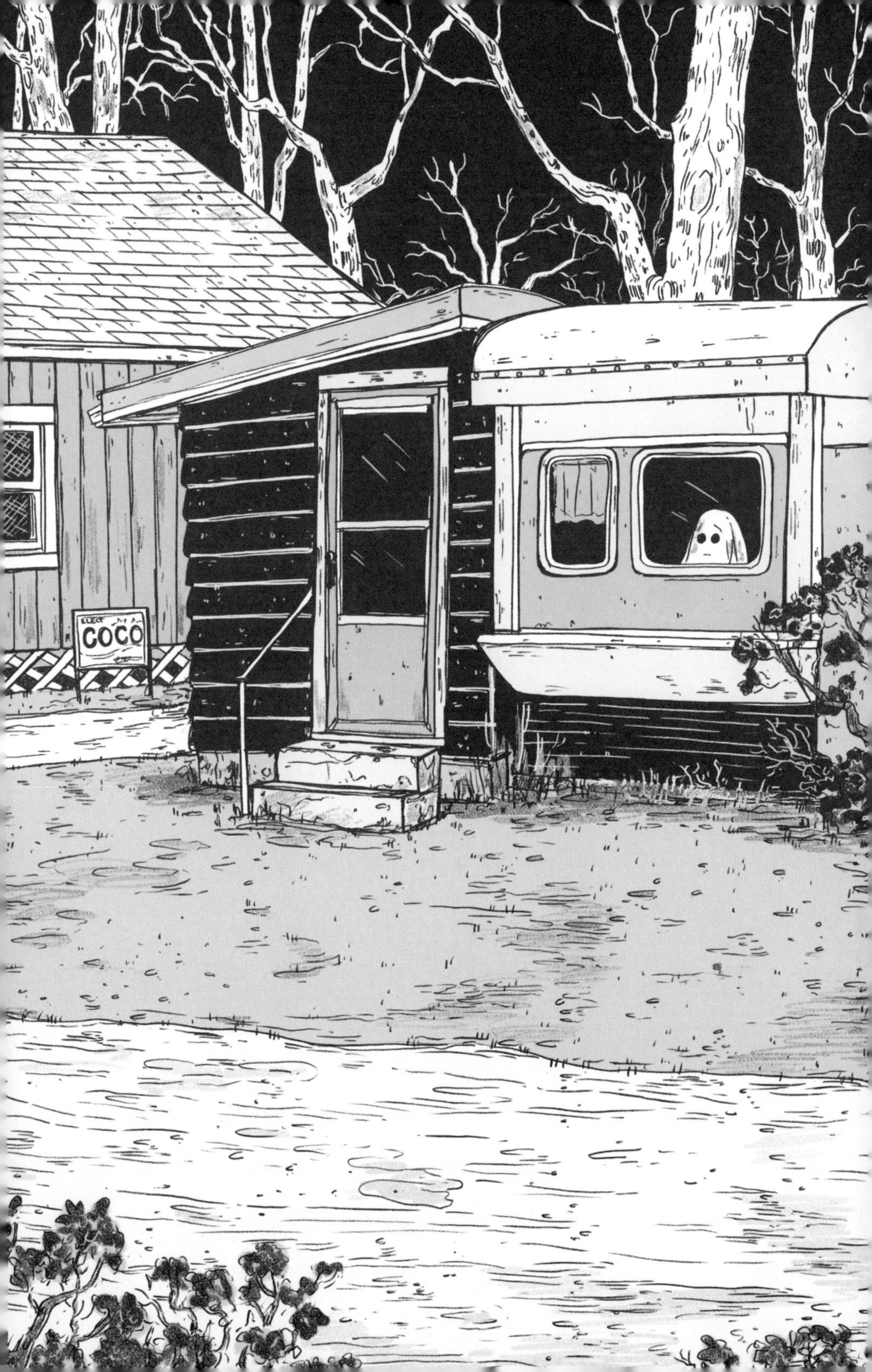
ELECT
COCO

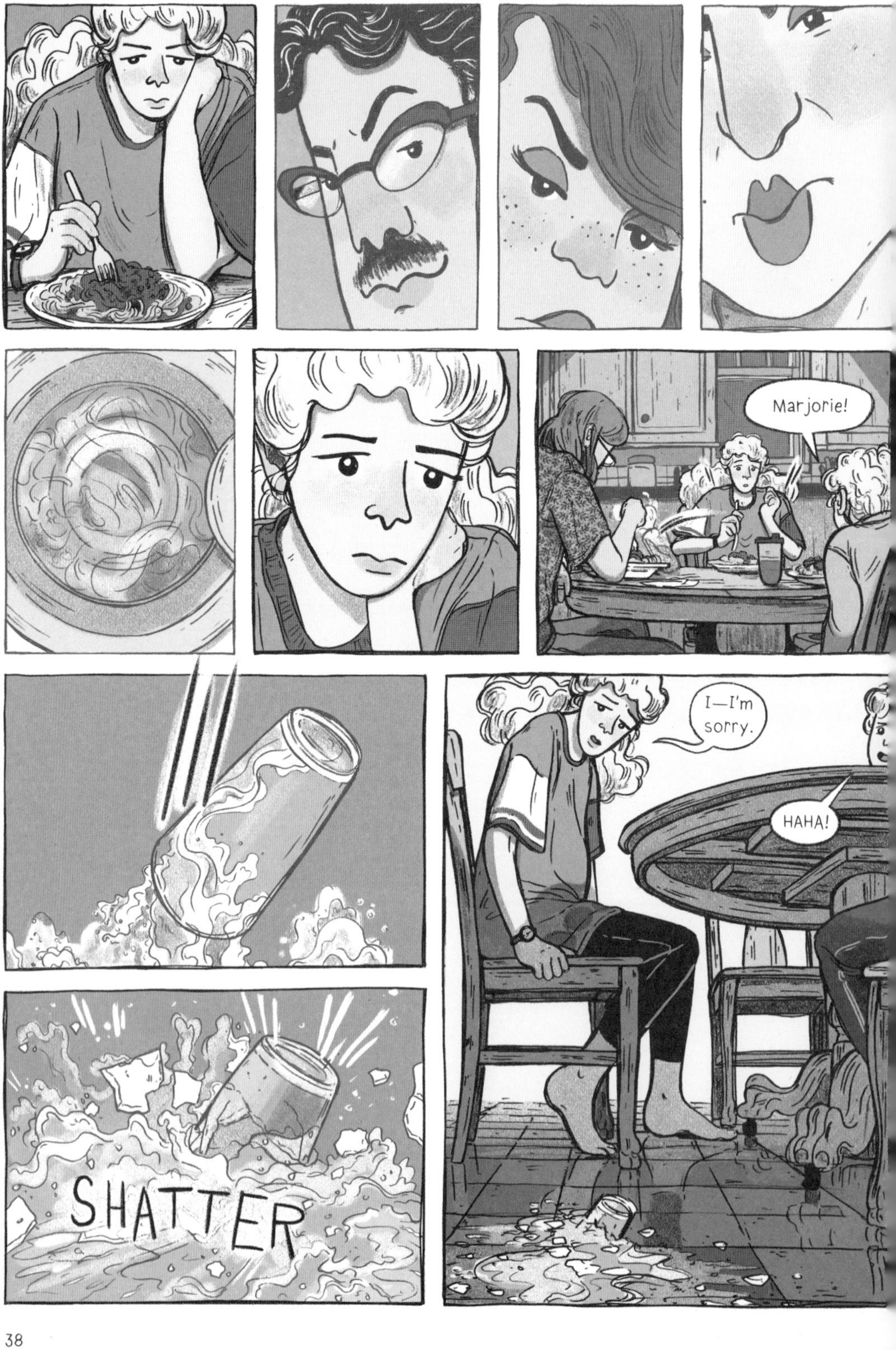
Marjorie!
SHATTER
I—I'm sorry.
HAHA!

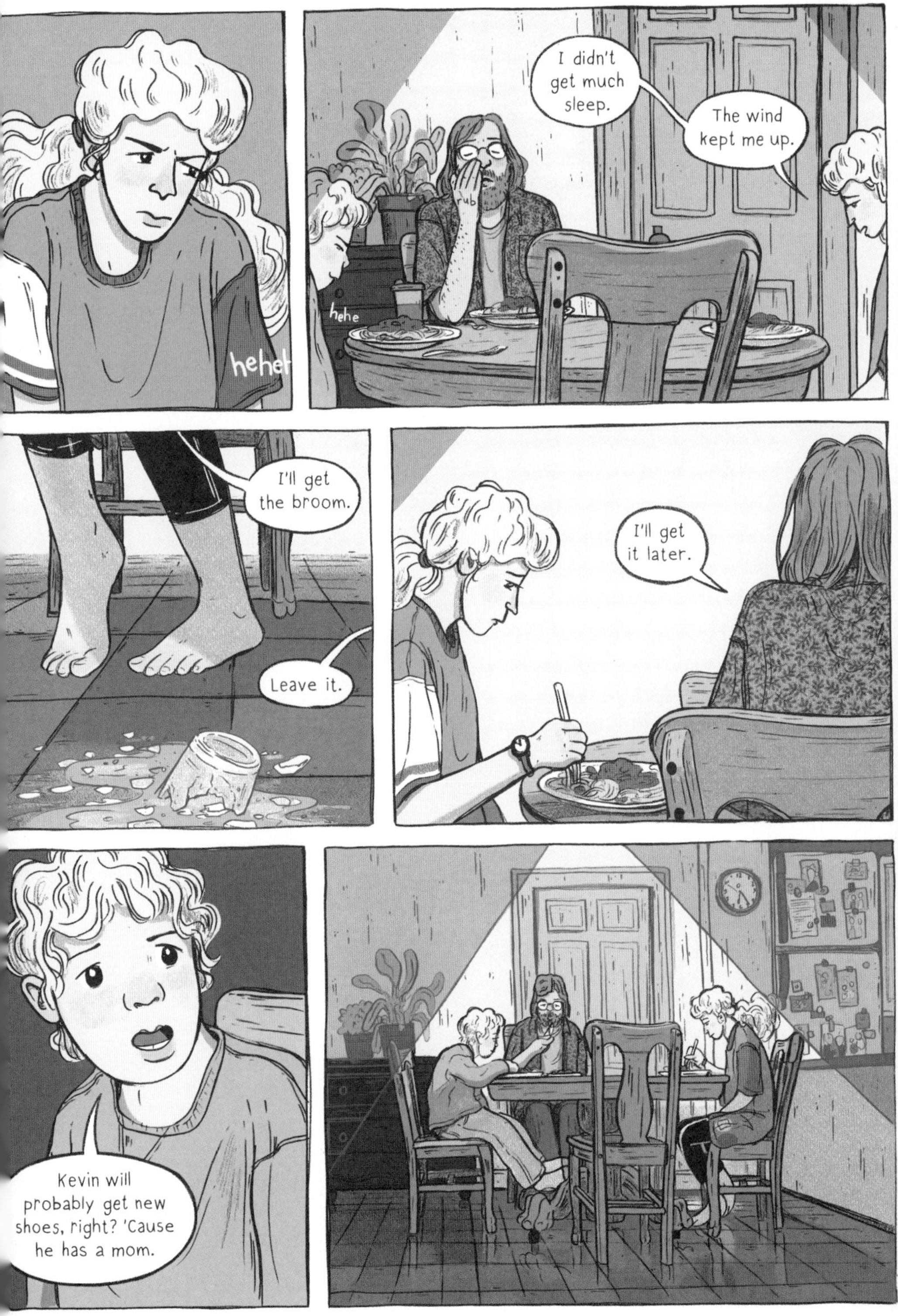
hehe
hehe
I didn't get much sleep.
The wind kept me up.
rub
I'll get the broom.
Leave it.
I'll get it later.
Kevin will probably get new shoes, right? 'Cause he has a mom.

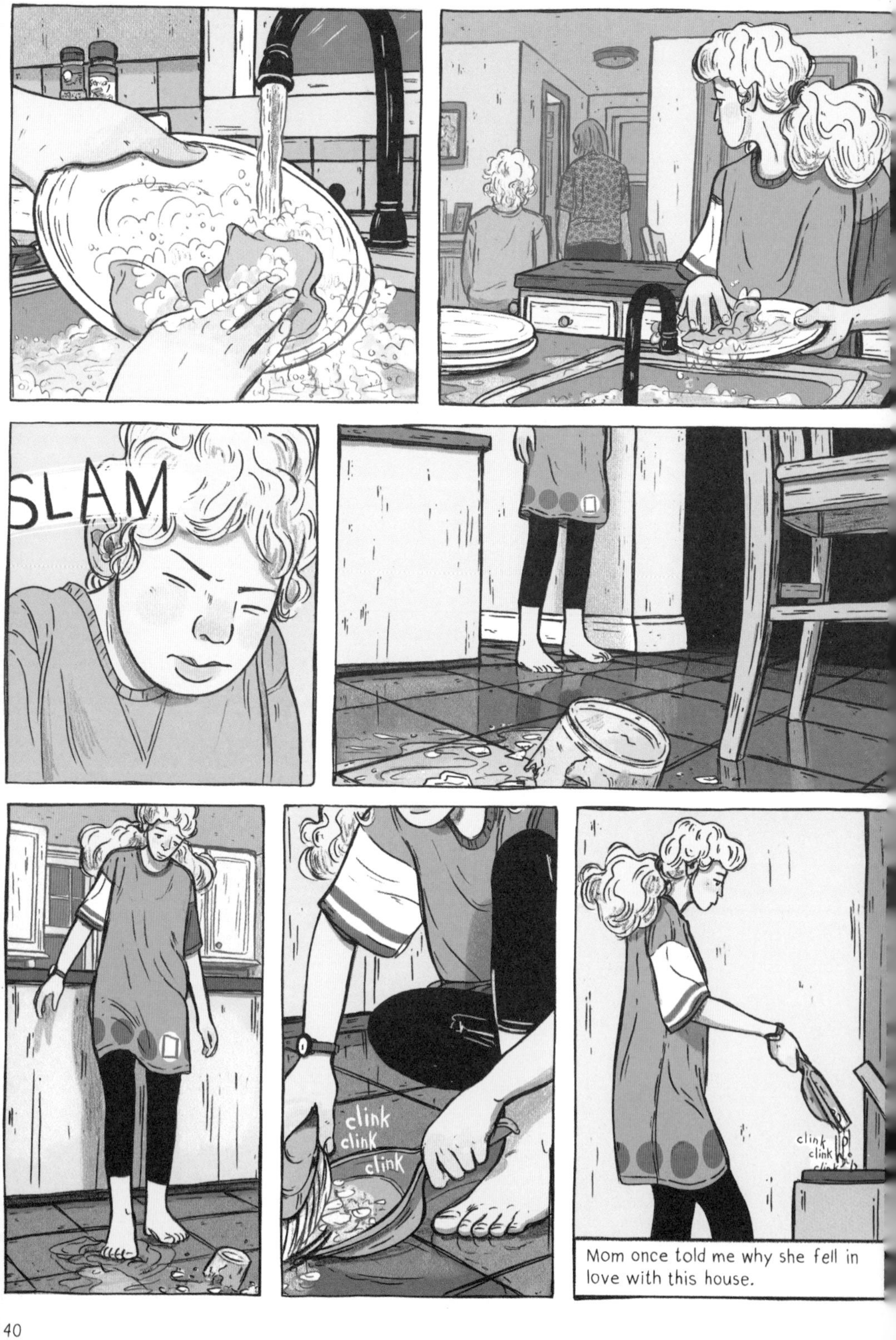
SLAM
clink
clink
clink
clink
clink
Mom once told me why she fell in love with this house.

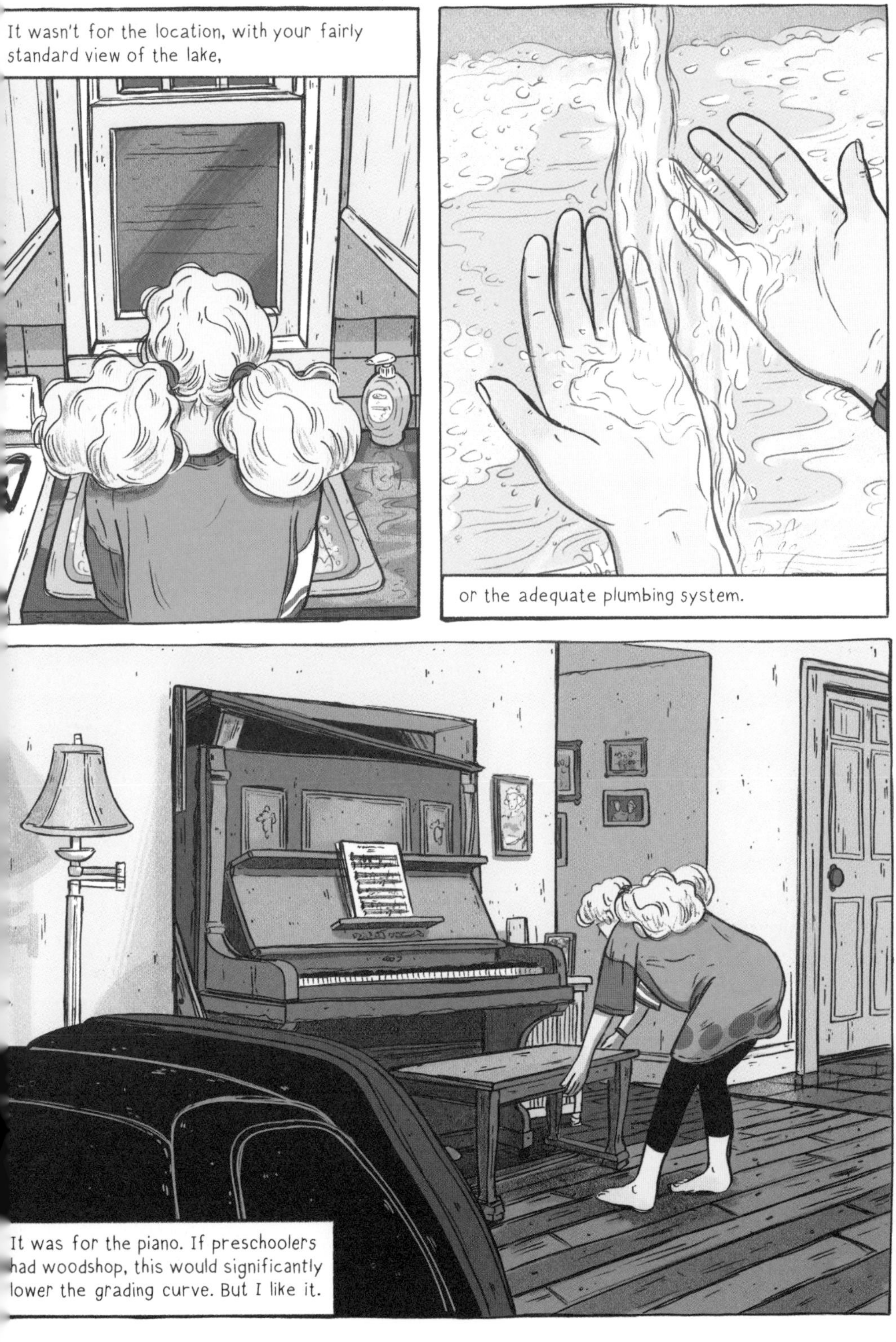
It wasn't for the location, with your fairly standard view of the lake,
or the adequate plumbing system.
It was for the piano. If preschoolers had woodshop, this would significantly lower the grading curve. But I like it.

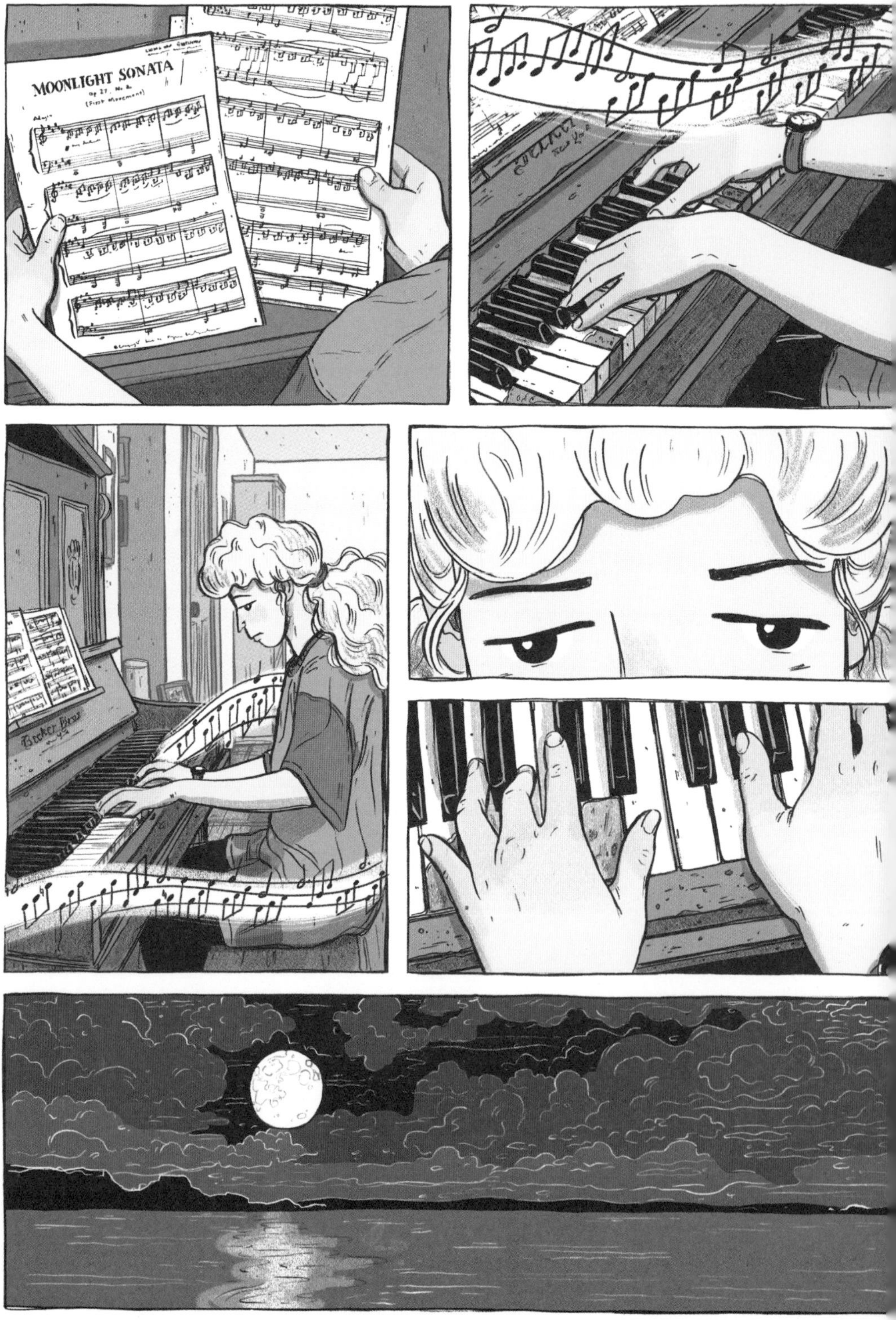
MOONLIGHT SONATA
Op 27, No 2
(First Movement)
Becker Bros

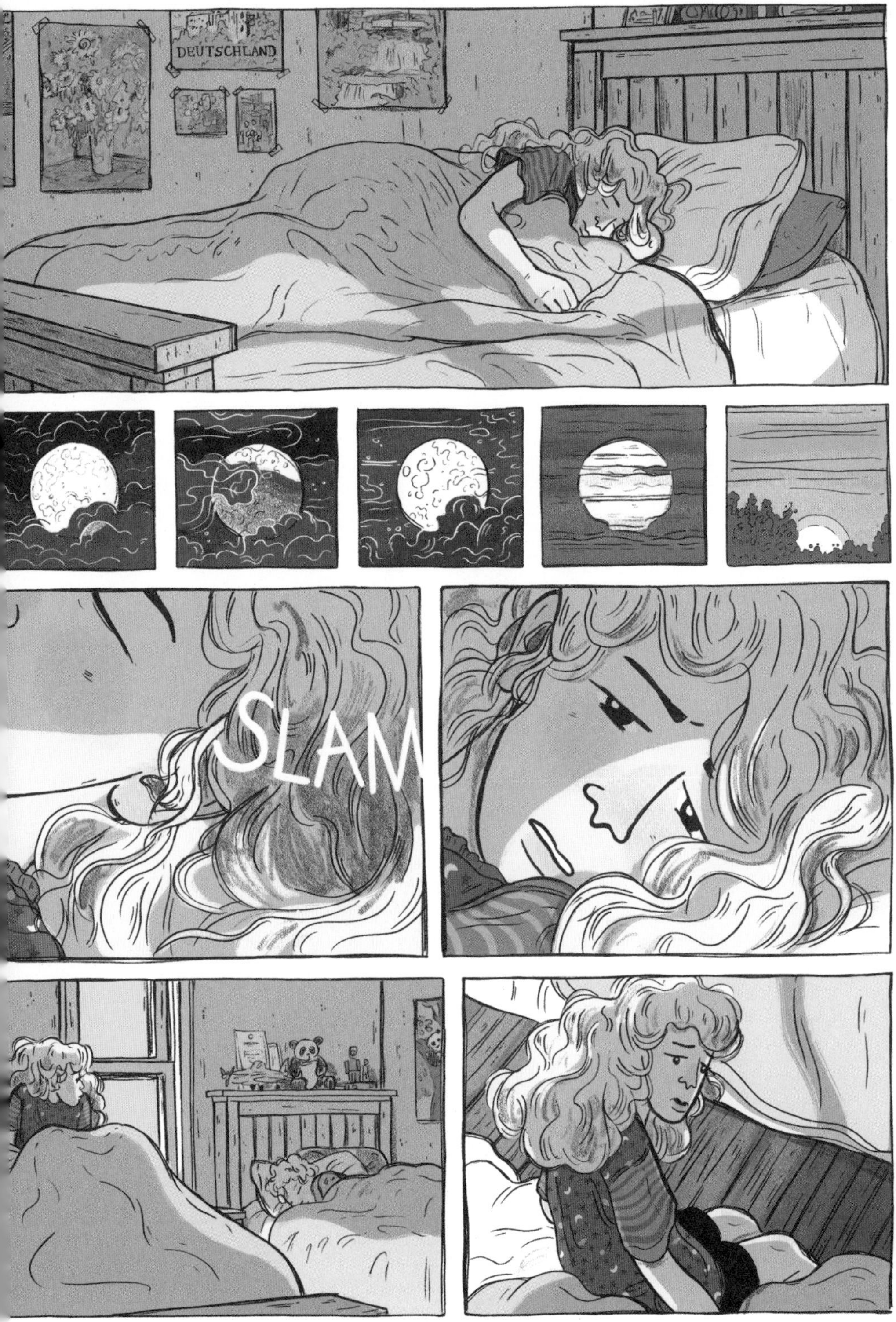
DEUTSCHLAND
SLAM

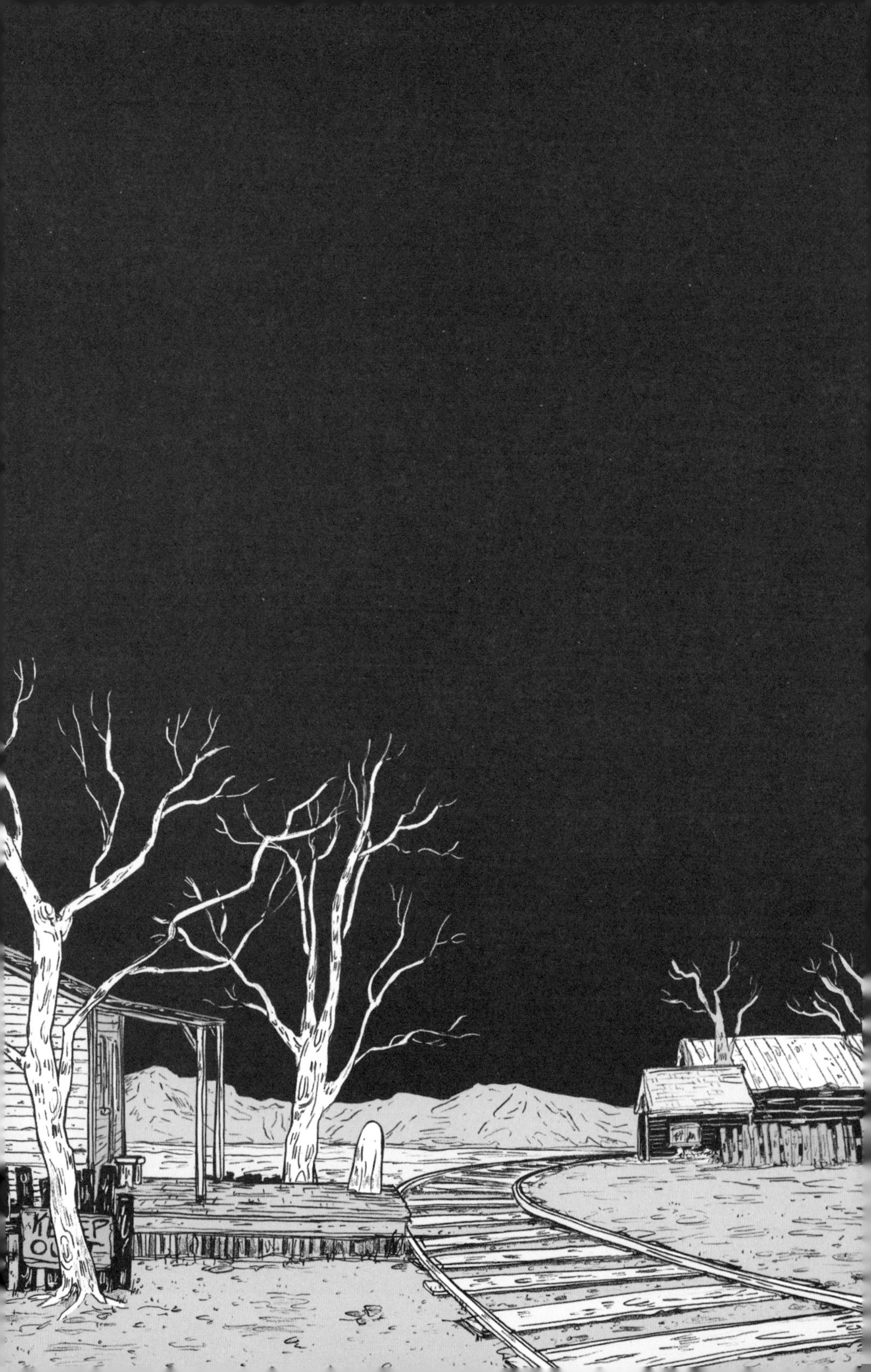

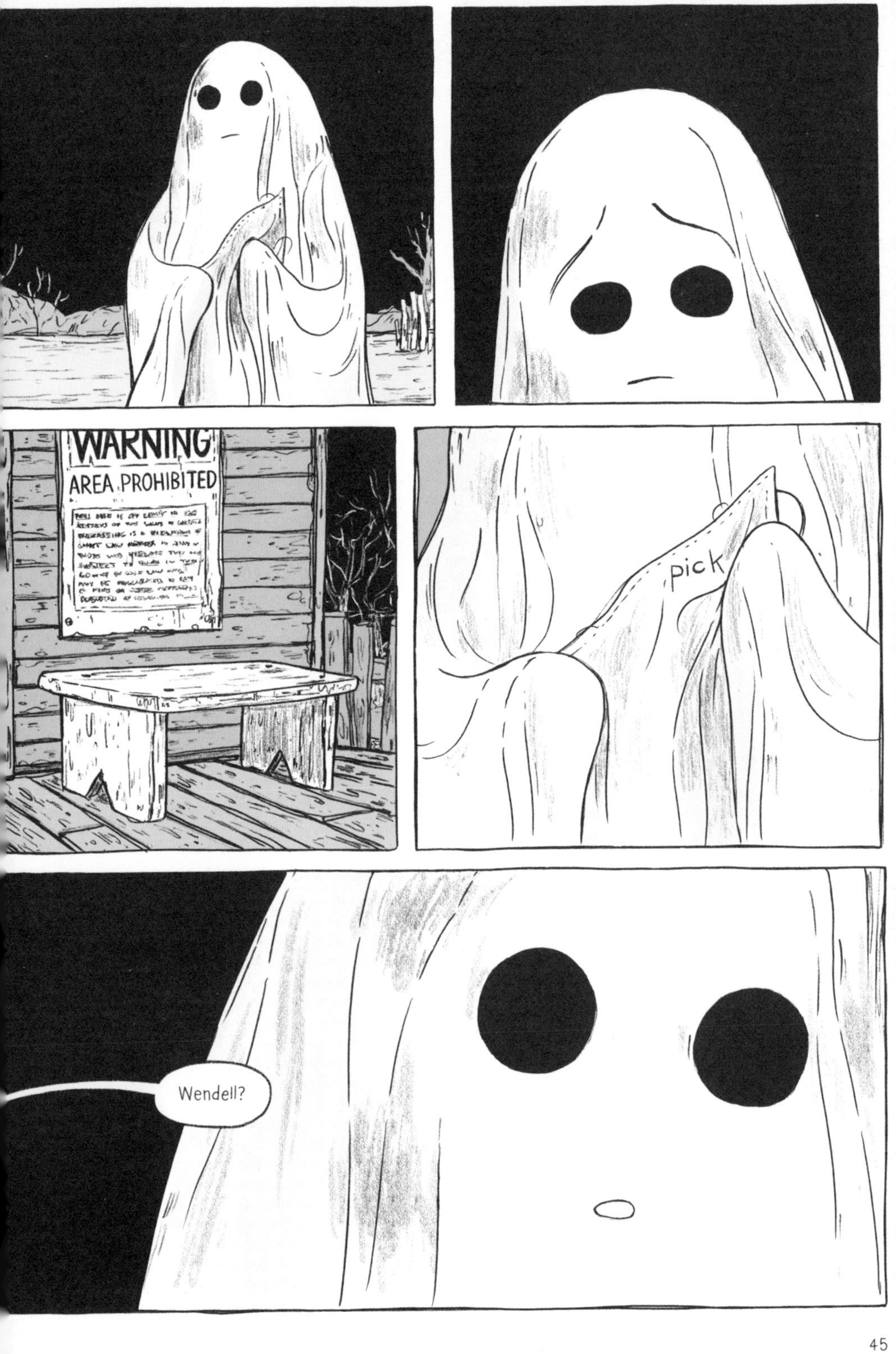
WARNING
AREA PROHIBITED
pick
Wendell?

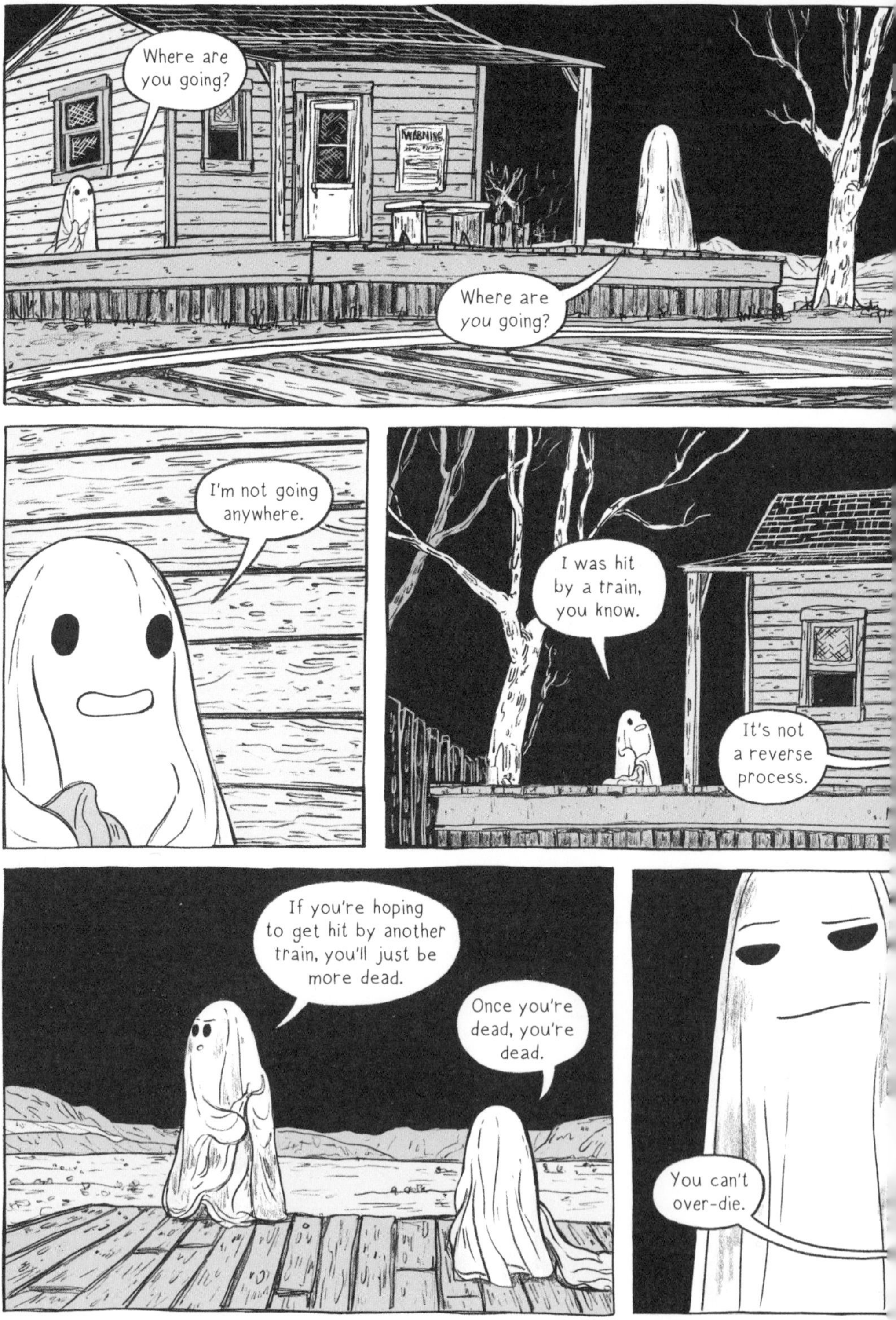
Where are you going?
Where are you going?
I'm not going anywhere.
I was hit by a train, you know.
It's not a reverse process.
If you're hoping to get hit by another train, you'll just be more dead.
Once you're dead, you're dead.
You can't over-die.

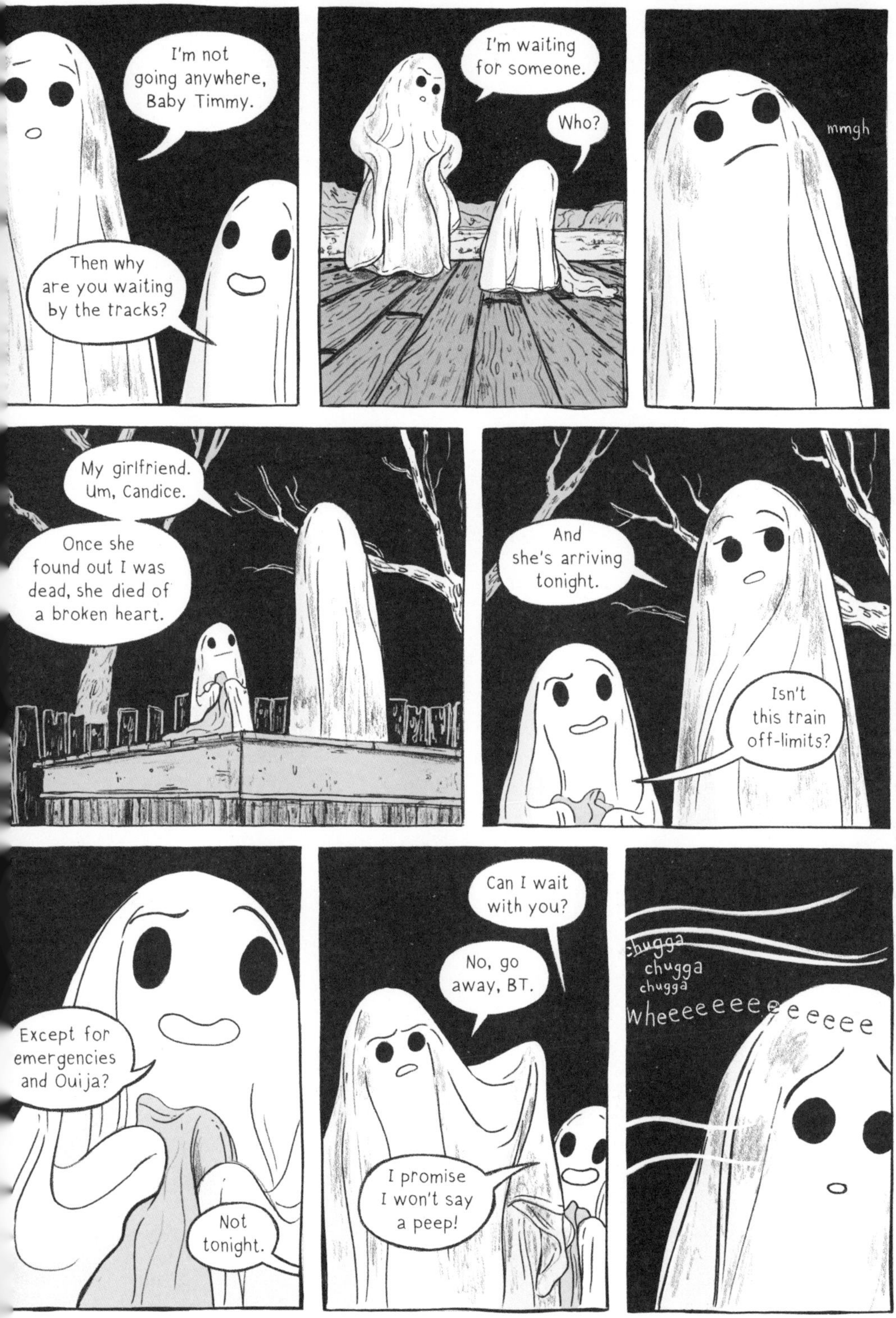
I'm not going anywhere, Baby Timmy.
Then why are you waiting by the tracks?
I'm waiting for someone.
Who?
mmgh
My girlfriend. Um, Candice.
Once she found out I was dead, she died of a broken heart.
And she's arriving tonight.
Isn't this train off-limits?
Except for emergencies and Ouija?
Not tonight.
Can I wait with you?
No, go away, BT.
I promise I won't say a peep!
chugga
chugga
chugga
Wheeeeeeeeeeeee

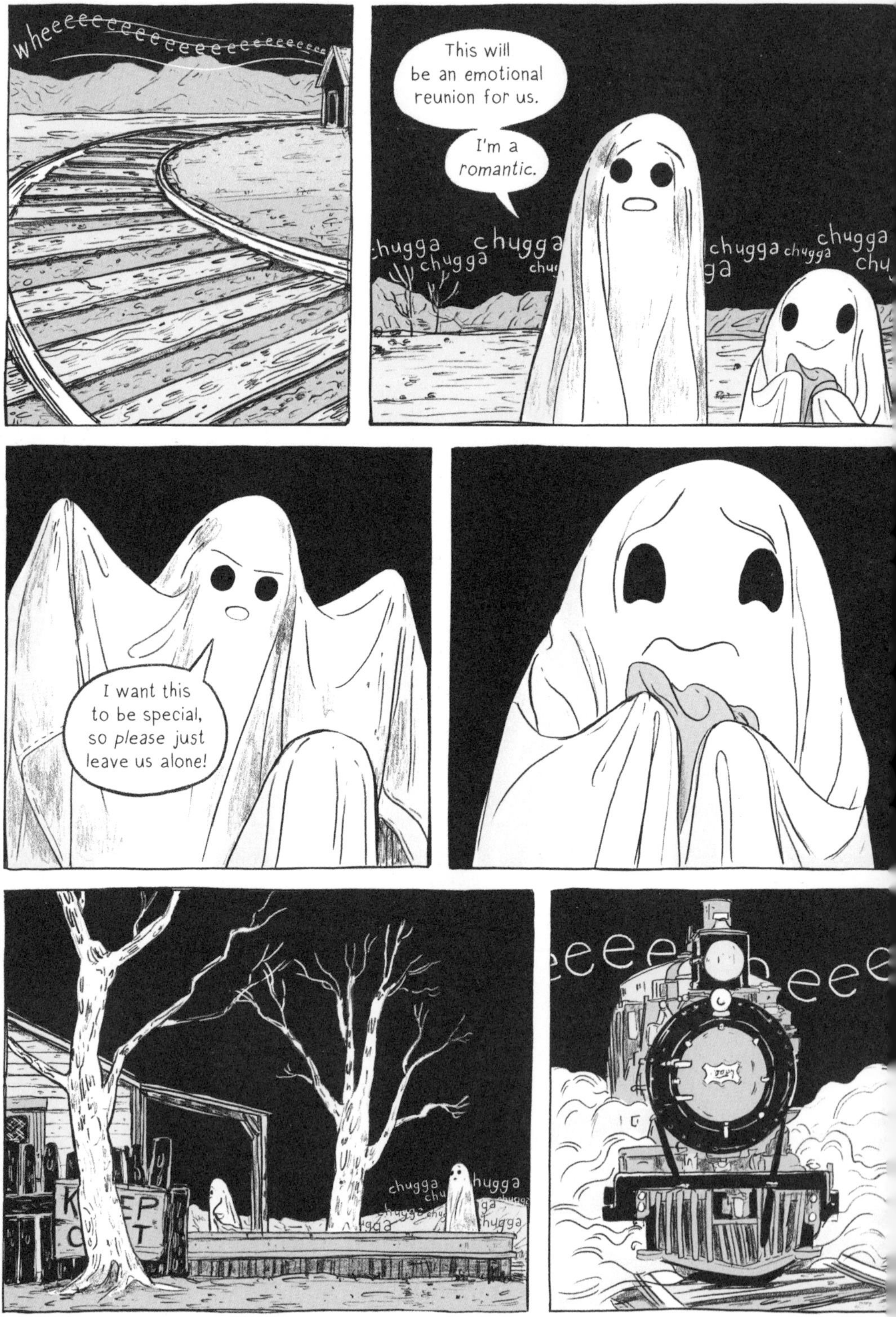
wheeeeeeeeeeeeeeeeeeeeeee
This will be an emotional reunion for us.
I'm a *romantic.*
chugga chugga chugga
chugga chugga chugga
I want this to be special, so *please* just leave us alone!
chugga chugga hugga
eeee eee

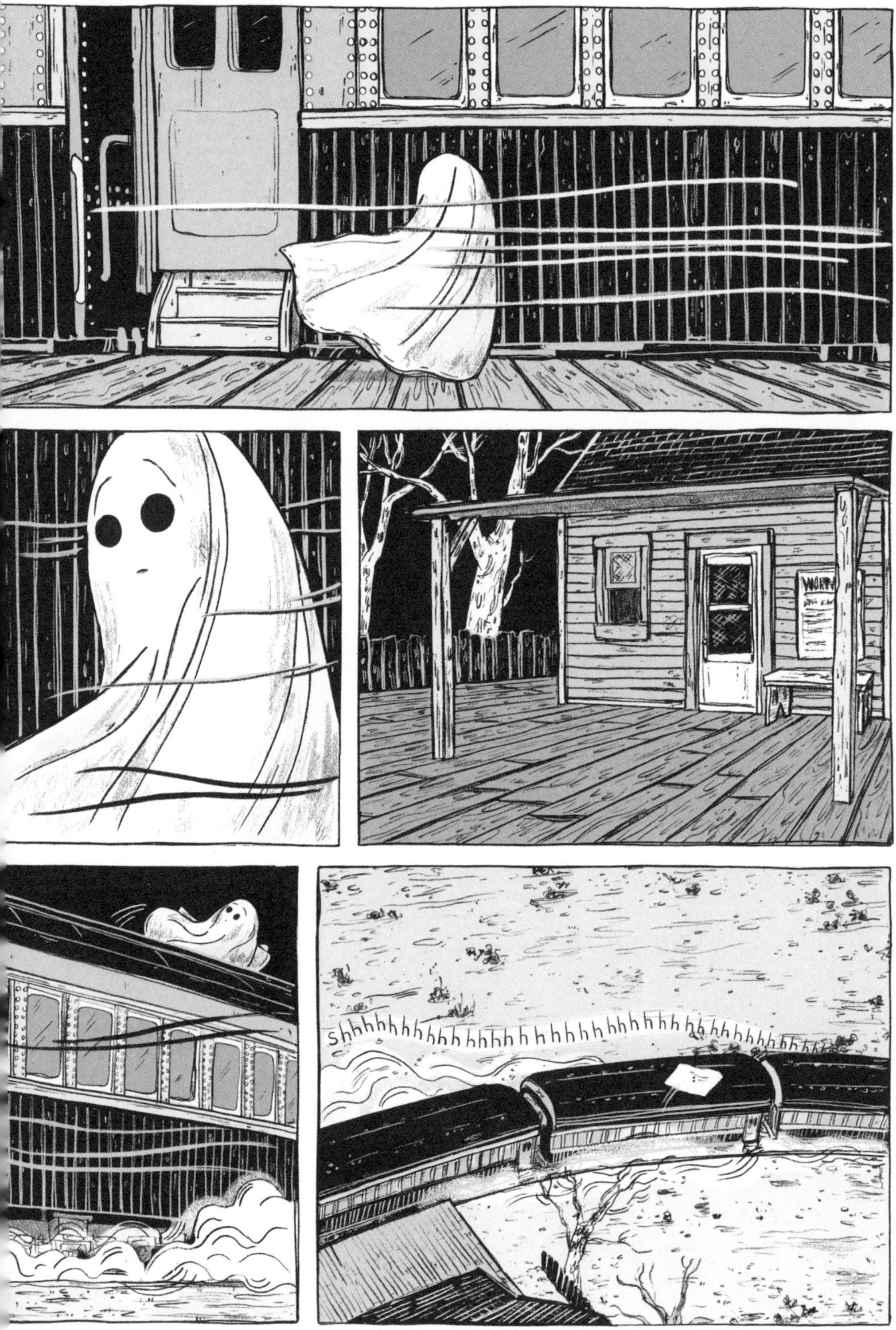
Shhhhhhhhhhhhhhhhhhhhhhhhhhhhhhhhhhhhhh

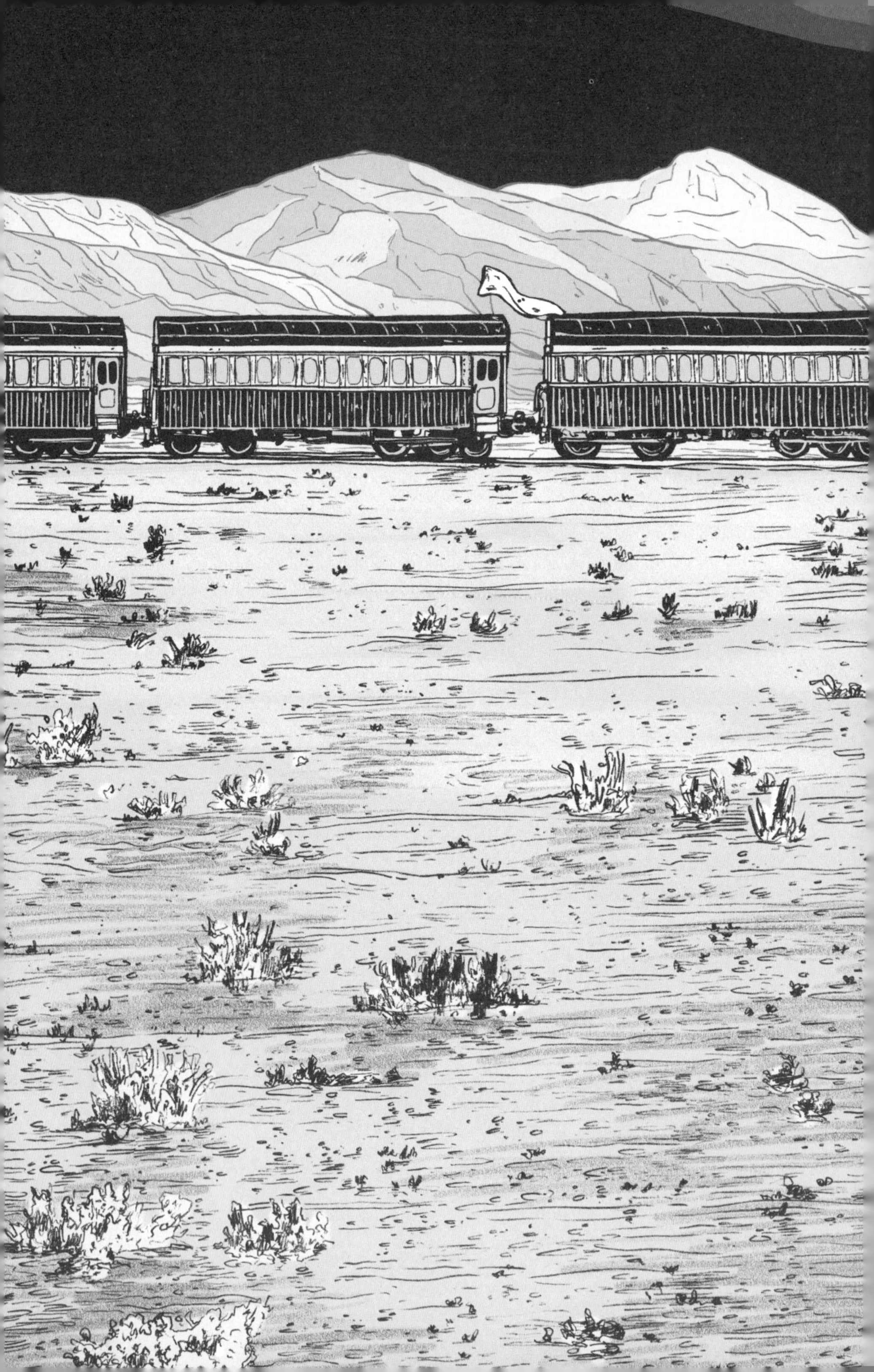

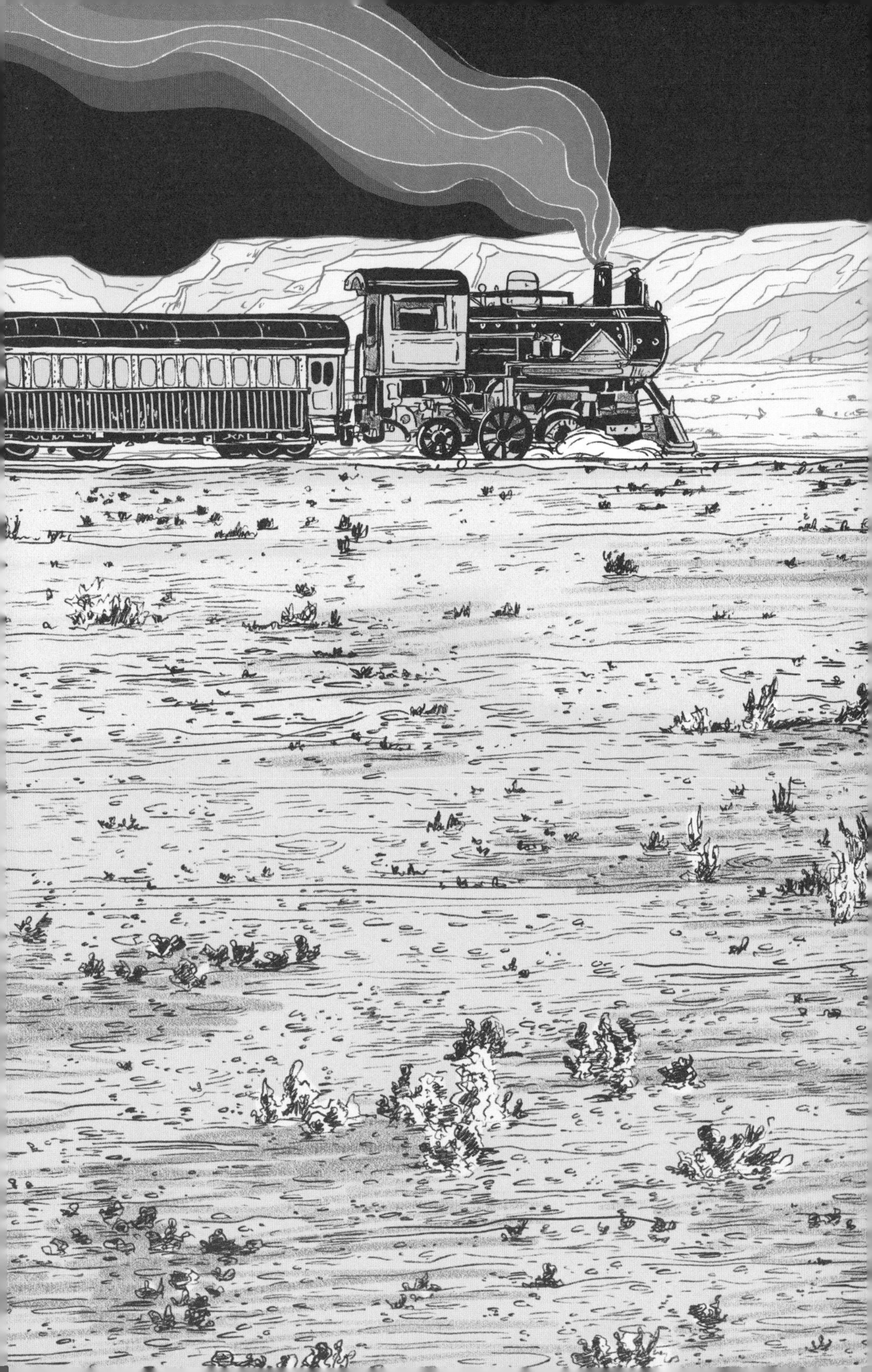

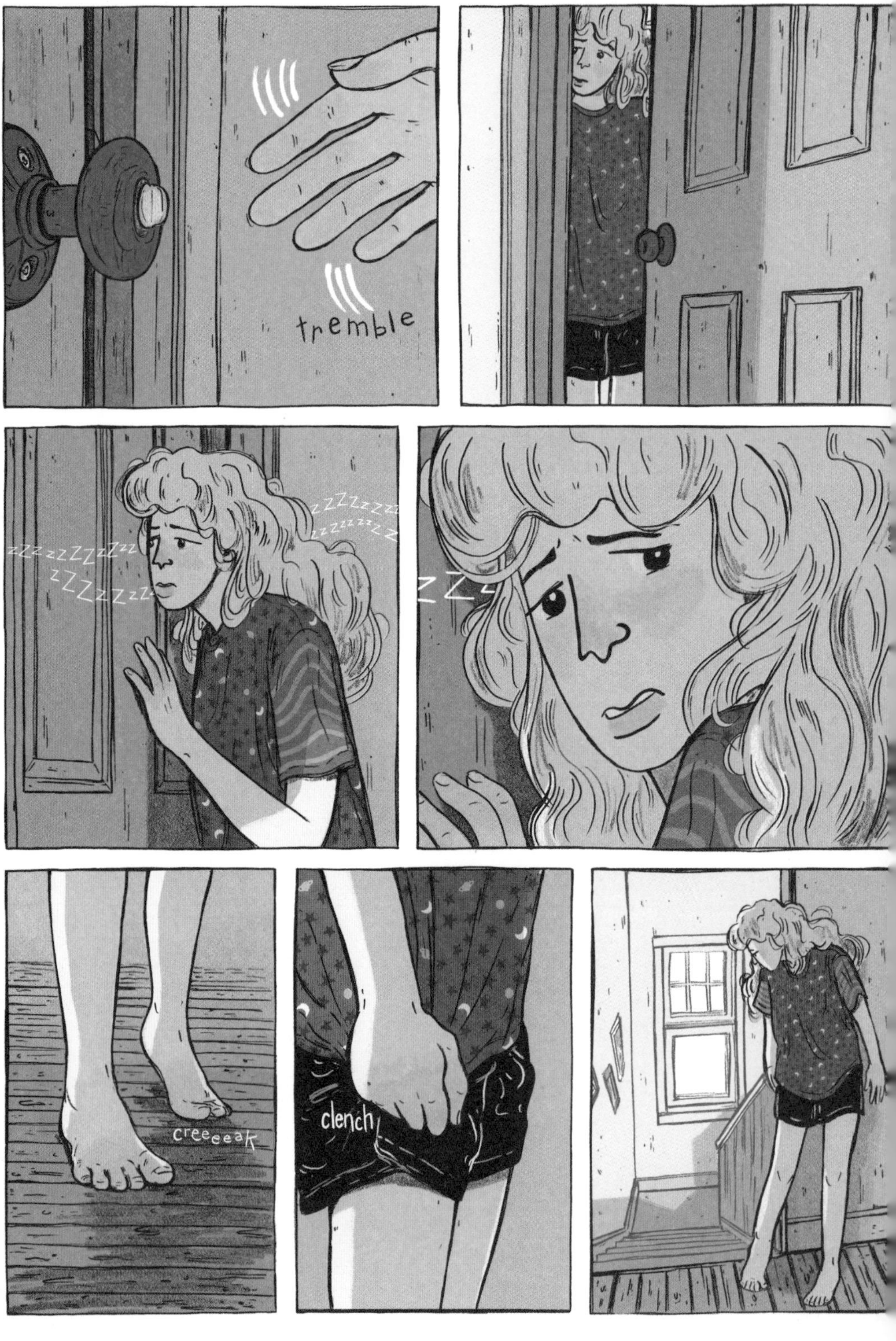
tremble
zzzzzzZzZzz
zZZzzZzzz
zzZZzzzzz
zzzzzzzzzz
creeeeak
clench

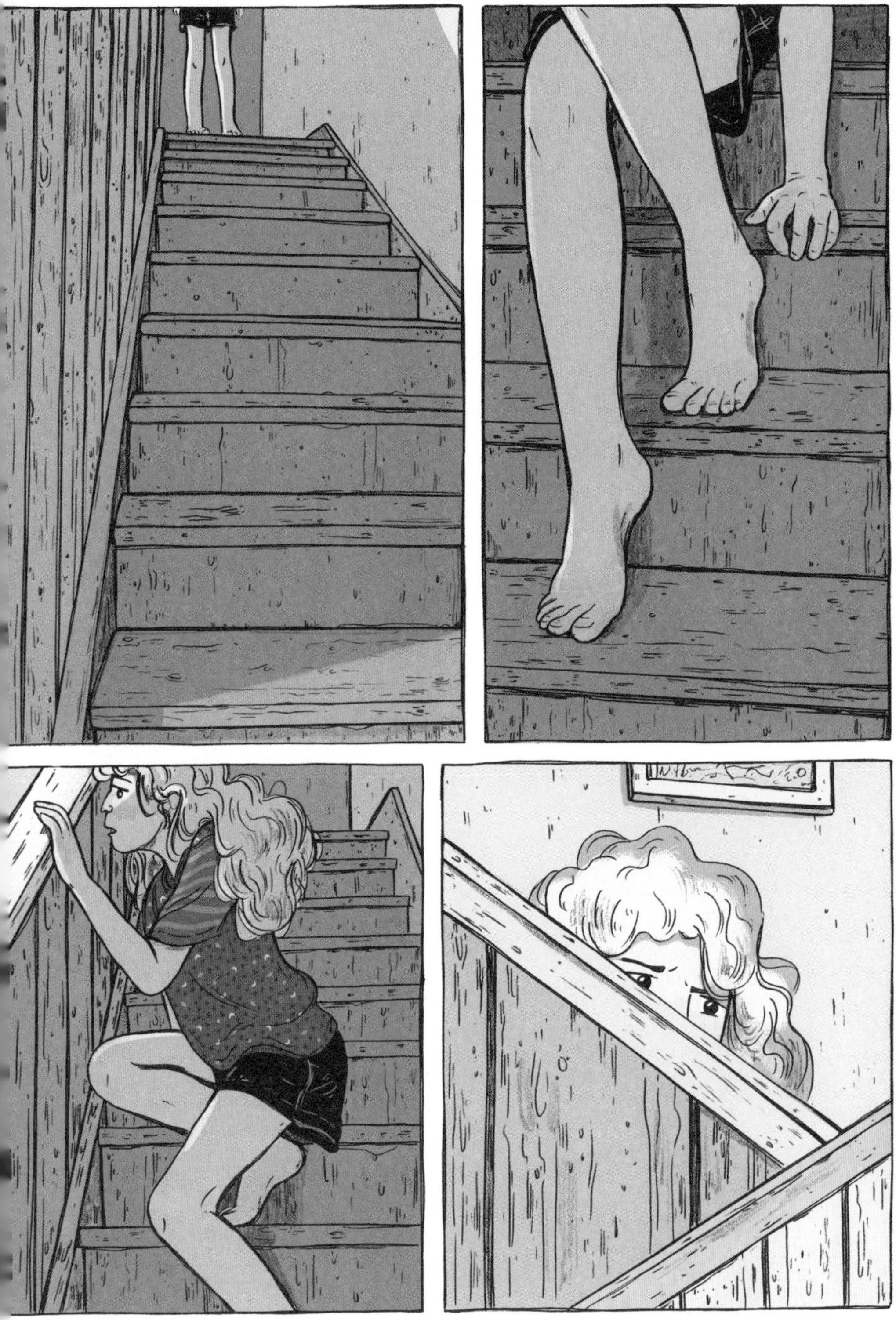

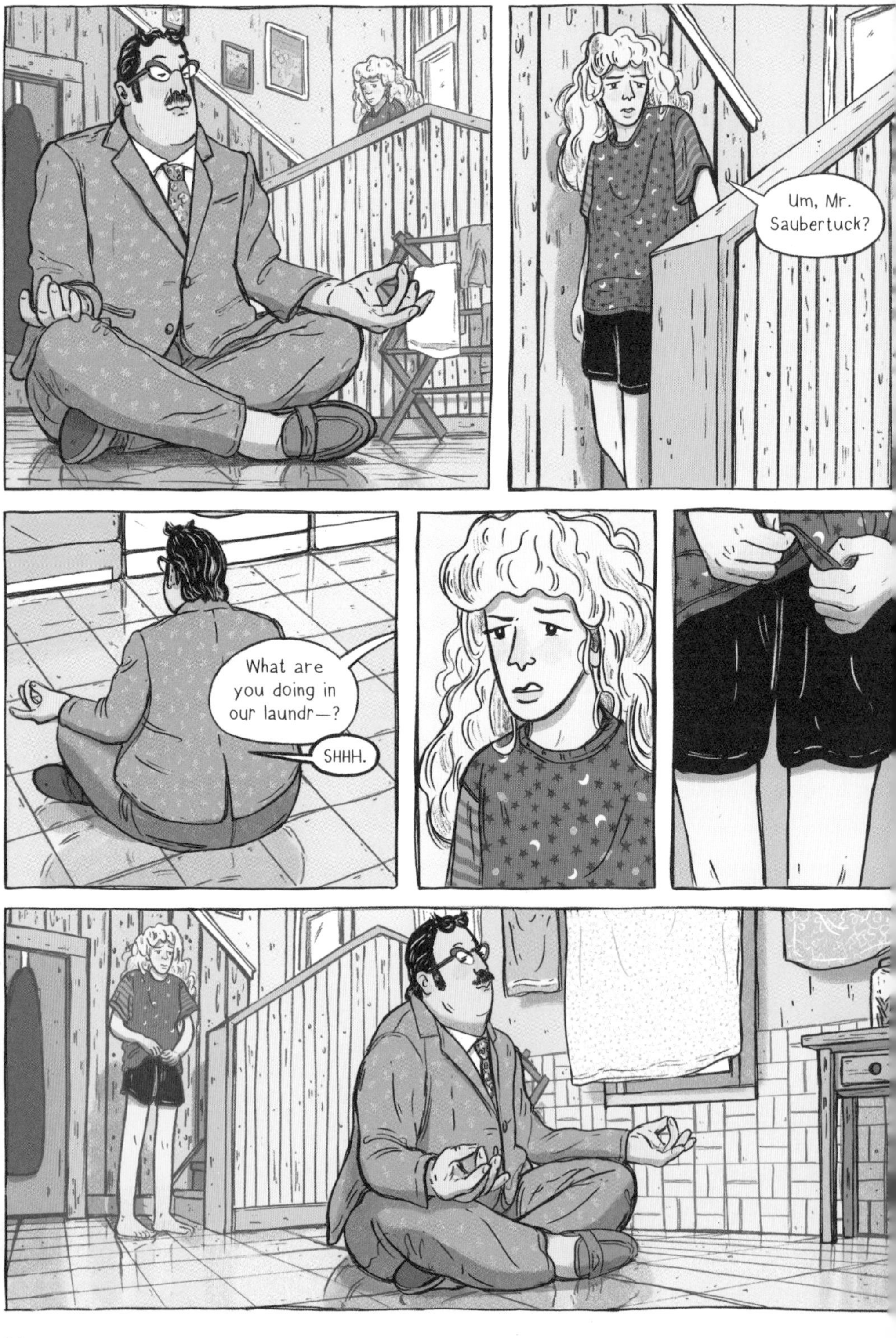
Um, Mr. Saubertuck?
What are you doing in our laundr—?
SHHH.

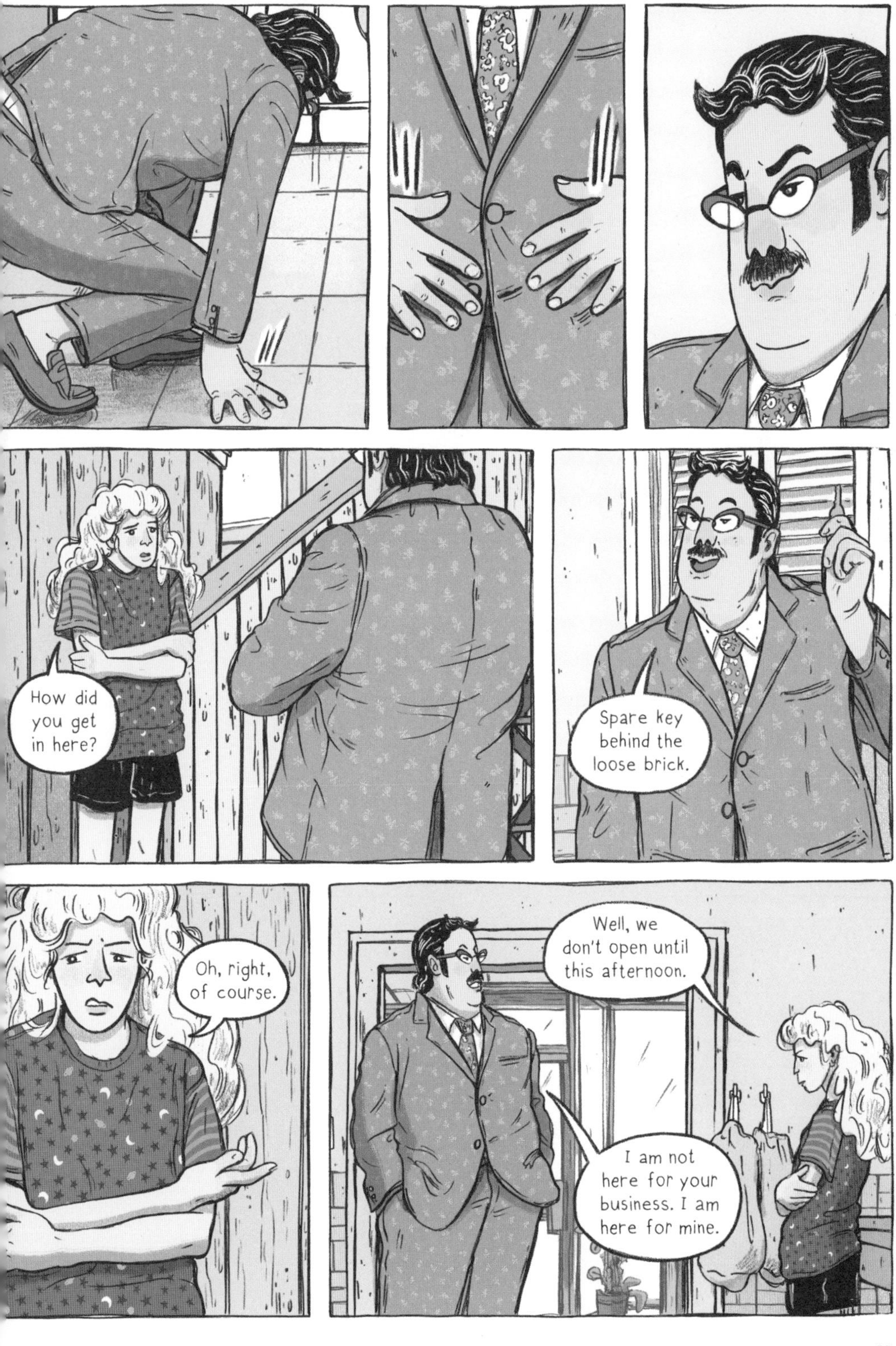
How did you get in here?
Spare key behind the loose brick.
Oh, right, of course.
Well, we don't open until this afternoon.
I am not here for your business. I am here for mine.

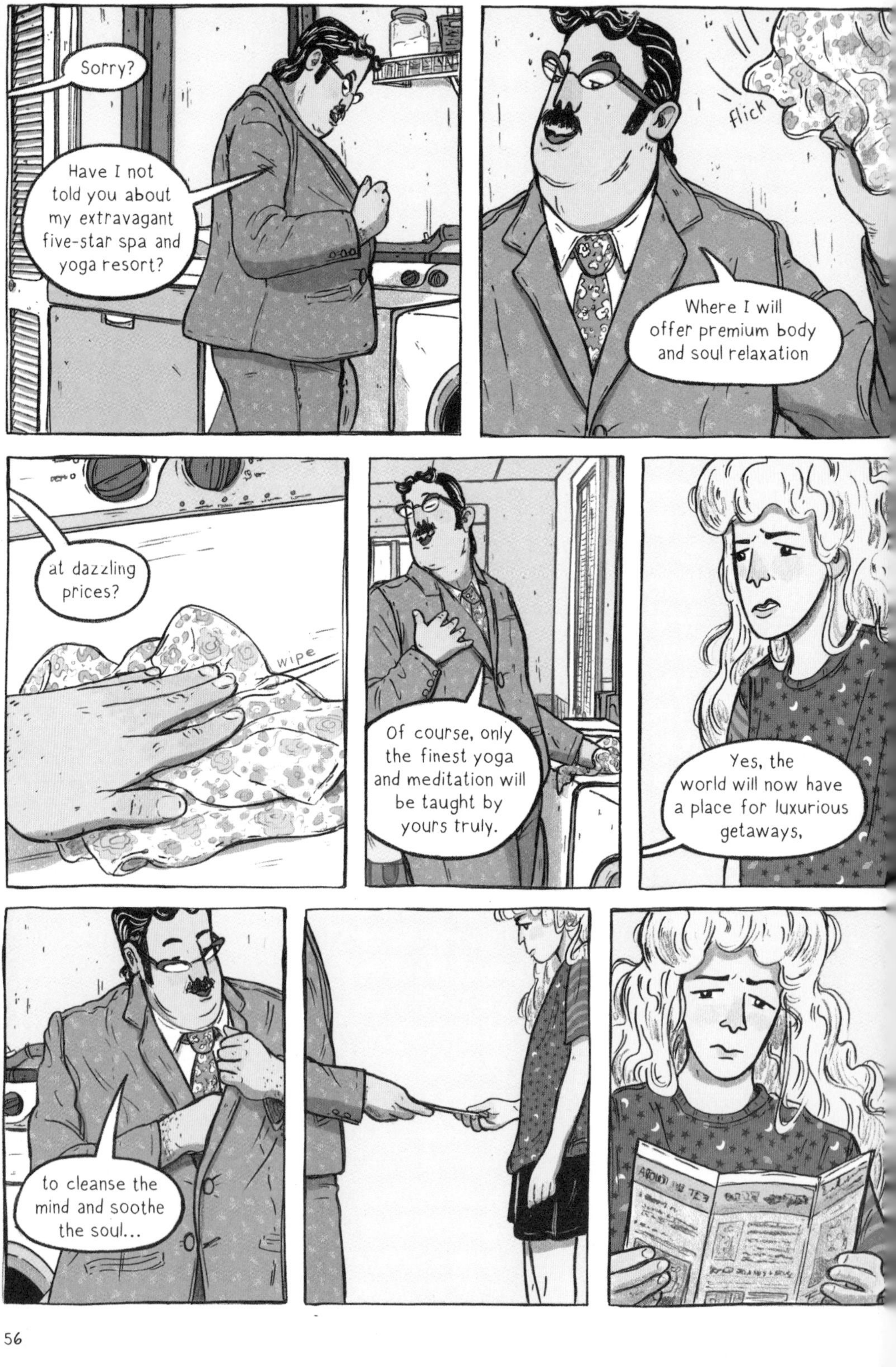
Sorry?
Have I not told you about my extravagant five-star spa and yoga resort?
flick
Where I will offer premium body and soul relaxation
at dazzling prices?
wipe
Of course, only the finest yoga and meditation will be taught by yours truly.
Yes, the world will now have a place for luxurious getaways,
to cleanse the mind and soothe the soul...

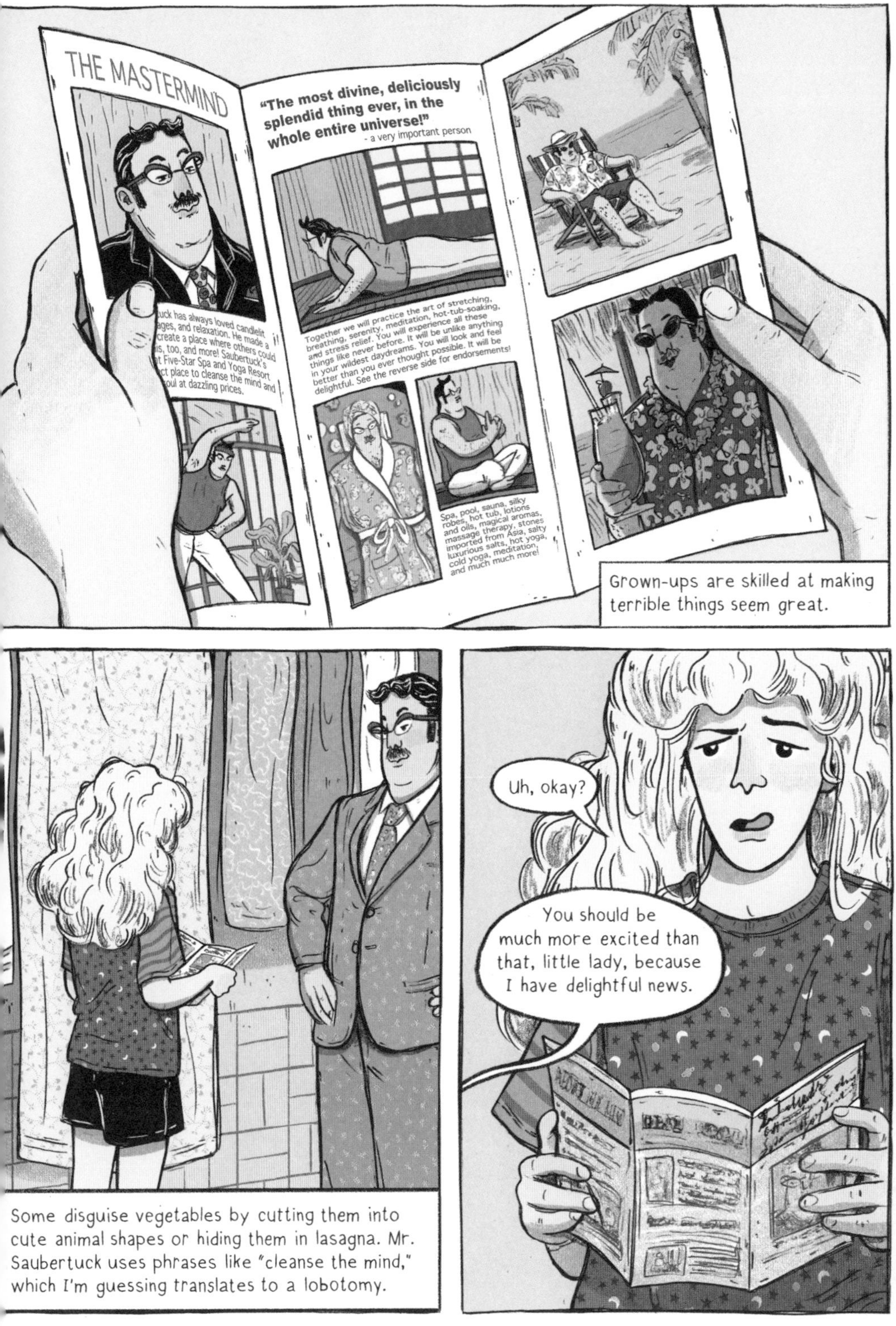
THE MASTERMIND
has always loved candlelit
and relaxation. He made a
create a place where others could
too, and more! Saubertuck's
Five-Star Spa and Yoga Resort
place to cleanse the mind and
at dazzling prices.
"The most divine, deliciously splendid thing ever, in the whole entire universe!"
- a very important person
Together we will practice the art of stretching, breathing, serenity, meditation, hot-tub-soaking, and stress relief. You will experience all these things like never before. It will be unlike anything in your wildest daydreams. You will look and feel better than you ever thought possible. It will be delightful. See the reverse side for endorsements!
Spa, pool, sauna, silky robes, hot tub, lotions and oils, magical aromas, massage therapy, stones imported from Asia, salty luxurious salts, hot yoga, cold yoga, meditation, and much much more!
Grown-ups are skilled at making terrible things seem great.
Some disguise vegetables by cutting them into cute animal shapes or hiding them in lasagna. Mr. Saubertuck uses phrases like "cleanse the mind," which I'm guessing translates to a lobotomy.
You should be much more excited than that, little lady, because I have delightful news.
Uh, okay?

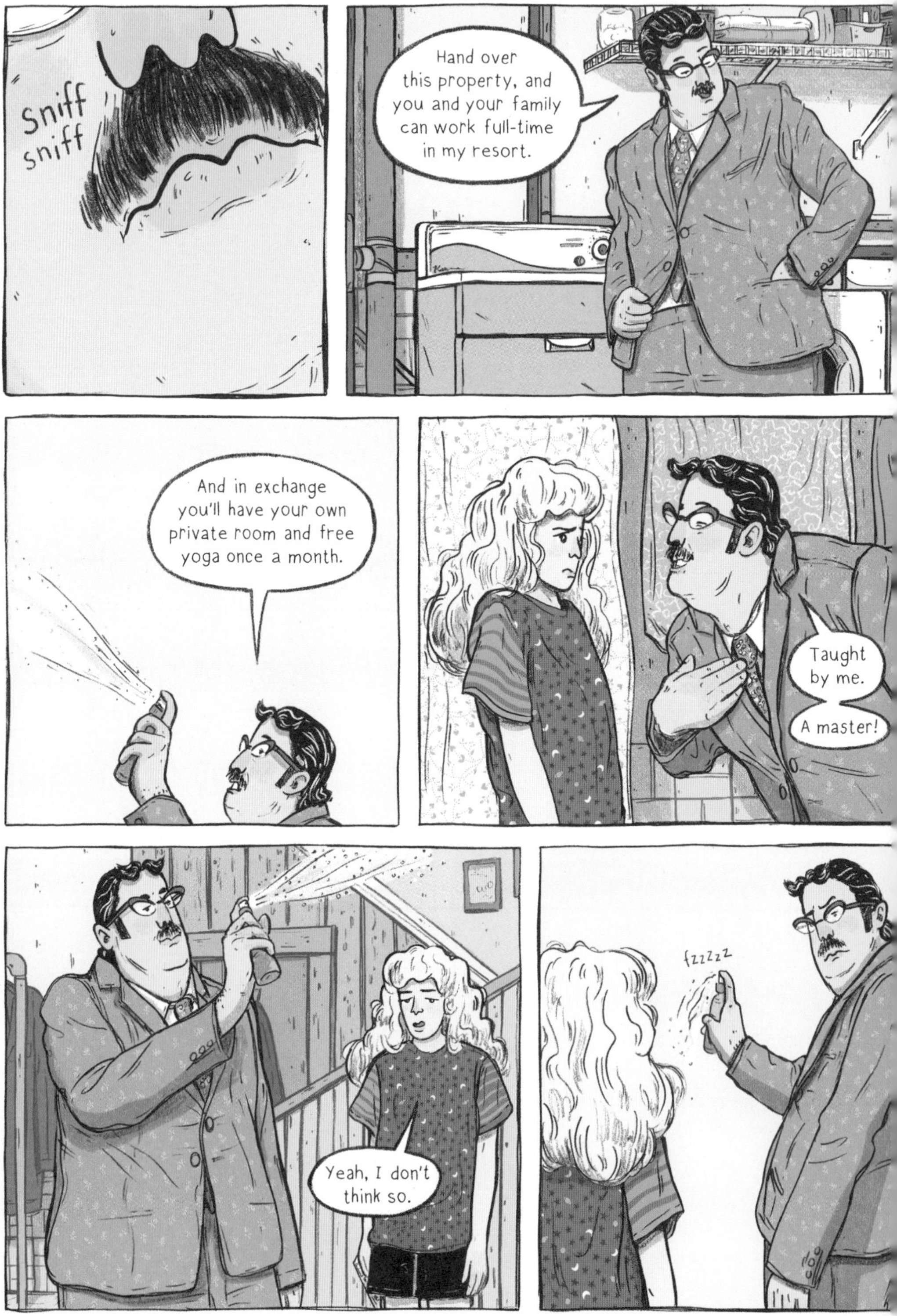
Sniff sniff
Hand over this property, and you and your family can work full-time in my resort.
And in exchange you'll have your own private room and free yoga once a month.
Taught by me.
A master!
Yeah, I don't think so.
fzzzzz

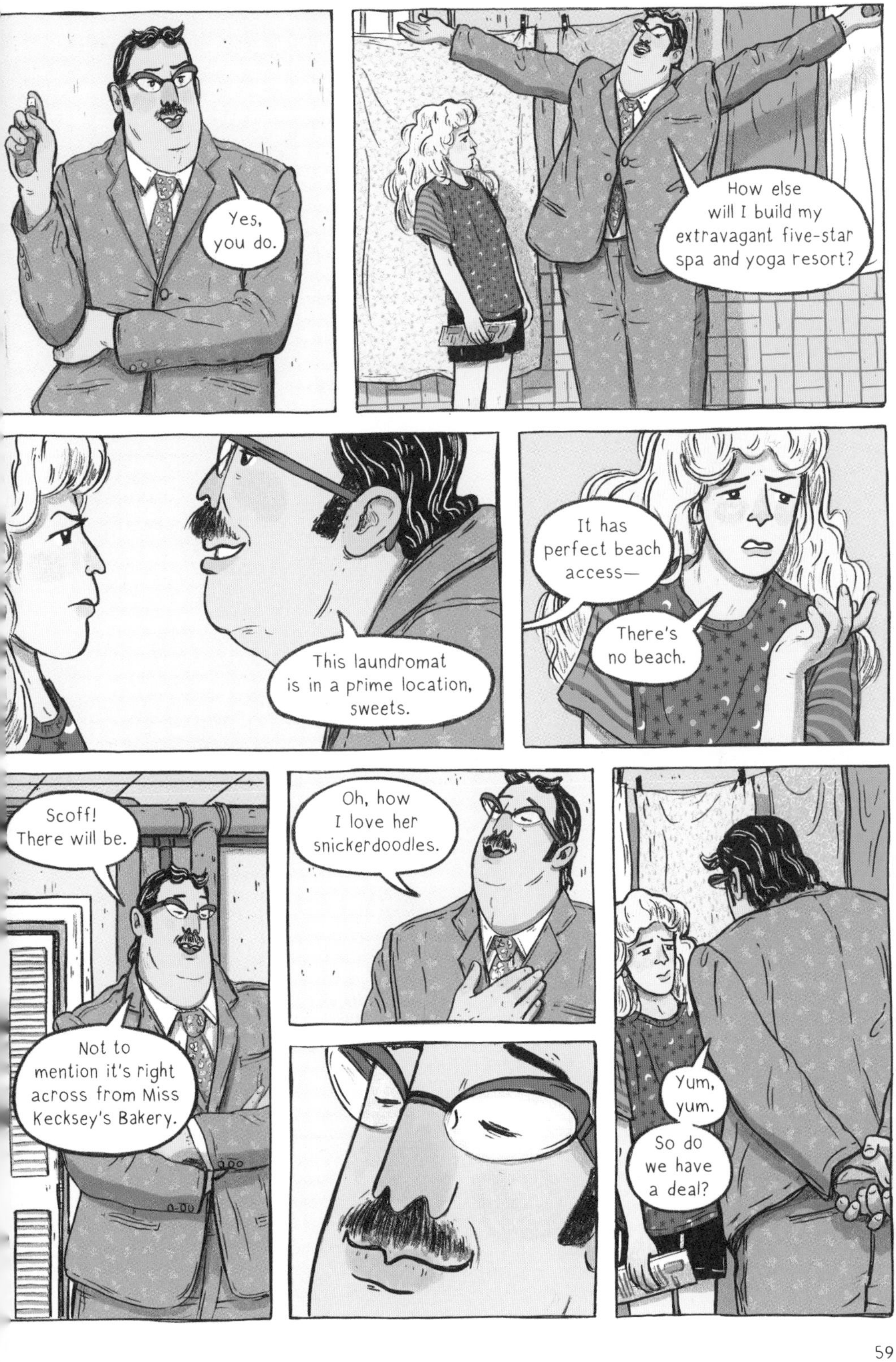
Yes, you do.
How else will I build my extravagant five-star spa and yoga resort?
This laundromat is in a prime location, sweets.
It has perfect beach access—
There's no beach.
Scoff! There will be.
Not to mention it's right across from Miss Kecksey's Bakery.
Oh, how I love her snickerdoodles.
Yum, yum.
So do we have a deal?

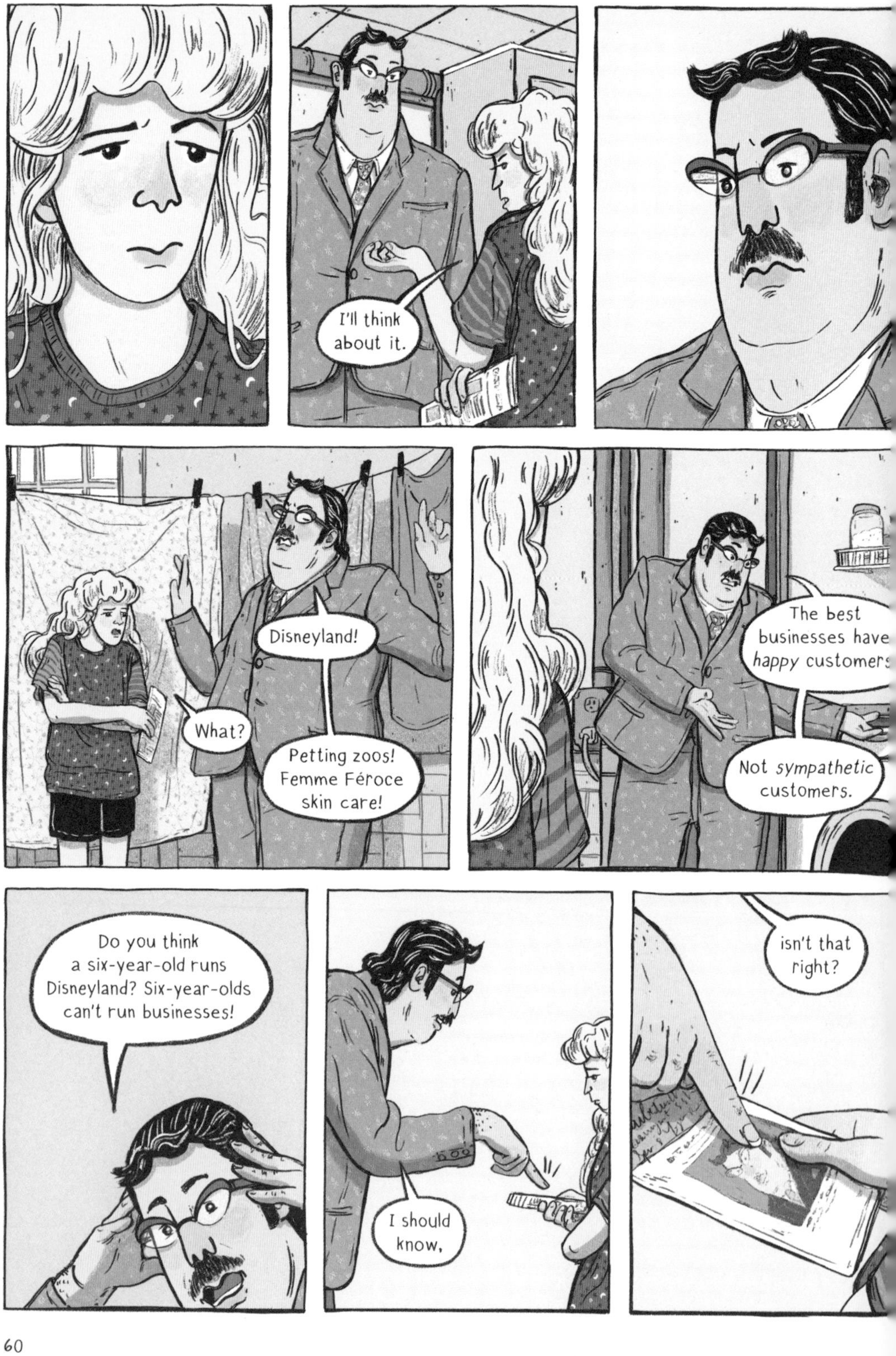

I'll think about it.
Disneyland!
What?
Petting zoos! Femme Féroce skin care!
The best businesses have happy customers.
Not sympathetic customers.
Do you think a six-year-old runs Disneyland? Six-year-olds can't run businesses!
I should know,
isn't that right?

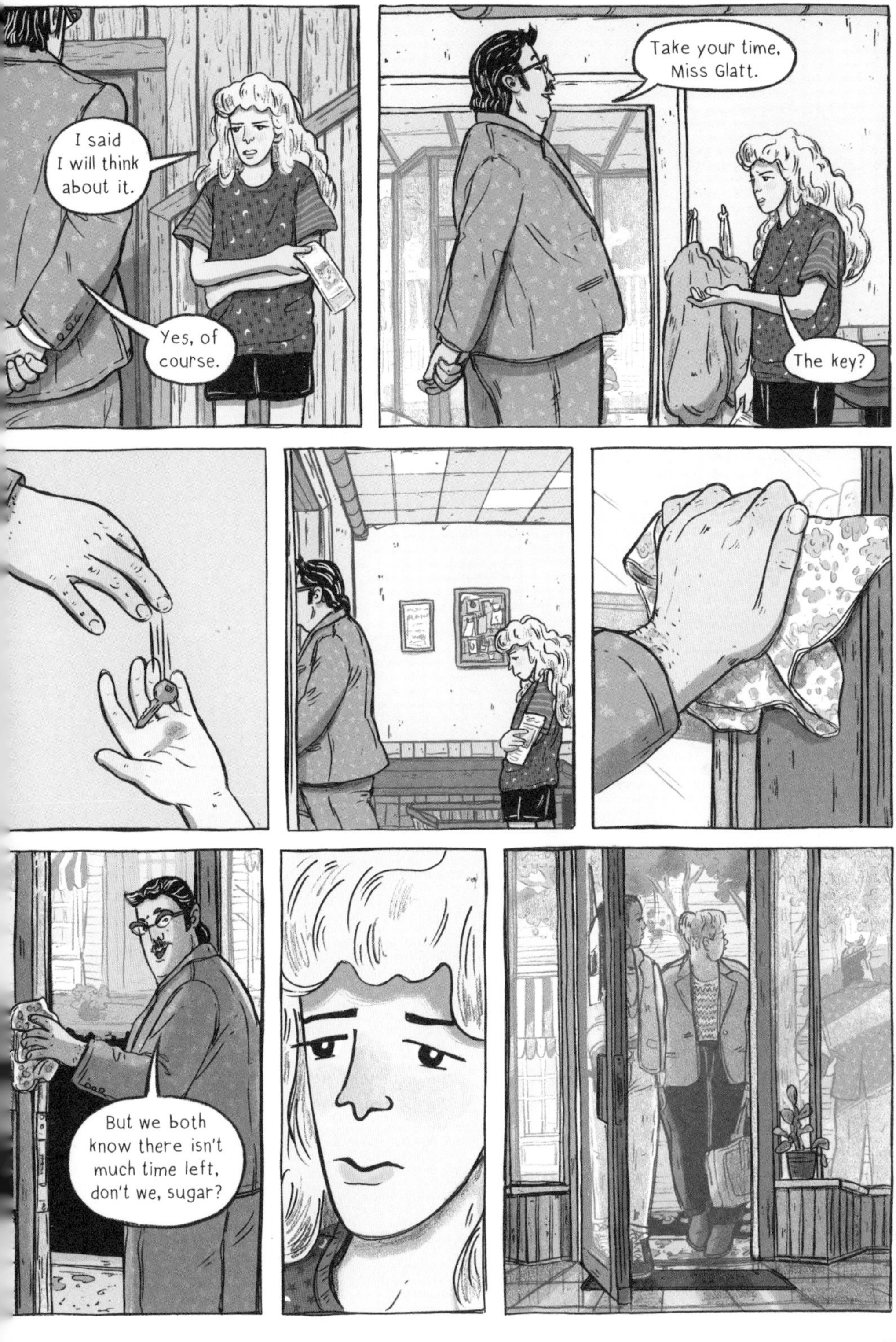
I said I will think about it.
Yes, of course.
Take your time, Miss Glatt.
The key?
But we both know there isn't much time left, don't we, sugar?

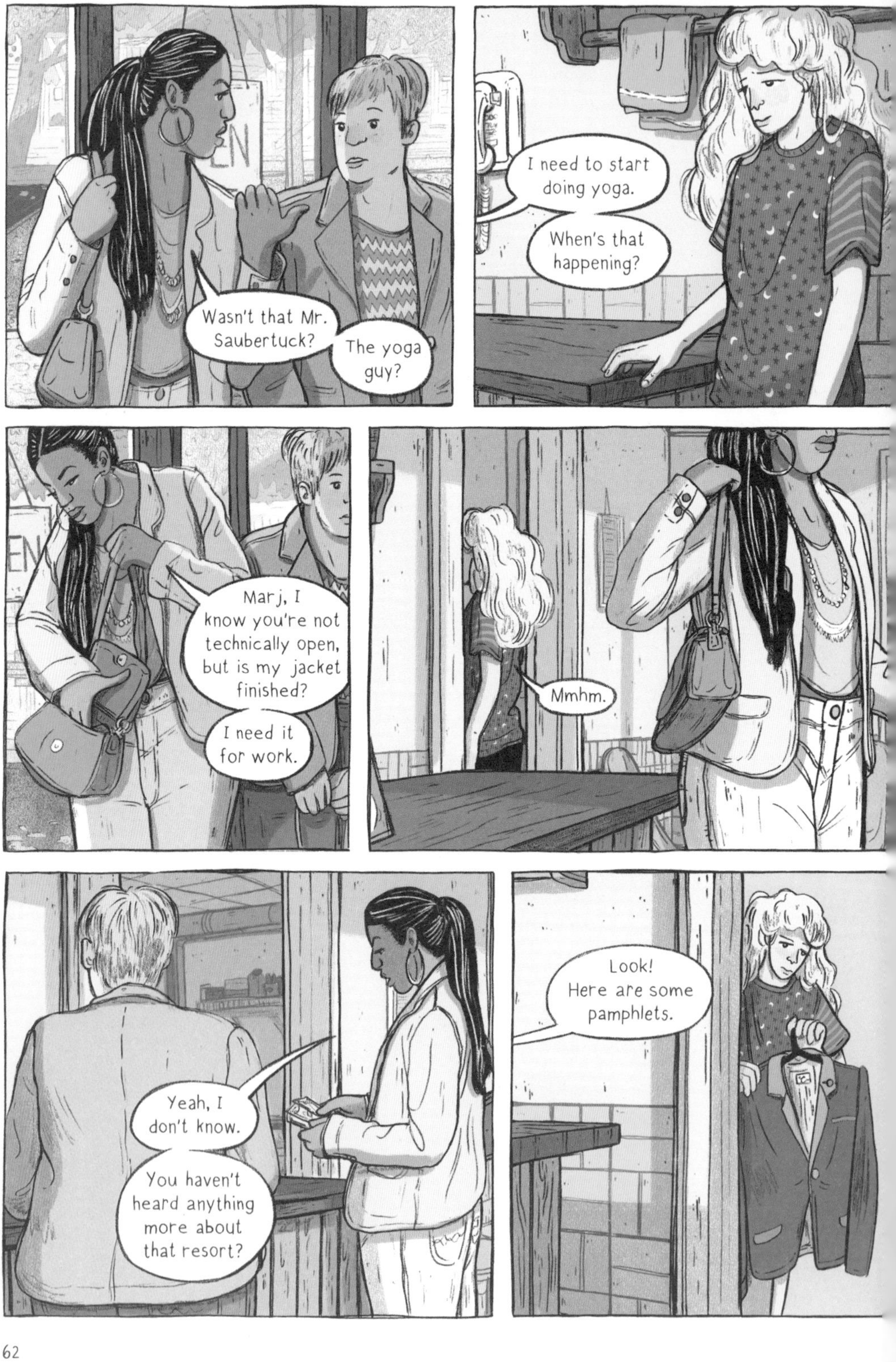
Wasn't that Mr. Saubertuck?
The yoga guy?
I need to start doing yoga.
When's that happening?
Marj, I know you're not technically open, but is my jacket finished?
I need it for work.
Mmhm.
Yeah, I don't know.
You haven't heard anything more about that resort?
Look! Here are some pamphlets.

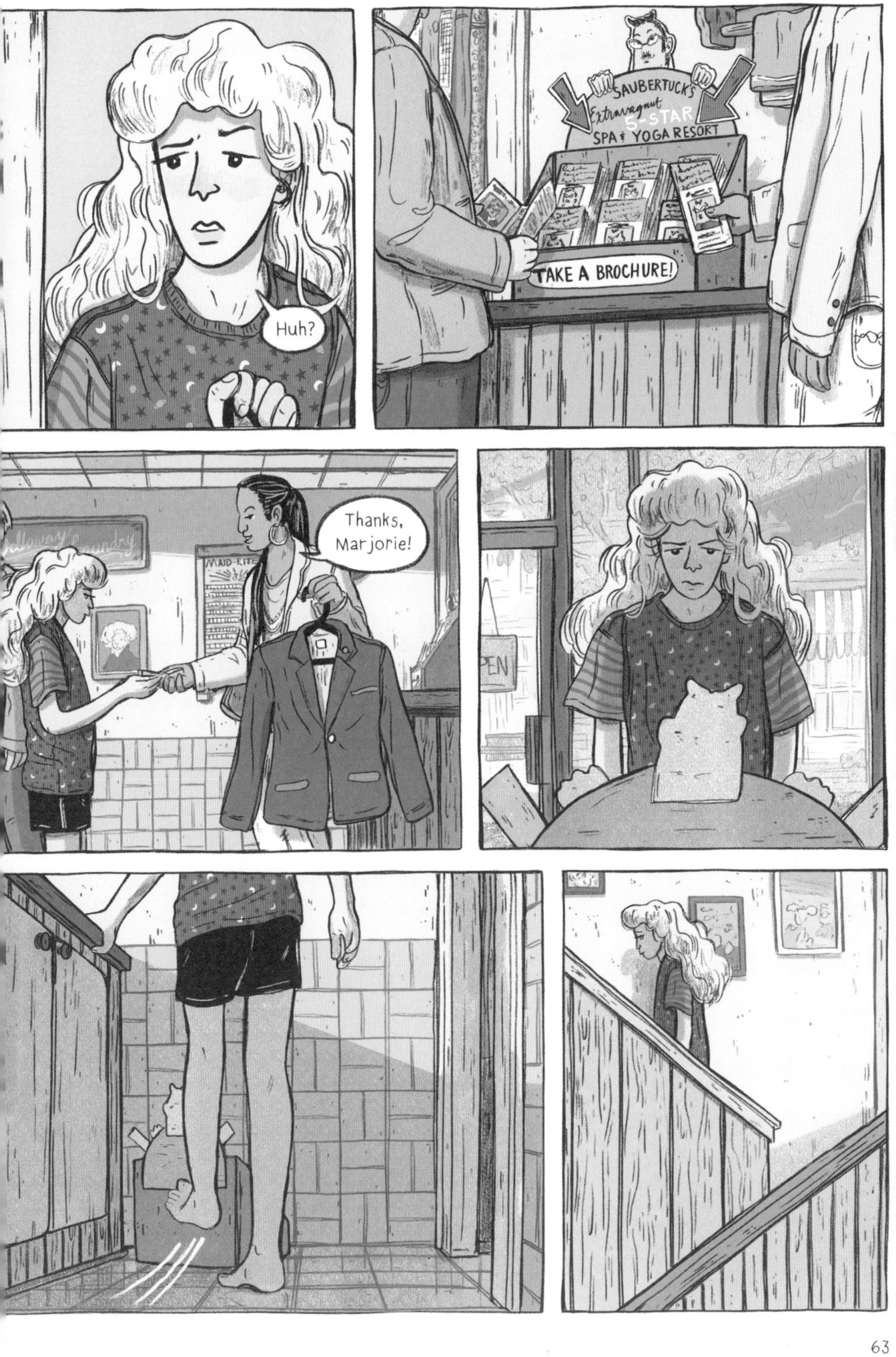
Huh?
SAUBERTUCK'S
Extravagant
5-STAR
SPA & YOGA RESORT
TAKE A BROCHURE!
Thanks, Marjorie!

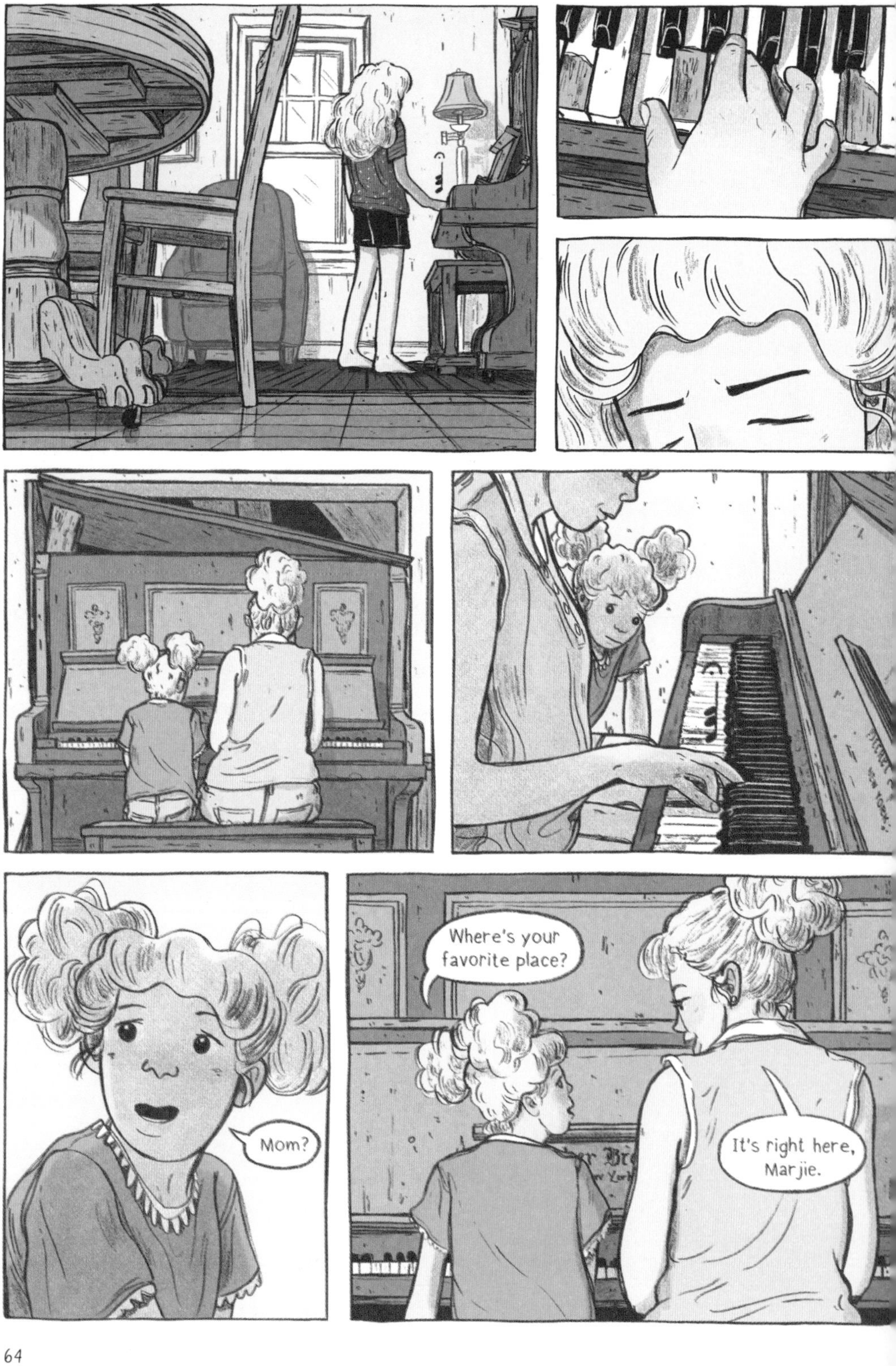
Mom?
Where's your favorite place?
It's right here, Marjie.

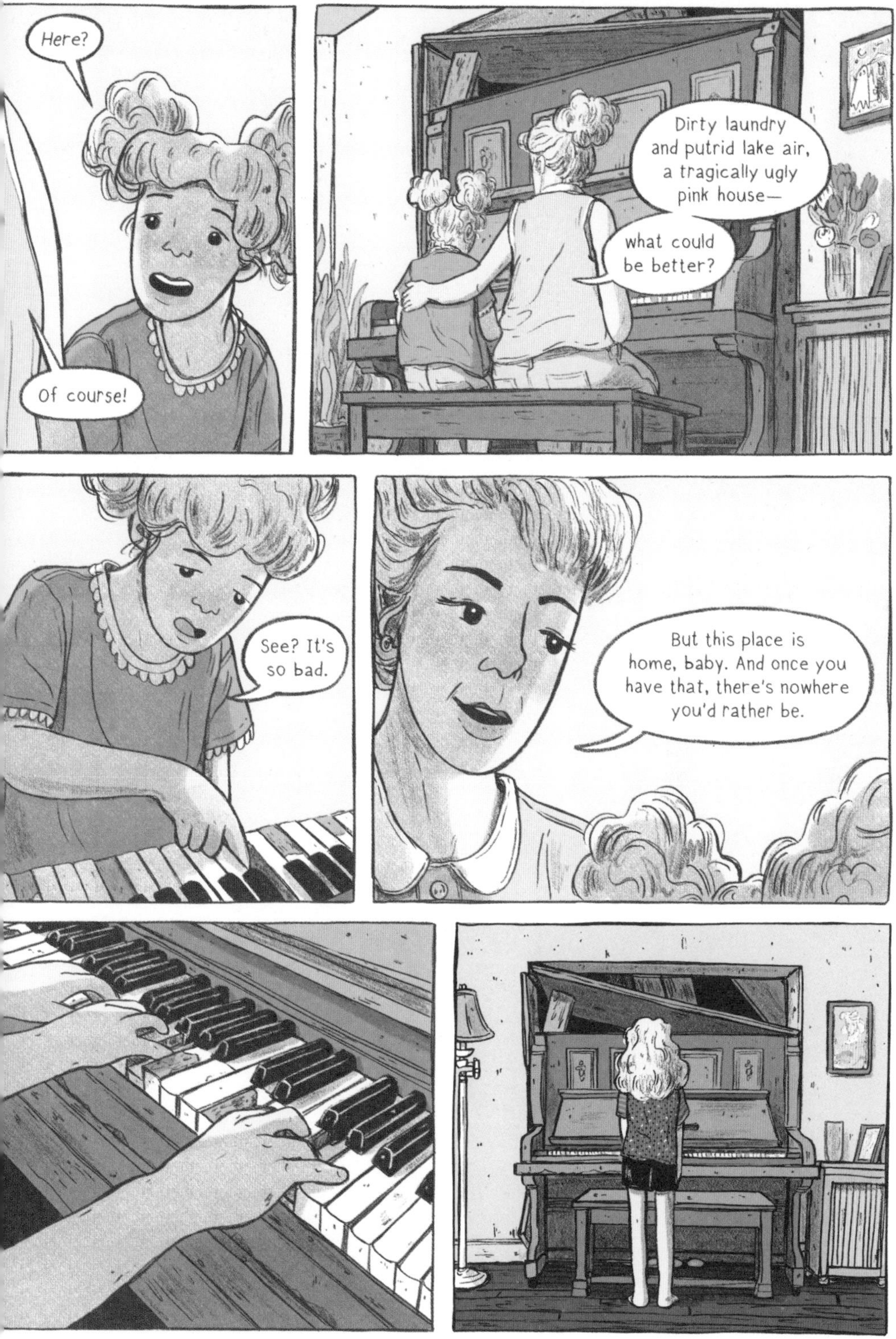
Here?
Of course!
Dirty laundry and putrid lake air, a tragically ugly pink house—
what could be better?
See? It's so bad.
But this place is home, baby. And once you have that, there's nowhere you'd rather be.

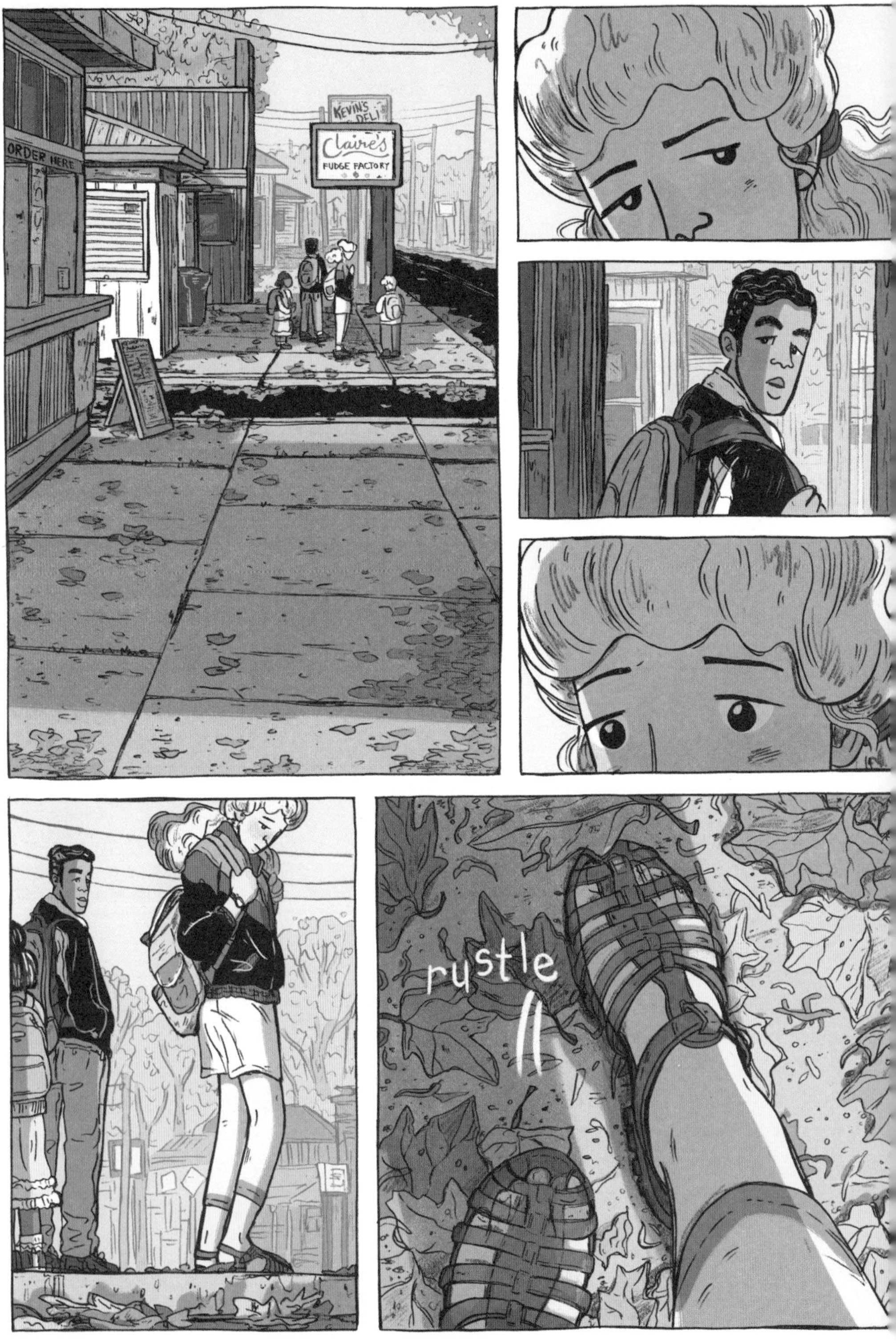

ORDER HERE
KEVIN'S DELI
Claire's
FUDGE FACTORY
rustle

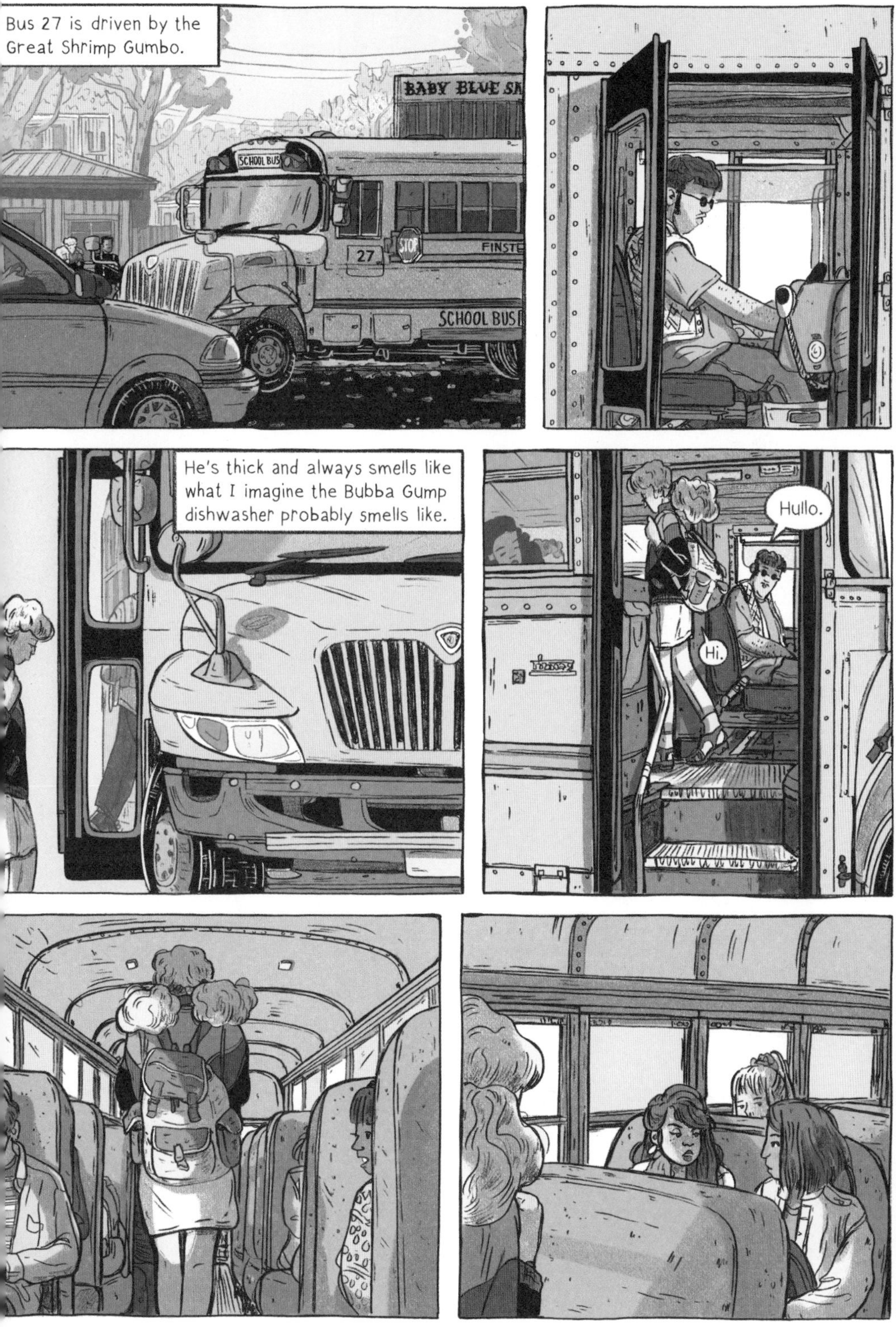
Bus 27 is driven by the Great Shrimp Gumbo.
BABY BLUE SN
SCHOOL BUS
STOP
27
FINST
SCHOOL BUS
He's thick and always smells like what I imagine the Bubba Gump dishwasher probably smells like.
Hullo.
Hi.

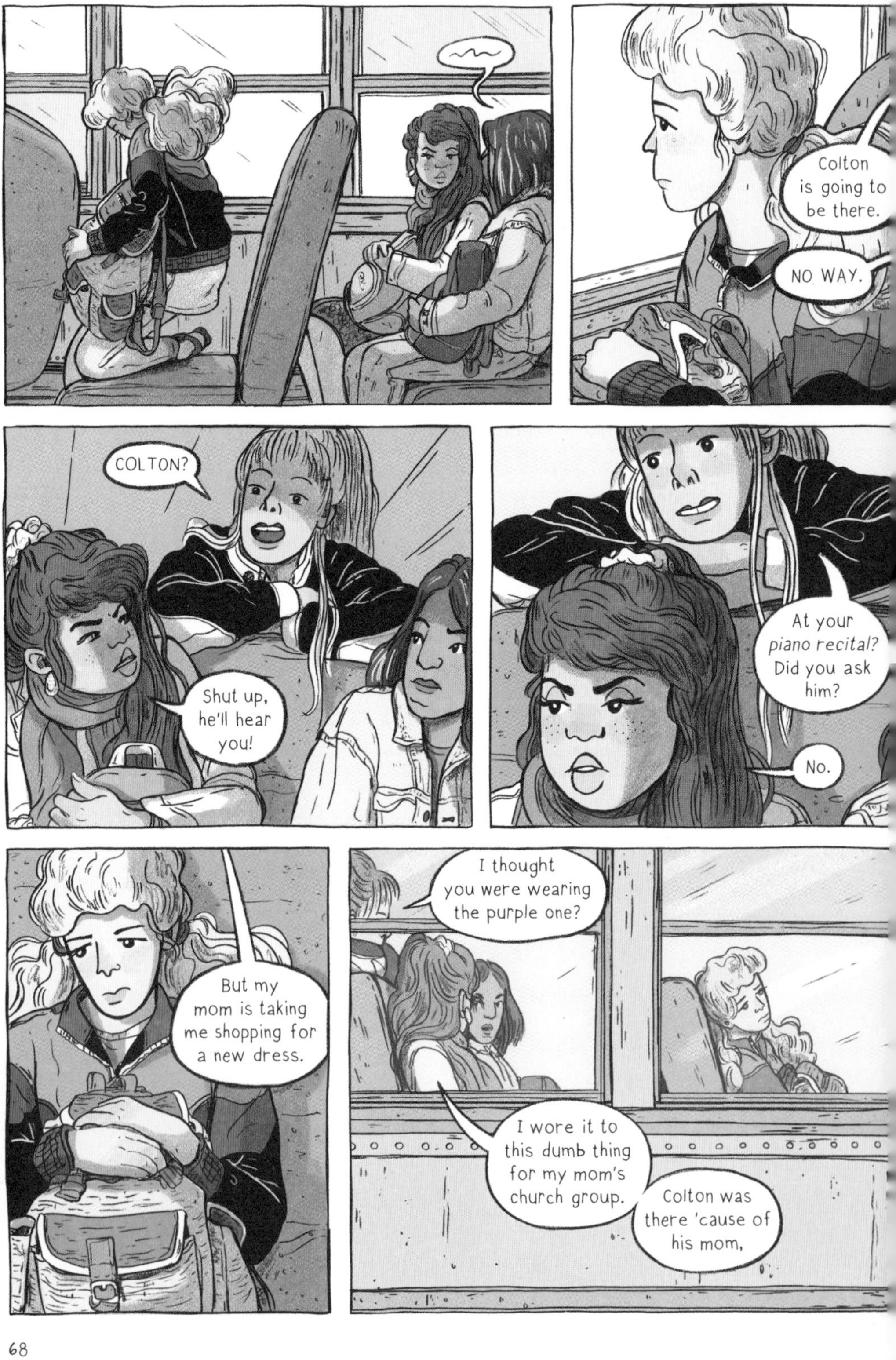
Colton is going to be there.
NO WAY.
COLTON?
Shut up, he'll hear you!
At your *piano recital?* Did you ask him?
No.
But my mom is taking me shopping for a new dress.
I thought you were wearing the purple one?
I wore it to this dumb thing for my mom's church group.
Colton was there 'cause of his mom,

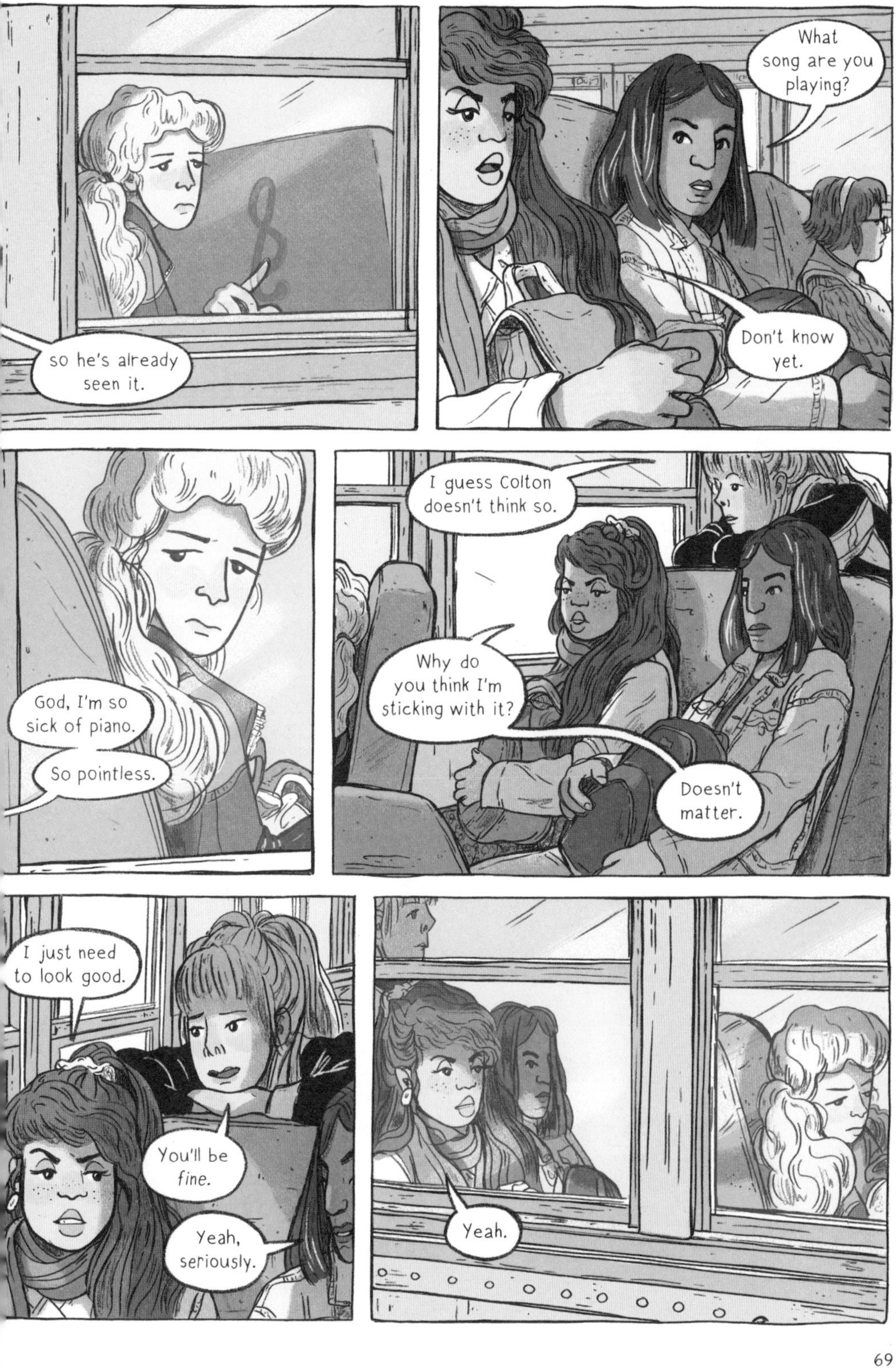
so he's already seen it.
What song are you playing?
Don't know yet.
God, I'm so sick of piano.
So pointless.
I guess Colton doesn't think so.
Why do you think I'm sticking with it?
Doesn't matter.
I just need to look good.
You'll be fine.
Yeah, seriously.
Yeah.

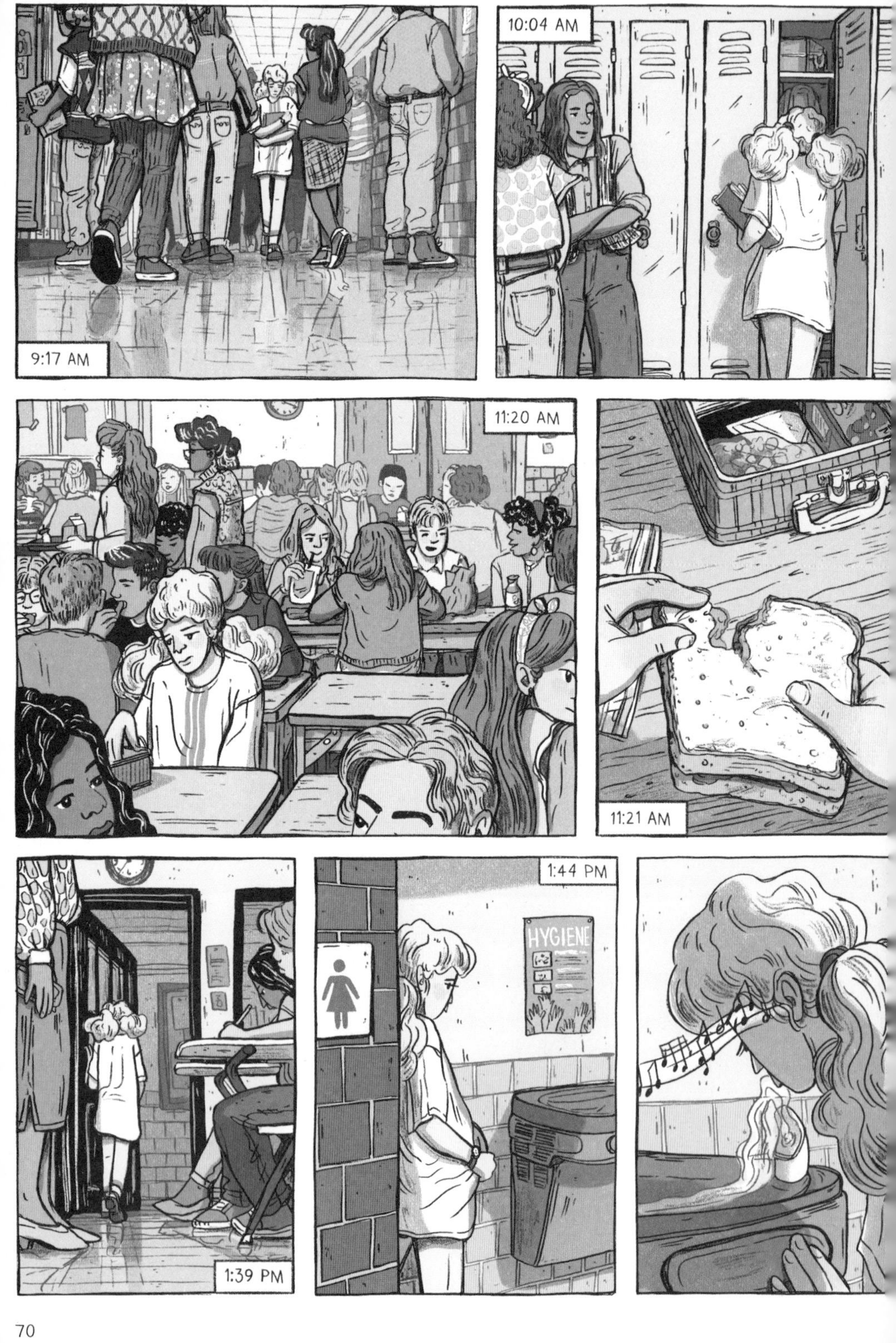
9:17 AM
10:04 AM
11:20 AM
11:21 AM
1:39 PM
1:44 PM
HYGIENE

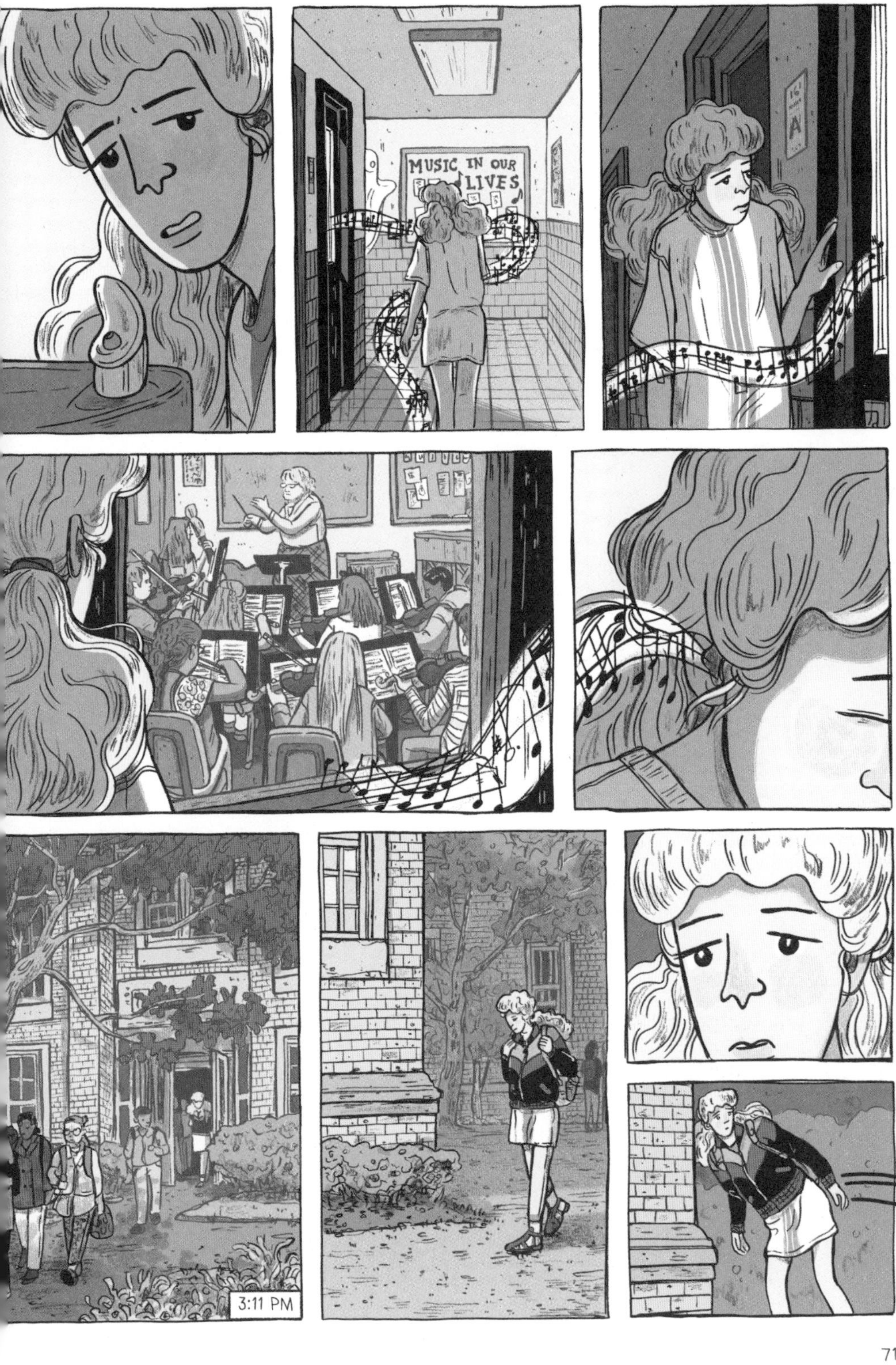
MUSIC IN OUR LIVES
3:11 PM

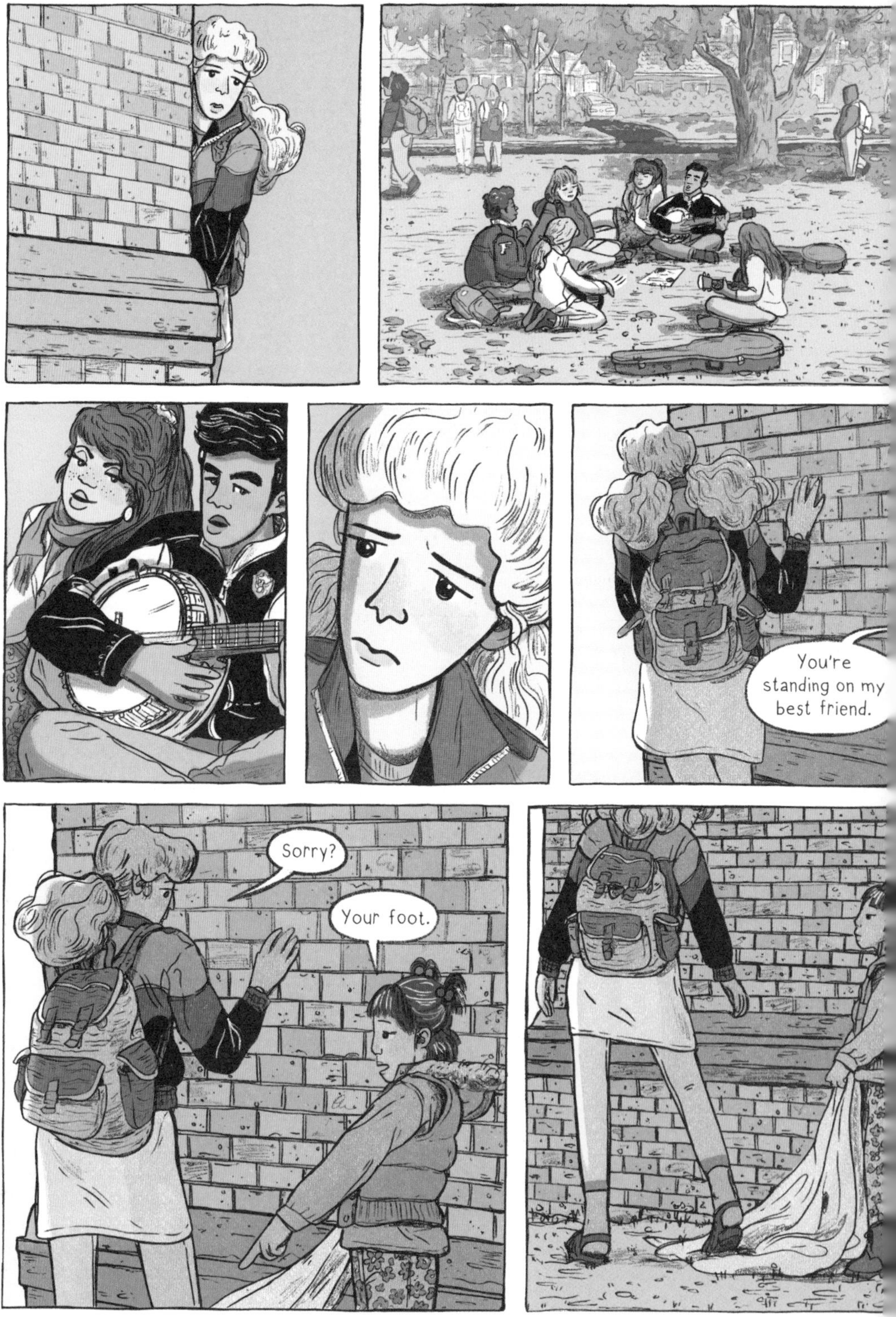
You're standing on my best friend.
Sorry?
Your foot.

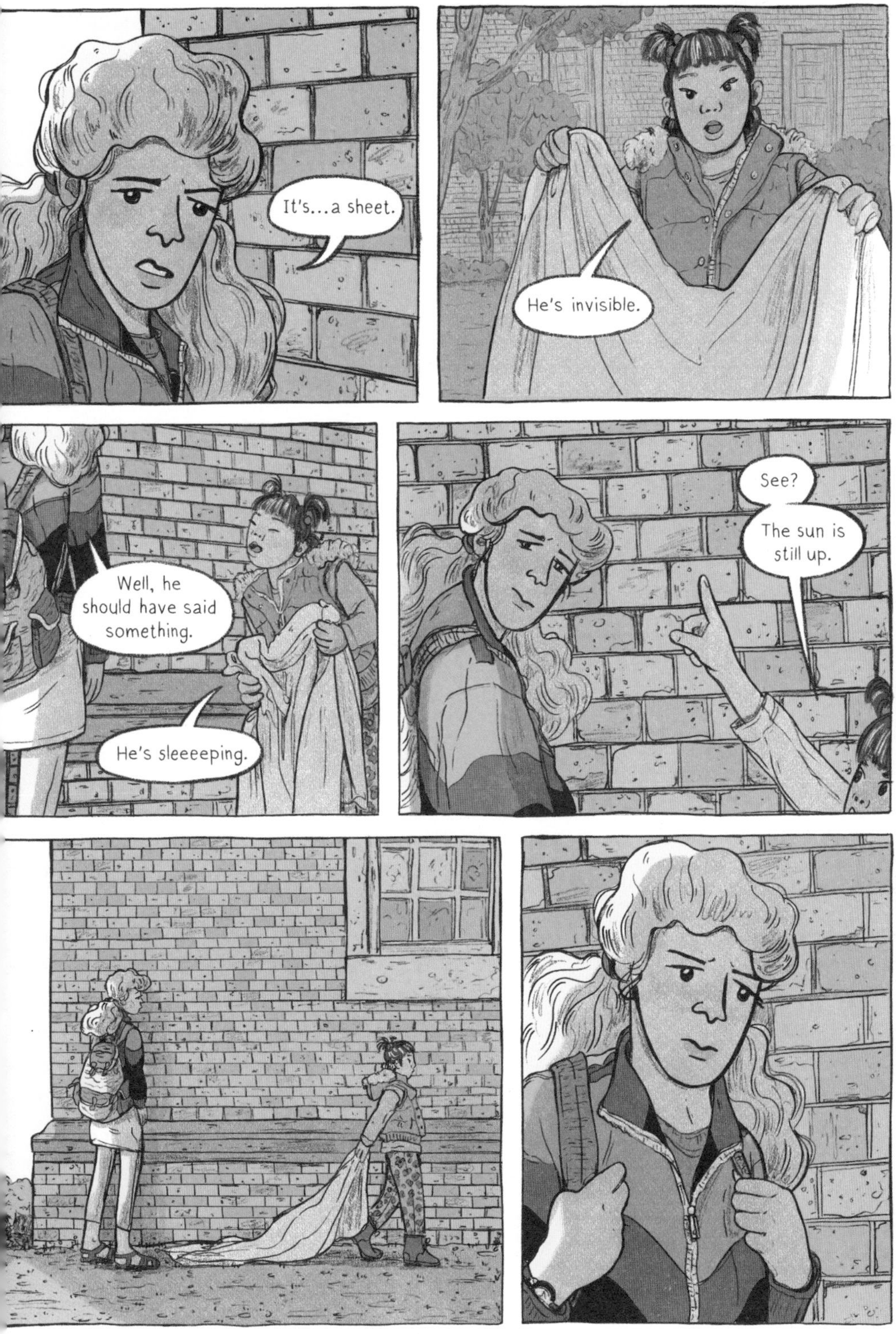
It's...a sheet.
He's invisible.
Well, he should have said something.
He's sleeeeping.
See?
The sun is still up.

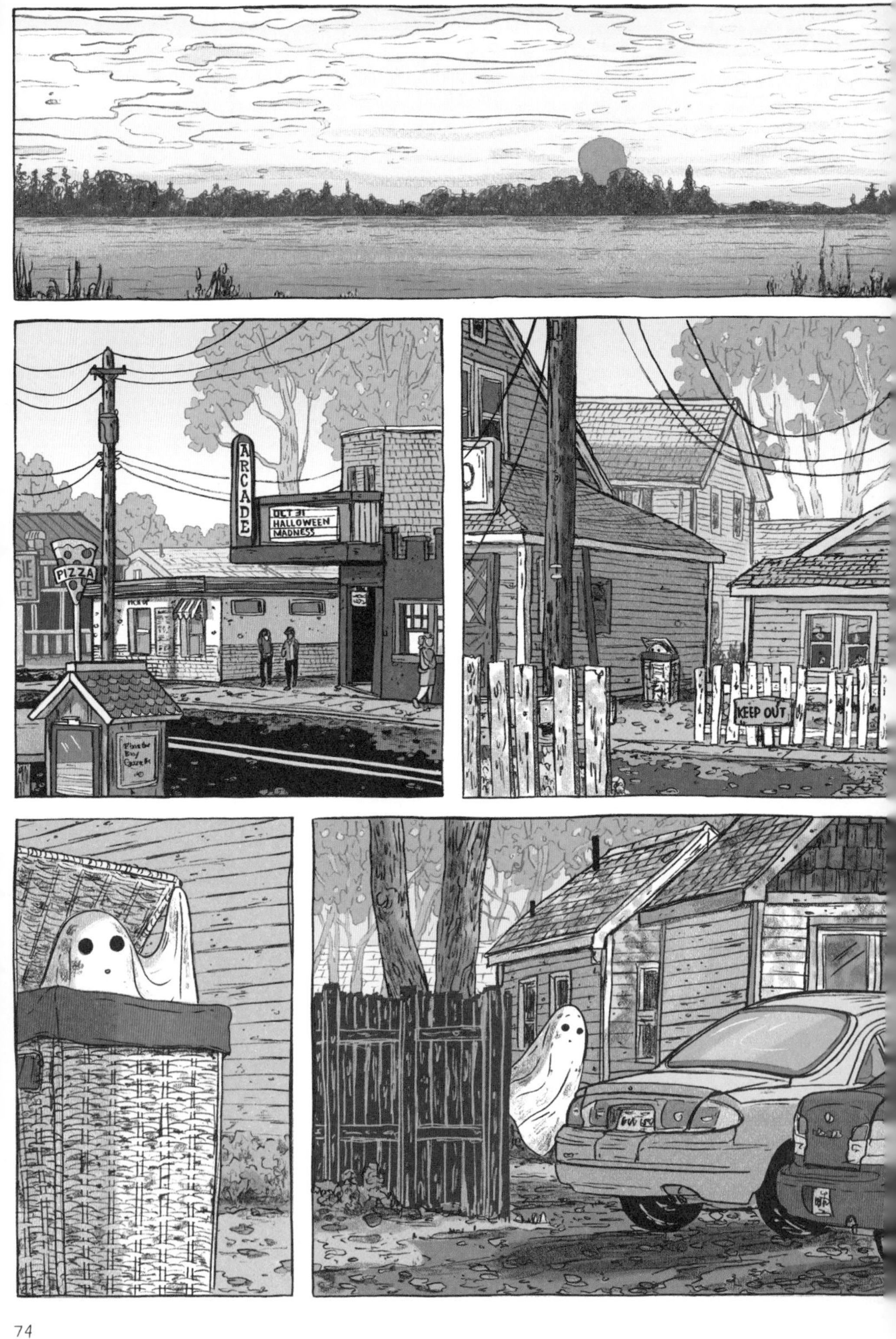
ARCADE
OCT 31
HALLOWEEN
MADNESS
PIZZA
KEEP OUT

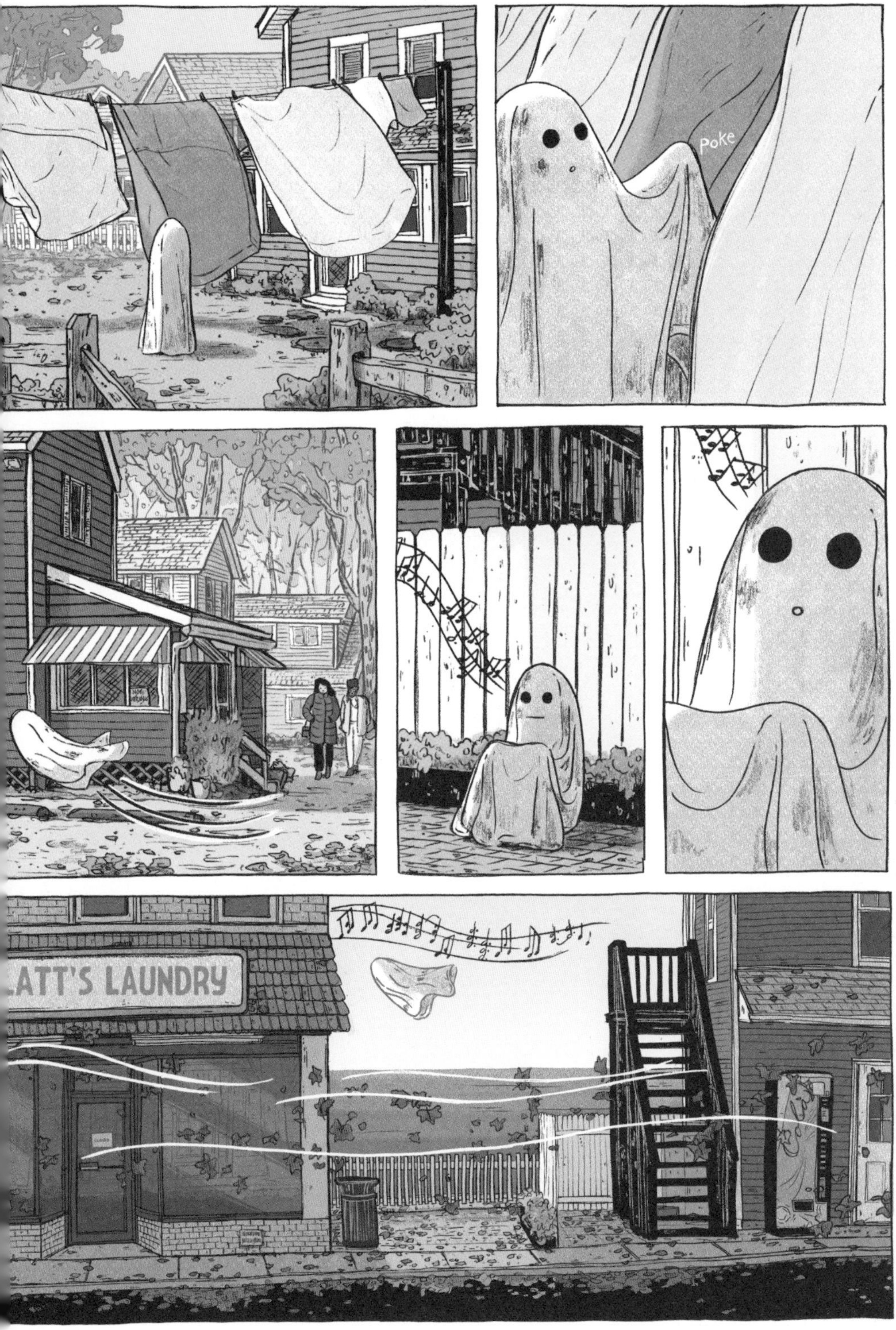
Poke
LATT'S LAUNDRY

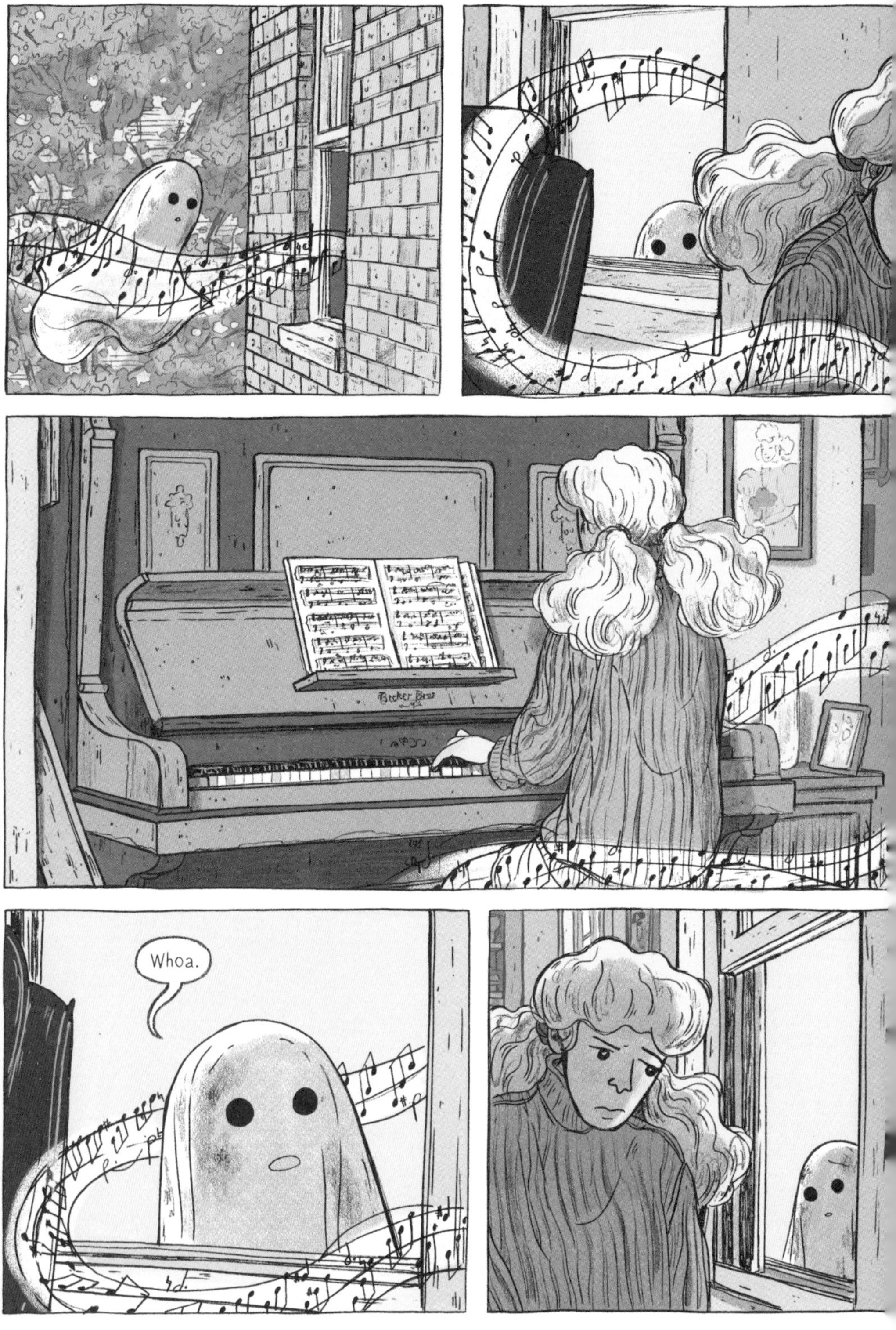
Whoa.

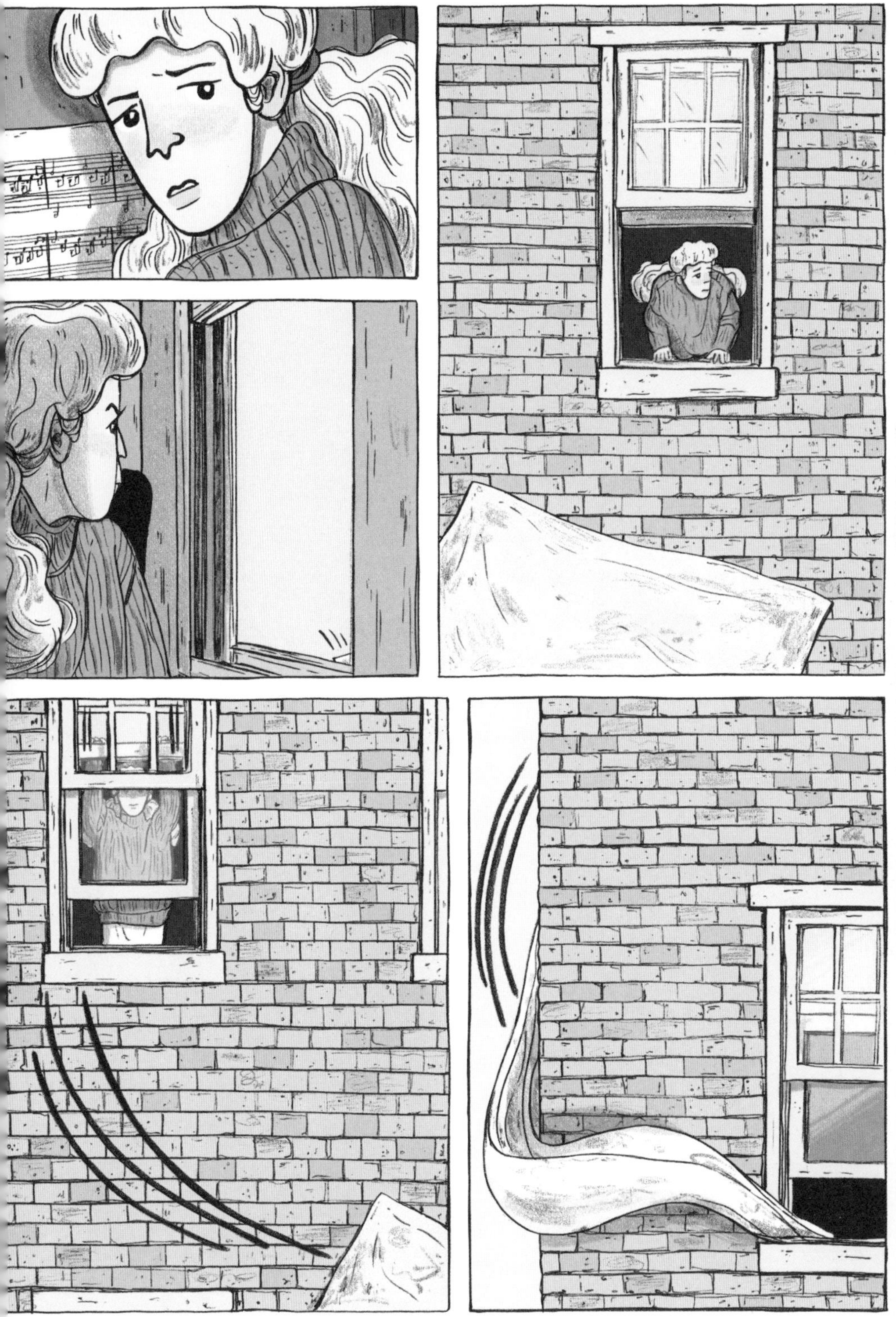

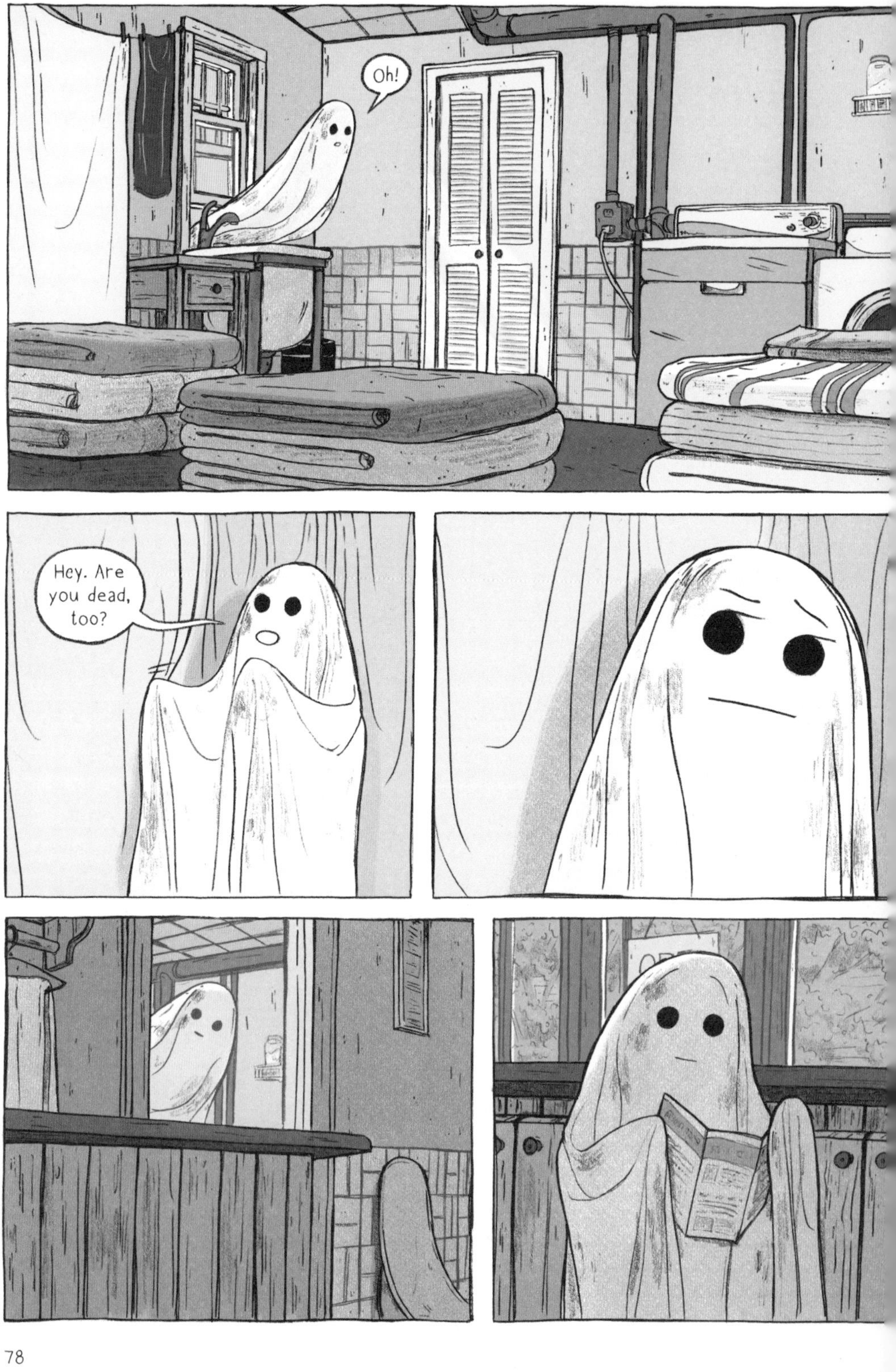
Oh!
Hey. Are you dead, too?

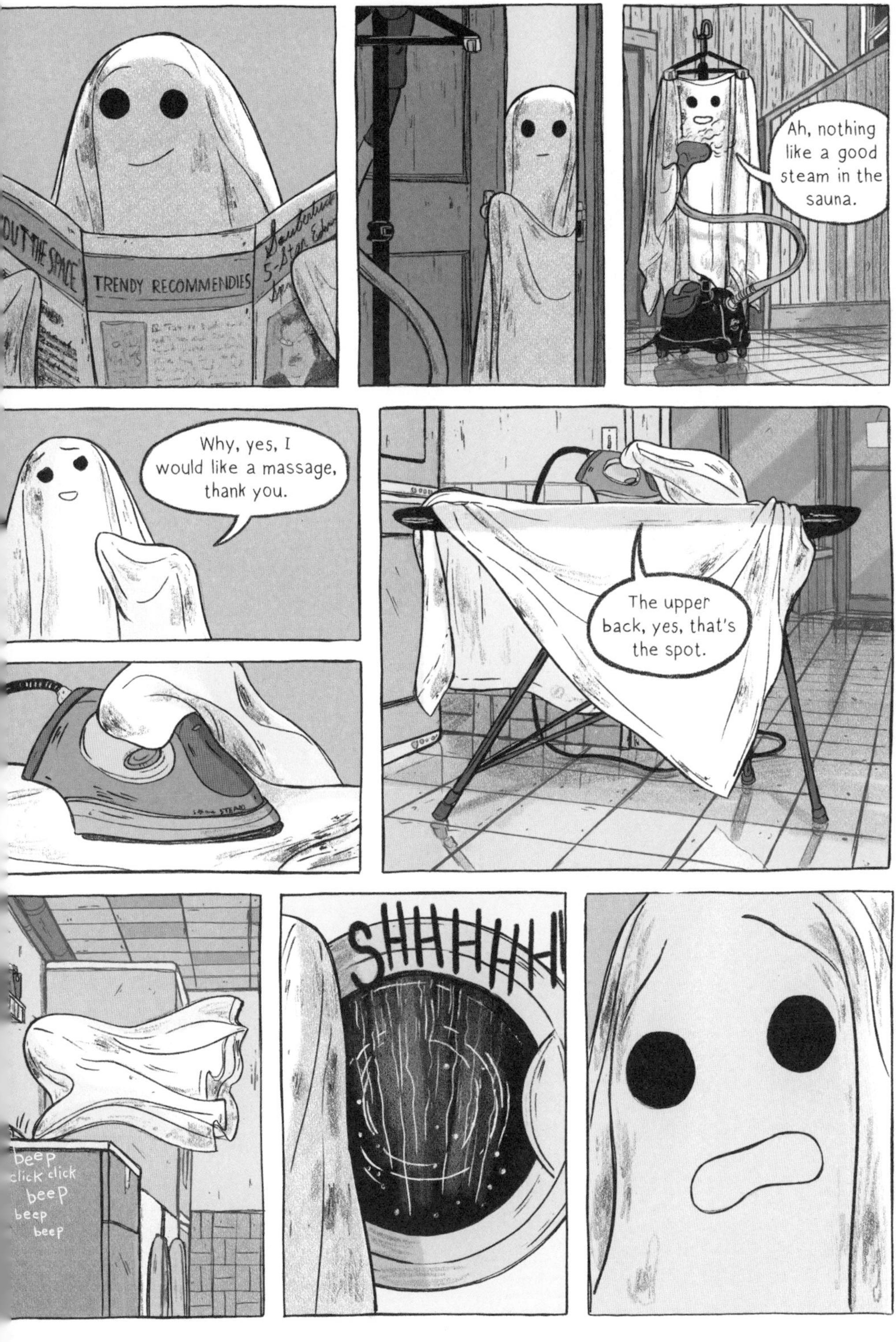
OUT THE SPACE
TRENDY RECOMMENDIES
Ah, nothing like a good steam in the sauna.
Why, yes, I would like a massage, thank you.
The upper back, yes, that's the spot.
beep click click beep beep beep
SHHHHH

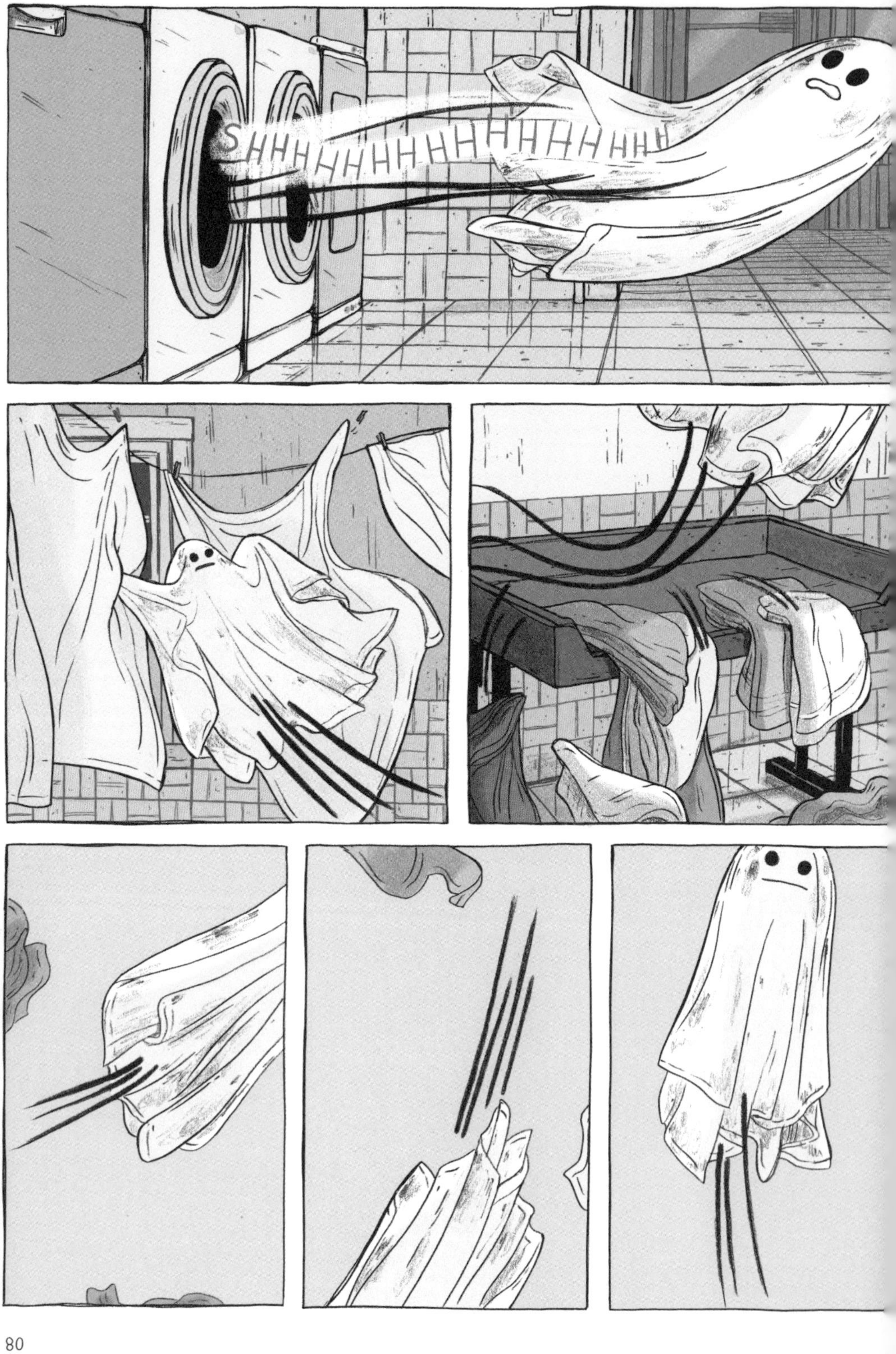
SHHHHHHHHHHHHHHHHHH

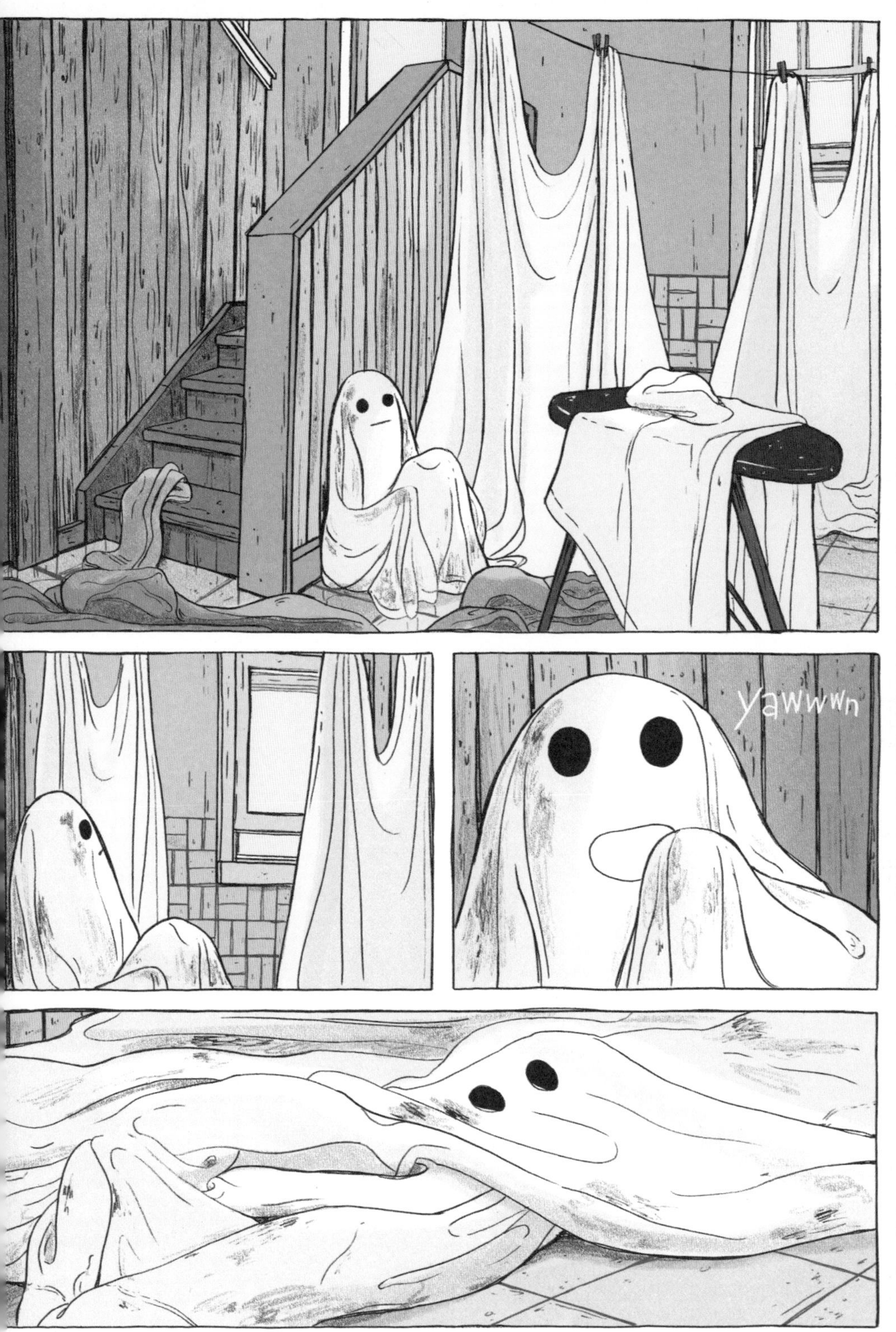
yawwwn

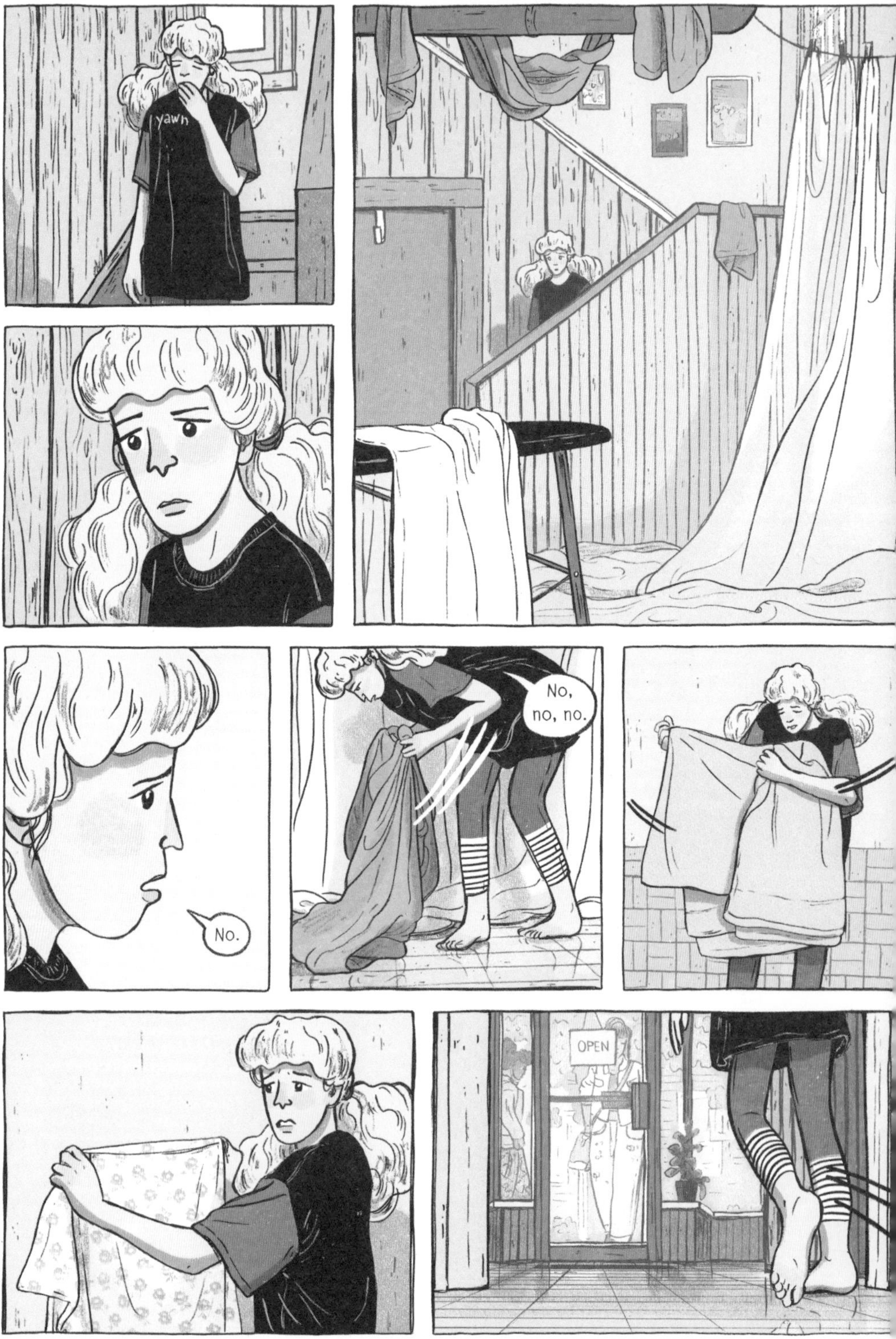
yawn
No.
No, no, no.
OPEN

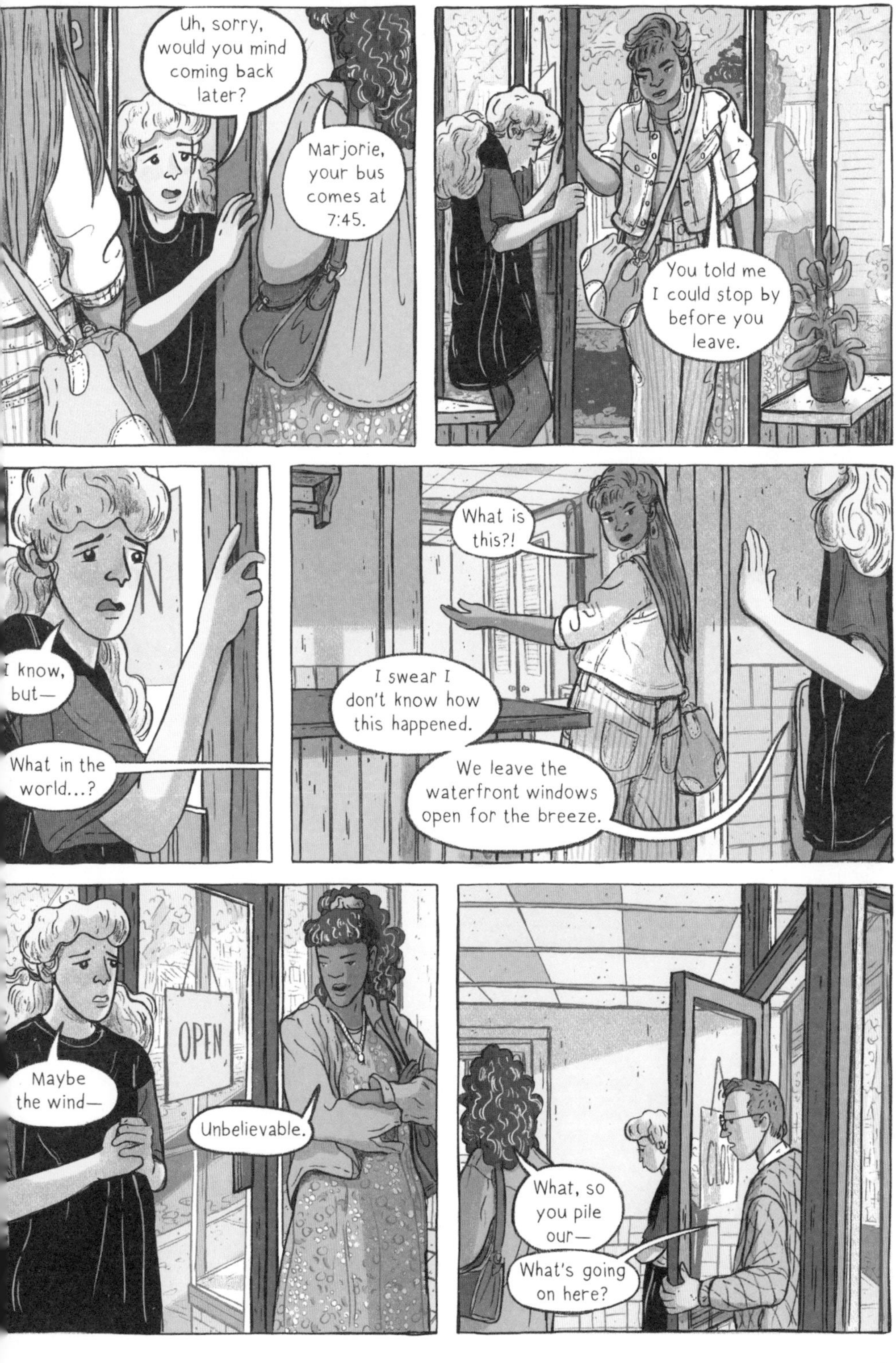
Uh, sorry, would you mind coming back later?
Marjorie, your bus comes at 7:45.
You told me I could stop by before you leave.
I know, but—
What in the world...?
What is this?!
I swear I don't know how this happened.
We leave the waterfront windows open for the breeze.
OPEN
Maybe the wind—
Unbelievable.
What, so you pile our—
What's going on here?

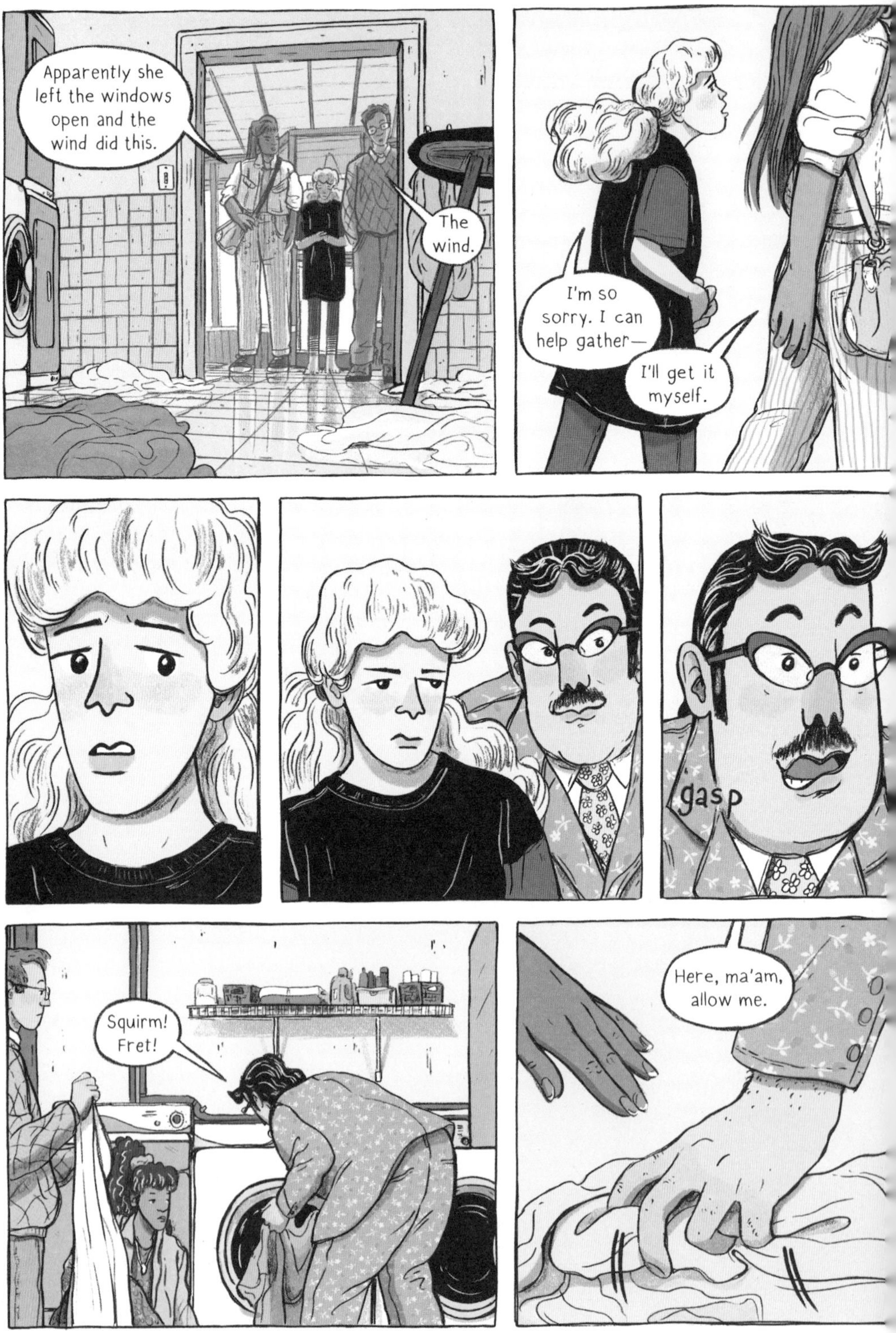
Apparently she left the windows open and the wind did this.
The wind.
I'm so sorry. I can help gather—
I'll get it myself.
gasp
Squirm! Fret!
Here, ma'am, allow me.

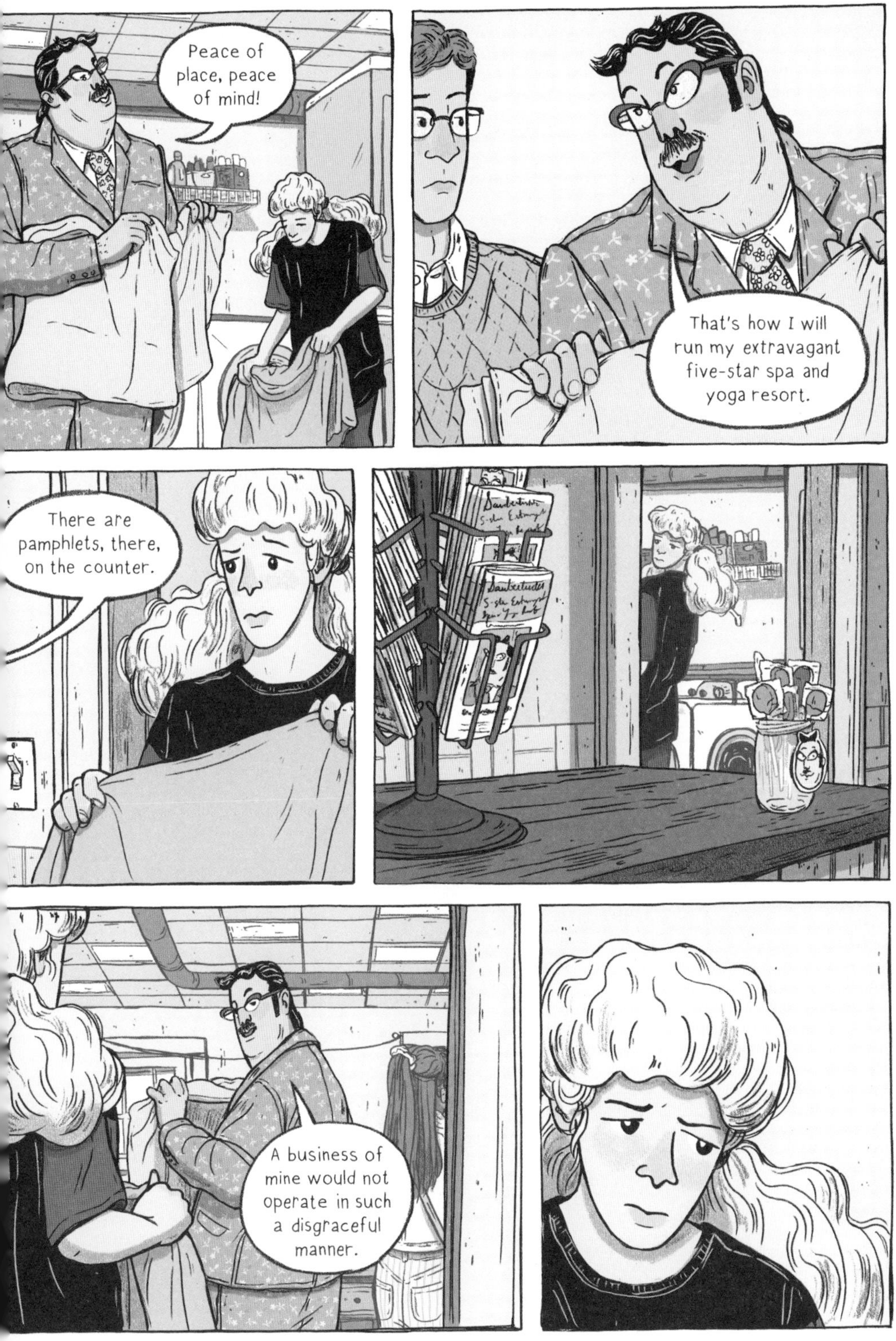

Peace of place, peace of mind!
That's how I will run my extravagant five-star spa and yoga resort.
There are pamphlets, there, on the counter.
A business of mine would not operate in such a disgraceful manner.

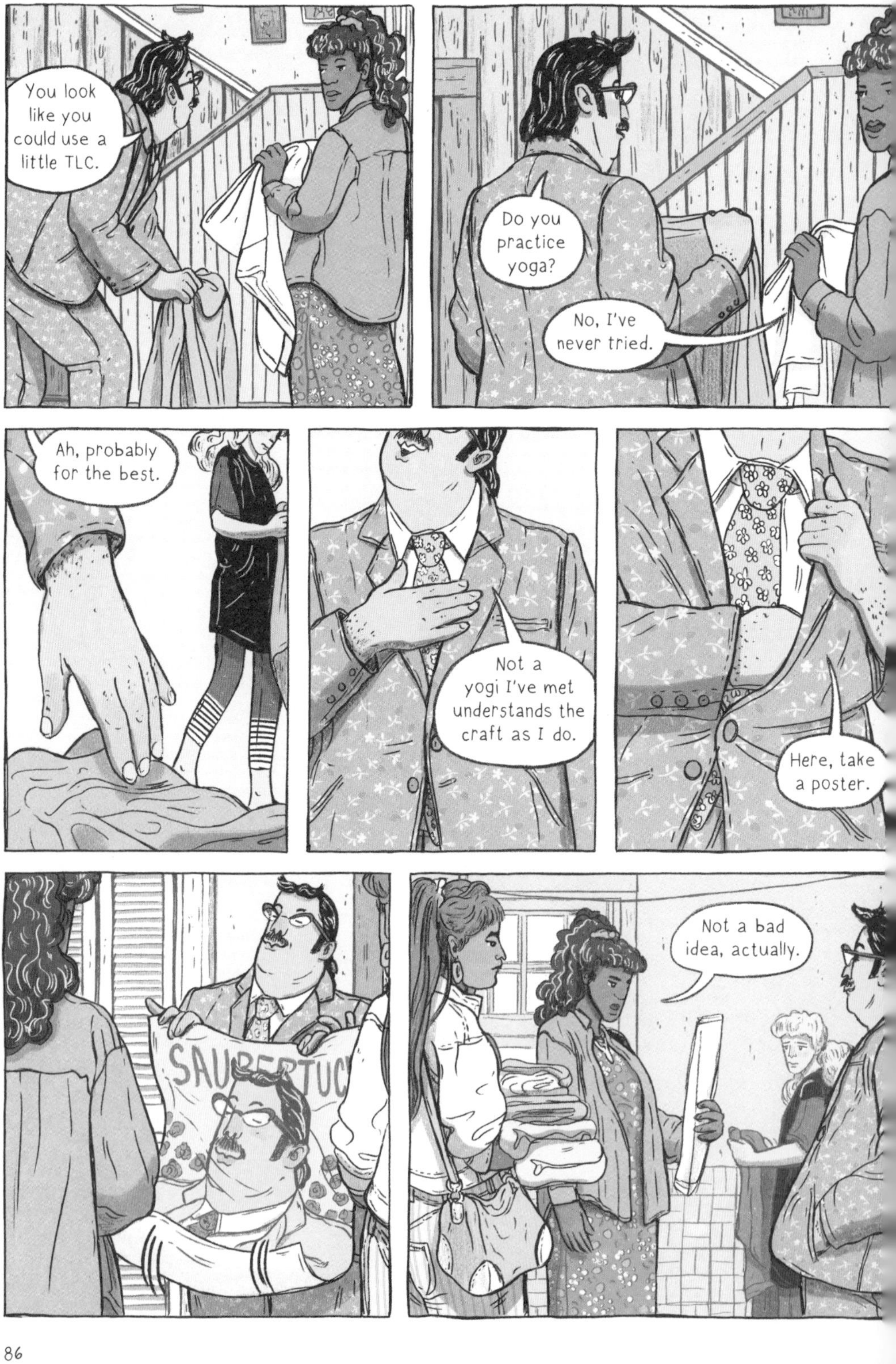
You look like you could use a little TLC.
Do you practice yoga?
No, I've never tried.
Ah, probably for the best.
Not a yogi I've met understands the craft as I do.
Here, take a poster.
SAUBERTUCK
Not a bad idea, actually.

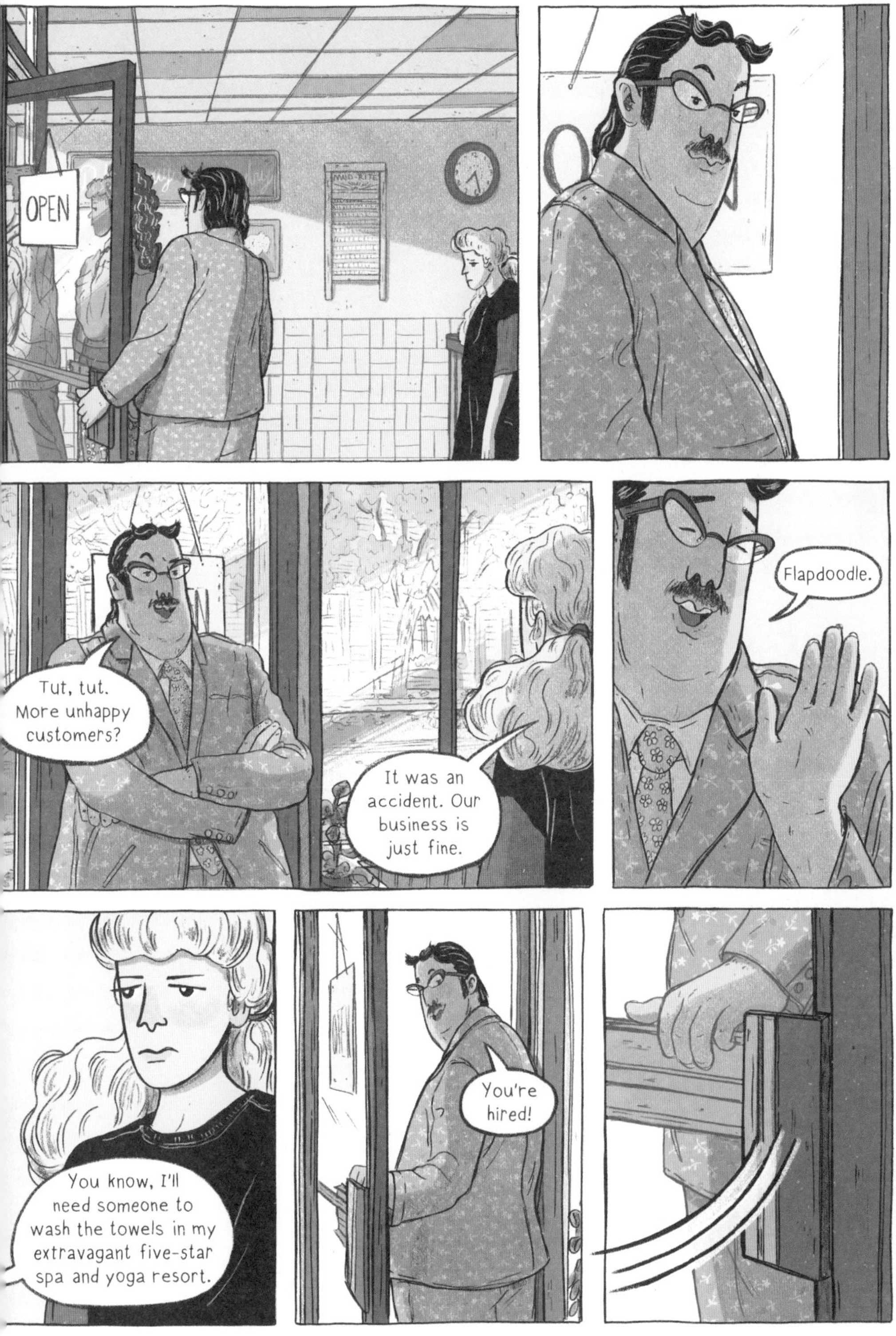
OPEN
Tut, tut. More unhappy customers?
It was an accident. Our business is just fine.
Flapdoodle.
You know, I'll need someone to wash the towels in my extravagant five-star spa and yoga resort.
You're hired!

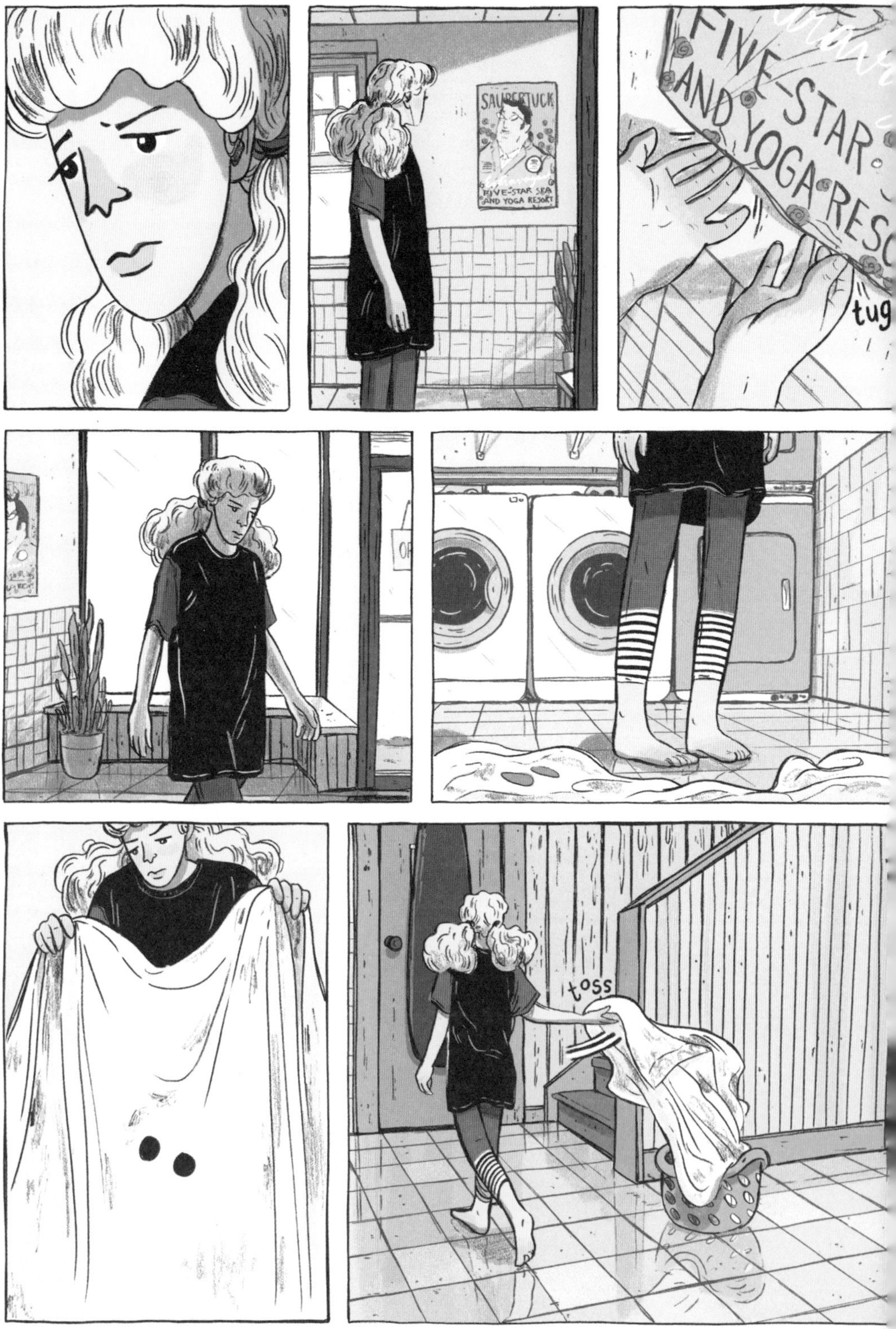
SAUERTUCK
FIVE-STAR SPA
AND YOGA RESORT
FIVE-STAR
AND YOGA RESO
tug
toss

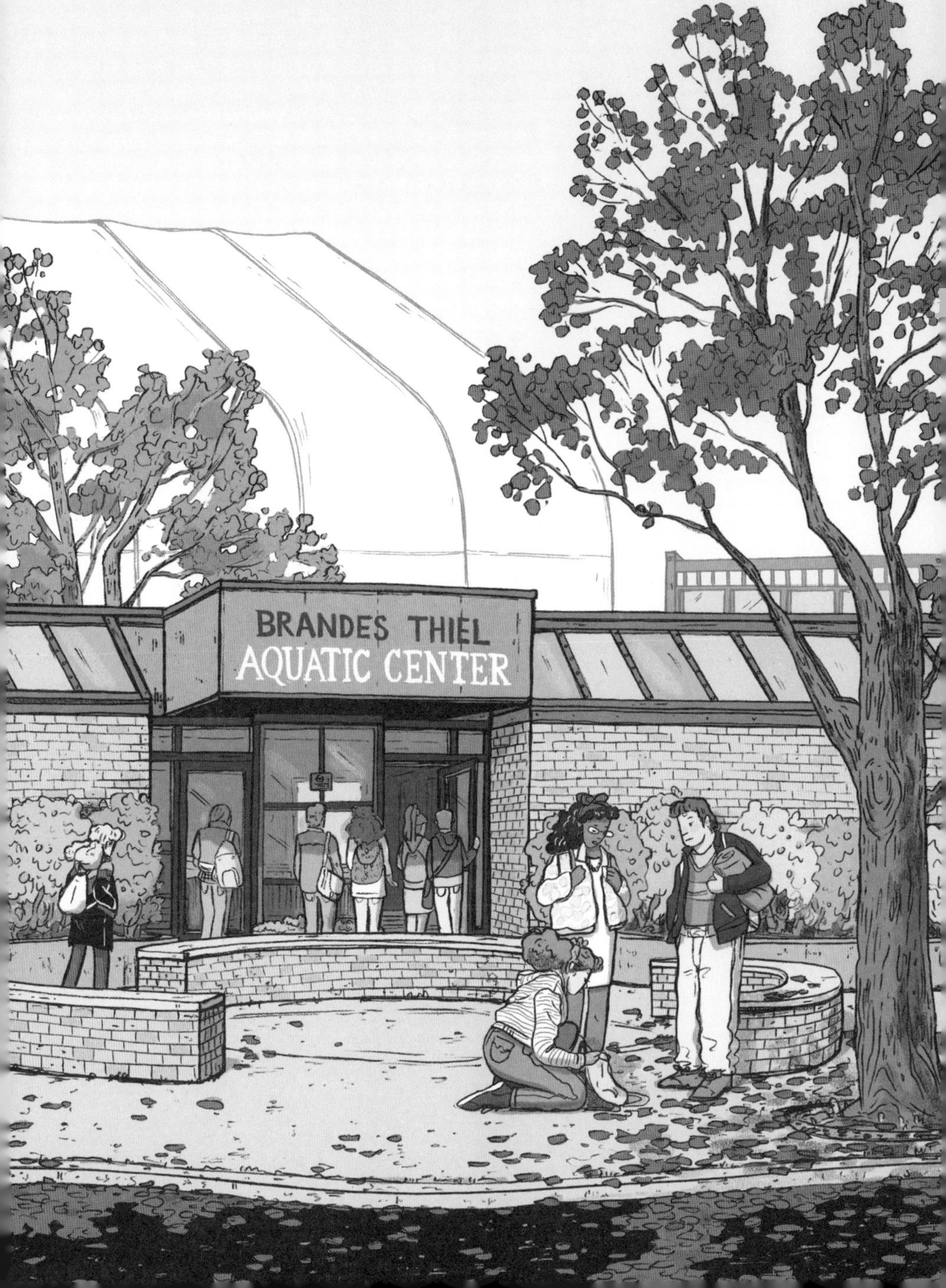
BRANDES THIEL
AQUATIC CENTER

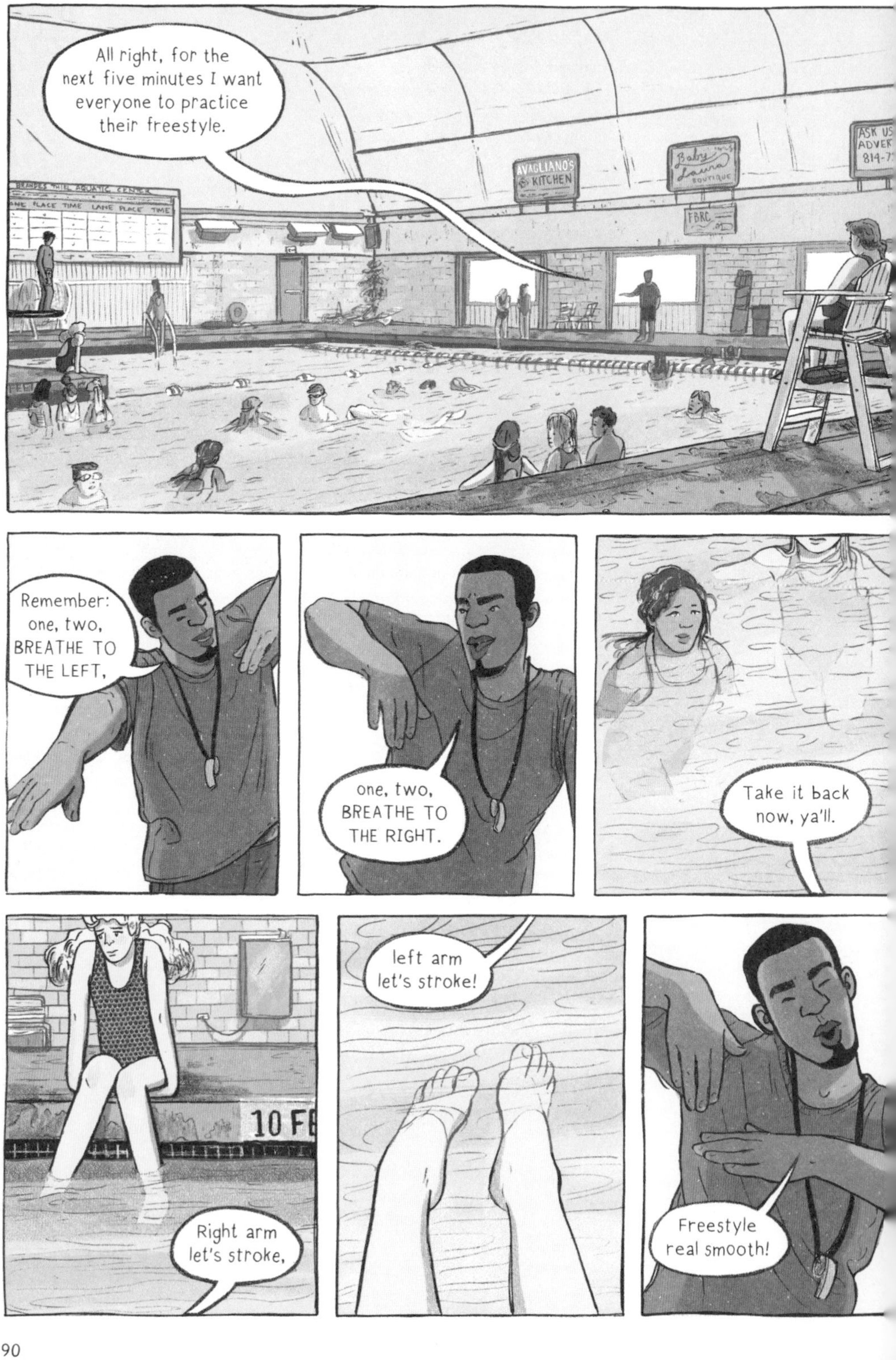
All right, for the next five minutes I want everyone to practice their freestyle.
AVAGLIANO'S KITCHEN
Remember: one, two, BREATHE TO THE LEFT,
one, two, BREATHE TO THE RIGHT.
Take it back now, ya'll.
Right arm let's stroke,
left arm let's stroke!
Freestyle real smooth!

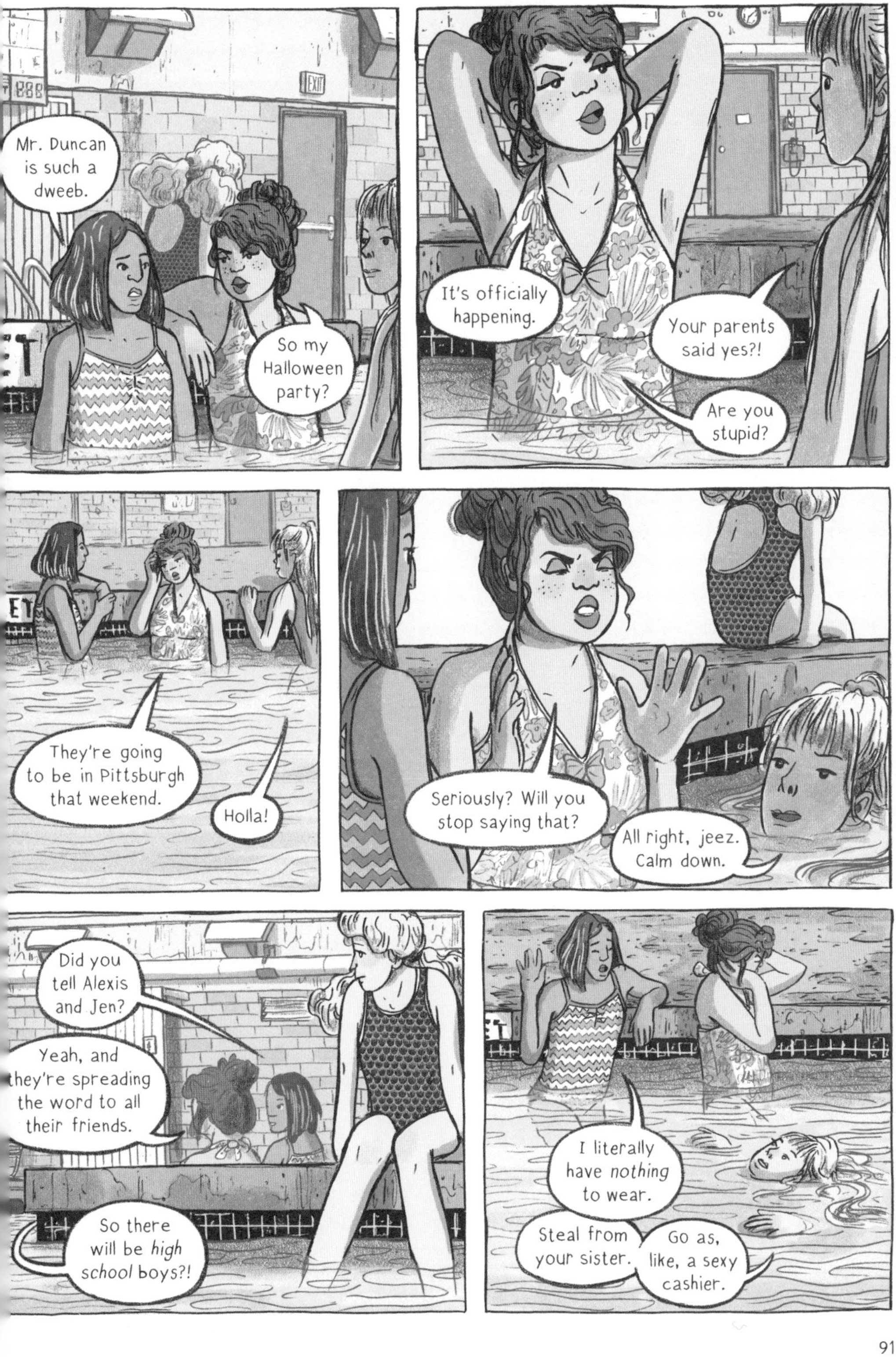
Mr. Duncan is such a dweeb.
So my Halloween party?
It's officially happening.
Your parents said yes?!
Are you stupid?
EXIT
They're going to be in Pittsburgh that weekend.
Holla!
Seriously? Will you stop saying that?
All right, jeez. Calm down.
Did you tell Alexis and Jen?
Yeah, and they're spreading the word to all their friends.
So there will be *high school* boys?!
I literally have *nothing* to wear.
Steal from your sister.
Go as, like, a sexy cashier.

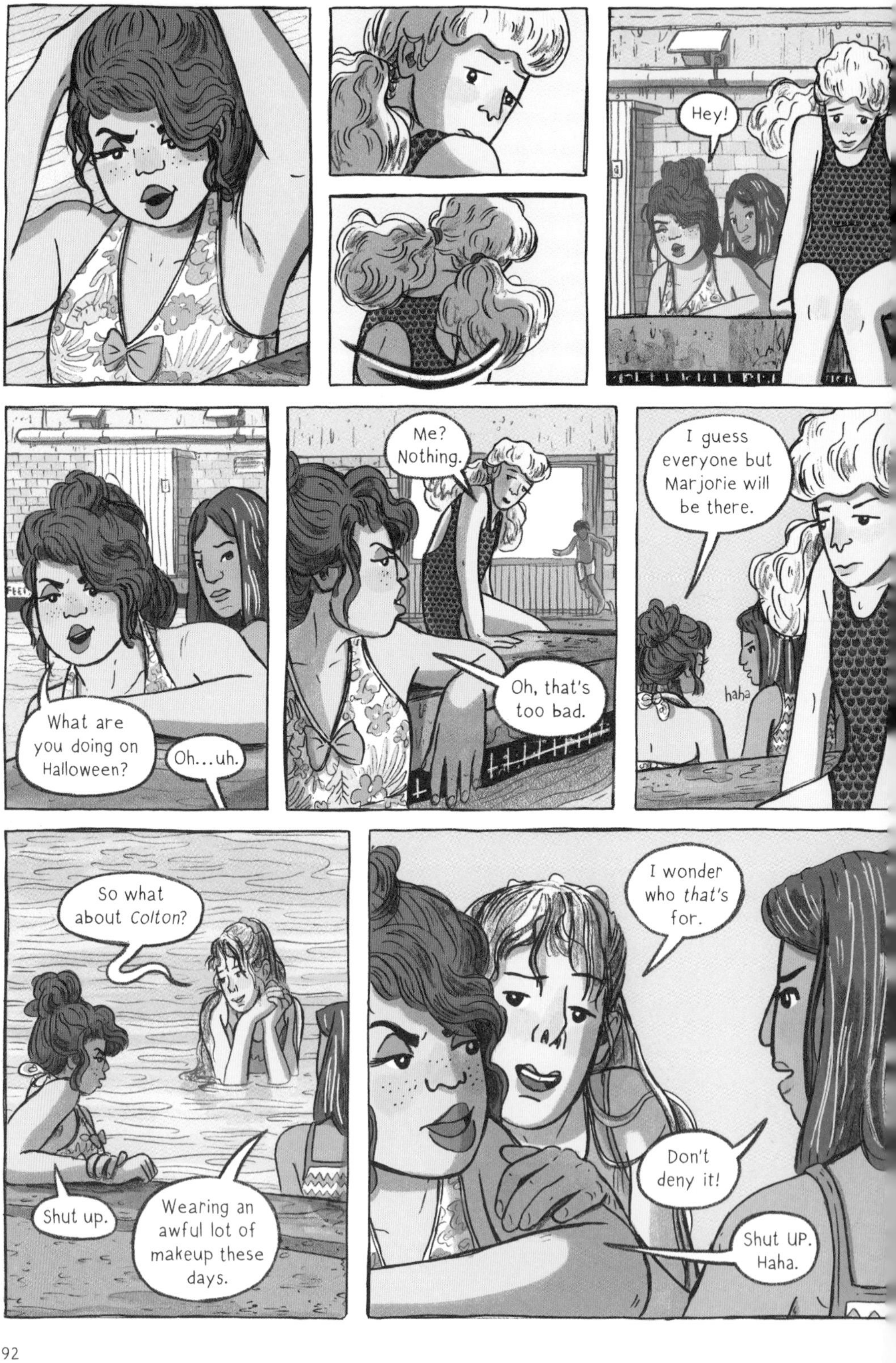
Hey!
What are you doing on Halloween?
Oh...uh.
Me? Nothing.
Oh, that's too bad.
I guess everyone but Marjorie will be there.
haha
So what about *Colton*?
Shut up.
Wearing an awful lot of makeup these days.
I wonder who *that's* for.
Don't deny it!
Shut UP. Haha.

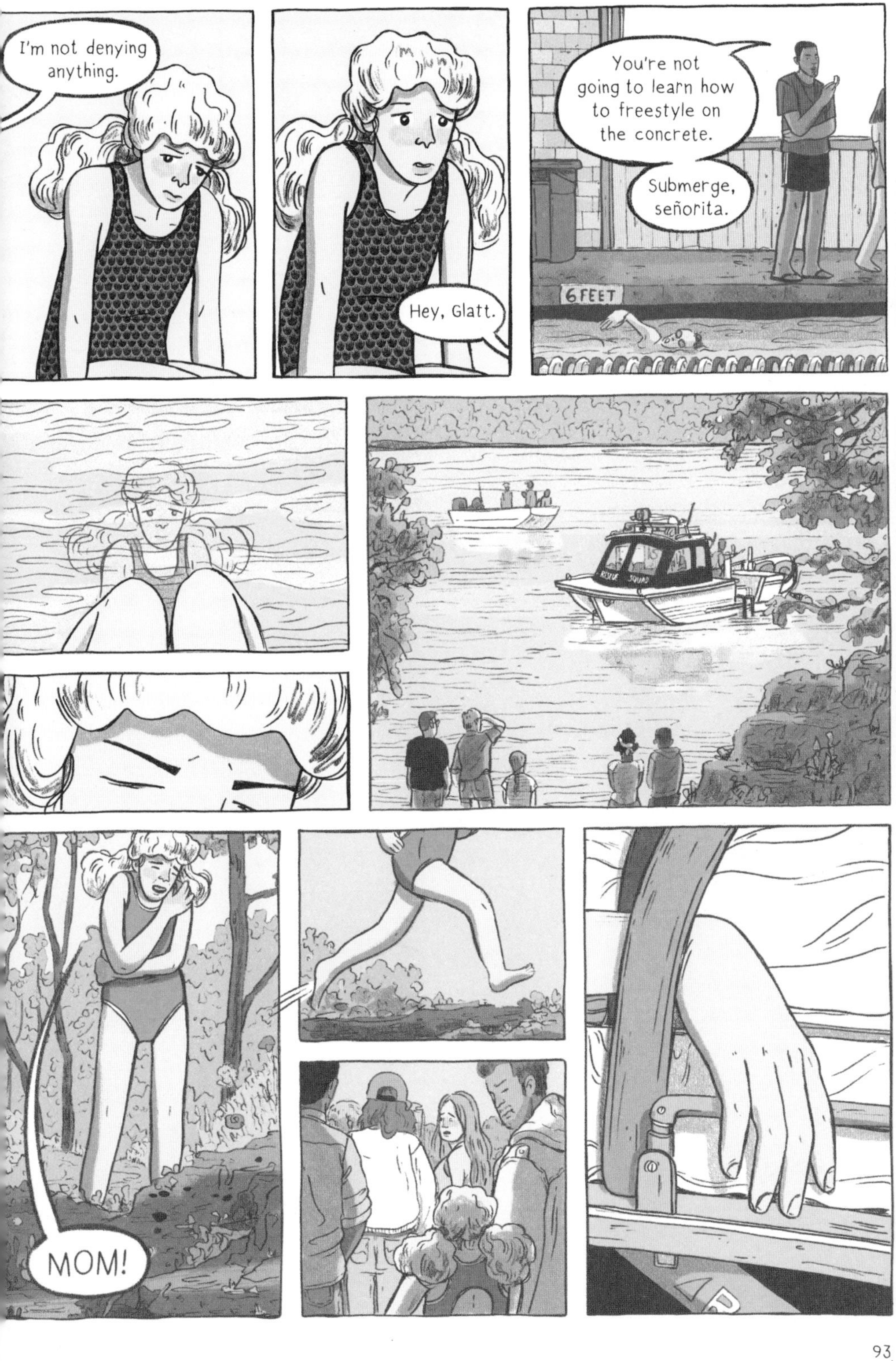
I'm not denying anything.
Hey, Glatt.
You're not going to learn how to freestyle on the concrete.
Submerge, señorita.
6 FEET
MOM!

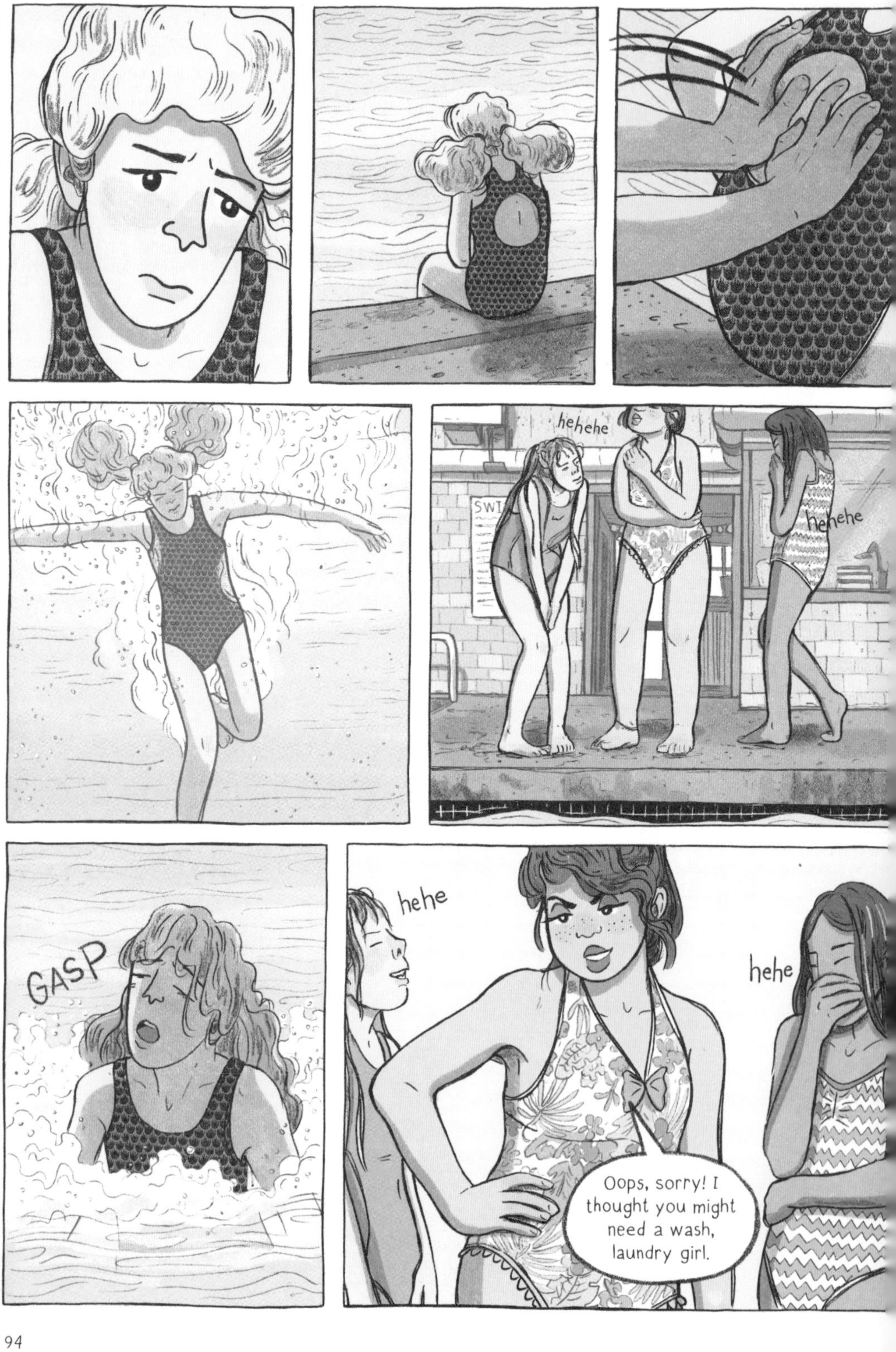
hehehe
hehehe
GASP
hehe
hehe
Oops, sorry! I thought you might need a wash, laundry girl.

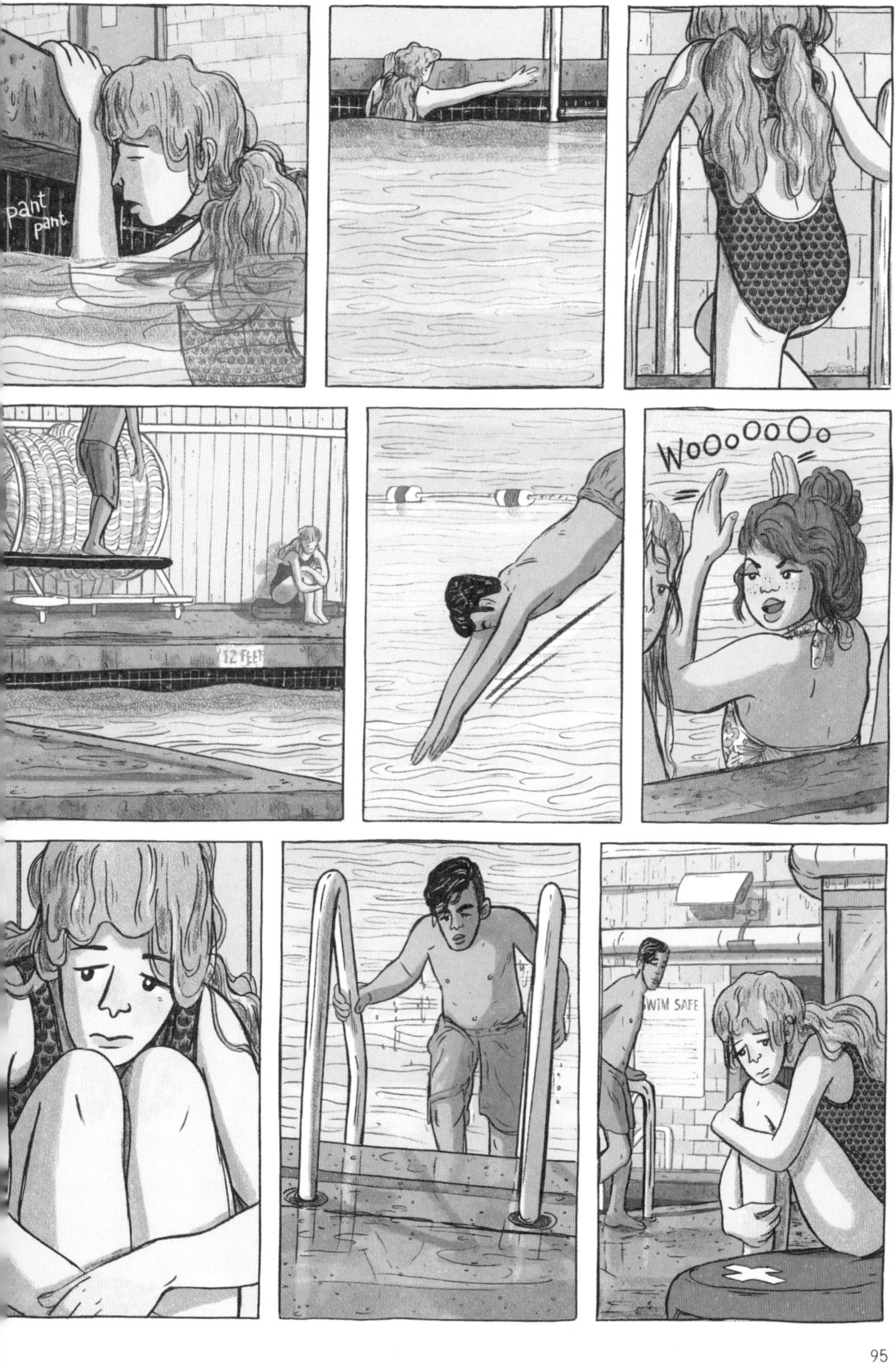
pant pant
12 FEET
WoooOOOo
WIM SAFE

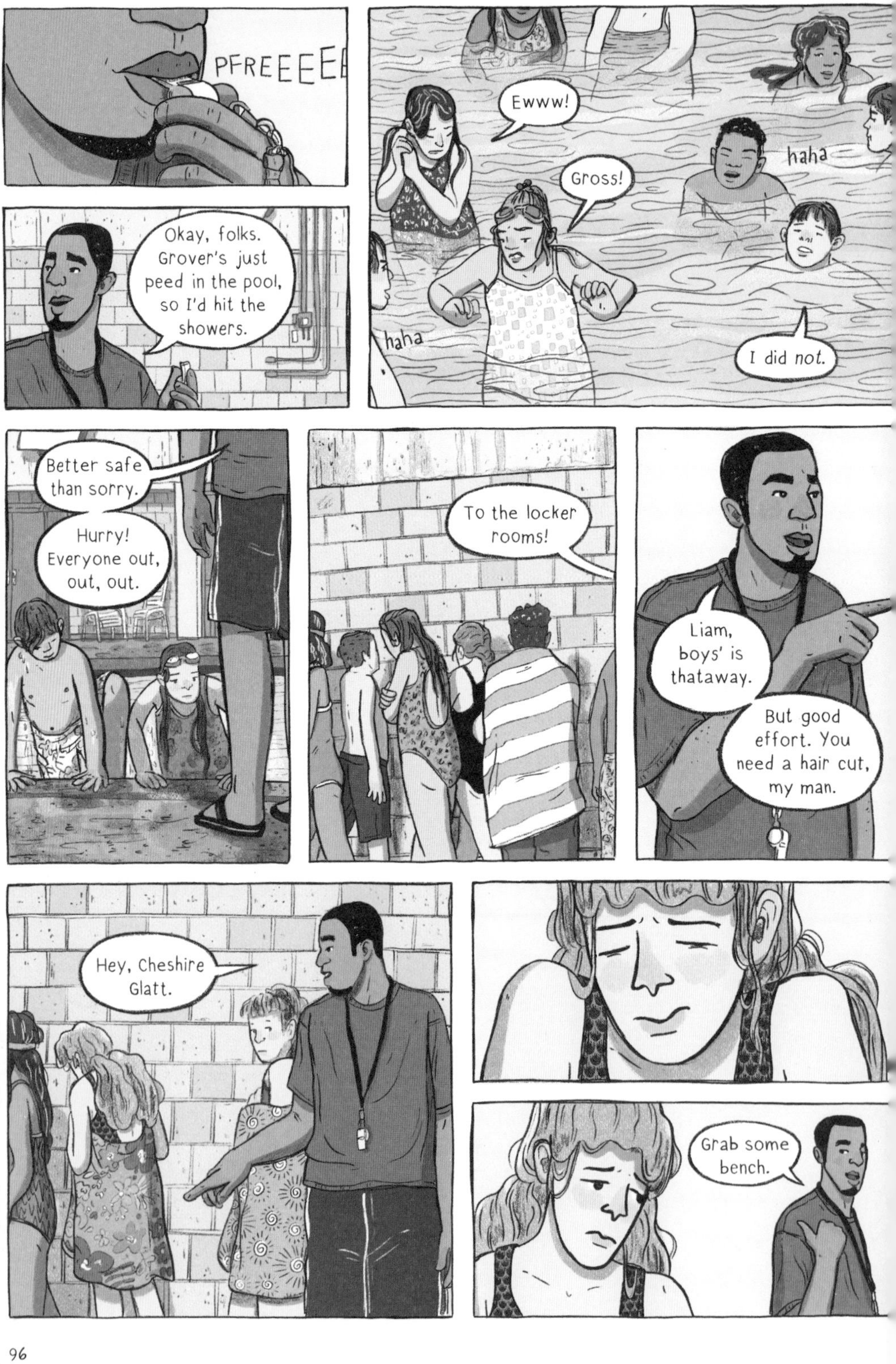
PFREEEEE
Okay, folks. Grover's just peed in the pool, so I'd hit the showers.
Ewww!
Gross!
haha
haha
I did *not*.
Better safe than sorry.
Hurry! Everyone out, out, out.
To the locker rooms!
Liam, boys' is thataway.
But good effort. You need a hair cut, my man.
Hey, Cheshire Glatt.
Grab some bench.

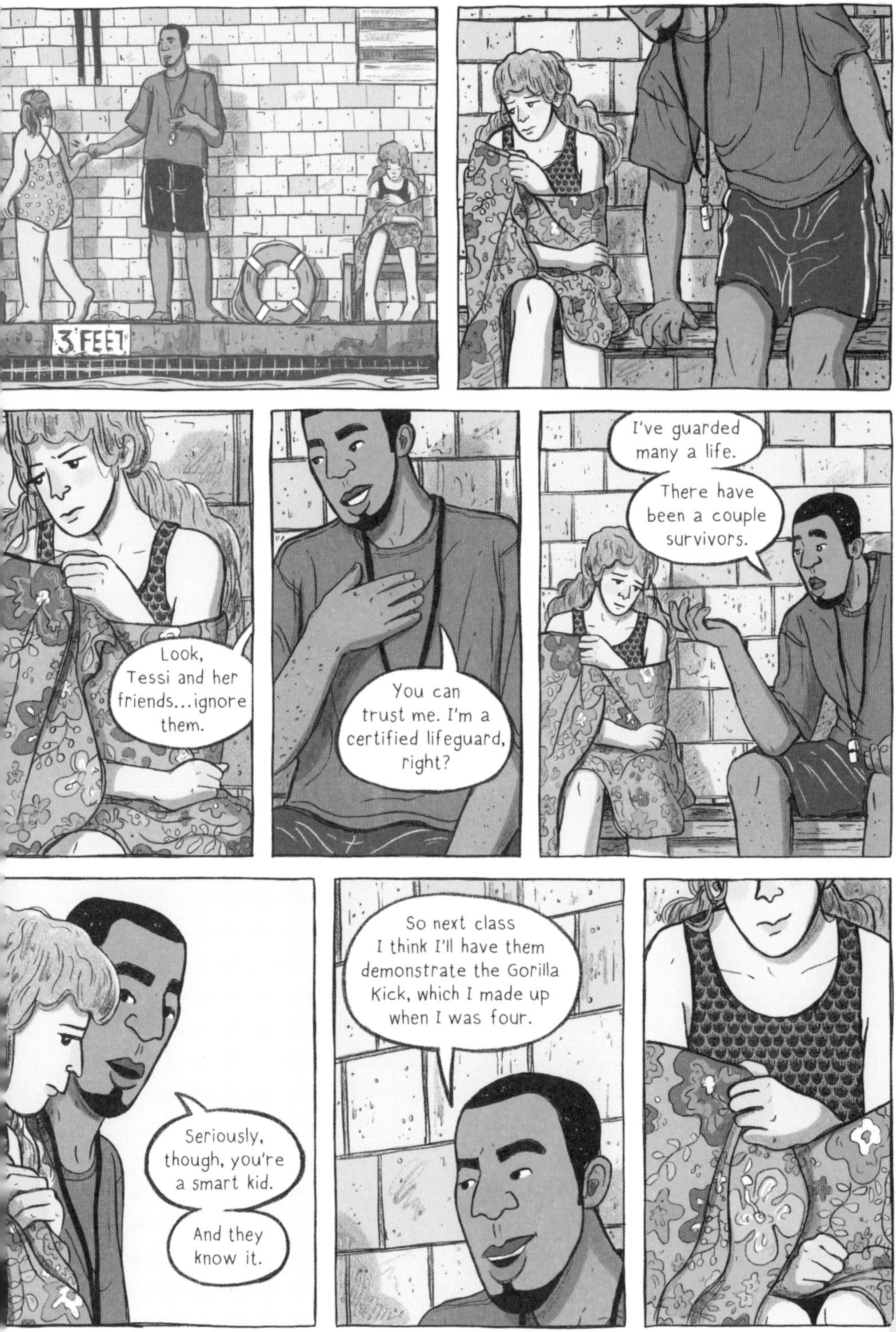
3 FEET
Look, Tessi and her friends...ignore them.
You can trust me. I'm a certified lifeguard, right?
I've guarded many a life.
There have been a couple survivors.
Seriously, though, you're a smart kid.
And they know it.
So next class I think I'll have them demonstrate the Gorilla Kick, which I made up when I was four.

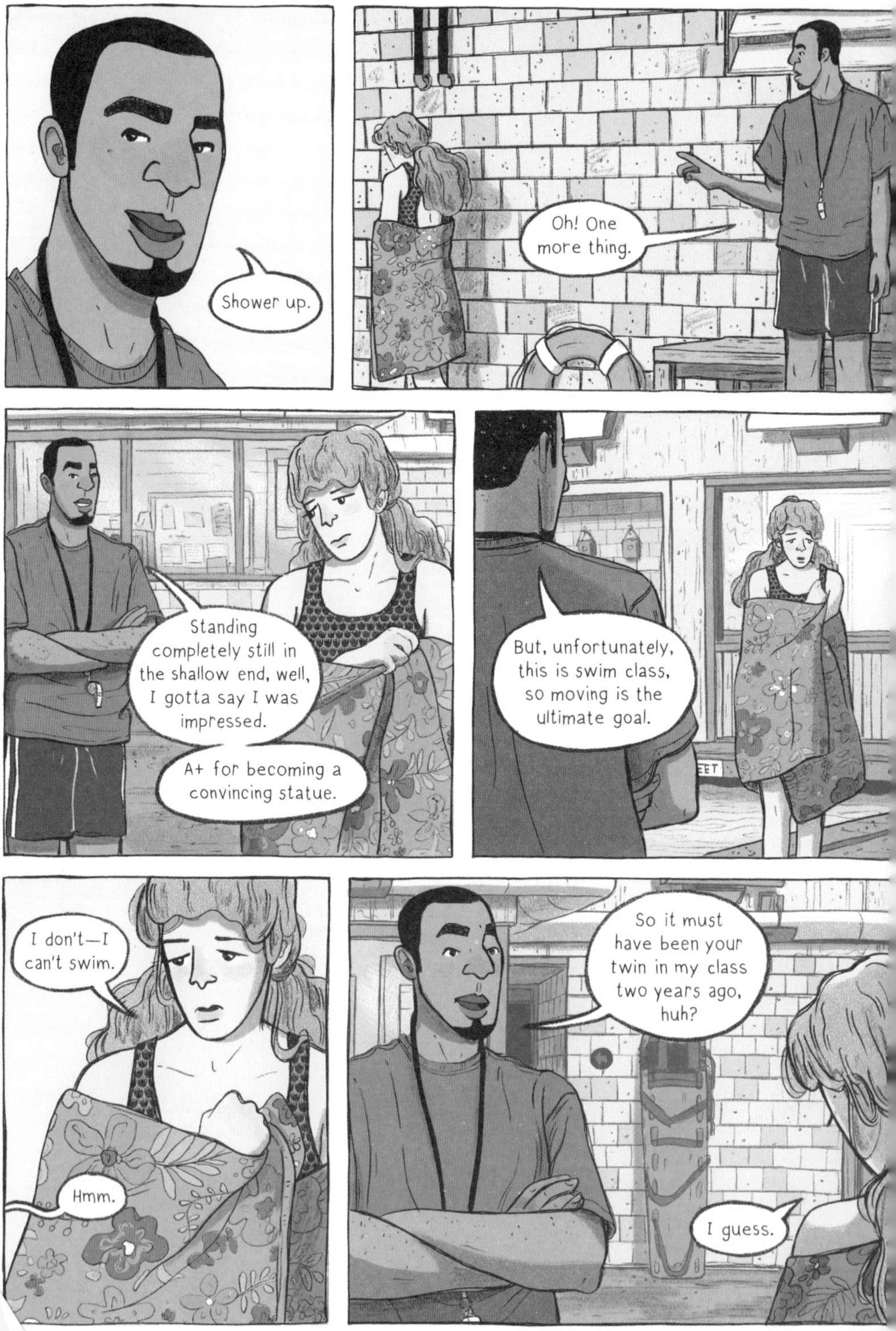
Shower up.
Oh! One more thing.
Standing completely still in the shallow end, well, I gotta say I was impressed.
A+ for becoming a convincing statue.
But, unfortunately, this is swim class, so moving is the ultimate goal.
I don't—I can't swim.
Hmm.
So it must have been your twin in my class two years ago, huh?
I guess.

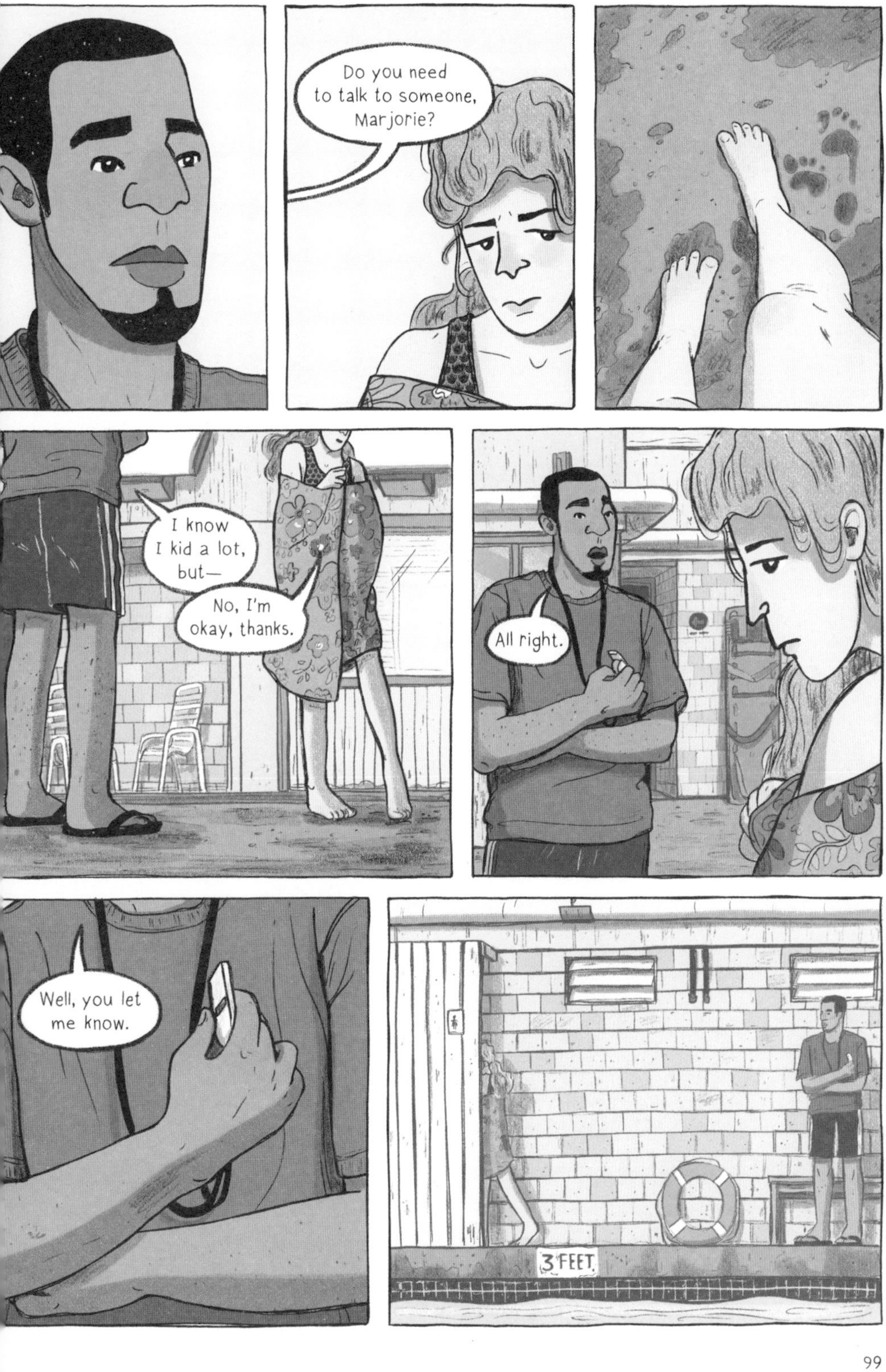
Do you need to talk to someone, Marjorie?
I know I kid a lot, but—
No, I'm okay, thanks.
All right.
Well, you let me know.
3 FEET

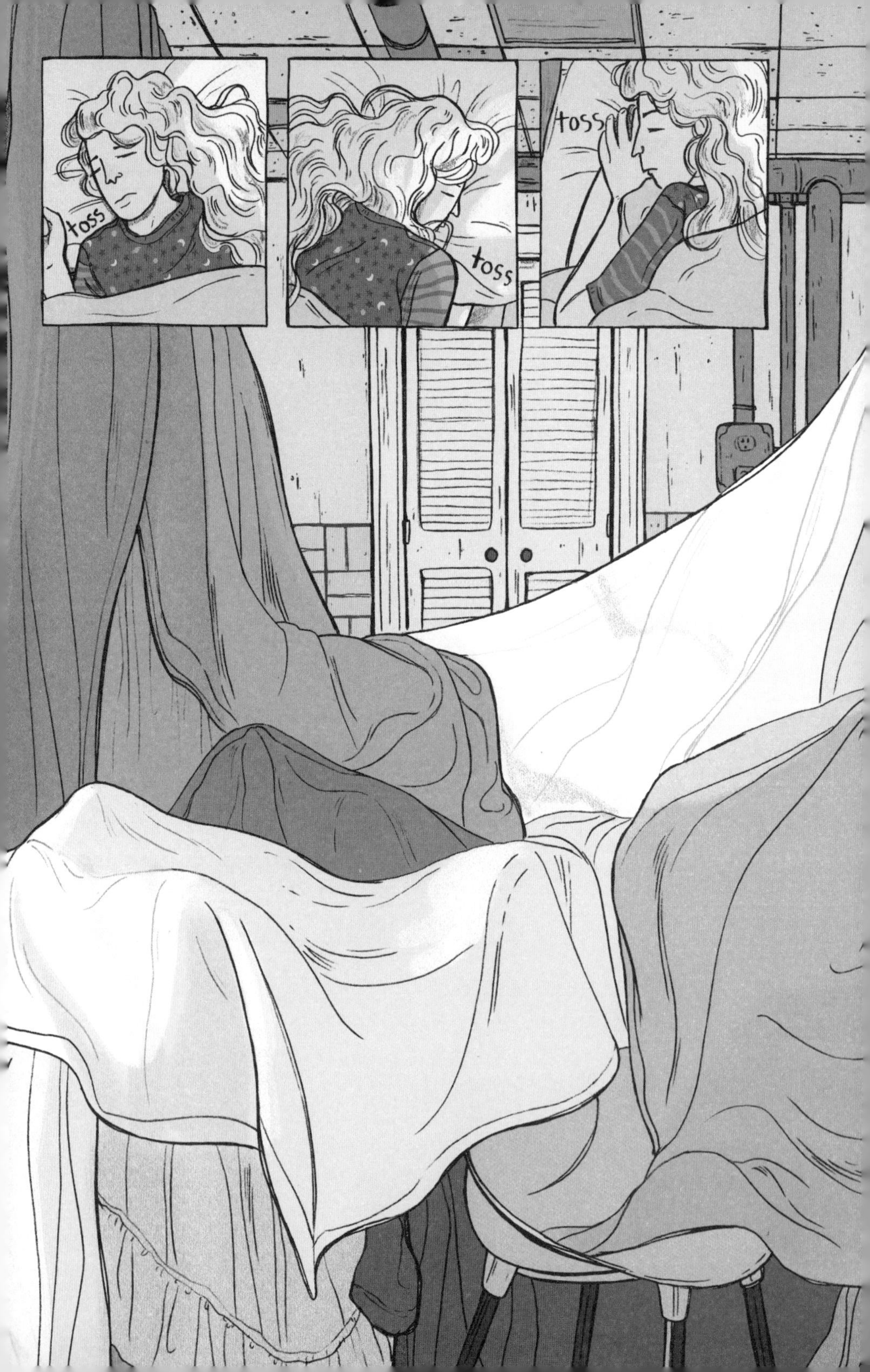
toss
toss
toss

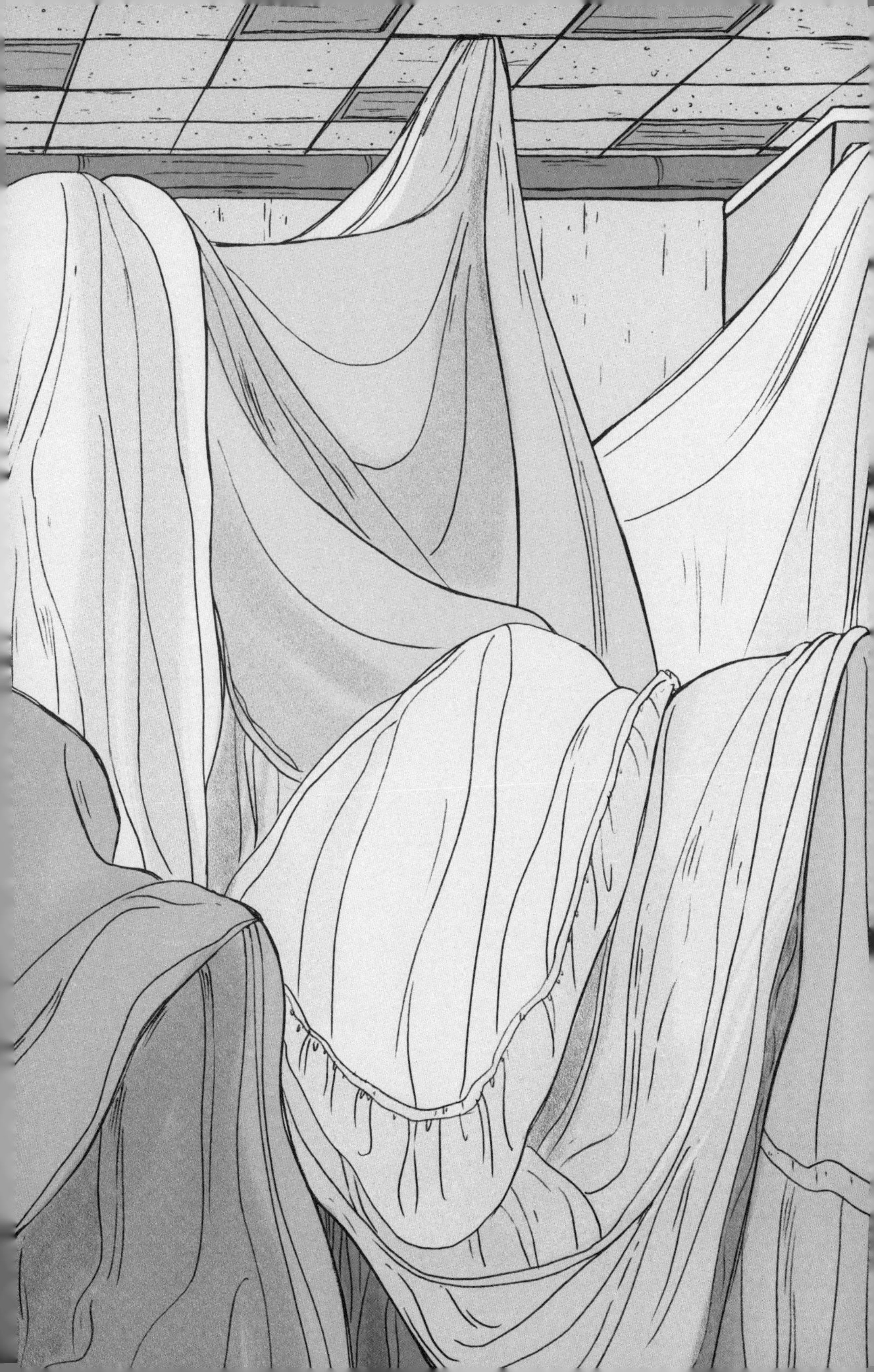

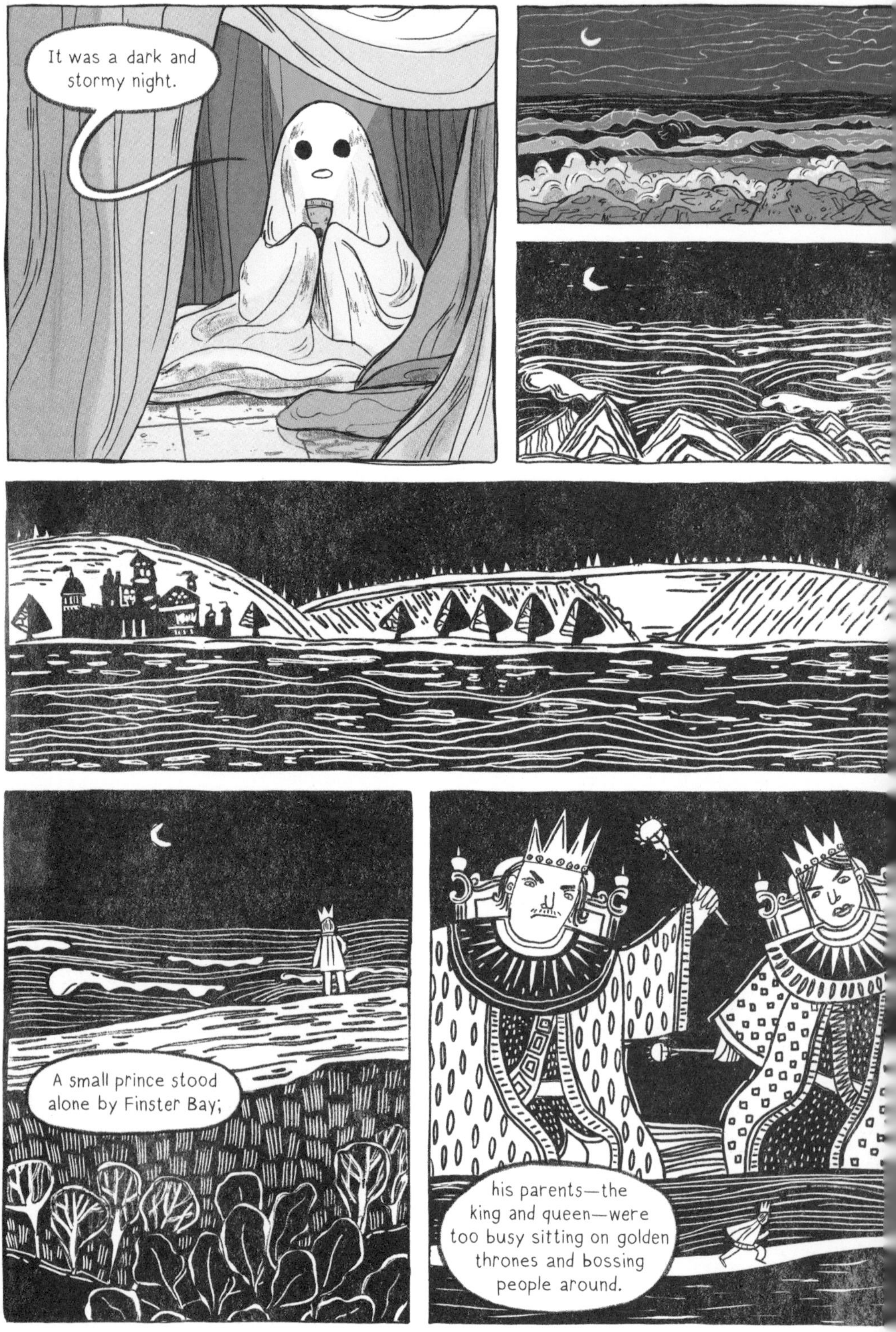
It was a dark and stormy night.
A small prince stood alone by Finster Bay;
his parents—the king and queen—were too busy sitting on golden thrones and bossing people around.

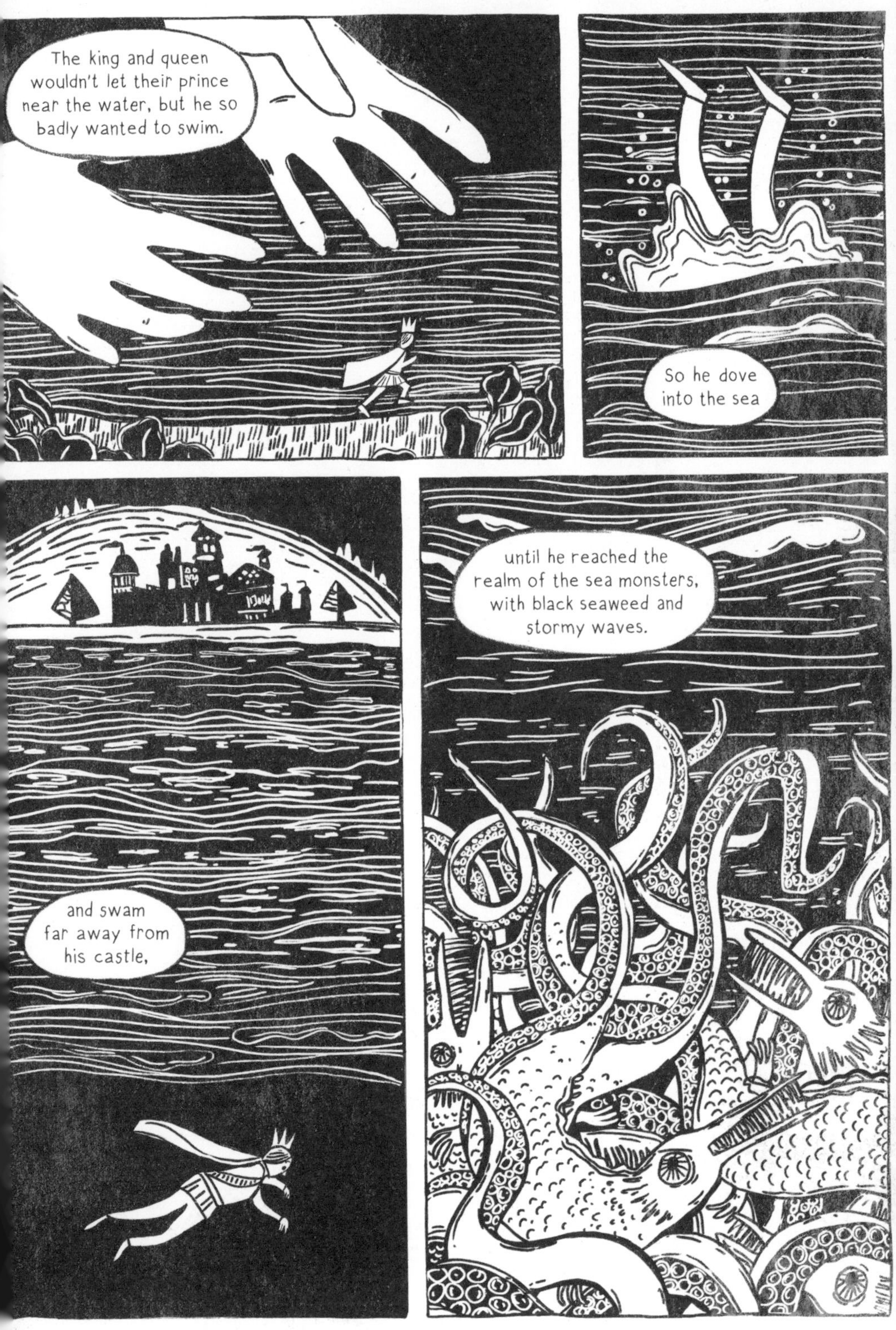
The king and queen wouldn't let their prince near the water, but he so badly wanted to swim.
So he dove into the sea
and swam far away from his castle,
until he reached the realm of the sea monsters, with black seaweed and stormy waves.

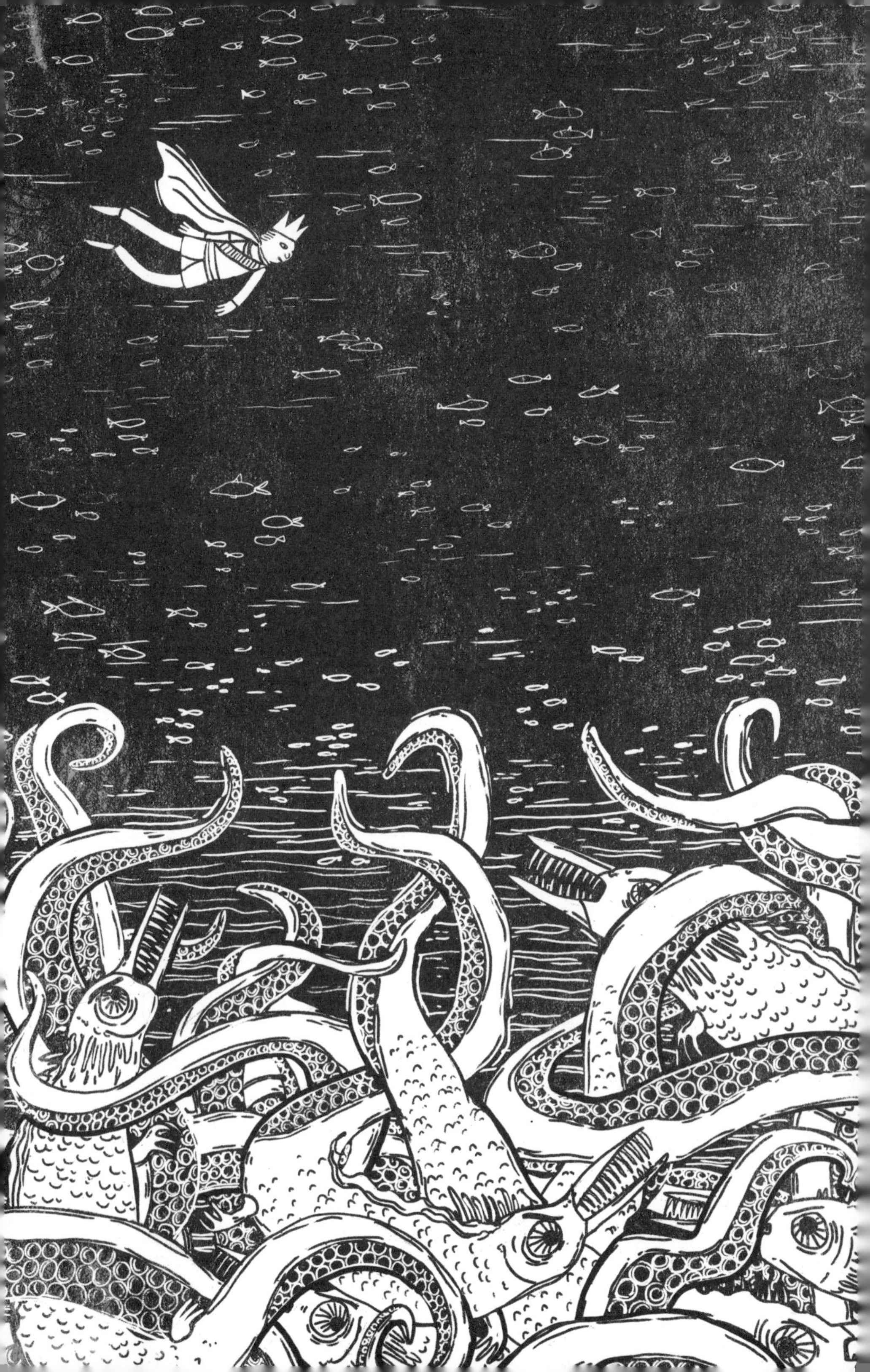

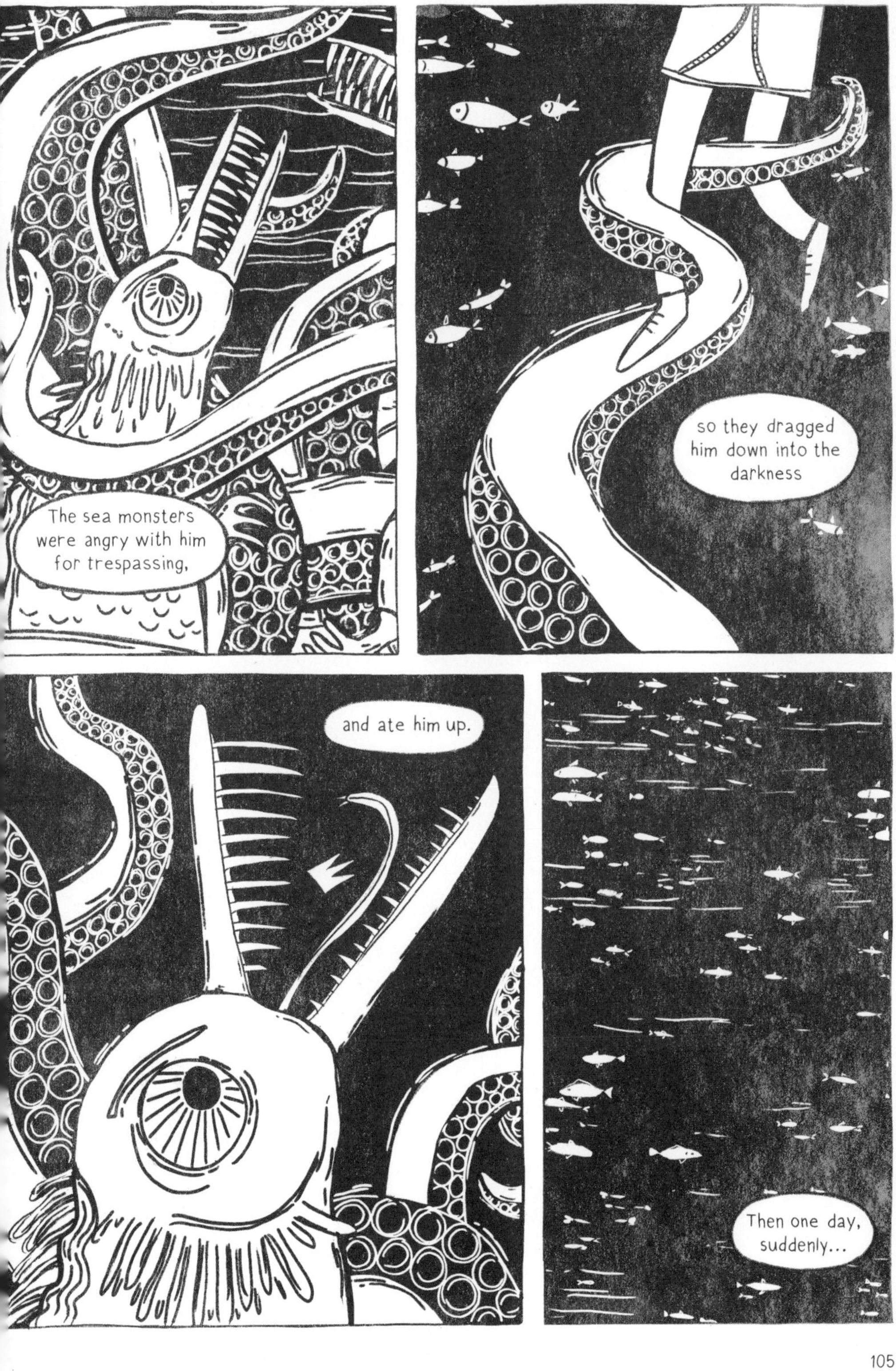
The sea monsters were angry with him for trespassing,
so they dragged him down into the darkness
and ate him up.
Then one day, suddenly...

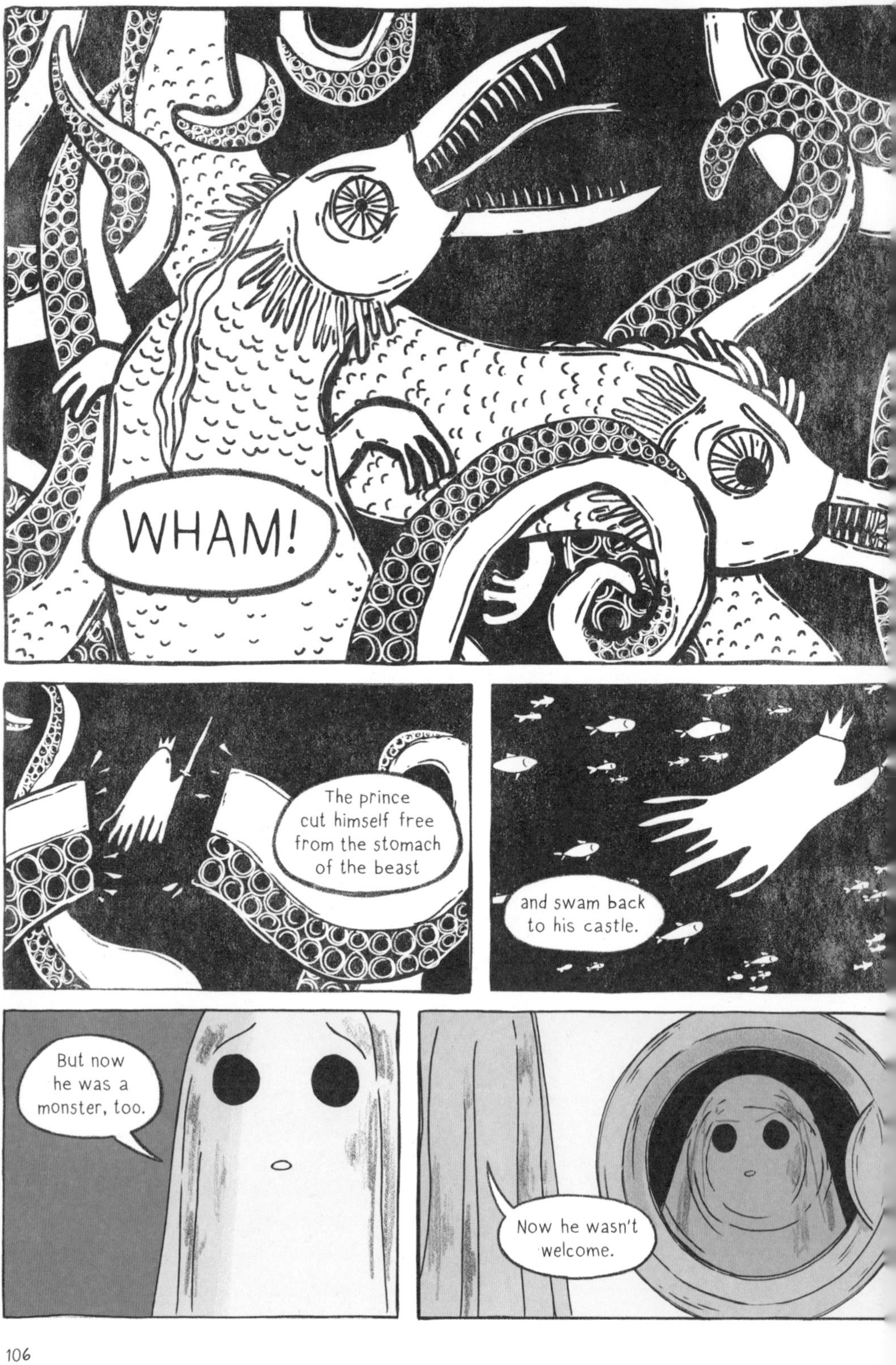

WHAM!
The prince cut himself free from the stomach of the beast
and swam back to his castle.
But now he was a monster, too.
Now he wasn't welcome.

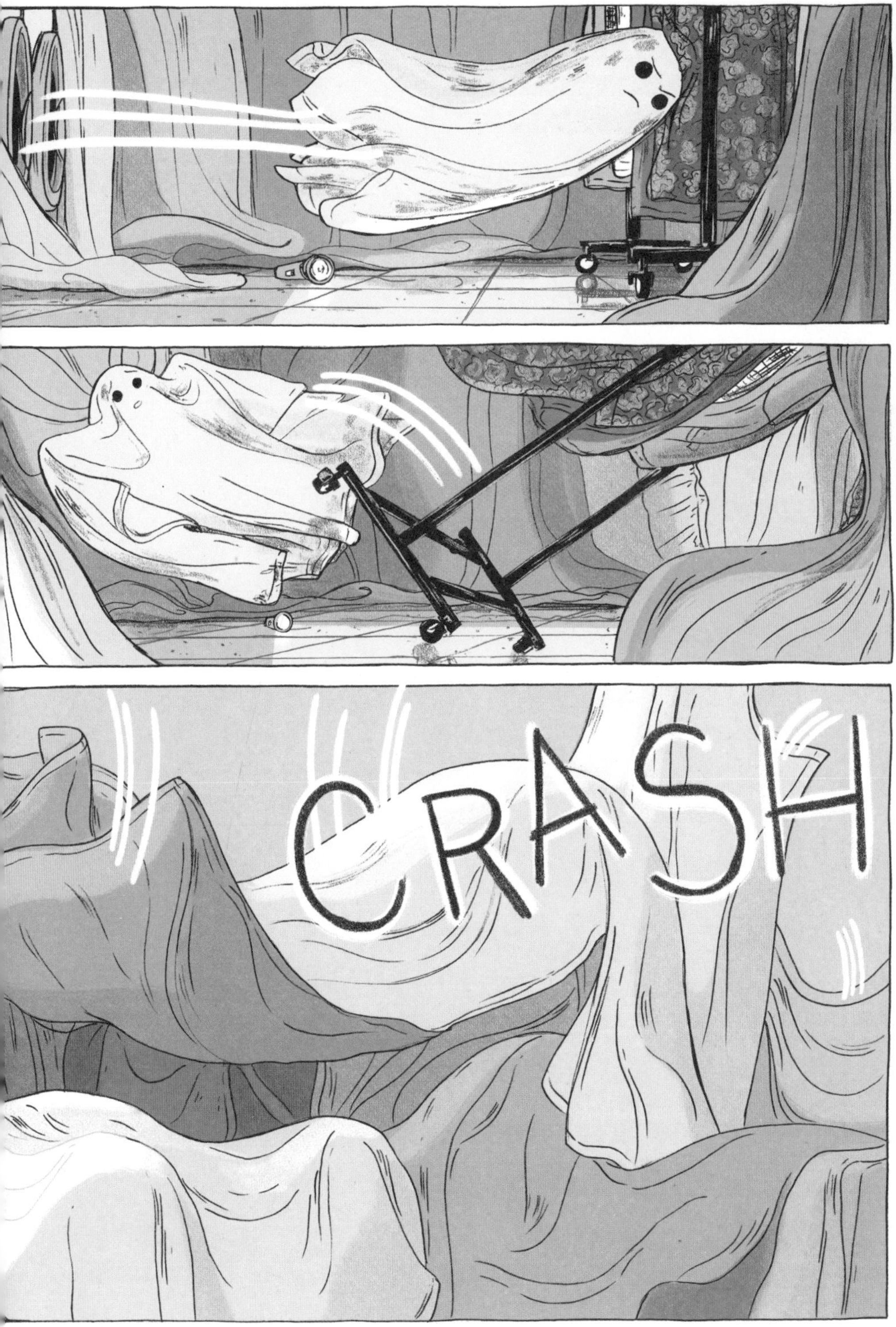
CRASH

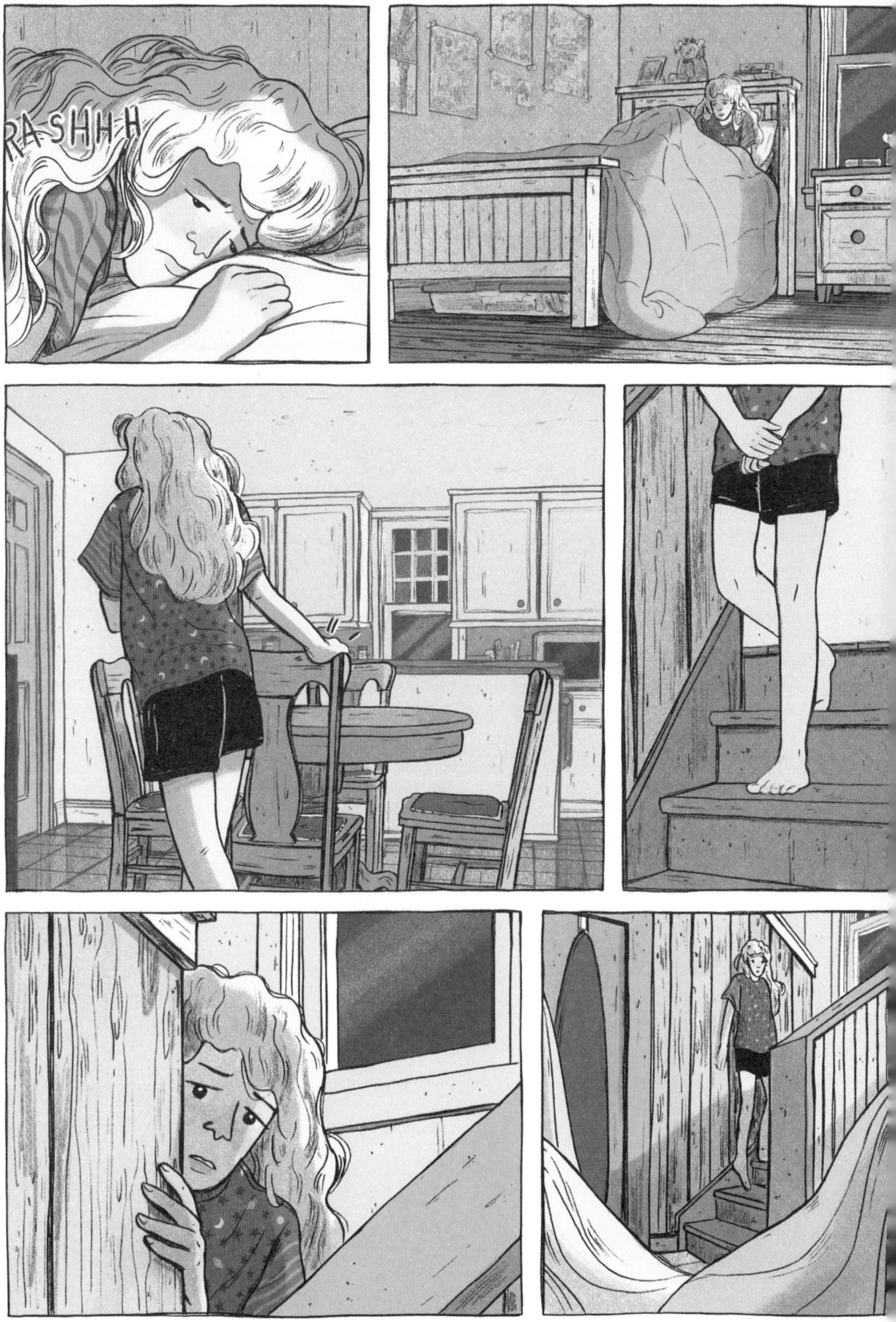
RASHHH

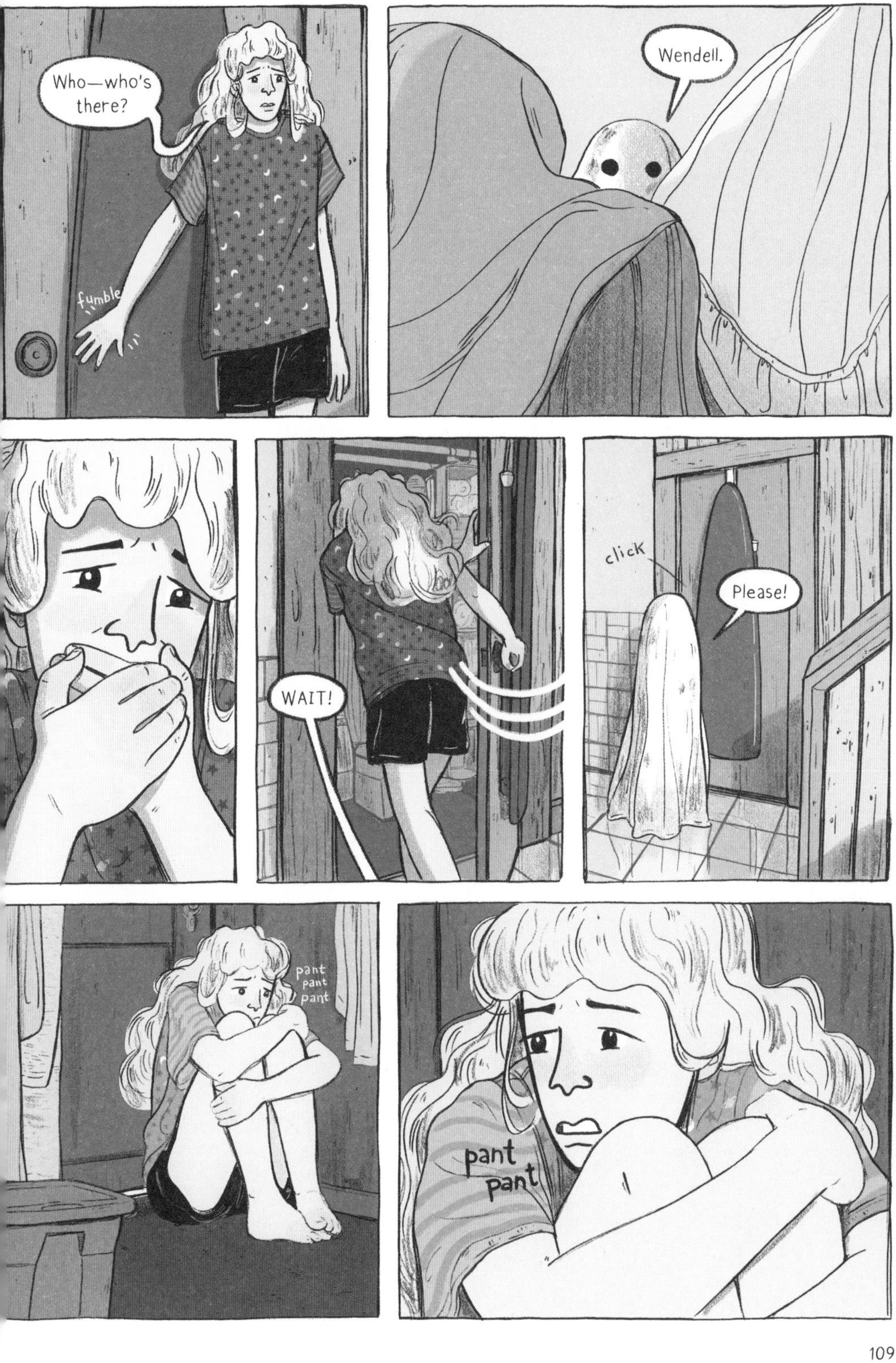
Who—who's there?
fumble
Wendell.
WAIT!
click
Please!
pant pant pant
pant pant

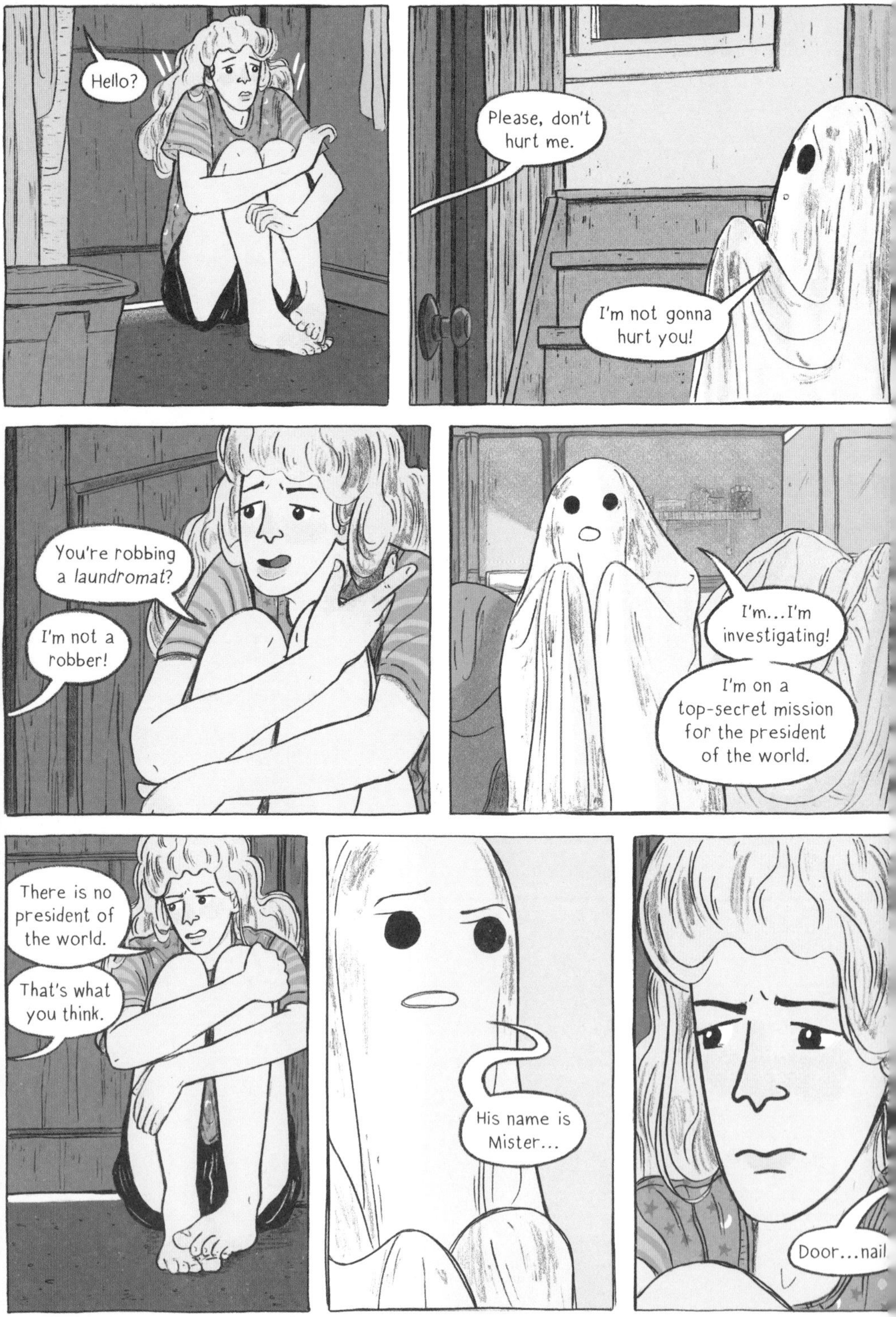
Hello?
Please, don't hurt me.
I'm not gonna hurt you!
You're robbing a *laundromat*?
I'm not a robber!
I'm...I'm investigating!
I'm on a top-secret mission for the president of the world.
There is no president of the world.
That's what you think.
His name is Mister...
Door...nail

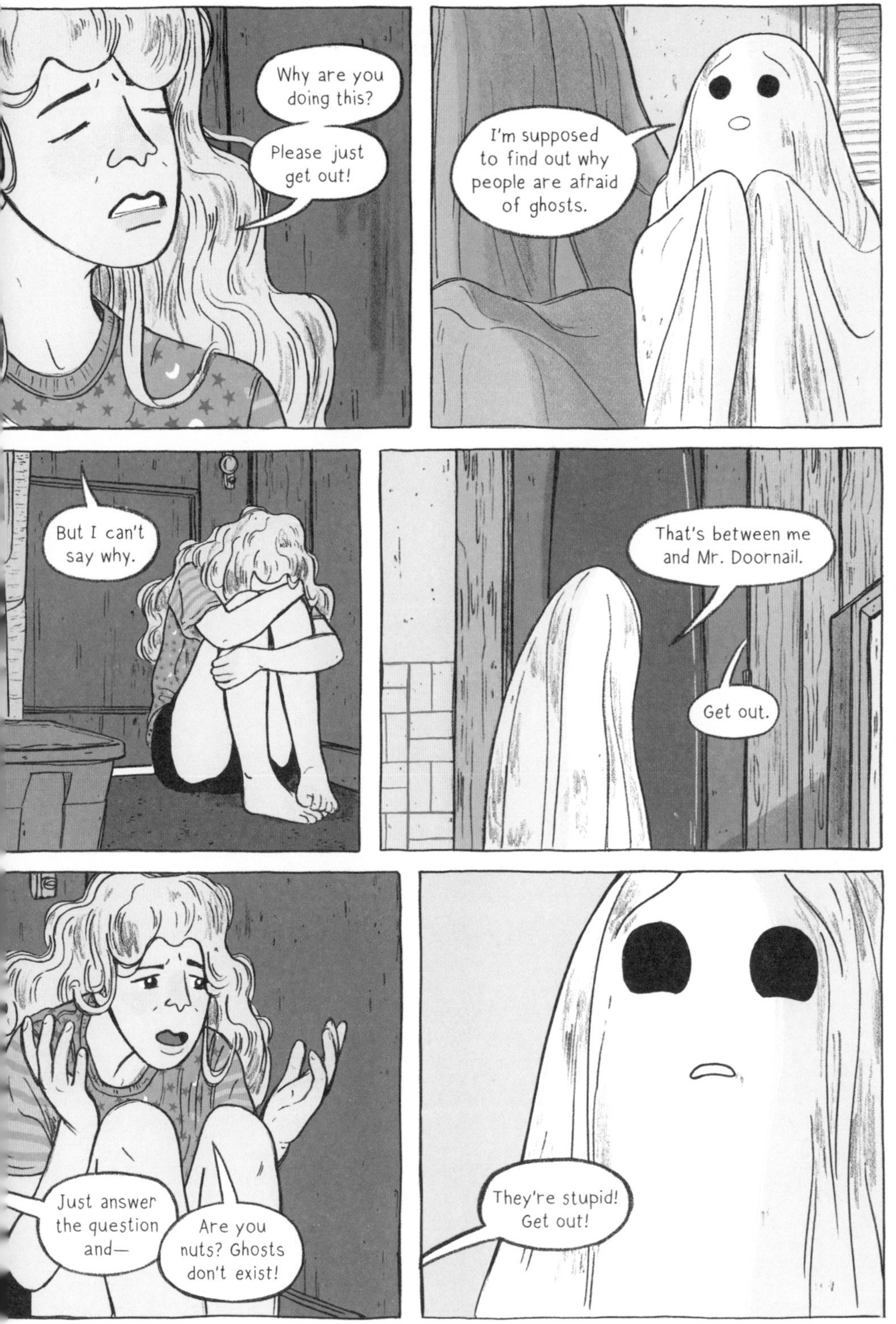
Why are you doing this?
Please just get out!
I'm supposed to find out why people are afraid of ghosts.
But I can't say why.
That's between me and Mr. Doornail.
Get out.
Just answer the question and—
Are you nuts? Ghosts don't exist!
They're stupid! Get out!

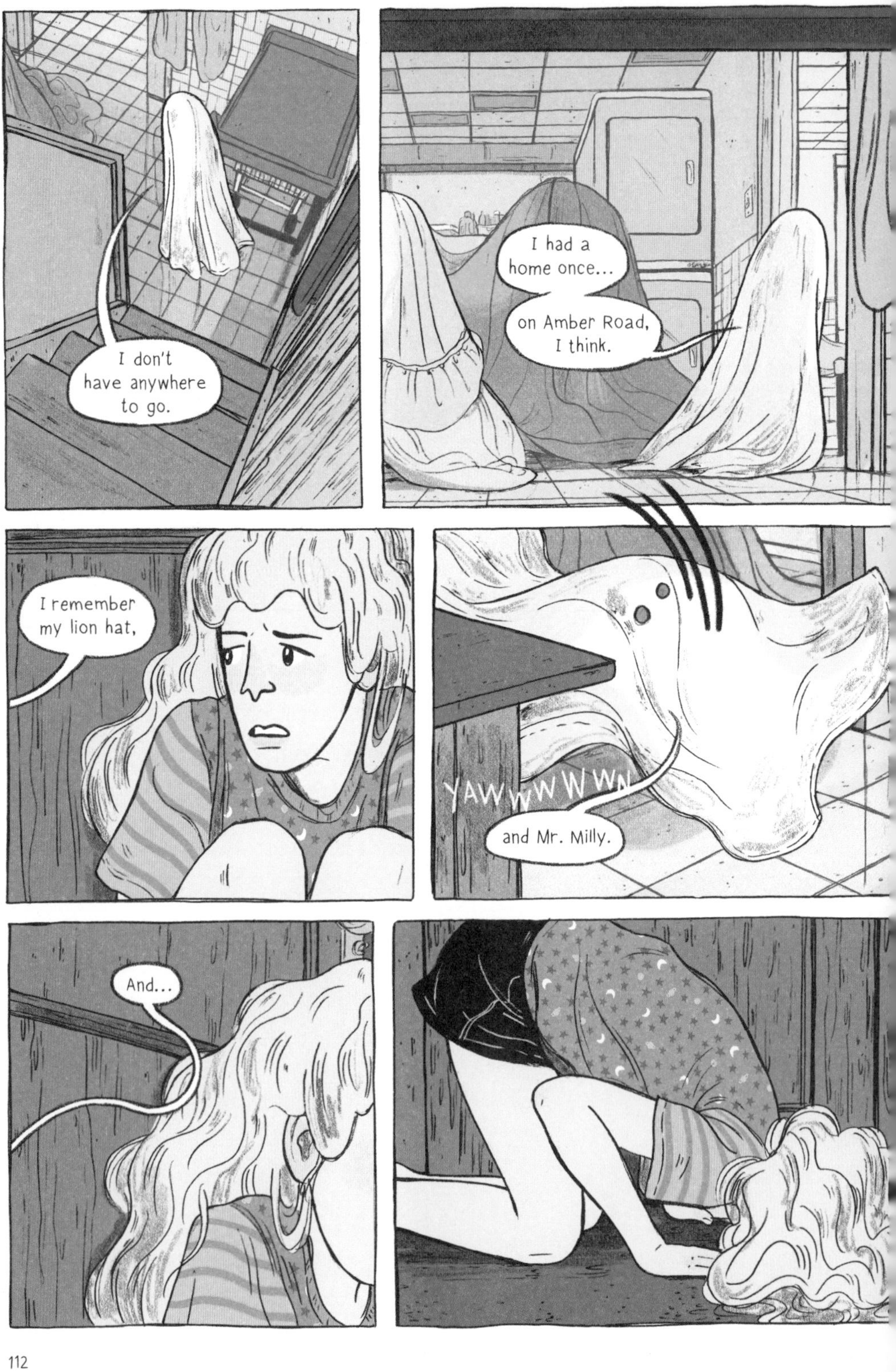
I don't have anywhere to go.
I had a home once...
on Amber Road, I think.
I remember my lion hat,
YAWWWWWN
and Mr. Milly.
And...

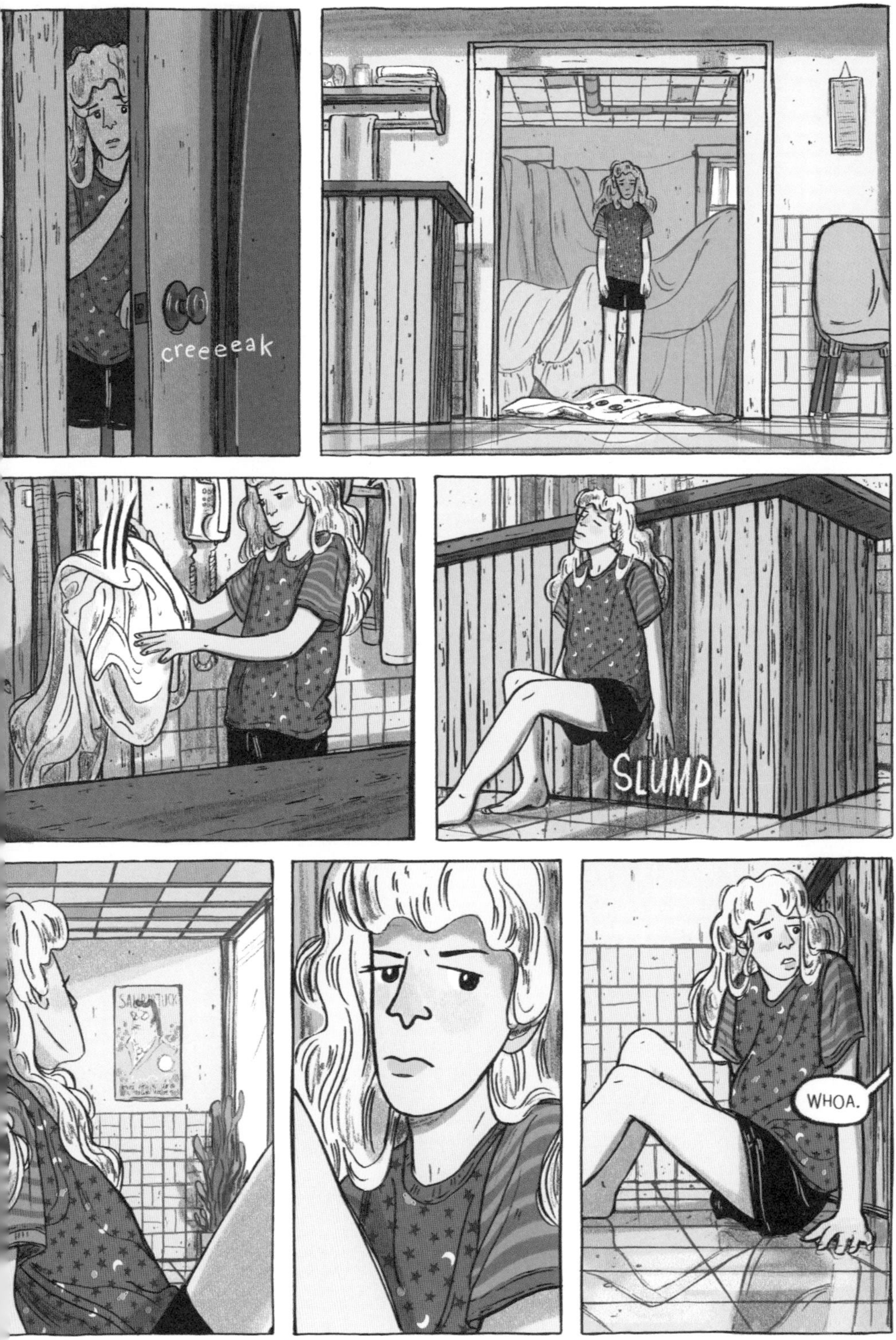
creeeeak
SLUMP
WHOA.

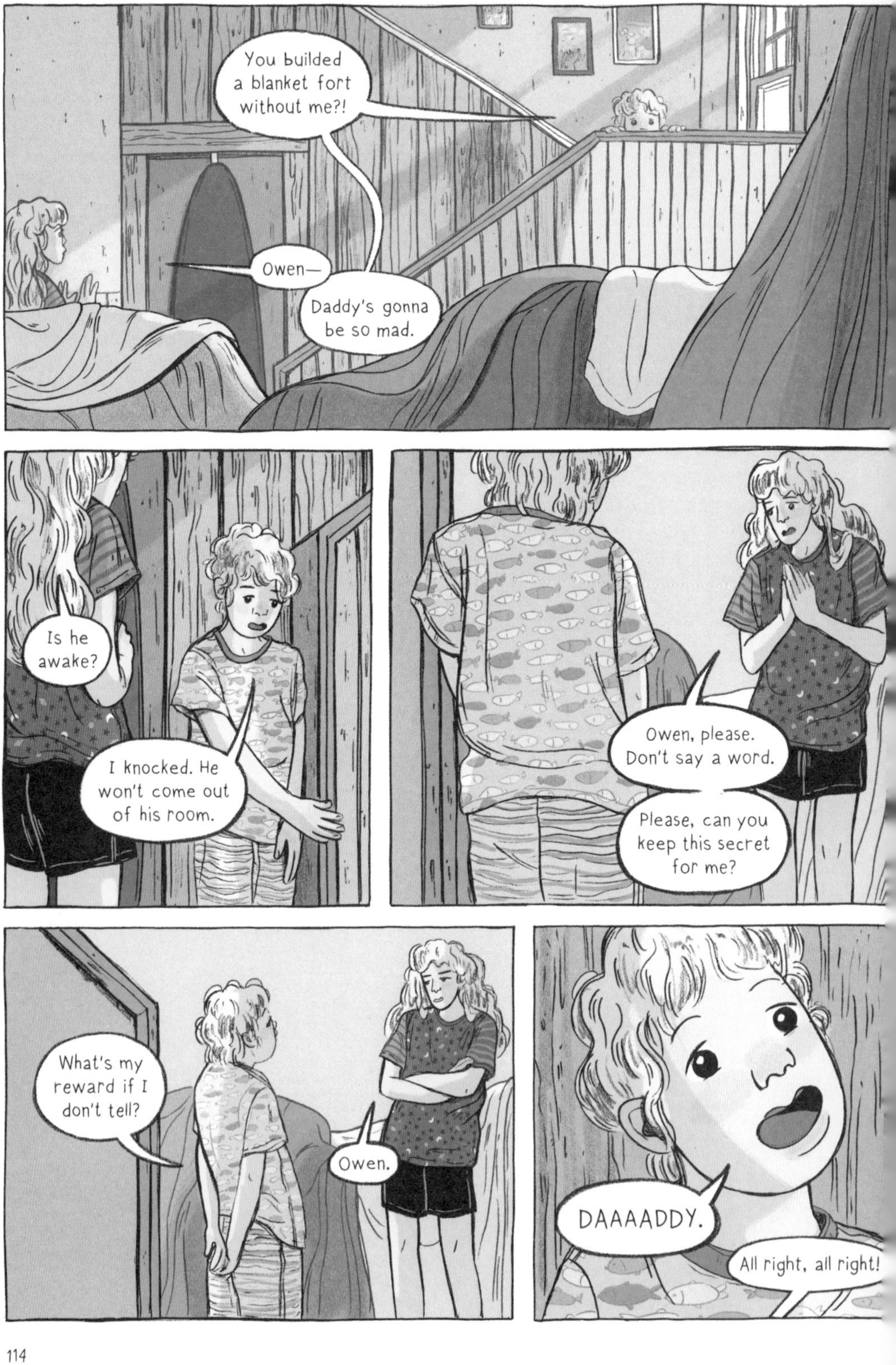
You builded a blanket fort without me?!
Owen—
Daddy's gonna be so mad.
Is he awake?
I knocked. He won't come out of his room.
Owen, please. Don't say a word.
Please, can you keep this secret for me?
What's my reward if I don't tell?
Owen.
DAAAADDY.
All right, all right!

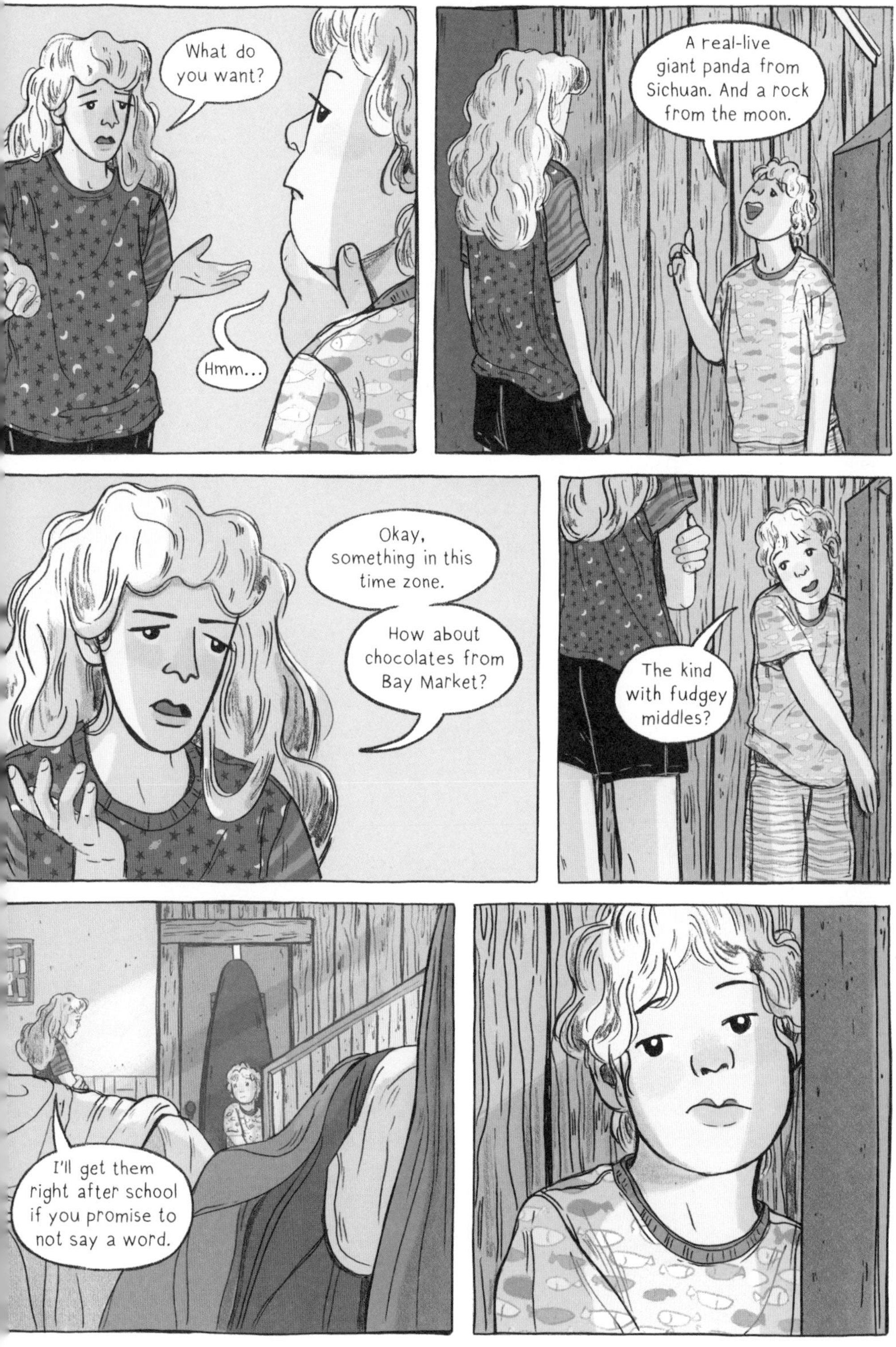
What do you want?
Hmm...
A real-live giant panda from Sichuan. And a rock from the moon.
Okay, something in this time zone.
How about chocolates from Bay Market?
The kind with fudgey middles?
I'll get them right after school if you promise to not say a word.

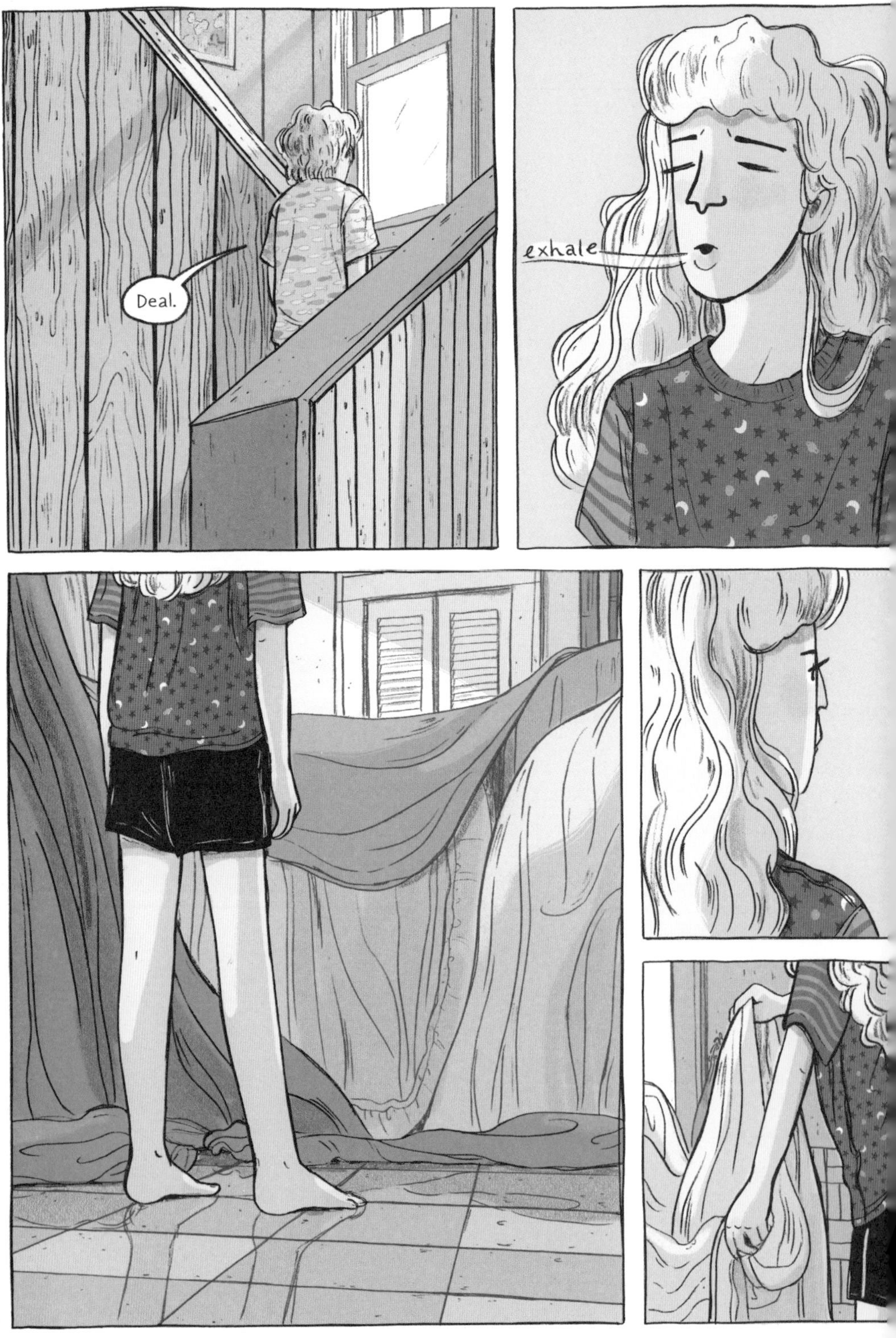
Deal.
exhale

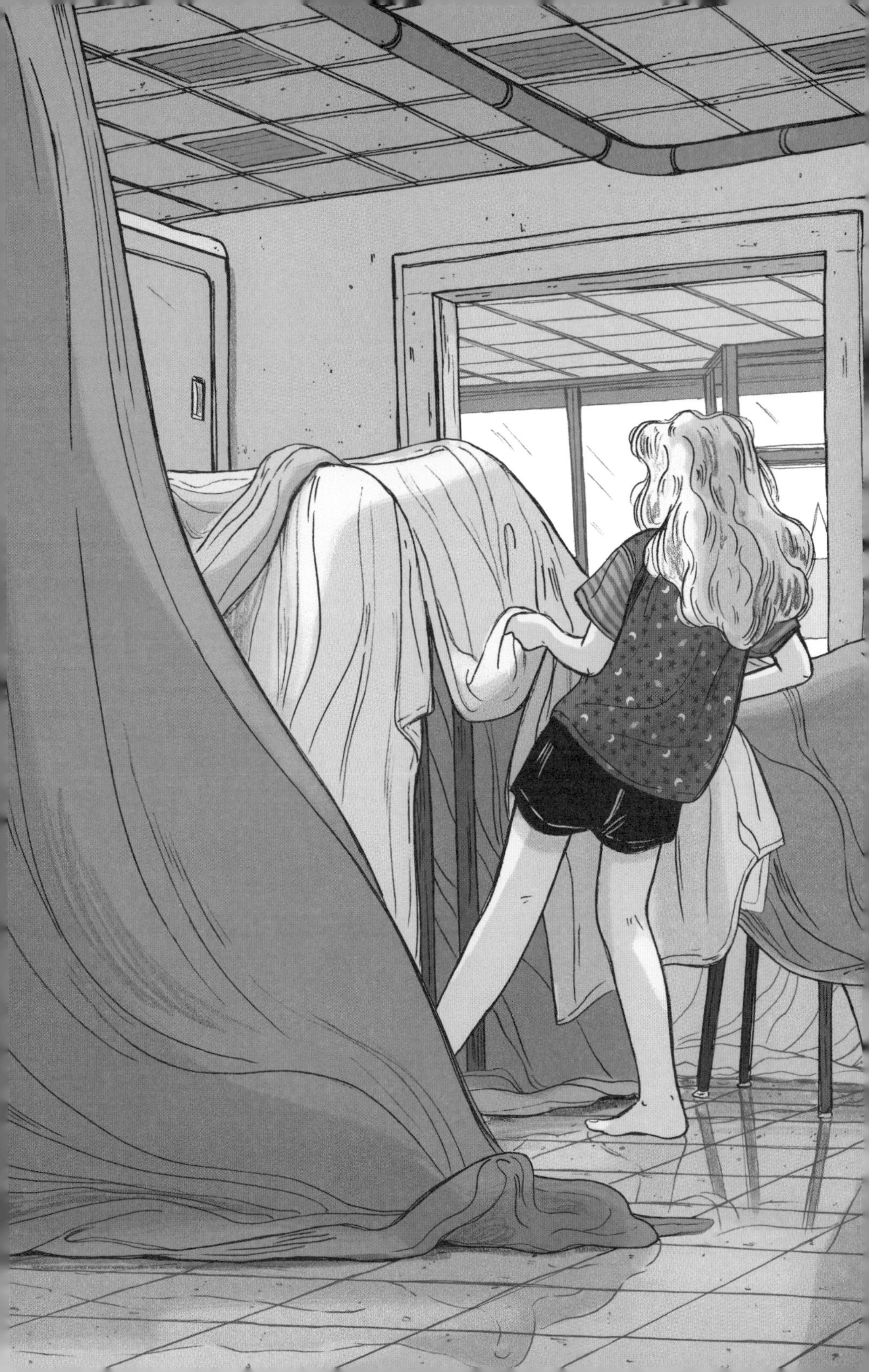

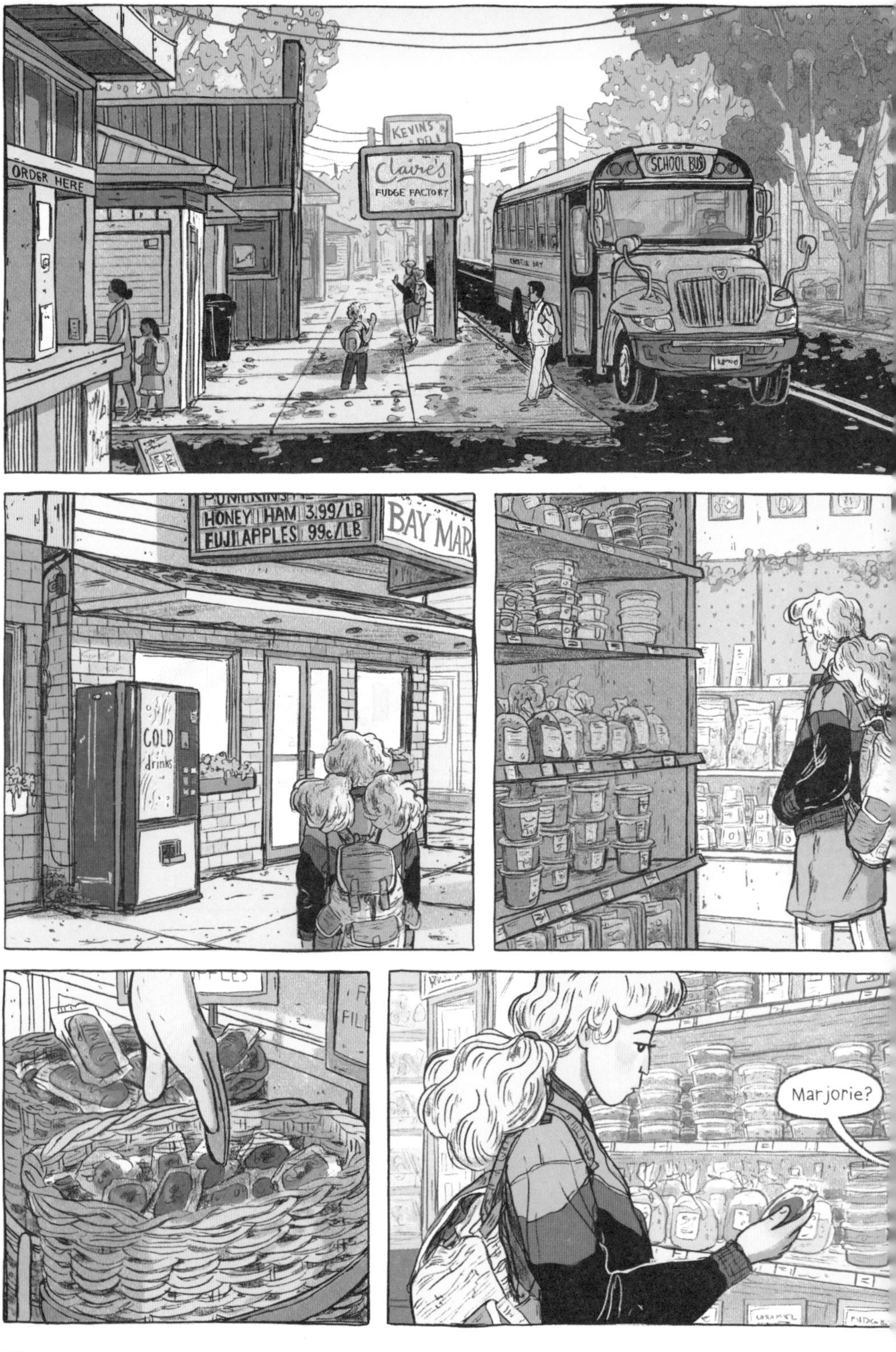
ORDER HERE
KEVIN'S DELI
Claire's
FUDGE FACTORY
SCHOOL BUS
HONEY HAM 3.99/LB
FUJI APPLES 99¢/LB
BAY MAR
COLD
drinks
Marjorie?

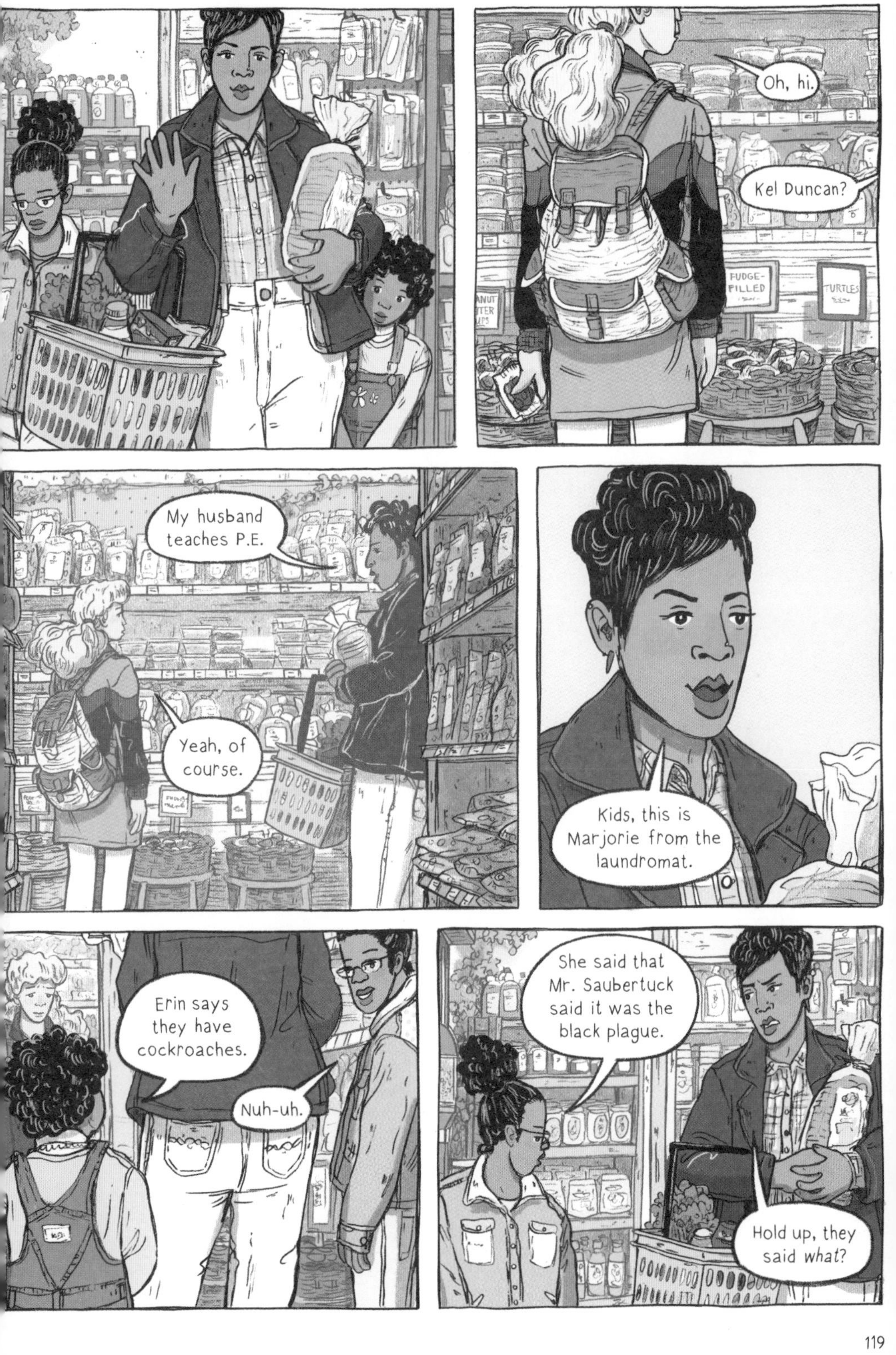
Oh, hi.
Kel Duncan?
FUDGE-FILLED
TURTLES
My husband teaches P.E.
Yeah, of course.
Kids, this is Marjorie from the laundromat.
Erin says they have cockroaches.
Nuh-uh.
She said that Mr. Saubertuck said it was the black plague.
Hold up, they said *what*?

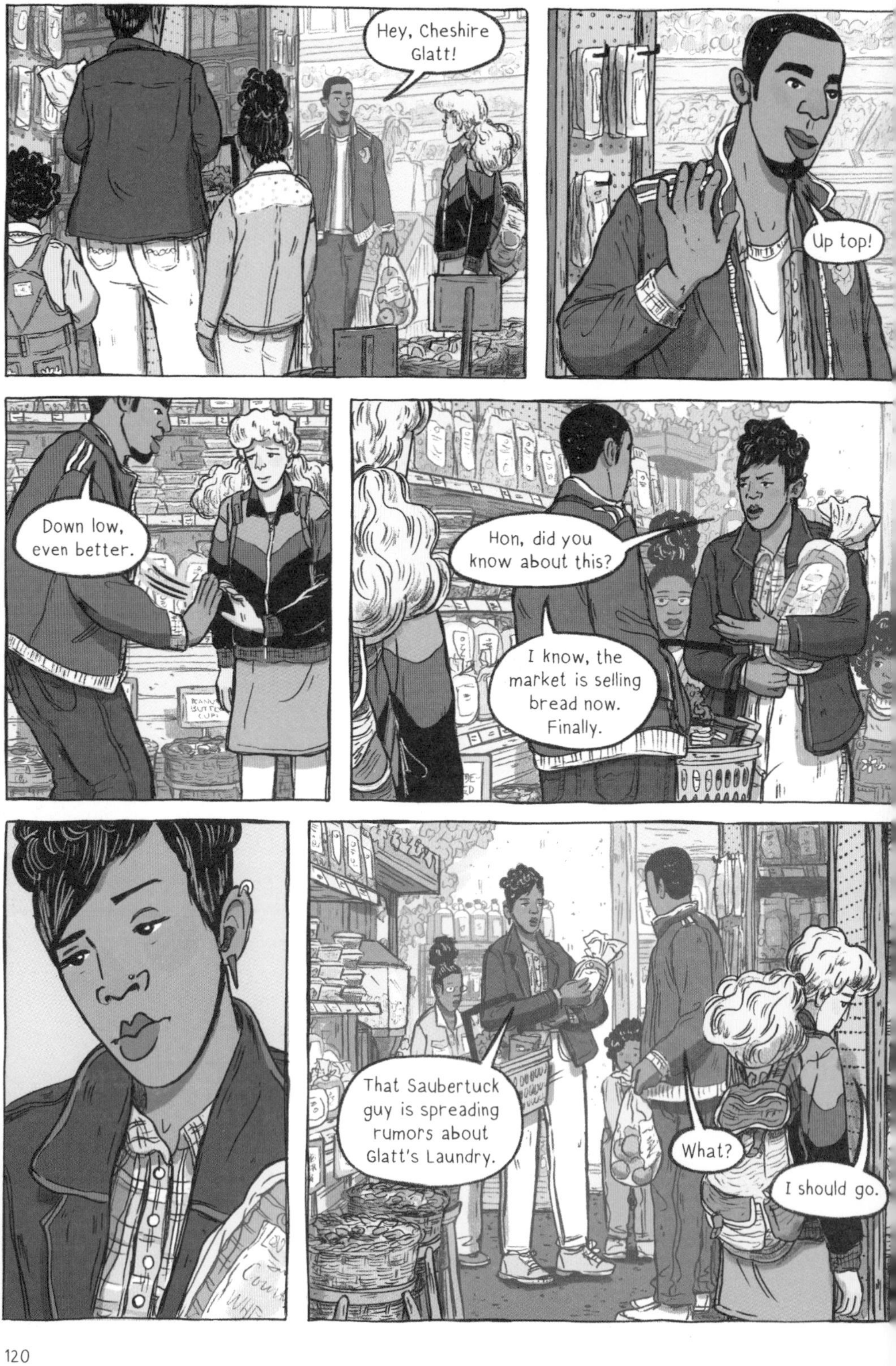
Hey, Cheshire Glatt!
Up top!
Down low, even better.
Hon, did you know about this?
I know, the market is selling bread now. Finally.
That Saubertuck guy is spreading rumors about Glatt's Laundry.
What?
I should go.

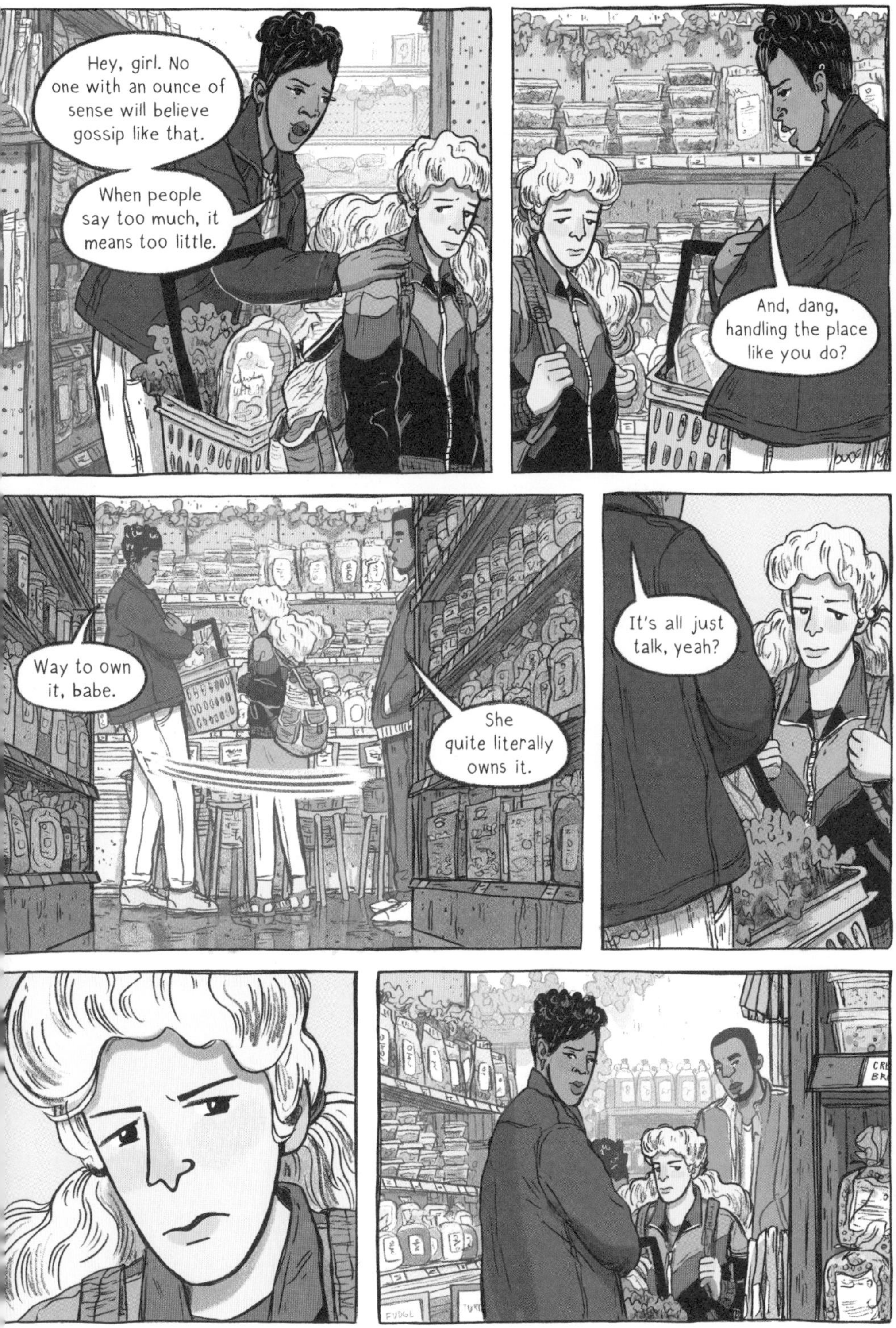
Hey, girl. No one with an ounce of sense will believe gossip like that.
When people say too much, it means too little.
And, dang, handling the place like you do?
Way to own it, babe.
She quite literally owns it.
It's all just talk, yeah?
FUDGE

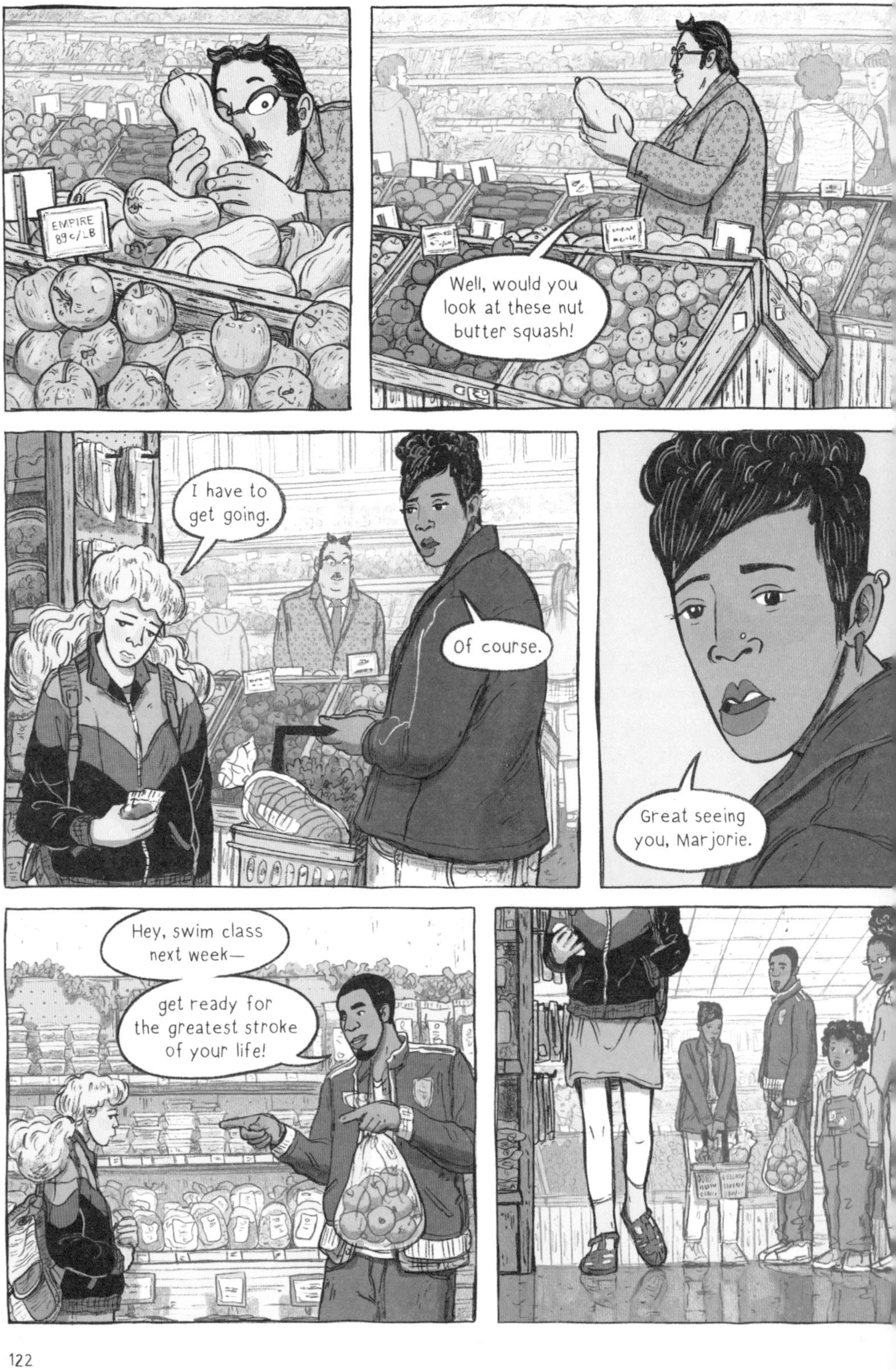
EMPIRE
89¢/LB
Well, would you look at these nut butter squash!
I have to get going.
Of course.
Great seeing you, Marjorie.
Hey, swim class next week—
get ready for the greatest stroke of your life!

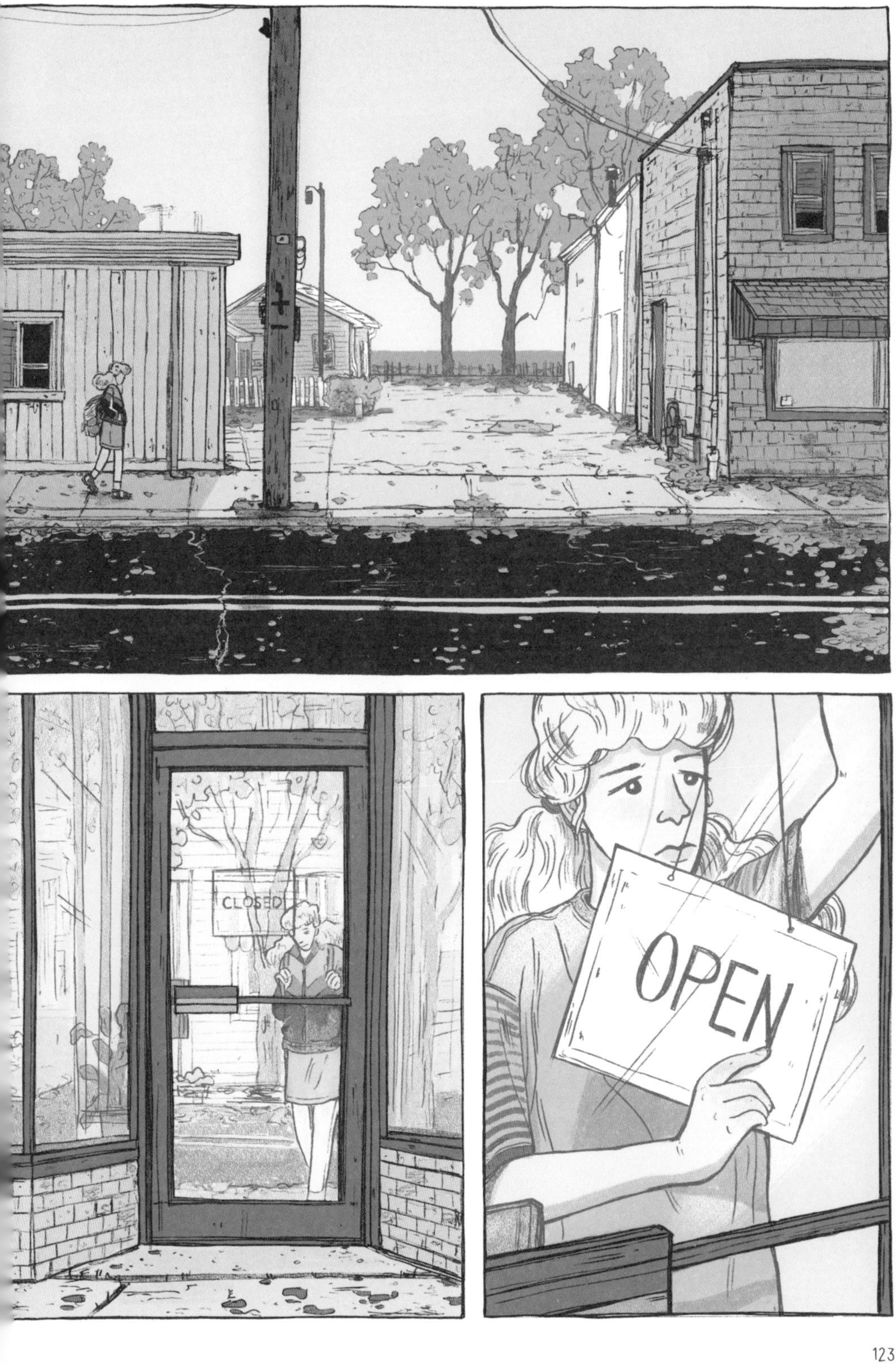
CLOSED
OPEN

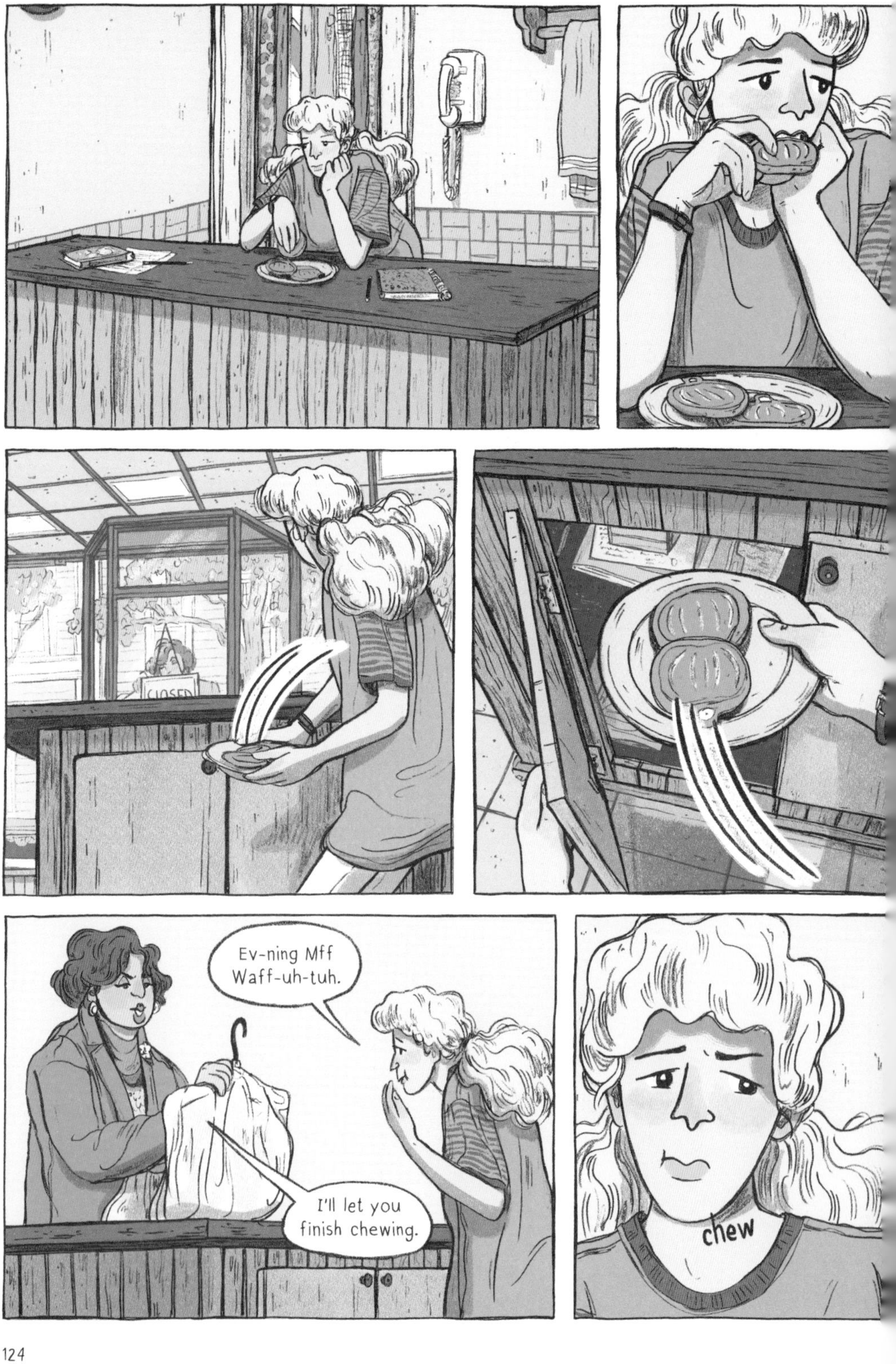
Ev-ning Mff Waff-uh-tuh.
I'll let you finish chewing.
chew

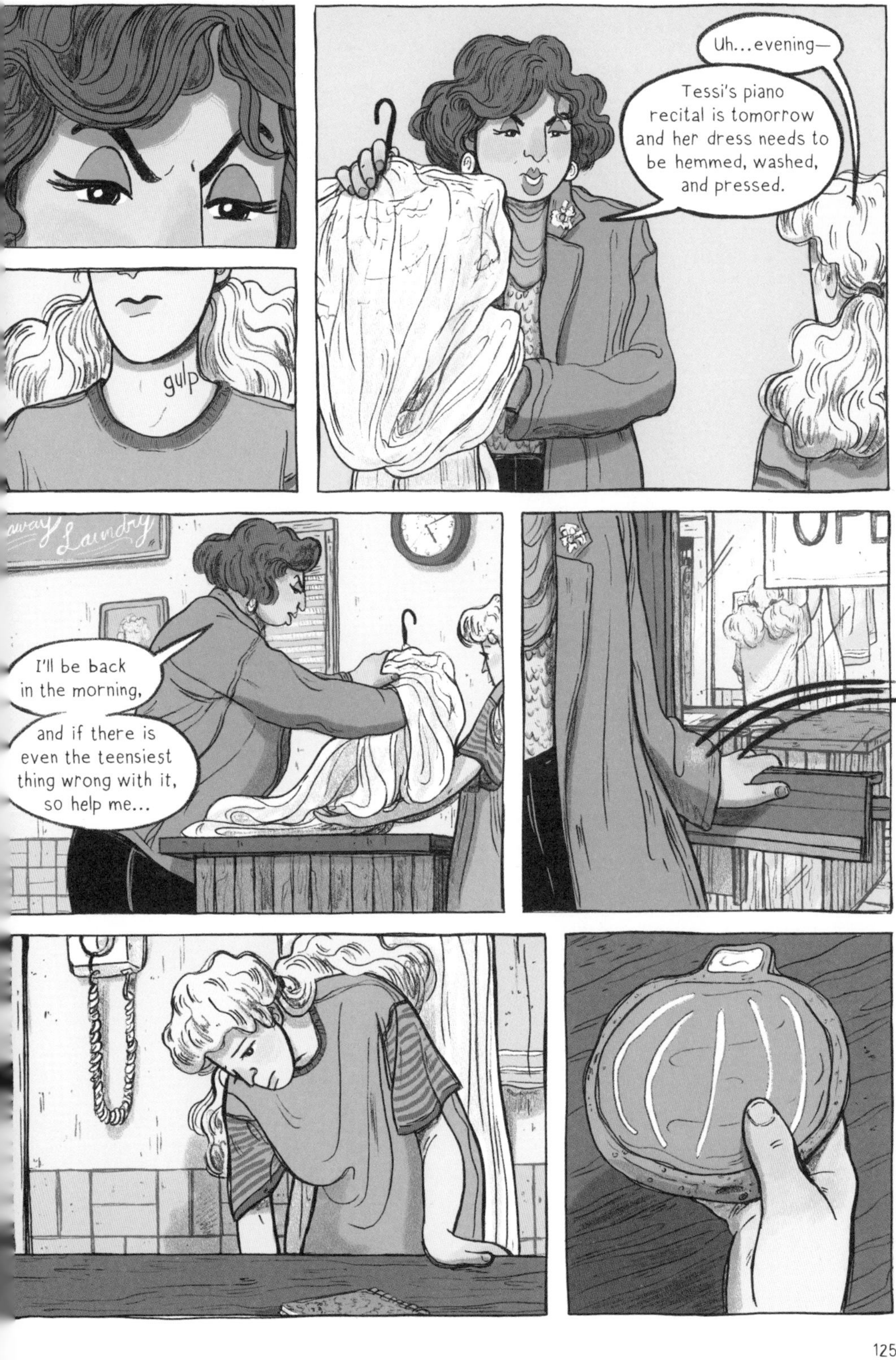
gulp
Uh...evening—
Tessi's piano recital is tomorrow and her dress needs to be hemmed, washed, and pressed.
Laundry
I'll be back in the morning,
and if there is even the teensiest thing wrong with it, so help me...

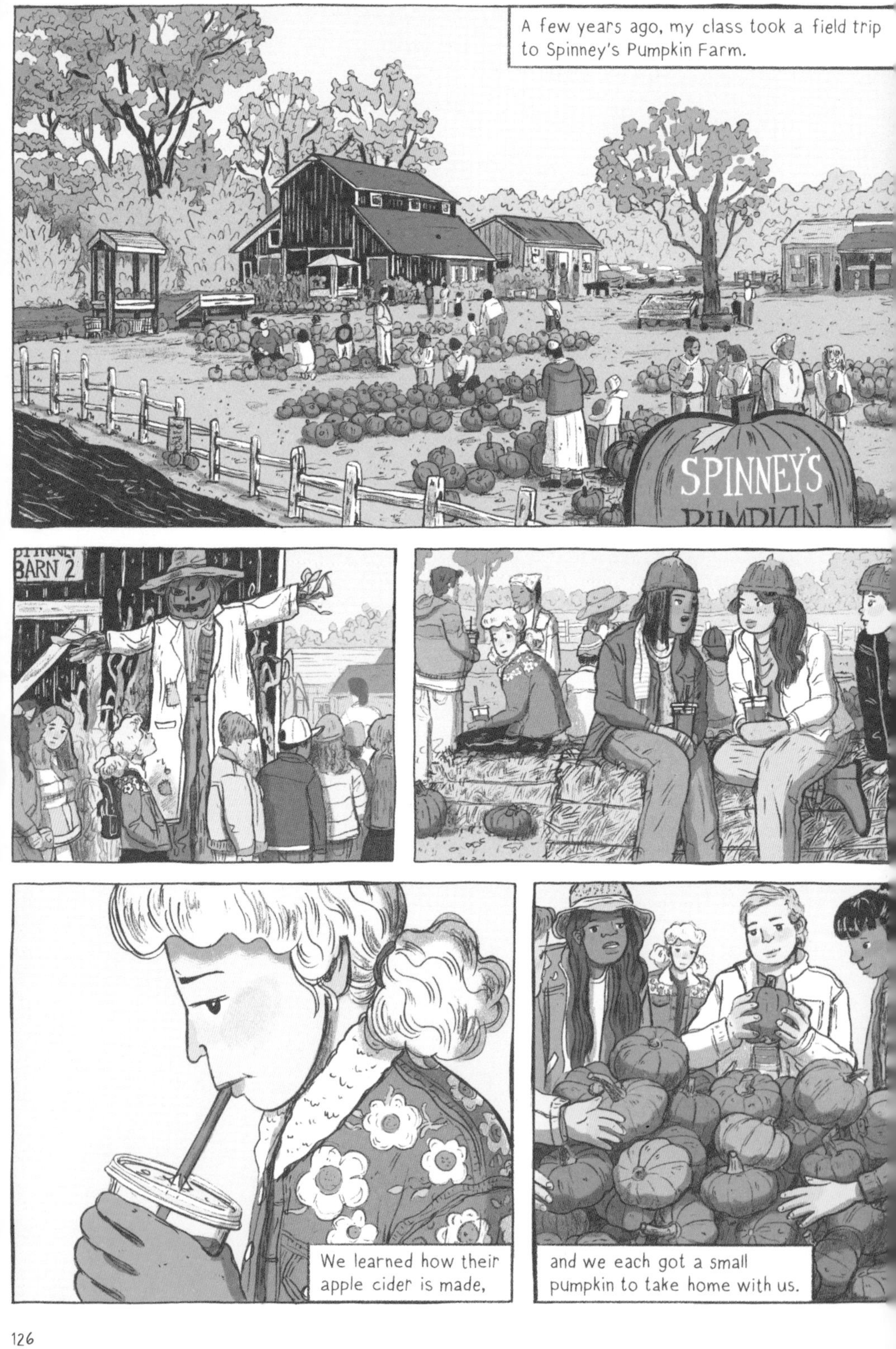
A few years ago, my class took a field trip to Spinney's Pumpkin Farm.
SPINNEY'S
BARN 2
We learned how their apple cider is made,
and we each got a small pumpkin to take home with us.

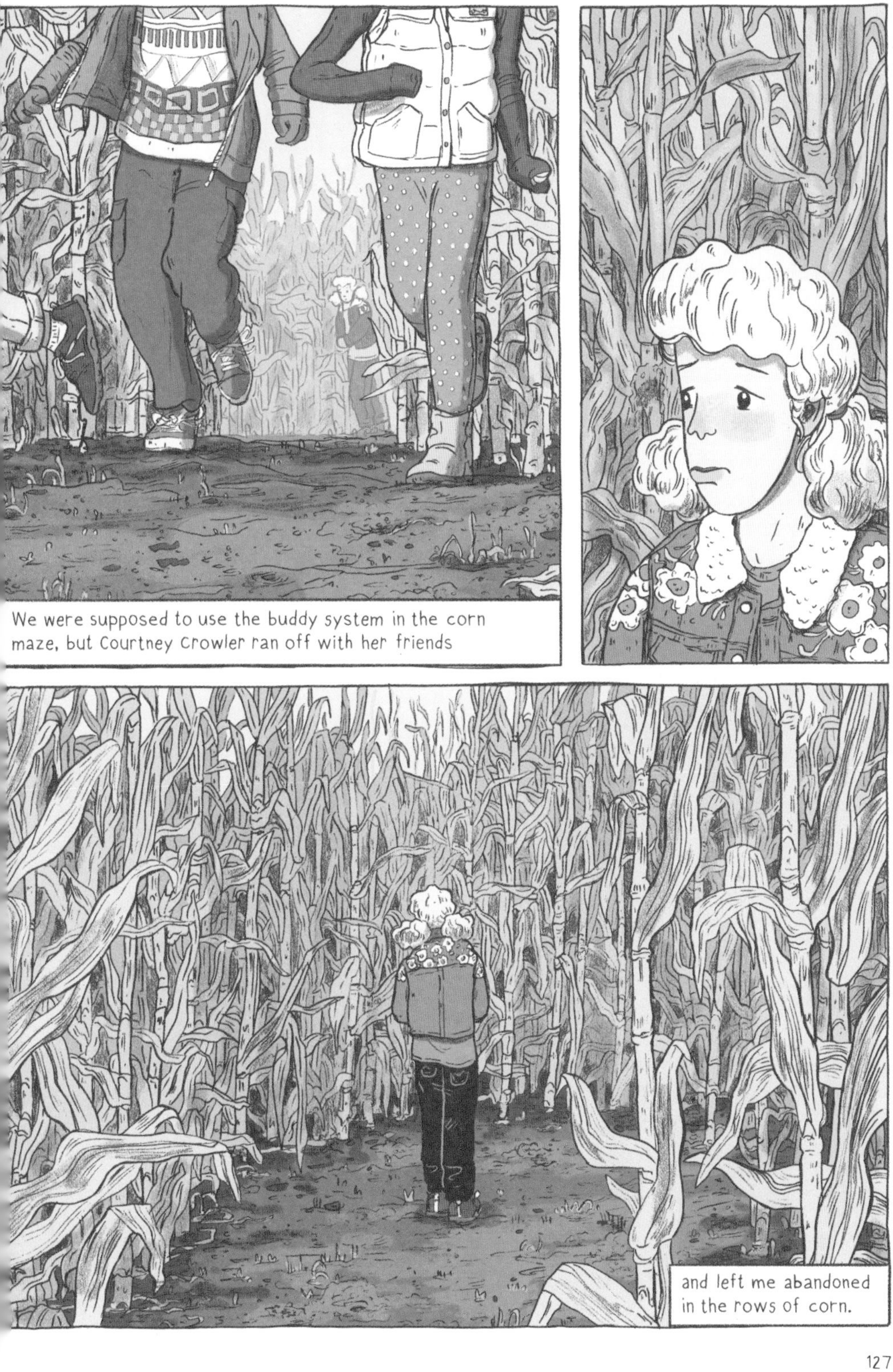
We were supposed to use the buddy system in the corn maze, but Courtney Crowler ran off with her friends
and left me abandoned in the rows of corn.

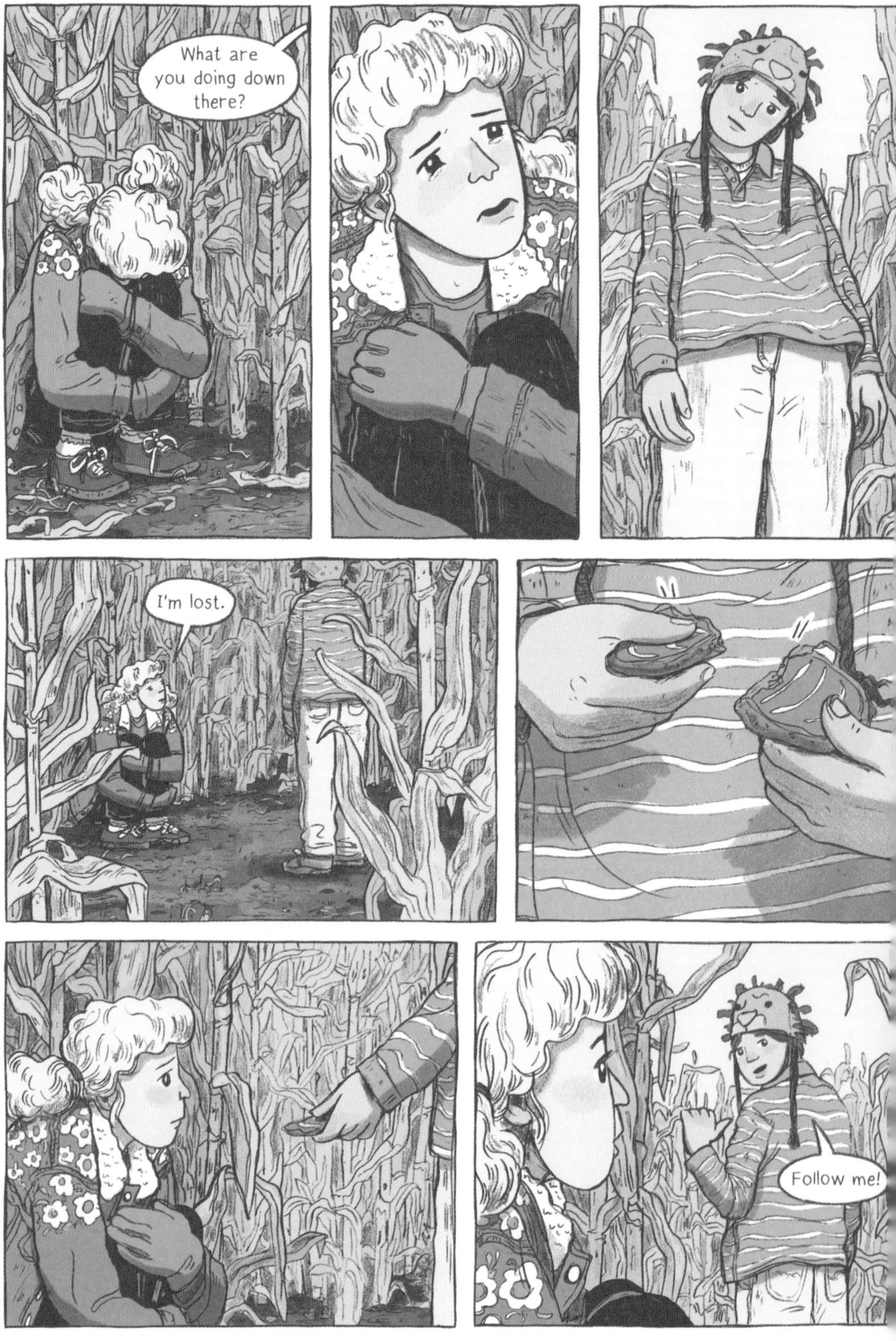
What are you doing down there?
I'm lost.
Follow me!

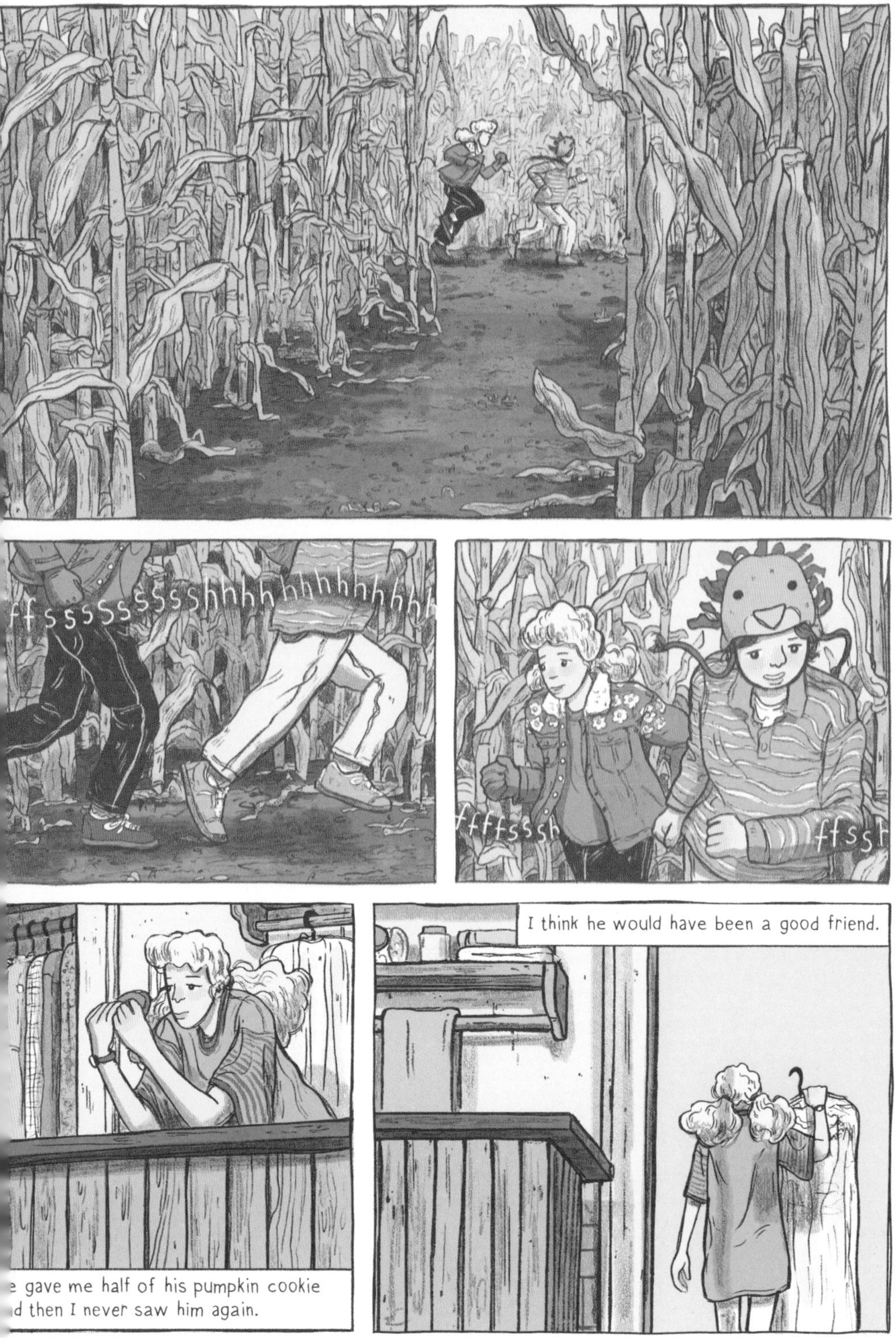
ffsssssssshhhhhhhhhhhhh
fffsssh
ffssh
e gave me half of his pumpkin cookie
d then I never saw him again.
I think he would have been a good friend.

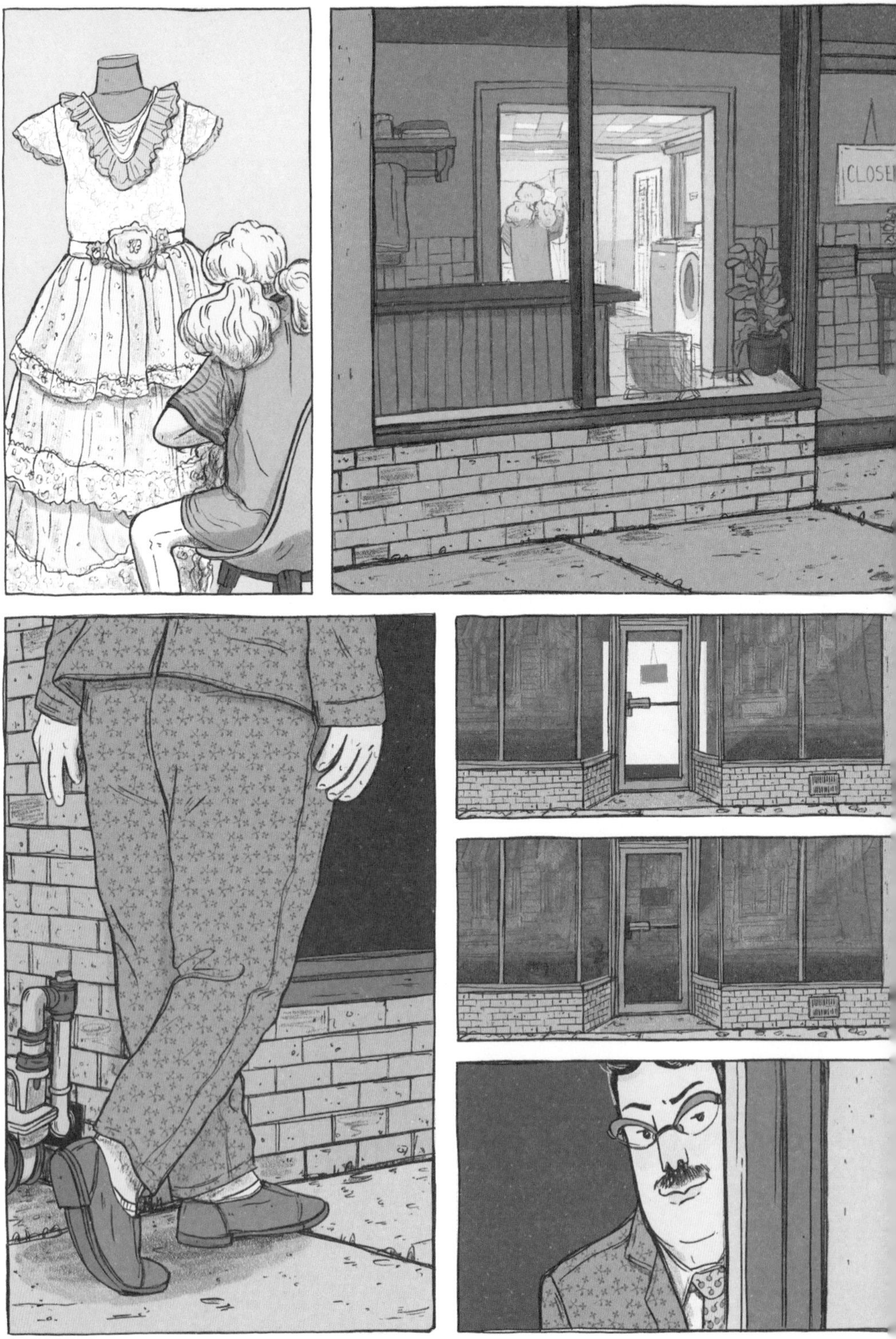
CLOSE

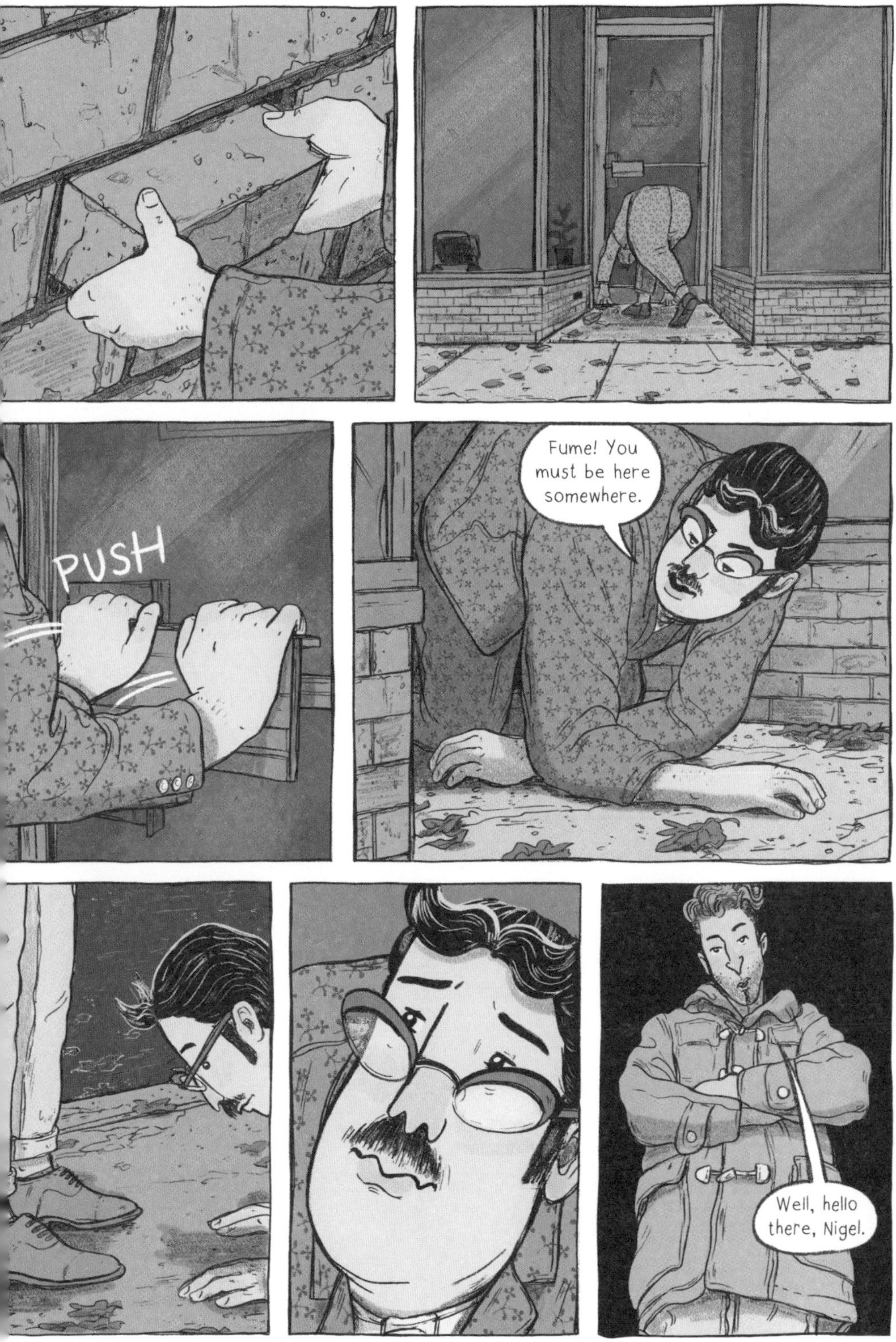
PUSH
Fume! You must be here somewhere.
Well, hello there, Nigel.

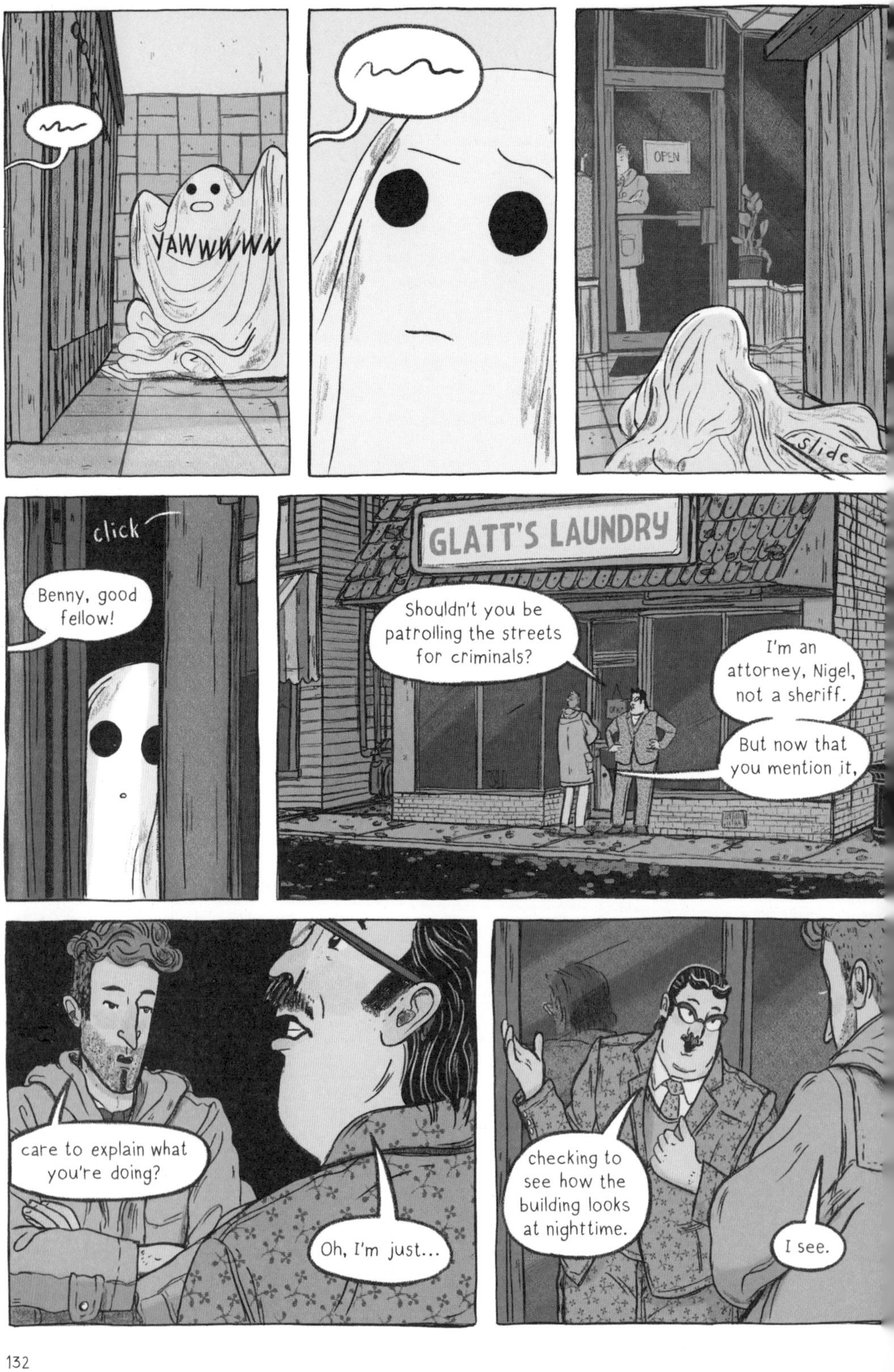
YAWWWWN
OPEN
slide
click
Benny, good fellow!
GLATT'S LAUNDRY
Shouldn't you be patrolling the streets for criminals?
I'm an attorney, Nigel, not a sheriff.
But now that you mention it,
care to explain what you're doing?
Oh, I'm just...
checking to see how the building looks at nighttime.
I see.

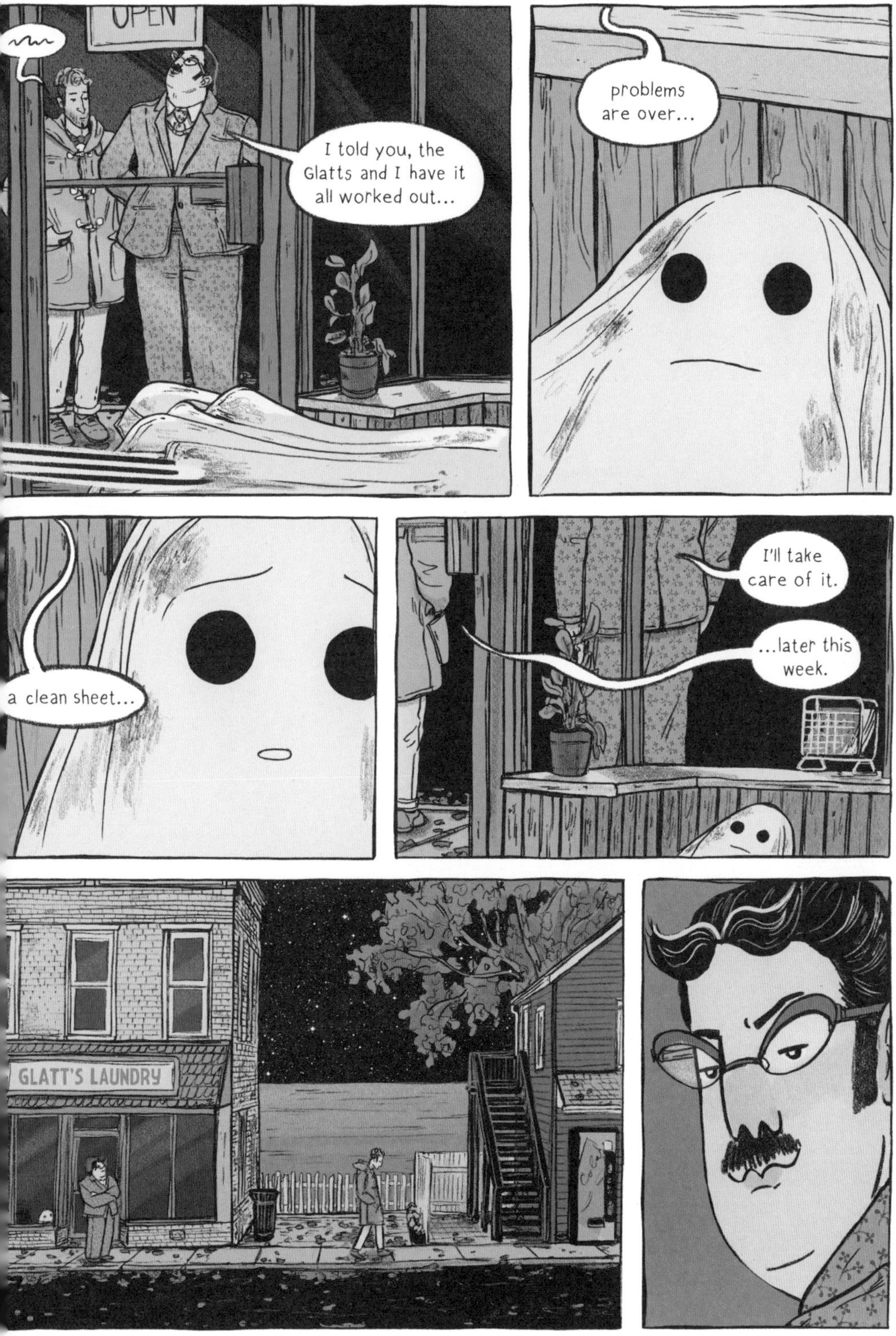
OPEN
I told you, the Glatts and I have it all worked out...
problems are over...
a clean sheet...
I'll take care of it.
...later this week.
GLATT'S LAUNDRY

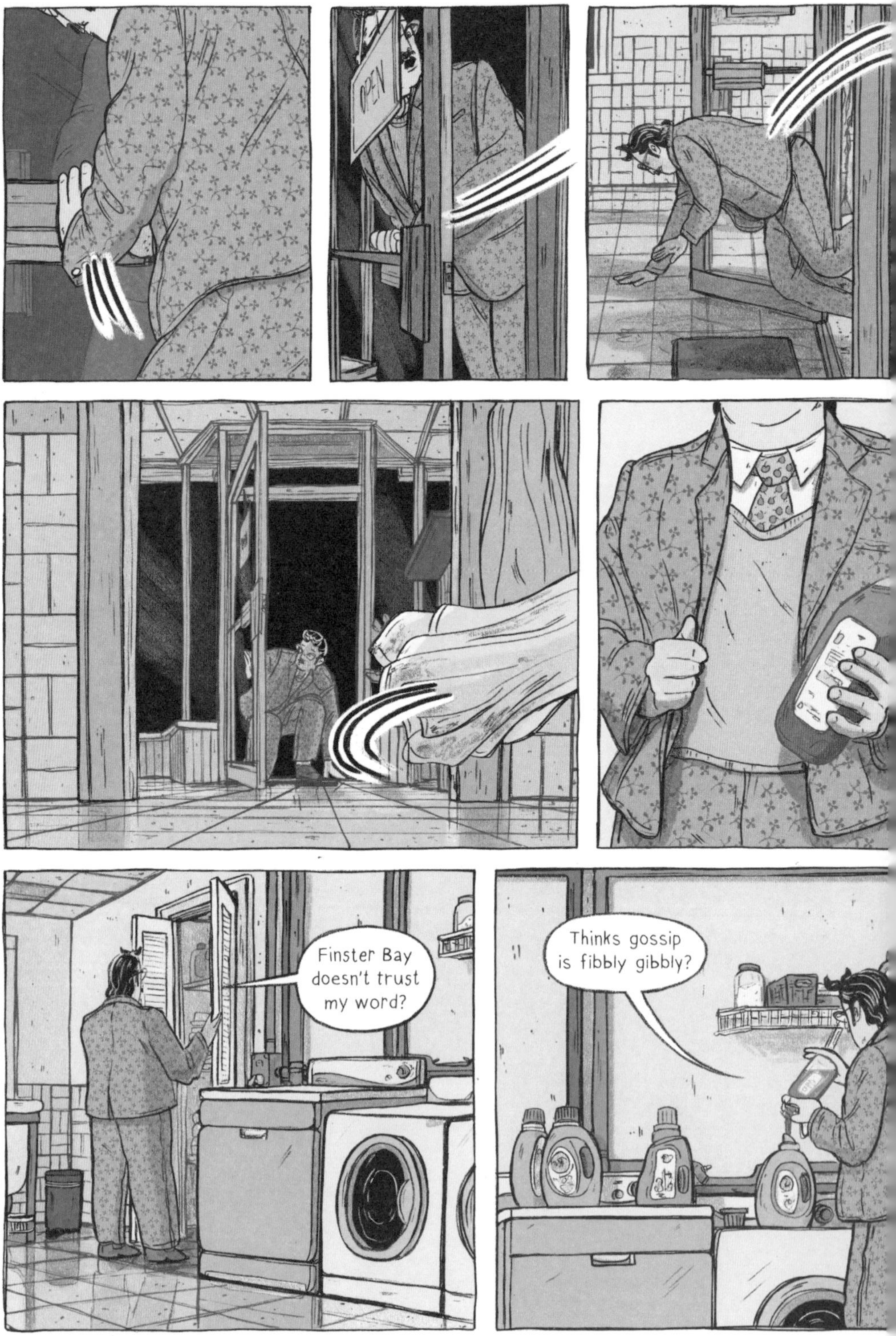
OPEN
Finster Bay doesn't trust my word?
Thinks gossip is fibbly gibbly?

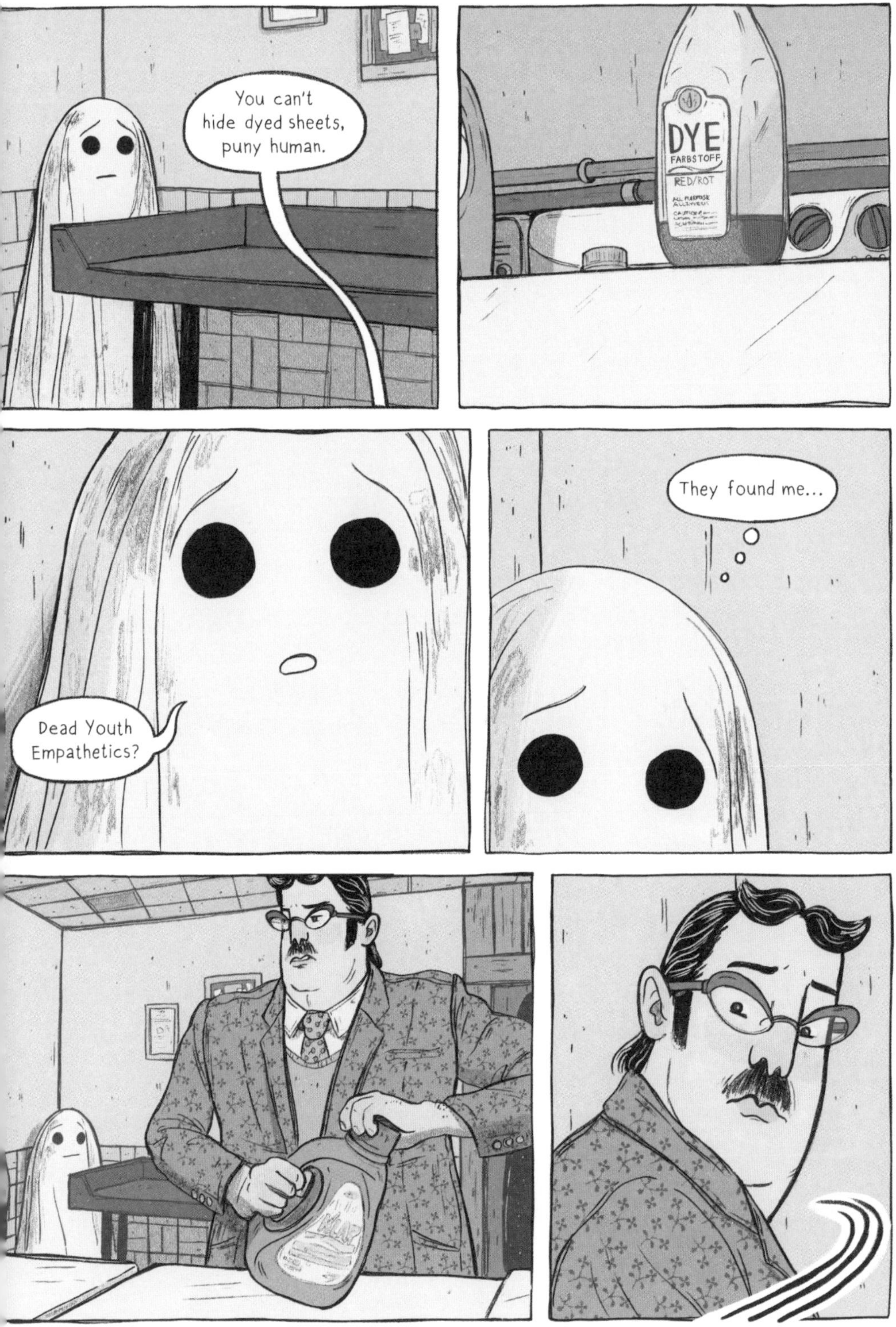
You can't hide dyed sheets, puny human.
DYE
FARBSTOFF
RED/ROT
Dead Youth Empathetics?
They found me...

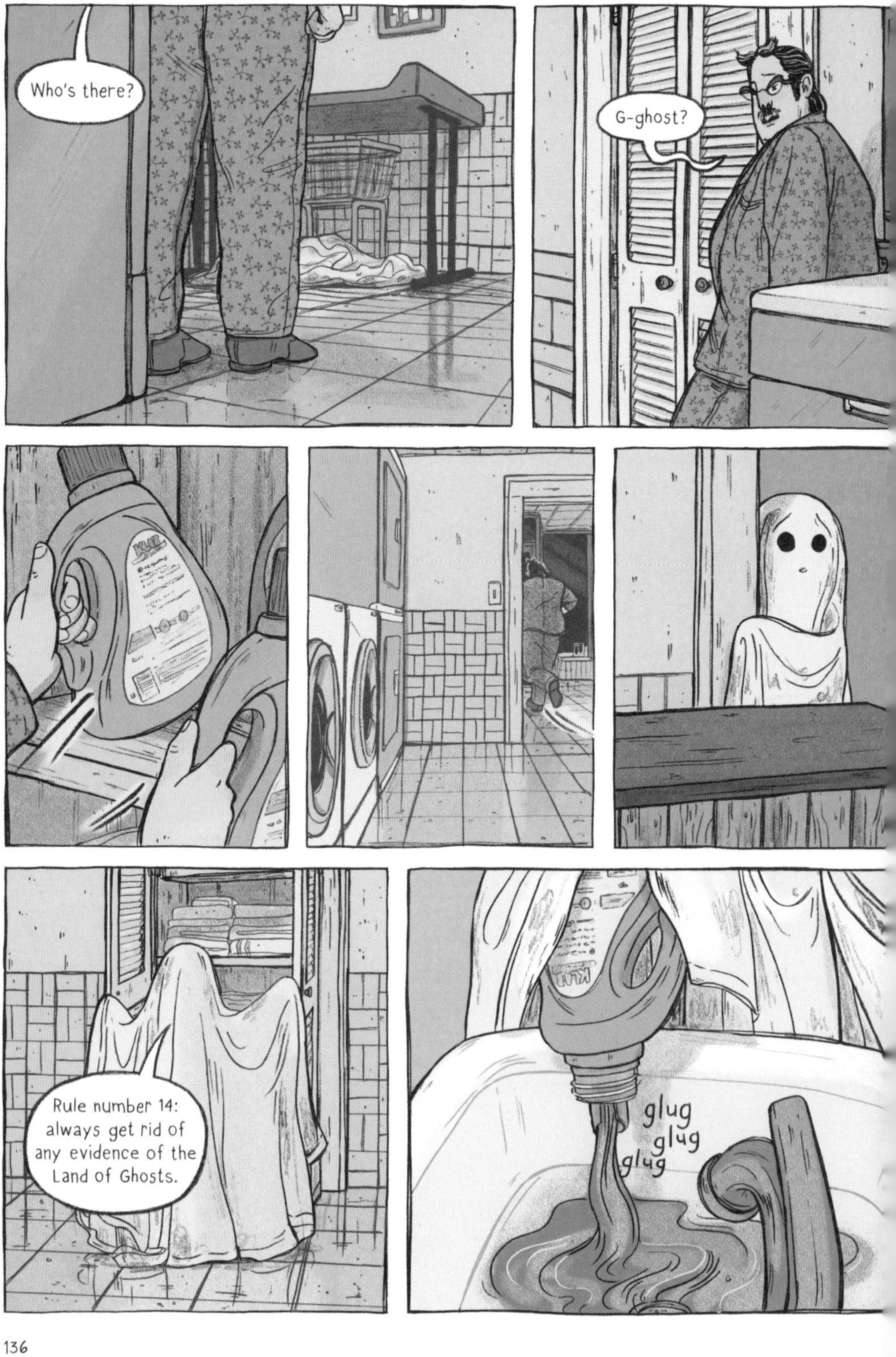
Who's there?
G-ghost?
Rule number 14: always get rid of any evidence of the Land of Ghosts.
glug glug glug

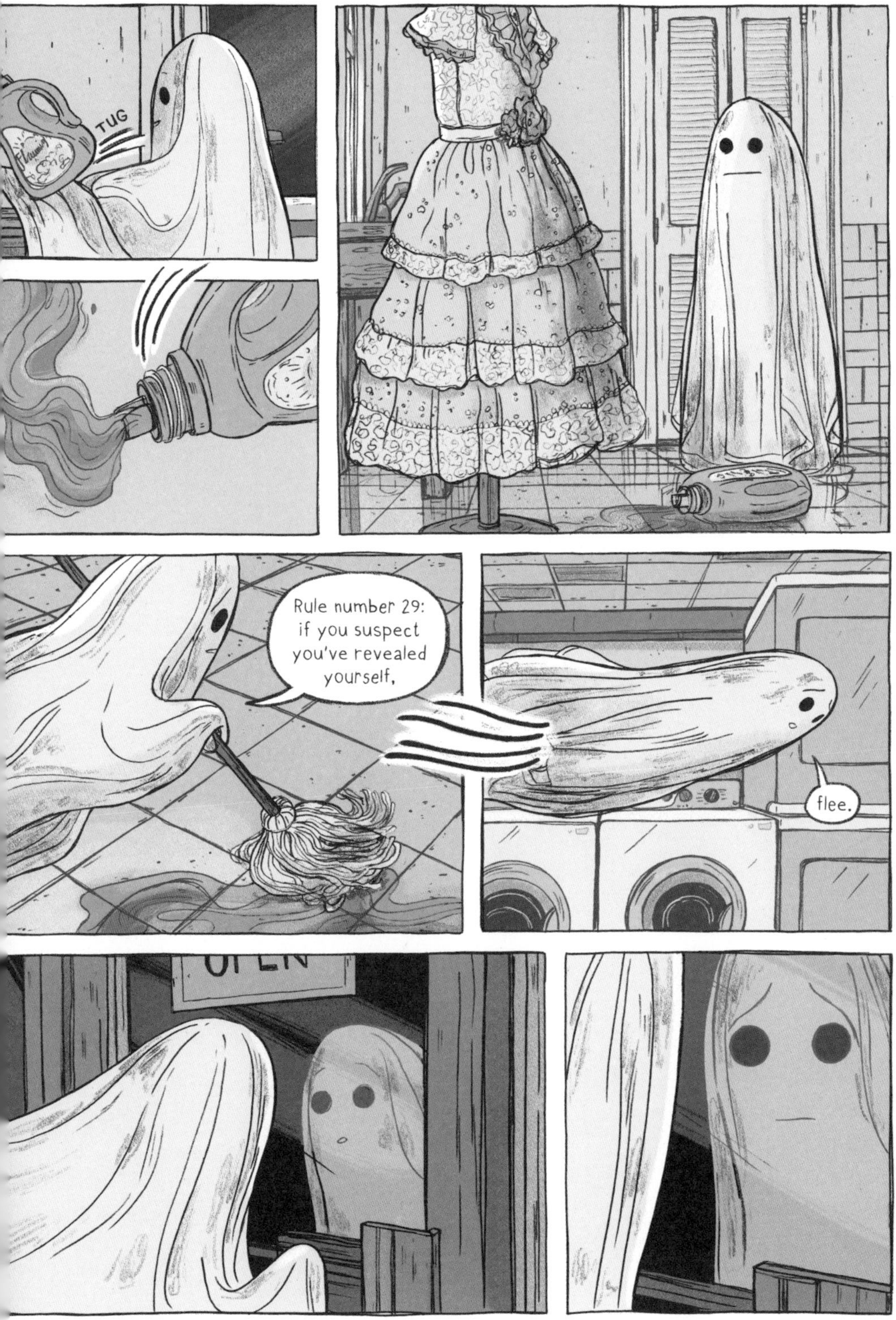
TUG
Rule number 29: if you suspect you've revealed yourself,
flee.
OPEN

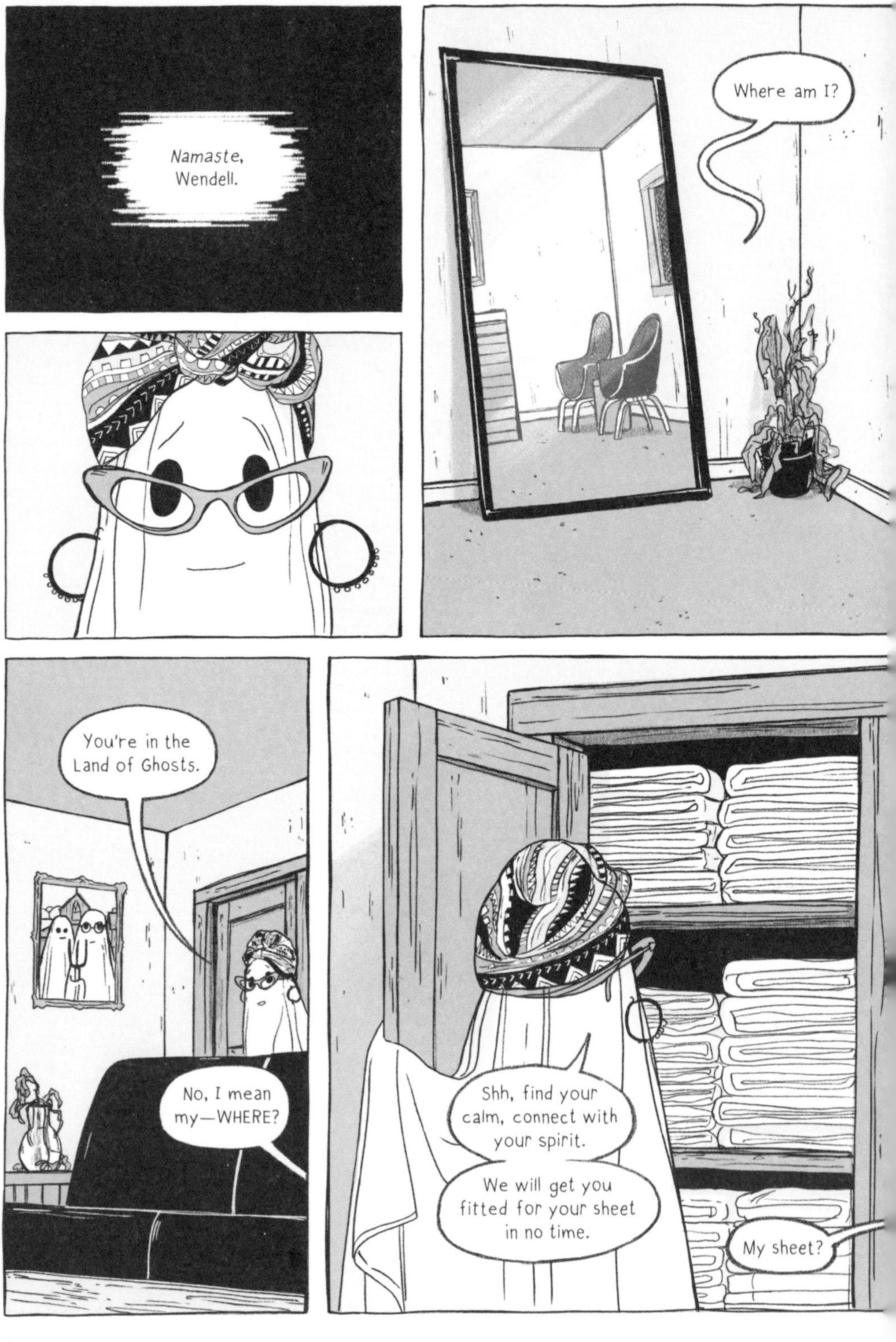

Namaste, Wendell.
Where am I?
You're in the Land of Ghosts.
No, I mean my—WHERE?
Shh, find your calm, connect with your spirit.
We will get you fitted for your sheet in no time.
My sheet?

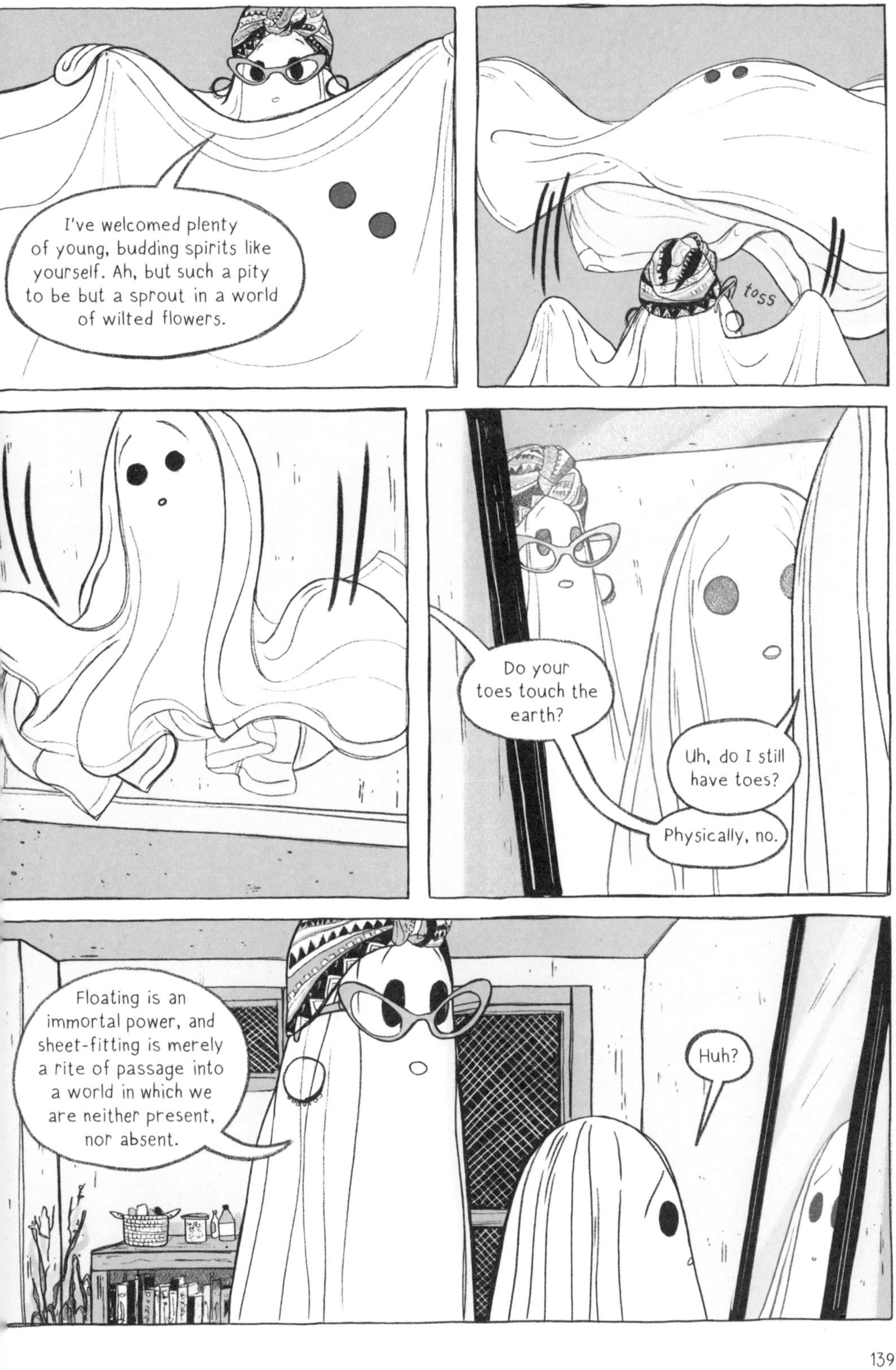
I've welcomed plenty of young, budding spirits like yourself. Ah, but such a pity to be but a sprout in a world of wilted flowers.
toss
Do your toes touch the earth?
Uh, do I still have toes?
Physically, no.
Floating is an immortal power, and sheet-fitting is merely a rite of passage into a world in which we are neither present, nor absent.
Huh?

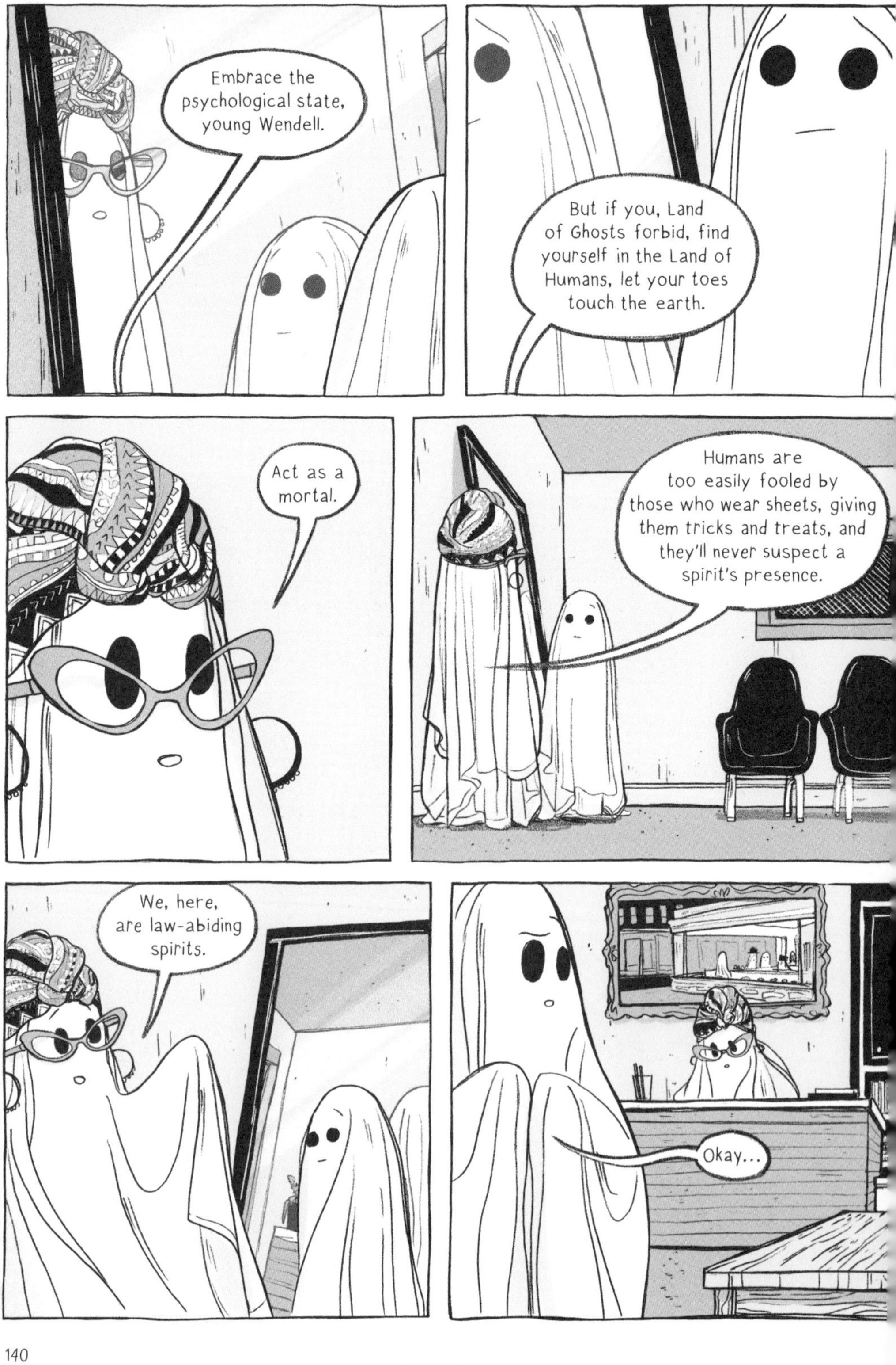
Embrace the psychological state, young Wendell.
But if you, Land of Ghosts forbid, find yourself in the Land of Humans, let your toes touch the earth.
Act as a mortal.
Humans are too easily fooled by those who wear sheets, giving them tricks and treats, and they'll never suspect a spirit's presence.
We, here, are law-abiding spirits.
Okay...

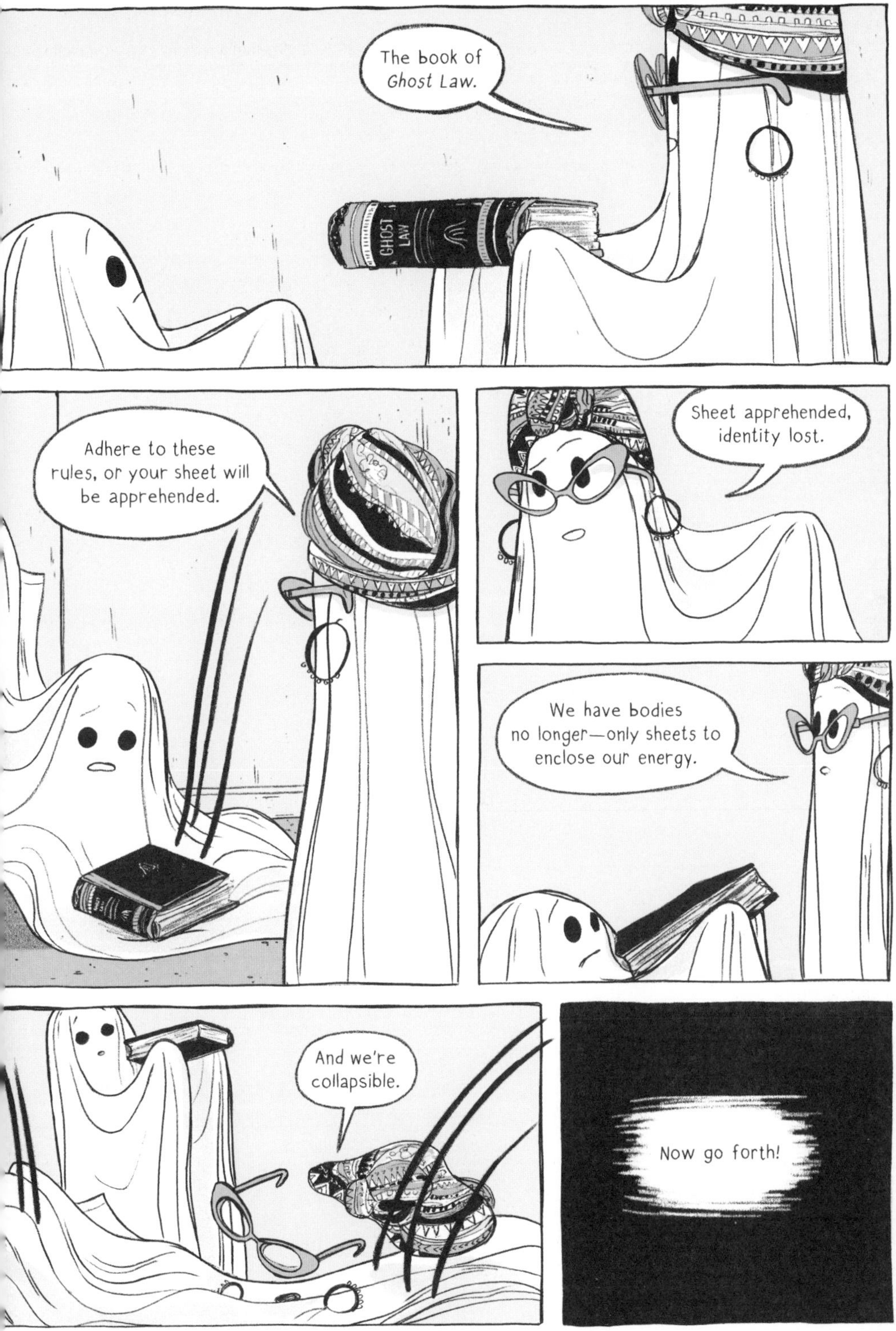
The book of *Ghost Law*.
GHOST LAW
Adhere to these rules, or your sheet will be apprehended.
Sheet apprehended, identity lost.
We have bodies no longer—only sheets to enclose our energy.
And we're collapsible.
Now go forth!

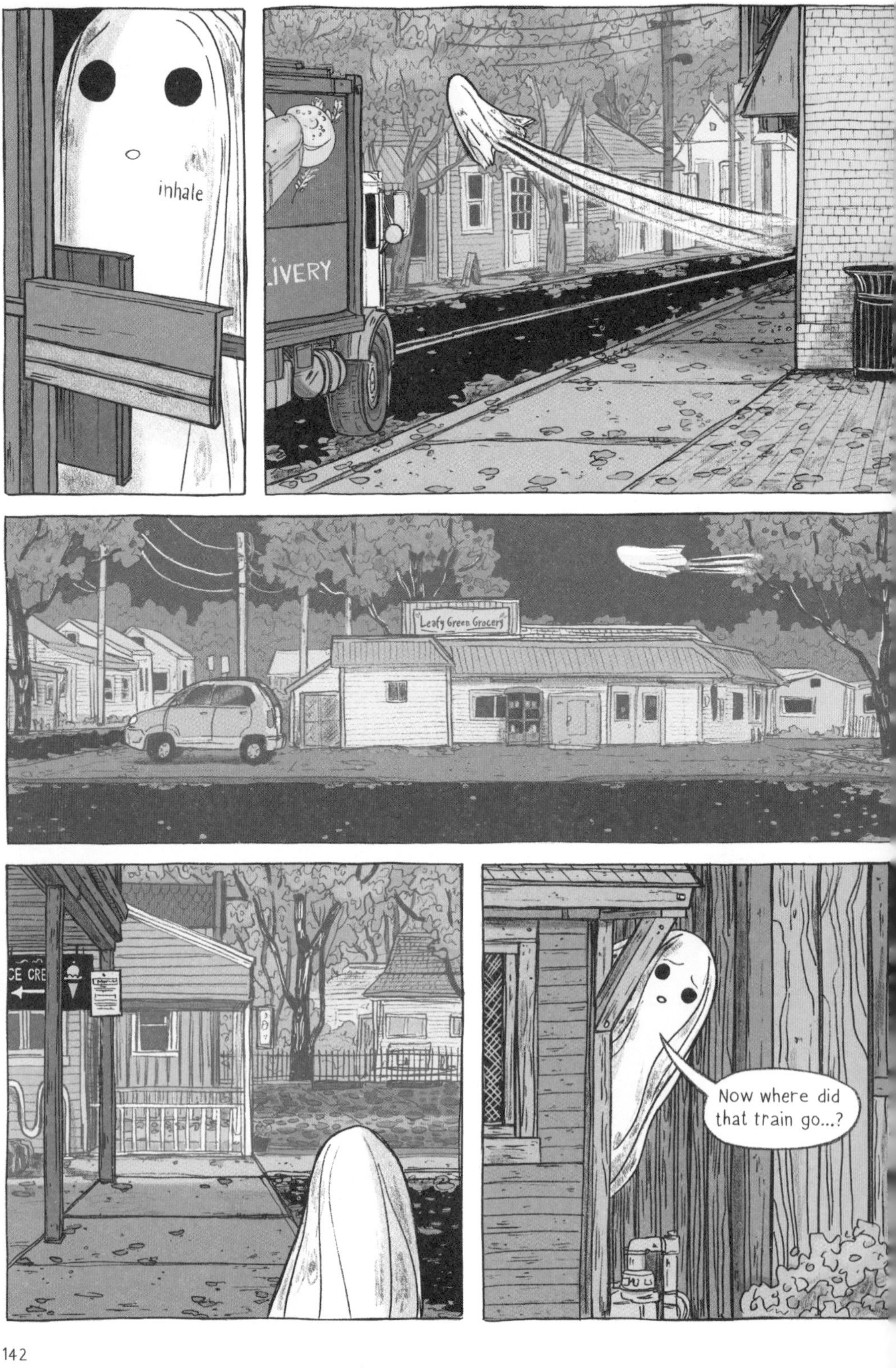
inhale
LIVERY
Leafy Green Grocers
CE CRE
Now where did that train go...?

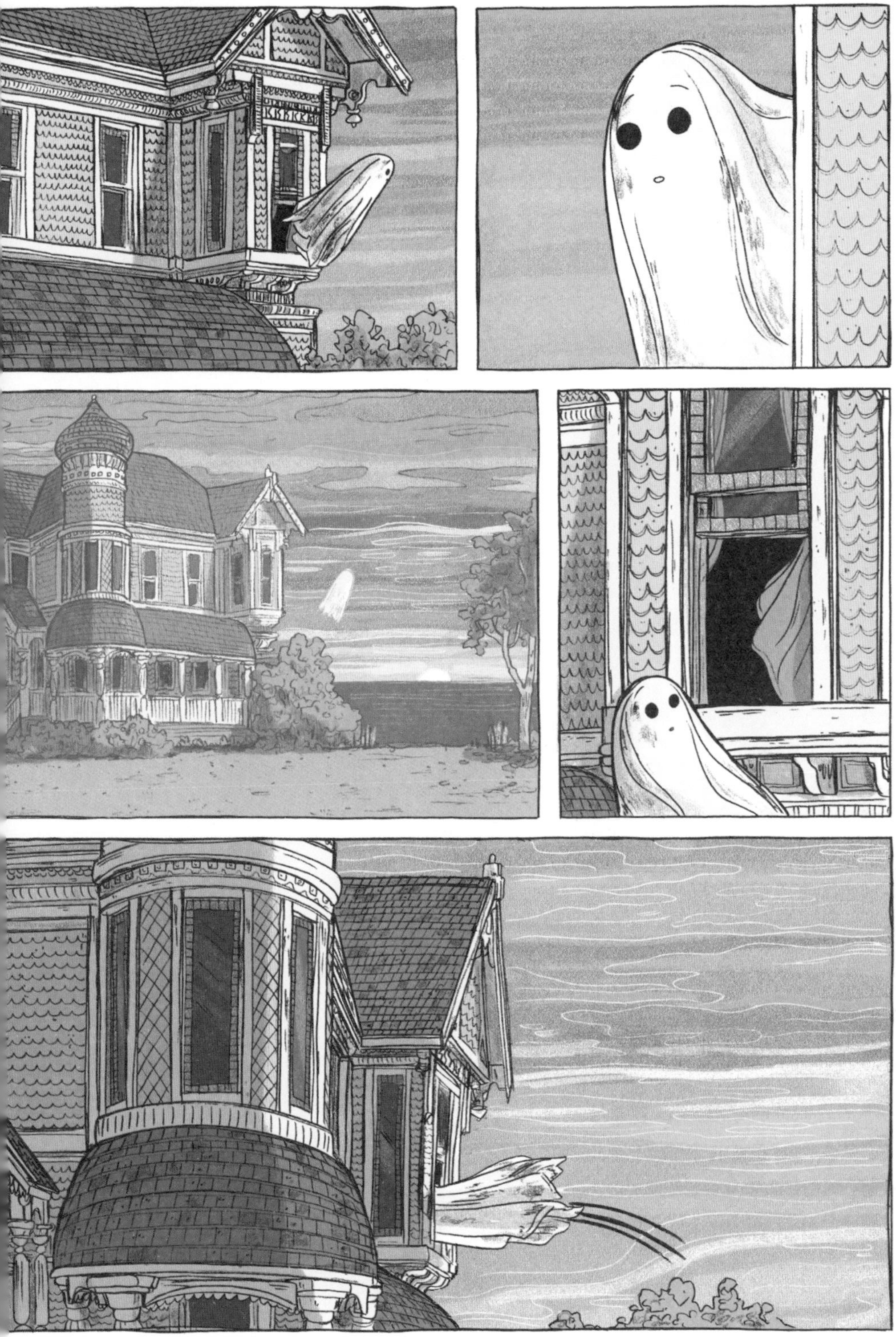

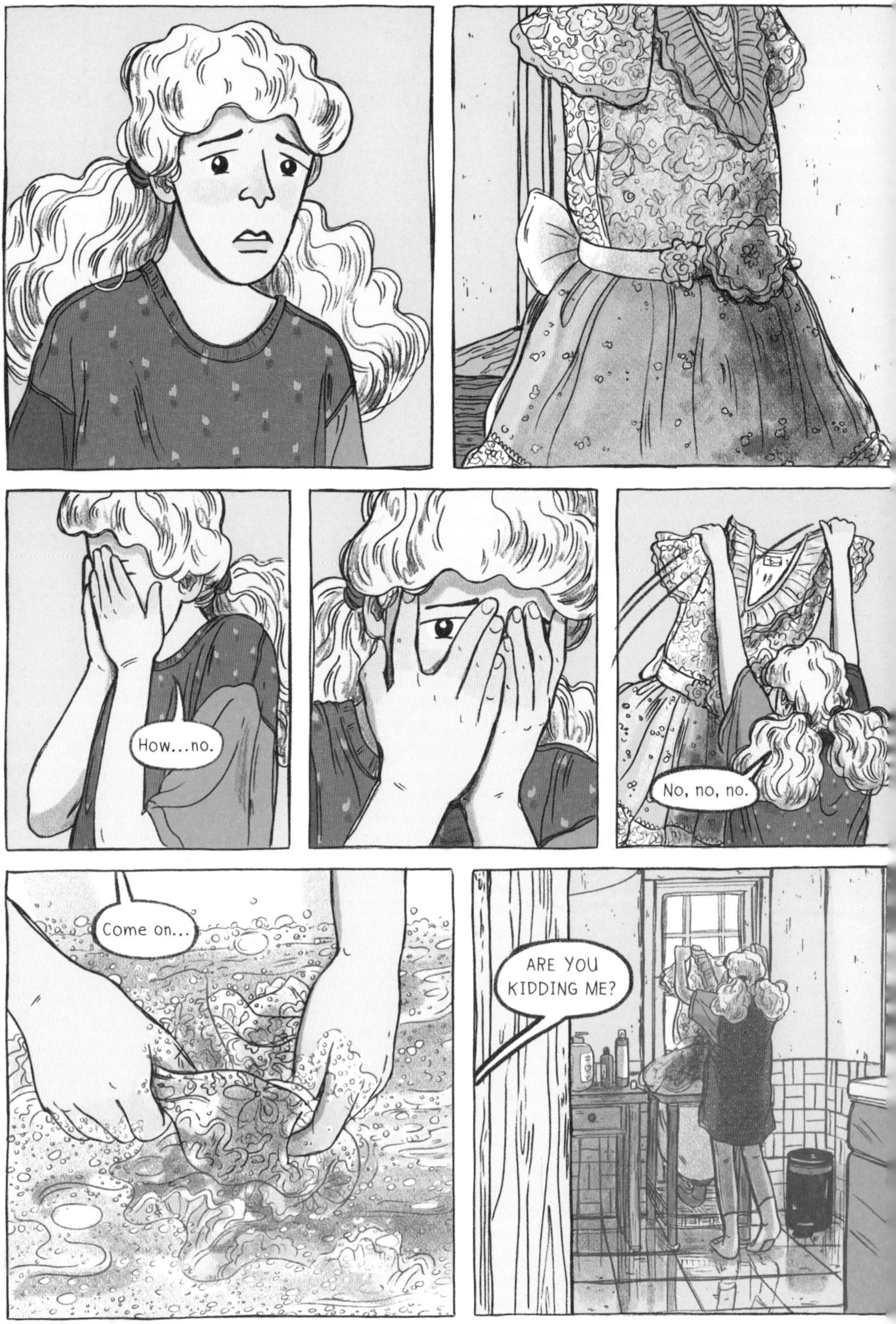
How...no.
No, no, no.
Come on...
ARE YOU KIDDING ME?

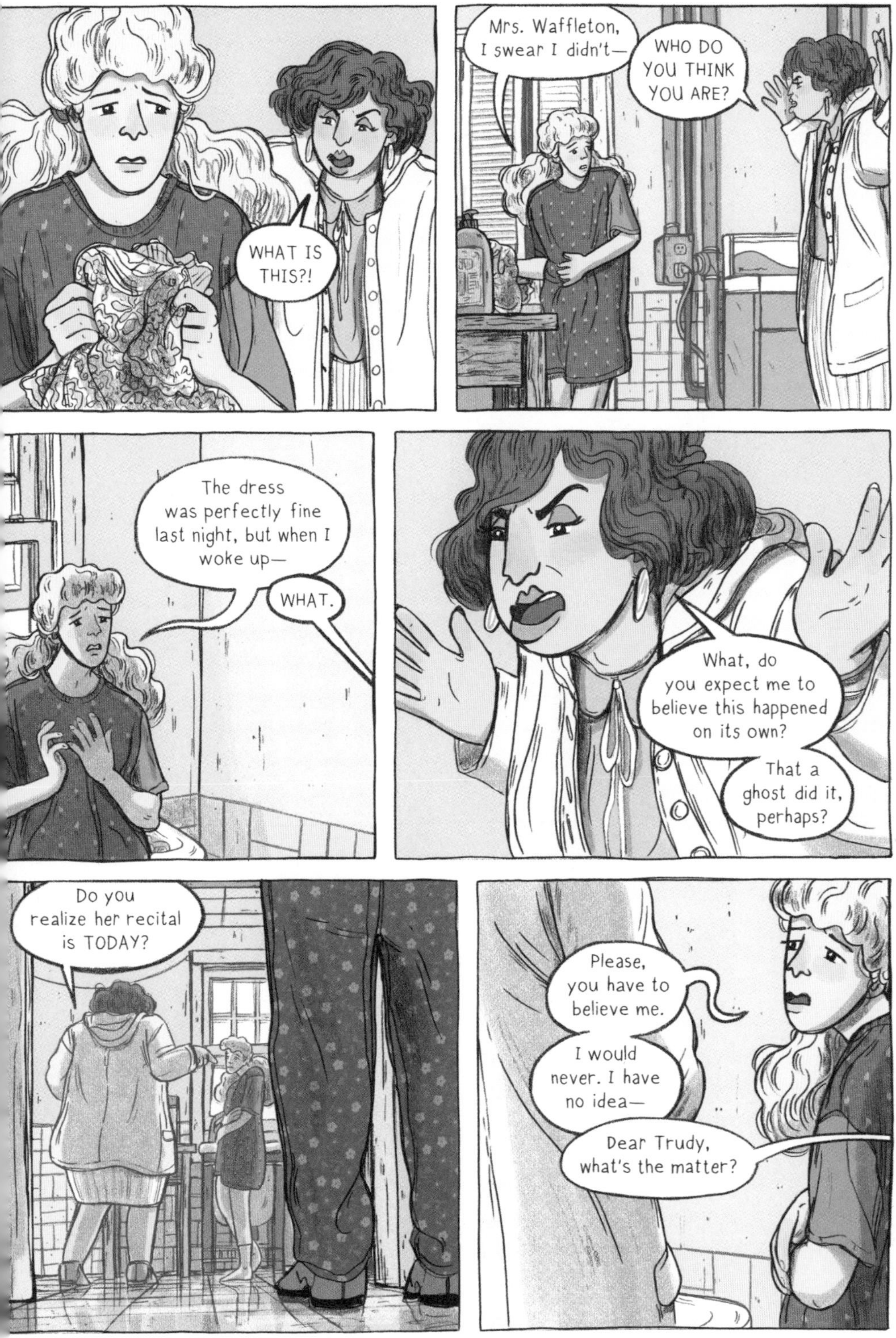
WHAT IS THIS?!
Mrs. Waffleton, I swear I didn't—
WHO DO YOU THINK YOU ARE?
The dress was perfectly fine last night, but when I woke up—
WHAT.
What, do you expect me to believe this happened on its own?
That a ghost did it, perhaps?
Do you realize her recital is TODAY?
Please, you have to believe me.
I would never. I have no idea—
Dear Trudy, what's the matter?

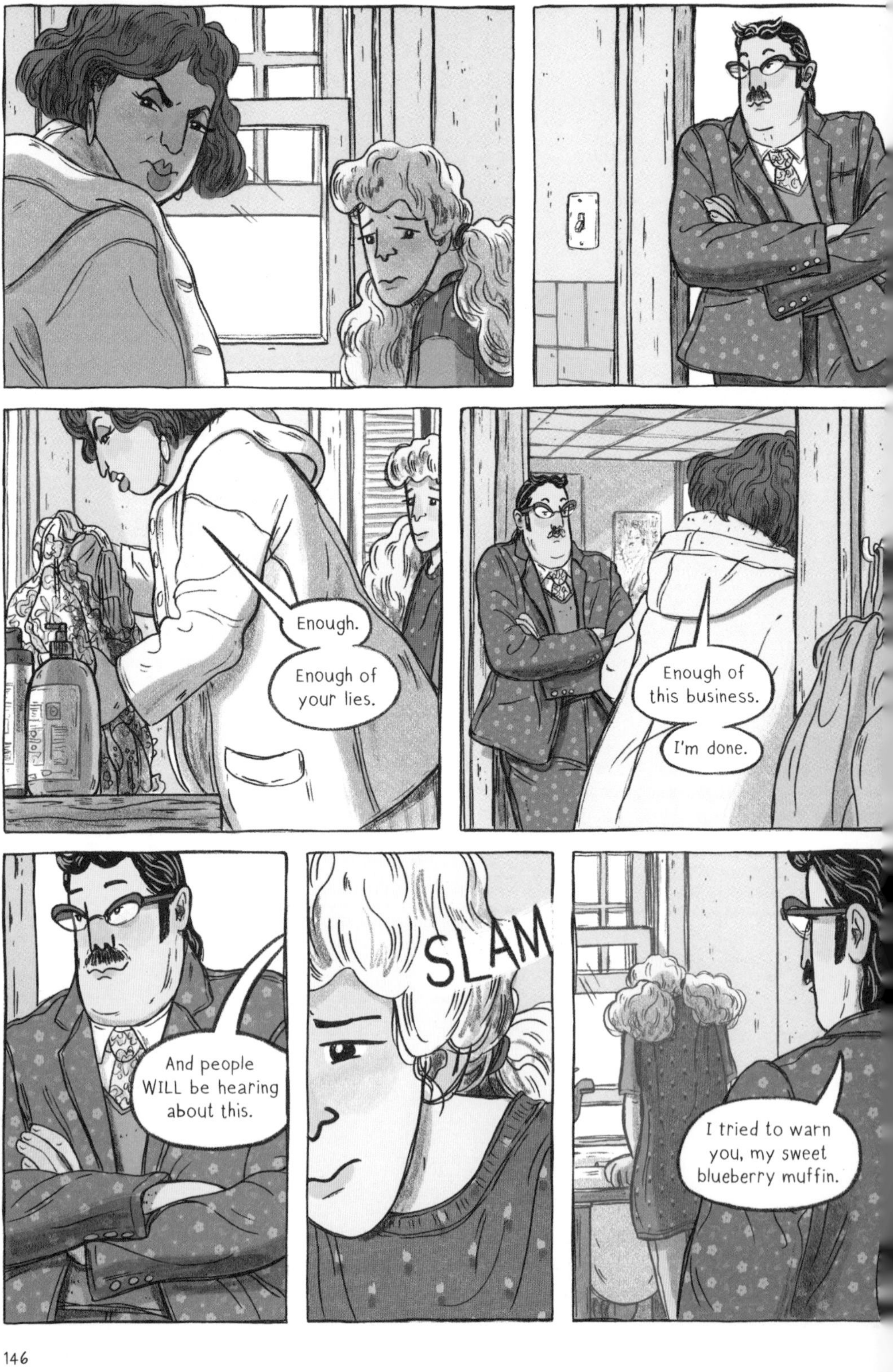
Enough.
Enough of your lies.
Enough of this business.
I'm done.
And people WILL be hearing about this.
SLAM
I tried to warn you, my sweet blueberry muffin.

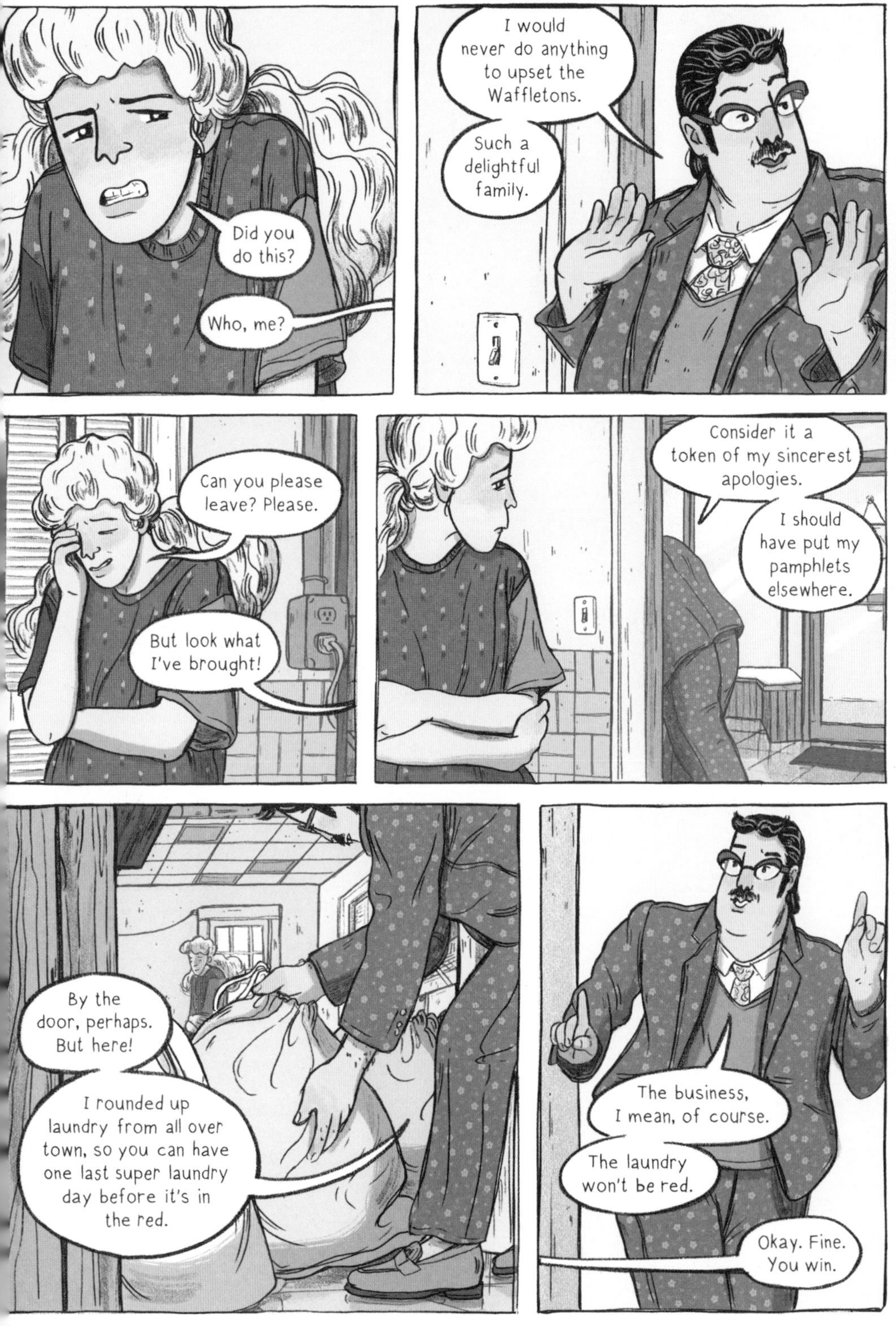
Did you do this?
Who, me?
I would never do anything to upset the Waffletons.
Such a delightful family.
Can you please leave? Please.
But look what I've brought!
Consider it a token of my sincerest apologies.
I should have put my pamphlets elsewhere.
By the door, perhaps. But here!
I rounded up laundry from all over town, so you can have one last super laundry day before it's in the red.
The business, I mean, of course.
The laundry won't be red.
Okay. Fine. You win.

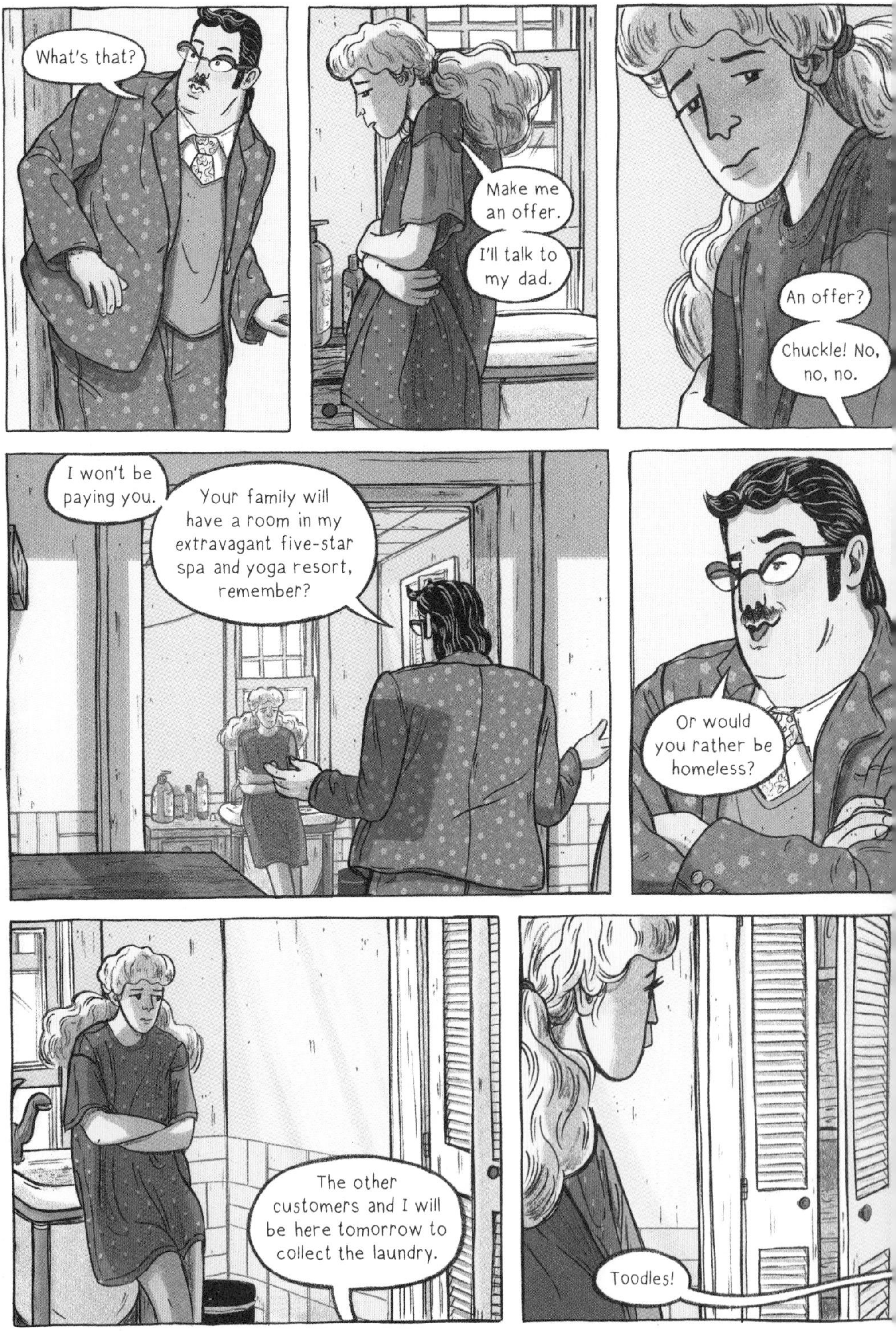
What's that?
Make me an offer.
I'll talk to my dad.
An offer?
Chuckle! No, no, no.
I won't be paying you.
Your family will have a room in my extravagant five-star spa and yoga resort, remember?
Or would you rather be homeless?
The other customers and I will be here tomorrow to collect the laundry.
Toodles!

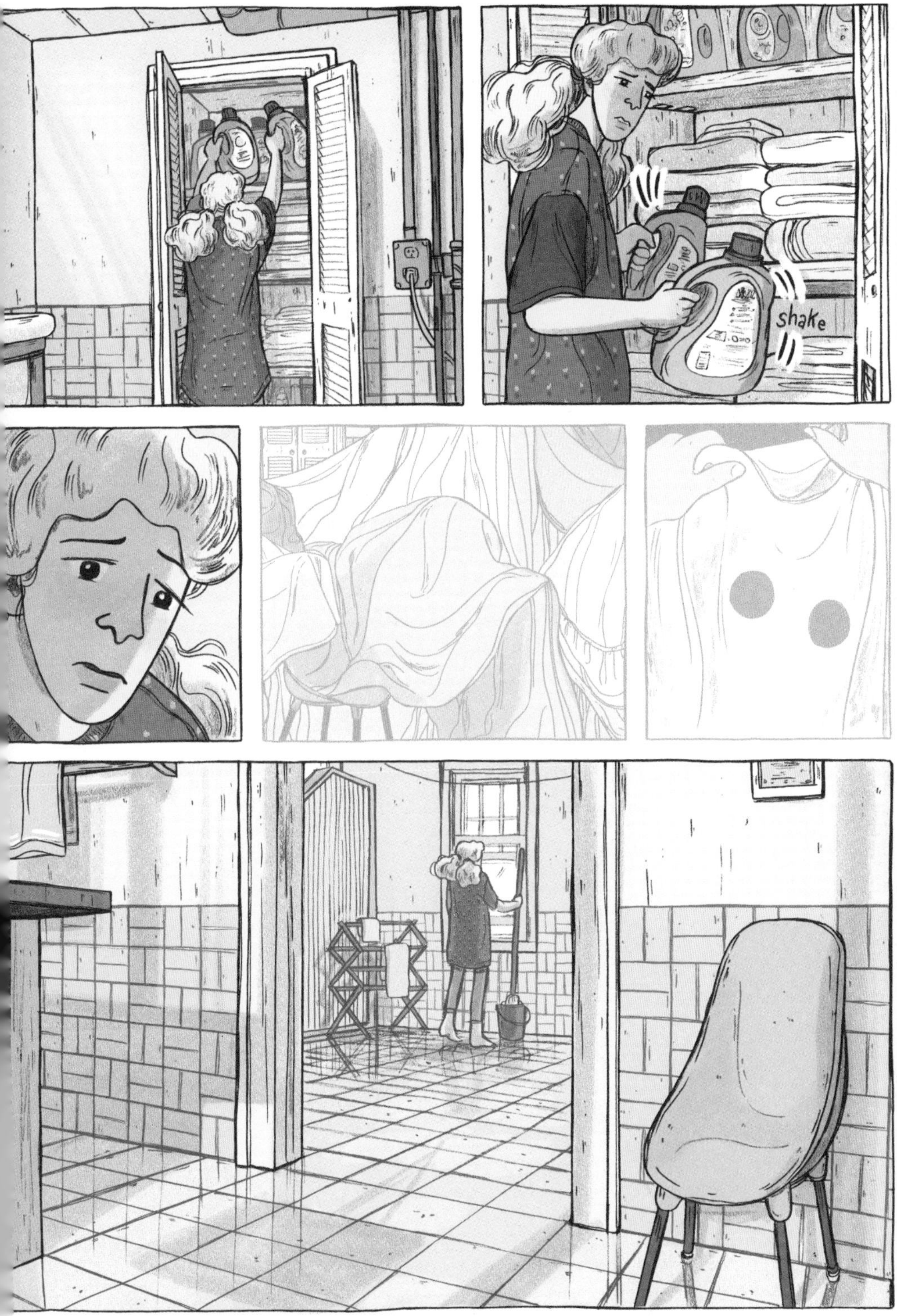
shake

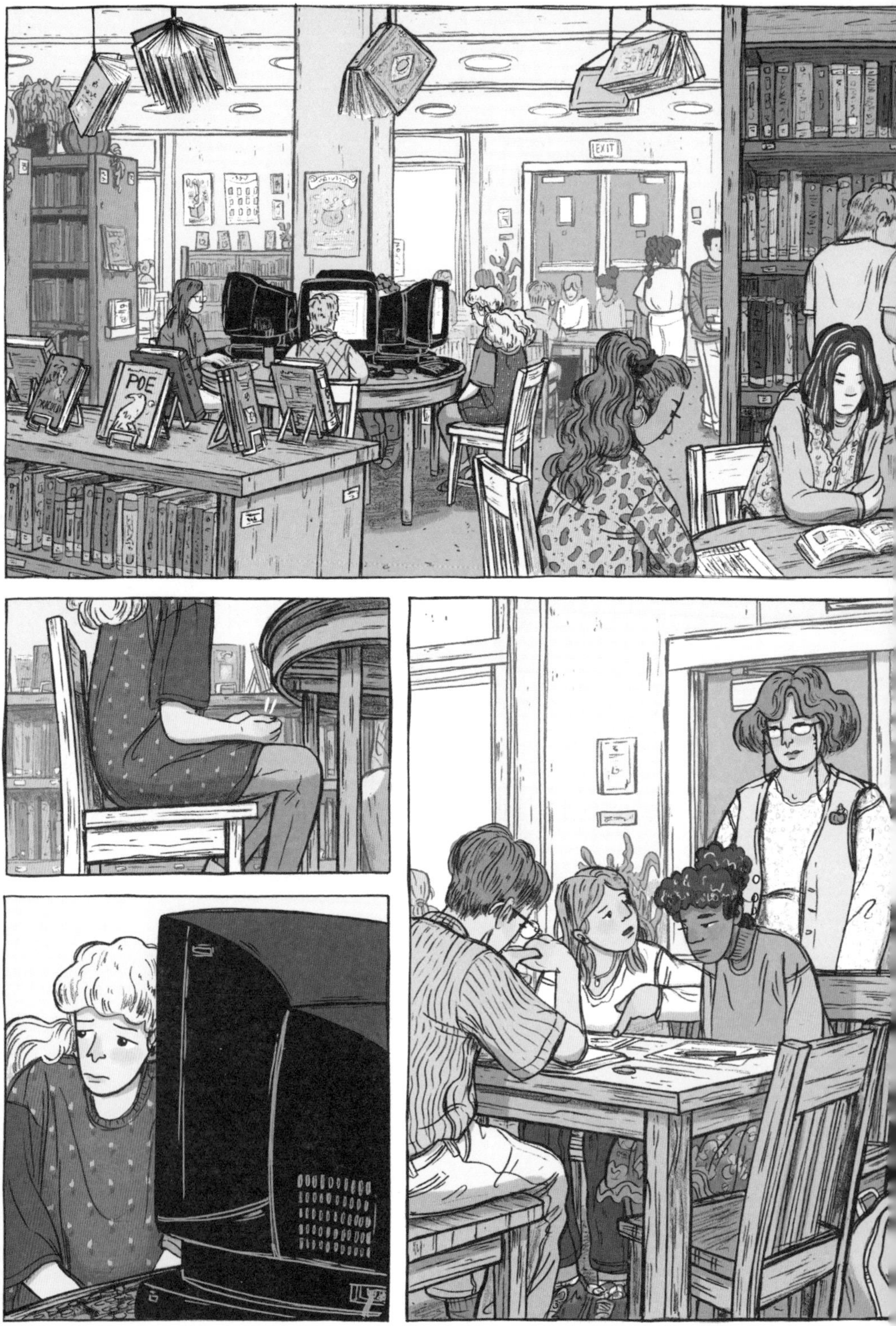
EXIT
POE

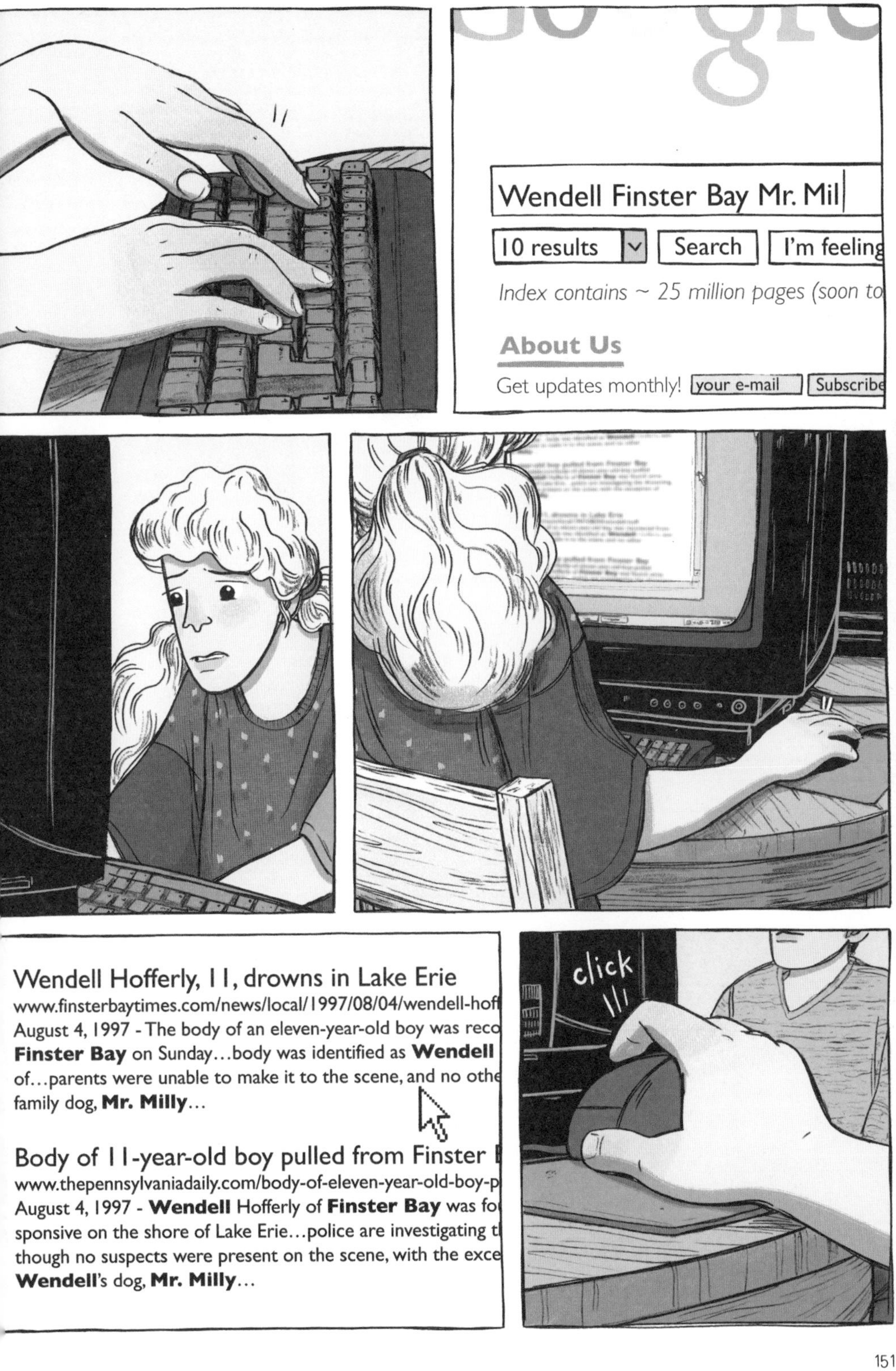
Wendell Finster Bay Mr. Mil
10 results
Search
I'm feeling
Index contains ~ 25 million pages (soon to
About Us
Get updates monthly! your e-mail Subscribe
Wendell Hofferly, 11, drowns in Lake Erie
www.finsterbaytimes.com/news/local/1997/08/04/wendell-hoff
August 4, 1997 - The body of an eleven-year-old boy was reco
Finster Bay on Sunday…body was identified as Wendell
of…parents were unable to make it to the scene, and no othe
family dog, Mr. Milly…
Body of 11-year-old boy pulled from Finster
www.thepennsylvaniadaily.com/body-of-eleven-year-old-boy-p
August 4, 1997 - Wendell Hofferly of Finster Bay was fo
sponsive on the shore of Lake Erie…police are investigating t
though no suspects were present on the scene, with the exce
Wendell's dog, Mr. Milly…
click

WENDELL HOFFERLY, 11, DROWNS IN LAKE ERIE

AUGUST 4, 1997

The body of an eleven-year-old boy was recovered from Finster Bay on Su ternoon, after police responded to complaints of a barking dog. The body tified as Wendell Hofferly, son of business tycoon Louis Hofferly and his business partner, Hellen. For reasons presently unknown, the parents we to make it to the scene, and no other witnesses were present, with the exc

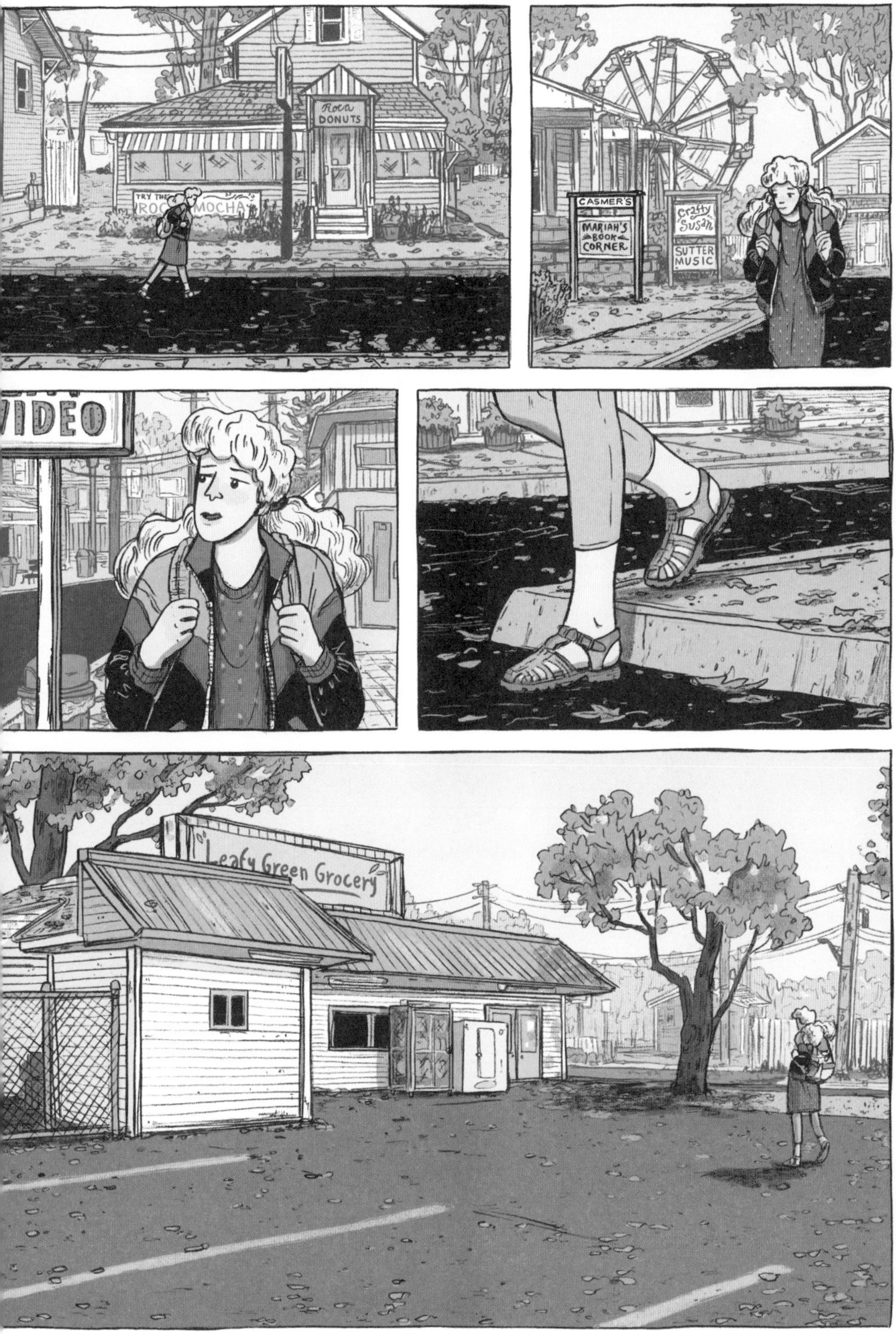
Roca
DONUTS
TRY THE
ROC
MOCHA
CASMER'S
MARIAH'S BOOK CORNER
Crafty Susan
SUTTER MUSIC
VIDEO
Leafy Green Grocery

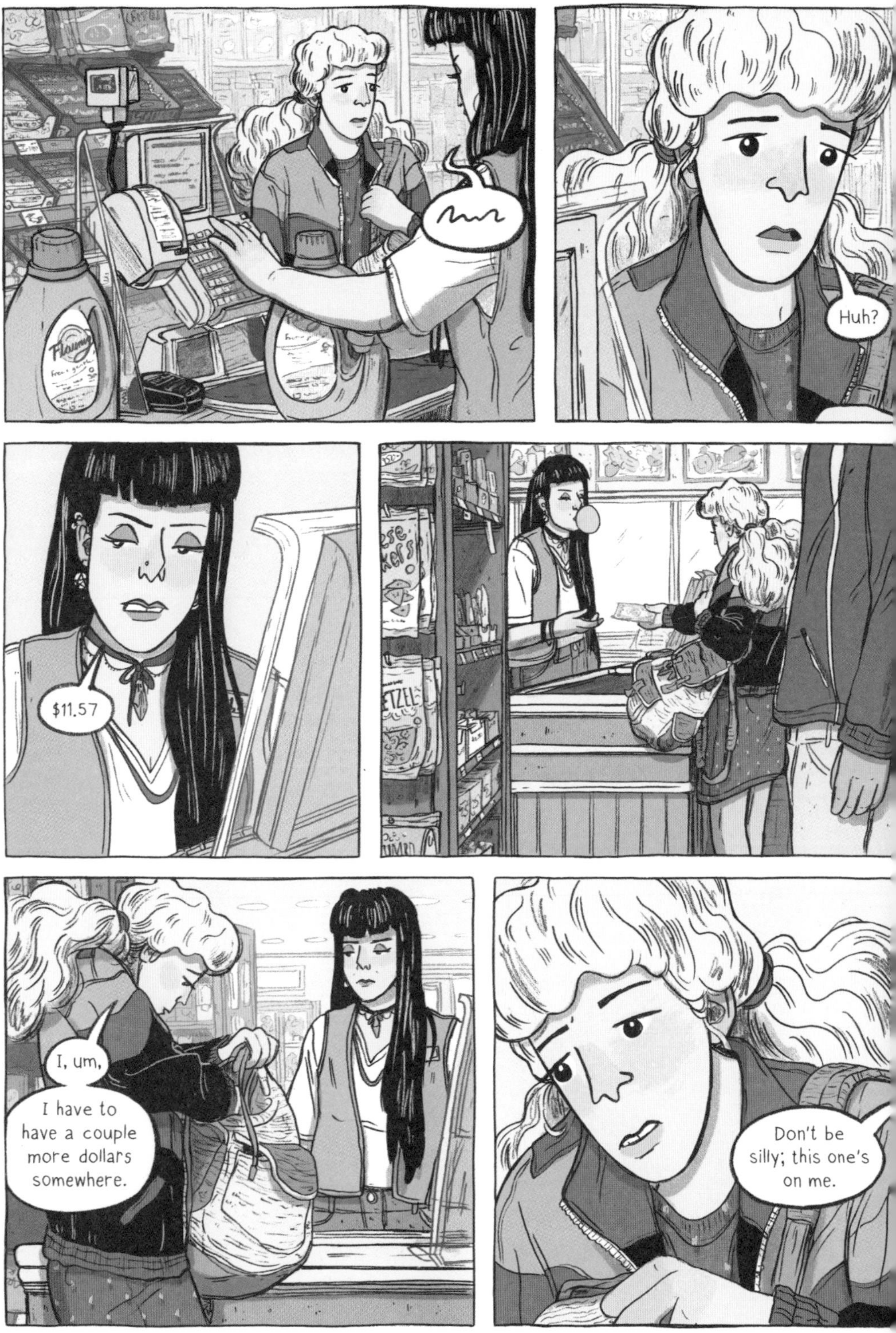
Huh?
$11.57
I, um,
I have to have a couple more dollars somewhere.
Don't be silly; this one's on me.

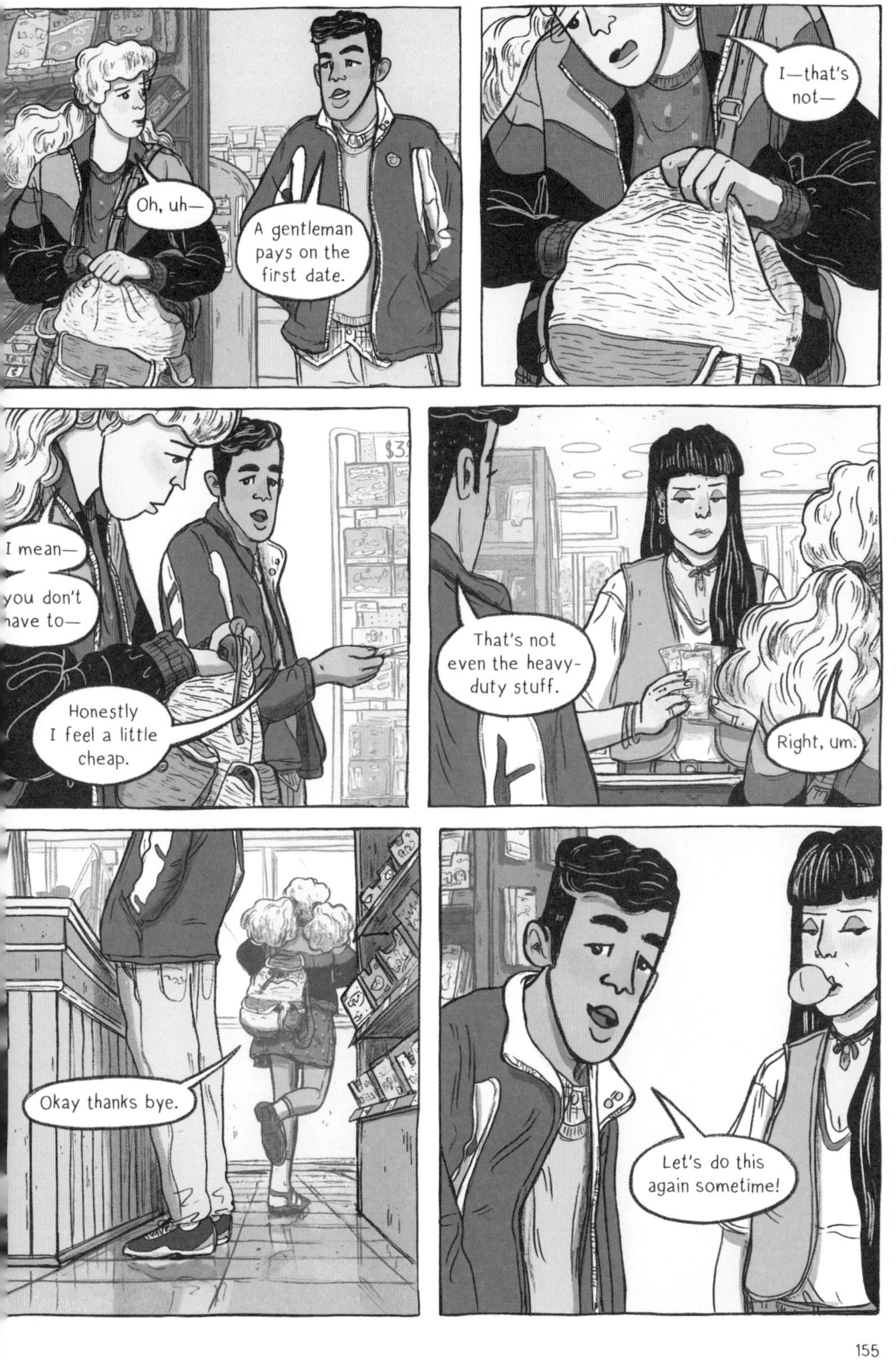

Oh, uh—
A gentleman pays on the first date.
I—that's not—
I mean—
you don't have to—
Honestly I feel a little cheap.
That's not even the heavy-duty stuff.
Right, um.
Okay thanks bye.
Let's do this again sometime!

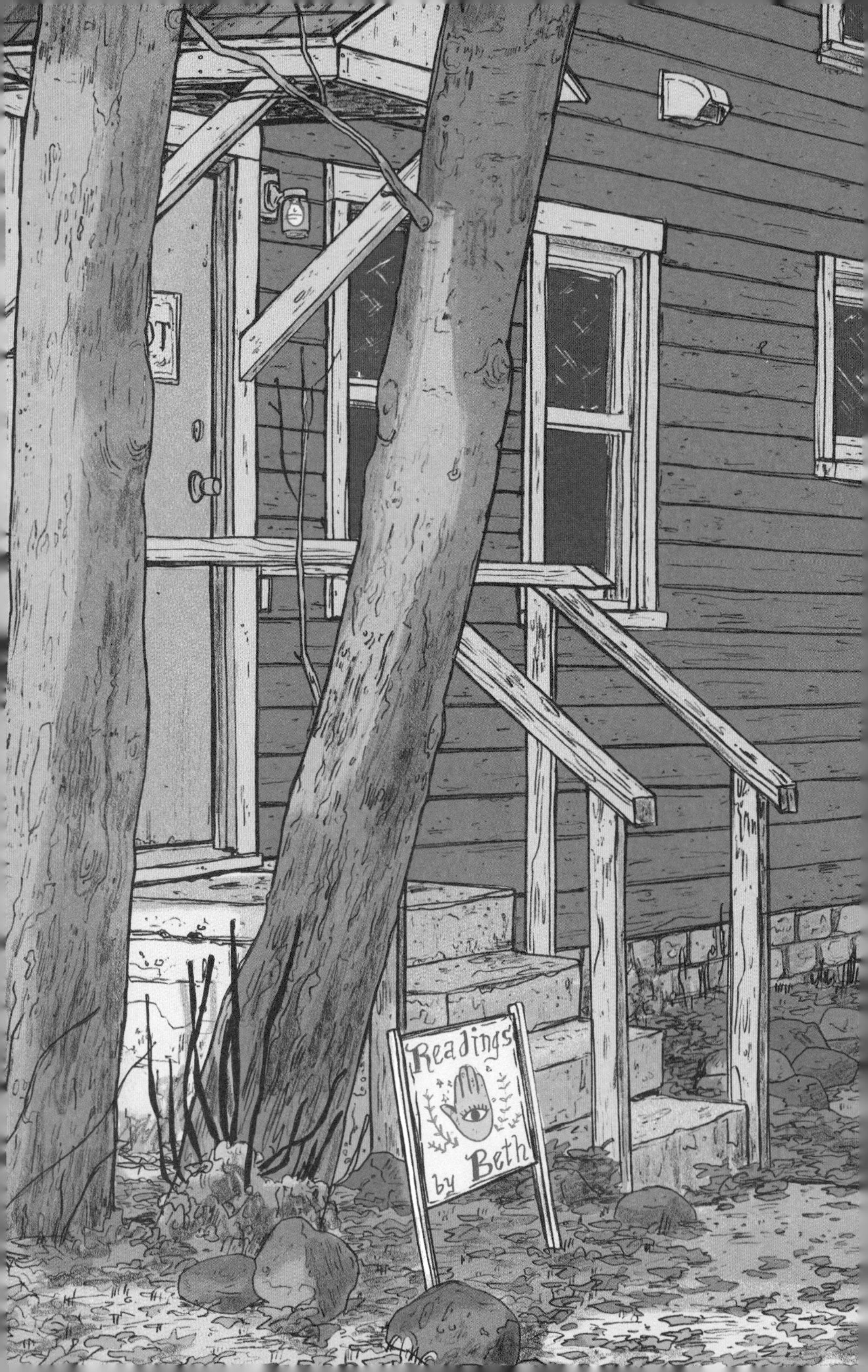
Readings by Beth

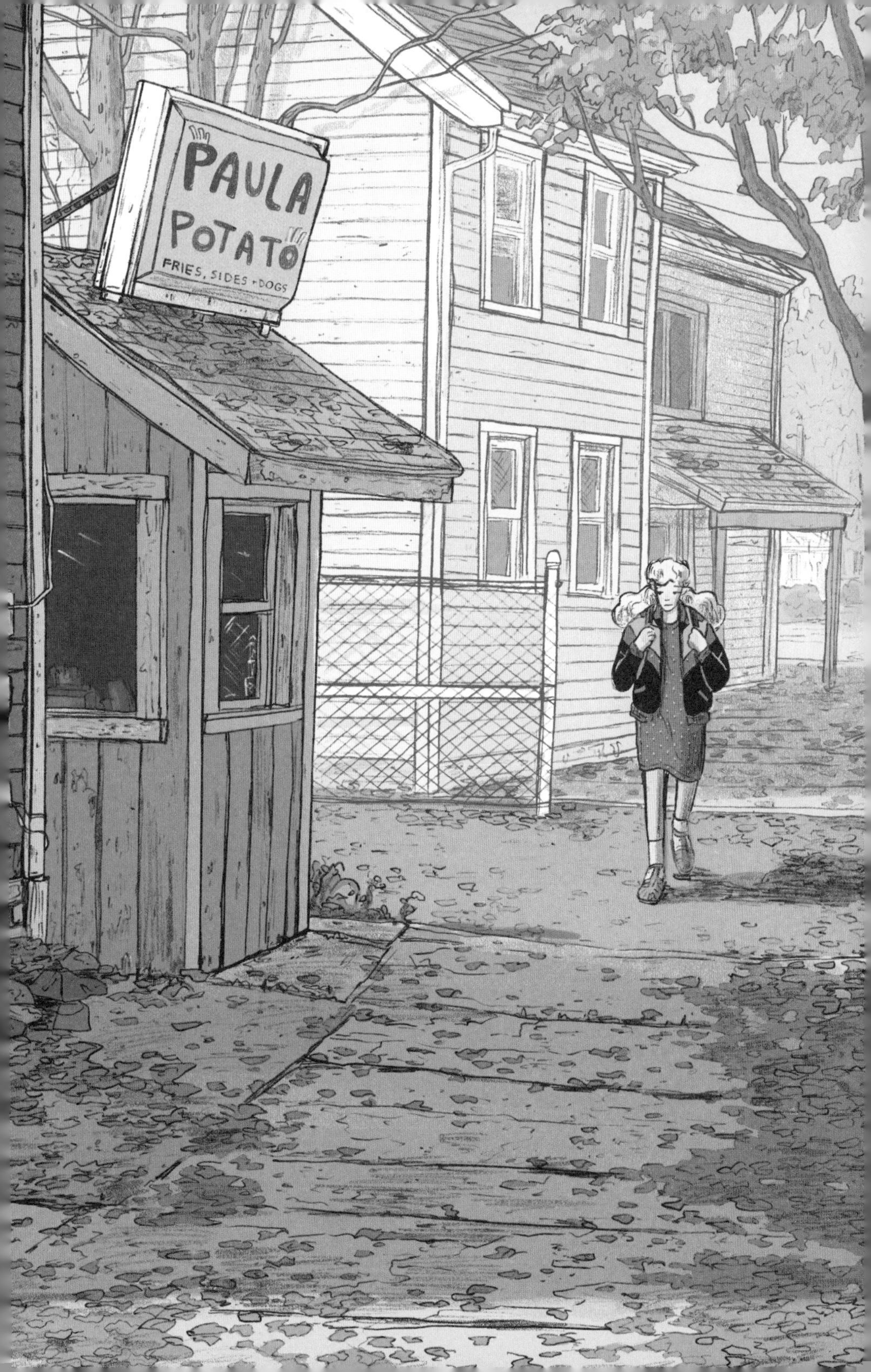
PAULA
POTATO
FRIES, SIDES + DOGS

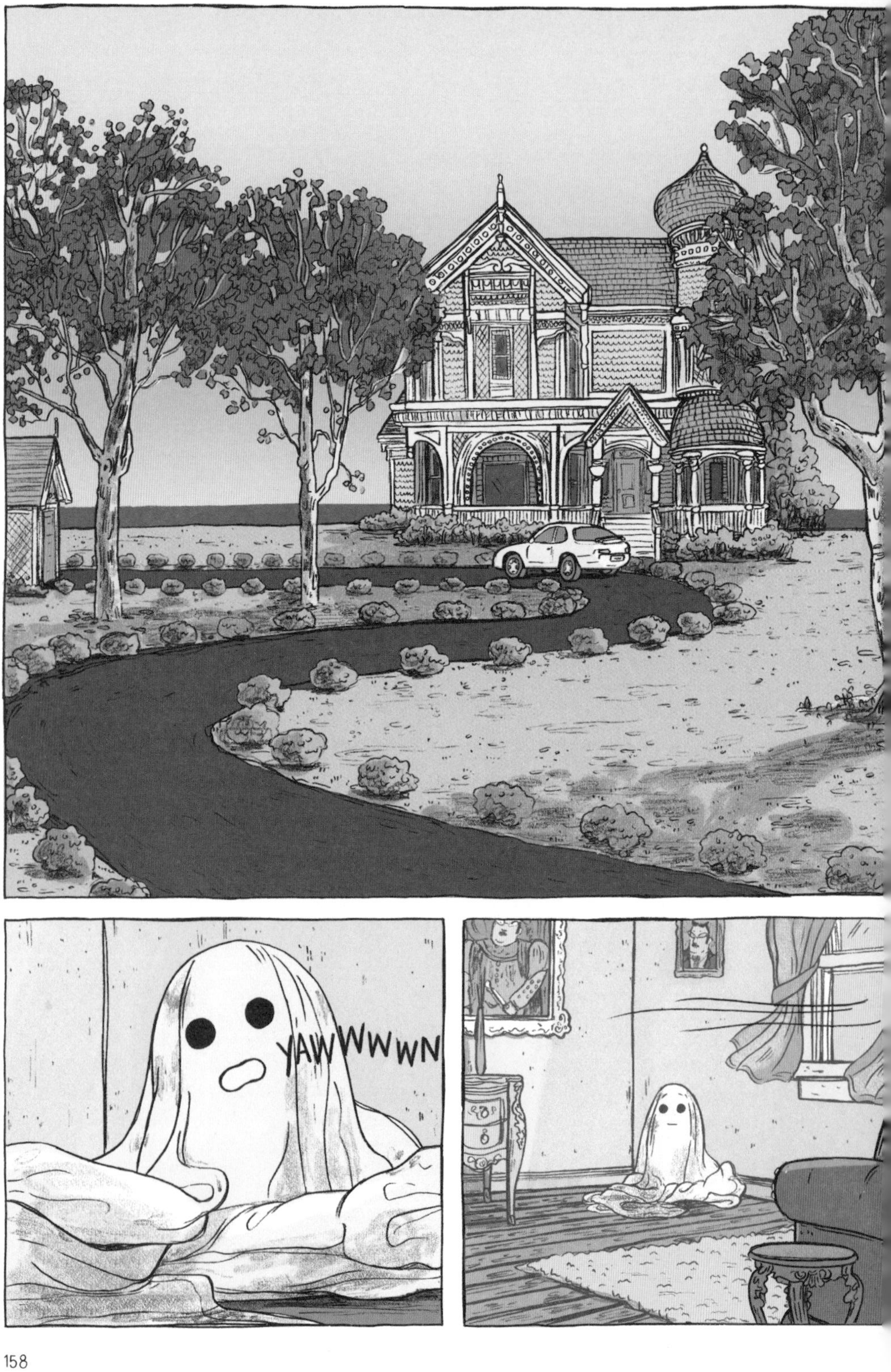
YAWWWWN

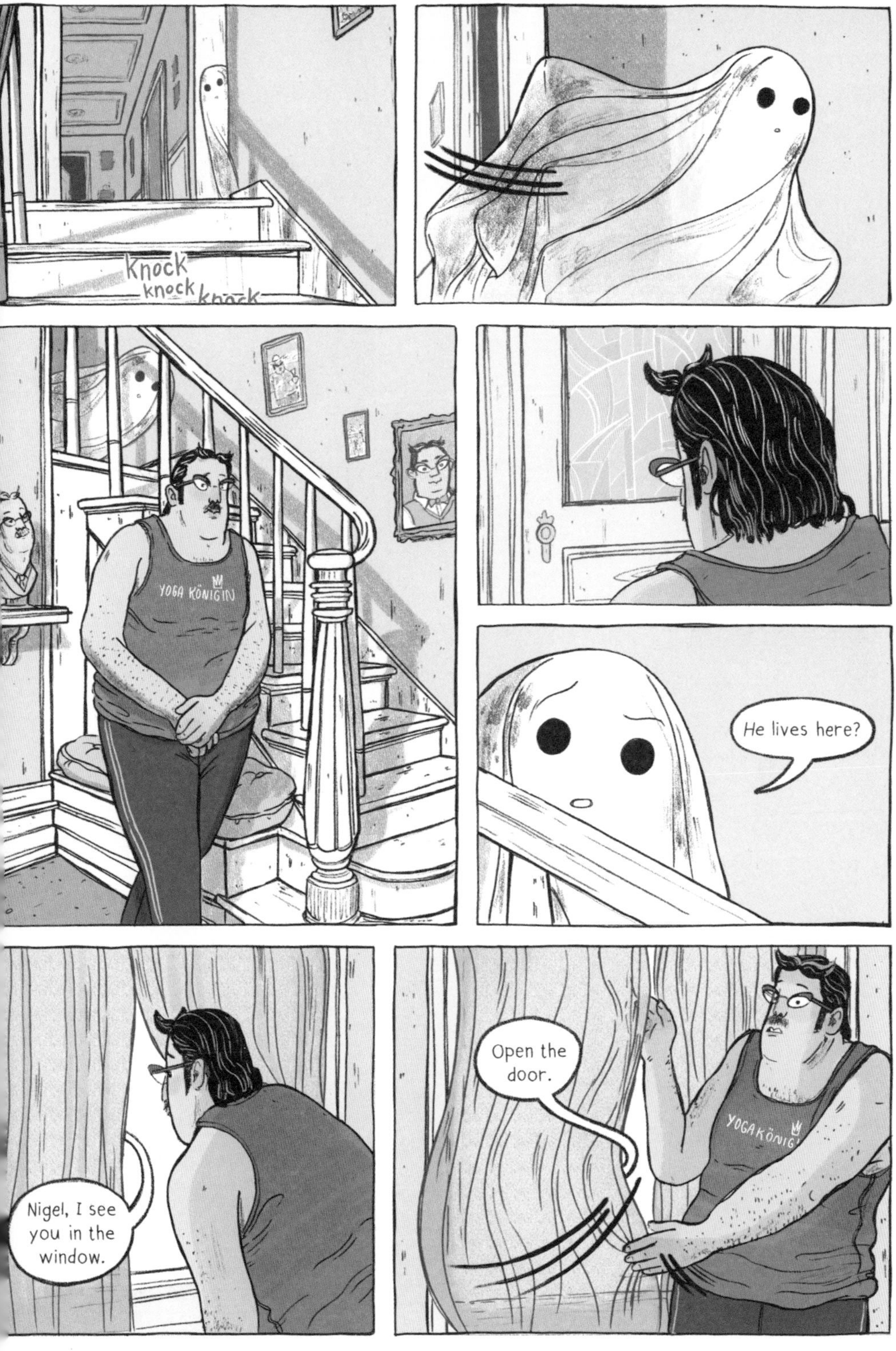
knock
knock
knock
He lives here?
Nigel, I see you in the window.
Open the door.

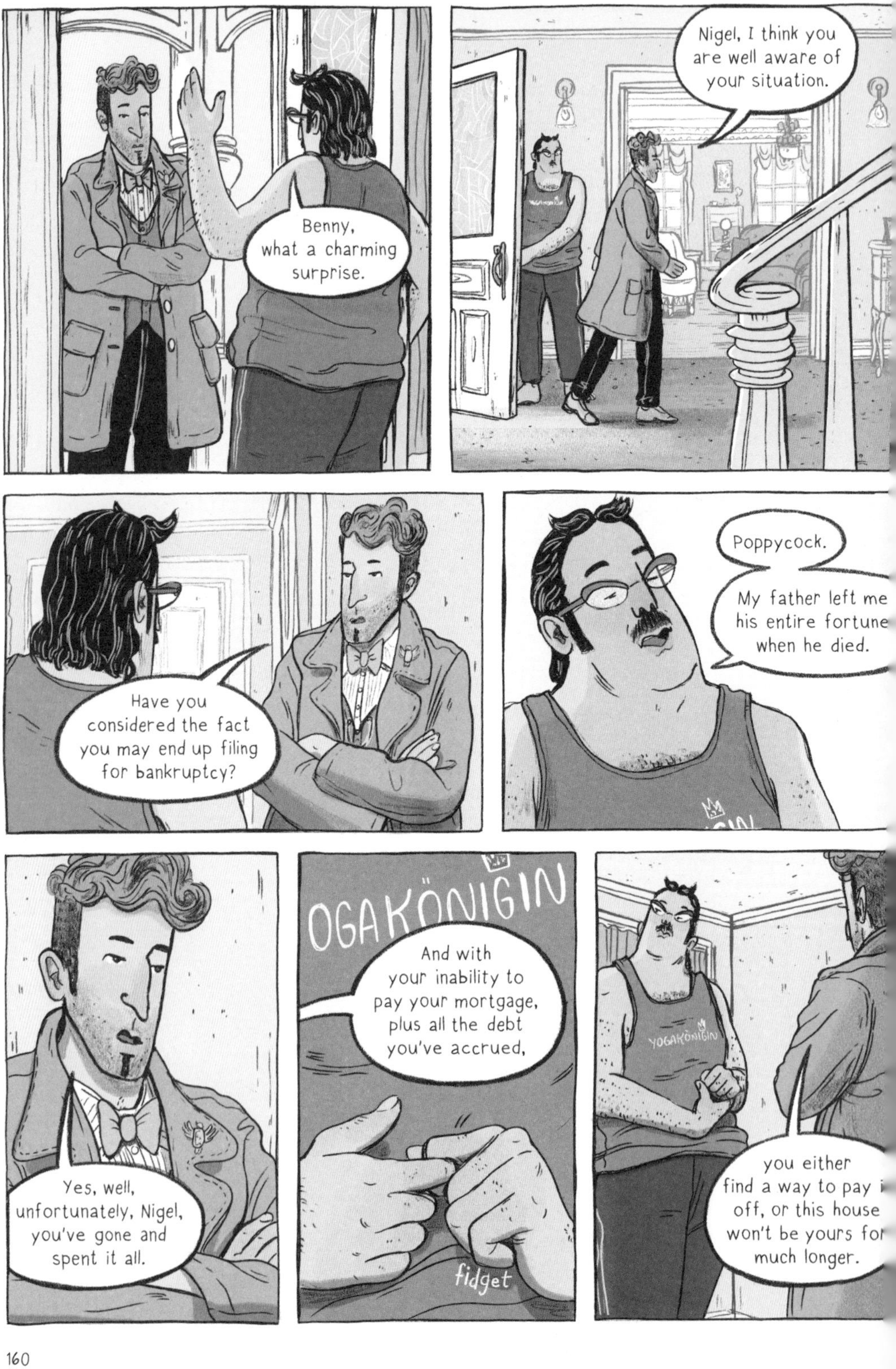
Benny, what a charming surprise.
Nigel, I think you are well aware of your situation.
Have you considered the fact you may end up filing for bankruptcy?
Poppycock.
My father left me his entire fortune when he died.
Yes, well, unfortunately, Nigel, you've gone and spent it all.
OGAKÖNIGIN
And with your inability to pay your mortgage, plus all the debt you've accrued,
fidget
YOGAKÖNIGIN
you either find a way to pay i off, or this house won't be yours for much longer.

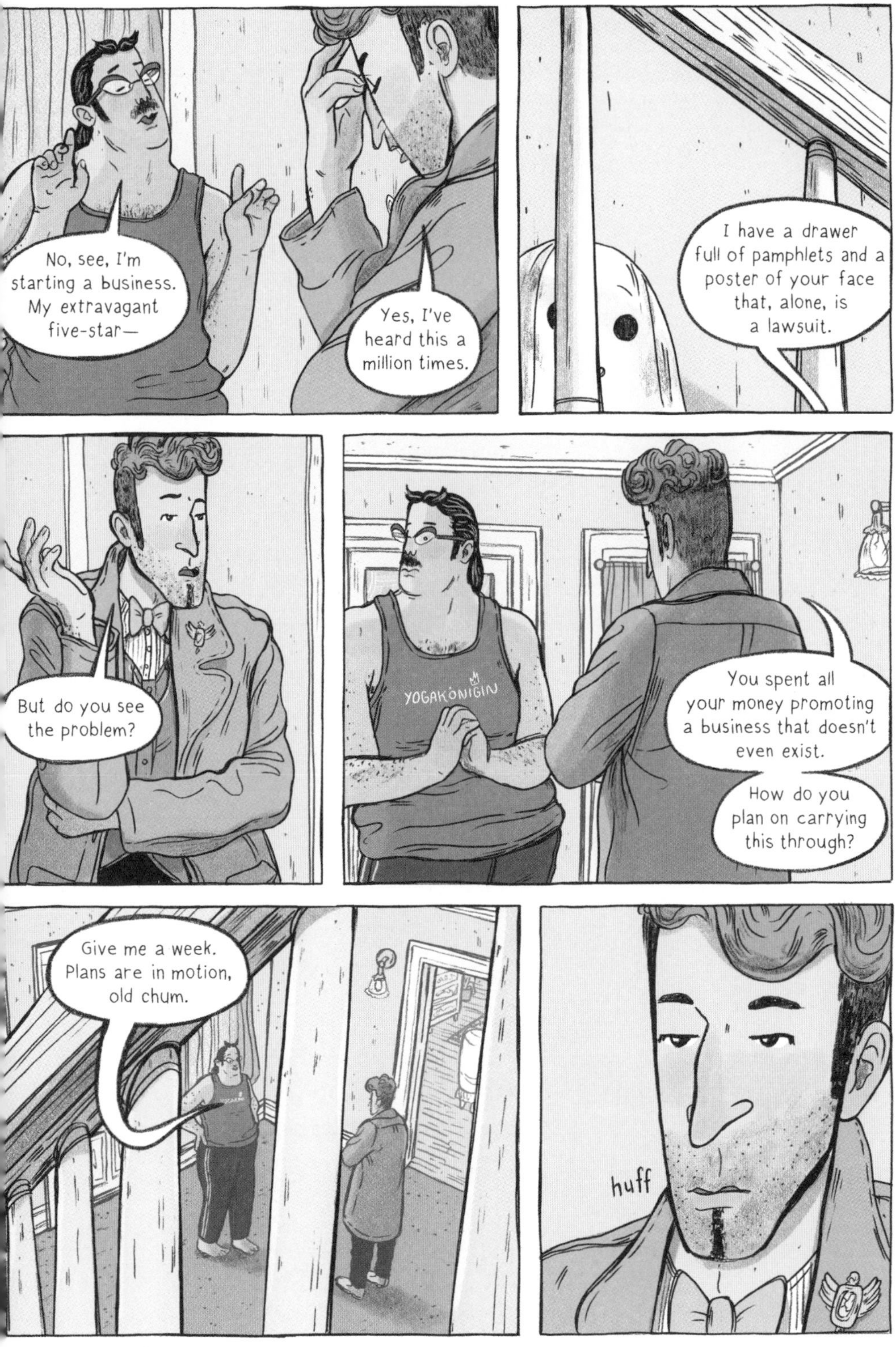
No, see, I'm starting a business. My extravagant five-star—
Yes, I've heard this a million times.
I have a drawer full of pamphlets and a poster of your face that, alone, is a lawsuit.
But do you see the problem?
YOGAKÖNIGIN
You spent all your money promoting a business that doesn't even exist.
How do you plan on carrying this through?
Give me a week. Plans are in motion, old chum.
huff

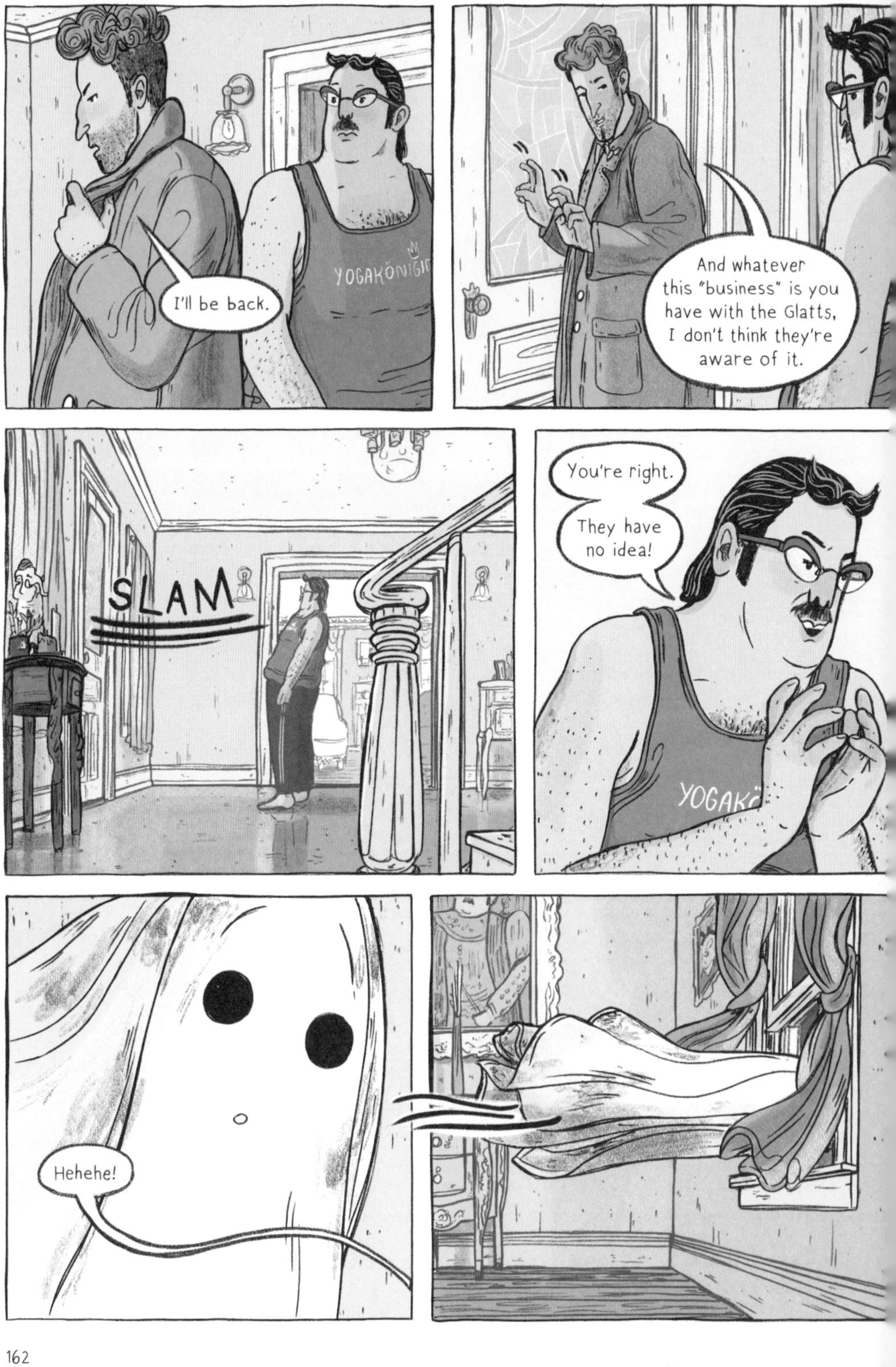
I'll be back.
YOGAKÖNIGIN
And whatever this "business" is you have with the Glatts, I don't think they're aware of it.
SLAM
You're right.
They have no idea!
YOGAKÖ
Hehehe!

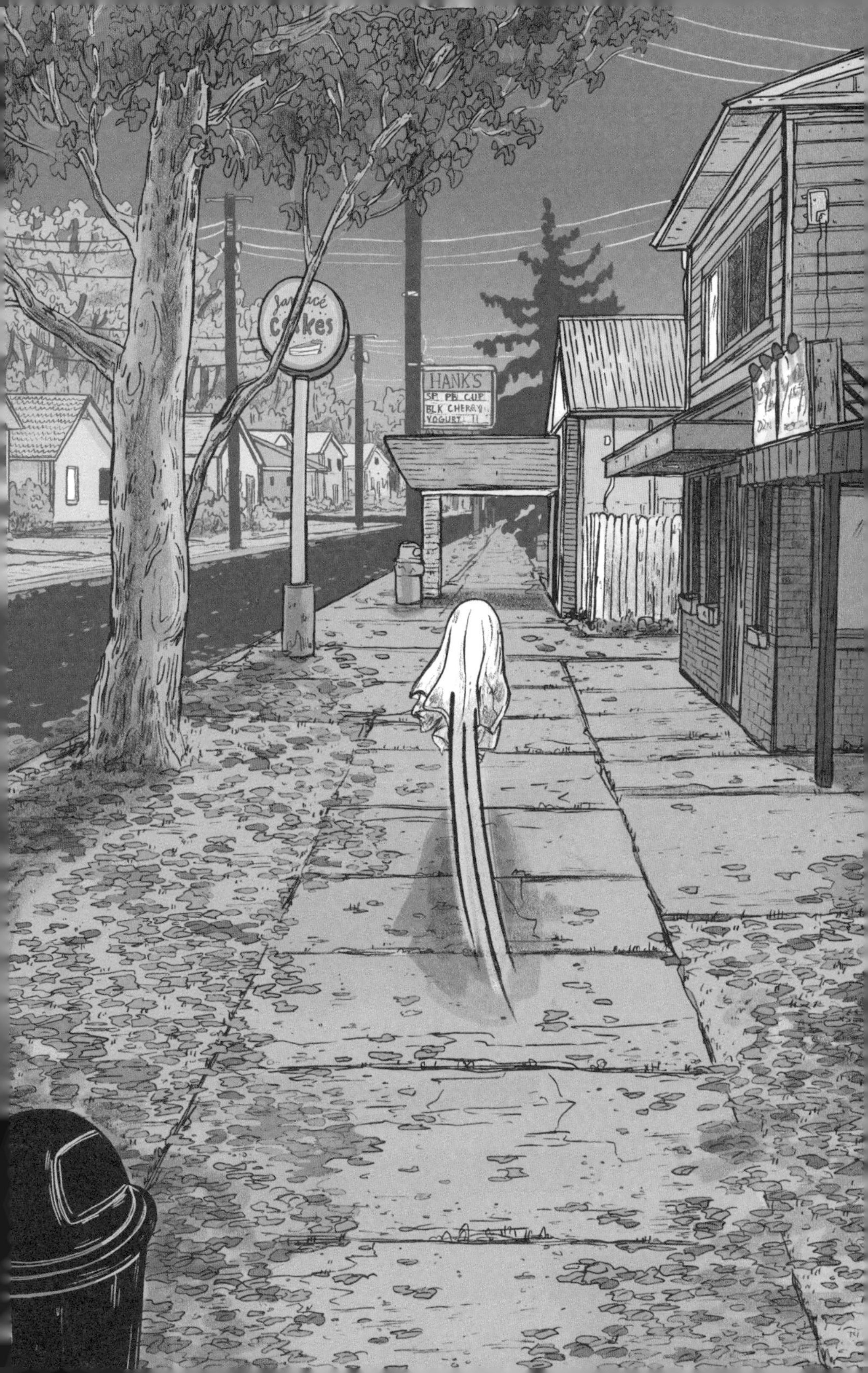
HANK'S
SP. PB CUP
BLK CHERRY
YOGURT

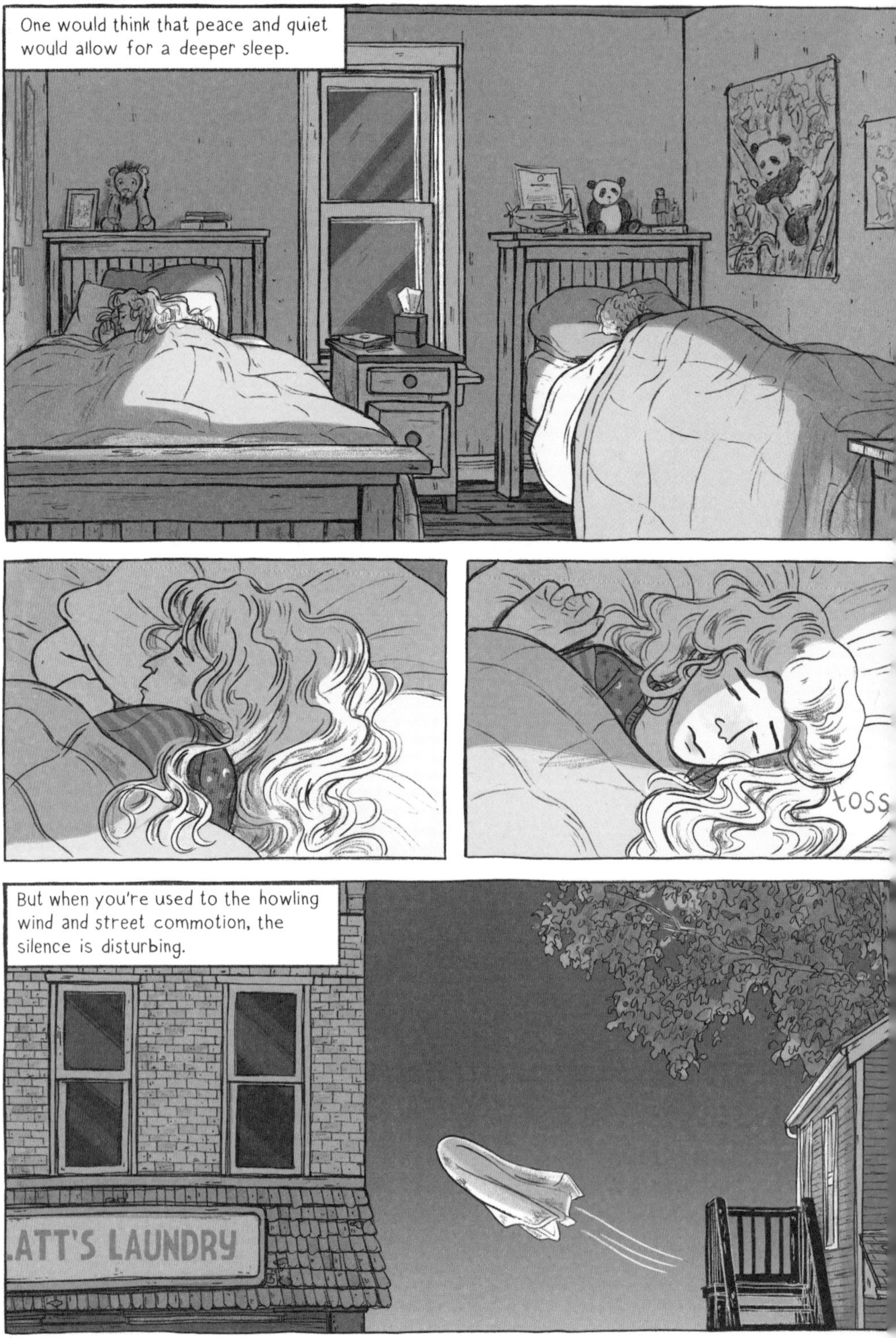
One would think that peace and quiet would allow for a deeper sleep.
toss
But when you're used to the howling wind and street commotion, the silence is disturbing.
ATT'S LAUNDRY

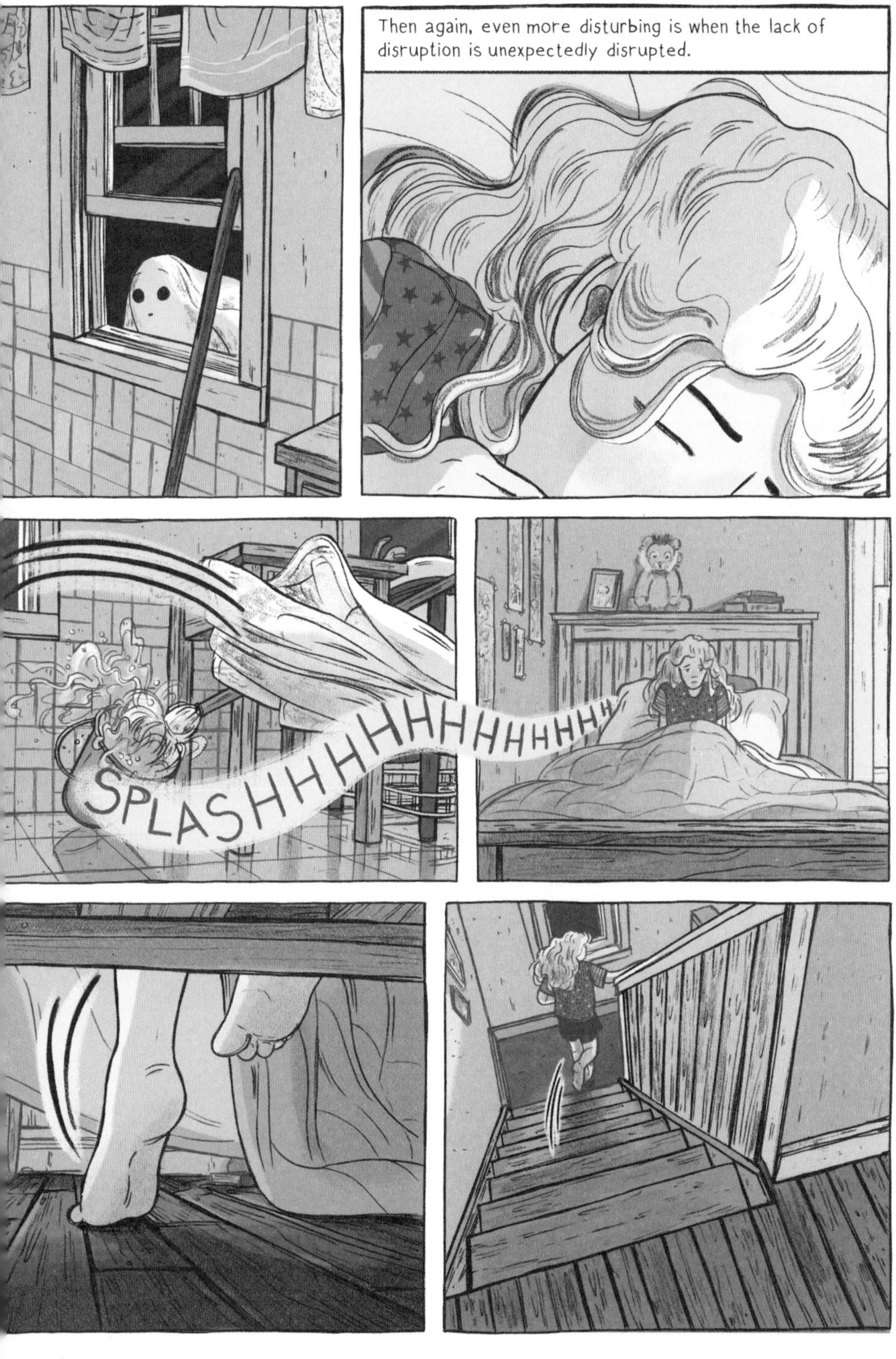
Then again, even more disturbing is when the lack of disruption is unexpectedly disrupted.
SPLASHHHHHHHHHHHHHH

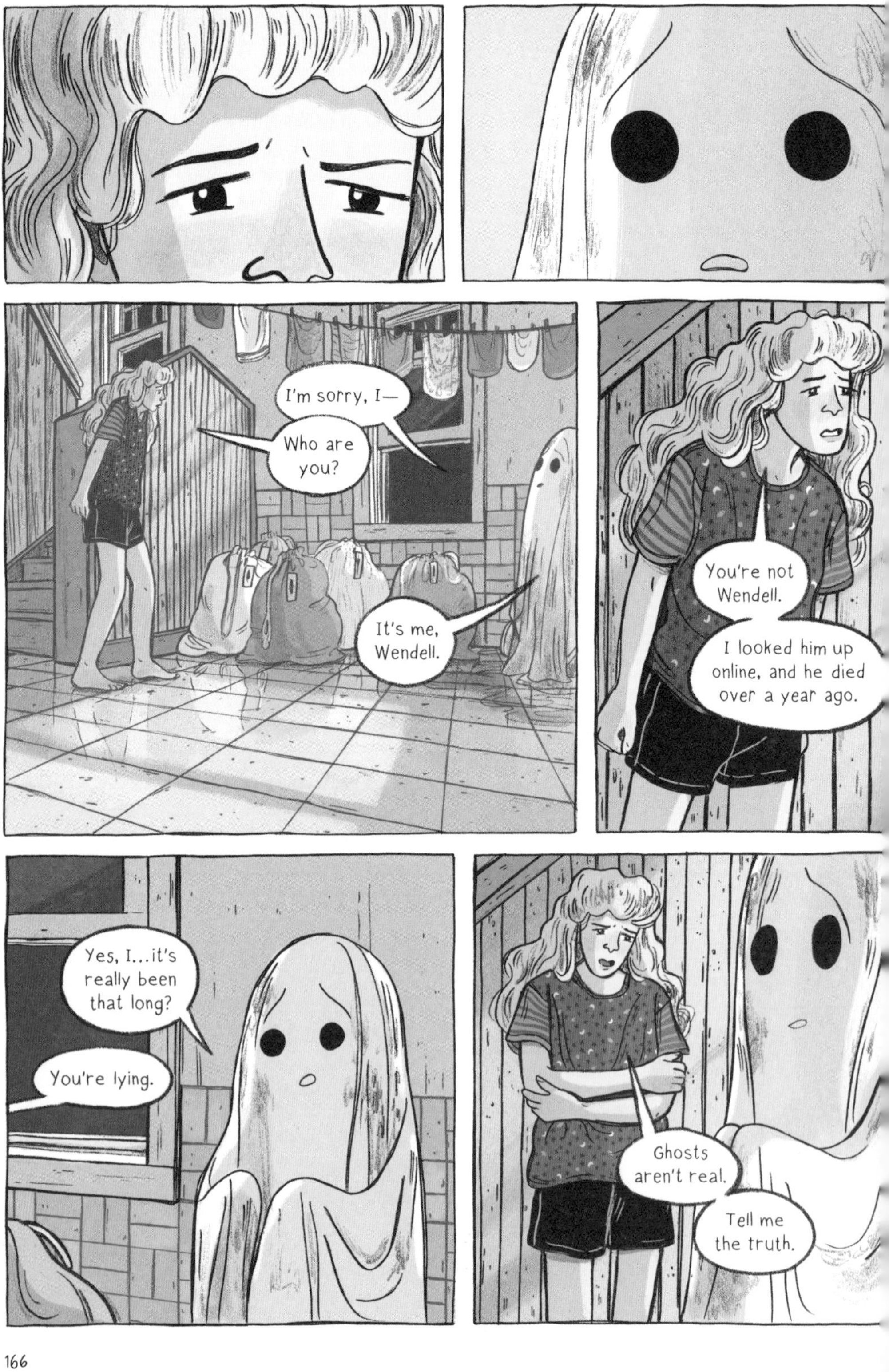
I'm sorry, I—
Who are you?
It's me, Wendell.
You're not Wendell.
I looked him up online, and he died over a year ago.
Yes, I...it's really been that long?
You're lying.
Ghosts aren't real.
Tell me the truth.

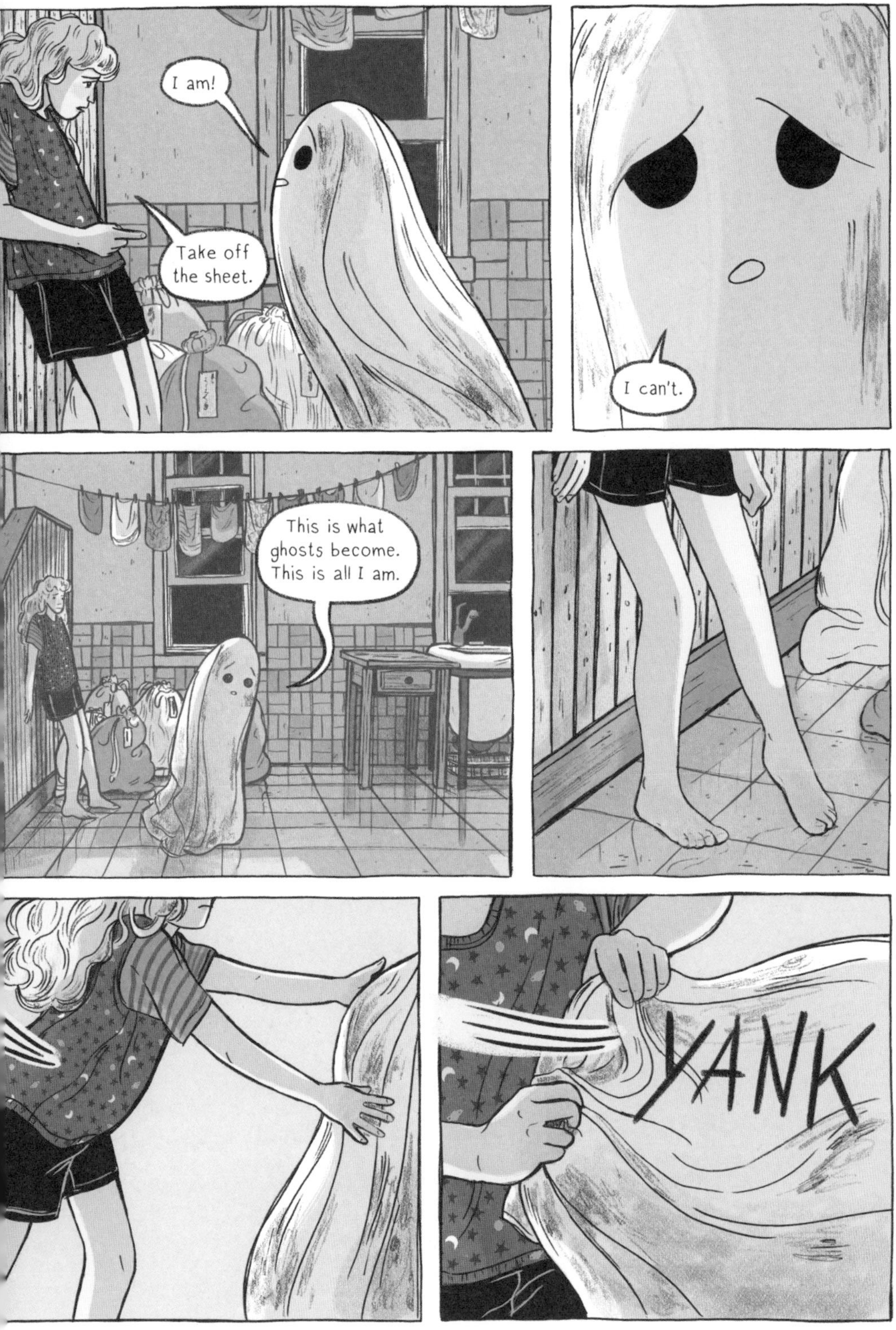
I am!
Take off the sheet.
I can't.
This is what ghosts become. This is all I am.
YANK

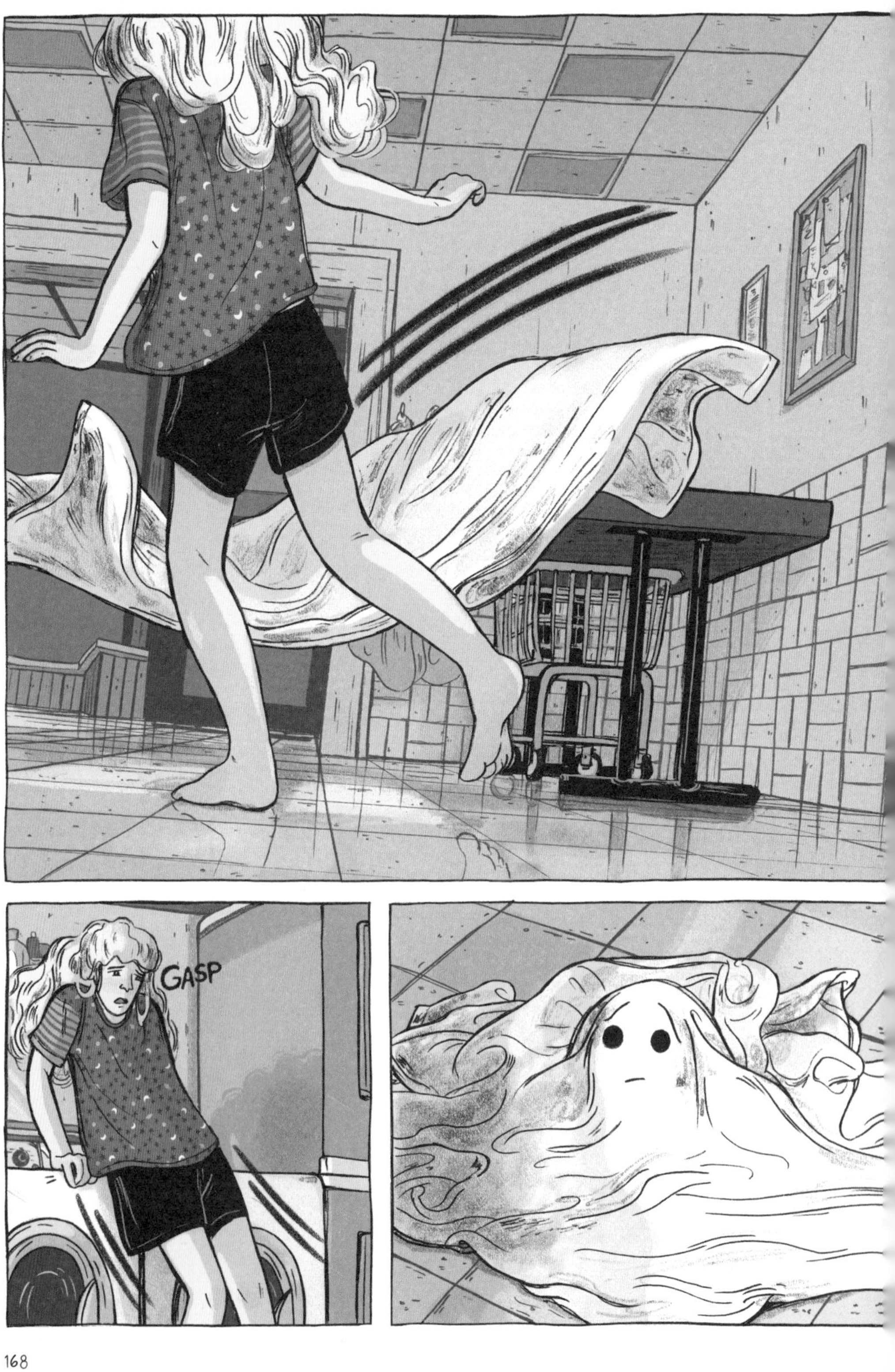
GASP

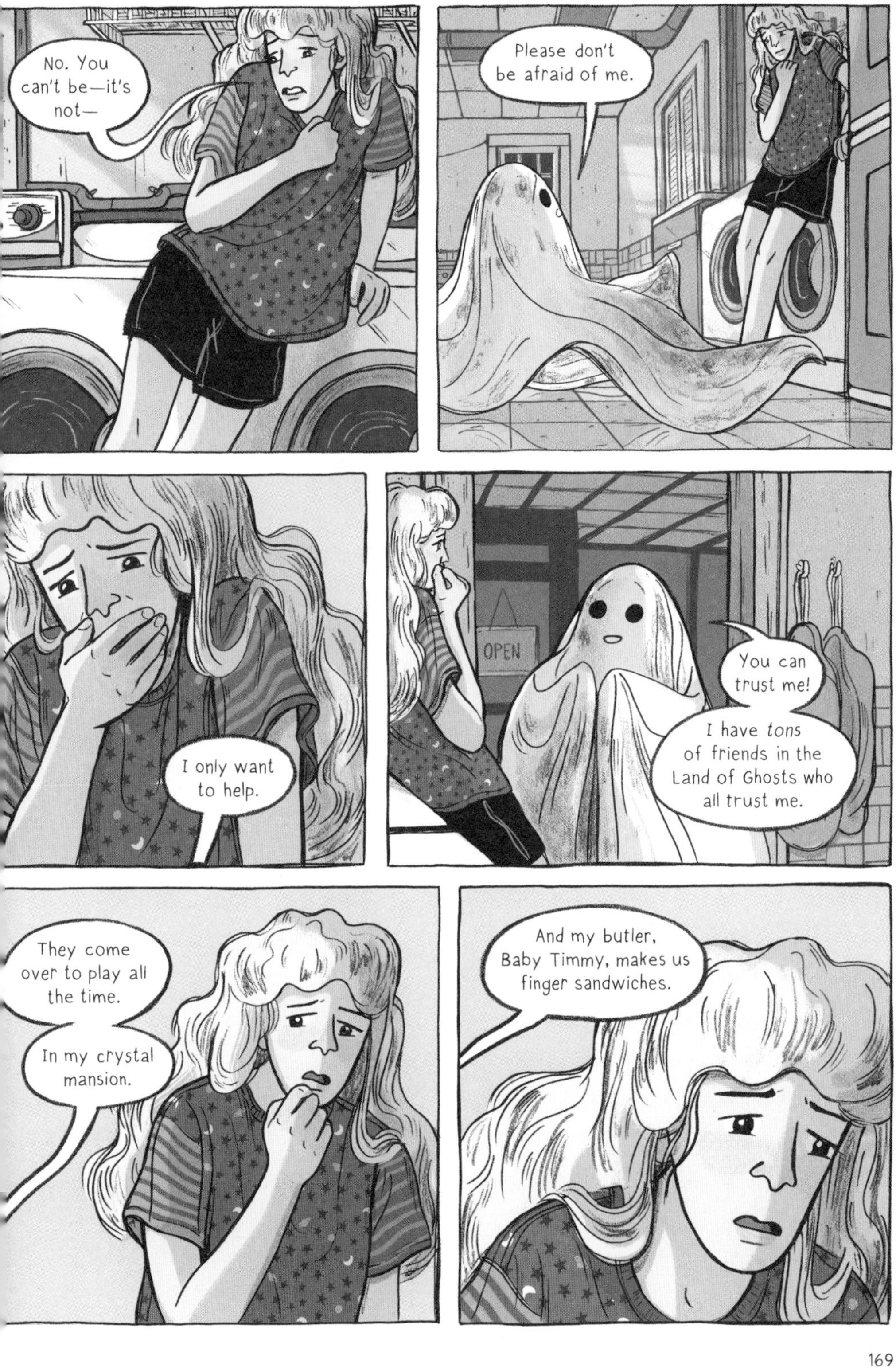
No. You can't be—it's not—
Please don't be afraid of me.
I only want to help.
OPEN
You can trust me!
I have *tons* of friends in the Land of Ghosts who all trust me.
They come over to play all the time.
In my crystal mansion.
And my butler, Baby Timmy, makes us finger sandwiches.

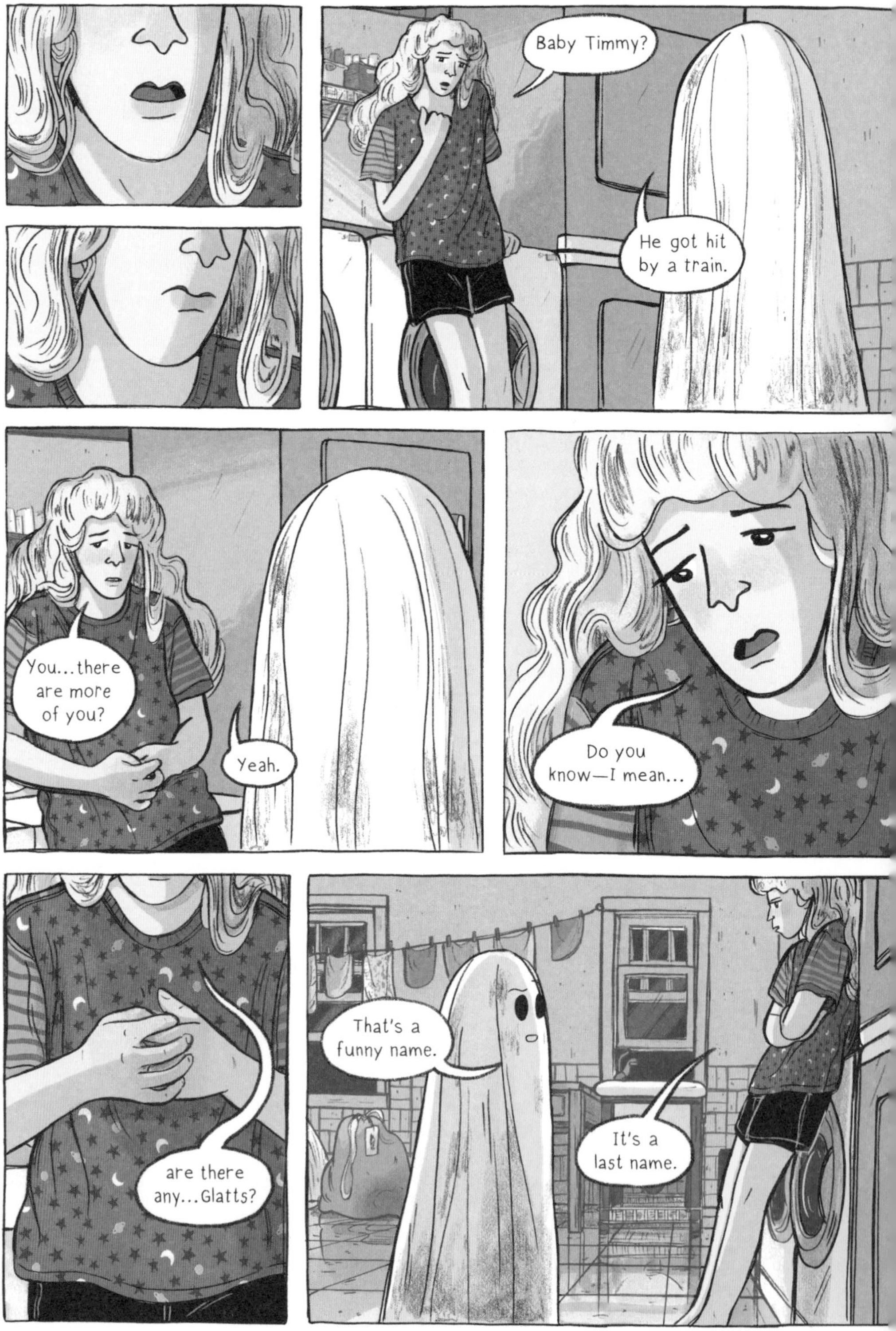
Baby Timmy?
He got hit by a train.
You...there are more of you?
Yeah.
Do you know—I mean...
are there any...Glatts?
That's a funny name.
It's a last name.

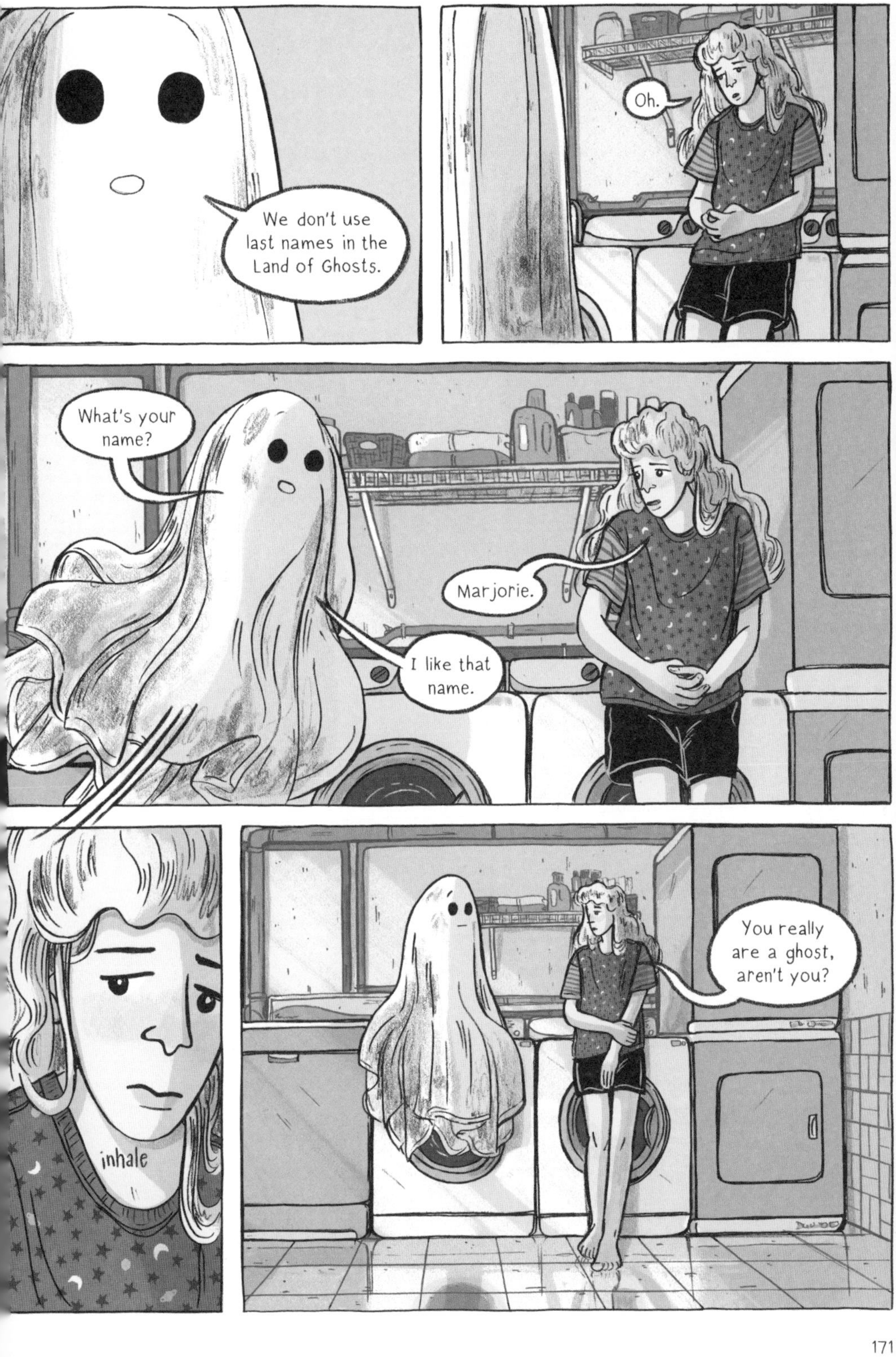
We don't use last names in the Land of Ghosts.
Oh.
What's your name?
Marjorie.
I like that name.
inhale
You really are a ghost, aren't you?

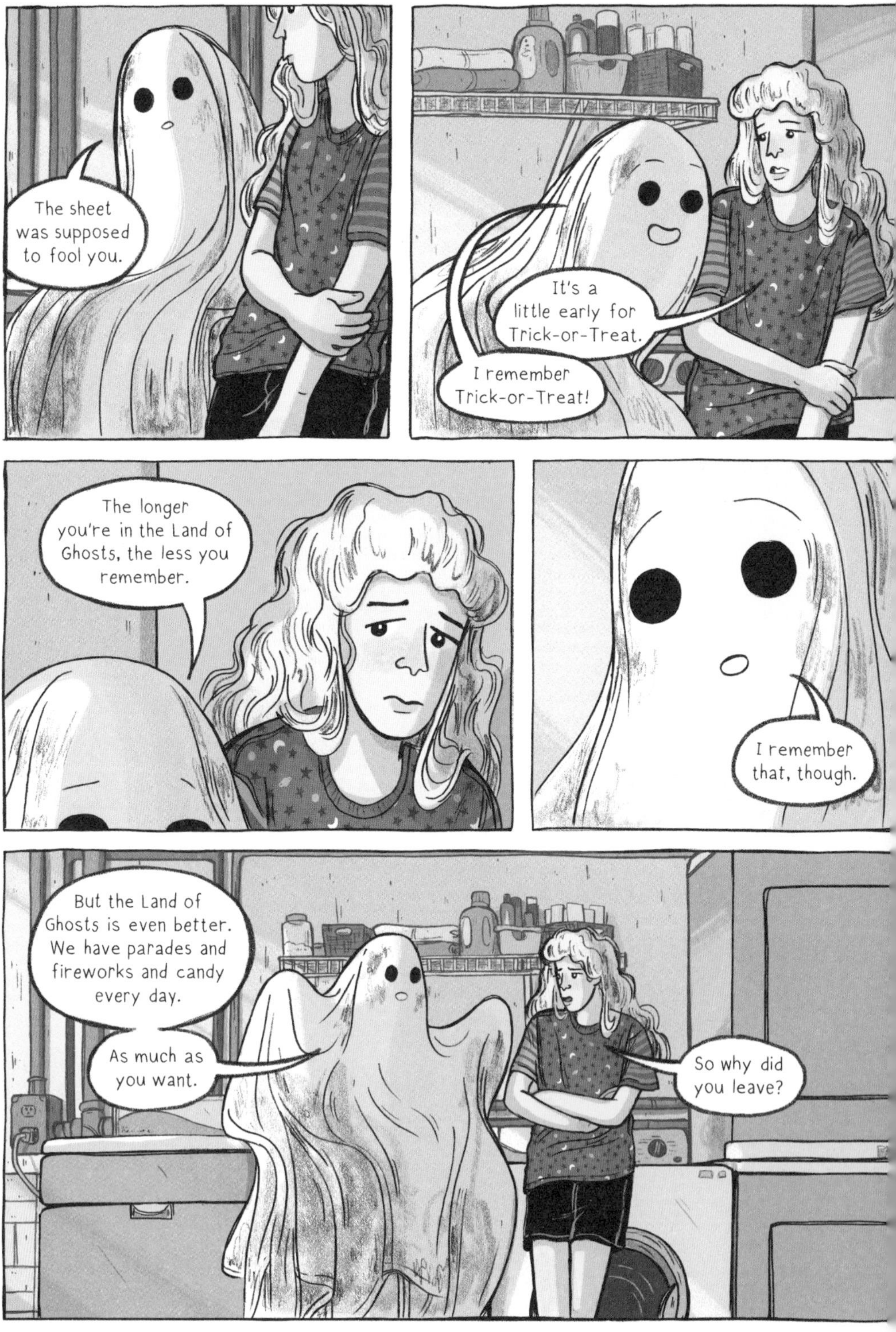

The sheet was supposed to fool you.
It's a little early for Trick-or-Treat.
I remember Trick-or-Treat!
The longer you're in the Land of Ghosts, the less you remember.
I remember that, though.
But the Land of Ghosts is even better. We have parades and fireworks and candy every day.
As much as you want.
So why did you leave?

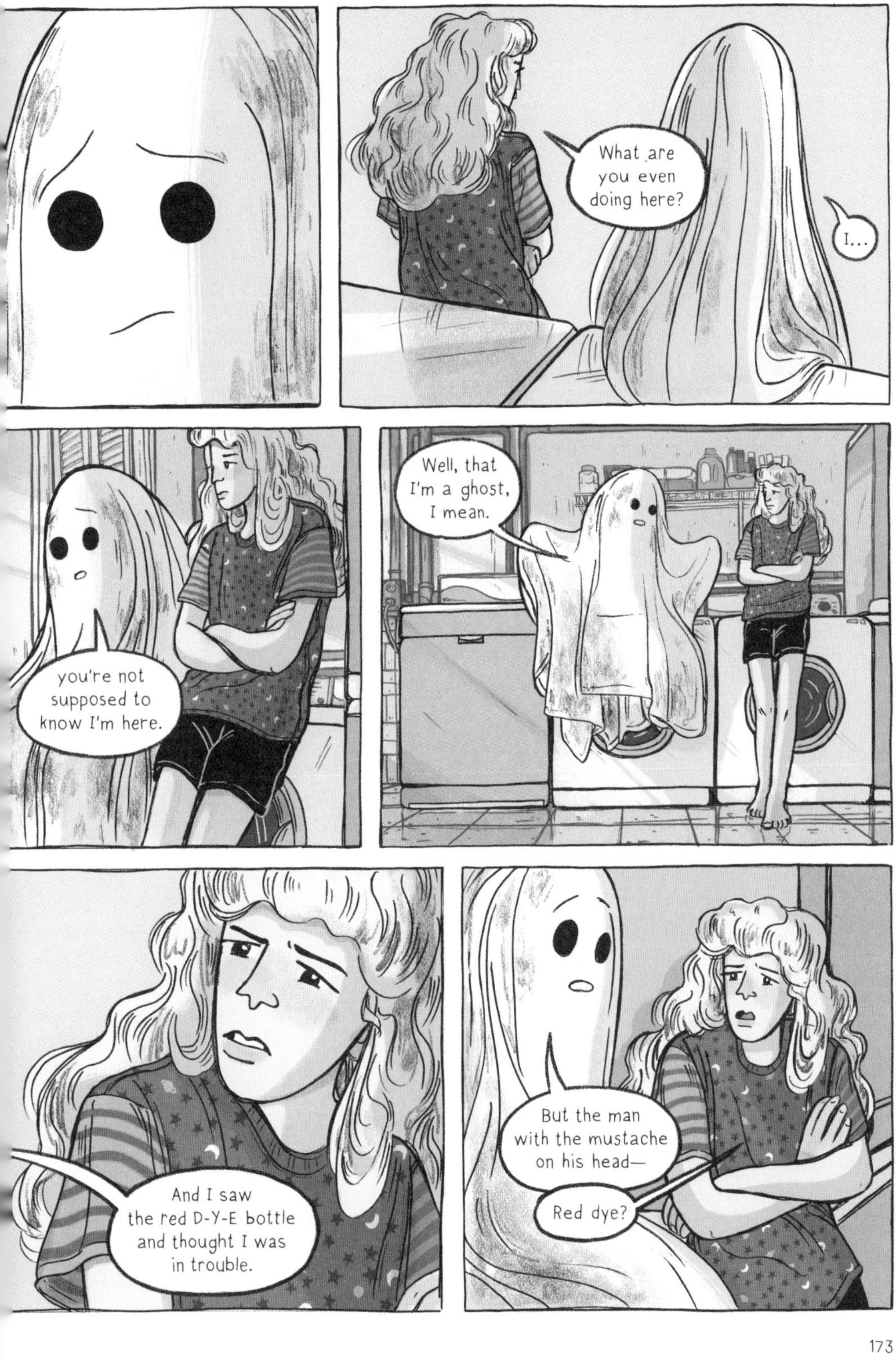
What are you even doing here?
I...
you're not supposed to know I'm here.
Well, that I'm a ghost, I mean.
And I saw the red D-Y-E bottle and thought I was in trouble.
But the man with the mustache on his head—
Red dye?

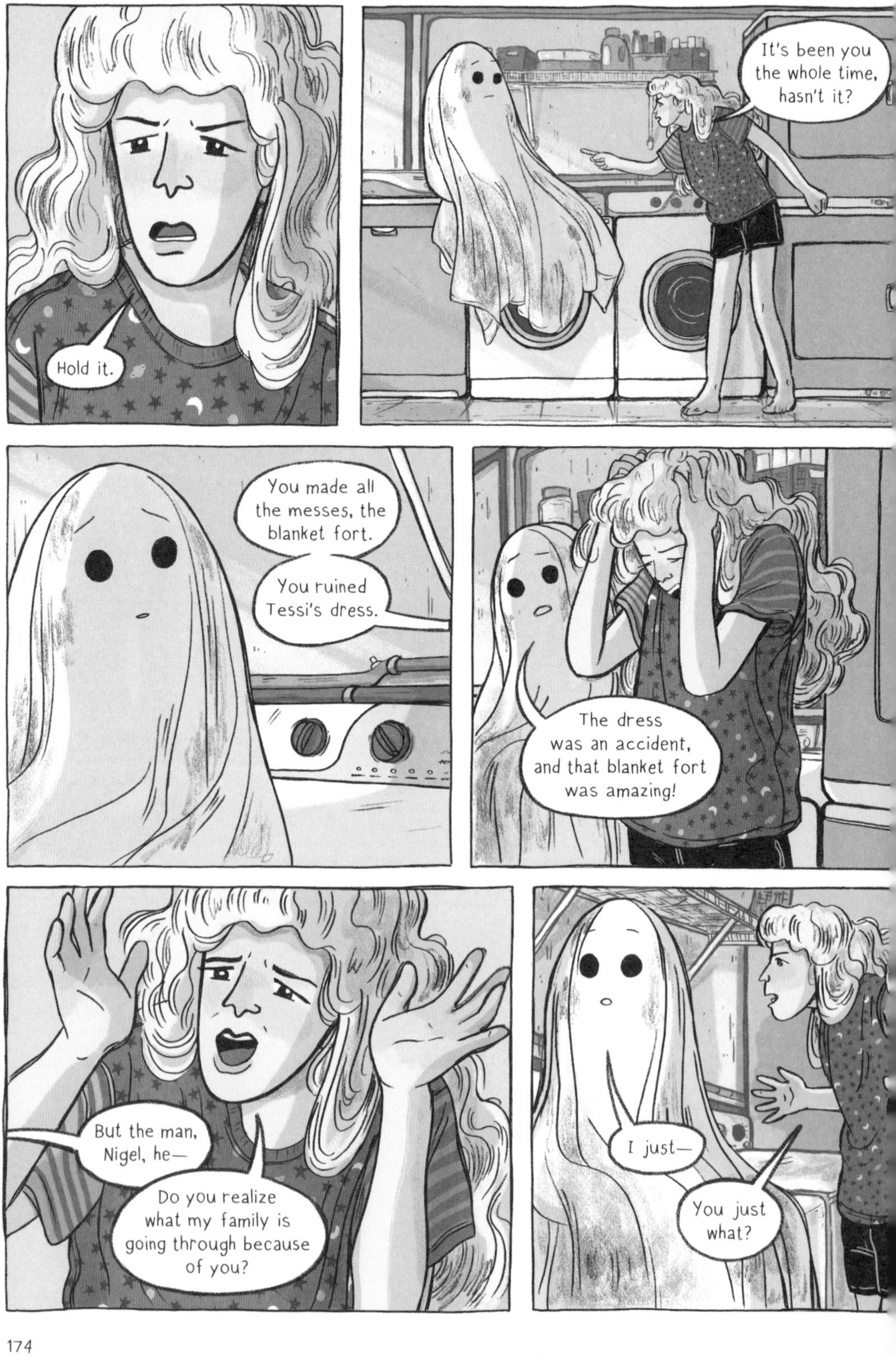
Hold it.
It's been you the whole time, hasn't it?
You made all the messes, the blanket fort.
You ruined Tessi's dress.
The dress was an accident, and that blanket fort was amazing!
But the man, Nigel, he—
Do you realize what my family is going through because of you?
I just—
You just what?

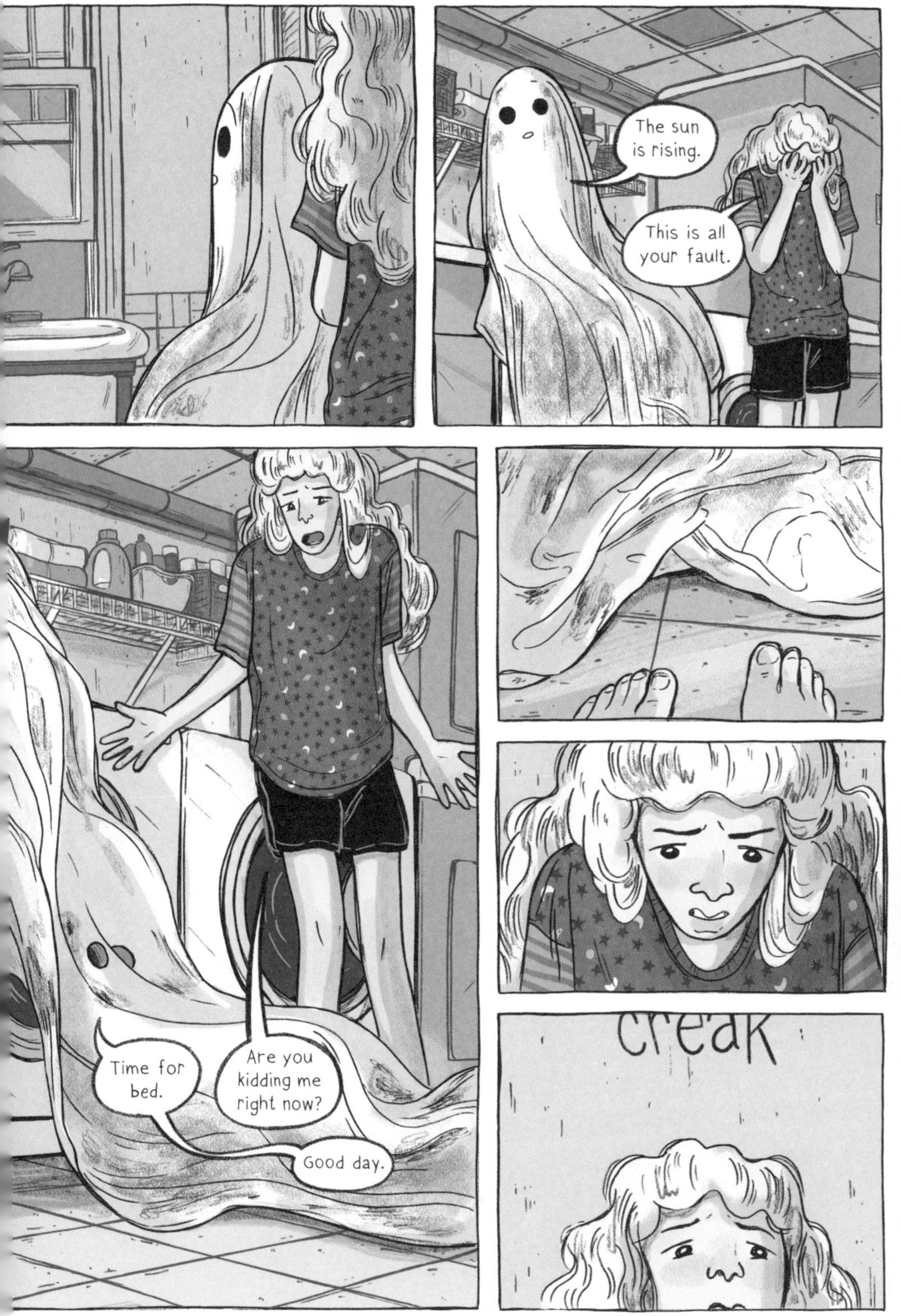
The sun is rising.
This is all your fault.
Time for bed.
Are you kidding me right now?
Good day.
creak

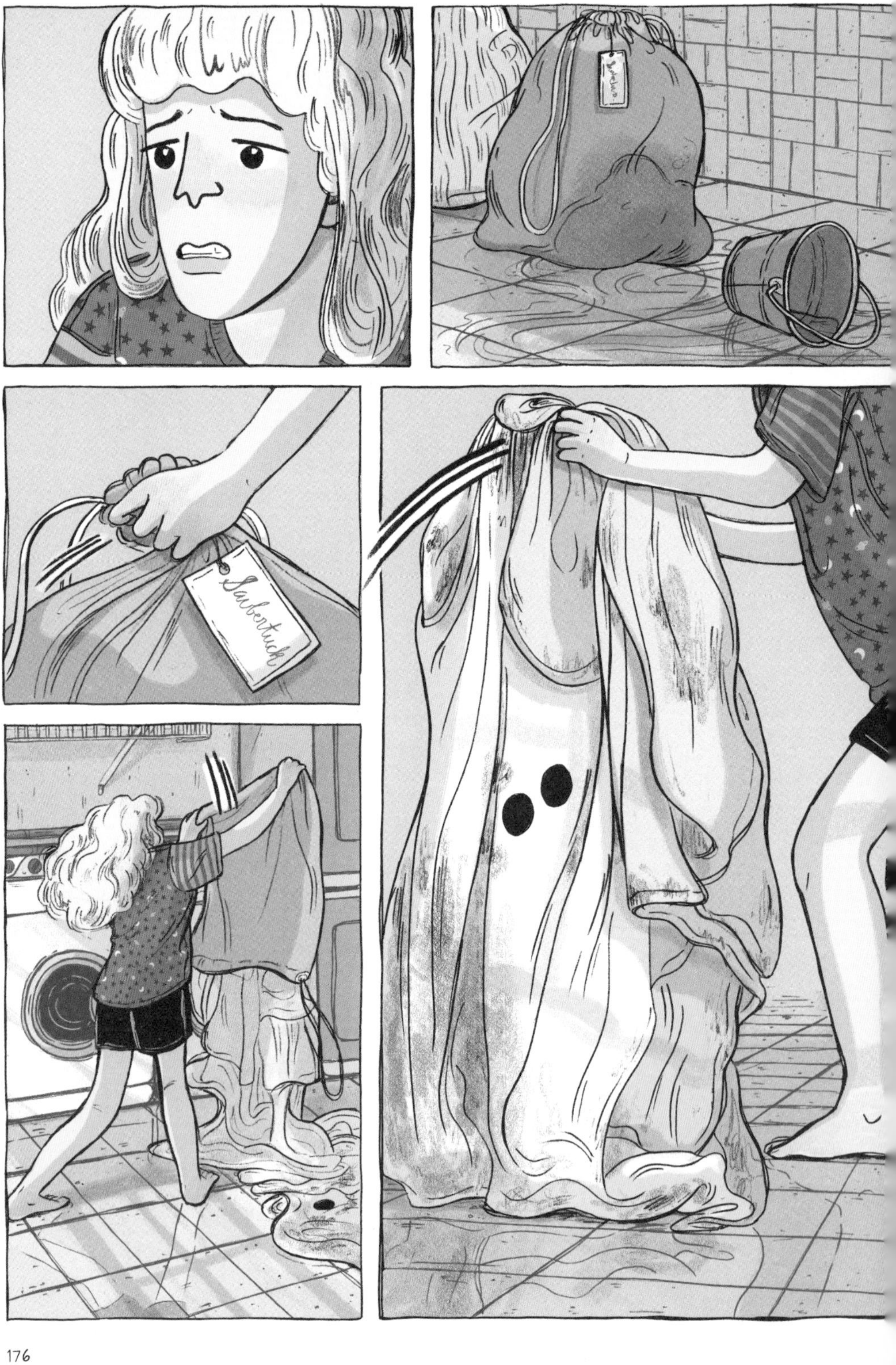
Saubertuch

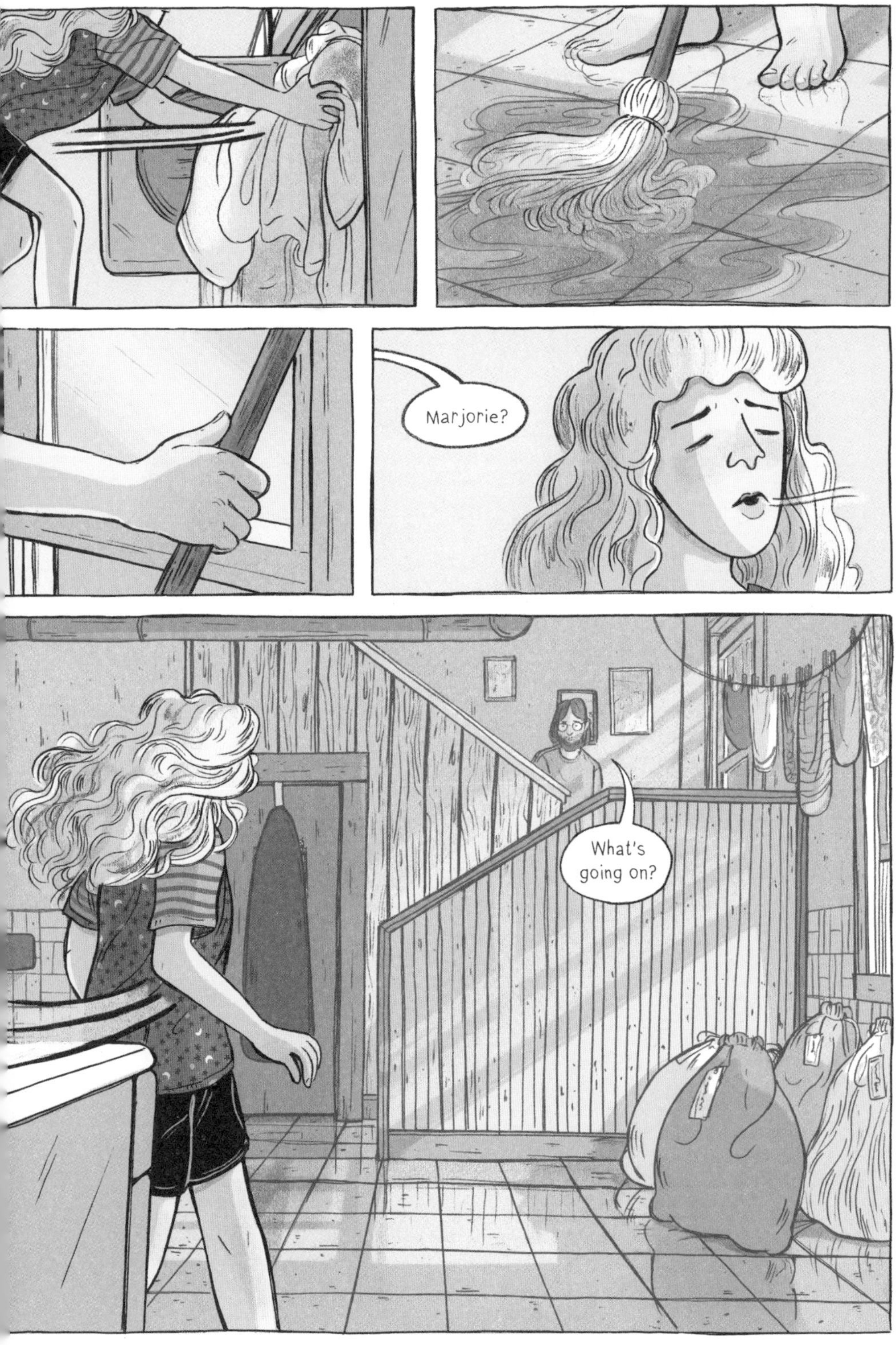
Marjorie?
What's going on?

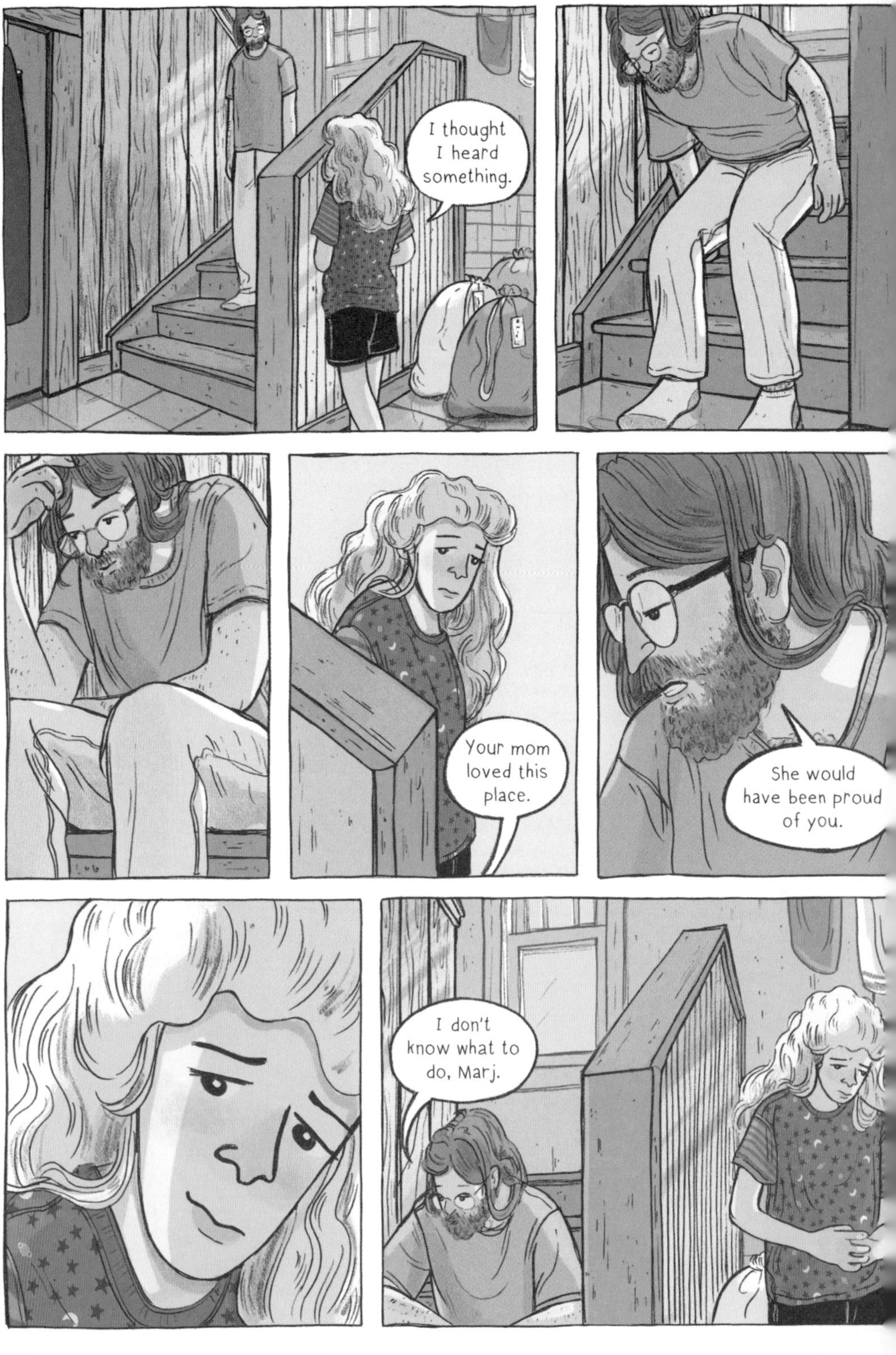
I thought I heard something.
Your mom loved this place.
She would have been proud of you.
I don't know what to do, Marj.

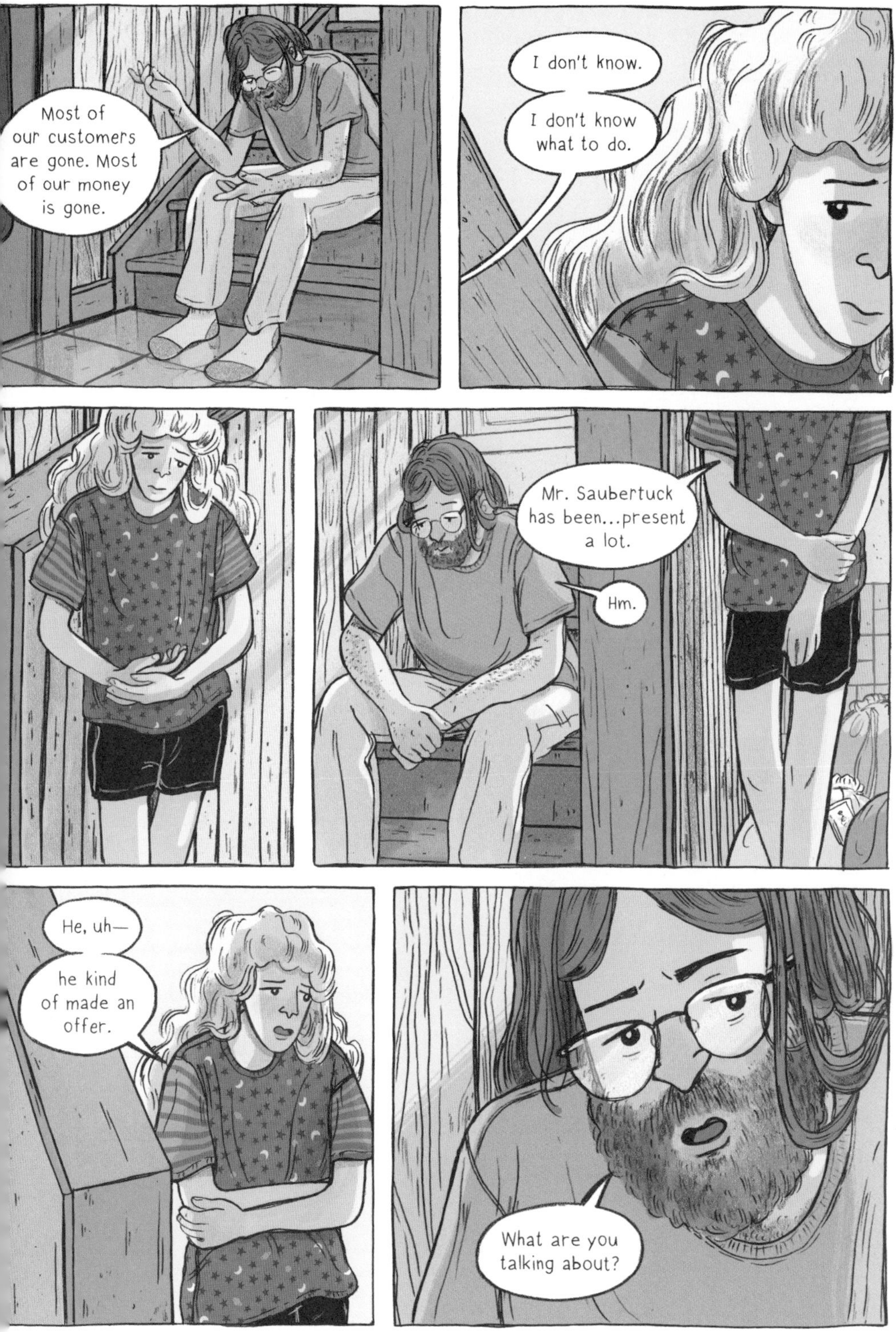
Most of our customers are gone. Most of our money is gone.
I don't know.
I don't know what to do.
Mr. Saubertuck has been...present a lot.
Hm.
He, uh—
he kind of made an offer.
What are you talking about?

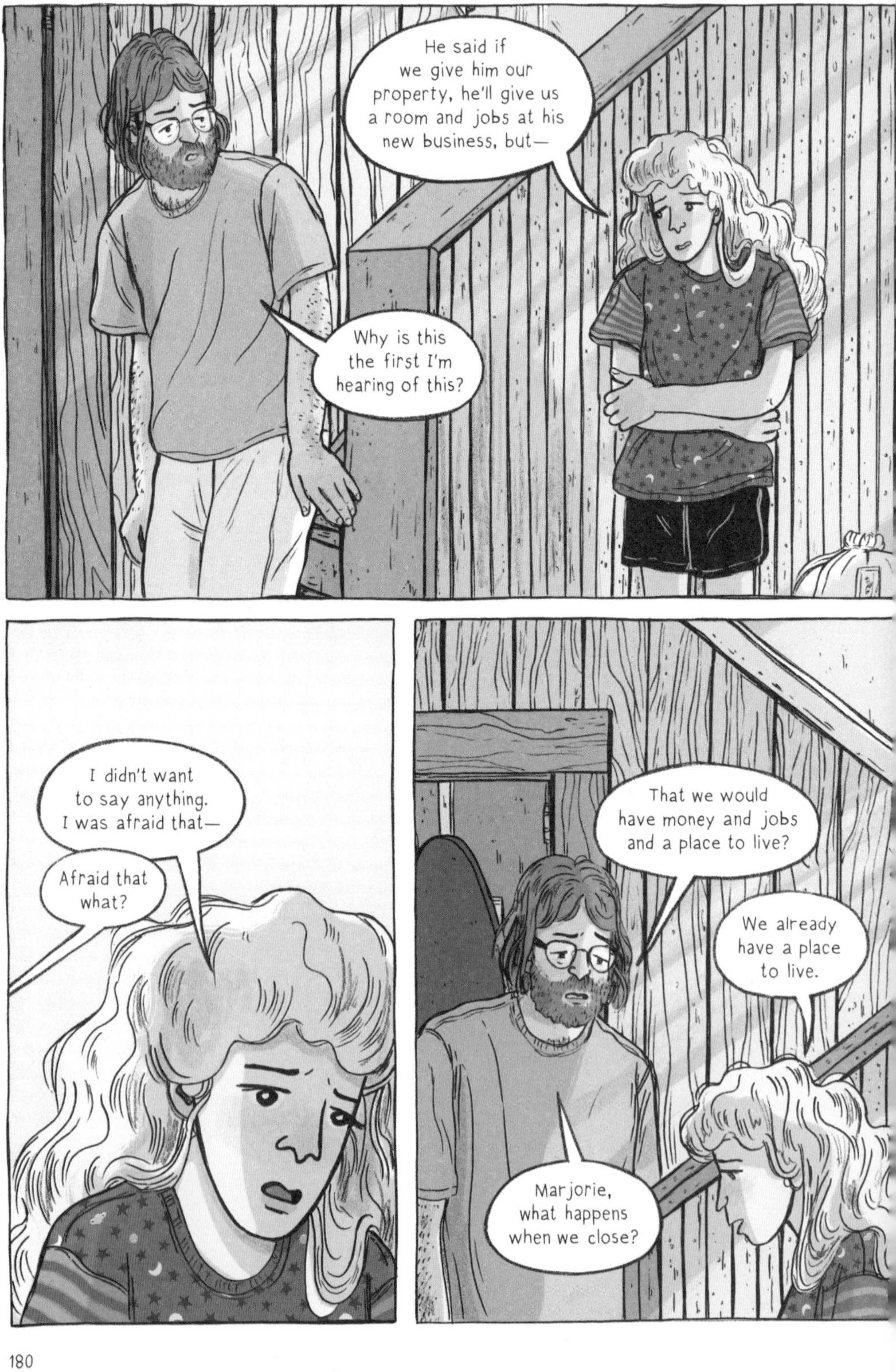
He said if we give him our property, he'll give us a room and jobs at his new business, but—
Why is this the first I'm hearing of this?
I didn't want to say anything. I was afraid that—
Afraid that what?
That we would have money and jobs and a place to live?
We already have a place to live.
Marjorie, what happens when we close?

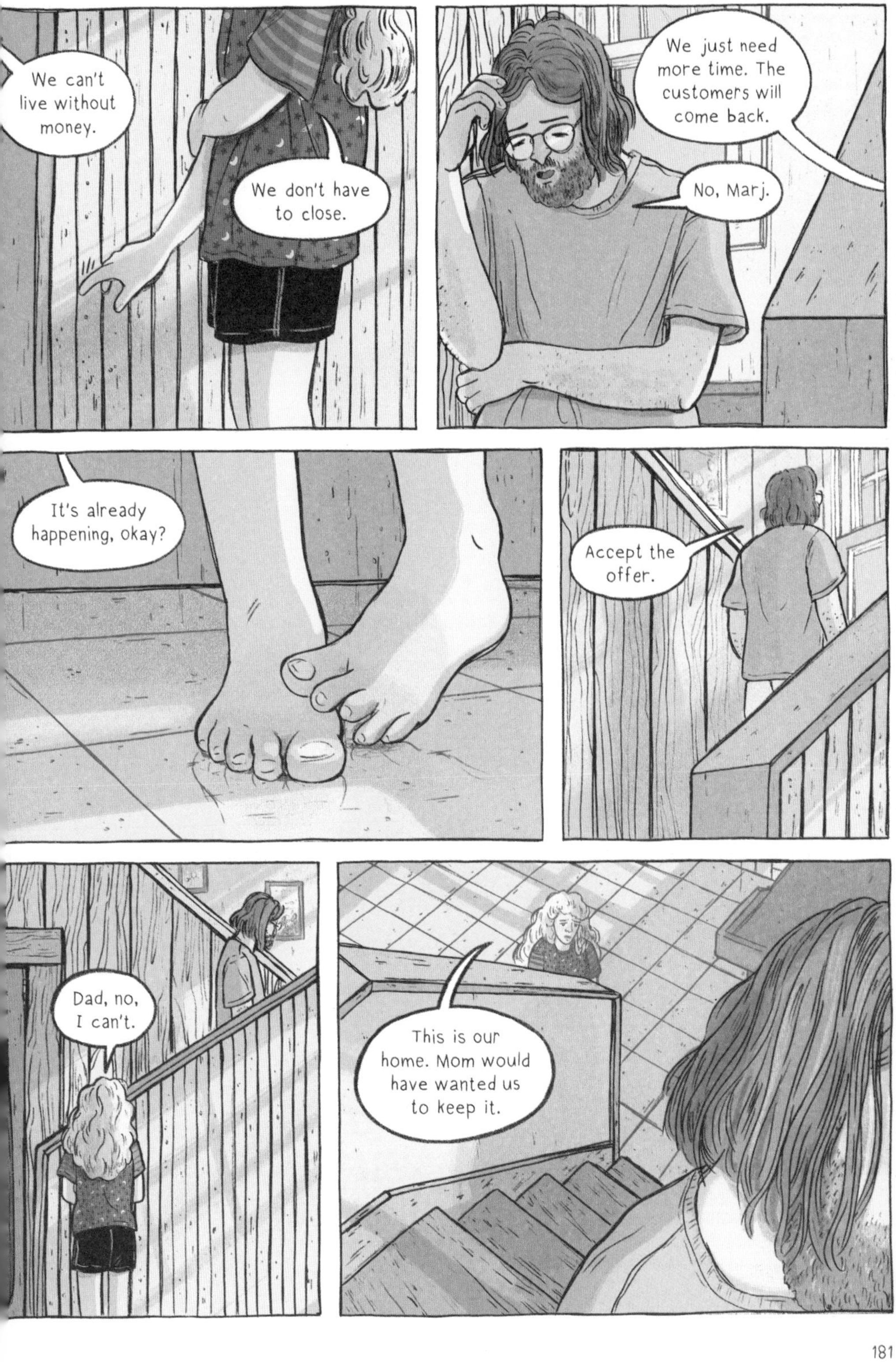
We can't live without money.
We don't have to close.
We just need more time. The customers will come back.
No, Marj.
It's already happening, okay?
Accept the offer.
Dad, no, I can't.
This is our home. Mom would have wanted us to keep it.

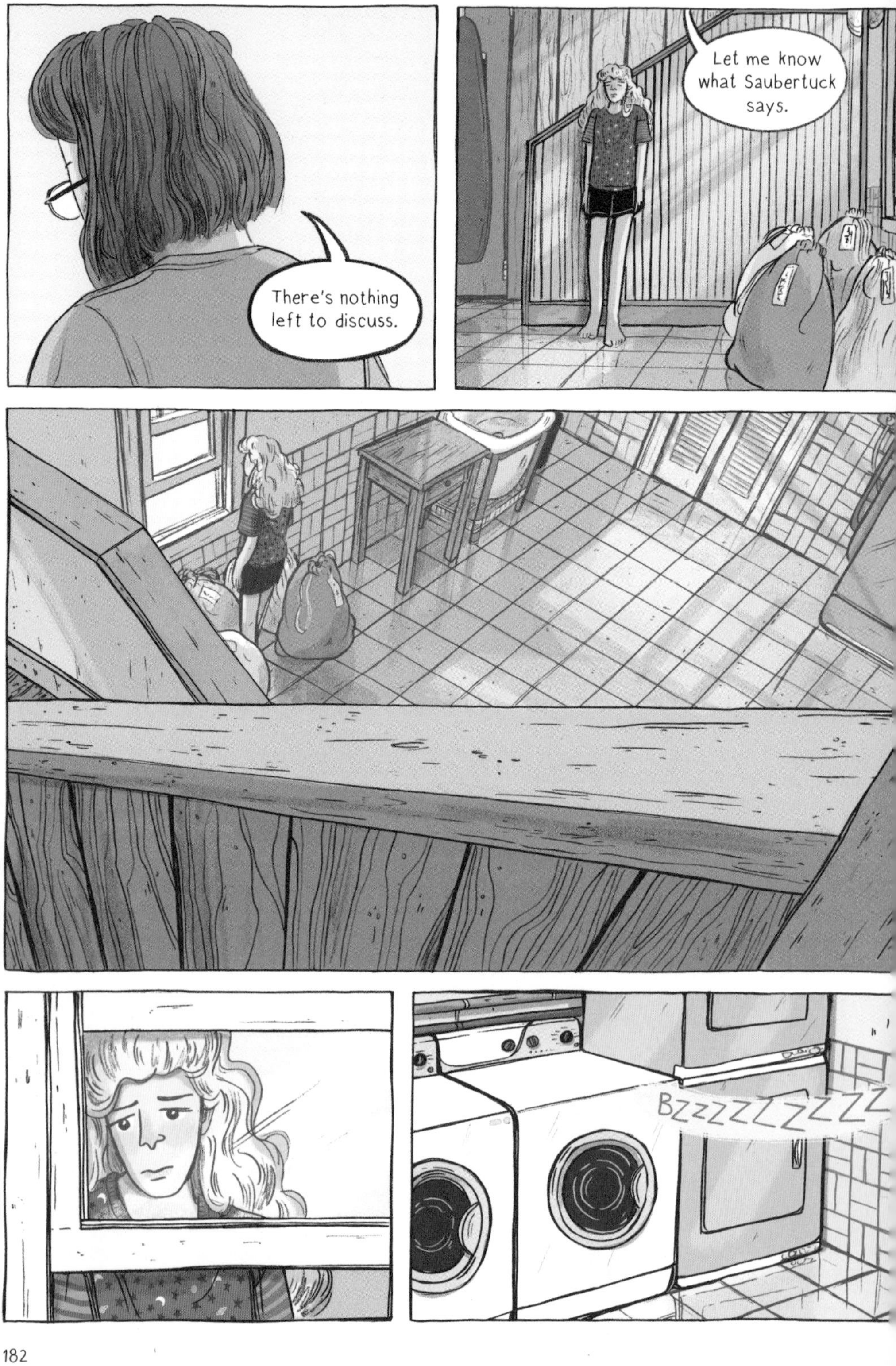
There's nothing left to discuss.
Let me know what Saubertuck says.
Bzzzzzzzzz

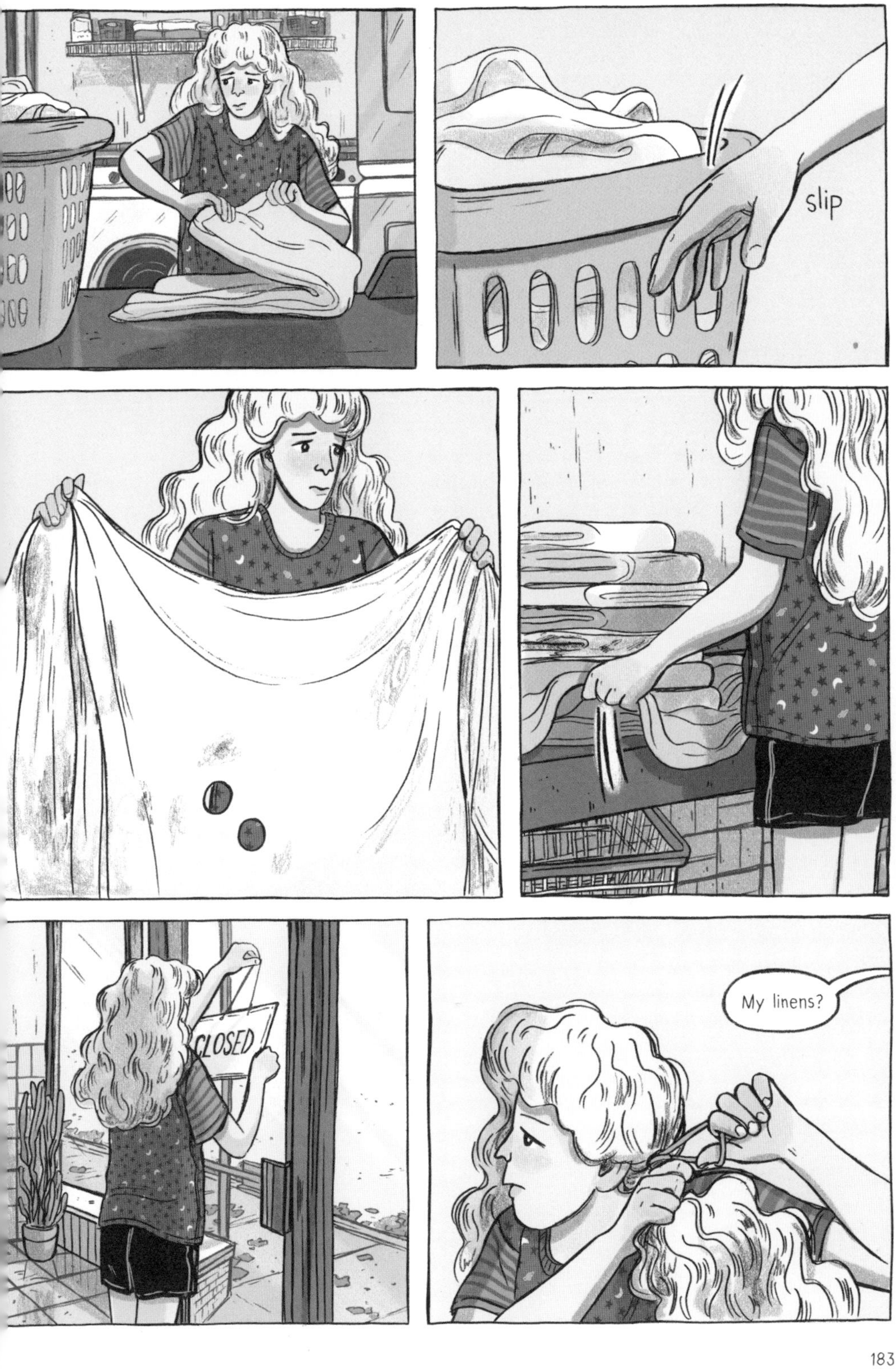
slip
CLOSED
My linens?

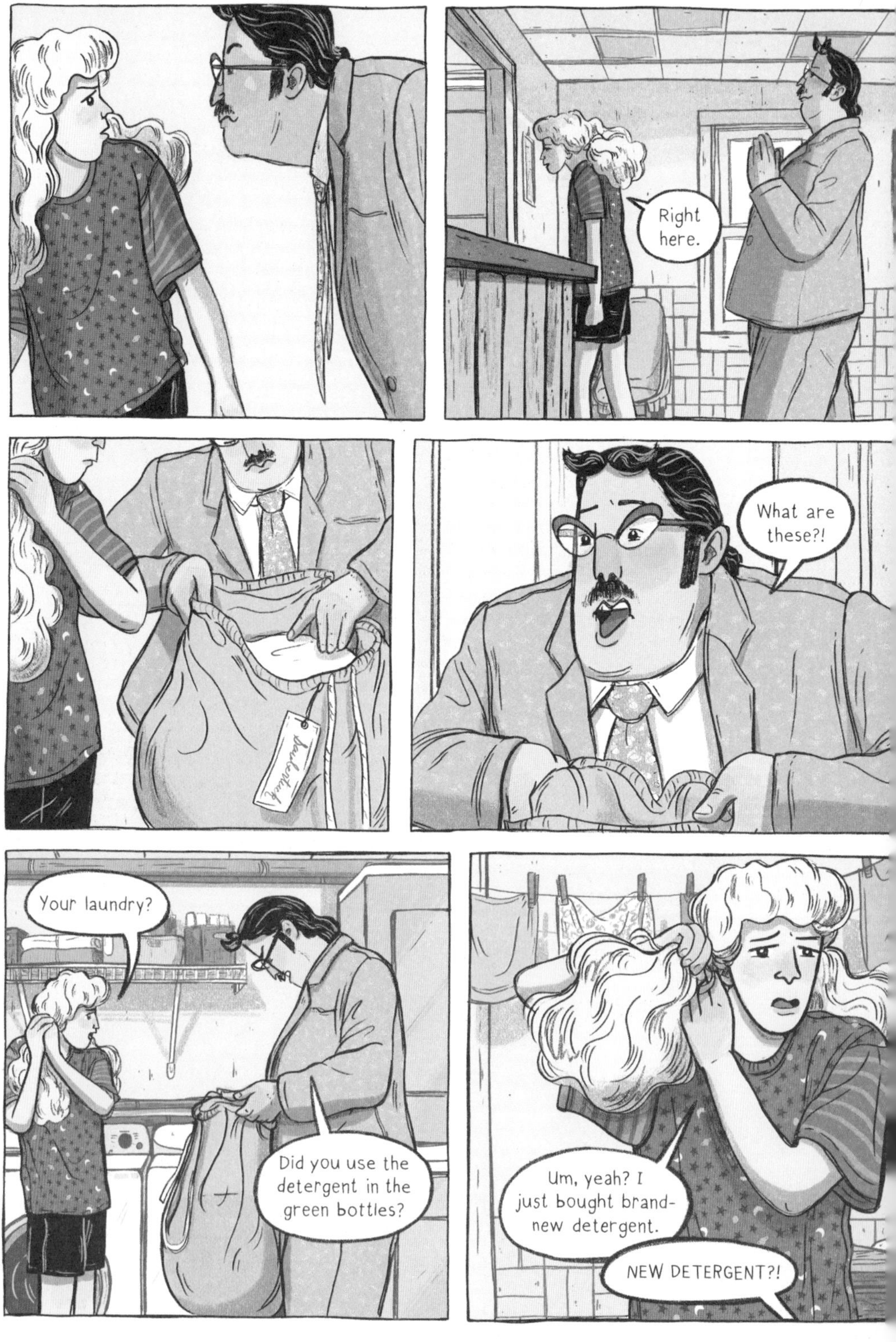
Right here.
What are these?!
Your laundry?
Did you use the detergent in the green bottles?
Um, yeah? I just bought brand-new detergent.
NEW DETERGENT?!

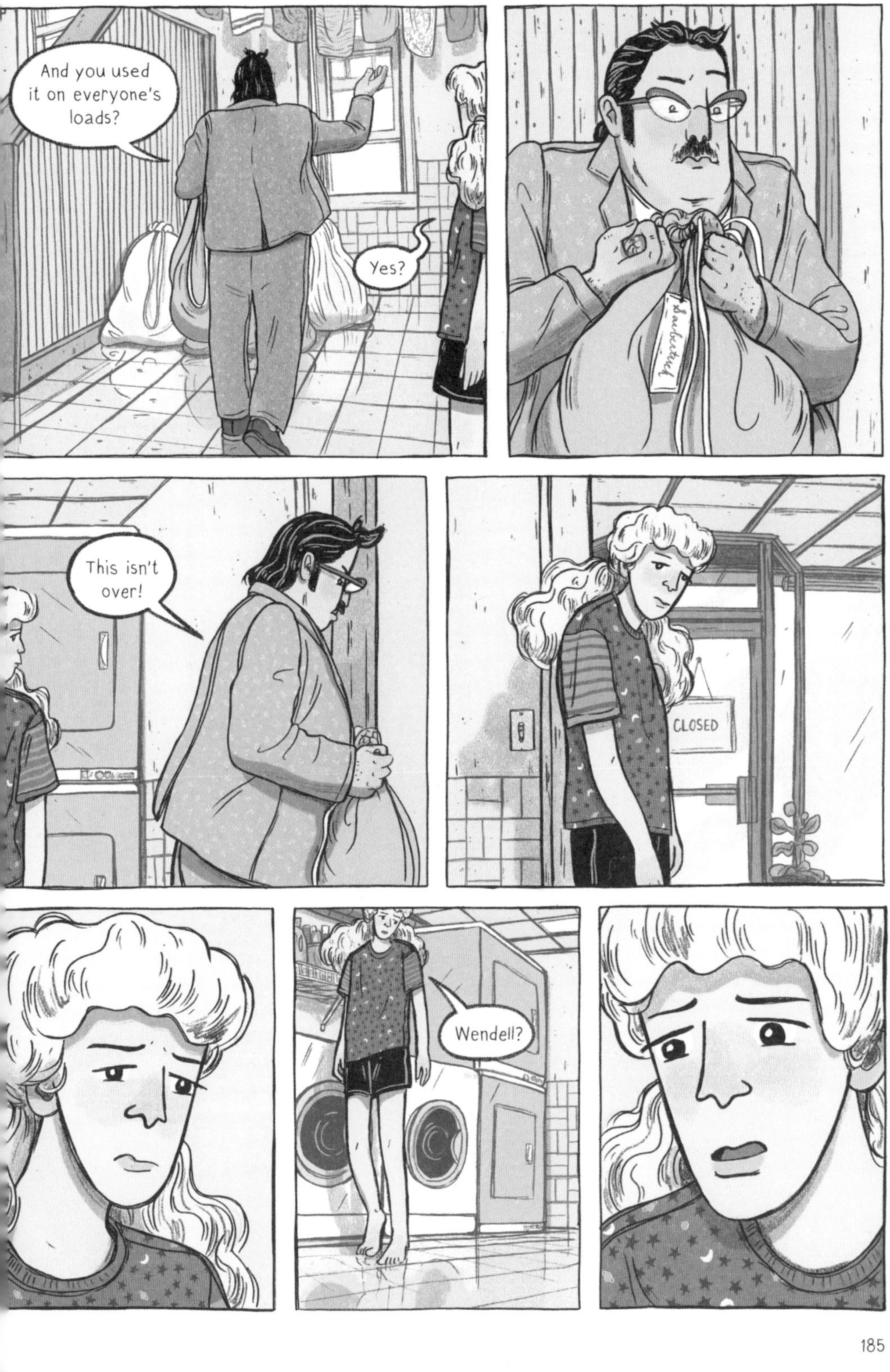

And you used it on everyone's loads?
Yes?
This isn't over!
CLOSED
Wendell?

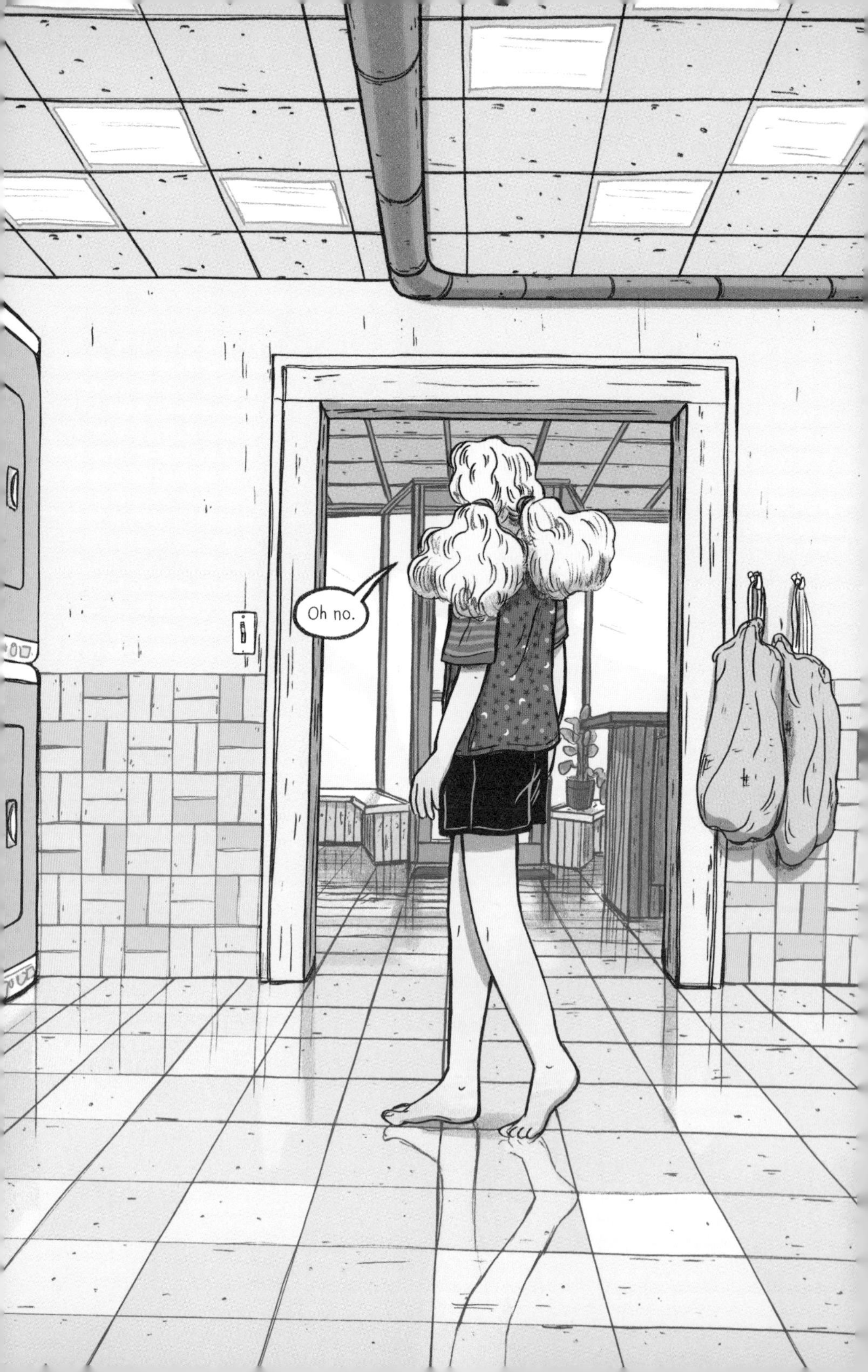
Oh no.

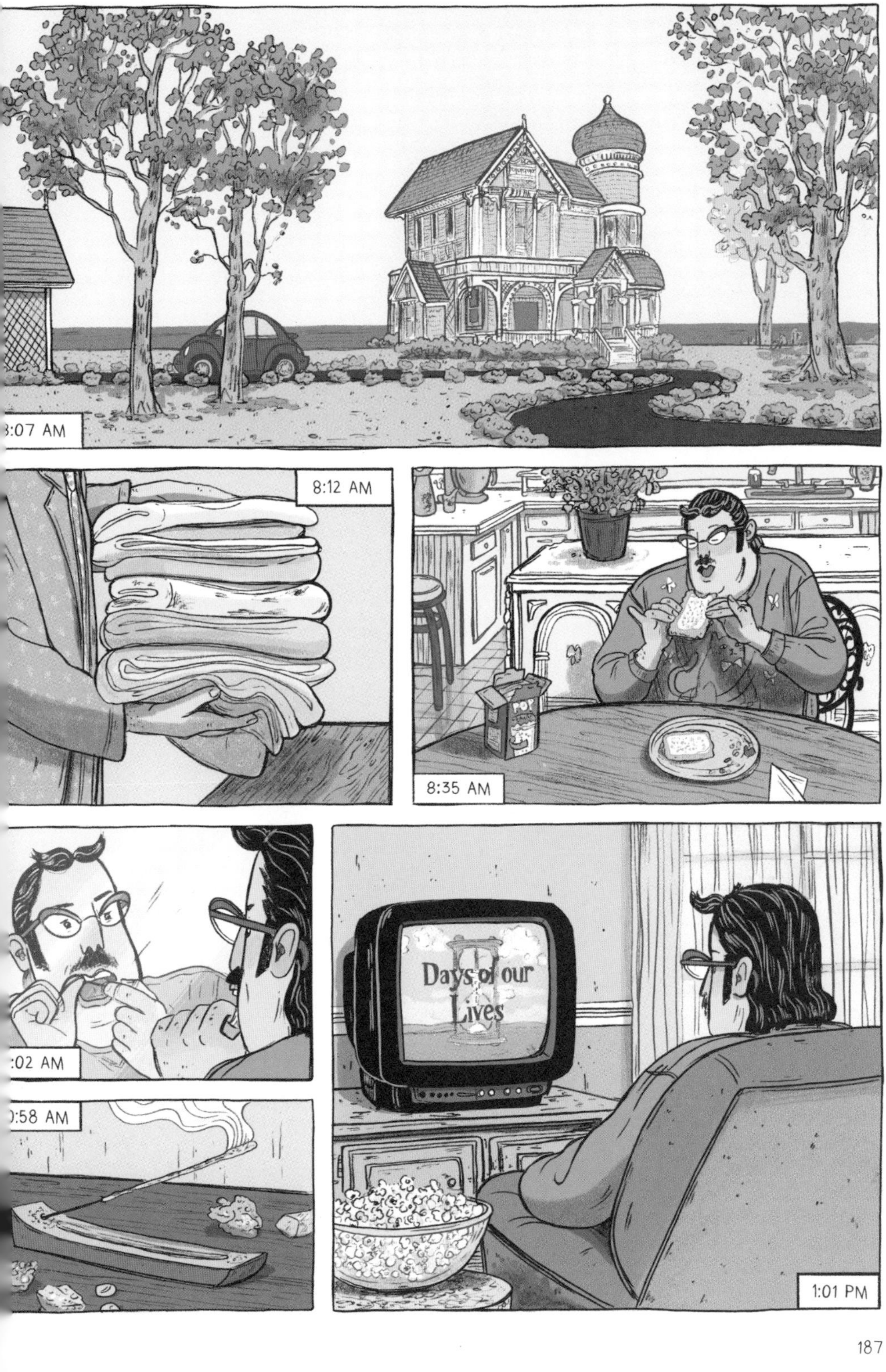
:07 AM
8:12 AM
8:35 AM
POP
:02 AM
:58 AM
Days of our Lives
1:01 PM

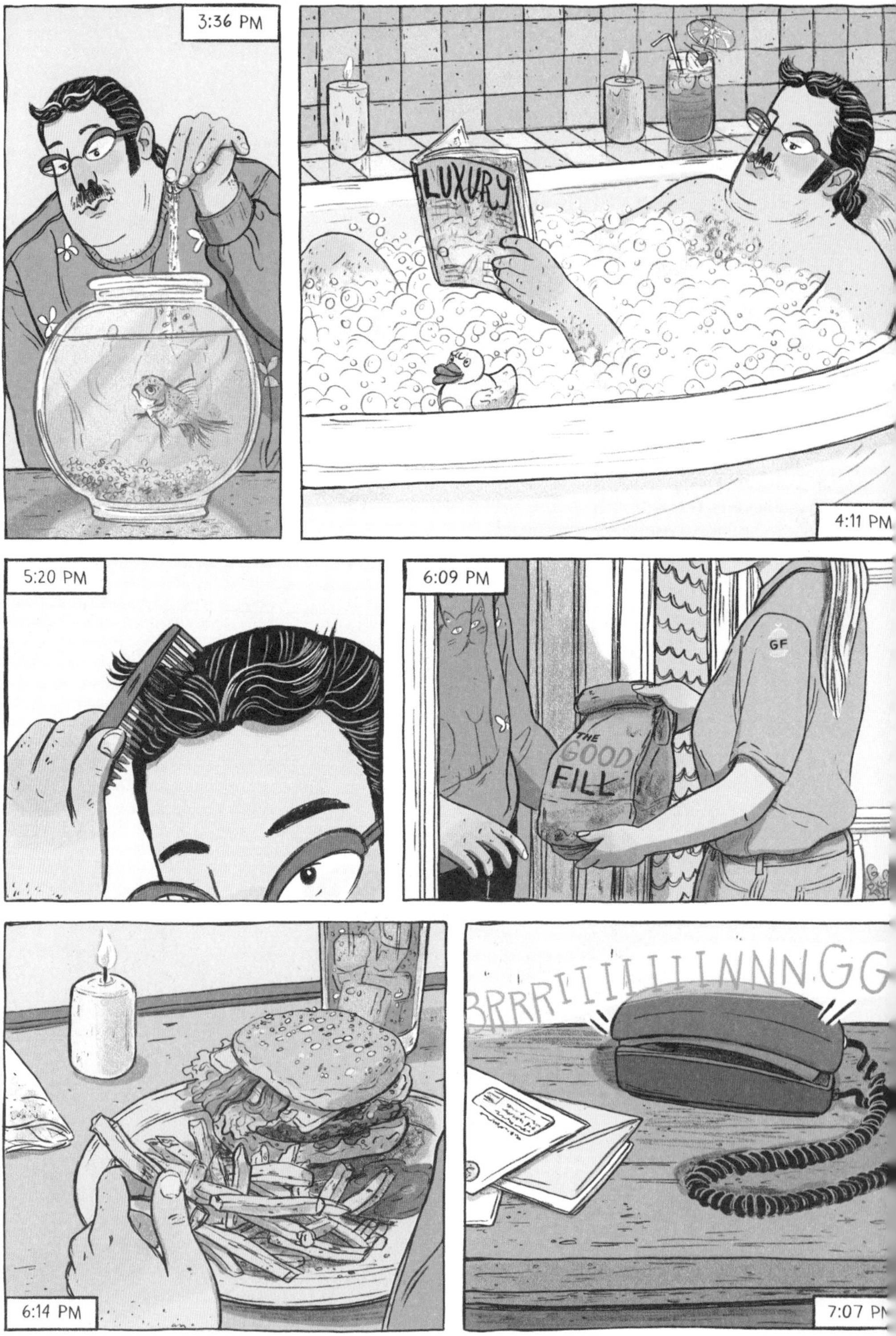
3:36 PM
LUXURY
4:11 PM
5:20 PM
6:09 PM
GF
THE GOOD FILL
6:14 PM
BRRRIIIIIIIINNNGG
7:07 PM

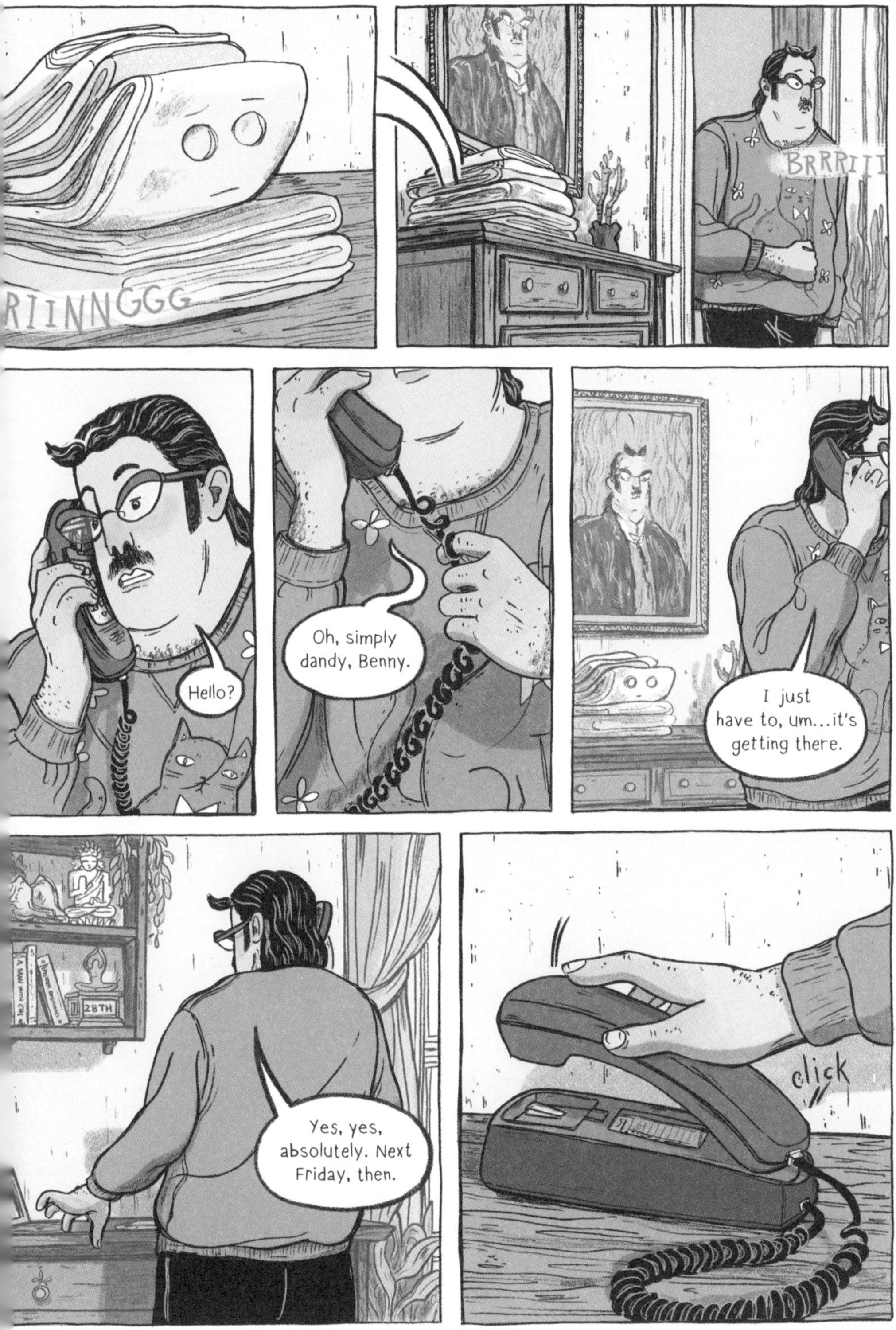
RIINNGGG
BRRRIII
Hello?
Oh, simply dandy, Benny.
I just have to, um...it's getting there.
28TH
Yes, yes, absolutely. Next Friday, then.
click

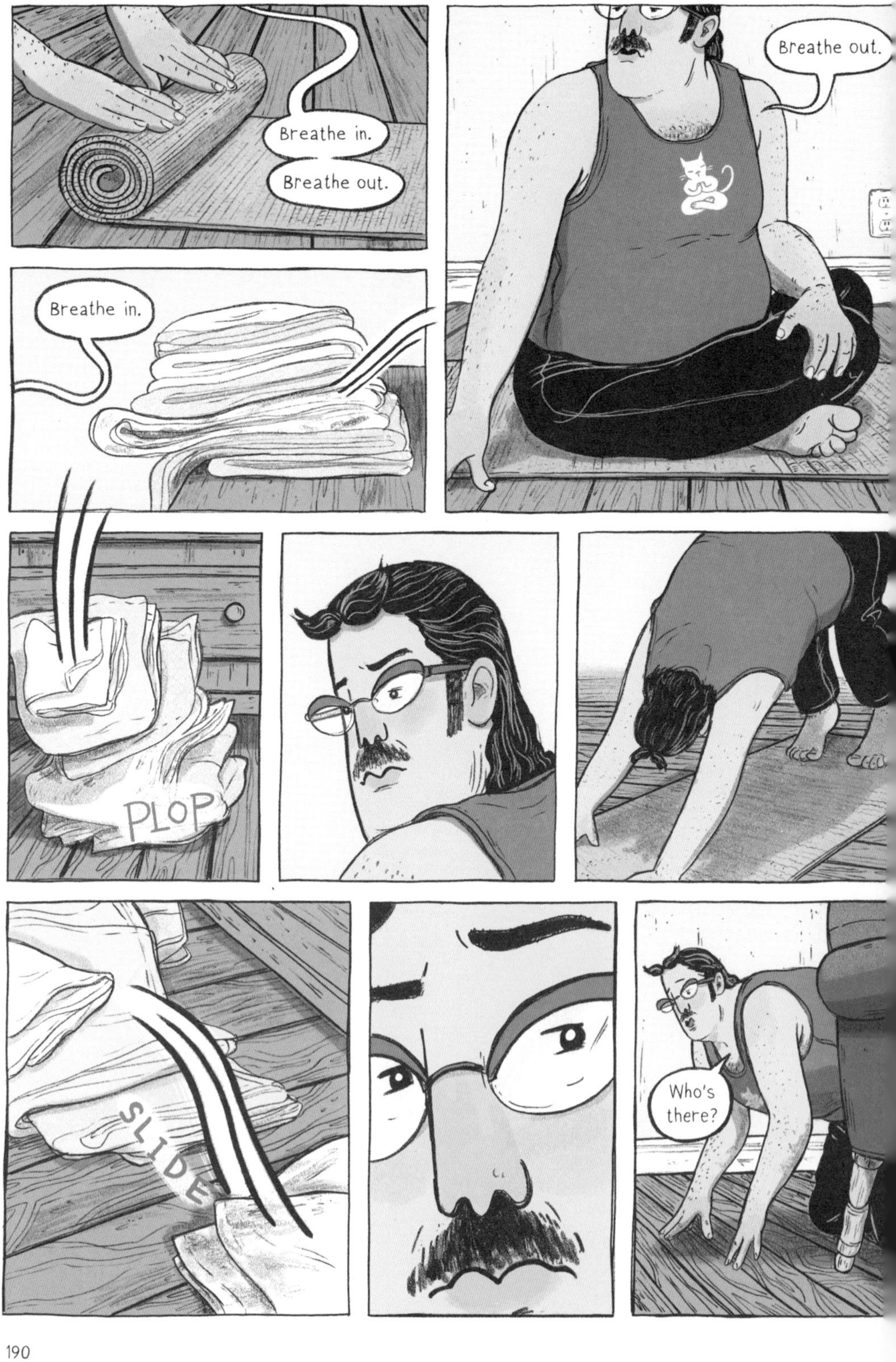
Breathe in.
Breathe out.
Breathe out.
Breathe in.
PLOP
SLIDE
Who's there?

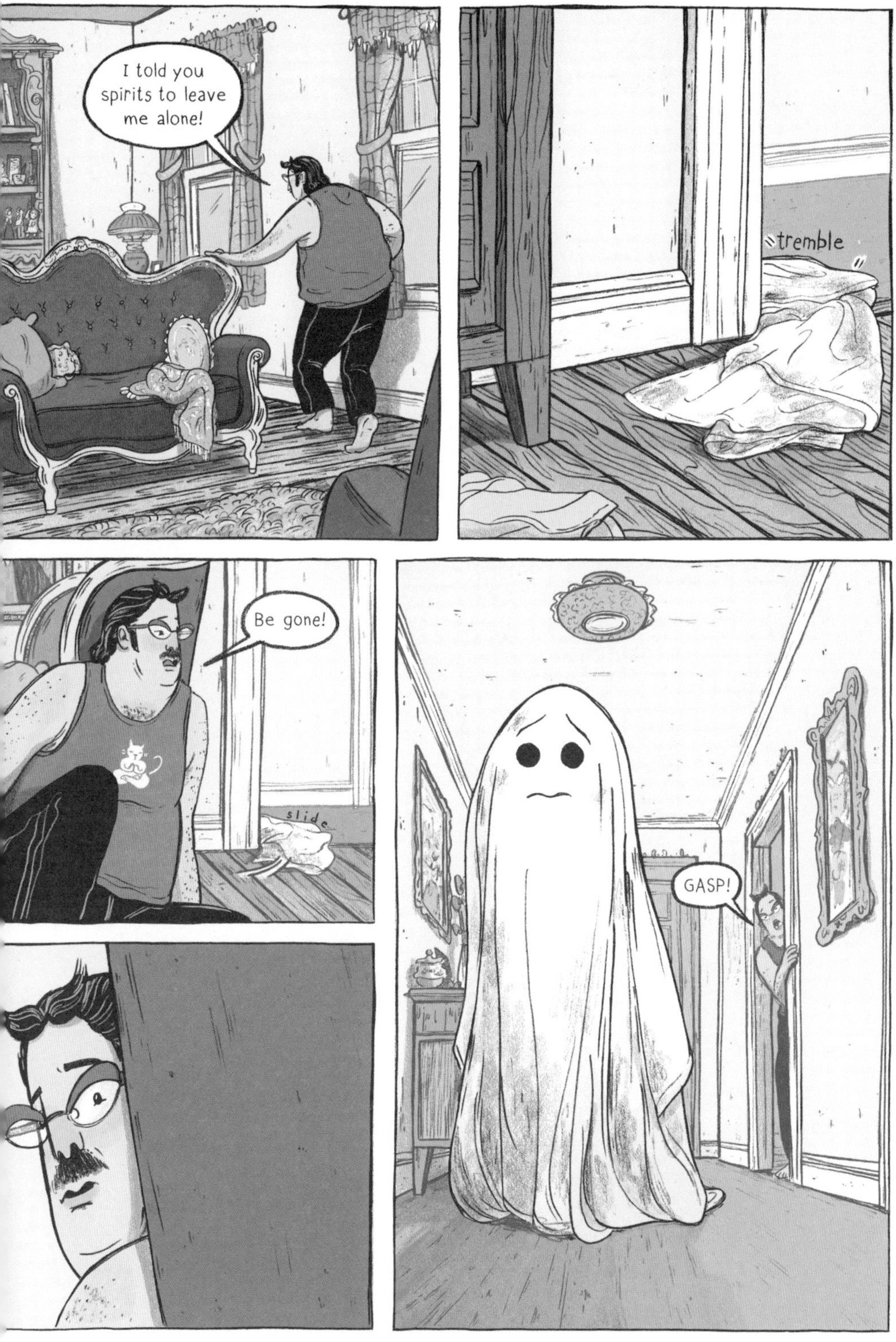
I told you spirits to leave me alone!
tremble
Be gone!
slide
GASP!

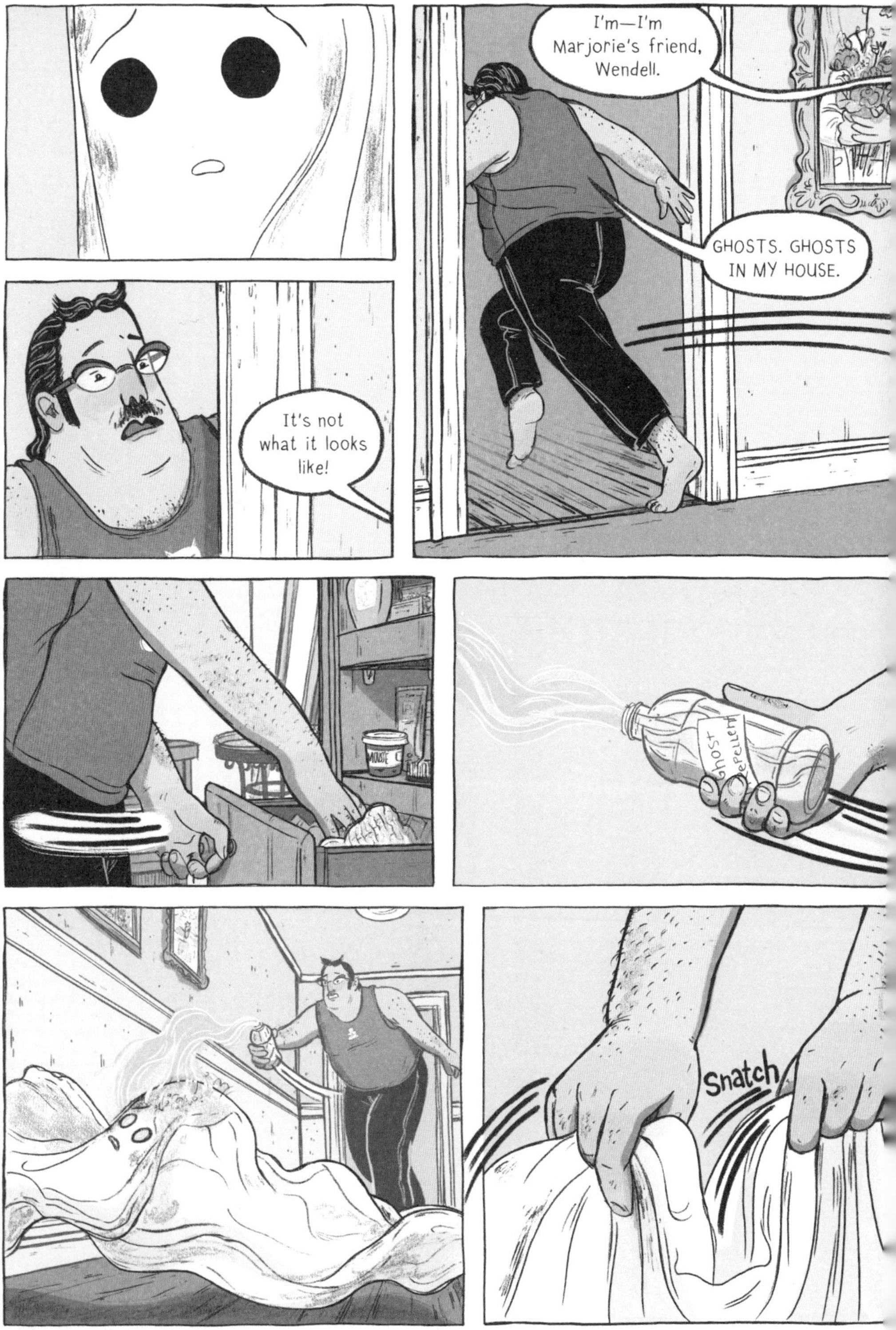
I'm—I'm Marjorie's friend, Wendell.
GHOSTS. GHOSTS IN MY HOUSE.
It's not what it looks like!
MOUSSE
Ghost Repellent
Snatch

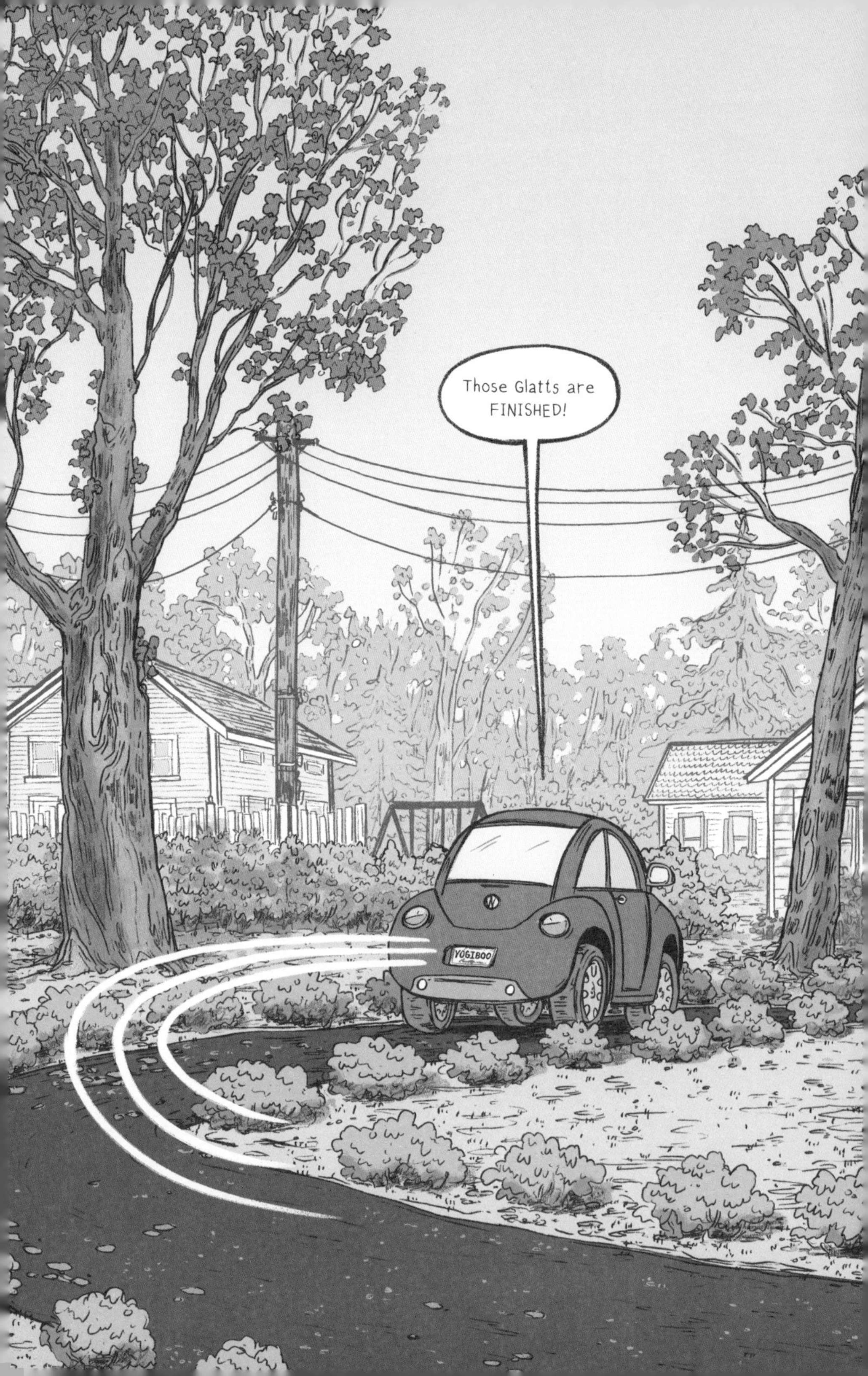
Those Glatts are FINISHED!
YOGIBOO

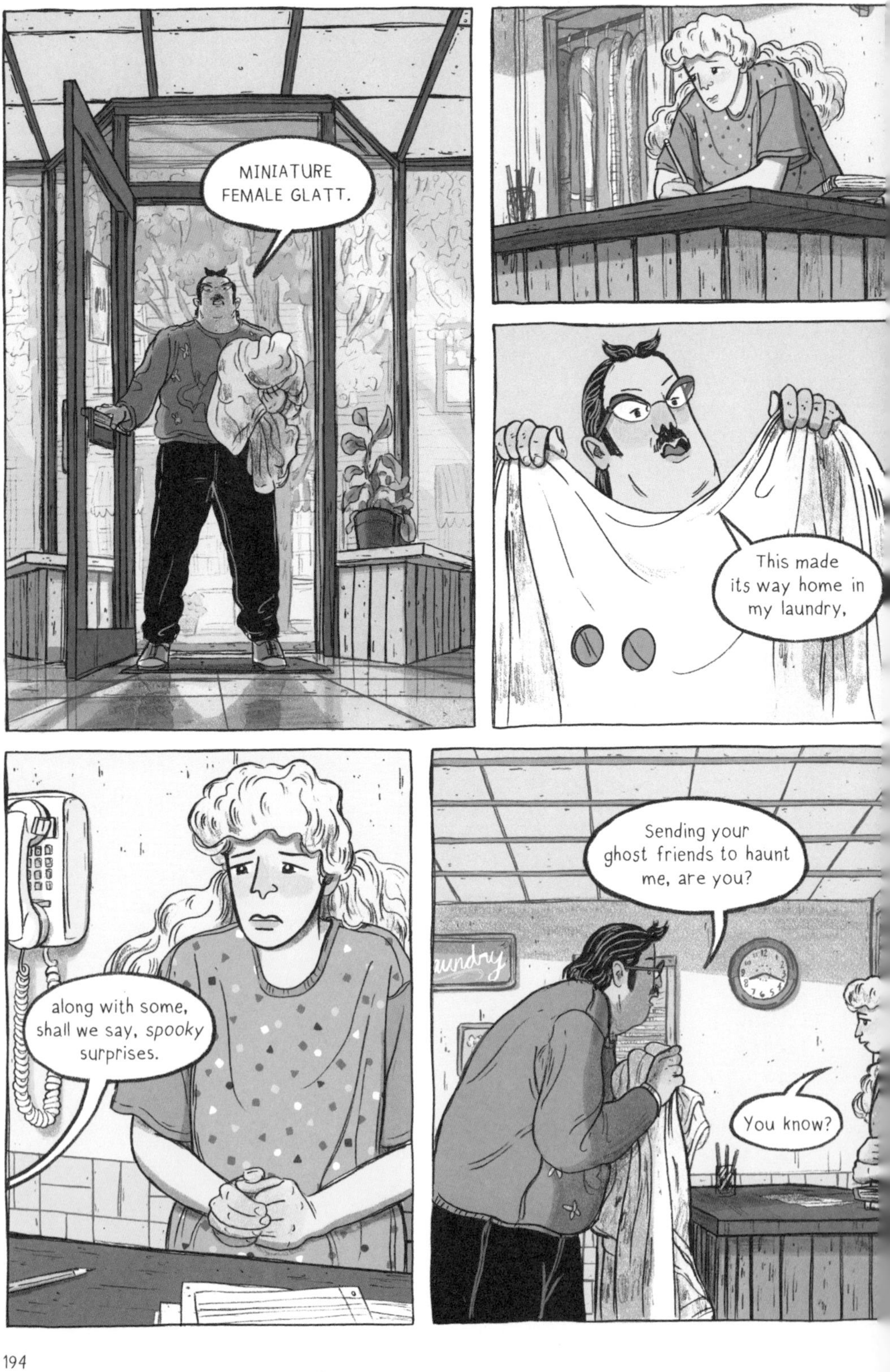
MINIATURE FEMALE GLATT.
This made its way home in my laundry,
along with some, shall we say, *spooky* surprises.
Laundry
Sending your ghost friends to haunt me, are you?
You know?

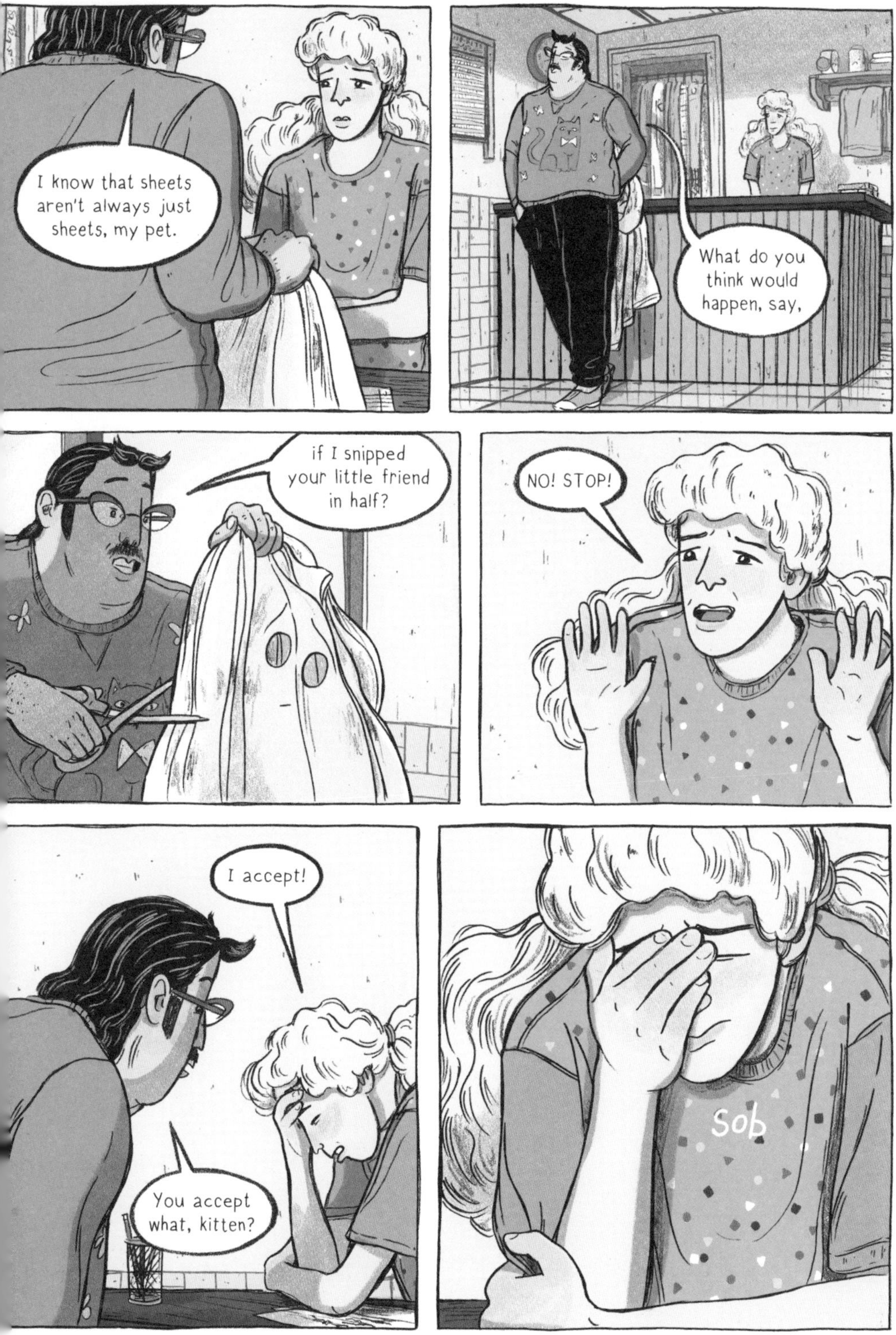
I know that sheets aren't always just sheets, my pet.
What do you think would happen, say,
if I snipped your little friend in half?
NO! STOP!
I accept!
You accept what, kitten?
sob

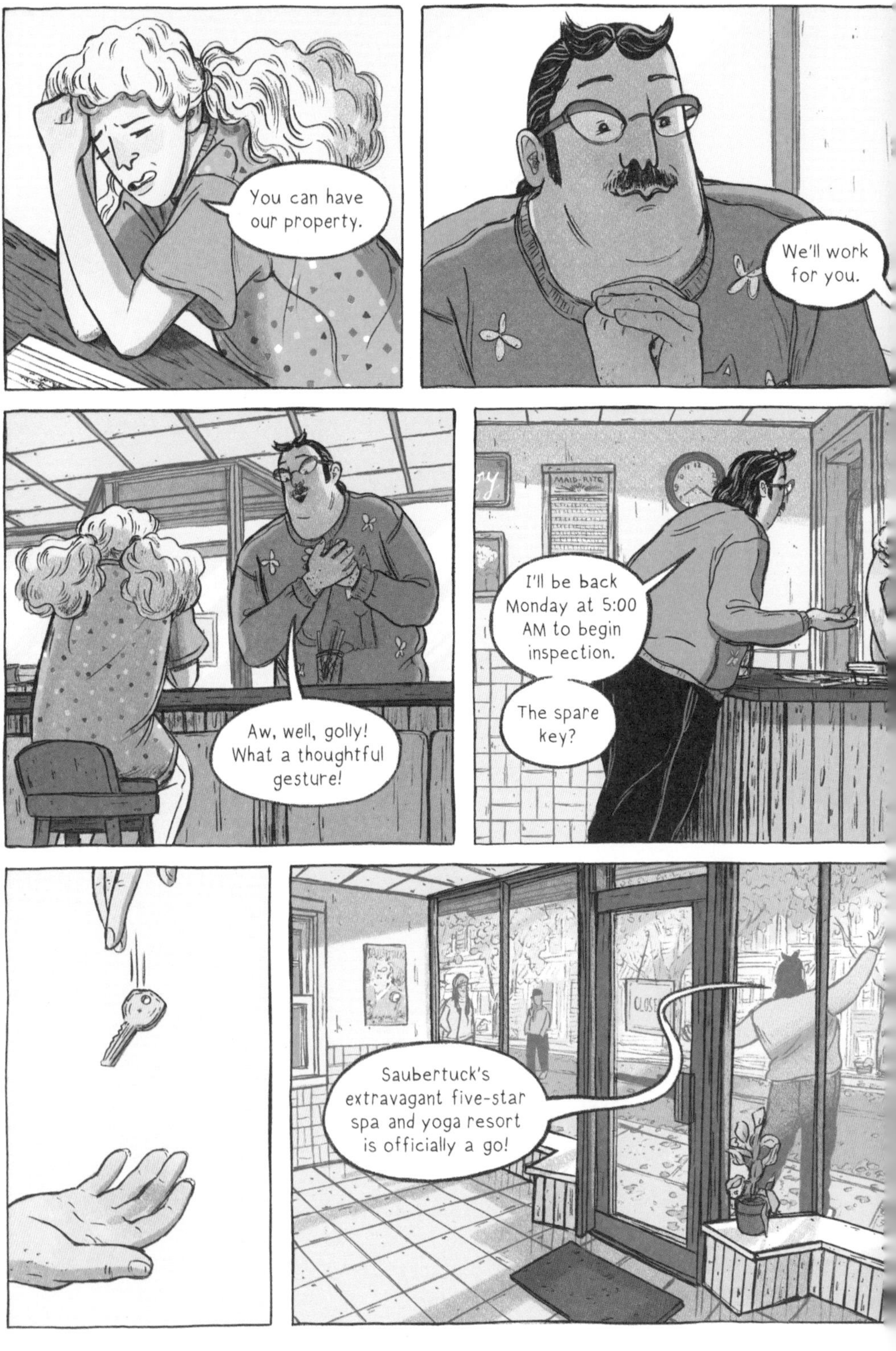
You can have our property.
We'll work for you.
Aw, well, golly! What a thoughtful gesture!
I'll be back Monday at 5:00 AM to begin inspection.
The spare key?
Saubertuck's extravagant five-star spa and yoga resort is officially a go!

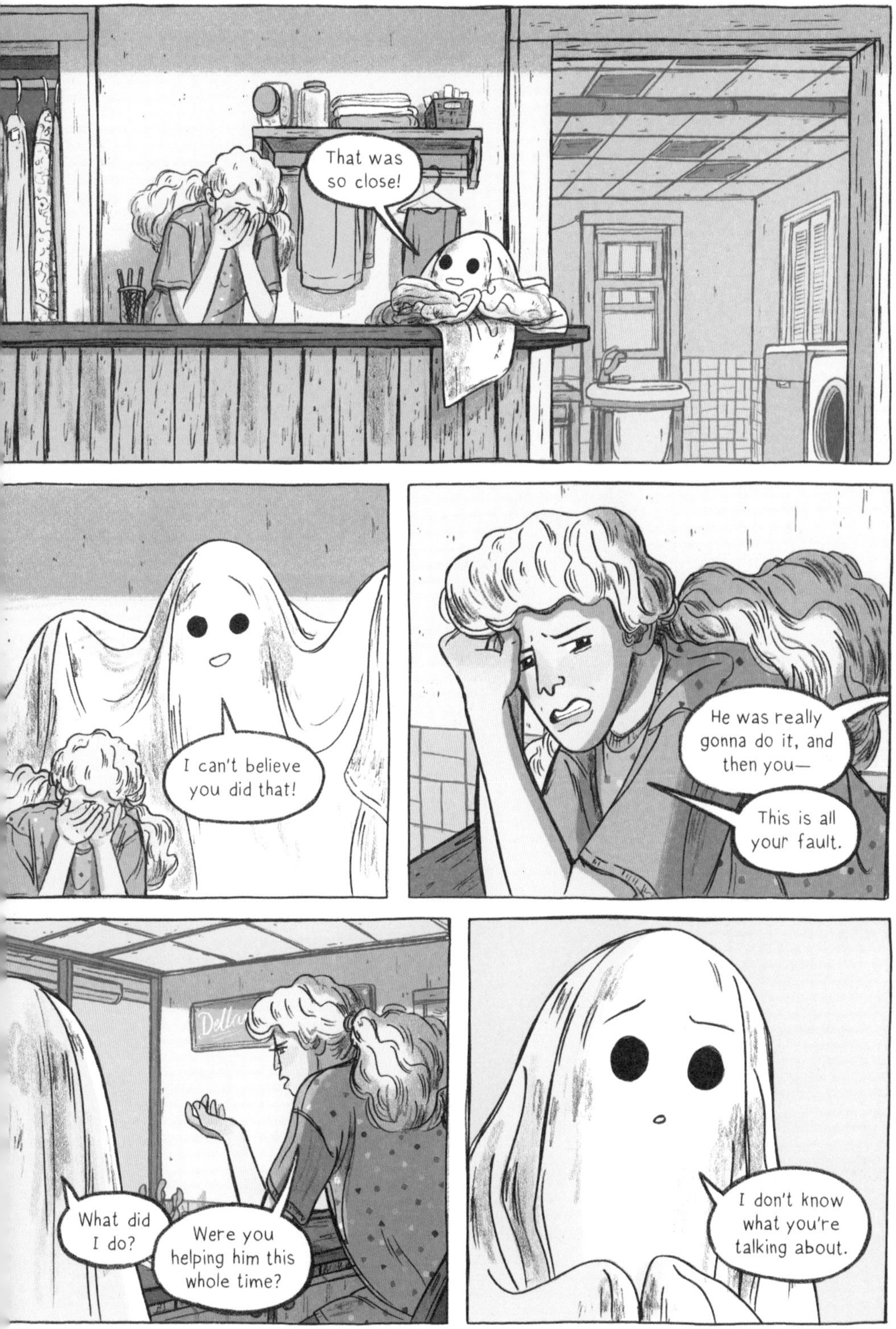

That was so close!
I can't believe you did that!
He was really gonna do it, and then you—
This is all your fault.
What did I do?
Were you helping him this whole time?
I don't know what you're talking about.

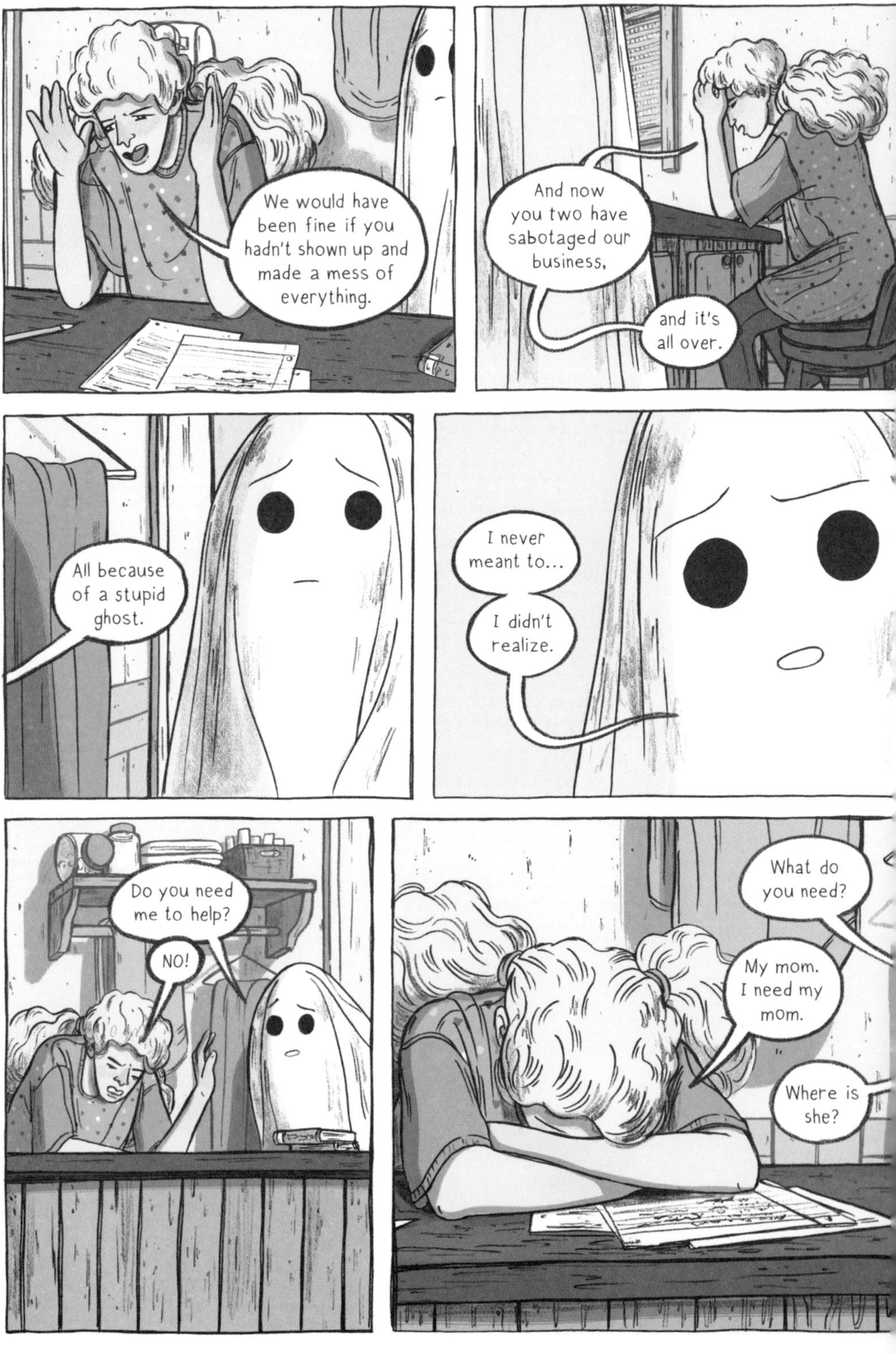
We would have been fine if you hadn't shown up and made a mess of everything.
And now you two have sabotaged our business,
and it's all over.
All because of a stupid ghost.
I never meant to...
I didn't realize.
Do you need me to help?
NO!
What do you need?
My mom. I need my mom.
Where is she?

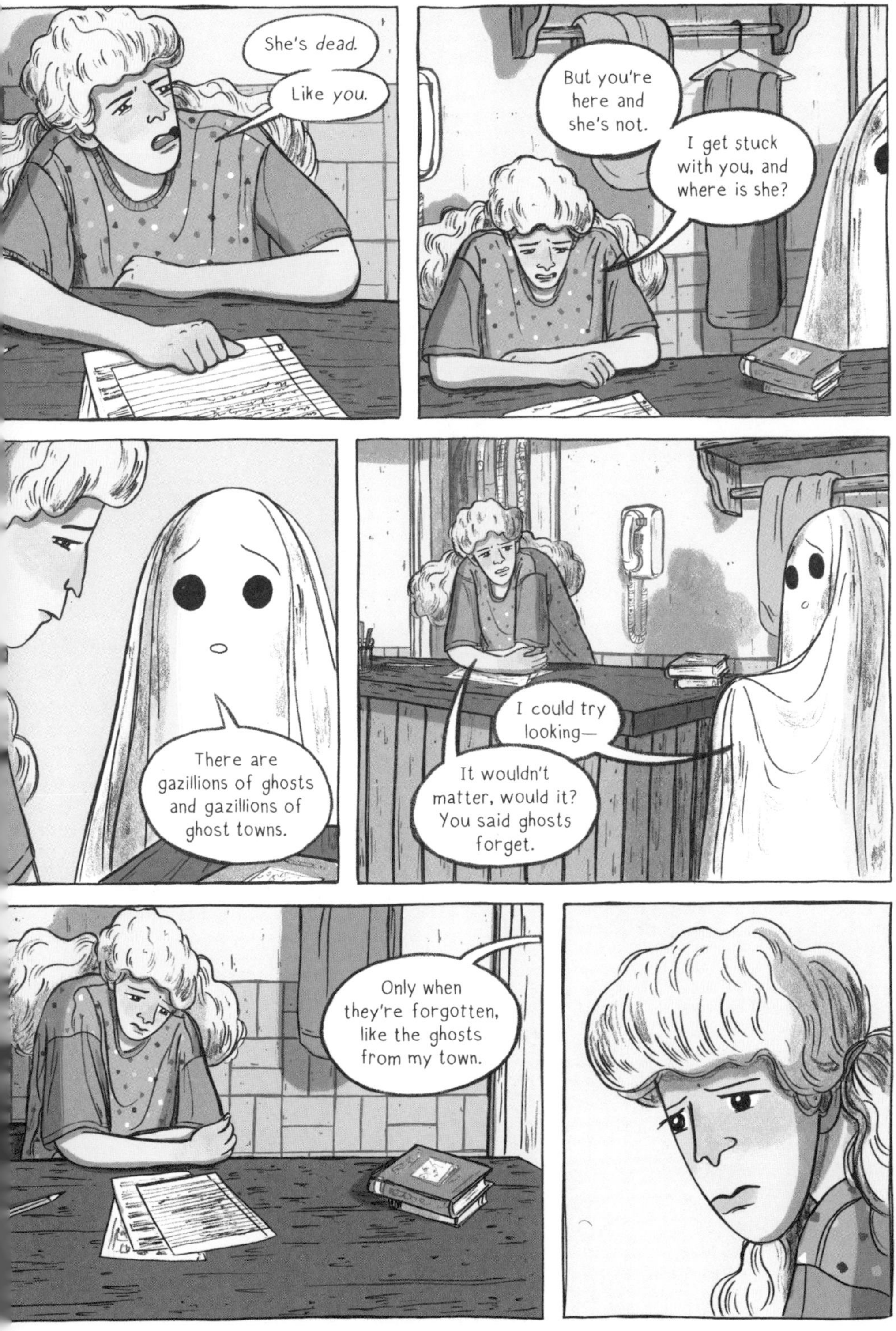
She's *dead.*
Like *you.*
But you're here and she's not.
I get stuck with you, and where is she?
There are gazillions of ghosts and gazillions of ghost towns.
I could try looking—
It wouldn't matter, would it? You said ghosts forget.
Only when they're forgotten, like the ghosts from my town.

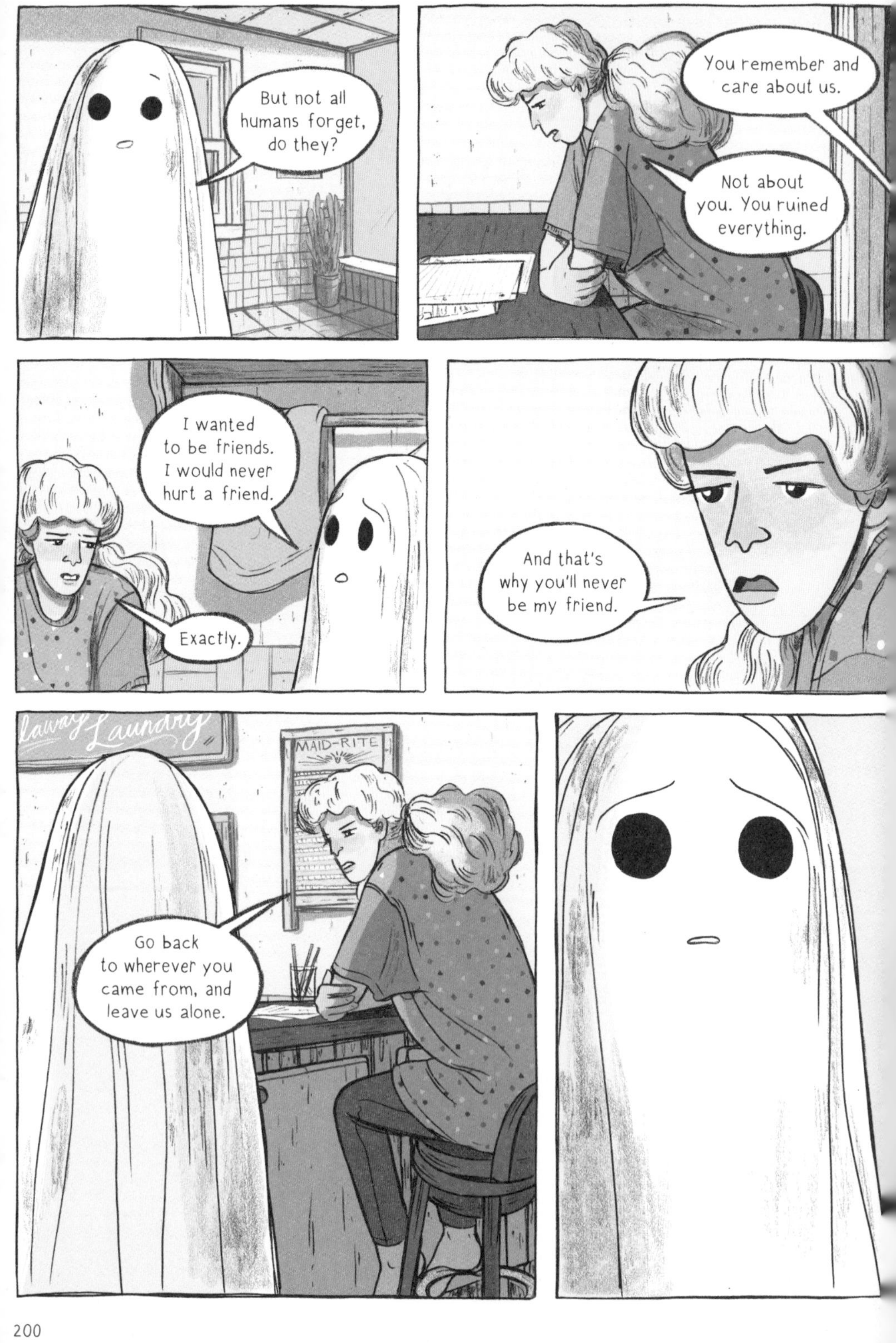
But not all humans forget, do they?
You remember and care about us.
Not about you. You ruined everything.
I wanted to be friends. I would never hurt a friend.
Exactly.
And that's why you'll never be my friend.
Laundry
MAID-RITE
Go back to wherever you came from, and leave us alone.

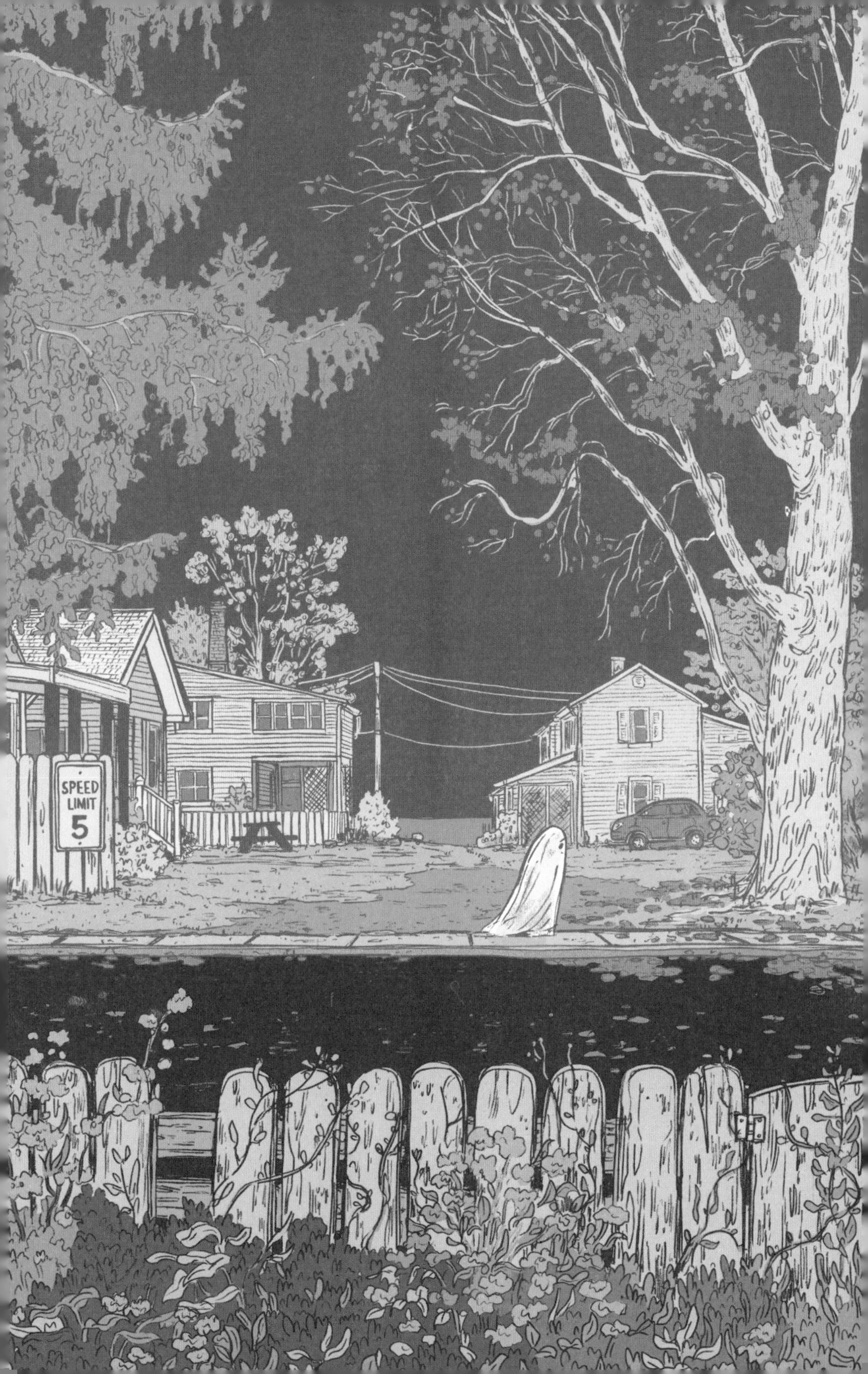
SPEED
LIMIT
5

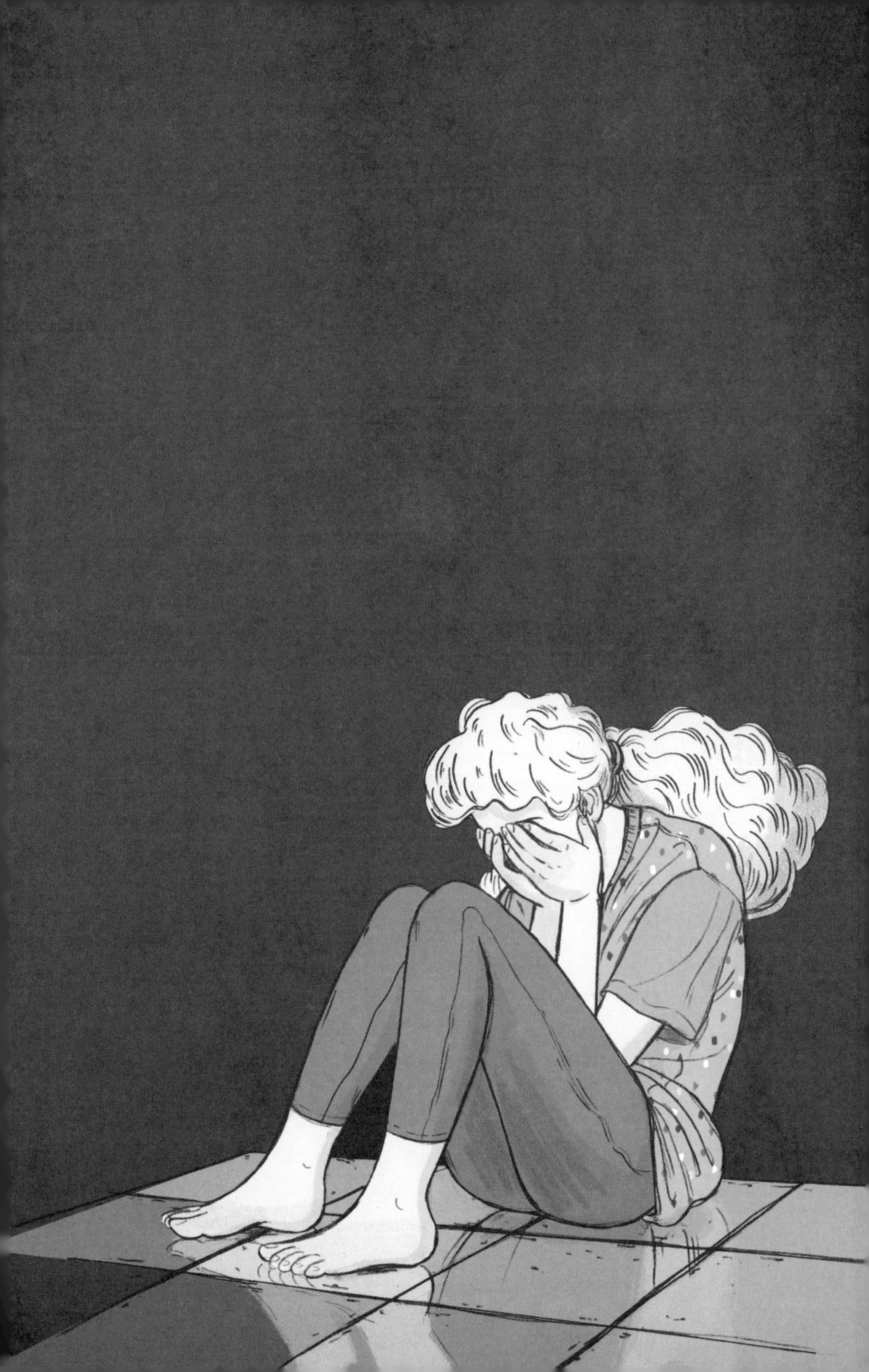

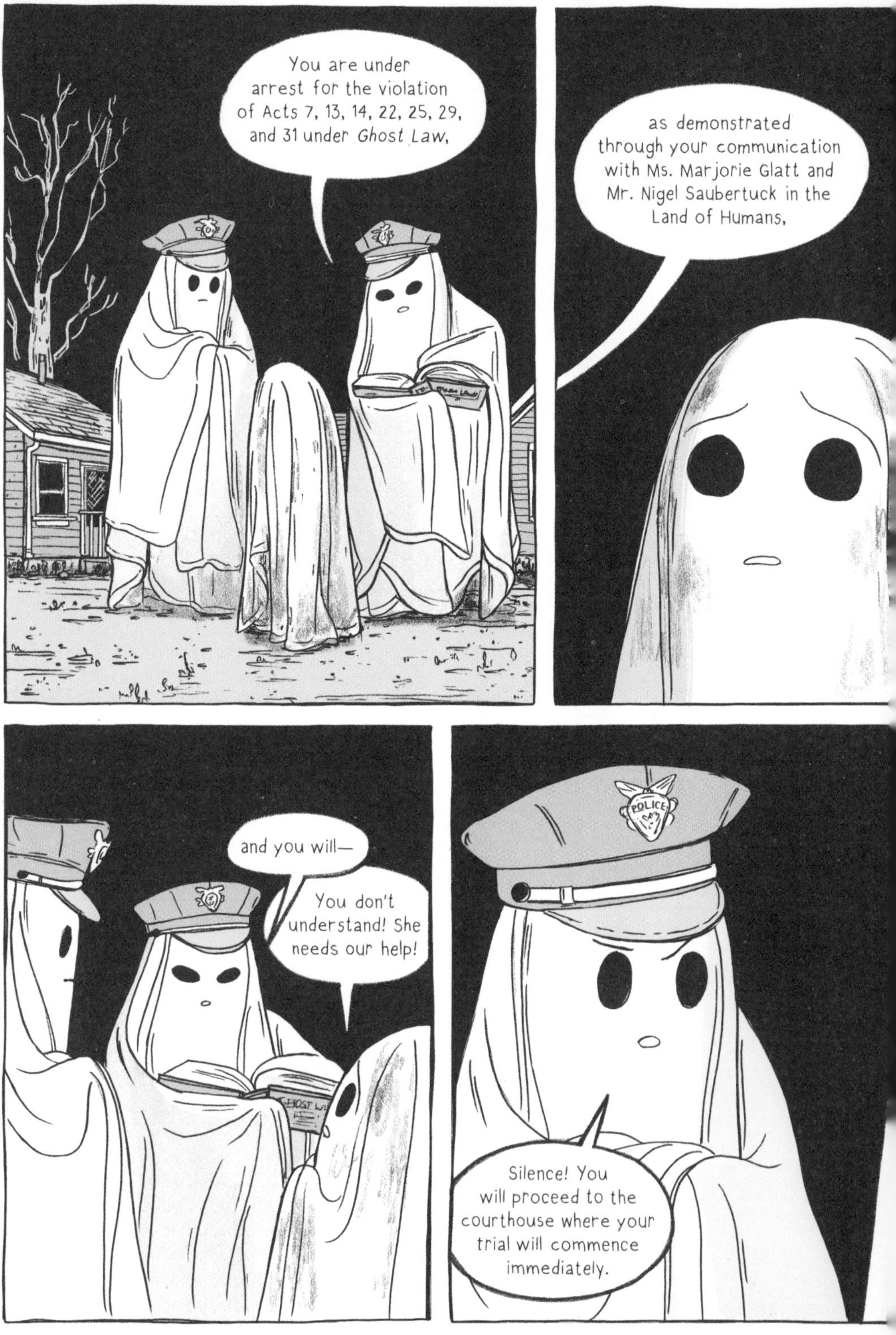
You are under arrest for the violation of Acts 7, 13, 14, 22, 25, 29, and 31 under *Ghost Law*,
as demonstrated through your communication with Ms. Marjorie Glatt and Mr. Nigel Saubertuck in the Land of Humans,
and you will—
You don't understand! She needs our help!
POLICE
Silence! You will proceed to the courthouse where your trial will commence immediately.

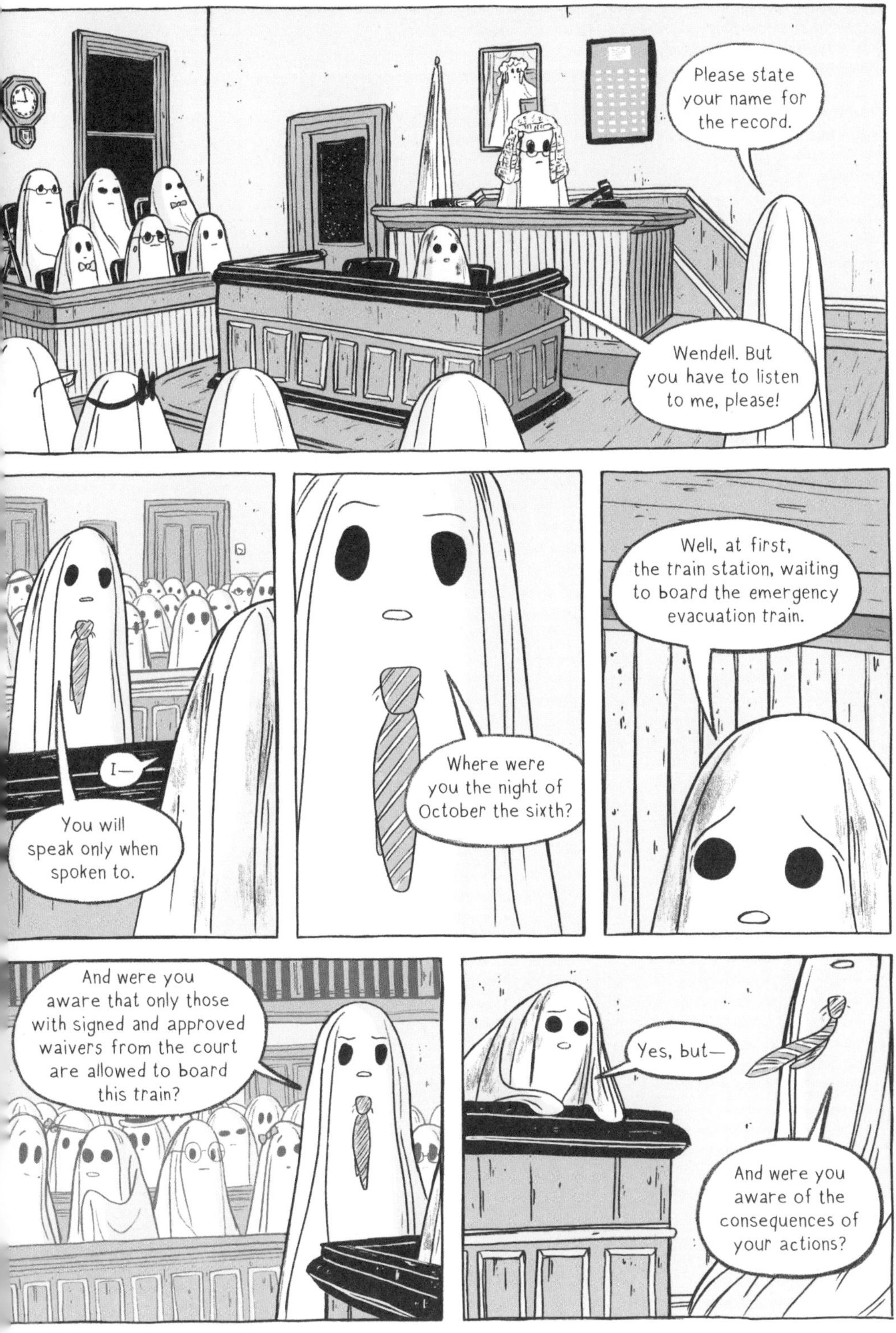
Please state your name for the record.
Wendell. But you have to listen to me, please!
I—
You will speak only when spoken to.
Where were you the night of October the sixth?
Well, at first, the train station, waiting to board the emergency evacuation train.
And were you aware that only those with signed and approved waivers from the court are allowed to board this train?
Yes, but—
And were you aware of the consequences of your actions?

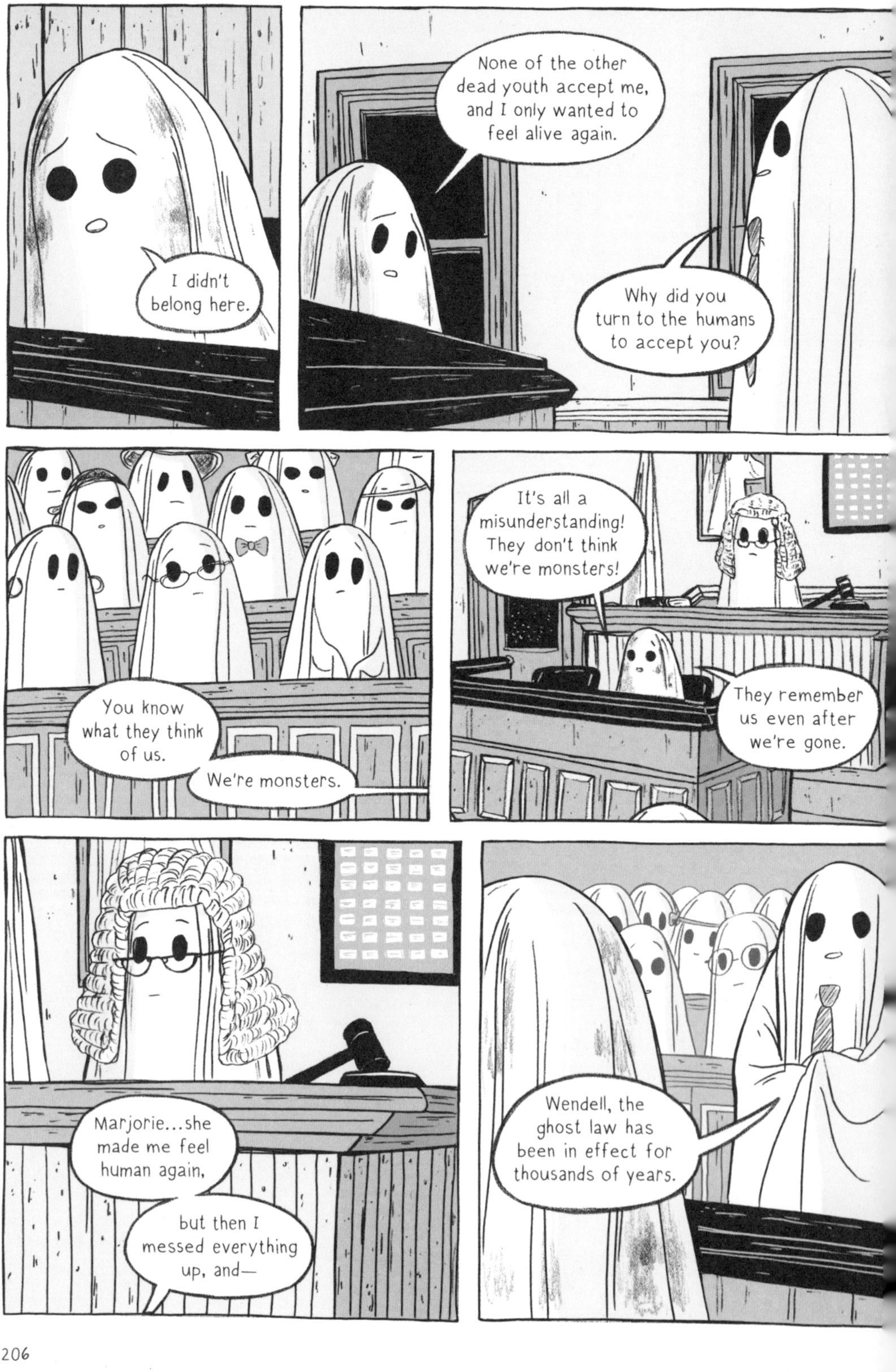
I didn't belong here.
None of the other dead youth accept me, and I only wanted to feel alive again.
Why did you turn to the humans to accept you?
You know what they think of us.
We're monsters.
It's all a misunderstanding! They don't think we're monsters!
They remember us even after we're gone.
Marjorie...she made me feel human again,
but then I messed everything up, and—
Wendell, the ghost law has been in effect for thousands of years.

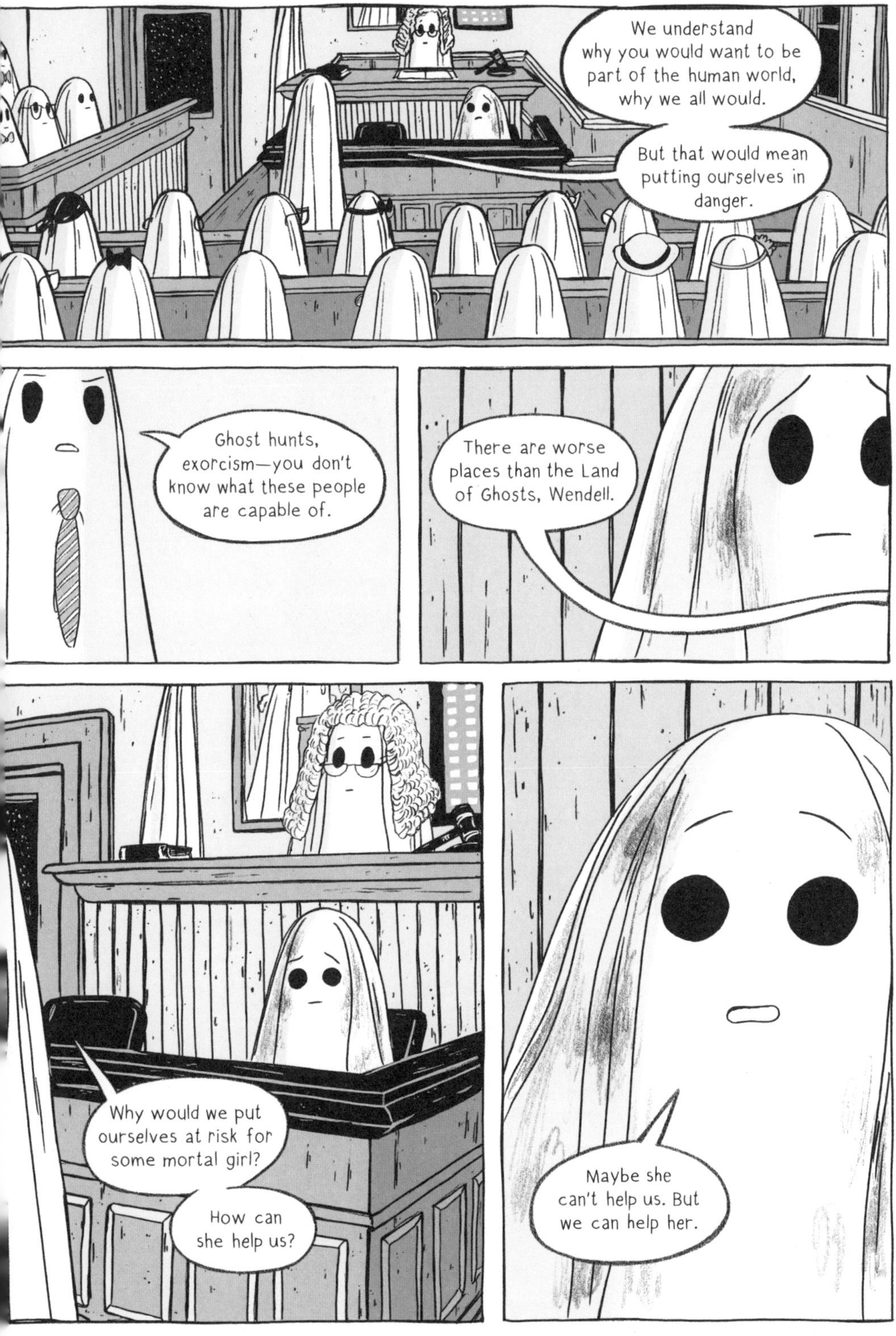
We understand why you would want to be part of the human world, why we all would.
But that would mean putting ourselves in danger.
Ghost hunts, exorcism—you don't know what these people are capable of.
There are worse places than the Land of Ghosts, Wendell.
Why would we put ourselves at risk for some mortal girl?
How can she help us?
Maybe she can't help us. But we can help her.

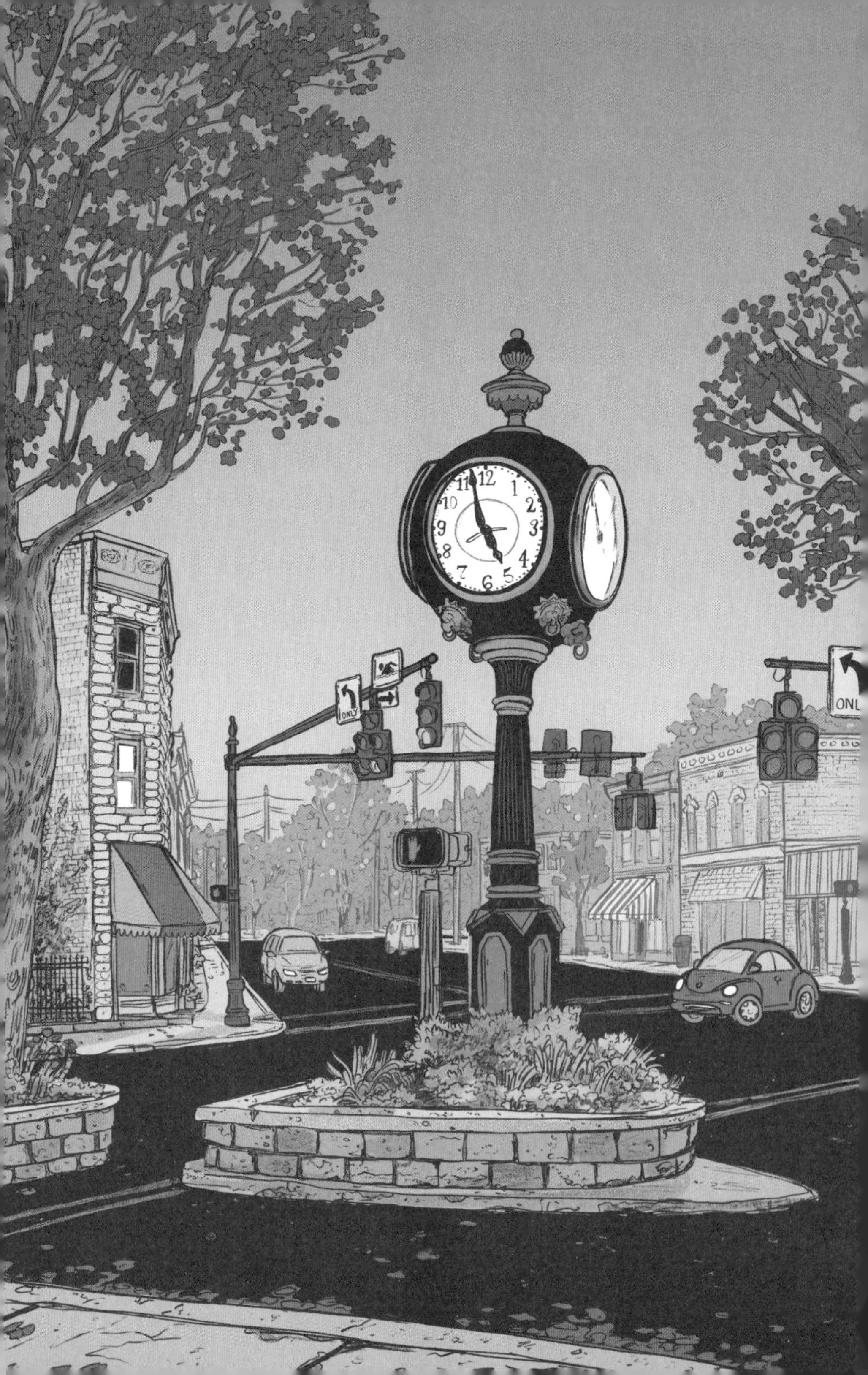
ONLY

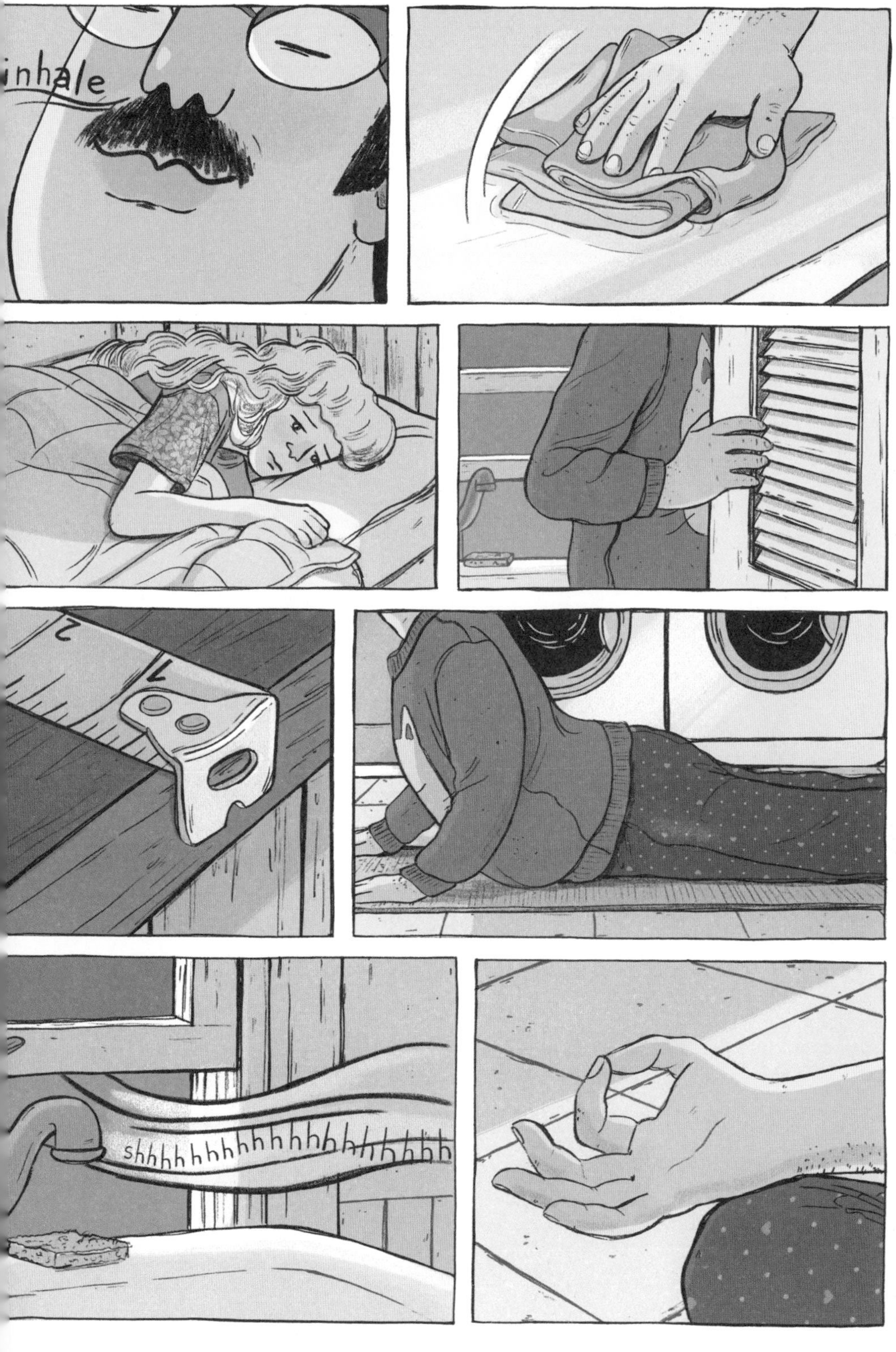
inhale
shhhhhhhhhhhhhhhhhh

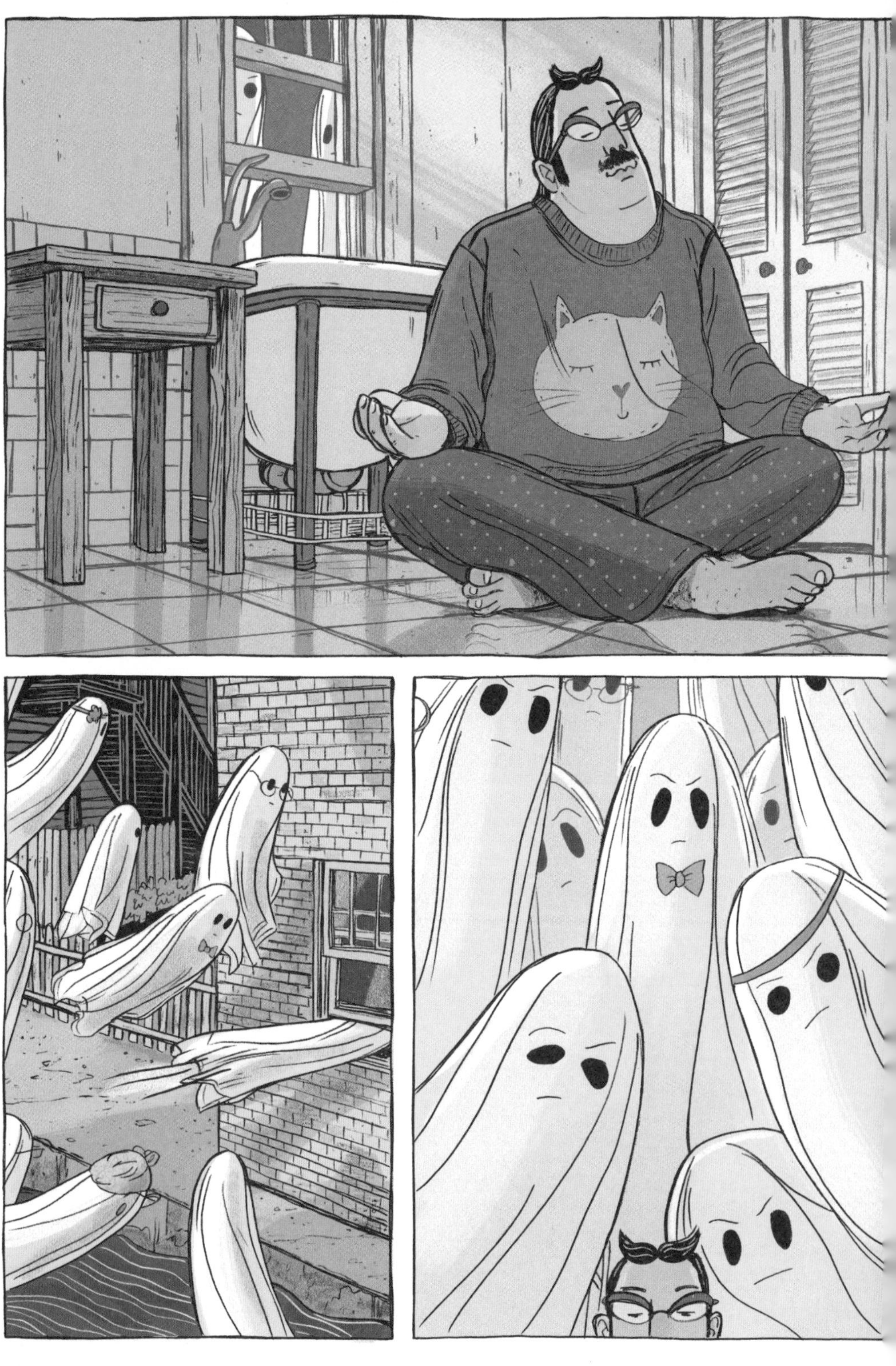

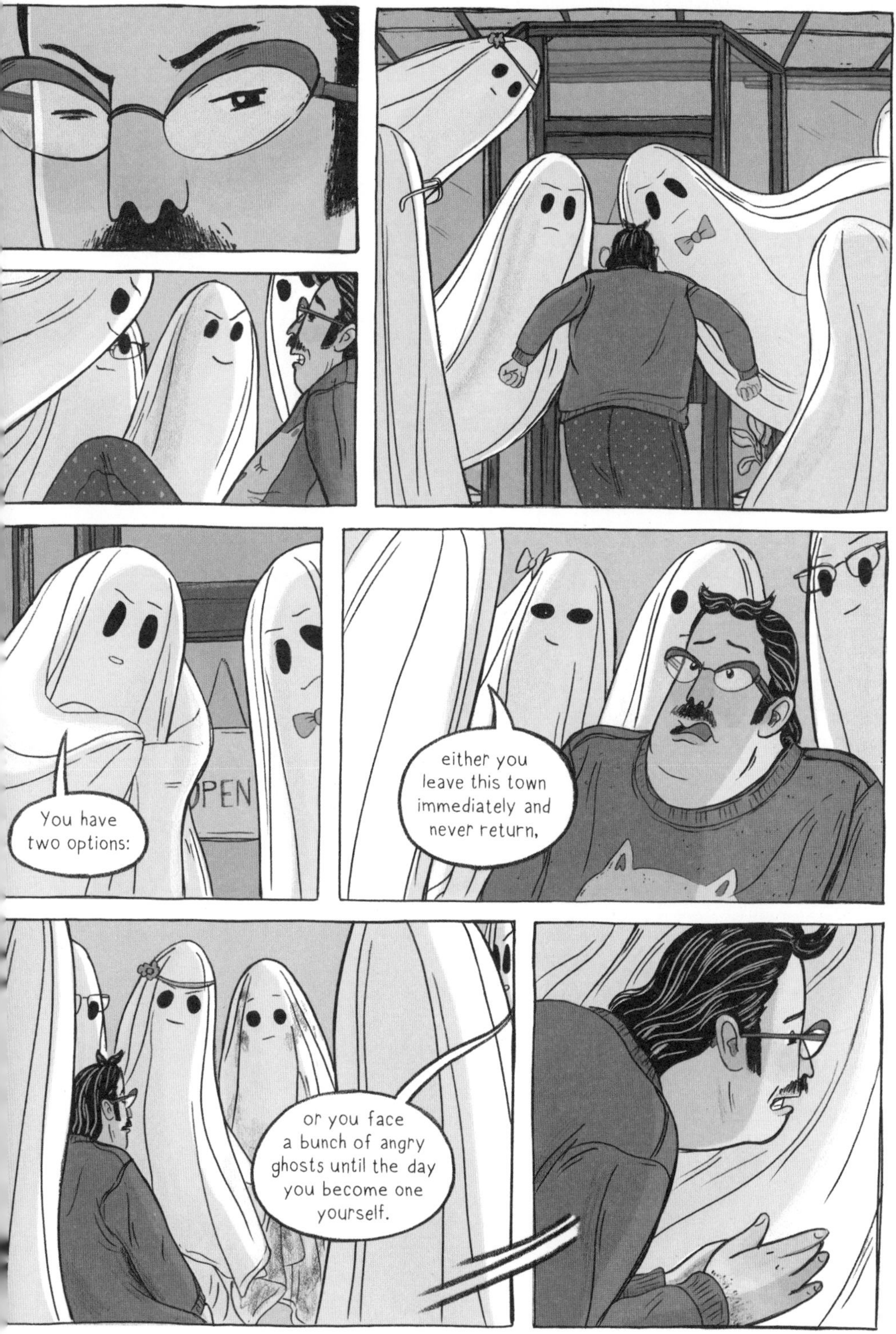
OPEN
You have two options:
either you leave this town immediately and never return,
or you face a bunch of angry ghosts until the day you become one yourself.

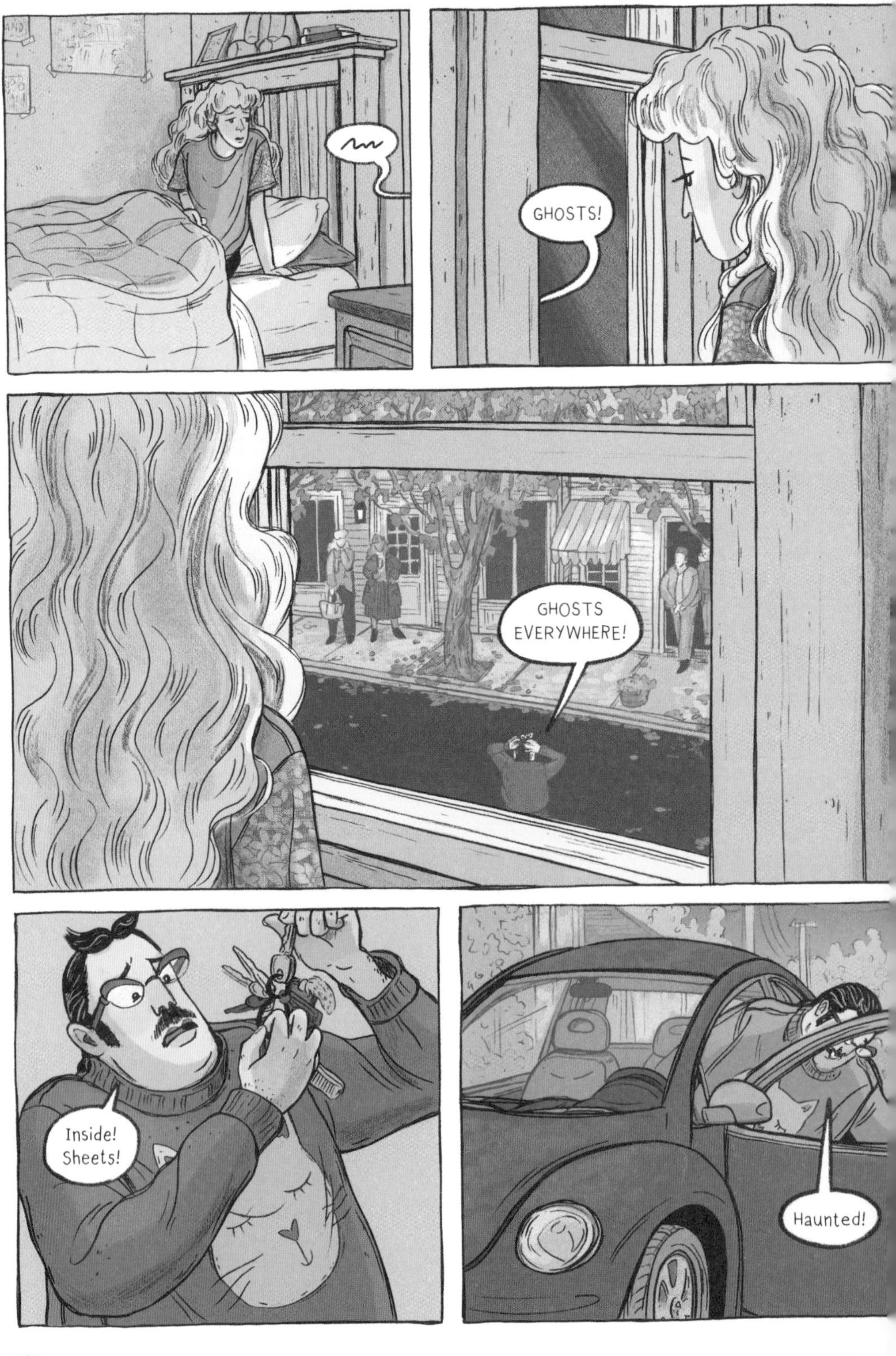
GHOSTS!
GHOSTS EVERYWHERE!
Inside! Sheets!
Haunted!

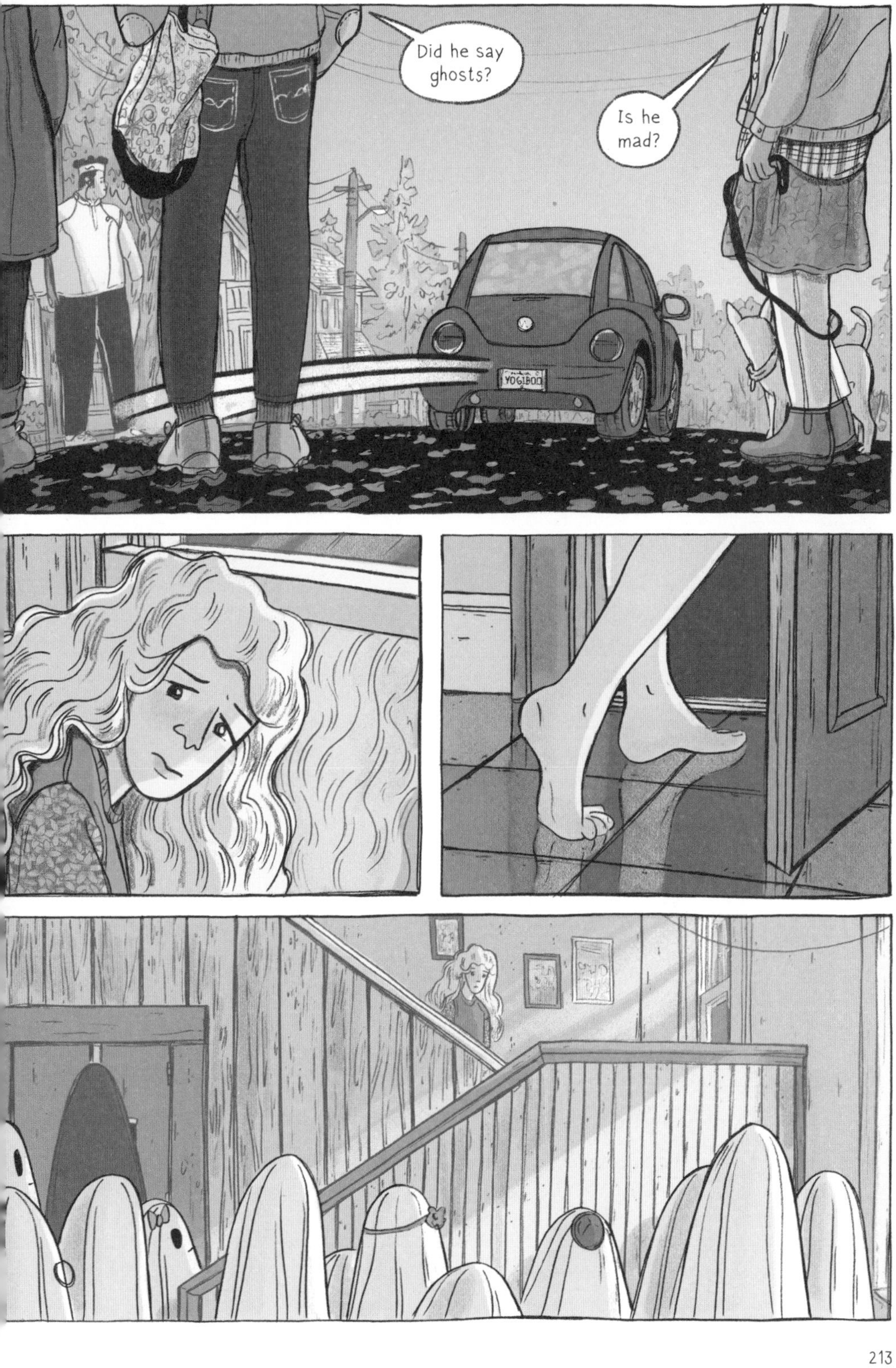
Did he say ghosts?
Is he mad?
YOGIBOO

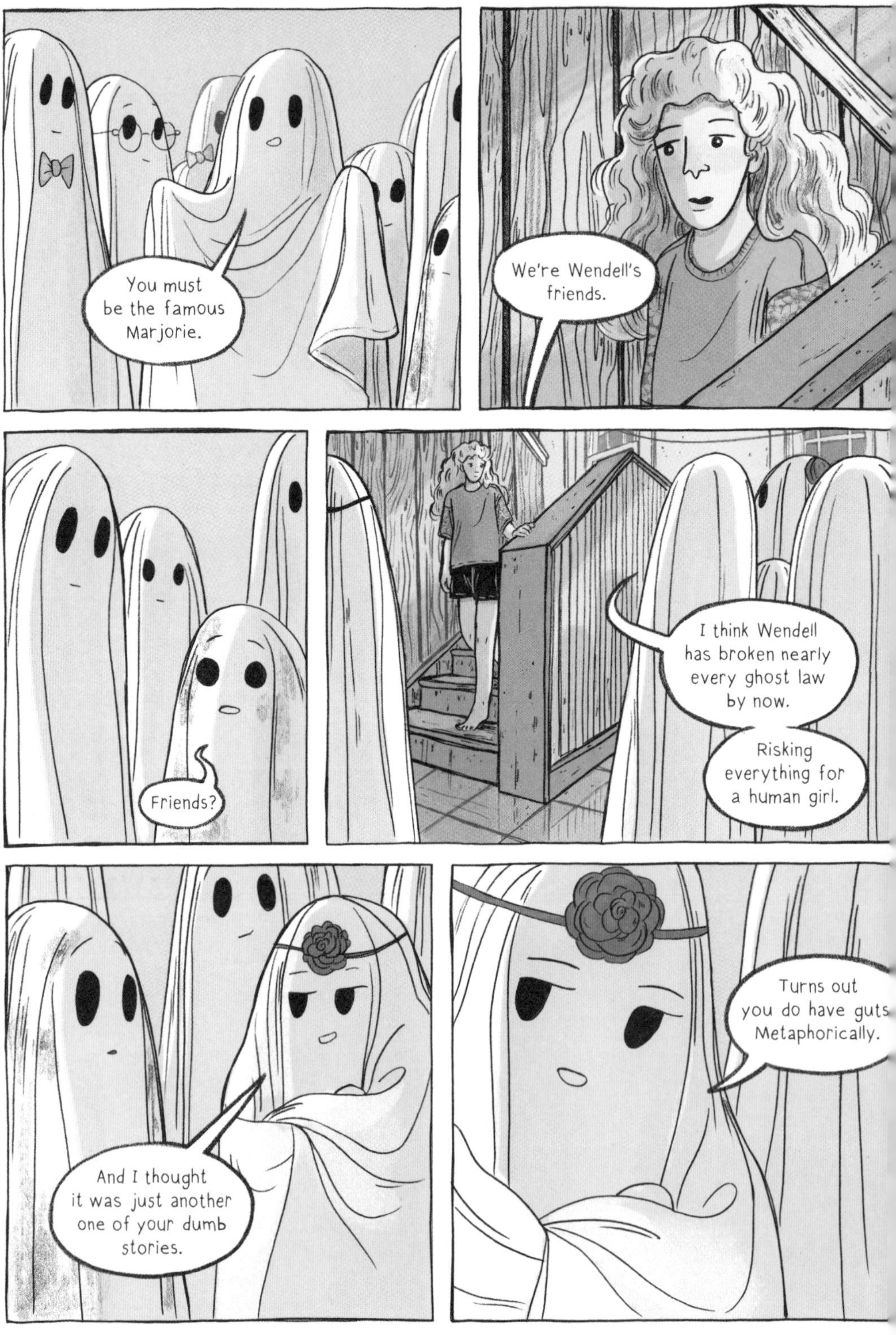
You must be the famous Marjorie.
We're Wendell's friends.
Friends?
I think Wendell has broken nearly every ghost law by now.
Risking everything for a human girl.
And I thought it was just another one of your dumb stories.
Turns out you do have guts Metaphorically.

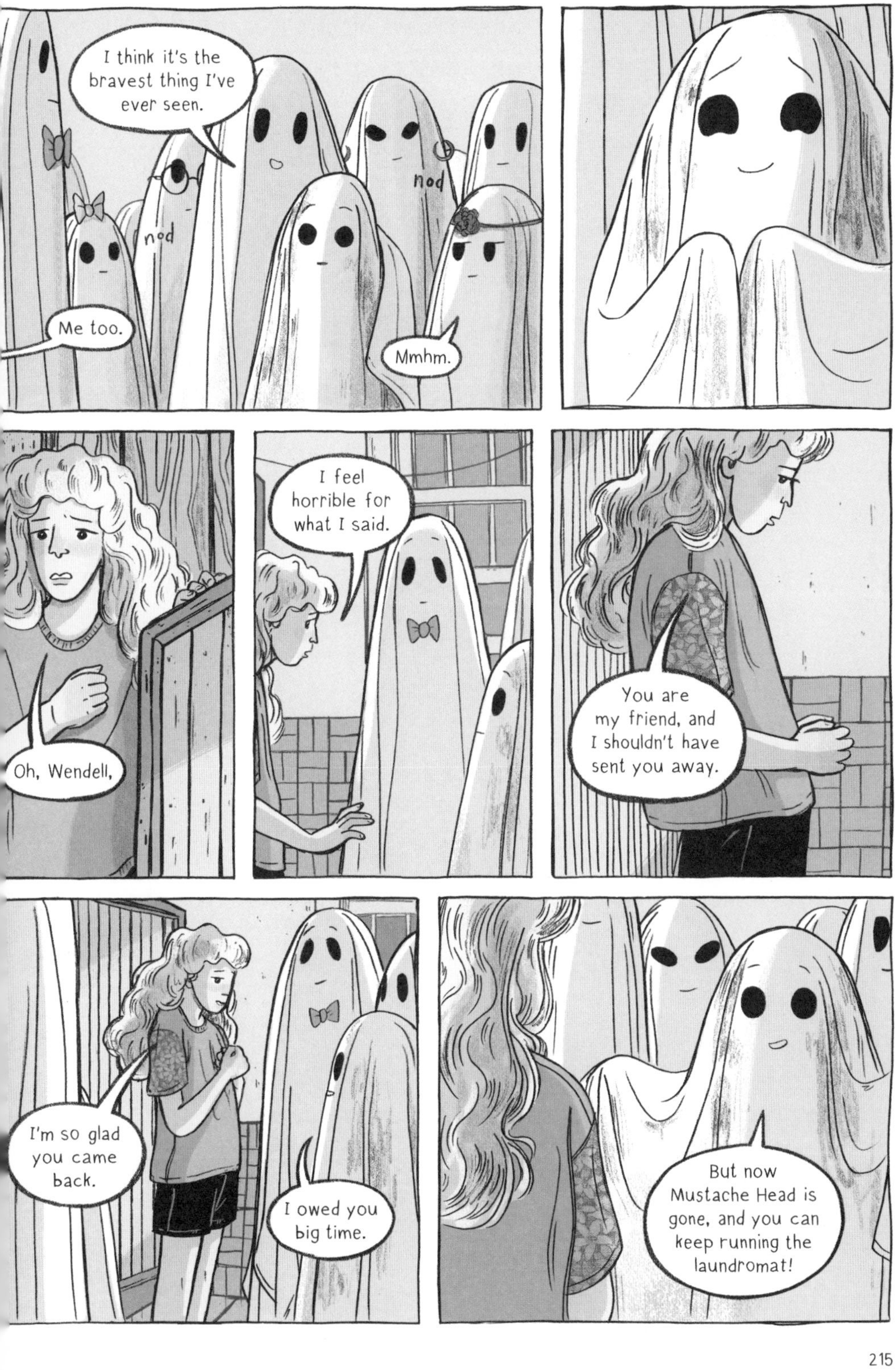
I think it's the bravest thing I've ever seen.
nod
nod
Me too.
Mmhm.
Oh, Wendell,
I feel horrible for what I said.
You are my friend, and I shouldn't have sent you away.
I'm so glad you came back.
I owed you big time.
But now Mustache Head is gone, and you can keep running the laundromat!

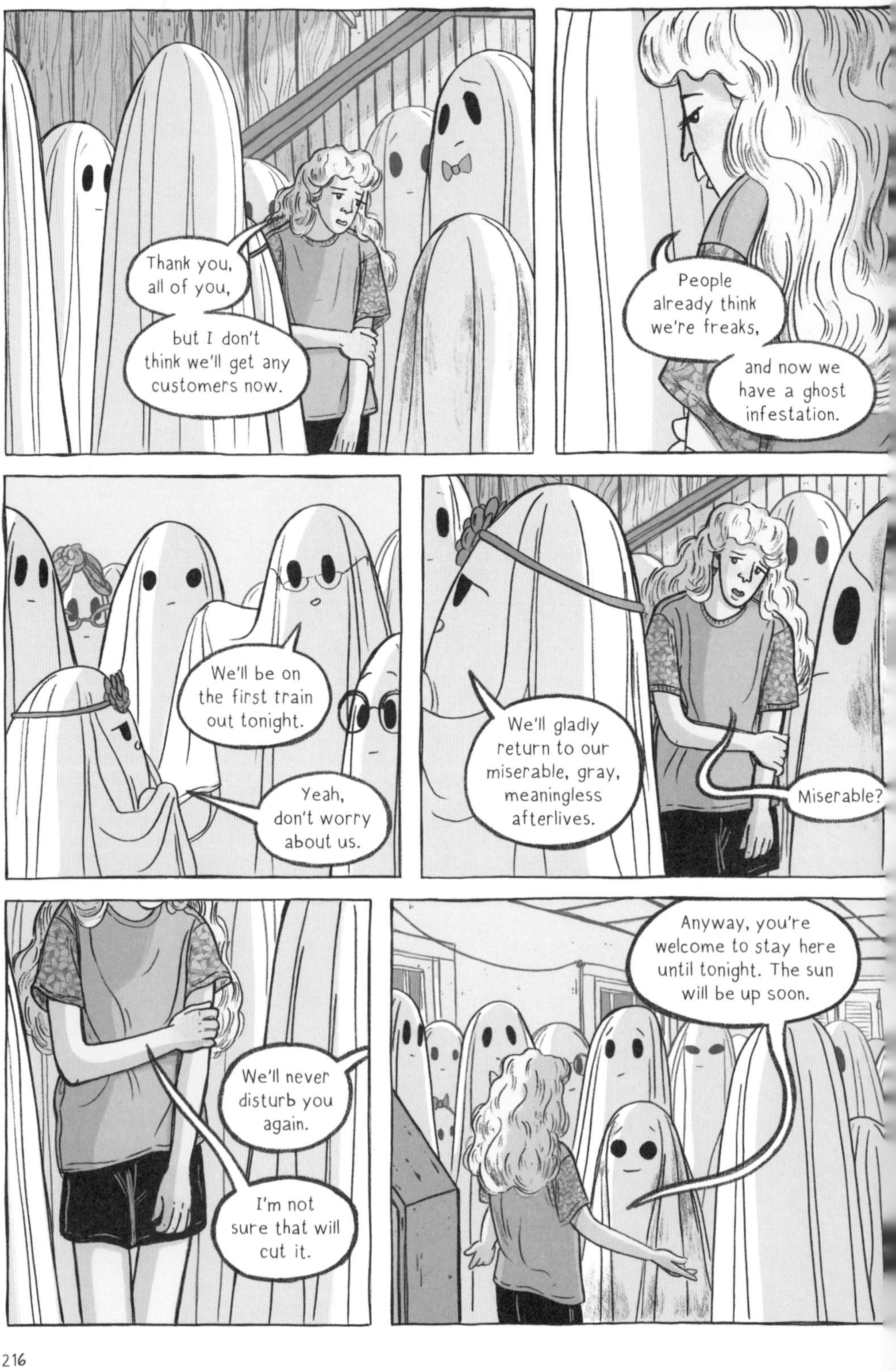
Thank you, all of you,
but I don't think we'll get any customers now.
People already think we're freaks,
and now we have a ghost infestation.
We'll be on the first train out tonight.
Yeah, don't worry about us.
We'll gladly return to our miserable, gray, meaningless afterlives.
Miserable?
We'll never disturb you again.
I'm not sure that will cut it.
Anyway, you're welcome to stay here until tonight. The sun will be up soon.

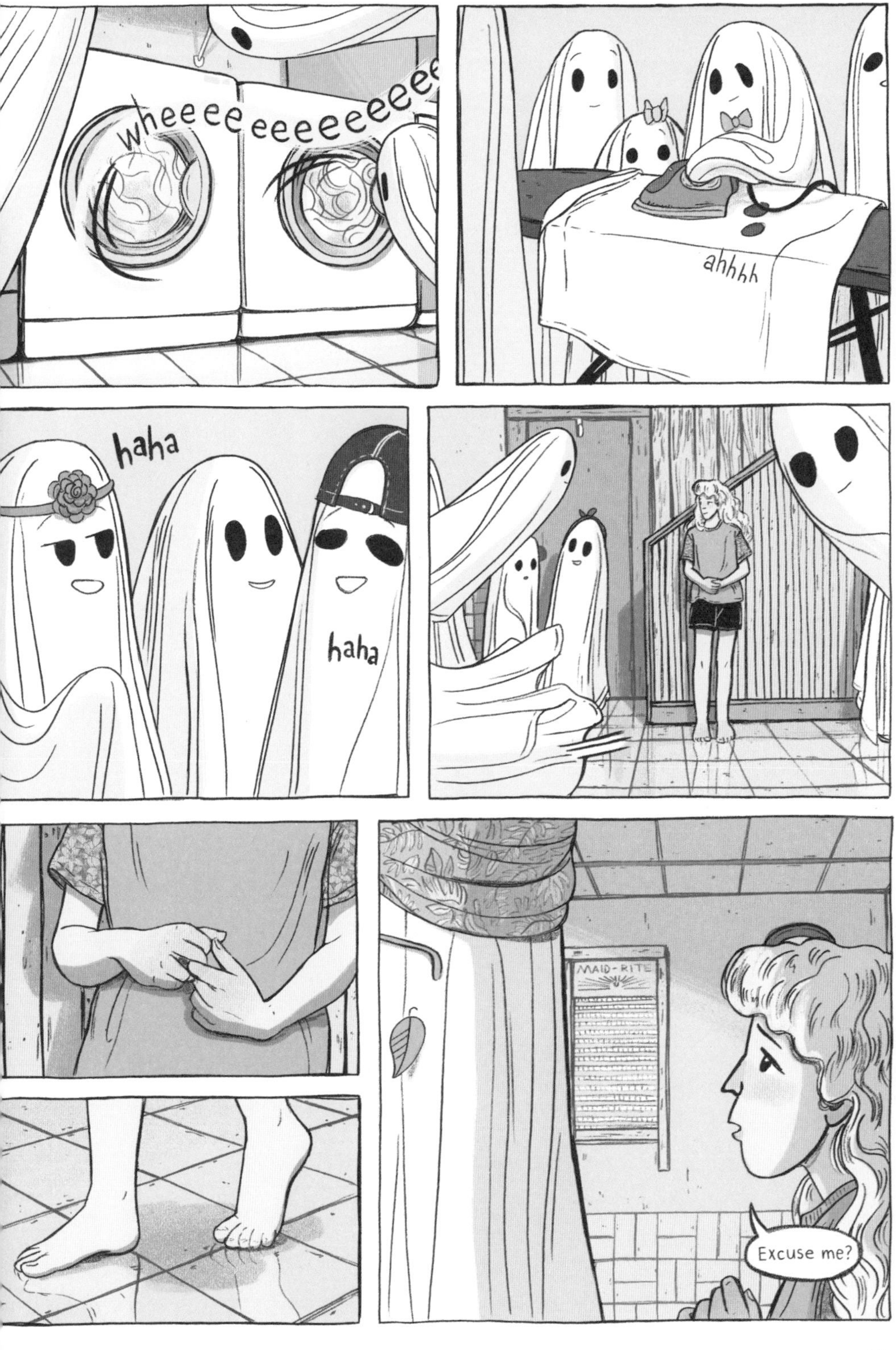
wheeeeeeeeeeeeeee
ahhhh
haha
haha
MAID-RITE
Excuse me?

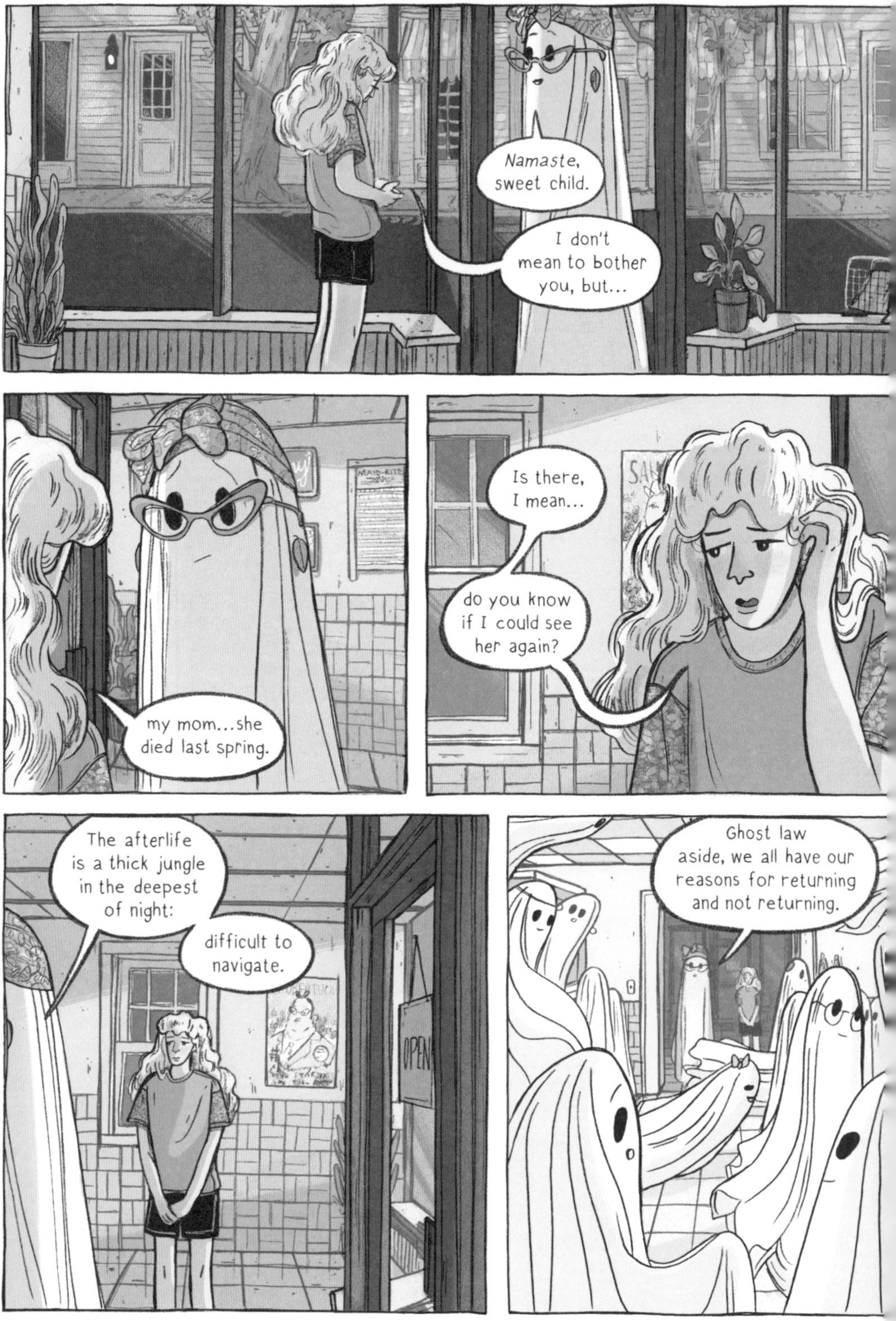
Namaste, sweet child.
I don't mean to bother you, but...
my mom...she died last spring.
Is there, I mean...
do you know if I could see her again?
The afterlife is a thick jungle in the deepest of night:
difficult to navigate.
OPEN
Ghost law aside, we all have our reasons for returning and not returning.

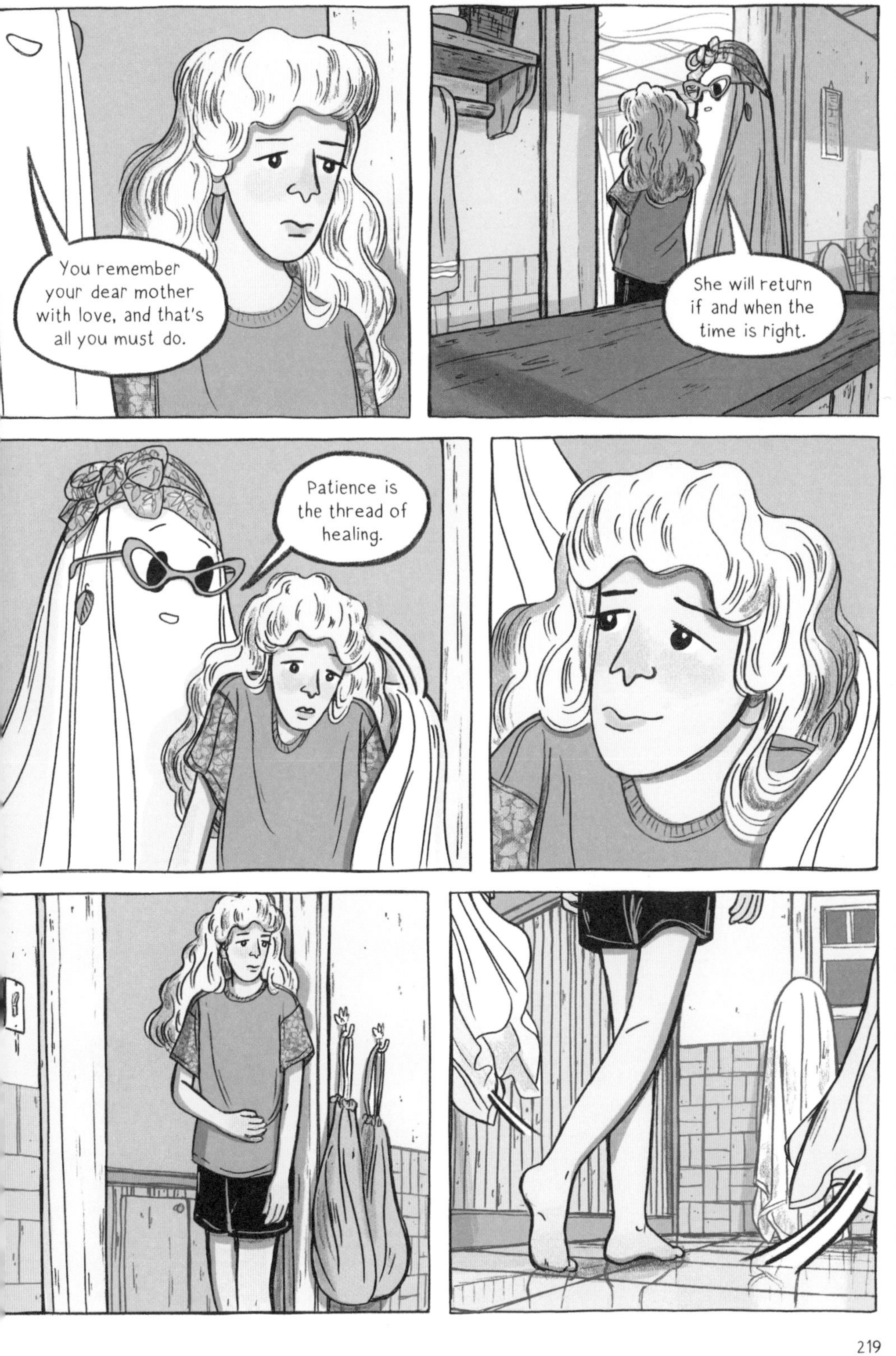
You remember your dear mother with love, and that's all you must do.
She will return if and when the time is right.
Patience is the thread of healing.

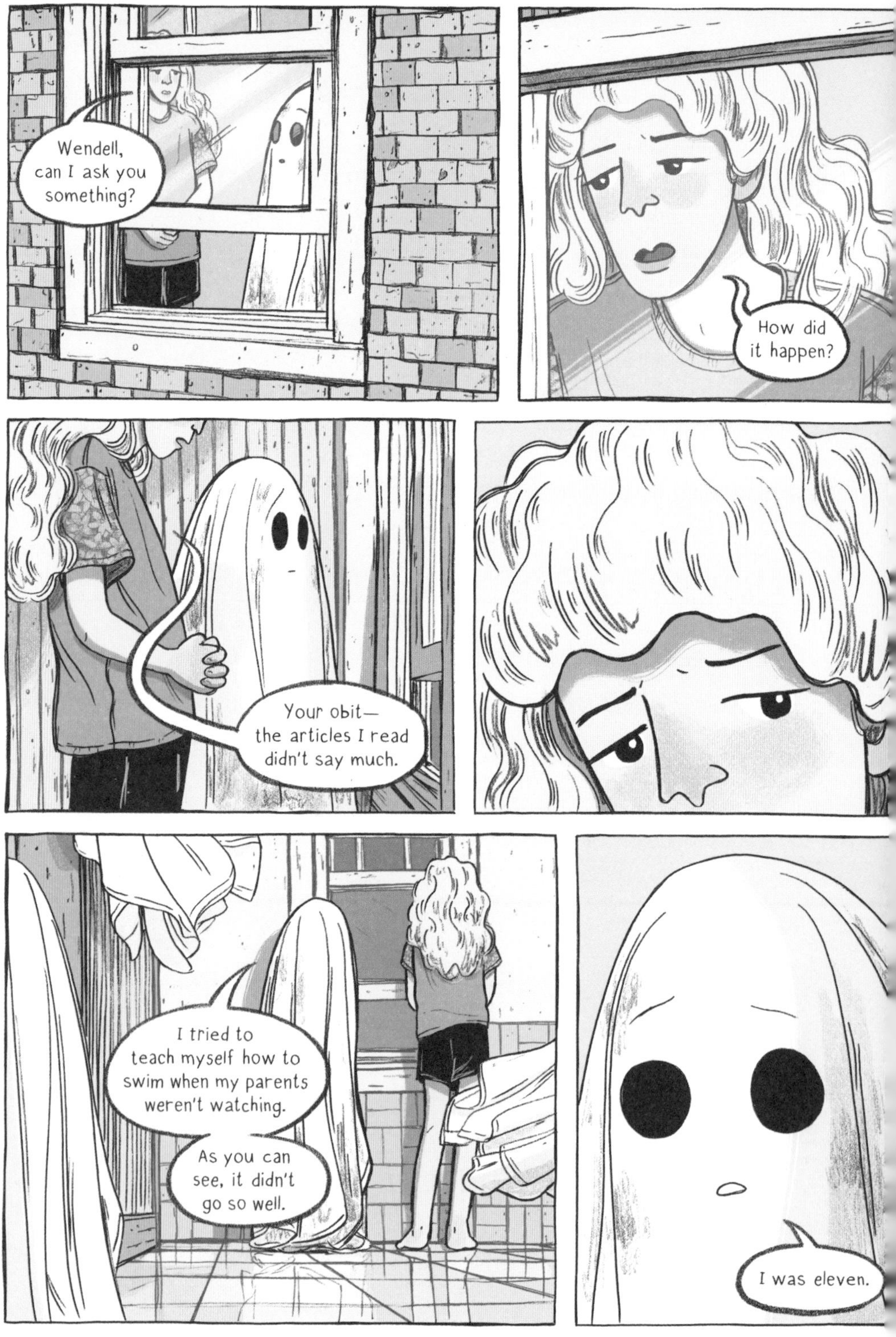
Wendell, can I ask you something?
How did it happen?
Your obit— the articles I read didn't say much.
I tried to teach myself how to swim when my parents weren't watching.
As you can see, it didn't go so well.
I was eleven.

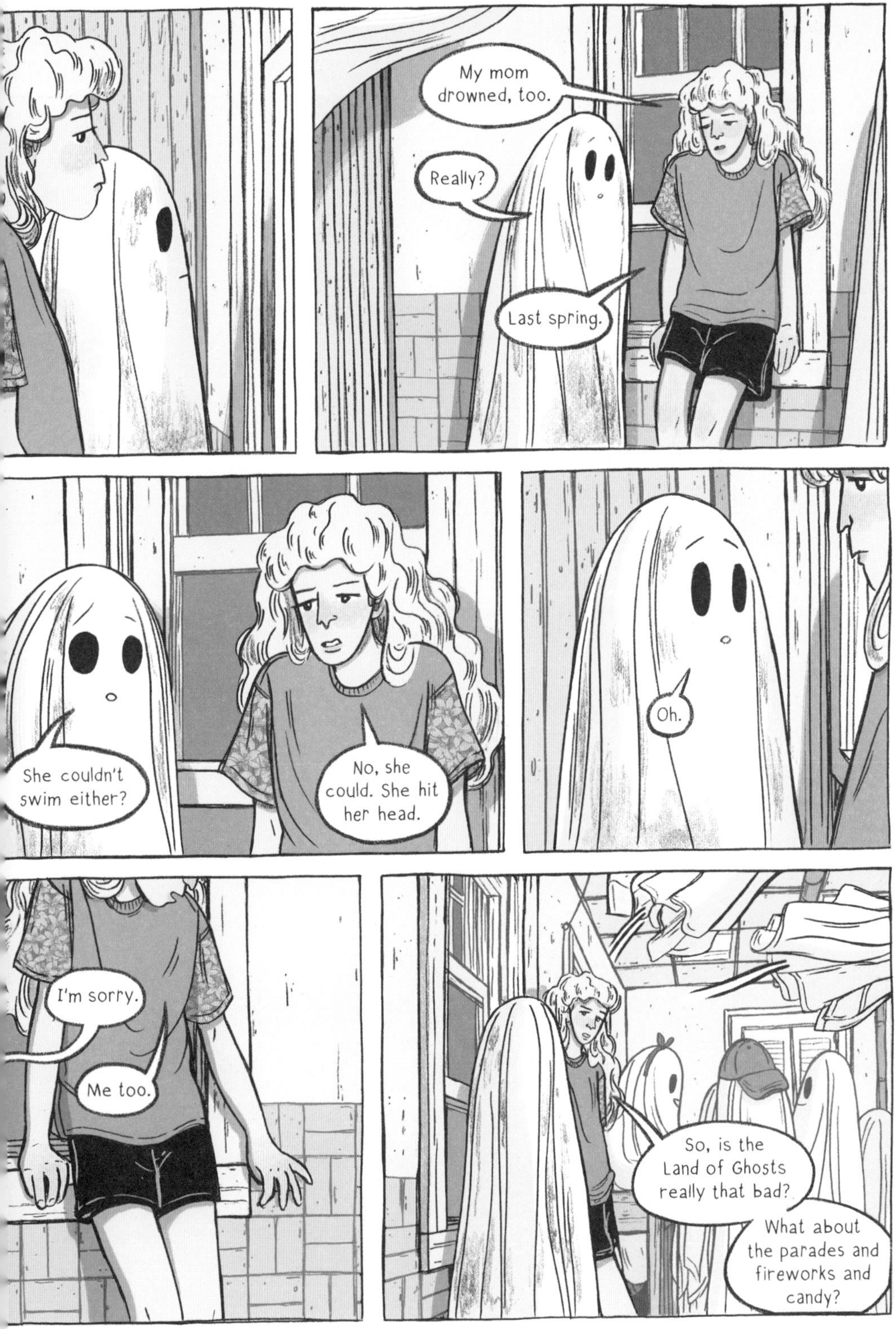
My mom drowned, too.
Really?
Last spring.
She couldn't swim either?
No, she could. She hit her head.
Oh.
I'm sorry.
Me too.
So, is the Land of Ghosts really that bad?
What about the parades and fireworks and candy?

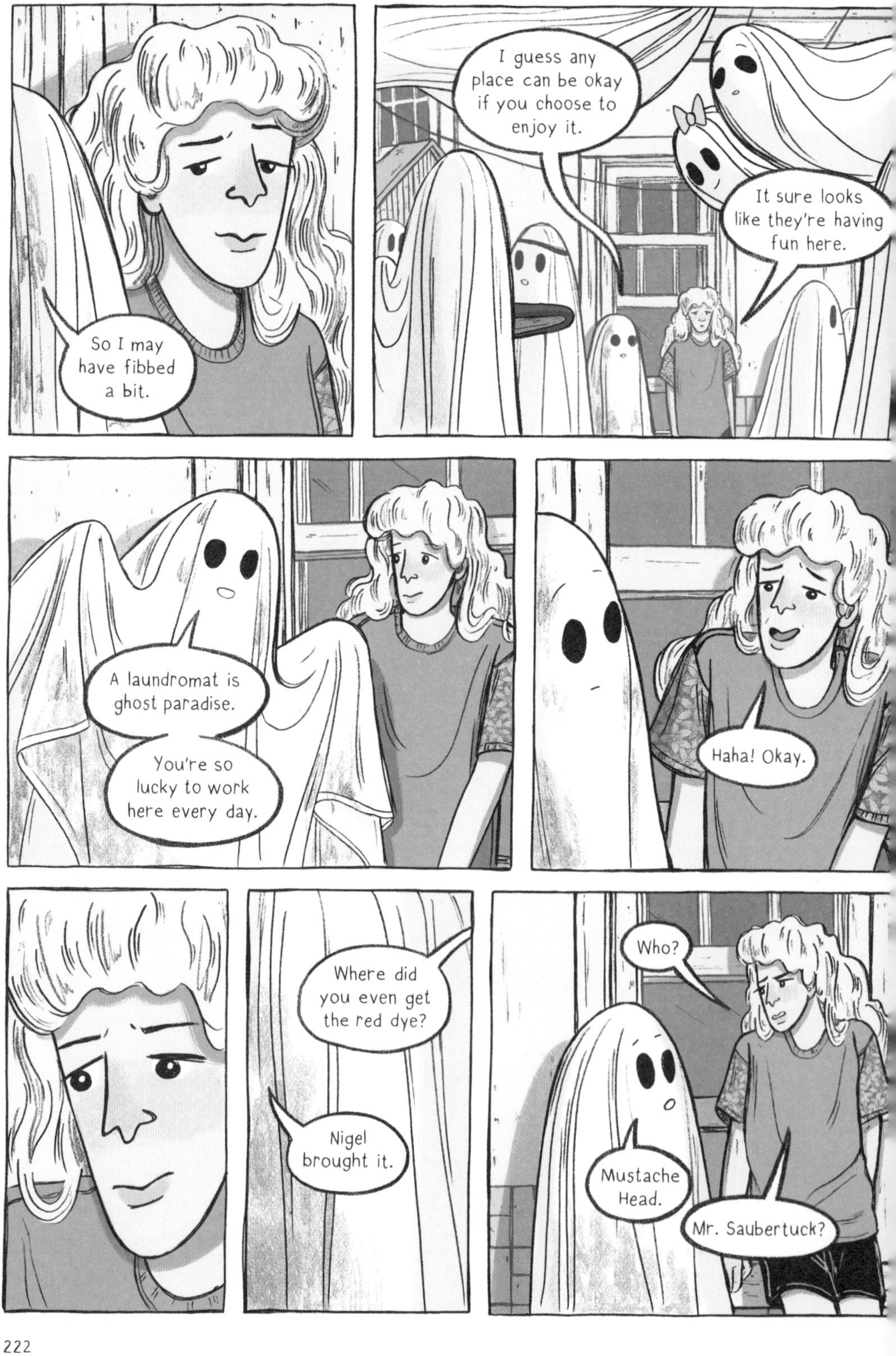
So I may have fibbed a bit.
I guess any place can be okay if you choose to enjoy it.
It sure looks like they're having fun here.
A laundromat is ghost paradise.
You're so lucky to work here every day.
Haha! Okay.
Where did you even get the red dye?
Nigel brought it.
Who?
Mustache Head.
Mr. Saubertuck?

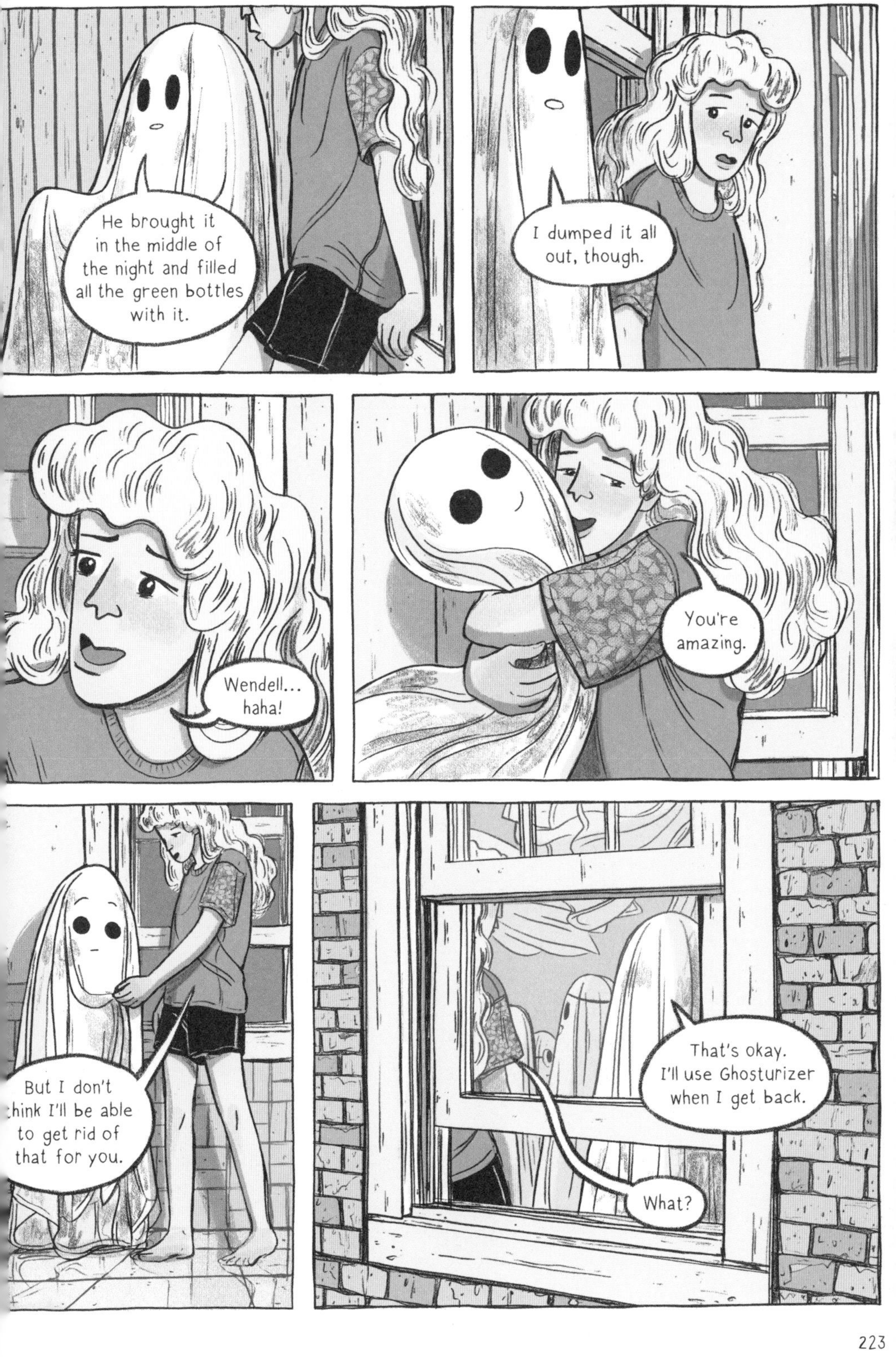
He brought it in the middle of the night and filled all the green bottles with it.
I dumped it all out, though.
Wendell... haha!
You're amazing.
But I don't think I'll be able to get rid of that for you.
That's okay. I'll use Ghosturizer when I get back.
What?

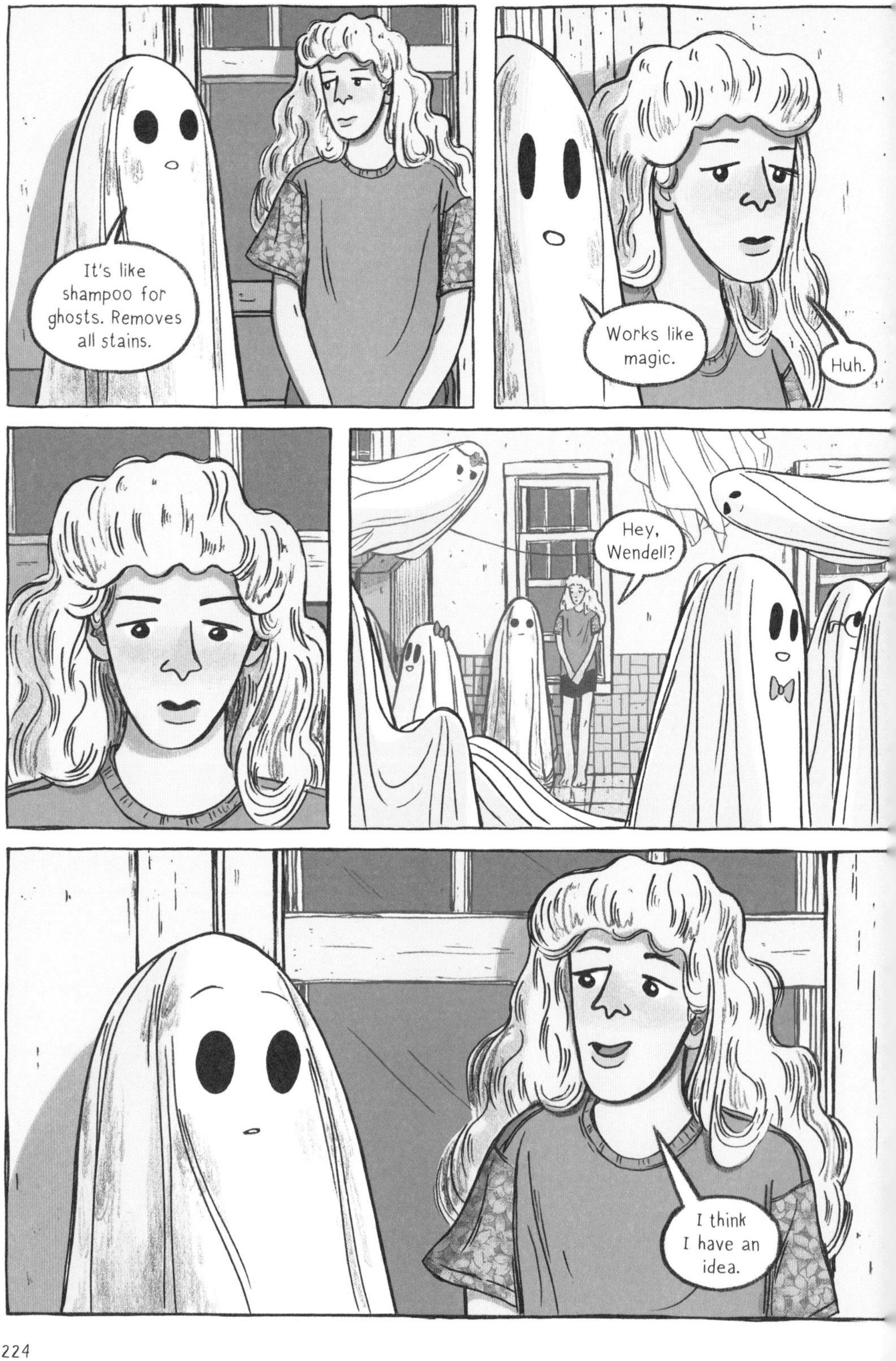
It's like shampoo for ghosts. Removes all stains.
Works like magic.
Huh.
Hey, Wendell?
I think I have an idea.

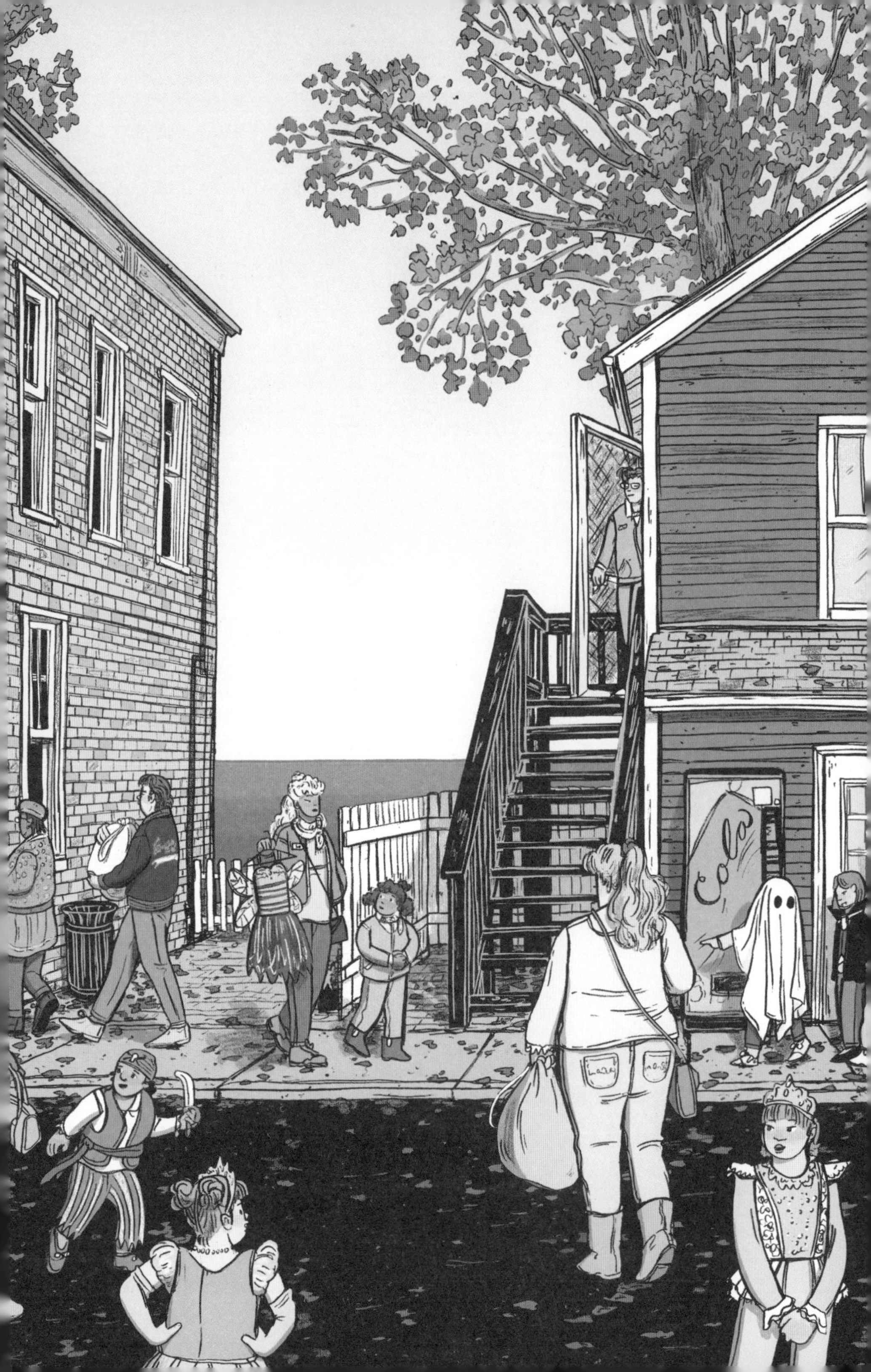
Cola

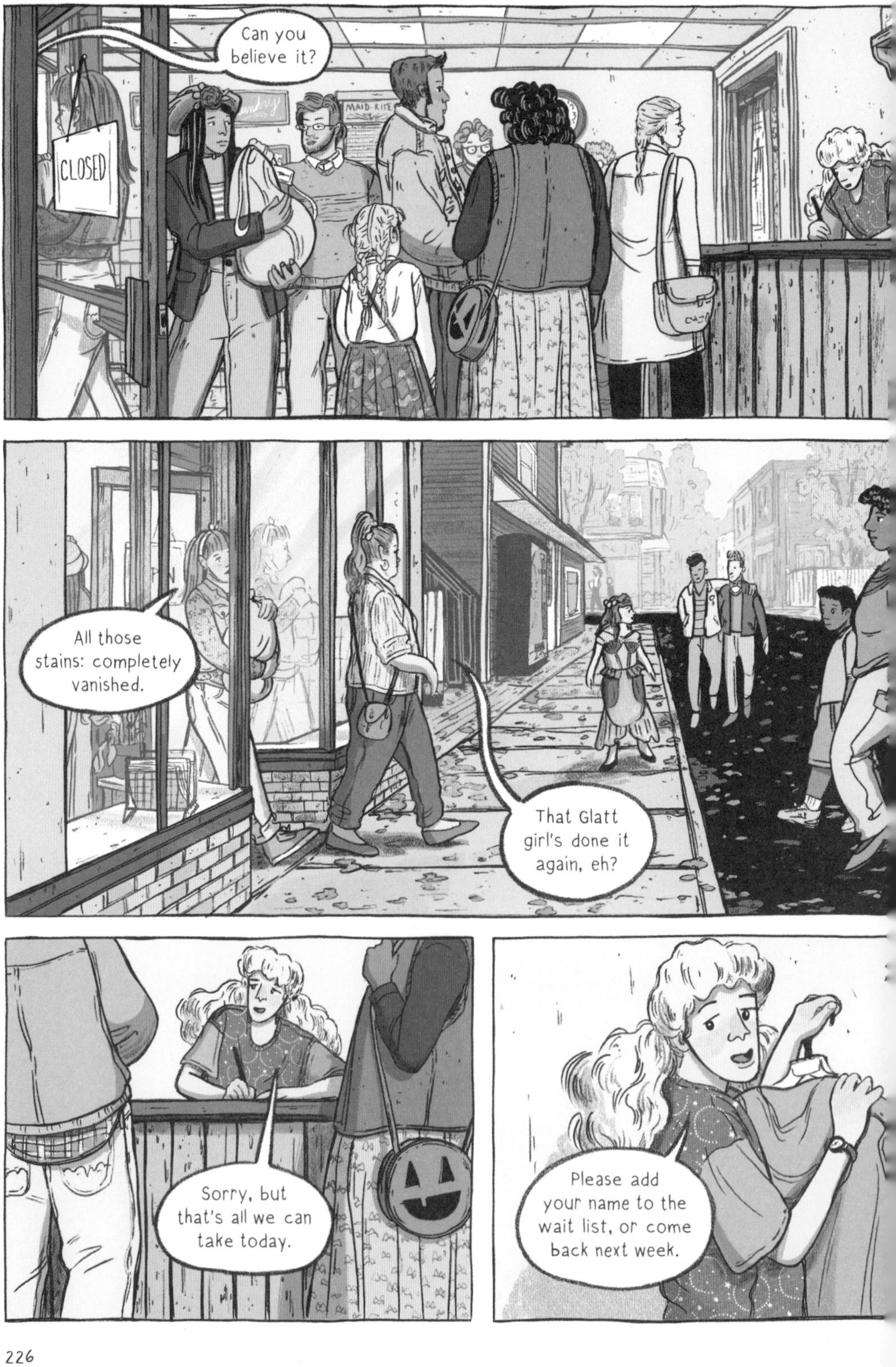
CLOSED
Can you believe it?
All those stains: completely vanished.
That Glatt girl's done it again, eh?
Sorry, but that's all we can take today.
Please add your name to the wait list, or come back next week.

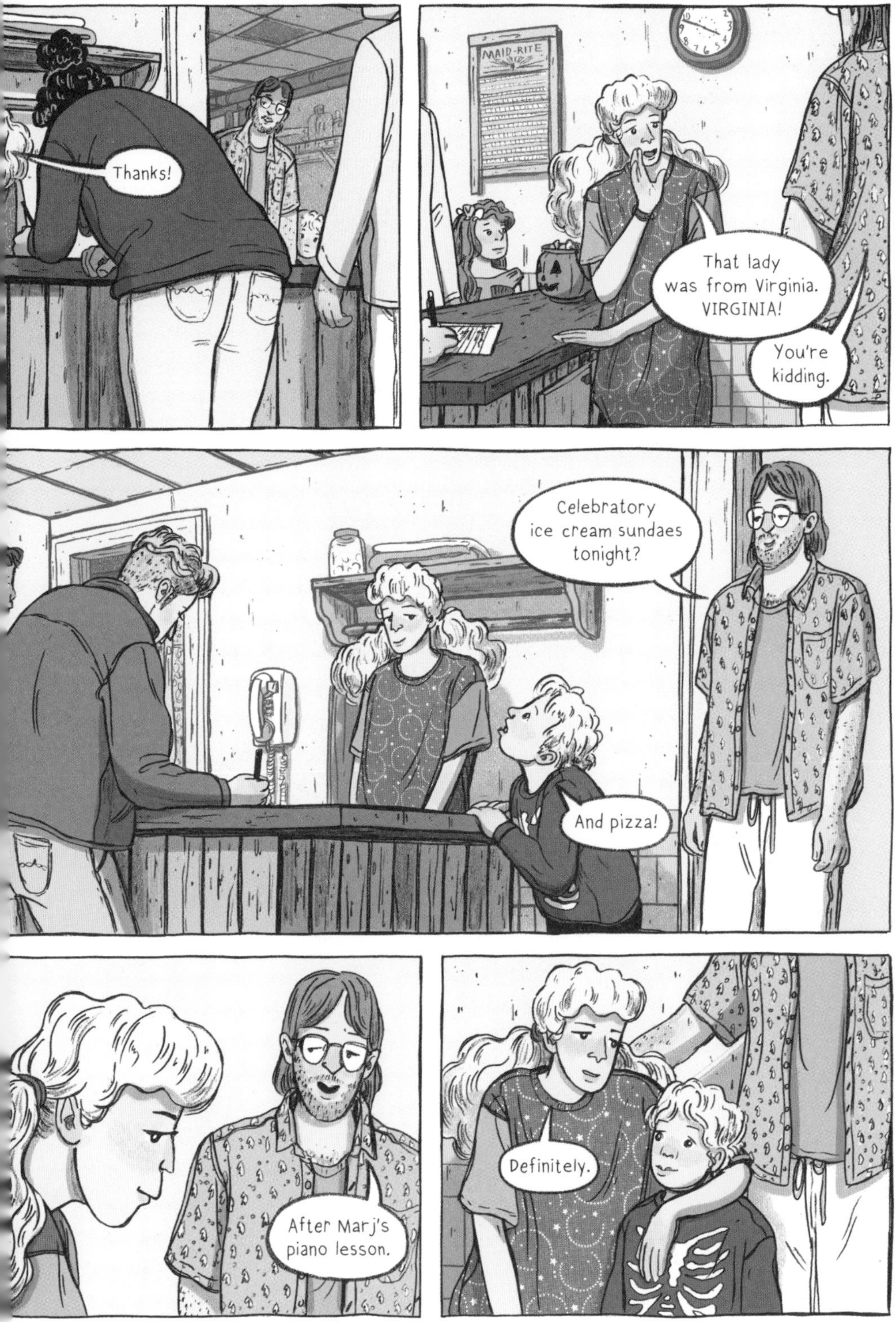
Thanks!
MAID-RITE
That lady was from Virginia. VIRGINIA!
You're kidding.
Celebratory ice cream sundaes tonight?
And pizza!
After Marj's piano lesson.
Definitely.

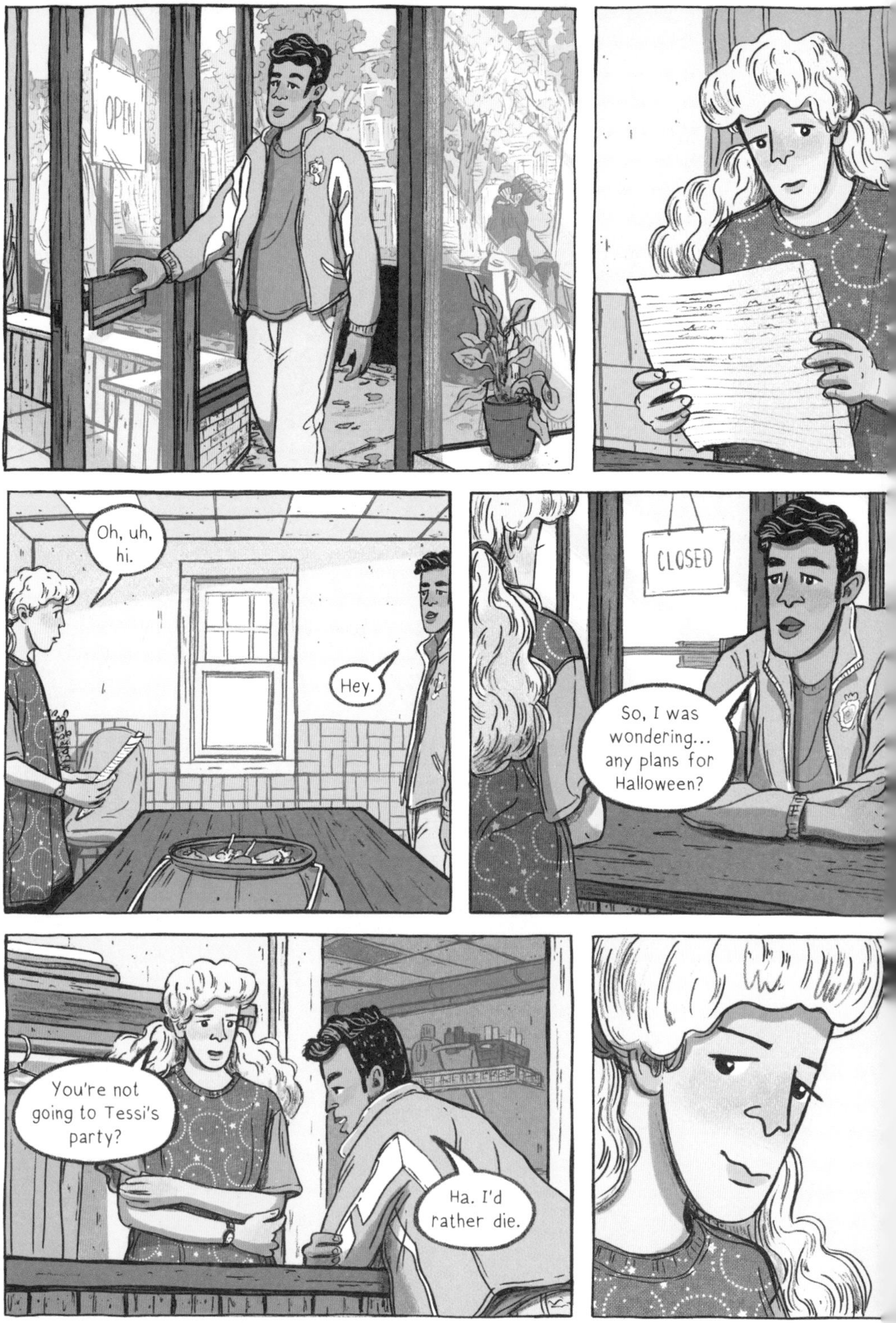
OPEN
Oh, uh, hi.
Hey.
CLOSED
So, I was wondering... any plans for Halloween?
You're not going to Tessi's party?
Ha. I'd rather die.

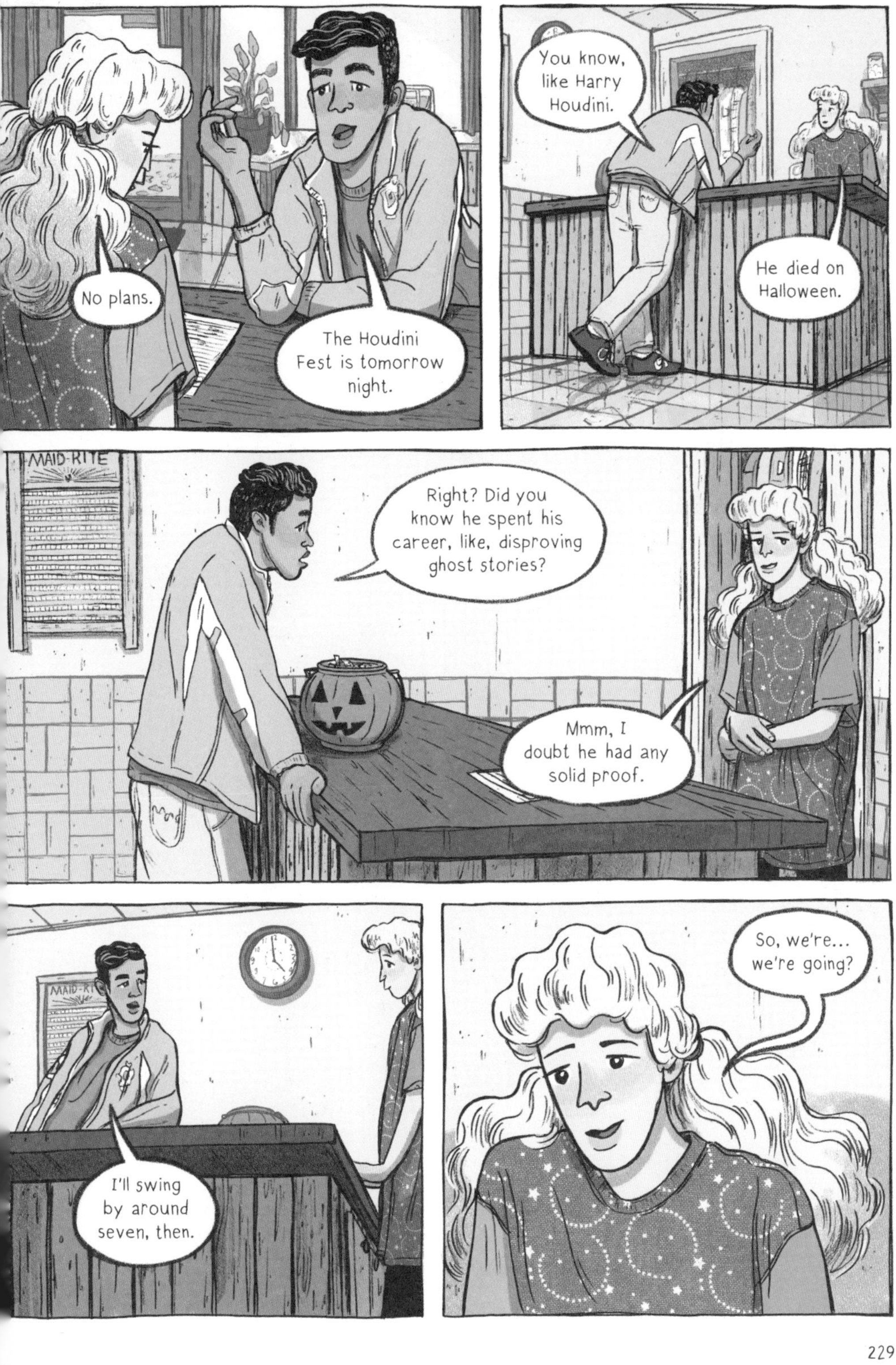
No plans.
The Houdini Fest is tomorrow night.
You know, like Harry Houdini.
He died on Halloween.
MAID-RITE
Right? Did you know he spent his career, like, disproving ghost stories?
Mmm, I doubt he had any solid proof.
I'll swing by around seven, then.
So, we're... we're going?

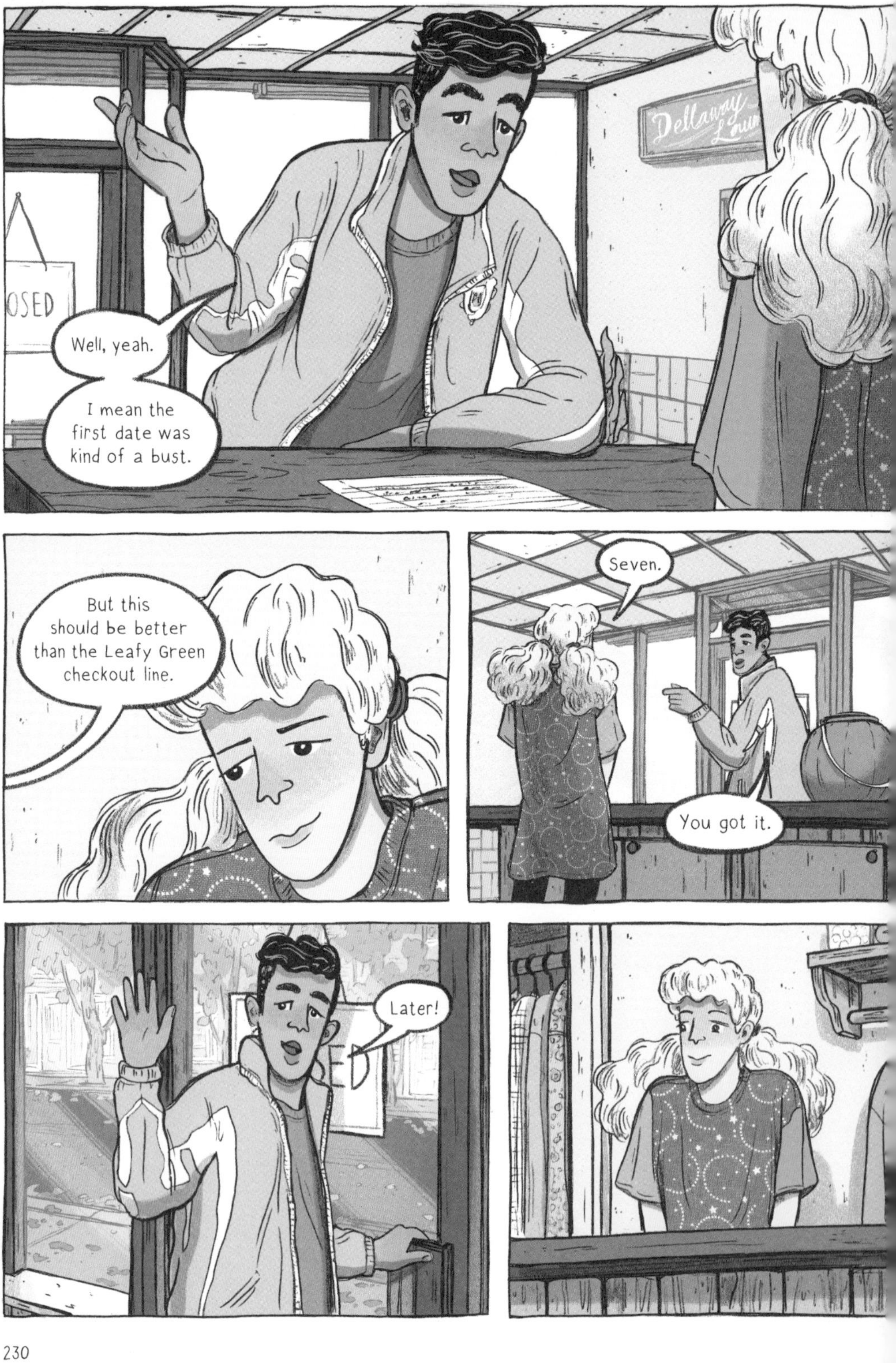
OSED
Dellaway Loun
Well, yeah.
I mean the first date was kind of a bust.
But this should be better than the Leafy Green checkout line.
Seven.
You got it.
Later!

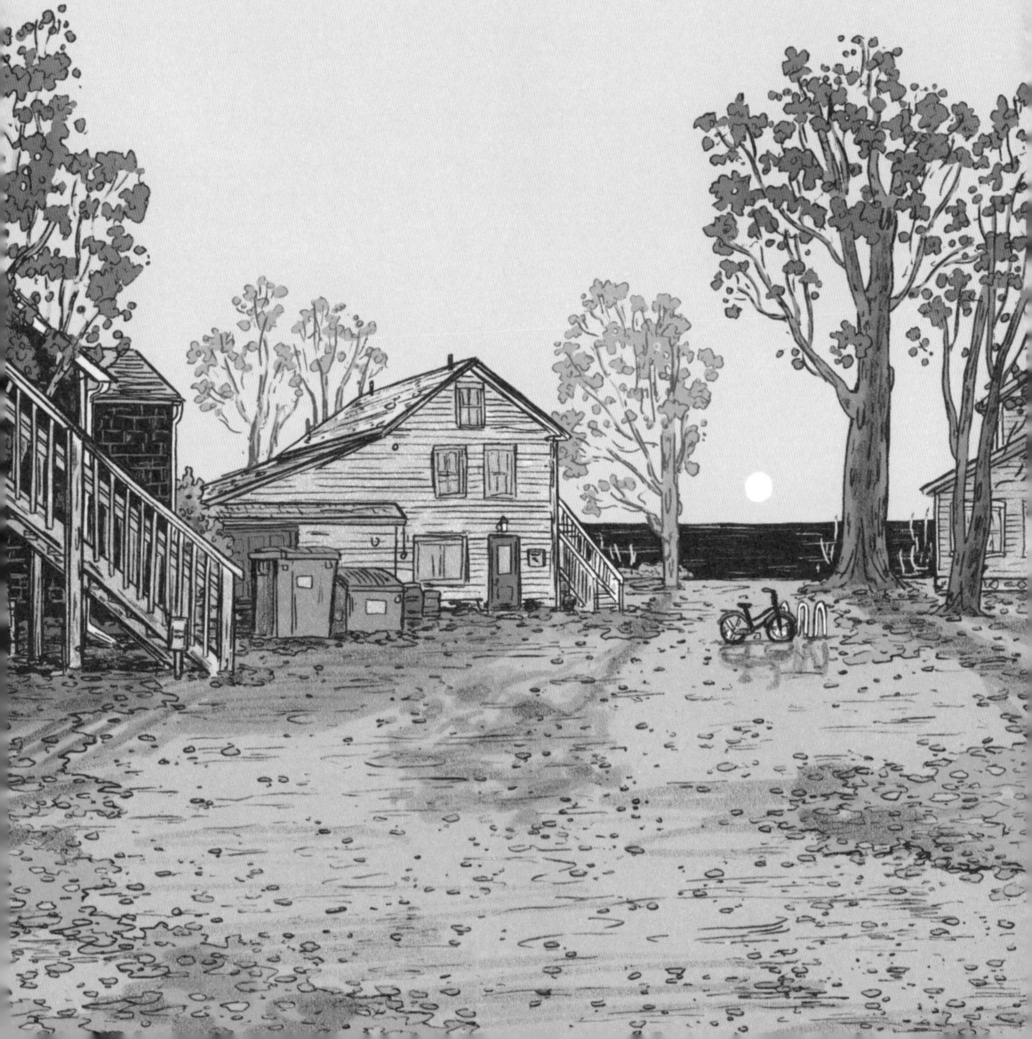

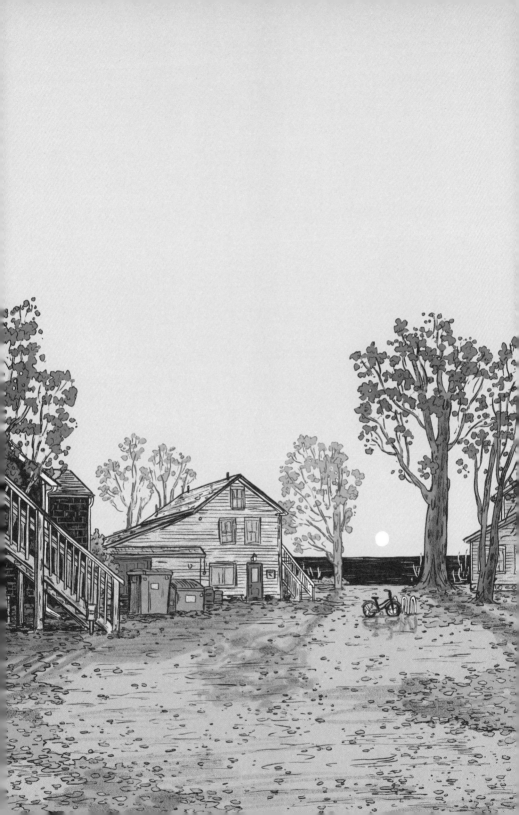

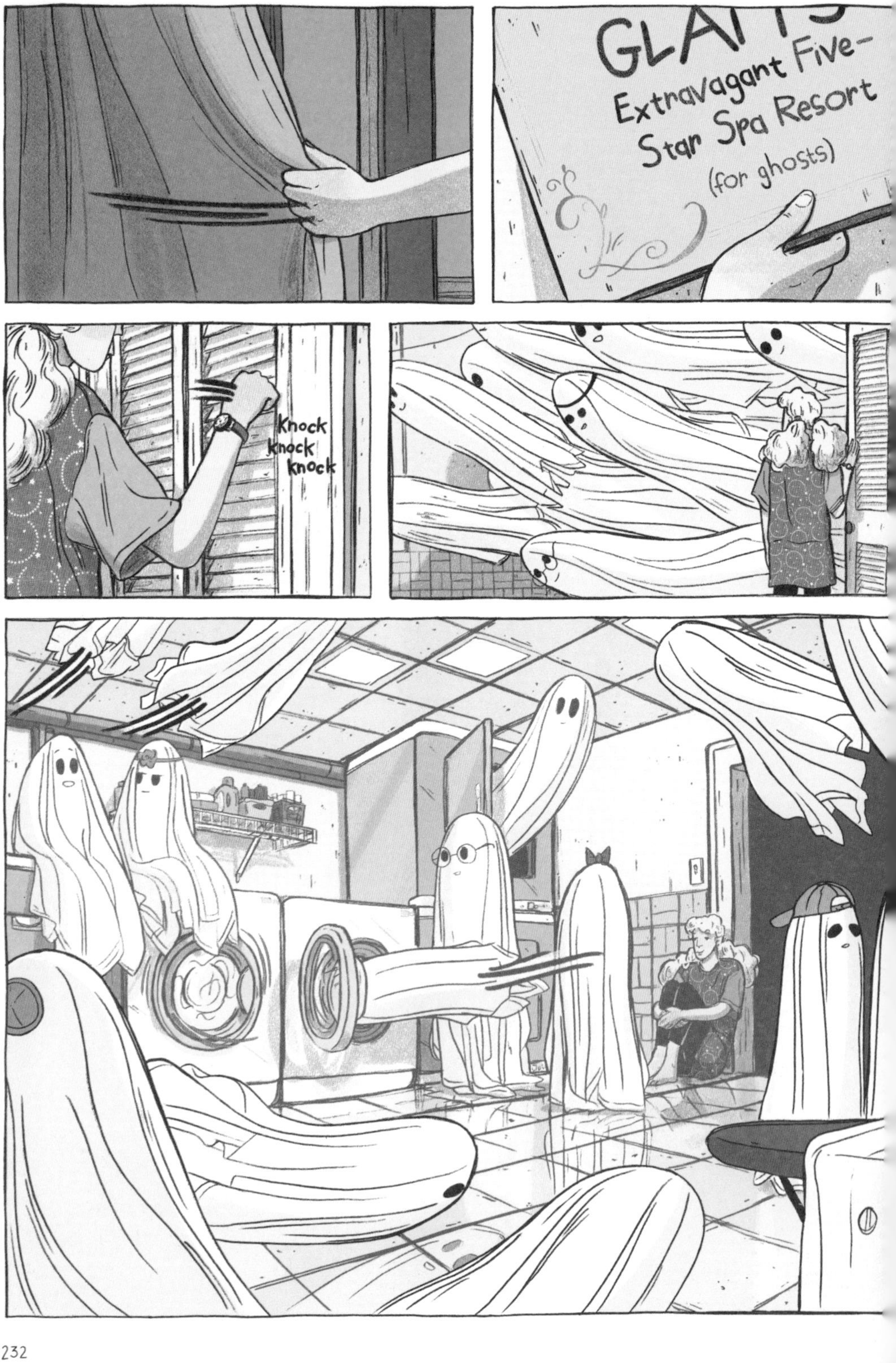
GLAM'S
Extravagant Five-Star Spa Resort
(for ghosts)
Knock
knock
knock

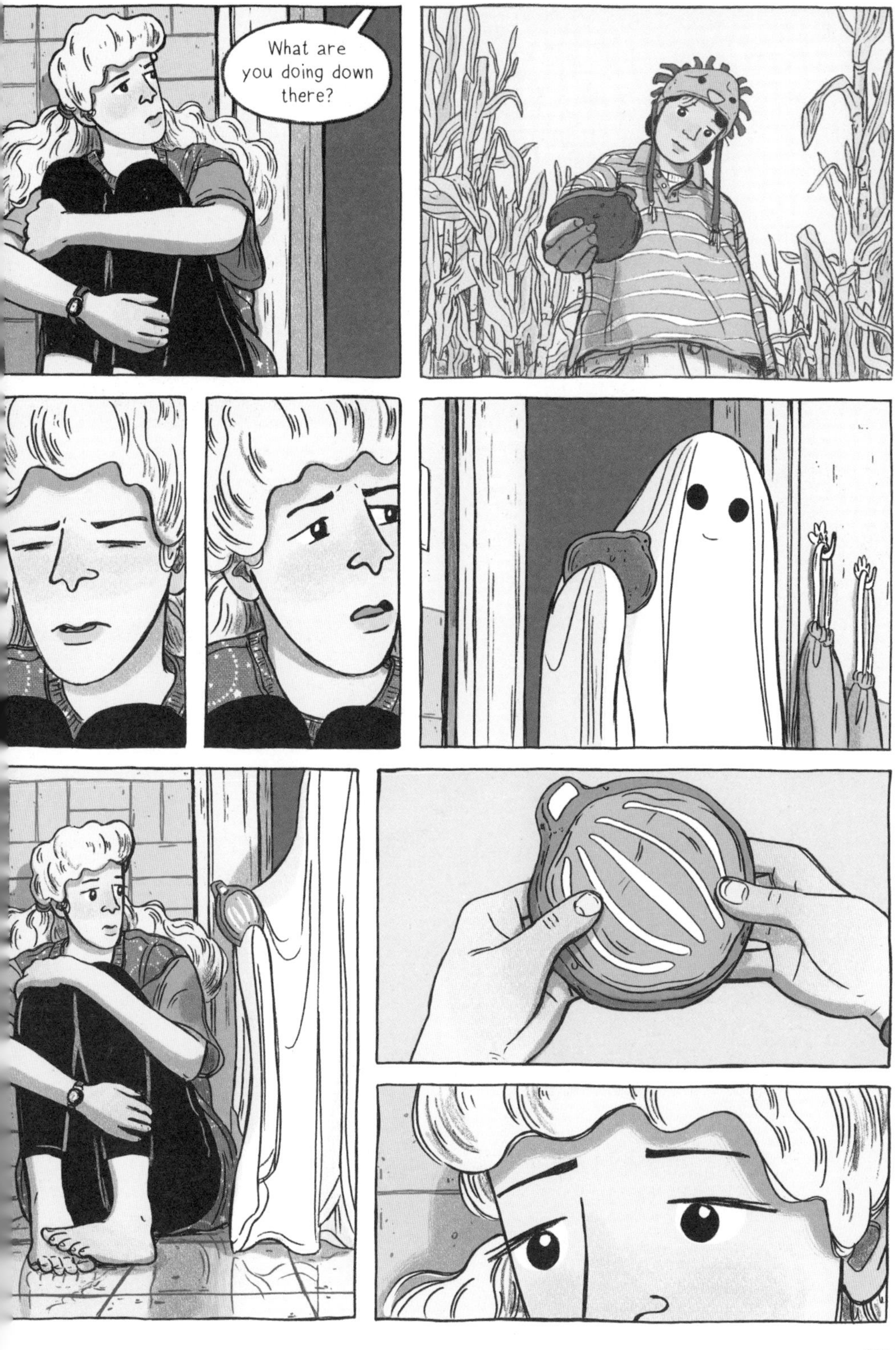
What are you doing down there?

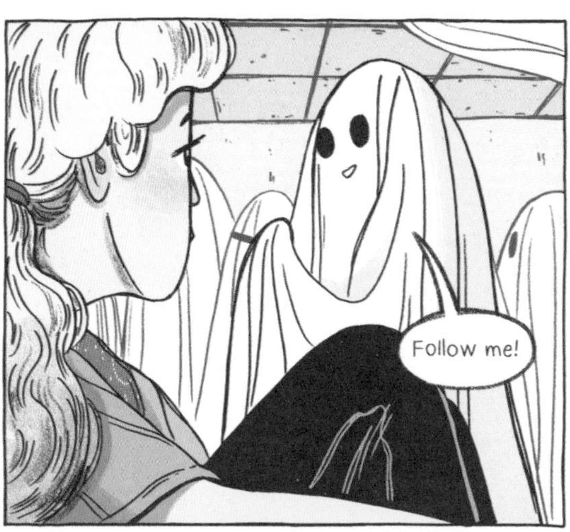
Follow me!
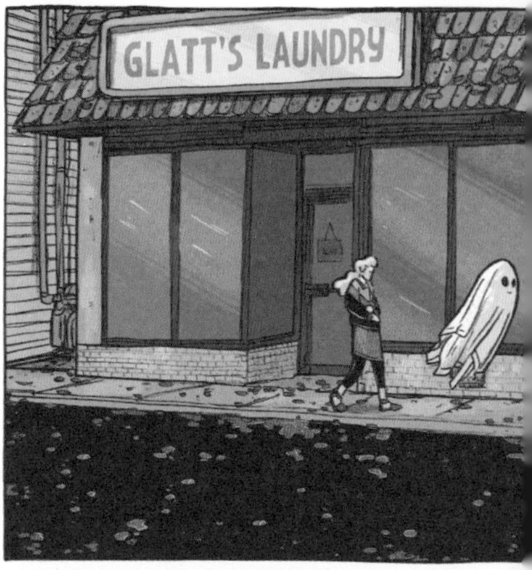
GLATT'S LAUNDRY
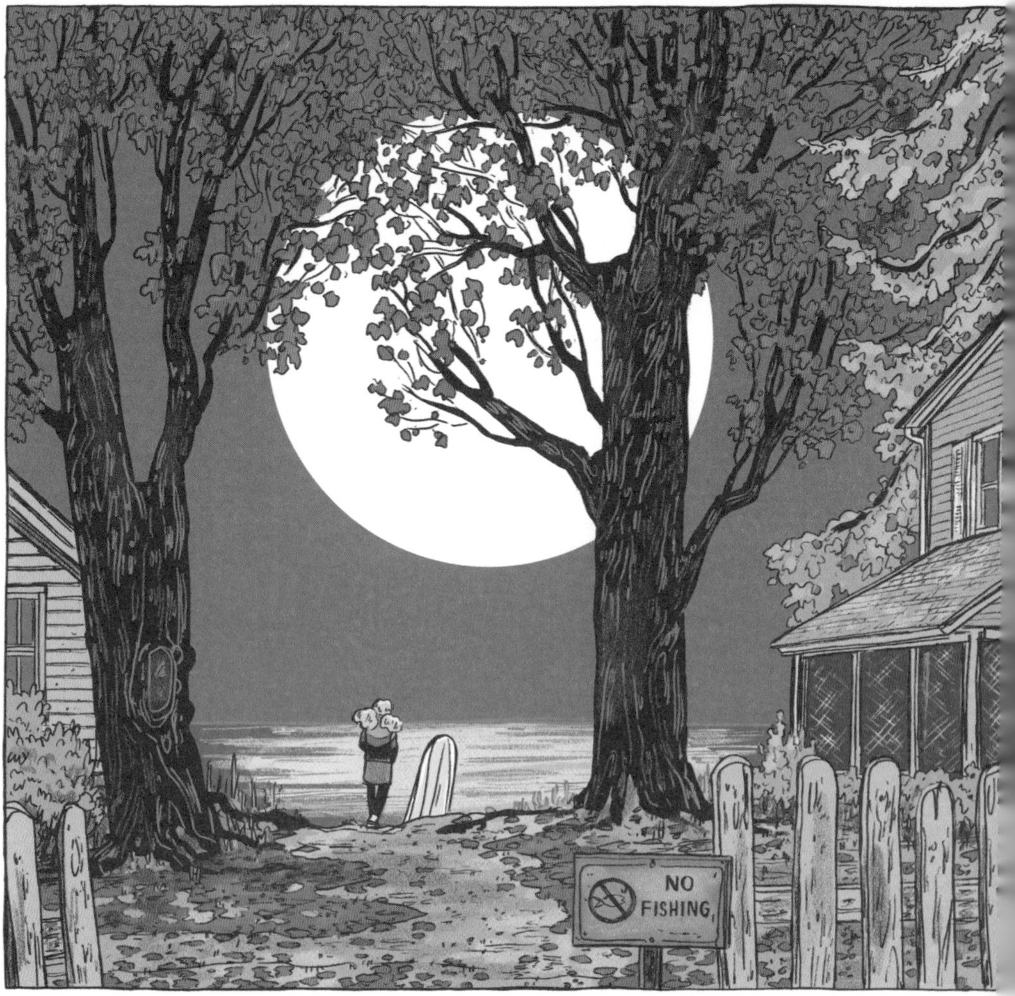
NO FISHING

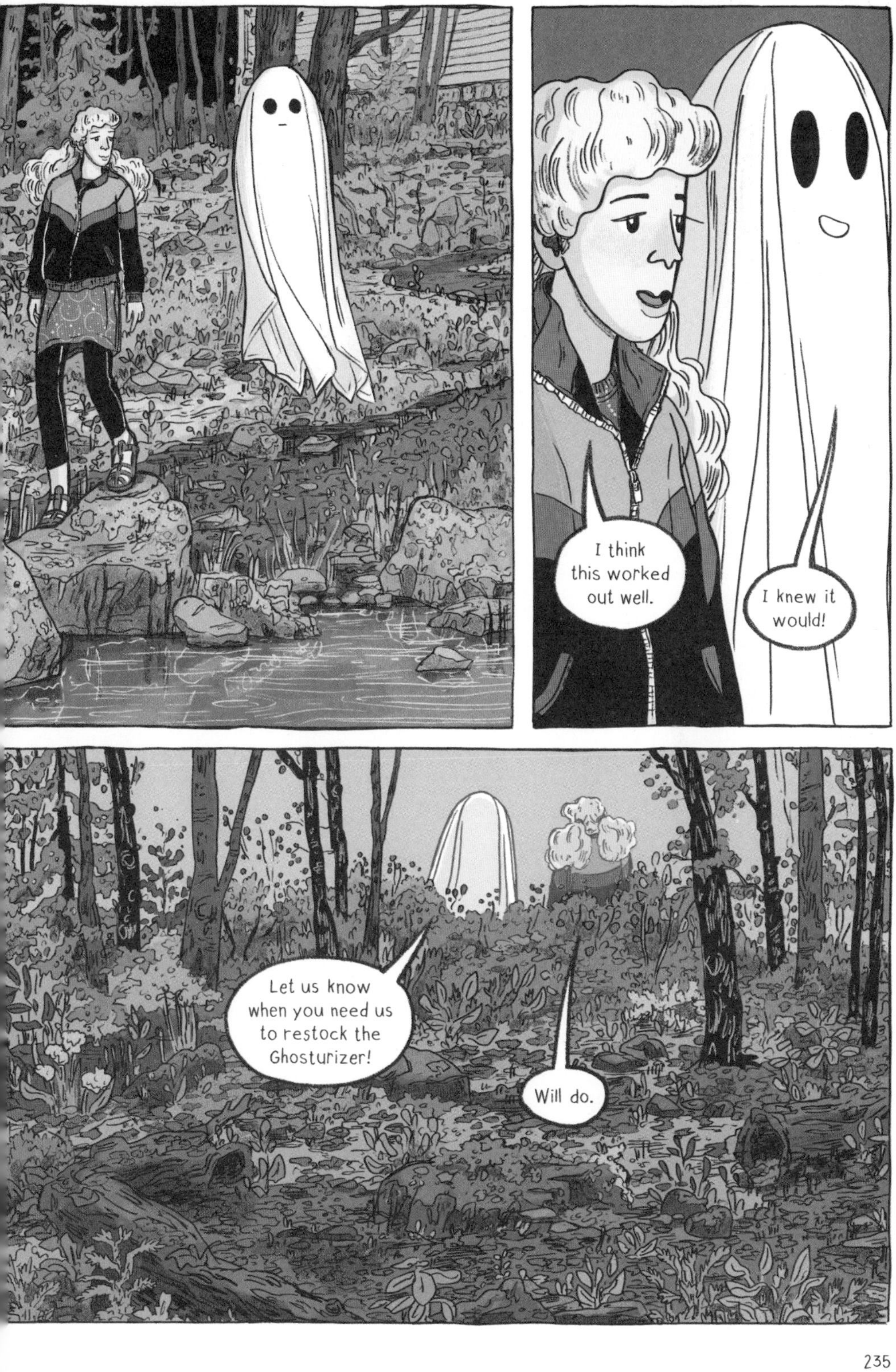
I think this worked out well.
I knew it would!
Let us know when you need us to restock the Ghosturizer!
Will do.

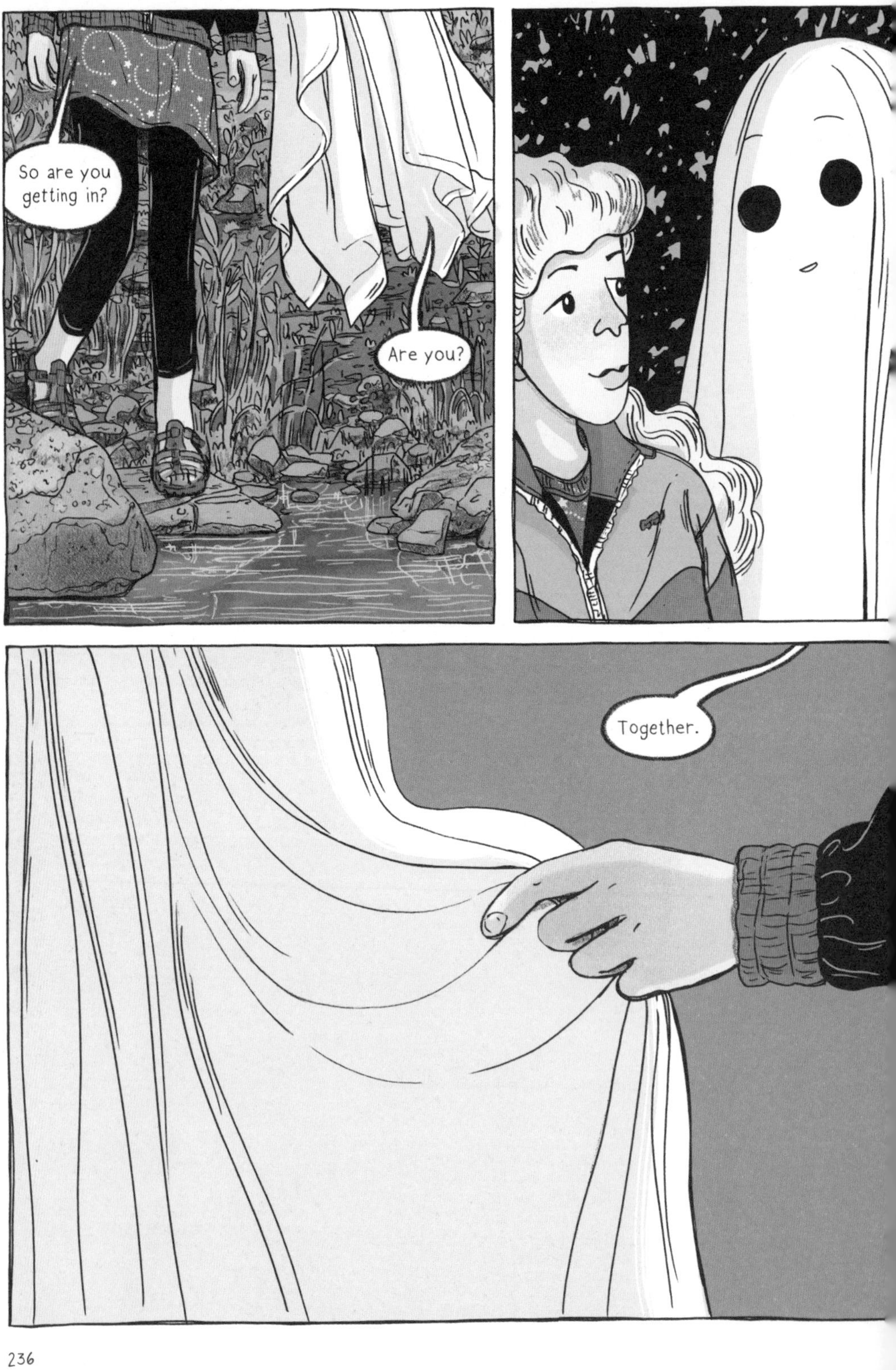
So are you getting in?
Are you?
Together.

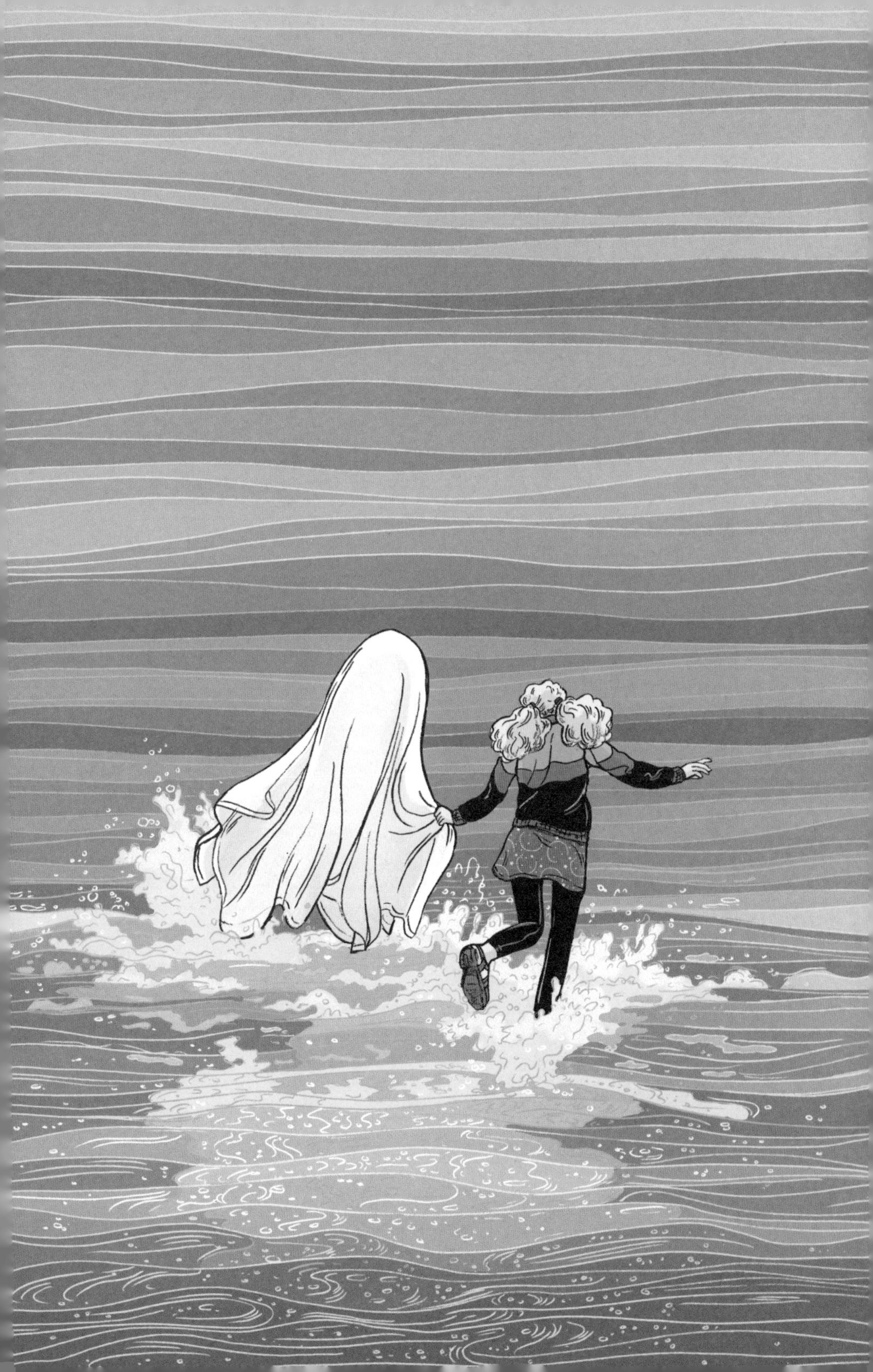

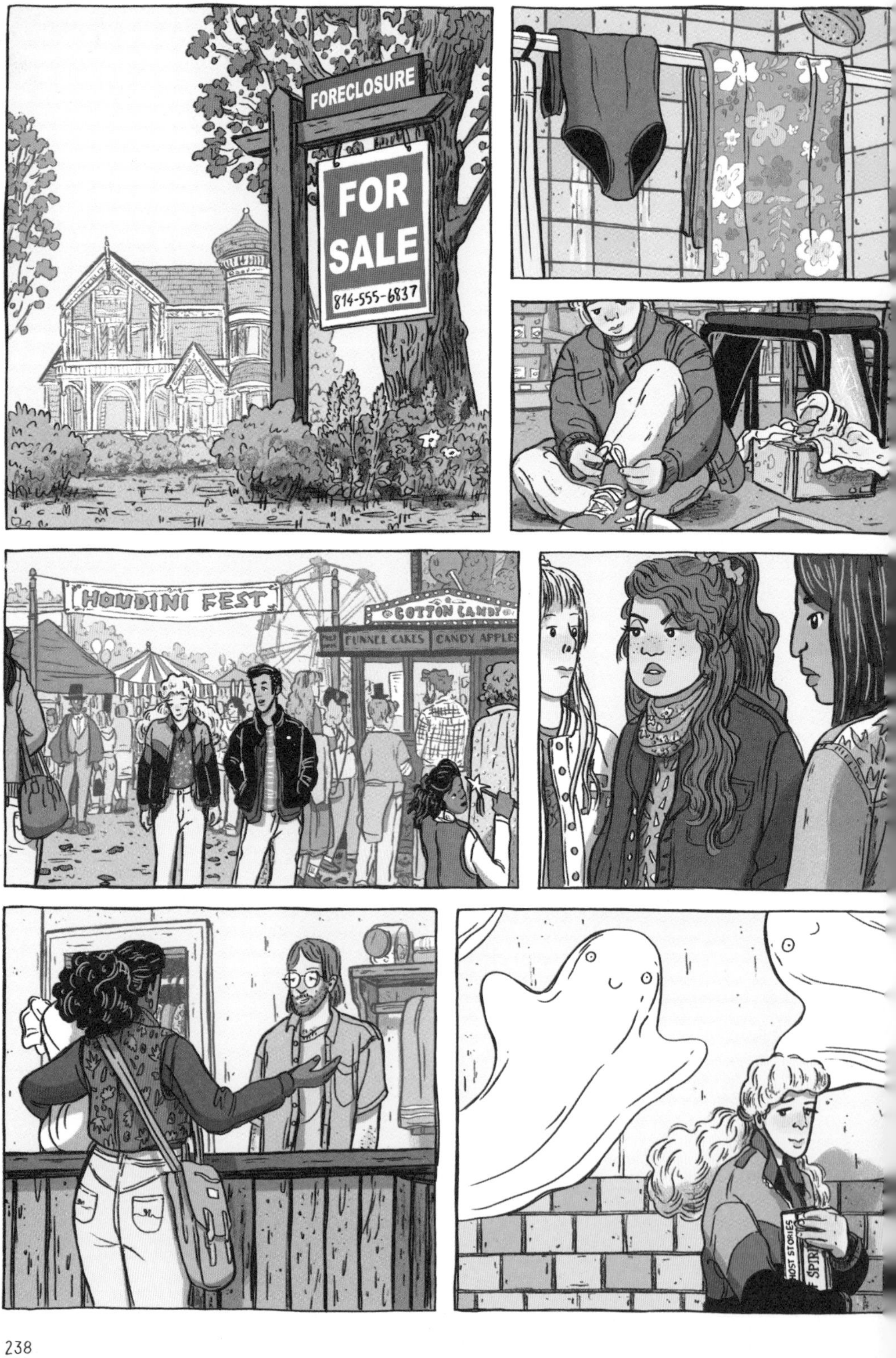
FORECLOSURE
FOR SALE
814-555-6837
HOUDINI FEST
COTTON CANDY
FUNNEL CAKES
CANDY APPLES

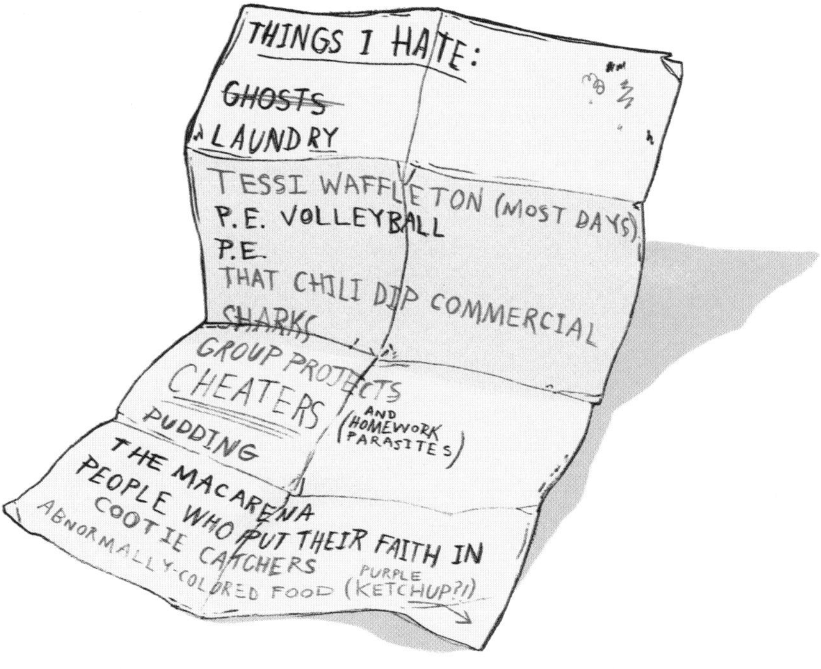
THINGS I HATE:
GHOSTS
LAUNDRY
TESSI WAFFLETON (MOST DAYS)
P.E. VOLLEYBALL
P.E.
THAT CHILI DIP COMMERCIAL
SHARKS
GROUP PROJECTS
CHEATERS
AND (HOMEWORK PARASITES)
PUDDING
THE MACARENA
PEOPLE WHO PUT THEIR FAITH IN COOTIE CATCHERS
ABNORMALLY-COLORED FOOD (PURPLE KETCHUP?!)

THE *SHEETS* STORY CONTINUES...

in Brenna Thummler's newest
graphic novel, *DELICATES!*

Enjoy a sneak preview now.
IN STORES MARCH 2021.

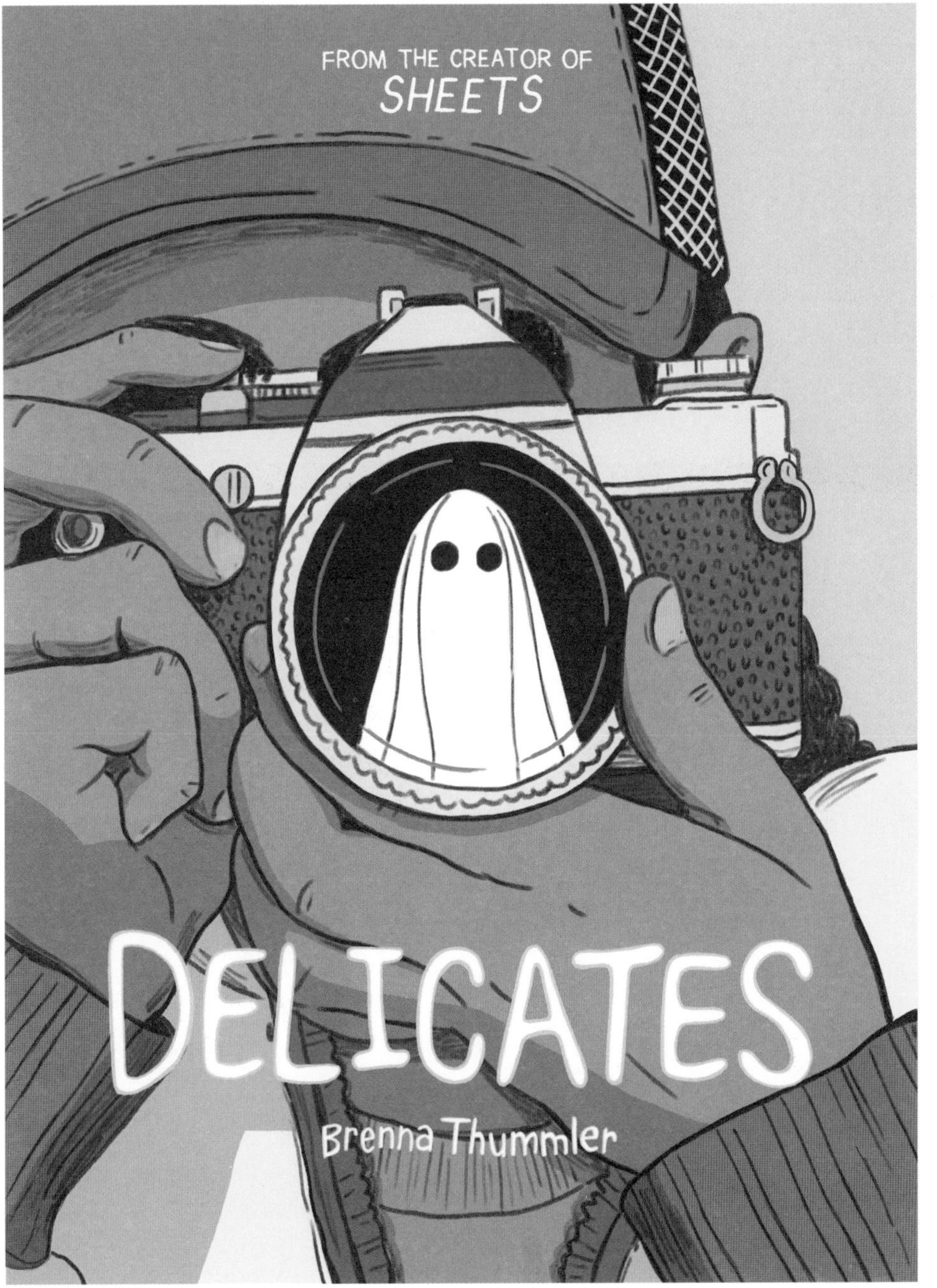
FROM THE CREATOR OF
SHEETS
DELICATES
Brenna Thummler

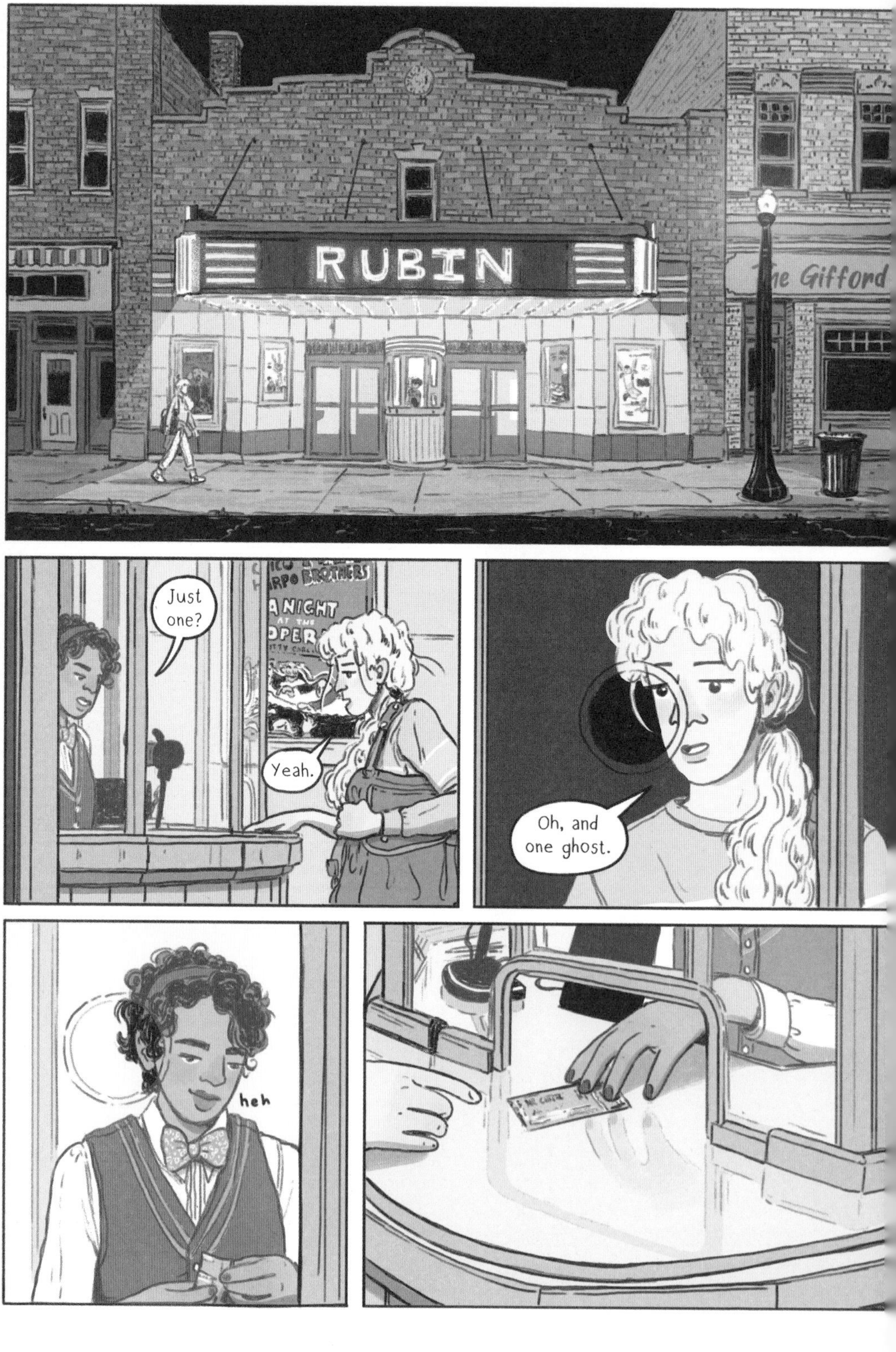
RUBIN
The Gifford
MARX BROTHERS
A NIGHT AT THE OPERA
Just one?
Yeah.
Oh, and one ghost.
heh

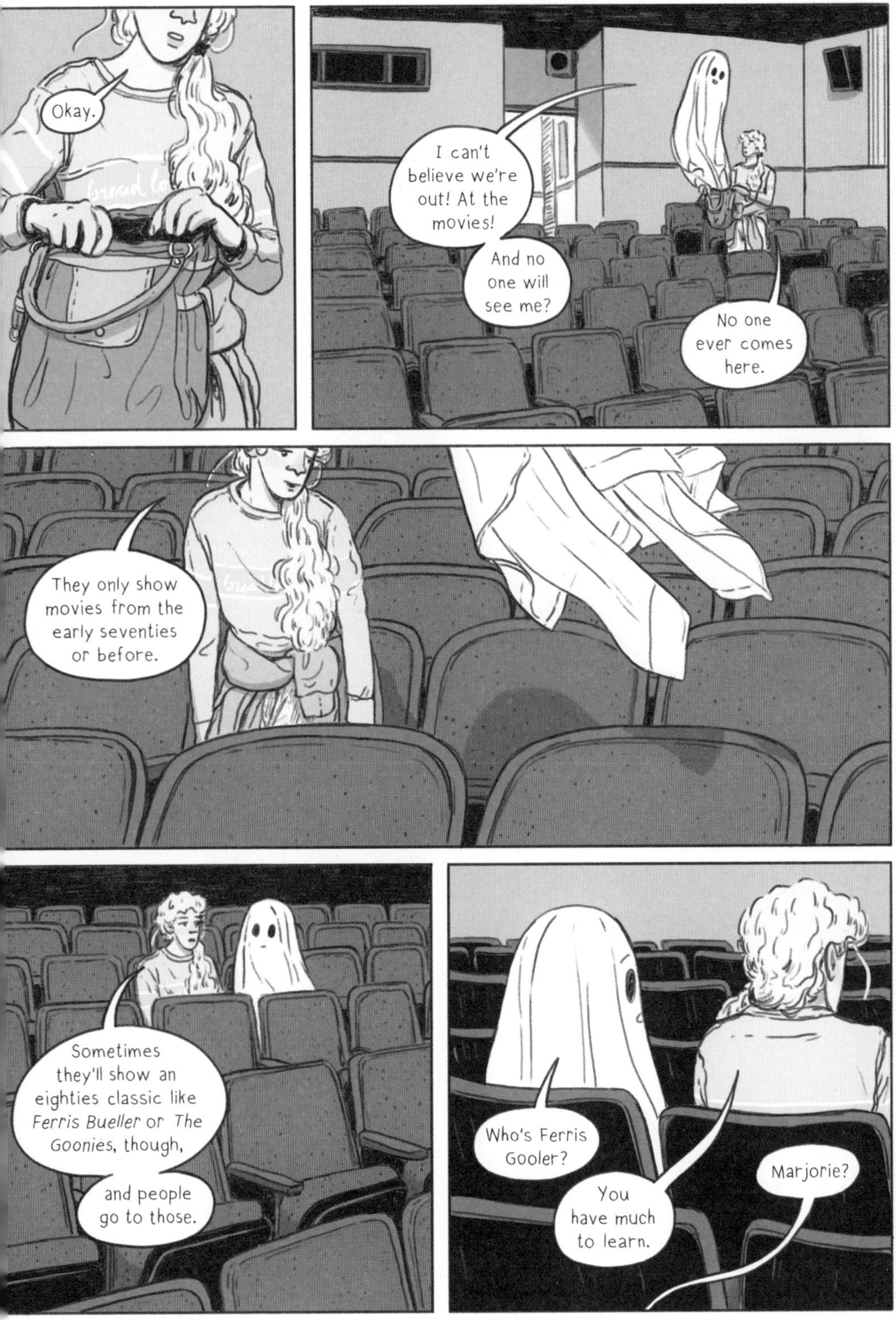
Okay.
I can't believe we're out! At the movies!
And no one will see me?
No one ever comes here.
They only show movies from the early seventies or before.
Sometimes they'll show an eighties classic like *Ferris Bueller* or *The Goonies*, though,
and people go to those.
Who's Ferris Gooler?
You have much to learn.
Marjorie?

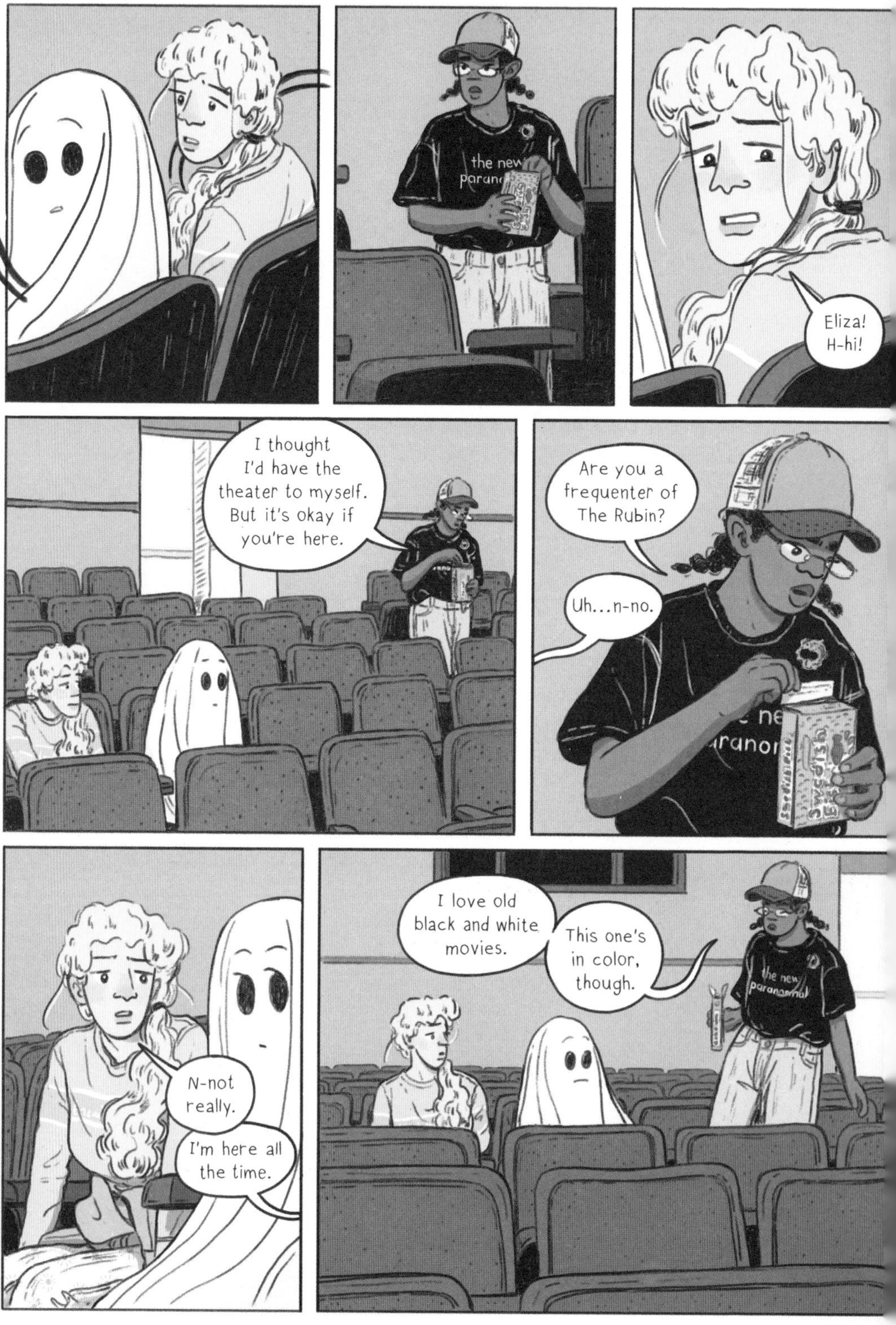

the new paranormal
Eliza! H-hi!
I thought I'd have the theater to myself. But it's okay if you're here.
Are you a frequenter of The Rubin?
Uh...n-no.
N-not really.
I'm here all the time.
I love old black and white movies.
This one's in color, though.
the new paranormal

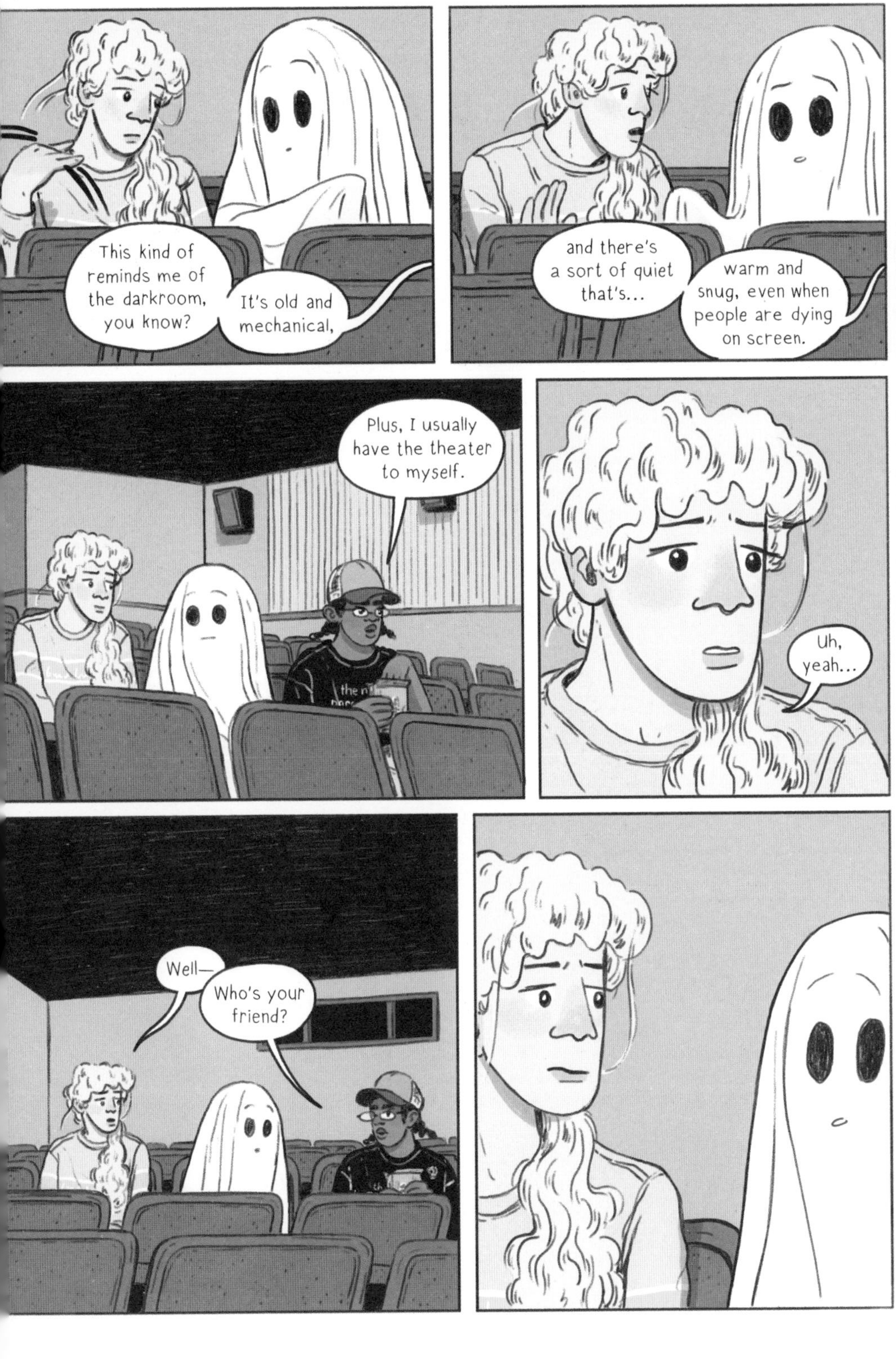
This kind of reminds me of the darkroom, you know?
It's old and mechanical,
and there's a sort of quiet that's...
warm and snug, even when people are dying on screen.
Plus, I usually have the theater to myself.
Uh, yeah...
Well—
Who's your friend?

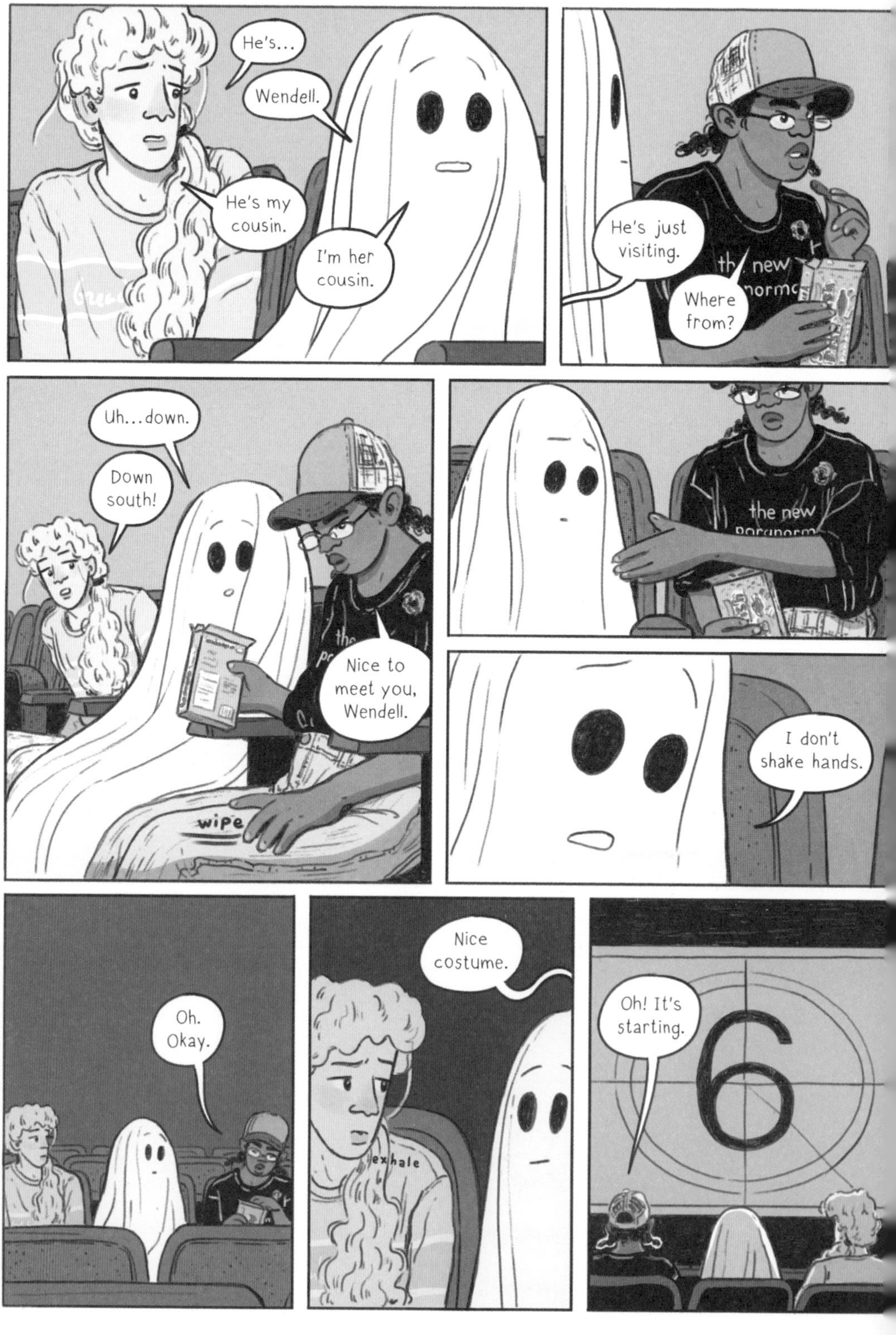

He's...
Wendell.
He's my cousin.
I'm her cousin.
He's just visiting.
Where from?
Uh...down.
Down south!
Nice to meet you, Wendell.
wipe
I don't shake hands.
Oh. Okay.
Nice costume.
exhale
Oh! It's starting.
6

ACKNOWLEDGMENTS

The exceptional Andrea Colvin and the Lion Forge
team for their endless support and overall existence.

My friends at Andrews McMeel, with a special
shout-out to Tim Lynch for getting me here.

Nick Galifianakis, Dave Apatoff, and Daniel Miyares
for their kindness and professional insight.

Professor Paula Jawitz, in whose classroom
the story of *Sheets* began.

Brandes, Thiel, Casmer, Matteo, and all of my
Ringling professors for their inspiration and critique.

Kendra Phipps, Erika Kuster, and Mariah Marsden
of "Team Anne," the loveliest sisterhood.

Mr. O for his wisdom and belief in me.

My family and friends for their constant love,
encouragement, and Facebook shares.

onipress.com • lionforge.com
facebook.com/onipress • facebook.com/lionforge
twitter.com/onipress • twitter.com/lionforge
instagram.com/onipress • instagram.com/lionforge

brennathummler.com • instagram.com/brennathummler

First Edition: August 2018

ISBN 978-1-941302-67-5
eISBN 978-1-5493-0179-7

Printed in China.

Library of Congress Control Number: 2018932765
4 5 6 7 8 9 10